GOOD THINGS COME

BOOKS 1–3

LINDA SHANTZ

Good Things Come: Digital Box Set Books 1–3

Cover Photo by Linda Shantz

www.lindashantz.com

This is a work of fiction. Names, characters, businesses, places, events, locales and incidents are either the products of the author's imagination or used in a fictitious manor. Any resemblance to actual person, living or dead, or actual events is purely coincidental.

Print ISBN: 978-1-990436-06-2

THE GOOD THINGS COME SERIES BY LINDA SHANTZ

Book 1: Good Things Come

Book 2: All The Little Things

Book 3: All Good Things

Book 4: This Good Thing

Join my mailing list to stay up to date on news and release information:

www.lindashantz.com/writes

GOOD THINGS COME

BOOK 1

For my parents.
I'm sorry I didn't become a vet, but at least I outgrew my dream of being a jockey! Raising a horse girl isn't easy!

1

JANUARY

There was a weight to the stillness, the tangerine band streaking across the inky horizon holding something contrary to the promise of a new day. Liv's nostrils stuck together as she drew in a breath. *So cold.* Maybe not as cold as the winters she remembered as a child *à Montréal,* but the record-breaking polar vortex sweeping Southern Ontario made her forget some of her hardy *Québécois* pride. She tugged her hood down and pushed gloved hands deeper into the pockets of her down-filled jacket, the squeak of her boots on the laneway's hard-packed snow like Styrofoam to her ears.

She'd take these frigid mornings over what was to come. Inventing creative ways to keep her fingers from freezing as she legged up feisty two-year-olds in the indoor arena was still preferable to hours spent imprisoned in the University of Guelph's stuffy lecture halls and labs. Just three more days of winter break, and that's what she'd be back to—pursuing a degree she wasn't convinced she wanted.

Back to reality. Back to expectations.

Light spilled from the barn's overhead apartment, and she almost expected to feel warmth as she sliced through the bright pool of light in her path. She slid through the side door, frost condensing on her eyelashes, her face starting to thaw, and a chorus of whinnies greeting her even before she switched on the lights.

"'Morning girls," she called, inspiring another singsong as she ducked into the feed room and scooped the breakfast ration of grain into a pail. When she turned the corner to the well-lit aisle, the faces of two mares jutted out of boxes on either side. The third, though...

"Hey, 'Tisse, what's up?"

Sotisse stood in the corner of the deeply bedded straw, oblivious. The mare took a deliberate turn, huge belly swollen with the life she carried; her tail slightly raised, patches of sweat on her flank and neck darkening her bright chestnut coat to liver. Liv's heart rate took off, and she scrambled to feed the other two horses.

Nerves and muscles were at odds with her brain, but she summoned enough self-control to keep from racing back to the feed room, the grain bucket clattering to the ground. Vapour from the hot water flushed her face as she filled a stainless steel pail. In her other hand she scooped up the foaling kit she'd prepared—just in case—and power-walked back to the stall.

Hold it together, Liv. Her hands were trembling so badly she fumbled with the elastic bandage as she wrapped Sotisse's long golden tail, something she should be able to do in her sleep.

Three weeks. Sotisse was three weeks early. Not technically premature, but still.

She glanced at the time on her phone, then up at the ceiling. Both she and the exercise rider who lived upstairs were due at the training barn for seven, but she definitely wasn't going to make it now. Calling on an extra set of hands was the sensible thing to do, even though complications were rare. This was Sotisse, Papa's favourite racemare, having her first foal, by none other than Just Lucky. And she could be as practical as she wanted about the breeding business, but there was no denying she'd been waiting for this foal. This foal was special.

Foaling was messy, and fast. But there was something intimate about it too, ushering a newborn into this world, and part of her didn't want to share it with a stranger. Because even though Nate Miller had been working on the farm since September, he was really still a stranger to her.

She'd just get him to hold Sotisse while she checked the foal's position and washed under her tail and udder. Once she knew all was well, he could go. Taking two steps at a time, she flew up the stairwell.

Meaning to knock softly, she rapped a staccato beat on the apartment door. There was no hiding the welling combination of panic and excitement in her eyes. The whole being professional and under control thing was definitely not coming off at the moment. She was ready to knock again when the door swung open.

"Everything okay?" Nate stepped back to let her inside, eyebrow tweaked, but she stayed where she was, and dodged his eyes when they landed on hers.

Damn the way her stomach tumbled. Normal, physiological response, right? Sure he was good-looking, but she had enough trouble being taken seriously because she looked fourteen without acting it. She'd leave the gushing to her younger sister Emilie, and the girls who worked on the farm—all of whom had applauded her for hiring him to break yearlings last summer. She'd given him the job because of his experience and references, not because a hot guy would be a welcome addition to the female-dominated staff.

"Sotisse is in labour. I need someone to hold her while I check the foal's position. I won't keep you long." Words ran together, the heat wafting from the apartment threatening to turn her into a puddle of sweat. *Winter? What winter?*

"She's pretty early, isn't she?"

Liv nodded, already dashing back down the stairs.

Sotisse was sinking to her knees in the straw, glancing uncomfortably at her side before rocking back to roll as she tried to adjust the uncomfortable pressure inside her. The mare righted herself, resting, her well-sprung rib cage heaving with laboured breaths before she pitched into another roll, hooves clattering against the wall's wooden boards. She lurched back to her feet, circling with head low, steam rising.

Liv discarded her coat and adjusted her dark ponytail before sliding on a sterile sleeve, aware of Nate's appearance beside her. She waited, balanced on the balls of her feet, shaking her arms loose at her sides like a runner ready to step into the starting block.

"No…"

The word caught in her throat; the sac appearing under the mare's bandaged tail gleaming red instead of pearly white. Nate was already dragging open the door, like he must know what this meant. *Red bag delivery, placenta previa, premature detachment of the placenta…*more importantly, the foal wasn't getting oxygen.

Liv grabbed the sharp scissors from the foaling kit, Nate already at Sotisse's head. She sliced through the thick membrane, a pungent soup of blood, faeces and amniotic fluid sluicing out, soaking her through jeans and long johns and coursing down the mare's hocks. Reaching inside the birth canal to find the foal, her chest seized—one tiny foot was missing from the expected triad of two hooves and a nose.

"You need to get this going," Nate said, his eyes locking onto hers.

"I know that," she snapped, stepping back and ripping off the sleeve. "There's a leg caught."

She peeled off layers until she was stripped to a tank top, beyond any memory of cold, and drew on a fresh sleeve. Sotisse's contractions were powerful, closing in on her arm as she eased it inside the mare, following the foal's neck past the pelvic rim to the shoulder wedged against it. How could such a tiny baby get it so wrong? Not that it wasn't a good thing the foal was small, because it might be what made the difference between getting it out alive instead of dead. Braced against the mare's hindquarters, she pushed the shoulder back and found the uncooperative limb, stretching farther to cup the soft hoof in her hand, struggling to flip it up to join its mate. *Got it.*

Liv withdrew her arm and stepped back, still humming with adrenaline. Now they needed to get it out. Fast. "Turn her loose."

Sotisse lumbered around the stall, sweat and straw matting her thick coat, then buckled into the bedding and flattened herself with a grunt. Liv dropped to her knees, Nate right with her, the foal's tiny feet inching out with every contraction. They each grasped a leg, and Liv looked at him sideways. Nate nodded, and when the next contraction came, they pulled.

"C'mon, 'Tisse." Liv tried not to give in to the desperation creeping into her voice.

"You got this, momma," Nate murmured. "Just one more push to get those shoulders clear and we'll do the rest, promise."

He sounded a lot calmer than Liv felt. They strained with the mare, Liv clenching her jaw and putting her bodyweight behind one last heroic heave, and the foal's shoulders popped through. Another grunt from all three of them, and Nate and Liv drew the foal out onto the straw with a slippery mess of blood and membrane and fluid. Liv fretfully looked for signs of life.

Nate reached for the towels, passing her one, and started to vigorously rub the small, still, body. Liv lifted the foal's head, propping its shoulder against her own hip as she cupped the tiny muzzle to clear the nostrils.

"Filly," Nate said with a quick peek under the wispy tail.

"She's not breathing," Liv responded flatly, overwhelming dread paralyzing her as she cradled the foal's head in her lap.

"Get out of the way."

She was too dumbfounded to protest as he double-checked the foal's airway, stretched out the neck, then closed off the far nostril to start resuscitation. The foal's delicate rib cage rose and fell with the timing of his breaths, and as much as it irked Liv that she wasn't the one doing it, it made no sense to interrupt him. She crept closer to check the filly's pulse, and noticed Nate had stopped, his lips moving soundlessly, eyes fixed on the filly's side. They both saw the faint flutter.

"You got her." Liv pressed her eyes shut, opening them again to assure herself it hadn't been her imagination.

"Welcome to the planet, baby girl," Nate said softly.

Neither of them moved, watching as each breath came more strongly than the last. Sotisse stirred with a low rumble, rocking up onto her sternum and curling her neck towards the foal. Liv turned to Nate, at a loss as to how to express the emotions flooding her, so she pushed herself to her feet instead.

She grabbed the door frame as her legs cramped, then reached down for a dry towel and tossed it to him. "Stay with her?"

Her legs slowly regained function as she shuffled to the office, heartbeat tempering. The newborn foal's heritage surrounded her on the walls of the small room—framed images of their stallion, Just Lucky, winning the Queen's Plate, and Sotisse's victory in the Canadian Oaks. A large oil painting of the pair posing on either side of farm manager Geai Doucet dominated the room from behind a huge old desk. Liv paused—

she could never just ignore that painting—then picked up the landline, not trusting the reception of her cell phone, and put in a call to Geai, leaving a message.

By the time Liv returned, the foal was alert, her long forelegs stretched in front of her. Nate still rubbed the baby with the towel, a huge grin on his face as the filly shook her head and struck out with a hoof, trying to get her hind end underneath her. Sotisse was on her feet, supervising anxiously over his shoulder. While it got old, the way Emilie and the girls went on about Nate—the charm, the sandy blond hair, the azure eyes—he looked pretty good at the moment.

A rush of incoming air from the door interrupted the sentiment, Liv glancing up the aisle. A fresh smile took over her face as Geai appeared around the corner. "You must not have been far away."

The old man ambled towards her and threw a well-bundled arm around her shoulders, pulling her into him as he squeezed. "Put some clothes on! It's freezing!"

"I'd forgotten," Liv said wryly, bending down to scoop up the discarded pile. She eased her shirt on, everything aching.

Geai peered through the stall door. "A filly?"

Nate nodded and draped the towel over his shoulder as he climbed stiffly to his feet, hand outstretched. Geai grasped it firmly.

"All good?" The farm manager turned back to Liv.

"I could have done without the drama, and some oxygen would have been nice…but yeah, now, so far." The list of things that could still go wrong lurked in her brain.

Geai crossed his arms, the corners of his eyes crinkling as they went from Liv to Nate. "Great work, you two. But who's getting on the horses this morning while our two exercise riders are here playing midwife?"

Nate glanced at Liv with a smirk. "I'll get going. Don't expect I'll see you over there anytime soon."

"I think you're on your own this morning, sorry." Her sweater hid the upward curve of her lips as she pulled it over her head, the adrenaline wearing off and leaving her with a chill. "Thank you," she said, which was totally inadequate, but she wasn't good at putting feelings into words.

He flashed an easy grin, zipping his jacket and extracting a toque from the pocket. "Pleasure was all mine."

Maybe it was a good thing she was going back to school, because that, there, was a distraction, and there was no room for distraction in any of her plans.

"At least her early arrival means you'll get a few days to dote on her before your classes start, eh?" Geai's voice pulled her back to the filly in the stall.

She wasn't going to think about classes right now. She fished a tiny cup out of the foaling kit and filled it with chlorhexidine, then went back in, interrupting Sotisse's devoted cleaning of her new daughter to douse the foal's umbilical stump. Sotisse rumbled worriedly, bumping Liv with her nose.

"Don't worry, momma, I'll just be a second."

The filly kicked and struggled, amazing Liv with her rally. There were no markings on the jumble of legs, and only a few white hairs on her small wedge of a head, bobbing as her mother resumed her doting. A defiant whinny escaped from the filly's throat.

"Those lungs seem to be working fine now." Liv grinned at Geai.

"On dirait une p'tite chique," Geai said, lapsing back into French now that Nate was gone.

Chique—that name was going to stick. The comparison was amusing, but fitting—the filly kind of looked like a little quid of tobacco someone had chewed up and spit out on the straw. Liv went in once more to give the foal an enema, and started removing the soiled bedding, replacing it with a deep, dry, bed, banked up the walls.

Geai's steady gaze landed on her when she rejoined him. "You will make a great vet. But I'm not sure you can practice veterinary medicine and be ready to ride this one in the Plate in three and a half years."

"They're all Plate horses at this stage," Liv scoffed, deflecting the way he pinpointed her real dream with logic. Because that was the dream—to ride races, the Plate the ultimate goal, this filly worthy of a place in her fantasy. She'd made it this far, overcoming her first hurdle and moving on to the next, all legginess and hope.

Geai chuckled and pushed up the sleeve of his heavy coat to check his watch. "I'll leave you to it. Keep me posted." He gave Liv a pat on the back and ambled off.

She tossed Sotisse a flake of hay and shrugged into her coat, hugging it around herself as she headed to the feed room to make the mare a hot mash. Then she left mare and foal to bond, and in the warmth of the office collapsed into the chair behind the desk to write up the foaling report, the painting of Lucky and Sotisse overseeing.

The Queen's Plate—Canada's most prestigious race, restricted to three-year-old Thoroughbreds foaled north of the forty-ninth parallel. Twelve hundred foals might be born across this country that spring; a hundred might be nominated for the classic; as many as twenty might go postward. Only one would get their picture taken in the winner's circle under the royal purple and gold blanket of flowers. One winning team would be on the podium accepting the fifty gold sovereigns from the Queen's representative. *Many are called, few are chosen*...and only one comes home first.

Liv wrote it down like a prophecy: *SOTISSE: January 2, 7:05AM, dk.b./br.filly by Just Lucky...*

Breed the best to the best, they said. And hope for the best.

Her own future was as mapped out as Chique's. She'd gone along with the assumption she'd become a vet for so long; now here she was, with a year and a half left of the DVM program and a surgical internship hers for the taking after she graduated, questioning the whole thing. Sure, it would be an asset to have a vet in the family, between the farm, and the string of racehorses at the track, currently wintering in Florida. Liv's heart was with those horses, her passion pitch perfect on their backs, not at the end of a scalpel or reading radiographs. There was no doing both, because both were all-or-nothing paths.

She finished up the foaling report and went back to the stall. The little filly struggled with determination to get to her feet.

"Let's see if I can help you out."

Positioning herself behind the foal's rump, she wrapped her fingers around the base of Chique's tail, and when the filly's next scrambling effort came, Liv scooped an arm under the narrow ribcage for added support. The filly bobbled, but with Liv steadying her, parked a leg at each corner. Chique gave a definitive snort and minced forward, instinctively looking for her first meal.

"You're a fighter, *ti-Chique.*"

Being a vet was a responsible choice. A safe choice. Giving up what she'd spent years in school for? Was crazy. Period. But Liv had done sensible her whole life. Maybe this filly was her chance to break free.

2

MAY

The clock on the tack room wall read ten to six, and outside Woodbine's Barn Five, it was beginning to get light. A radio that was probably older than he was hung in the doorway, playing painful top-40 shit to which Nate found himself humming along, in spite of himself. He sat on top of the cupboards with *The Daily Racing Form* in his lap, worn brown boots beneath his faded jeans, waiting for his first mount of the morning. The light jacket and sweatshirt over his safety vest and t-shirt would be gone by the time they were finished with the last set of horses.

"'Morning."

Trainer Roger Cloutier's lengthy shadow appeared in front of the door beneath one of the covered light bulbs illuminating the shed, his back to Nate as he reviewed the whiteboard training schedule.

"Hey, Rog."

"Claire ready to go?"

The question wasn't directed at Nate—he glanced up to see Liv at Roger's side.

Claire was a bay two-year-old—officially, *L'Éclaircie*—the only one Nate hadn't started last fall when he was breaking the yearlings. Liv's father, Claude Lachance, had purchased Claire at the Keeneland Breeding

Stock Sale as a scruffy little weanling with no pedigree, apparently because he'd felt sorry for her, getting her for cheap. Liv had taken Claire on as her own project, somehow working around her insane school schedule to break the filly with the help of the farm manager, Geai. Claire had gone to Florida—without her—and came back last month with the rest of the Triple Stripe string, transformed over the winter into an athletic Amazon of a filly.

Since Liv had finished her exams, she was here each morning to get on her share of the twelve horses Roger trained for her father, but she arrived way before Nate to muck Claire's stall, take off her bandages, and clean her feed tub and water bucket—just like the grooms did for each of their charges. After she was done for the morning, she went on rounds with Roger's vet, or helped out at the nearby equine hospital. She was definitely a novelty when it came to owners' daughters.

"'Morning Liv," Nate said when she walked into the room.

She smiled at him briefly, finding her Kroops in the corner and kicking off her shoes to slip into the tall black boots. He'd gotten used to that reserved, almost aloof smile. Small talk was definitely not her thing.

"All set?" She twisted in his direction as she tied a kerchief over her dark hair and covered it with her helmet.

Nate nodded, leaving *The Form* on the counter. He pushed his own helmet on with one hand and picked up his whip.

"Michel's on the shed with your filly, Nate." Jo St-Laurent, Roger's assistant trainer, emerged from the stall next to the office with Claire towering beside her, bay coat shimmering.

Claire was flashy, the kind of filly that stopped people in their tracks. Legs for days with high white on three of them; a big star connecting to a wide stripe that covered her face before falling off her nose into one nostril; a little bit of a wall eye that made you wonder if you could trust her. Wall eyes weren't often attractive, but Claire pulled it off.

Michel came around the corner leading a smaller, stockier, bay filly, and the groom greeted Liv with a lazy grin as he went by. He stopped in front of Nate.

"How's Gemma today, Mike?" Nate checked the tack, the last overplayed pop song loitering, unwelcome, in his head.

"Good to go, Miller." He legged Nate up and walked Gemma off, turning them loose.

Gemma bounced as Nate took her a short turn, cutting through the middle of the barn. *Small but mighty.* Maybe she didn't have Claire's height, but Gemma was a full sister to Just Lucky, Claude's horse-of-a-lifetime, with the associated high hopes. Heir apparent, while Claire was auditioning as Cinderella.

He picked up the slack in his lines when they caught up to Claire back on the Triple Stripe side, Gemma's quarters swinging out as they stopped. Claire curled her head around and bumped Jo in the shoulder, knocking her off balance, while Roger threw Liv up.

"Meet you outside," Roger called over his shoulder, walking down to the stable pony's stall as Claire marched off, Jo leaning into her while Liv got tied on—knotting her reins, tightening the girth, adjusting her stirrup irons.

The gradually rising sun cast a golden glow over the landscape, picking up brilliant highlights in the gleaming coats of both fillies as Roger steered Paz, the pony, between them. Liv reached forward and scratched Claire under her flip of black mane, Claire stretching her neck down and snorting happily.

Gemma jigged a few strides, flinging her head and crowding Paz before Nate reeled her in. "See how nice Claire is being?" he chided. "Why can't you be more like that?"

They joined a growing stream of horses on the tree-lined path to Woodbine's main oval. Toronto's racetrack was the largest in Canada, one of the top racing venues in North America. Nate's hometown Calgary didn't have anything close.

He'd told people that was why he'd left—it sounded reasonable. If he never went back, it would be too soon. He'd lucked out, getting this job. Claude had nice horses, and he'd even let Nate keep the apartment on the farm, though he'd been full time at the track since the Florida horses had returned.

"L'Eclaircie and Just Gemma, a half." Roger called the pair of fillies in to the clocker as they reached the tunnel to the main, just as it opened.

The cadence of aluminum-shod hooves on the rubberized paving stones echoed off the concrete walls as they passed under the turf course.

Claire was alert, head up and ears zeroed forward, and when they came out the other end, Liv let her jog up the slope to the on-gap. Gemma matched her enthusiasm, and even Paz sprang to life.

"Meet you at the pole," Roger said before turning off to the right and nudging Paz into a canter down the backstretch.

Nate glanced over his shoulder and laughed as he and Liv jogged off the other way. Paz gave Roger a hard time, bouncing like a spring horse, ready to take up the chase when he saw horses already on the track ahead of him. Every. Single. Day. The old sprinter loved his job.

Claire and Gemma jogged the wrong way along the outside rail—backing up—until they reached the wire, stopping with the towering grandstand behind them as they faced the infield. The sun coming across the track was blinding, bathing the surface. Horses galloped by while they stood: Claire a statue, Gemma bowing her neck and pawing impatiently.

"Are you ready to get your ass kicked?" Liv smiled nonchalantly, with a rare outward display of confidence in her filly.

Nate held back a laugh. Liv was so bloody serious most of the time. The only time she loosened up was when she was with Claire. "Oh yeah?"

"You have the privilege of being among the first to view the sight that will frustrate many a jock this year." She slapped Claire's well-rounded rump.

"We'll see who's watching what."

"Dream on, Miller. Let's go."

They turned, both fillies leaping into a gallop—Claire on the inside, Gemma close beside her. Nate relaxed, standing in the irons and keeping Gemma next to Claire in the middle of the track, rounding the clubhouse turn and entering the straight. Liv glanced ahead at Roger's silhouette astride Paz, standing on the outside rail a furlong away from the red and white half-mile marker that would be their starting point. Nate pulled down his goggles, and when Liv dropped Claire to the rail, Gemma locked onto her like a missile onto a target.

The fillies matched strides, figuratively—Gemma was taking two for every one of Claire's. Claire dragged Liv around the turn, when Nate didn't have anywhere near that much filly beneath him. As they came down the stretch, Claire's ears flickered forward and she accelerated, each thrust of her hindquarters dismissing the smaller filly, Liv still poised motionless in the tack. Nate sent Gemma after them with a chirp and a crack of his stick, Gemma inching up on Liv's boot bravely, but with the wire looming, Claire cleanly changed leads, regaining a length advantage on her stablemate by the time the watches stopped.

Gemma caught up as they galloped out. Nate ran his eyes over Claire, the easy bunching and extending of her muscles, then Liv. The smile she gave him lacked her usual restraint.

"Nice ass," he called, and ducked the look she shot back. *Real original, Miller.*

They pulled up and turned in on either side of Roger and Paz. The trainer looked his two charges up and down.

"That looked pretty easy," Roger said to Liv.

She shrugged, but the slight curve of her lips and the way her grey eyes shone belied her indifference.

Roger glanced at his stopwatch. "She's something else. If she turns out to be as good as I think she is, she'll look like quite the bargain."

Liv withdrew back into herself as the endorphin rush subsided on the walk back to the barn. That's the way it went—Nate had learned not to take it personally. She intrigued him, sure. Under different circumstances, he'd be into figuring that out. *I mean, why not?* She wasn't hard to look at, and had that whole dark and mysterious thing going on. But there was a whole list of reasons why it stopped there, not the least of which was, owner's daughter? Definitely off limits.

Michel and Jo met them in front of the barn, exchanging halters for bridles and taking the fillies a turn while Nate and Liv set the tack for the next two horses. Back outside, Nate took the lead shank from Michel as Liv started to douse Claire's neck with suds while Jo held, leaving the tall bay glimmering beneath a slick film.

"So when do we head to New York, Rog?" Michel dipped a sponge in his own pail of steaming water, squeezing it over Gemma's crest when the trainer rejoined them after putting Paz away.

Roger crossed his arms. "A couple of weeks. Your father wants to send Claire now, too, Liv."

Nate arched an involuntary eyebrow and noticed the sharp turn of Liv's head in Roger's direction. News to her too, apparently. Claire shook her head and lashed her tail, Jo cursing while Liv wiped her face on her sleeve before carrying on like she hadn't just been christened with bathwater…or had that boulder of information dropped in front of her.

"Why the hell do you get to go, Mike?" Nate grumbled once he'd passed Gemma over to a hotwalker. Of course it made sense to send a groom—Roger was planning to ship three horses to Don Philips, Claude's trainer at Belmont. *I wouldn't mind rubbing horses for a bit if it meant going to Belmont Park.*

"Think it's called seniority, Miller." Michel flicked the sponge at him before dropping it in the empty bucket.

Nate dragged the back of his hand over his face. "Obviously not maturity."

"Boys," Jo reprimanded. "Don't worry, Nate, he'll only be gone for a couple of weeks."

Liv actually smiled, though her eyes were on Claire as another hotwalker relieved Jo and started walking the Amazon.

"I've never been to Belmont." Nate stopped himself. No whining. One thing at a time. Woodbine was already a move up.

"I'll send you a postcard." Michel slapped him on the arm as Nate followed him into the barn.

Jo pulled out his next mount, a dark bay three-year-old. "Throw Nate up, will you, Michel?"

Nate gathered the lines, and Michel thrust him aboard carelessly.

"Miss you already, Mike." Nate grinned as the colt walked off.

Liv waited outside, circling her colt to keep him moving. The colt tried to bite Nate's gelding playfully, and she smacked him on the neck with her stick and pulled him away, chasing him forward. Roger jogged Paz up and inserted the pony in between the two three-year-olds.

Liv glanced at Roger, a slight furrow to her brow. "So I guess I'm going to New York."

Napoleon's whole hind end wagged in welcome as Liv pushed through the door of Geai's bungalow. Rubbing the black Lab's head helped still the nerves her sprint here hadn't.

Geai appeared from the kitchen, ushering her into the living room. "So? How'd the filly work?"

Liv tucked a leg under herself as she perched on the sofa, pulling a cushion to her midriff. "She was brilliant. Forty-five flat, just breezing. Put Just Gemma away without even trying."

Geai frowned. "Gemma? Roger worked them together?"

"She's the only one in the barn who can go with Claire."

"Who was on her? She must have an excuse." Geai was ever loyal to their homebreds.

"Nate Miller."

"Ah, you should have had a rider on her, then you'd be telling me something different."

"He can ride all right."

"I'll get you some water. You must be light-headed from your run."

Liv grinned as she and Napoleon followed him to the kitchen, fellow devotees.

Geai poured a glass from a jug in the fridge. "He's really as good on a horse as I hear he is?"

"I think he probably is."

"You obviously like him, then."

With Geai, Liv had no fear her words of praise for Nate would be misinterpreted—Geai would realize her admiration was limited merely to his way with horses. The same conversation with her sister Emilie or her best friend Faye would quickly get twisted.

"Did you know about New York?" Napoleon rested his chin on her knee when she sat at the kitchen table, and she stroked his well-padded side to try and settle herself again. Back-up therapist, when her stress was related to her usual one—Claire.

Geai nodded, silently, setting the glass in front of her.

"A little warning would have been nice." Liv abandoned the disappointed Labrador to take a gulp, like the water offered fortitude. "I'm going with her."

Geai's eyebrows peaked. "Have you discussed that with your parents?"

"No, but I'm twenty-three, what can they say?"

"Well, your father owns the filly, I think he could say a lot."

"You and I both know it's not my father who'll be the problem."

Geai chuckled, and parked himself opposite her. "Have you actually thought this through?"

Liv pressed her lips into a line, hands encircling the glass. "Still processing."

"You want to get your apprentice license down there."

"Is that crazy? It's crazy, isn't it?" She went back to stroking Napoleon. Science, right? Petting an animal was supposed to lower blood pressure. At this rate, poor Napoleon would be bald by the time she left.

"Completely." *You weren't supposed to agree with me, Geai.* "But I doubt that will stop you." *True.* "You'll need a good agent." Like he'd already thought about it, and had it figured out. "I hear Kenny O'Connell is looking for a new bug rider. He handles Ricky Acosta's book."

"Ricky Acosta?" Liv squeaked. Only the leading rider at Belmont, not to mention movie star good-looking, fangirl-worthy. *Poor, poor Napoleon.* "He's like an idol, Geai."

"I'll give Don a call and have him mention you. Acosta rides for him a lot."

Her stomach spasmed. This was making it all the more real and terrifying.

"You should eat something, you're looking pale." Geai pushed himself up, grinning.

Liv choked on a laugh. "I'm not feeling so hungry at the moment, thanks. Besides, I guess I need to watch that now."

He glanced over his shoulder as he opened a cupboard. "You don't eat nothing as it is. You be careful."

"It's just a couple of pounds." She waved off his concern. "Any more advice?"

Geai opened a bag of potato chips and started nibbling. She shook her head when he offered it to her. She ate better than he did, that was for sure.

"You see those French riders when they come over for the International? They come, they go in suits. You be like that. It shows class. It shows respect for your profession. The sport of kings, eh?"

"Kings?" The corner of her mouth curved up.

"Would you prefer Princess? See how you like that, because that's what you're going to get. They'll say the only reason you have the mount on Claire is because your father owns her."

"Which is true, but too bad for them, right?" Claire made all the other stuff fade away. Claire was her secret weapon. Napoleon scrambled, dancing beside her on the hardwood as she rose. "Sorry, I can't sit still, I'd better go. Please tell me I'm not crazy?"

Geai followed her to the door, and he patted her on the shoulder as he smiled. "Only a little bit."

"Is my mother going to kill me?"

"Probably. Find some nice young man in New York to sweep you off your feet, and maybe she'll forgive you."

"Like that's going to happen."

"You must be such a disappointment to her."

She laughed, putting her arms around him and squeezing. She just needed Geai and Napoleon to come with her, and everything would be fine. She skipped down the steps and broke into a run to chase away a fresh flutter of nerves, following the path through the woods that separated the stallion barn from the mares' paddock.

Mares and foals milled by the gate, waiting to be brought in. It wasn't hard to locate Sotisse's little filly, dodging the girl who sought to catch her while Sotisse waited patiently at the end of a rope shank. Chique didn't seem to care that the rest of her companions were on the way to the barn—she tore off, showing admirable athleticism as she threw bucks and leaps into her performance.

"Cheeky little bitch, eh?"

Liv started, her head snapping to the side. Nate Miller, slowing from a jog in shorts and a good pair of shoes, his blond hair damp.

He pulled the back of one wrist across his brow. "Sorry."

No he wasn't. Not one bit. It was as if he liked to make her squirm, with his nice arms and easy grin. She glanced at him sideways when he joined her at the fence.

Chique was losing interest in her game, her circles getting slower and smaller. She finally lapsed into a jaunty walk, shaking her head and snorting happily, short tail flapping. When she sidled up to her mother, doing a perfect turn on the forehand to line herself up alongside the mare to nurse, the girl crept up and snapped the rope to her halter.

Nate fell in beside Liv as she began walking towards the barn. It would probably be rude to tell him to go away. Besides, she couldn't just run and hide every time someone made her uncomfortable. She had to get better at this. *Think of it as training.*

"So, New York." His eyes caught hers, pulling them away from the filly's progress. "Why New York?"

Yes, why? She'd been working on that since Roger had announced it this morning. "My father likes to have a couple horses with Don. He spends a lot of time in New York with work. I galloped there a few summers ago, actually." Some kids went to Europe after graduating high school; she'd gone to Belmont Park. "Claire is New York-bred, and they have a good incentive program. She really only came here from Florida because…well…because I asked." She glanced at him quickly, tucking a flyaway strand of hair behind her ear. "I should know better than to get attached in this business."

"Some of them get to you no matter how much you tell yourself that, don't they?"

She tilted her head. It wasn't the reaction she'd expected from the guy who always had a quick comment.

"It takes guts, what you're doing," he went on. "Quitting school."

"You did." She stopped by the empty paddock gate and crossed her arms.

The way he shifted his weight and his eyes was uncharacteristically self-conscious. "I'm surprised you remember that."

"Not many people come to an interview for a farm job with a resumé, not to mention a university education."

"Like you said, I dropped out."

"Still."

"Not vet school."

She rolled her eyes. "It's so cliché. Smart horse girl has to go to vet school, right? Don't get me wrong, I'm a total science geek. I love it. I just love this more."

"So with what, a year left, I'm betting you'll be pissing off a lot of people by bailing?" He threw her that grin.

"Right?" Those connections who'd supported her, the faculty, the relatives who'd told her for as long as she could remember she was going to be a vet, so much so she'd finally believed it herself. At least Geai was on her side. And, it would appear, Nate. Only because of his similar aspirations, she was sure. "Do you think it would make my mother feel better if I told her one of my classmates is dropping out to pursue his drug addiction?"

He choked on a laugh. "Seriously? Not sure, though. Riding racehorses is its own addiction."

She sighed and started walking towards the barn again. "Yeah. Exactly."

It was weird, this. Almost comfortable. She didn't do comfortable. Especially not with guys anywhere near her own age. It wasn't as if there were men lining up to ask her out in vet school, where her class was 80 percent female. Which was fine, because keeping her focus on her studies, and now her career, was her shield; an easy excuse to put off things that, she had to admit, scared her. Not that she thought Nate was coming on to her. Maybe that was what made him bearable.

They found the dark filly nose-deep in the corner feed tub next to her long-suffering mother. She still wasn't very big, and was losing her foal coat in patches, leaving her with a decidedly moth-eaten look.

Liv would miss Geai and Napoleon, that was a given. But she'd also miss seeing Chique change and grow. "You'll keep an eye on this filly for me?"

Nate arched an eyebrow—it was an odd request, considering there were farm staff responsible for such things, but he'd been there from day one—a big part of the reason the little filly was here to torment them all.

"For sure."

Back outside in the daylight, she faced him, folding her arms across her body. "Can you do me one other favour? Can you check on Geai from time to time?"

There was a glint of curiosity in his eyes. "Sure. Can I ask why? Is he all right?"

"I just worry about him getting lonely—not that he'd admit to it. And you're easy to talk to." When she actually got over herself enough to have a conversation. They'd worked together every day since the middle of April, but this was the longest they'd talked since last August's interview.

Nate reflected her posture, one corner of his mouth twisting up. "No problem. I'm guessing he's got a story or two to share."

"Geai's forgotten more about horses than you or I will ever know." She made no attempt to hide her affection. "And by the way, he calls Sotisse's filly Chique, so you two are on the same page already."

"You know I'm still going to call her Cheeky, right?"

She backed away a few steps before leaving him with an amused look, breaking into a run towards the woods. Nate Miller was definitely safer left behind.

Liv slipped in the front door, her courage bolstered, and kicked off her shoes. She skipped down into the sunken living room, grabbing the new copy of *The Blood-Horse* resting on the coffee table with the day's mail. The clinking of dishes in the kitchen brought her tension right back. She flipped through pages of coloured ads and reports from tracks across the world…stalling.

Just get it over with.

Taking the magazine with her, she sat on the bench at the kitchen table, pressing it open at the article about this year's Preakness Stakes. "Hi *Maman.*"

Anne Lachance reached up with the clean glass she'd just taken from the dishwasher, placing it in the cupboard before bending down for the next. Her dark hair, peppered with grey, brushed her jaw where it fell, and she tucked it behind her ear. She always looked as if she belonged in the pages of a women's magazine; that mother who had it all together—raising kids, keeping an immaculate house, looking good doing it.

"Have a good run?"

Liv nodded, fingering the edge of the page.

"Ready for New York?"

Liv's eyes shot from the magazine, meeting Anne's. "Am I the only one who didn't know about this?"

"When your father told me he was sending L'Éclaircie, I assumed you'd want to go and gallop for Don until your externship starts. I'm sure you can find a vet to work for at Belmont while you're there."

At least her mother wasn't totally clueless. Liv turned the page and tried to sound casual. "I'm going to get my apprentice license down there."

Anne closed the cupboard and turned slowly. "I'm sorry, what did you say?"

"I'm not going to let someone else ride Claire when I'm perfectly capable."

The silence was so loud it pierced her eardrums; the weight of her mother's realization terrifying.

"You're dropping out." Her mother's words were like an accusation. "You can't be serious."

"I am. Completely. I've always wanted to do this. I didn't plan for it to be now. That's just the way it worked out."

"But—vet school, Olivia. You only have a year left! And the internship! I thought that's what you wanted."

It's what you *wanted*...but she bit back the retort. "Roger thinks this filly is good. You know there's nothing like being on these horses. You can't tell me, if you'd had this kind of a chance thirty years ago, you honestly could have turned it down?"

She couldn't tell if there was more than displeasure in her mother's dark brown eyes. It was because of horses her parents had met—but marrying Claude Lachance had ironically been the end of Anne's aspirations as a rider, as instead she chose to raise a family. That wouldn't be Liv's story. A man wasn't going to derail her dreams.

"There's so much more to life than horses, Olivia," Anne said—reading her mind, if not her heart.

Was there, though?

3

JUNE

Sometimes when he ran, it all came back. At work it was easy to believe he'd reinvented himself, but here the solitude and calm of the farm exposed his raw and busted parts, and it was as if he was running away all over again, trying to put distance between past and present, but getting nowhere.

He stopped and forced himself to look around. To look up at the huge maples towering on either side of the lane, the perfectly clear blue sky peeking through cloaked branches, down to where leaves cast dappled shadows beneath his feet. He breathed in their oxygen, and sent some CO_2 back. He had this job. He had a plan, of a fashion, even if today he felt like he was standing still. Or worse, left behind.

The maples gave way to a clearing, tall double fence lines forming the stallion paddocks in front of him. Even though the busiest part of the breeding season was done, Geai still had both stallions in this time of day.

Wasn't doing something for someone else the best way to get your sorry-ass thoughts off yourself? Even if that someone was the one who'd inadvertently induced this current frame of mind. The interior of the barn was cool and dark after the brightness outside. He walked down the aisle as his eyes adjusted, following up on a promise.

"Ah, Mr. Miller. To what do I owe the honour?"

Geai was in the stall with a small bay horse, currying dried mud off into clouds of dust. The sign on the door told Nate what he knew already —this was Just Lucky, the farm's pride and joy. The stallion wasn't very big, but the look he gave you when you entered his presence warned you not to be fooled by that. As a sire, he was still unproven, Chique the first foal of his first crop.

"Figured maybe now things were slowing down around here, I'd pop in and say hi to my fellow Chique guardian." He'd barely seen Geai since he'd started at Woodbine. Most days he just ran by the stallion barn, because there was inevitably a trailer pulled up outside, bringing a visiting mare to be bred.

Lucky grabbed the chain—doubled up so he was tied short, no doubt to keep him from using those teeth on his handler. The stallion stepped abruptly into Geai, who hopped spryly out of the way before reprimanding him with a deft poke behind the shoulder and a short verbal rebuke in French.

"Everything go smoothly this morning?"

Nate nodded, even though Geai's back was to him. "The van left around nine, with Liv right behind it."

Geai laughed and slipped around Lucky's hindquarters to the other side. Geai wasn't all that tall, but he could still look over the stallion's back. Just Lucky was what, maybe fifteen-two? Chique had come by at least some of her lack of size naturally.

"Of course she would. She'd ride in with the horses if they'd let her."

The old man's accent was heavy, but you didn't grow up watching *Hockey Night in Canada* without learning how to understand a French-Canadian. Geai ducked under Lucky's neck and picked up a set of brushes, then started knocking off the layer of fine dust that left both him and Lucky sneezing.

After turning the stallion loose, Geai slid the stall door shut behind him and left the halter on the door. "You want a drink? Water? Pop? Beer?"

Nate followed him to the tack room at the end of the barn, stopping in the doorway. It was a big room, one corner of it breeding lab, another mini office. No-nonsense, like the man who spent the most time there. The fridge looked like a typical farm fridge—all three of the beverages on offer, half a sandwich and some snack-size yogurts, plus an assortment of injectable medications. He didn't want to know what else.

When Nate didn't give him an answer, Geai held out a beer. "Don't tell me you're all healthy like Livvy."

Nate grabbed the bottle. "Thanks." So much for the rest of his run.

Geai led the way to a picnic table on the lawn outside the barn and unscrewed the cap on his bottle. "Has Roger hired another exercise rider?"

"Not yet." Nate settled across from him. "It'll be okay for a couple of days, with those three horses leaving. Emilie will help on the weekend. I'm sure Rog will fill those stalls with some two-year-olds pretty quick though." He shrugged. "I can get on twelve if I have to. I don't mind."

"How long before you run off and start riding races too?"

The old man propped his bottle in front of him with both hands, and Nate could practically hear the whizzing in his brain as questions queued up.

"I agreed to babysit a foal, I'm not going anywhere." He threw out a grin.

"Probably below your paygrade, though."

Nate picked at the label, the sodden paper peeling easily in his fingers. "I admire her, going off to New York like that. Admire her conviction." *Envy it.* "I'm not in a hurry myself. Still sizing things up around here."

"Patience is a virtue?"

"Something like that."

The old man was still sizing him up, like he saw right through the casual excuses to the doubt beneath.

"Livvy says you're good. She's stingy with compliments."

"She's stingy with words," Nate quipped dryly. What did she know? But she *was* good. And she had connections. He should probably just be content staying on the sidelines. Career exercise rider, that was him.

"She asked you to watch Chique. Don't take that lightly. She doesn't like to let people help her."

"Should I be honoured, or scared? I'm pretty sure your crew here on the farm is perfectly capable of looking after that filly." This visit had been inspired by the fact she'd asked him to keep tabs on Geai, too, but Nate didn't mention that. He didn't know if he wanted the responsibility of Liv's trust. It didn't fit with his goal of underachiever.

"It's just her way of showing respect. You stepped up when she foaled Chique. She won't ever forget that."

"I think I pissed her off as much as anything. I'm sure she knows how to resuscitate a foal."

Geai chuckled. "Kind of hard to stay mad when you saved the filly's life. She froze, and she knows it."

"There's a reason they don't let doctors treat kin, right?"

Geai tipped the bottle to his lips. "You were in the right place at the right time. If you have ambitions to be a rider, it won't hurt to have Livvy as a friend. She may be young, but she does have a fair bit of influence around here."

He'd let her believe that's what he wanted, at the interview. Once, at least, it had been true, before he'd tried to rewrite his life into what he thought would please someone else. Which had backfired, big-time. Deep down, that was what he envied most about Liv. That she'd gone after what she wanted, everyone else's expectations be damned.

"She's one of those really smart kids who has trouble dealing with humans, isn't she? Does she even have friends?"

Geai's eyes narrowed slightly, and it was a moment before he responded. "So like I said…don't take her loyalty lightly."

Nate stewed when he left, crossing the lawn in front of Geai's cottage to the trailhead through the woods. The beer left him with a mild buzz…*lightweight*…but he broke into a run anyway. Running away again, the confusion that conversation left him with piled on top of the same old broken record in his head. He always thought if he went fast enough, he could outrun it all, but it always caught up.

He didn't stop today, merely identifying Chique as he ran past the mares and foals, back to his apartment. Maybe a glass of cold water would dilute what remained of the alcohol in his bloodstream and clear his head.

The piano under the big picture window in the main room had been there when he'd moved in. He'd never asked what the hell it was doing in a barn apartment, let alone how they'd got it up here, but it was what made him think this job had been meant to be. That piano was his best friend. He slid onto the bench and placed the glass on a coaster next to a picture frame, resting his fingers on the keys and playing a few bars from a song that had kept him company in his beat-up old Mustang last summer as he drove east.

The photo always won, though. He stared at it—he and his two brothers, and a blonde girl who still gave his heart a jolt. He didn't know why he tortured himself, keeping that photo out. It would be better off at the bottom of a box somewhere. Except when it didn't pitch him into misery, it fueled a fire.

Ambition. It wasn't that he didn't have it. His was just a slow burn, eating away at him. One day, he'd show them all—when he figured out what exactly that meant.

"GIVE HER BACK, LIV."

The voice broke through her self-absorption, coming from behind her as she walked Claire down Don Philips' shedrow at Belmont. Liv glanced over her shoulder and slowed, Don's assistant, Jeanne, standing there with hands on hips.

"You're going to have to start acting more like a rider if you want to be taken seriously around here."

Liv relinquished the shank to the hotwalker, and with it, a portion of her sense of security. "The track's not even open yet."

"So don't show up so early tomorrow." Jeanne's face softened, and Liv followed her to the training board. "Kenny said he'd be here at six. Sit down and have a coffee or something."

She didn't do caffeine; besides, she was jittery enough. She forced herself to study the win pictures decorating the walls around Don's messy desk, then, perched on the spare chair, flipped distractedly through status updates on her phone.

Footsteps jolted her back to reality. Kenny O'Connell didn't acknowledge her as he walked over to the coffee maker and filled a Styrofoam cup. Liv rose slowly, waiting while he took his time adding generous portions of cream and sugar, then slurped carefully. He gave a satisfied nod, and finally turned to her.

The way he looked her up and down made her leery, but she squared her shoulders and offered her hand. When he grasped it, he didn't let go.

"Harder," he said, with the faint lilt of an Irish accent.

"I'm sorry?" She pulled back, but he hung on.

"You're going to have to work on that handshake, darlin', if you want trainers to believe you're stronger than you look."

She flinched, pressing her lips together as he finally released her. "Thanks for agreeing to take me on." Though she wasn't completely convinced of it, at the moment.

"Thank Don. He's the one who talked me into it. I could use a good bug, so guess we'll see if we can make you into one." Kenny took another sip of his coffee. "Girl jocks do well at Woodbine. Why didn't you stay there?"

There it was again. Why New York? She couldn't answer without discrediting herself by bringing up Claire, so she returned his challenging gaze, channeling assertiveness she didn't feel. "What matters is I'm here now, so why don't we just go with that?"

"Fair enough. How 'bout we go meet some people, darlin', and we'll talk."

"How about you stop calling me darling?"

Kenny cracked a wide smile and put an arm around her shoulders. "You might be all right. Put your helmet on, so you look the part."

She wriggled out from under his arm, suppressing a shudder, and followed him to a shiny black Lexus, feeling conspicuously like a child being lured with the promise of candy. *Come with me, darlin', and I'll make your dreams come true.*

He set the coffee cup in the console and poked the start button. "How's your weight?"

Right to it—good thing she hated small talk. "Almost there."

"Well get on that, 'cause almost ain't good enough." He reached across and grabbed her bicep beneath the sleeve of her polo shirt, and she winced, resisting the urge to slap his hand away. "Start by laying off the weights. You're never actually going to be as strong as the guys, and muscle weighs too much. You need finesse, not power. I'll get Ricky to help you with the rest."

She nodded, even though it was counterintuitive to sacrifice strength—not to mention health. That was the whole warped truth of this profession. It's what she'd signed up for.

He pulled up to a barn, and she walked behind him, her eyes on the horses reaching heads out of the stalls with radar ears. *Yeah, I'm not sure what I'm doing here either.* She tried to smile pleasantly and think about her grip as Kenny introduced Rod Milotski. *That's Mister to you.*

Milotski's eyes skimmed over her, finally resting on her face. "She's better looking than your last bug, at least, huh Kenny? I hope this one can ride."

Talking like she wasn't even there. Was a little respect too much to ask? The Woodbine backstretch wasn't Disneyland—but compared to this? No one at home acted like this to her face. But her father was somebody at Woodbine. Here, once she left Don's barn, if they even knew who Claude Lachance was, they didn't care. It was starting to hit her just how sheltered—and privileged—she'd been.

"Why don't you see for yourself, Rod? What about that little filly of yours? She might like a lighter touch. When you gonna breeze her again?"

"How 'bout you gallop her this morning?" Rod finally spoke directly to Liv.

And she had to defer to Kenny. He nodded.

In a few minutes the groom brought a pale chestnut filly around, and after legging Liv up, Rod took over the shank.

"What's her name?" Liv stroked the filly's neck, her washed-out colour tending towards pink instead of orange or red.

"Blush. She's a bit of a nervous thing. Back her up as best you can, then go once around."

As soon as she was on the filly, Liv's edginess dissolved, sitting quietly as they jigged their way to the track. When Rod turned them loose at the gap, Blush jumped ahead, then settled into Liv's cross when she realized no one was going to fight with her. They eased to a walk just past the wire, but only for a second, Blush rocking back on her hocks and doing a half-pirouette. Liv decided not to push the whole standing thing, and let the filly go.

Blush leapt forward, feeling like she wanted to run off, giving Liv visions of barreling around the clubhouse turn in front of the trainer. Not a good first impression. Liv concentrated on keeping still, and the filly started to trust. She tried to trust back, praying Blush didn't duck out the on-gap.

The trainer was waiting at the off-gap when they were done, Kenny beside him still nursing his coffee. Rod snapped the shank to the bit and Blush tossed her head and started to jig again.

"She looked good," Rod said, not hiding his surprise.

"She was great once she started to relax. She'd be a lot happier if you took that ring bit off her and put something kinder in her mouth."

"You gonna come gallop her every day, then?" Rod glowered up at her.

Liv looked beyond him to Kenny, whose face was telling her to shut up. She leaned forward and rubbed Blush under her flouncing mane, lower lip between her teeth. "She's a nice filly."

Back at the barn, her tension returned as soon as her boots hit the ground, like it was crawling up from the mats under the straw in Blush's stall. She slid off the tack, thanking the groom. Now to see if she'd blown it.

Kenny and Rod stopped talking as she approached. Rod still didn't look happy.

"She breezes Wednesday. Six AM work?"

Liv caught herself—it was easy enough to transform her disbelief into a smile—and endured the handshake ritual again. "Thank you."

"I'll be sure to put a rubber D on her," Rod crowed as he walked away.

Liv allowed herself a skip step once she and Kenny were out of sight. "He asked me back to work her."

"Don't get excited until your name's in the entries, or you'll find yourself a glorified gallop girl," Kenny countered. "And maybe wait till people get to know you a bit before you start saying stuff about the equipment."

"It was the truth, though. I'd think they'd want feedback."

"You come off a little like a snob, darlin'." He raised his hands in surrender as she grimaced at the endearment. "They have to like you a little, at least until you prove you can ride. Try and show some personality."

Her teeth hurt, she clenched them so hard. "Is there a book I can buy? Or maybe I could hire a life coach." An online course, maybe.

He howled. "Maybe some less sarcastic personality."

She left Kenny to chat up trainers with his stereotypical Irish gift of the gab—selling the ten-pound weight advantage she'd receive as a shiny new apprentice; gambling on his reputation until she built her own. It was up to her to ignore the affront of every sneer and derogatory comment. Smile anyway, practice a killer handshake, laugh at their jokes, say nice things about their horses, and keep the other stuff to herself. *Get yourself some mounts so you make them forget you're a* girl. She lost track of time and barns visited.

"One more stop." Kenny pulled up outside of Don's shed, and it felt like coming home.

Don sat behind piles on his desk in the office. Under normal circumstances, between his impressive build and brusque demeanor, she found him totally intimidating, but after being plugged to strangers all morning, Liv could have hugged him.

"How'd it go?" Don sat back in his chair.

"It's a start," Kenny said. "What have you got for our girl?"

"I'll enter that gelding Roger sent from Woodbine for Friday and give you the call, assuming you get the all-clear from the stewards and starter. Get your feet wet."

Kenny put an arm around her shoulders, and the muscles in her neck ratcheted tighter, but she kept her feet planted. "Don't worry, before you know it, I'll have you swimming in the deep end."

"Speaking of..." Don pushed an open booklet towards her.

The current condition book, listing the races written for the next two weeks. There was Claire's name, scribbled at the top of a maiden special weight for two-year-old fillies. Her chest tightened at the sight.

"All right, darl —" Kenny stopped himself with an unapologetic grin. "See you in the morning. Call me if you need me."

LIV HAD ALWAYS BEEN LUCKY, naturally lightweight, but this was a whole new dimension. She stepped off the scales—scales that would rule her life, at least as long as she had the ten-pound bug. It was a significant allowance for a racehorse—*one pound equals one length,* the saying went —but to ask that kind of a reduction from an already slim human was…inhumane.

She looked up, finding Ricky Acosta watching her. Another step closer to real now, starstruck in the Belmont jock's room. He wouldn't remember the times they'd breezed horses together for Don—with helmet, kerchief and goggles on, she was just another no-name gallop girl to him—but each time was emblazoned on her memory.

He sauntered over, his face as hard and hollow as his body, an unlit cigarette hanging out of the corner of his mouth. He didn't look nearly as attractive as he did on TV. The camera added ten pounds, right? *Ten pounds*…that number haunted her.

"Kenny asked me to give you some tips."

Somehow it felt like he was looking down his nose at her, even though she had two inches on him. He slung an arm around her shoulders, paralyzing everything but her eyes, which shifted sideways to his leer.

"Here's one. Lasix isn't just for horses. It'll suck the water out of you. Works a treat." He tilted his head into hers, lips close to her ear. "But you look all pure, and I can think of a perfect drug-free way to work up a sweat. It'd be an honour to help you break your maiden."

The words crawled up her spine, working into her brainstem and igniting a signal that finally got through to her legs. She spun away, face burning, her still-frozen tongue thwarting a snappy comeback.

"Think she might be a bit of a slow starter, boys." Fed by their laughter, he called after her. "This ain't high school, princess. And this sure as shit ain't a team sport."

Whatever he said as she bolted was in Spanish, garnering more laughter, and it certainly wasn't anything she'd picked up in the intro course she'd taken as an elective during her undergrad. She crumpled onto the bench in the safety of the women's change room, her heart still pummeling against her chest wall.

Princess. Geai had called that one. It was clear: Acosta would never let her forget she was a woman. Not on the track, and not in ways in which she had even less experience. His physicality had made her shamefully aware of *that.*

She closed her eyes, controlling her breathing—crush officially crushed. *As it turns out, your idol is an asshole.*

The density of the safety vest under the nylon colours Liv wore gave her body an illusion of substance she didn't feel, arms folded to keep them steady. Just five wins, and the allowance would drop from ten pounds to five. It sounded straightforward enough, until you went two weeks riding nothing but also-rans. She was starting to understand why guys like Acosta were such bastards. Hangry. All the time.

"Riders up!"

She glanced at the trainer, and he threw her up on the walk.

"Stay out of trouble," was all he said.

She didn't know if her heart palpitations were from nerves or dehydration, grateful for the pony's steady influence escorting her mount through the post parade and warm up. They filed into the gate, the doors slamming shut behind them.

Her horse broke sideways, brushing the runner next to her—of course it was Acosta, Liv catching his dirty look as they were drawn along in the charge of bodies vying for position. In a blink she was trailing the pack.

The race was only six furlongs, and everything was happening so fast. They were already heading into the turn. Her horse moved up steadily, and the field swept into Belmont's broad stretch.

Going to the outside was the safest plan—making her own room wouldn't be following the trainer's instructions. But was staying out of trouble the best she could do? She wanted to win this race. *Needed* to, tired of finishing at the back of the pack all the time. Tired in general.

The leader was running out of gas, and Liv pulled her horse out a lane so they didn't get stuck behind the stopping pacesetter. One on the outside started to drift out, leaving room—but the hole left on the rail was the shortest path. Her horse was game, and Liv was determined to show these guys she had grit.

Her exhale came like a maniacal cackle as her horse bullied his way through. They scraped the rail, and her mount veered sideways, clobbering the horse next to her, the curses reaching Liv's ears unmistakably Acosta's —*again*. Liv drove on, throwing everything she had into the drive to the wire.

Acosta's horse caught up as Liv eased hers, galloping out.

"You're coming down, princess."

"Did we win?" she asked.

"Don't know. Don't matter." He pulled his horse up as Liv let hers go on.

She was the last to return to the front of the grandstand. Her heart soared seeing the tote board, her number on top, then plummeted at the bold red letters of the inquiry sign.

The groom peered up at her as he snapped a paddock shank to the horse's bit. "Acosta claimed foul."

"Of course he did."

Liv tossed her whip to her valet, hanging her head as they circled, and waited for the stewards' verdict. She didn't like her chances of it being in her favour.

FAYE: *Are you coming home for the Plate? Dean's running Playing Catchup!*

Liv: *Wouldn't miss it for the world.*

Faye: *What? Seriously? How?*

Liv: *Suspension.*

Faye: *That's the best news! I mean, sorry. See you Saturday!*

WOODBINE FELT like a heartening embrace after the harshness of Belmont, even on a day like today when it was dressed up almost beyond recognition. Liv felt that way herself, but the Plate was special. It was history and pageantry and pride, distinctly Canadian, and worth a little social discomfort.

She and Emilie threaded their way through the masses, pressing on to find Faye, who was, naturally, right in the middle of it. Faye didn't spend a lot of time around the track, even though her older brother was a trainer, but Queen's Plate was an event, so Faye was in her element.

Faye hugged her gingerly, as if she were afraid Liv would crumble. "You look fabulous—in an anorexic, runway model sort of way."

"Um, thanks?"

"I do have to applaud you for picking out that cute dress without my help, so something about this crazy New York thing has been worthwhile."

They were jostled, and Faye grabbed Liv's arm to steady herself, then steered them out of the crowd to a free bench.

"So who gets a suspension when they haven't even been riding three weeks?"

Liv smirked. The win had been taken away from her, but her actions had served a purpose. She'd shown Acosta she'd come to play. "I guess I got carried away trying to prove something."

"Brilliant." Faye didn't buy into the whole horse thing, but she was in full support of beating men at their own game, whatever game that happened to be. Her eyes dropped back to Liv's spare frame with a sweep of her hand. "This, not so much. There's nothing to you under normal circumstances. You're not doing anything stupid, are you?"

Liv dropped her eyes, crossing her legs and tugging at her skirt. "There's always some sort of compromise. Where's Nate, Em?" She needed to distract Faye from probing further into how she met the low weight assignments. "I thought he'd be here."

Faye's perfect eyebrows peaked. "He's real then, is he? I've been convinced he's a figment of Emilie's imagination."

Emilie tilted her head and stuck out her tongue. "He stayed at the farm to watch the race with Geai. Geai had a mare booked for a rebreed to Lucky this afternoon."

Faye's face fell to a frown, her lower lip jutting out. "So disappointing. I need to meet him."

Liv buried her own sense of letdown. Not that she'd been hoping to see him or anything. "Maybe Em wants to keep the exercise rider for herself."

"Chasing an older man," Faye teased.

"As tempting as that is, because he is completely gorgeous, and also super nice, I'm really just protecting him from you, Faye." Emilie gave Faye a pointed look. "Older man. Four years. Besides, you only date jocks."

Faye's mouth curled upward. "True. For future reference, though."

Liv's phone chimed, and she glanced at the screen. "Speak of the devil."

She opened the message, making out a selfie of little Chique nuzzling Nate's hair, Sotisse grazing passively behind them. *She's gonna come watch the Plate with me and Geai* he'd typed below it, as if the power of suggestion could fashion the filly's destiny. The word *adorable* came to mind—because of Chique, of course. She handed the phone to Faye.

Faye lifted the device, studying it approvingly. "How do I get on that list? You do have good taste, Emilie."

Faye gave the phone back and Liv glanced at the photo again, letting Emilie's crush be the decoy. She didn't know what to think of Nate, with his regular updates on Chique, and his faithfulness to Geai. Sure, she'd asked him to keep an eye out, but she didn't want to mistake his devotion for something it wasn't. As in, anything to do with her.

She felt Faye zero back in on her, and quickly turned the phone over.

"So, your agent's creepy, your idol's an asshole...you're still determined to do this riding thing?"

Liv shrugged. "Kenny's kind of grown on me."

"Like a fungus?" Emilie chirped.

Liv had to laugh. *Kind of.* "I haven't officially withdrawn from school yet."

Faye's eyebrows shot up. "Are you seriously thinking about going back?"

"I can't win a race to save my life, can I? Maybe this was a big mistake. I've still got time to decide."

Faye looped an arm through Liv's and pulled her to her feet. "Let's go up to the Turf Club and see Dean and have something to eat. Free lunch."

"I can't. If I got started on that buffet I might not be able to stop. I'll see Dean when he comes down for the Plate."

Emilie led the way as the horses left the paddock for the current race, taking the shortcut to the trackside apron at the west end of the grandstand.

"Hey Liv, how's it going in New York?" A voice behind them caught her attention as they climbed the stairs.

She couldn't remember the guy's name, or place him out of context—someone who worked on the backstretch—but she gave him a polite smile. "It's going."

"How's your filly?"

"Great. She runs next week. Don almost entered her a week ago, but decided to wait for a longer race."

"Acosta going to ride her? First time starter and all."

Liv curled her fingers into fists at the mention of Acosta's name, but sweetened her smile. "Nope, that one's mine."

"Well, good luck. Nice to see you."

Faye made a face, muttering under her breath, "Everyone's your friend when you're a big-time New York rider."

"Right." Liv rolled her eyes, but it reinforced her feeling of warmth for the home crowd, after weeks of being an outsider at Belmont.

The guy walked away with his buddy when they reached the apron, voices drifting.

"I thought they were pretty high on that filly when she was up here," the buddy said.

The first guy answered, "Yeah, me too. Can't be much if they're going to put Liv on her when Acosta rides the rest of the barn."

"Don't listen to them." Faye pulled Liv to the spot Emilie had secured on the rail.

Liv gazed across the track to the infield, flags billowing gently in front of the shrubs and lakes. "They're so wrong. Claire is the real deal."

Later, waiting at the gate to board the plane back to New York, she scrolled distractedly through the first photos and reports from the Plate—Dean's horse had run a gutsy third. The Plate magic lingered, reminding her of the whole point behind her decision to get her license at Belmont; her dream to be here with Chique in three years. She opened up Word and started drafting a letter to her academic advisor about her intention to withdraw from the DVM program.

She couldn't expect to be successful at this riding thing if she wasn't all in. It had only been three weeks; Claire hadn't even started yet.

Claire would change her luck.

4

JULY

When Liv had stood in this walking ring in the past month, she'd often questioned herself. But Claire was here this time, shimmering black and gold and white; the reason she'd come to New York. She flexed and extended her toes against the thin leather of her lightweight boots, little more than slippers. Suspension over. Recommitted. *All in.*

Her father stood on the other side of Don, but their conversation didn't register amid the hum in her brain. Had she expected her mother to be here? Not really. That might have been misconstrued as acceptance of this mad life choice. Just as well. Her mother wouldn't have ignored her drawn face, or the fact that a gust of wind could have blown her over. Don legged her up like she was a feather, and the groom led them into the tunnel, passing them off to the pony.

She shook off her guilt that Claire didn't have the benefit of a more seasoned rider for her first outing. It was Liv's job to make sure the filly had a good experience today, because this race could shape Claire's opinion on the whole game. Fillies weren't forgiving. She couldn't screw this up.

Behind the gate an assistant starter took over, Claire swinging her head and bumping him before Liv could stop her. He shoved back, and led them in. Liv reached down and touched the sheen of sweat on Claire's neck. Claire was feeling her tension. She needed to pull it together.

They missed the break, Claire popping out a beat behind the others when Liv had schooled her ad nauseam. Dirt flew back, pelting their faces as Liv parked the filly on the rail. Claire would either deal with it, or she wouldn't. She settled into her big stride, undeterred...*good girl.*

Even though they were at the back of the pack, they weren't all that far behind. The front-runners were flying—that would work in Claire's favour in the lane. One thing about Belmont's long homestretch, it would give them lots of time to get there. On the turn Claire passed a couple of fillies on her own, Liv still holding her. *Not yet.* The speed freaks on the lead would come back to her. She needed to be content to build momentum, wait for the right second to throw Claire into gear.

Turning for home, there was Acosta, ahead of her—elbows flying, cross thrown, the sound of his voice carrying back to her. Claire's ears flicked forward when Acosta's filly accelerated.

Yes. Now.

Claire launched, Liv's body mirroring the thrust of her neck as they drove for the wire. Claire's nose reached the other filly's saddle towel, then shoulder. But Acosta intentionally let his filly drift, nudging Claire wide. Liv gritted her teeth. *You don't get to mess with Claire.* She unsheathed her stick and struck Claire on the haunches—once, twice—and Claire dug in, pushed back, pulled even, and stuck her glorious pink nose in front.

Liv barely remembered the picture—or dismounting, or unsaddling, or weighing in—jogging back to the jock's room in a blissful daze. When the ice water drenched her, she welcomed it, letting herself think, just for that moment, she was one of them.

CHIQUE'S YELL pierced Nate's eardrums—for such a tiny thing, she had a voice on her. She contorted her body as only an indignant foal could while he attempted to stand her in the aisle of the broodmare barn for the blacksmith.

"She's right there, Cheeky."

Sotisse poked her head over the stall door with a mouthful of hay to check in, but went back to the pile with an unconcerned snort. The little filly braced all four legs solid as fence posts as the blacksmith sidled up to her shoulder, scratching under her spiky mane, trying to convince her they were friends. Chique rolled an eye, unconvinced.

"Whatever you're selling, she's not buying," Nate quipped.

"Each time I come it's like she's never seen me before." The blacksmith ran a hand down Chique's leg. She sighed and lifted it.

"She just has to make her point."

"Remember that when you're breaking her." Geai observed, amused, sitting on a bale of straw.

"I'm pretty sure Liv is going to be the one breaking her," Nate responded, stroking the filly's neck, her coat shiny and sleek now that the baby fuzz was gone.

"Ah, not if she's setting the world on fire in New York!"

"That filly of hers run huge the other day, eh?" The blacksmith rasped Chique's tiny hoof, then gently placed it down. Chique lifted it back up and stomped it to the ground for emphasis.

"It was a solid performance." Geai nodded. "Livvy kept her cool with that little bit of race-riding Acosta threw at her." The grin that overtook his face was all pride.

Geai opened the stall door for Nate when the blacksmith was finished. Chique shook her head once she was free, going immediately to Sotisse's side to nurse, like she'd just suffered an unthinkable injustice and her mother's milk would erase the memory.

"She says Don wants to run Claire in a stake at Saratoga next time out," Geai mused, pulling the door shut when Nate slipped out.

"We should go, Geai."

The old man looked at him like he was insane.

"Breeding season is over. The farm will survive without you for a couple of days."

Geai turned and walked away from him.

"I've got vacation days coming, and I'm guessing you've probably collected a few months' worth over the years." When the old man still ignored him, Nate played his trump card. "Think of how happy Liv would be. I bet she'd appreciate the moral support. It'd be nice to see Claire run, wouldn't it?"

"Shouldn't you be going home to see your folks or something?" Geai protested.

Hell no. He felt the recurrent pang of guilt knowing how much his mother wanted him to come back to visit, but she'd know it was impossible, that first anniversary looming, flaring like a gunshot wound in his chest.

"Not sure I'm welcome. My dad kicked me out when I quit school." That really wasn't enough to keep him away, but Geai didn't need to know he'd dropped out for less inspiring reasons than Liv had.

"Bah, parents get over stuff like that. You should go home. Why do you want to go to Saratoga?"

Nate handed the lead rope to the girl waiting to hold the next foal. "Everyone wants to go to Saratoga. It's like Mecca for racetrackers."

"You want to spend your holiday with an old man? Don't you have any friends?"

He put an arm around Geai's shoulders, grinning. "You're it."

Geai studied the next foal when the girl brought him out, assessing the sturdy chestnut colt's conformation. "I'll talk to Claude. No promises."

5

AUGUST

A year ago he'd climbed into his ancient Mustang, packed with as little as he could get away with, and started heading east. He'd had no business driving a car that night. Not a recollection he was proud of. Saratoga was as good a distraction as any.

They'd left before dawn, because Geai insisted they get there to see Liv ride in the first race. The playlist was carefully chosen to exclude anything that would stir the wrong memories, the timing of Eve 6's *Open Road Song* perfect, hitting the speakers as Nate accelerated onto the New York State Thruway. He started belting out the lyrics. Geai was a good sport about the music, though he'd spare the old man the Cursive and Three Days Grace that had featured prominently in his escape last summer.

"Is this song personal, Mr. Miller?" Geai yelled over the volume.

Nate threw Geai a grin, but only said, "It's the perfect road trip song," when it was almost as if it had been written for him. He could have looped it for the whole drive.

In just under four hours, they left the Thruway at Amsterdam. Forty-five minutes later, there it was: *Saratoga Springs*.

Geai complained about the sweltering heat as he and Nate walked toward the legendary racetrack—the closest lots were full, so they'd had to park on one of the sidestreets. Nate didn't mind, sauntering past stately old homes under towering trees before he recognized the sales grounds and pavilion, Saratoga's famous "Oklahoma" training track across the road, and the rustic barns beyond it. Geai left him behind. The old man couldn't disguise the excited glint in his eyes, the energetic swing in his step. Nate jogged to catch up before they crossed Union Avenue.

"I'm going to grab a program," he said once they were through the gates.

"They're just leaving the paddock." Geai didn't wait for him, swallowed up by the crowd.

Nate dodged bodies to catch up again. They passed tents of vendors—photographers and artists and fancy hats—before Geai led him through the grandstand, the smell of fresh pizza wafting from a concession stand. When they emerged at the trackside apron, Nate stopped and turned, bombarded by the history here.

"Why are you standing there?" Geai huffed, mopping sweat from his brow with a kerchief.

The old man pushed up to the chain link that kept the spectators from the outer rail, staring down towards where the green-coated outrider led the procession of horses onto the track. Before Nate could pick out Liv from her colours and program number, Geai had spotted her, dark hair braided down her straight back, focus absolute.

The horses warmed up off the other way, headed to the gate over in the chute. When the field came down the stretch minutes later, riders yelling and whips popping, Liv's horse was one of those struggling at the back of the pack. She probably rode a lot like that, though she'd won a couple of races at this meet, her tally resting at four. One more win and she'd be done with the ten-pound allowance. It put a whole new spin on the meaning of hungry.

Geai elbowed him and set off again. "We'll catch her coming back."

"Maybe I can get her autograph."

"Don't make fun."

"How do you know I'm not serious?"

Geai might've been stocky, but he nimbly darted around people with the single-mindedness of a forward intent on scoring a game-winning goal. They easily beat the jockeys back to the room.

Liv approached amid the bobbing helmets, aloof and businesslike—head down, stick under her arm, the goggles around her neck encrusted with dirt. When she finally glanced up, her eyes popped. She sprinted, launching herself at Geai, and clung to him like a homesick kid seeing her dad after a week at camp.

Liv grinned at Nate over Geai's shoulder, her cheeks flushed. "Hey, Miller!"

That smile wasn't meant for him, not at all, but it knocked him sideways. He pulled his eyes away and pushed his chin out, indicating behind her. "I think you've got another fan waiting."

Liv seemed almost as shy as the young girl as she accepted the pen and scribbled an autograph on the kid's program. The girl lit up as she took it back, holding both edges of the program and gazing at it, her father mouthing *thank you* as he ushered her away.

"Ah, my celebrity." Geai beamed.

"Hardly," Liv said, still looking unsettled by the girl's adoration. "I can't believe you made it for the first race. What time did you leave?"

"Dark o'clock." Nate elbowed Geai. "No traffic at the border, anyway."

"I can't believe you're actually here." She squeezed the old man again. "Gotta go."

Who was that? Definitely not a version of Liv Lachance he'd ever met; almost like a normal girl. She disappeared, and Nate smirked at Geai.

"You almost look happy I dragged you here, kicking and screaming." He ducked as Geai flicked him in the head with the back of his fingers.

Liv had one more mount between now and the Adirondack Stakes, in which she and Claire would make their stake debut. Her other mount looked like it had no chance.

"Must get pretty disheartening, riding all those longshots," Nate commented when they watched the horses load, the gate set up in front of them.

"It's horse racing. As long as you remember anything can happen, there's hope."

Especially in a maiden claimer. Liv's mount blasted out and assumed the lead. She was still on top when they came down the stretch, Geai rattling the chain link with both hands, screaming so loud Nate dissolved into laughter as Liv brought the 30-1 shot home first by five lengths.

"You're not allowed to leave!" Liv skipped up to them after she'd posed for the win photo and weighed in, pressing a finger to Geai's chest. She threw her arms around him and gave him a quick kiss on the cheek, then bounced to Nate and hugged him too before she realized what she was doing.

He caught her, hands on her impressively solid biceps, the body protector under her silks hard against him. *Put down the boss's daughter, Miller.* She pushed herself back looking mortified.

"Can I get you a slice of pizza?" He gave her a twisted grin.

"Ohmygosh, I could have pizza." Liv laughed. "Claire first."

LIV CHECKED HERSELF; checked Claire, reeling in the filly's enthusiastic gallop. Don had said it was okay to warm her up away from the pony, but getting run off with would be bad. She was still riding the high from the win—had she really hugged Nate? Thank goodness it had only been Geai there. The look on Nate's face, though.

There was no weight allowance for an apprentice in stake races, so she rode on equal terms with the journeymen. She probably could have eaten a whole pizza and still made weight.

They loaded into the gate, six and a half furlongs from the wire. Liv laced her fingers through Claire's mane, every muscle poised on the brink —Claire's too—every nerve under control, her focus unwavering between Claire's rigid ears.

Claire bounded out perfectly, but Liv sat back, convincing her to let the speed go. Claire's ears flickered, listening, and she settled into a big loping stride that carried her easily along the backstretch. The front-running grey started opening up on the turn, and Liv had a flash of indecision. Claire was on the bridle, pulling, asking. *No, just wait…*

They closed the gap as the field thundered into the stretch, Liv sighting the clear path before them. Claire took aim, wearing down the grey's lead until she drew even. But the grey eyeballed her, digging in, and fought back. Liv stopped herself from screaming as they blazed under the wire, beaten a head. Damn it! *Damn, damn, damn.*

She gritted her teeth. She should have moved sooner. She tried to talk herself down as they galloped out.

Placing in a stake earned Claire coveted black type designation, and in a Grade Two contest no less. This is where she belonged—she'd shown that today, and the way she'd come flying at the end, they'd just have to look forward to the longer fall championship races back at Belmont. And maybe…just maybe…did she dare think it? The Breeders' Cup.

When she got back to the barn, Geai was talking to Don, dwarfed by the trainer's commanding physique. Geai broke away, throwing his arms wide when he saw her. Nate stood off to the side with his hands jammed in the pockets of his chinos, watching.

"Ah, see? That was…*fantastique."* Geai pulled her close.

"I really wanted to win."

"So win next time."

"Black type for the big filly." Nate offered his hand, then recoiled as she gripped it. "Holy shit! Careful, I can't get hurt on vacation."

Kenny would be proud, Liv thought with satisfaction as he rubbed his fingers.

"You look nice, by the way," Nate said. "But that dress doesn't go with the handshake."

It was the same outfit she'd worn to the Plate, and definitely not out of place at Saratoga, but she had to stop herself from pulling at the hem of the skirt, having him notice her appearance. Instead, she swept the hair from her face with a sly smile. "That's the whole idea. The element of surprise."

When Claire returned from the test barn, the hotwalker walked her a few more turns before taking her out to graze, the sound of her teeth tearing the grass easing away the remnants of Liv's disappointment. At the end of the day, all that mattered was that the filly came back healthy and happy.

Nate appeared at her elbow. "Geai's right, she ran a big race."

"You're a miracle-worker, Miller. I owe you."

His forehead wrinkled in confusion. "What are you talking about?"

"Geai hasn't ventured very far from the farm since his wife died five years ago. I don't know how you talked him into this."

He shrugged, looking back to Claire. "He misses you. That's a pretty strong motivator."

"Thank you." She fought a sentimental urge to hug him again, and might have, if she hadn't thrown herself at him like a freak earlier.

He pushed his hands deeper into his pockets, still not looking at her. "It was nothing."

Nothing? It was everything.

6

SEPTEMBER

Blush was like a kid with no friends. Once upon another September, Liv had been that kid, climbing on the school bus for her first day in a new high school after moving to Ontario. Faye had adopted her introvert self, much like Liv had now adopted Blush.

Liv didn't normally buy into the chestnut filly stereotype, but Blush made a good case for it. Sore shins had set the filly back and delayed her debut, but if she got her gate card today, there was a race for her next week. Liv had earned that call—not that anyone else wanted it. Blush was a quick little thing though, and her trainer Rod was practical, running his horses where they belonged. They might get lucky with her first time out.

The filly quivered beneath Liv from the tip of her fiery forelock to the tail skirting her hocks. Not that Liv didn't understand—being locked in that huge metal contraption went against the most valued of equine instincts. She scratched the filly's rock-hard trapezius, hoping to relax the drum-tight muscle. Liv had lost track of how many times they'd gate schooled. Almost every day since she'd returned to Belmont after the Saratoga meet.

"All right, baby girl. Let's do this." The assistant starter at Blush's head led her forward.

Blush walked into the stall next to her workmate like a pro, save for the trembling. The starter's assistant climbed onto the frame beside them, turning Blush's head slightly and rubbing her forehead. The filly's heart pounded through her ribcage.

"We got one more," called another gate crew guy behind them.

Blush's ears flicked back as her head tilted, and the assistant gently straightened her.

"Can we just get these two on their way, please?" Liv begged. Blush was being so good, she hated to push their luck. Sure enough, the filly started sinking. "Don't you dare," she hissed, shifting her weight and tapping lightly with her stick.

Mistake. Blush rocked forward and pitched her head, dragging the assistant down and leaving him hanging precariously from the frame before he hauled her back up. As soon as the filly scrambled to her feet, she threw herself left, unbalancing the assistant before exploding vertically with a panic-driven twist. Liv crouched, ready to bail. She dropped the lines and grabbed at the frame, but Blush was tipping over, and the momentum sent Liv out the back of the gate without a chance to push herself away.

She heard the snap as her arm struck the ground first and cursed herself for not better controlling her fall. Someone grabbed her as she crumbled to the dirt, dragging her away from the filly's thrashing hooves.

"You okay?"

Searing pain siphoned the breath from her lungs as she cradled the limb against her body, but she forced a nod, her smile coming off more like a grimace. Somehow Blush was free of the gate, clambering to her feet, the crew on top of the filly before she realized she was loose.

"Is she all right?" Liv asked through clenched teeth, staggering to her feet and trying to shake off the hand on her elbow, even though her head was swimming. "Athletic little bitch, isn't she?"

"You don't look so good. You better sit down."

The voice seemed suddenly remote, Liv's ears ringing, and her legs abruptly gave way. The elbow-holder softened her landing as she collapsed.

Unbelievable. Taken out by a chestnut filly.

Silence, and more silence. Liv wasn't about to break it. All she had in her head were self-defeating thoughts. Only six more hours of this, and they'd be home, the trees and water of the Adirondacks in upstate New York flashing past like a movie on fast forward.

"I know this is hard for you," her mother finally said from behind the wheel, because of course driving a stick shift with one arm in a cast was impossible. So much for independence.

Which part did Anne mean? The six-week sentence this injury had served Liv? The part where she'd left Claire on a path leading towards the Breeders' Cup, and champion two-year-old filly? Or just being faced with relying on her mother for basic things like driving her car and pulling back her hair?

"But please tell me you're done now, with this riding madness. Tell me you'll finish your degree. It's only mid-September, surely —"

Liv's bitter laugh cut her off. "Do you really think I'd let a fluky gate accident scare me away?"

Her mother sighed. "It's just such a waste, Olivia."

"How embarrassing for you, to have a *pinhead* for a daughter." She spat out the slur, immediately ashamed Anne could so quickly reduce her to a petulant teenager.

"When I was your age…"

Here we go. Liv braced herself for the life lessons speech.

"…there was a boy, before I met your father. A rider."

Liv's eyes shot from the window. Her mother's remained fixed on the highway, fingers tightening and releasing on the wheel.

Anne glanced at her. "He lost his life in a spill. My not wanting you to ride...it's not just about quitting vet school."

Liv's gaze dropped to her lap. "I'm sorry, Maman. Why didn't you tell me?"

"It seemed better to make an argument out of logic than fear—though I think any rational parent would be terrified. I had a hard enough time watching you do cross-country on a pony, let alone seeing you out there on the track on a racehorse."

The smile Liv suppressed seemed wrong given the gravity of the conversation, but the memory of her pony—who'd actually been a small firecracker of an off-track Thoroughbred—inspired nostalgia.

"And I know this..." Anne looked down at Liv's cast quickly. "It's not going to stop you. But it doesn't help. So if I don't watch you ride, now you know why."

"You don't need to dry it. It's just going back up in a ponytail." Liv glanced at the stylist, itching to let Faye have her turn so she could watch the replay of the Frizette Stakes again.

"Yes you do, because no, it's not," Faye interjected. "We're going for dinner, because at least you can eat now, right? Then to a club to pick up guys. Kidding, of course," she added before Liv even reacted.

"What happened to Hot Bug Boy?"

Faye waved her hand airily. "I got bored."

Hacking a few inches off her hair made it more manageable with her cast, but she probably should have just chopped it off. Her mother was still going to have to braid it or pull it back. Her wrist ached constantly, and her fingers didn't want to move like they should.

She escaped from the chair as soon as the stylist removed the cape, trading places with Faye, then tuned their conversation out while she hit play on the video.

Claire running like she should, eating up the mile at Belmont, winning her first stake race by two. Without her. Worse yet, with Ricky Acosta. Okay, Acosta rode a lot of horses for Don, and he was Kenny's other rider, and still leading the standings at Belmont. So yes, not a hard call to make, but really? It just stung all the more.

But she had to be happy for Claire. The filly deserved it. Deserved better than her, obviously.

"You're still thinking about that race, aren't you?" Faye said when they were settled at the restaurant.

Liv asked for water to Faye's wine. Maybe she should take up drinking, only she didn't really like the stuff.

"The universe has it out for me. You know my dad is seriously talking Breeders' Cup now? Claire paid her way with that win. I should have just stayed in school and let Acosta ride her from the start like my mom said.

Then I wouldn't know what an ass he is and be that much more pissed about it all." She stabbed a chip into the bowl of salsa.

Faye smirked and pushed the glass of wine towards her. "Want some?"

Liv took a sip, then shook her head as the alcohol burned at the back of her throat. Nope. Not happening.

"Guess we don't have to worry about you turning to the bottle to drown your woes," Faye quipped. She set the glass to the side as the server came with their food.

"What am I even going to do for six weeks? Roger won't let me go into the track to help until the ortho is sure I won't need surgery."

"Maybe we could actually hang out." Faye smirked. "Between the horses and your crazy school schedule, I feel like I've barely seen you since undergrad. Some best friend you are. Remember that first day you got on the bus?"

"And you adopted the poor French girl?" Liv grinned, then sighed. "Sorry."

"That's okay. When you're famous, you can hire me as your image consultant."

Famous. Liv wasn't sure she wanted to be famous; she just wanted to be respected. This need of hers to be successful was at odds with the attention that went along with it. She wouldn't have to worry about that for a while, at least.

"We're having cake, right?" Faye tilted her head, perfect eyebrows quirked.

"Hell yes." That much she was sure of.

7

OCTOBER

Few people called Liv—anyone who knew her learned to use text, or email, because she hated answering the phone—but she picked up on the first ring when she saw Don's name on the screen. *Three weeks until Breeders' Cup.*

"Claire's caught that virus that's going around," the trainer said without preamble. "She's pretty sick."

The tone of his voice scared her, his pause loaded.

"I've already talked to your father, and we're sending her to the clinic for treatment. You know the drill. Fluids. Anti-inflammatories."

"I'll come down." She couldn't leave Claire to fight on her own while a deadly infection attacked her immature immune system.

"She'll be in isolation, so you won't be able to see her. It'll be easier for both of you if you stay put. Trust me. All you can do is hope for the best."

And plan for the worst, Liv finished in her head.

8

NOVEMBER

Claire pushed out her nose, twisting her neck first one way, then the other, upper lip contorted in a full-fledged peppermint appeal. Her two stablemates looked on with interest, but Claire was stealing the show—which Liv videoed with her phone. She reached into her pocket for Claire's inspiration, and the filly quickly lipped the candy up, the affection in Liv's eyes reserved for the leggy bay.

Claire gave him away with a low rumble, and Nate started down the aisle so he didn't feel so conspicuous for watching.

"Nice to see you embracing my suggestion. Give me the phone, I'll get one of both of you."

Liv frowned and shoved the phone into her pocket. "I'm not as photogenic as Claire."

"I doubt that. Your fans want to see you too."

She looked away, but handed over the device, self-consciously tucking her dark hair behind an ear.

Claire was happy to provide an encore. Liv loosened up when the filly started her performance again, her smile so sweet and natural Nate forgot himself for a moment.

"Maybe it's that block to having your picture taken that's getting in the way of you winning races."

"That's pretty woo, Miller." She smirked as she took the phone back and posted the new—in his mind, improved—video.

At first she'd scoffed at his idea to use social media to keep herself out there while she was off, but if her posts were any indication, she was actually enjoying it. She really did need more pics of herself in there, though. Cute bug girl needed to work that.

"I'm starting to think you might be the life coach I so obviously need." Her lips went a little less smirk and a little more smile, and he would have enjoyed that so much more if her comment hadn't inadvertently stirred something else.

"I'm hardly qualified for that." The slight furrow of her brow indicated she hadn't missed his flat tone. He pushed aside morose thoughts. "How'd it go this morning?"

She pulled back the sleeve of her coat to reveal her atrophied left arm, freshly cast-free, and rubbed it, opening and closing her fingers. "Rehab next."

"Maybe you'll be ready to ride the last couple weeks of the Woodbine meet."

"Because that would be so much fun. Spoken like someone who's leaving for Florida soon."

"Not my fault you're not bringing Claire down till January."

Liv touched the filly's pink nose, then let Claire lick her palm. "That was one scary virus. We could have lost her. She's going to need the time to gain back some weight before she trains again."

He'd felt Liv struggle, being away from Claire while she was so sick. There had been a couple of days when the reports from the clinic in New York had been grave, before the filly had turned a corner.

Nate checked the time. "Still coming to Geai's to watch the Breeders' Cup?"

"Yeah." She looked wistfully back to the big bay filly. "A few months ago I thought there was a chance we'd be there."

"It was hard enough having her win the Frizette without you, right? Can you imagine what it would have been like if you had to watch someone else ride her at Santa Anita?"

"If you're trying to cheer me up, it's not working."

"Next year. Everything happens for a reason."

"Any thoughts on what that might be?"

"Building a social media following?" He flashed a crooked grin. "Good things come to those who wait."

"Who knew you were such a philosopher, Miller."

He zipped up his coat, motioning in the direction of the door. "Shall we?"

Liv looked up at him quickly, then back to Claire, like she was searching for assurance from the filly, but Claire just stretched her neck back out looking for more treats. Nate almost laughed at her indecision—it wasn't like he was asking her out on a date.

"I was just going to walk," she said, and he had to stop himself from saying, *you're cute when you're all self-conscious.*

"I can walk."

A little smile tugged at the corners of her mouth. "Fine."

It was fun to push her, make her uncomfortable, try to get a reaction. He jumped ahead to open the door, standing back with a sweep of his arm. She rolled her eyes as she went through, pulling up her hood.

The farm's tall maples had lost most of their foliage, looking like skeletons against the grey sky, the paddocks reduced to mossy green scrub, and a cold wind stirred dead leaves around their feet making him wish he'd grabbed a toque. He glanced at Liv, her face hidden behind her hood as she held it tight to her cheeks.

She was a fast walker, but he wasn't going to complain—it would get them there sooner. He really should have just taken the car, left her to her exercise obsession. But this was kind of nice. That's what he liked about Liv. She wasn't afraid of silence. And he could throw out comments that poked at his past and she just let them go, never probed. Probably thinking *I'll stay out of your head, Miller, if you stay out of mine.*

The weanlings lived outside—colts in one big paddock, fillies in another. And cold as it was, when Liv stopped at the fence of the fillies' field, he didn't complain about that, either. Chique, never one to shun visitors, led the inquisitive group of youngsters over.

"Watch this." He dug into his jacket pocket.

Chique dropped her whiskery nose to his palm, and picked up the mini English mint with careful lips. She seemed to suck on it for a moment before working it back to her molars, grinding, then lifted her muzzle to blow a hot minty breath in his face. He planted a kiss between her nostrils.

"Impressive," she said. "I don't think I've ever known a weanling to figure that out. Let's hope peppermint-eating precocity is an indicator of racing prowess."

Talk nerdy to me, baby. But he stopped himself from saying that, too.

Chique leaned into his fingers as he scrubbed under her wild mane, then torqued her neck to try and grab his sleeve. He'd caught Liv smiling out of the corner of his eye when he'd kissed the filly. *C'mon, you like me, just a little, admit it.*

Napoleon gave them the royal welcome when they arrived at Geai's. There had been many afternoons here since Liv had come back, watching the racing channel; many days where she'd played restless spectator with her broken limb as he and Geai worked with the yearlings.

He couldn't help the flirting, or the things that popped into his head, but he didn't have any illusions. The only reason Liv even tolerated him was because of Chique and Geai. And he wasn't looking for anything more. There was still the owner's daughter thing—and the scar tissue holding together his heart.

9

DECEMBER

Liv was getting claustrophobic. Her mother was running true to form, preparing the traditional Christmas Eve *réveillon*. Geai, Faye, and Faye's brother Dean were over to join the celebration. Too many people, even if they were good friends and family. Time to escape.

Everything lay dormant around the farm, from huge maples to expectant mares. Solitary. Peaceful. Soft flakes drifted from the sky, melting on her face when she peered up into the blackness. The apartment over the office barn was dark, Nate in Florida with the rest of the Woodbine crew. Liv and Claire would join them in just over a week. The van was booked for New Year's Eve. That would put an end to her calm. She slipped through the barn door, flicking on the lights.

Three faces surfaced hopefully from the stalls when she looked down the aisle, but first she unlocked the office. She smiled at the painting as she went to the desk, picking up a small pile of mail and flipping through it. Business envelopes that were probably flyers advertising Ontario stallions; Christmas cards from some of the other stud farms. One card was addressed to Nate—glancing at the return address, she saw it was from Calgary, last name Miller. Odd they didn't have his Florida address, but she could take it with her when she went next week. She placed the envelopes back on the desk, glanced at the painting again, and locked the door behind her.

The water buckets were half-empty, so she topped them up, and threw all three horses more hay. Claire ignored hers, her toe tap-tap-tapping the mat until Liv unwrapped one of the starlight mints she'd stuffed in her pocket at the house. Claire inhaled it.

"See you later, Amazon filly." The Nate-assigned moniker had slipped into her own vocabulary. One last glance at the white-lined eye, the wide blaze—a face that never failed to give her heart a surge—and Liv turned off the lights, returning to the crisp darkness.

The weanlings came in at night now so they didn't become completely feral. Liv could pick Chique's voice from the chorus of whinnies that greeted her, the throaty declaration contradicting the dark filly's diminutive stature. Chique's head shot over the stall door at the crinkling wrapper, and Liv placed the red and white mint on her palm. The filly swept it up confidently, thanks to Nate's training, but spat the disc onto the ground, looking offended as she worked her lips and tongue.

"Fair. You're not used to the fancy ones."

Chique snuffled in her ear, then nibbled on her toque. Liv stepped out of reach and snapped a picture, sending it to Nate. *Cheeky Little Bitch says Merry Christmas.*

She pushed the filly back gently to peek at her bucket and started topping up waters with the hose. The click of the door latch made her jump, and she froze, until she recognized Geai's familiar bulk, hands deep in the pockets of his parka, stomping snow from his heavy boots.

"It's too early for night check," he reprimanded.

She dragged the hose to the next stall. "Well, whoever is supposed to do it will just have an easier time."

"That would be me."

Just like Geai to volunteer for the task so everyone else could enjoy Christmas Eve uninterrupted. Only a skeleton crew was on tomorrow—no one had to work Christmas Day if they didn't want to. The colt in the stall grabbed hold of the hose, and Liv poked him below a nostril to keep the stream going into the bucket instead of soaking the bedding.

"Your mother's getting twitchy."

"You're saying I have to go back?"

He chuckled. "I think you'd better. Your friend Faye is kind of miffed too. They're joining forces."

"Might as well finish what I started."

Geai started doling out flakes.

She rolled up the hose once the buckets were full, then wandered back to Chique, stalling. Chique was quick to leave her hay, and Liv ran a finger over the velvet between the filly's nostrils.

"It kind of feels like the calm before the storm." She felt Geai beside her, but kept her eyes on Chique, making sure the filly's investigation of her gloves didn't turn into a nip. "I'm ready to get back to it, but…it feels like I'm starting over."

"You don't have to go through the ten-pound bug again."

She laughed. "Thank goodness for that. But more expectations this year, right? For me and Claire." She'd been so restless while she was off—too much time to feed her doubts, relegated to social media posts that left her feeling like a fake. "It was hard to take, getting hurt when it seemed everything was finally going well."

"If this is what you want to do, it's not going to be the last time."

Chique latched onto the fabric at her elbow, tugging. "At least I got to know this monster better. You have developed some seriously bad habits, cheeky one." She pushed her finger into the corner of Chique's mouth and the filly let go.

"You kids spoil her." But there was fondness in Geai's eyes. Chique got to him as much as any of them.

"And I got to spend more time with you. Thanks for putting up with my whining." She gave him a sheepish grin.

Geai pulled a small box from his pocket, and held it out. "Might as well give this to you now."

Liv looked up at him, accepting it, and held it for a moment before removing the red bow and wrapping. She lifted a delicate medallion on a fine chain from its bed of tissue paper, and laid it in her gloved palm to study it.

The face of the medallion was decorated with a miniature painting of a bay horse with markings just like Claire, a woman in a nun's habit pressing her forehead devotedly to the animal's. Her eyes crinkled as the corners of her mouth turned up.

"I hope that's not supposed to be me," she joked, feeling a tiny bit bad that was her first response to something so exquisite.

"Ste-Anne. Patroness of horseback riders, protector from storms."

Liv bit her lip. So perfectly appropriate. "You and your Catholic superstitions." She blinked back a tear, closing it in her hand, and hugged him tight.

"Also the patron saint of unmarried women."

He chuckled as she pushed him back and smacked him in the arm, a lump constricting her throat.

10

JANUARY

It was just past ten PM when Liv pulled into the sandy driveway of Payson Park—in the Middle of Nowhere, Florida. The grounds were still, enveloped in the dark closeness—all except Barn Six. Jo waited, standing by with a lead shank in hand while the transport driver finished setting up the ramp.

Liv climbed out of the car, yawned and stretched, and accepted the shank when Jo offered it. No lectures from Jo about having to act like a rider to be taken seriously. Claire looked as bleary-eyed as she felt herself. Liv kissed her pink nose, and the filly shook her head half-heartedly.

"Grumpy girl." She smiled, winding the chain around the halter's sheepskin-covered noseband.

Claire stepped down the jute-lined ramp with exaggerated caution, and Jo held her while Liv dropped to her knees in the deep straw of the stall to remove the protective bandages and bell boots. The big filly took a languid drink from the pail of fresh water hanging by the door, then dribbled over Jo's arm before rubbing her face on the assistant trainer's elbow.

"Lovely, Claire." Jo wiped her arm dry with the hem of her t-shirt. "Just leave the bandages on the rail, Liv. I'll take care of them. Sleep in tomorrow. We'll bath and walk her for you."

"Thanks." She was exhausted enough not to turn down that offer. Liv gave one last touch to Claire's fuzzy bay shoulder before ducking out of the stall.

Shadowy orange groves and scrubby fields whizzed by her Nissan's open window on the way into the town of Stuart, and Liv checked into the first reasonable hotel she found. She'd be staying with Roger and his wife Hélène, but didn't want to disturb them this late. First she threw herself under the shower, washing away two days of sweat and hay and dirt, then she collapsed into bed.

SHE COULDN'T REMEMBER the last time she'd slept late enough to see daylight, rolling out of bed at eight AM. After the heavy winter clothing she'd needed at home, it was liberating to put on shorts and a tank top. The gloriously stifling air hit her as she stepped outside, sun shining through the haze, asphalt in the parking lot steaming from an earlier rainfall.

The final horse to train was cooling out when she got to the Triple Stripe barn. She passed Jo the box of doughnuts and tray of coffees she'd picked up for the crew, the card that had been delivered to the farm for Nate tucked under her arm. Claire looked happy and relaxed as she pulled at her haynet, bathed and walked as promised.

"How's my girl?"

"Temp's normal, no problems." Jo glanced at Liv's bare legs, her mouth twisting as she started for the tack room. "You're a brave one, walking on the shed your first day in Florida wearing shorts. I think you're going to wish you hadn't."

What a ridiculous thought. Liv touched the bay filly's nose lightly in parting, and Claire tossed her head, spraying her with alfalfa leaves.

She heard Nate's voice before she saw him, unmistakable as he sang along to the radio. Bridles and martingales moved on their hook in the doorway, Jo brushing by with a mouthful of doughnut, coffee raised in appreciation as she headed back to her stalls.

Liv stopped short. "Have you been doing any work down here, Miller, or do you spend all your time at the beach?"

Even in the dimness of the tack room the brown of his muscled arms against his light turquoise golf shirt added a beat to her pulse. The blue eyes, the sun-bleached hair, the tanned beach body—she caught herself. A normal girl might fall for that. But this wasn't spring break. She was here to get her career back on course, and falling of any sort wasn't part of the plan.

"Hey, Liv! How was the drive?"

"Fine, thanks. Just don't stand too close to me till I have a chance to catch up, all right?" She held out the card. "This came before I left."

He scanned the return address, then tossed it to the side and went back to work. *Well, that wiped the cheery expression from his face.*

"Where's Rog?"

Nate glanced at the clock to his left—he wasn't wearing a watch. Heaven forbid he should have a tan line. "He's around here somewhere."

As if on cue, Roger walked up behind Liv and gave her a gentle squeeze. "Welcome to Payson. Weather warm enough for you?"

"Clearly you've been having plenty of it." She tilted her head towards Nate.

"Your filly made it in good order."

"She'll feel much better when I get her clipped out. Maybe once Mr. Florida here is done his tack he'll give me a hand."

Nate fished a second sponge from his bucket and tossed it directly at Liv. She deftly caught it to avoid getting soaked, scowling as she squeezed the excess water out onto the sandy shed.

"Just thought if you helped me finish, we'd get to the big filly sooner."

Liv conceded, taking the bar of glycerin from him. "Now I know where you get the time to lie on the beach. You pawn off your work on everyone else." She started on the saddles resting on the rail.

"It's called delegating." He flashed his ever-ready grin.

Nate was hanging the last of the bridles when she pushed past with the final saddle, pads piled on top, and hoisted it onto the rack. He adjusted the bridle just so on the nail, the browband straight and the lines hanging evenly. Sometimes the simple things seemed to make Liv happiest, and the line of clean bridles, glowing rich Australian nut brown, was one of them. She took down the tack hook as Nate dumped the water pail, and found the clippers and an extension cord. Nate followed her to Claire's stall with a shank over his shoulder.

"Might actually be too hot out here," he said when he led Claire to the grassy expanse beside the barn.

Liv ran the extension from the closest outlet. "How could it possibly be too hot?"

The blades hummed to life, the thick fuzz of Claire's winter coat soon dropping in clumps around the filly's white feet. Fine hair tickled Liv's face and arms, but she wasn't about to give Nate the satisfaction of hearing her complain. She drew an arm across her brow and sneezed.

"Having fun yet?" he asked.

"I love clipping."

"Sure you do." He scratched Claire's white forehead. "So how come you didn't have my girl Cheeky stowed away somewhere?"

She took a moment to clean the blades, his fondness for the little yearling making her smile. "Next year."

"She'll be so mad I missed her birthday."

Liv laughed, stepping away as Claire shuddered, shaking loose the latest rows. "Where did you learn how to do respiration on a foal, anyway?"

He hesitated, eyes dropping to where he tickled the sensitive skin between Claire's nostrils with the end of the shank. Claire's lips flapped, trying to grab it.

"The trainer I worked for in Calgary had a few mares, and I did some nightwatching for him. One of them had a red bag delivery. Foal needed a bit of help when it came out, so Al taught me. Al was kind of my Geai."

"I'm surprised you didn't mention that, seeing you went to the trouble of putting together a resumé."

"Wasn't really relevant for breaking yearlings, was it?" He passed the loop of leather into his left hand, and brushed Claire's forelock to the side with his fingers. "Couldn't talk Geai into another road trip, eh?"

The abrupt change of both the subject and his manner was suspect, but she let it go. She didn't like it when people probed her, either. "That's your superpower, Miller. Maybe you could work on it. He has another month or so before breeding season starts."

She finished Claire's body, and exchanged large clippers for small, moving up beside Nate to do the filly's head. Sweat soaked through her tank top, clinging as she reached for one of Claire's ears to trim the protruding wisps.

"You know you're going to end up with a sunburn from this, right?"

Liv blew the hair out from the blades, not quite in his face, before continuing. He seemed aggravatingly acclimatized to the heat, considering he'd galloped the barn, while she was a disgusting, sweaty, mess. "I'm accepting the consequences of my choice, Miller. Unless you want to finish the job for me."

"I'd just wreck it, and Claire would be all embarrassed. We can't have that, can we?" He tickled the filly's nose again. Claire snorted. "You're almost done anyway."

Claire shook from head to haunches when Liv stood back to assess her work. "You're a pale girl now, Amazon filly."

"Don't you worry, Claire, in a couple of weeks no one will know you haven't been here since November like the rest of us." Nate slid Liv a sly smile.

She gave him a tired look, then fished her phone from her back pocket, composing a shot. "Thanks, Miller, you can put her away."

She glanced at the photo before writing the caption. Unlike her, the camera loved both of them. *Hey, pretty...*Mr. Florida would definitely help the post's engagement.

Liv followed him into the tack room as he hung the shank with the others. That card still rested where he'd tossed it.

"Not going to open that?" she couldn't help asking.

He glanced over his shoulder. "It's just a card."

Liv shrugged and leaned back against the doorframe. "Kenny's on me to get back riding again."

"That's good, right?"

"Well...yeah. Because I'll still have my apprentice allowance for most of the year, he thinks I have a shot at an Eclipse award. I think he might be dreaming. But either way...Claire."

Spending the better part of twenty-eight hours in the car had given her time to think, to accept reality—she couldn't be two places at once.

"I'm sure someone would have a stall at Gulfstream for her."

"I know...but she's better off here. I was jogging her back home, so she's ready to start galloping, but after being so sick last fall, we should really take our time bringing her back." She hesitated, hating that Gulfstream Park, where she'd be riding, was an hour and a half away. "You're going to have to get on her for me."

His eyebrow quirked, not hiding his surprise, and it reinforced her guilt, that she was abandoning Claire for her own career. Sure, like he said, they could get a stall for her at Gulfstream, but at Payson Claire could be turned out. She could go for hacks, she could gallop on the turf… there were so many alternatives to training on the track.

He recovered, the grin surfacing. "Is that supposed to be a hardship?"

"It's an extra horse."

"What's one more? I'll manage. Maybe not get to the beach as early. Too much sun isn't good for you anyway, right?" He sobered. "You know I'll take good care of her."

"It won't be right away. I'll gallop here for a couple of weeks to get back into shape." She found Nate's eyes. "I seem to be entrusting you with the things that matter most to me. Don't screw up, Miller."

He shifted uneasily, forcing a laugh. "No pressure."

It wasn't a big ask, not really. And maybe for the best, given how she wondered if Claire was actually better off without her. But it felt significant, somehow. Like she'd shared with him another part she'd always kept to herself.

11

FEBRUARY

Her old friend Blush minced around Gulfstream's paddock, washed out and showing the whites of her eyes as Liv tried to find something nice to say about her. Rod was one of the Belmont trainers who wintered at Palm Meadows, about an hour north. He seemed unexpectedly excited to have Liv back in the picture, quick to agree to a reunion with the filly to give Liv her first Florida ride. Blush's past performance was uninspiring—a few short lines summarizing lacklustre maiden claiming attempts at Aqueduct last fall when Liv had been off.

"See what you can do." Rod threw her up, with no other instructions. The groom led them out of the paddock, Blush's neck a dark sheen of sweat.

"Hey, little girl, sure you can handle that horse?"

"I never bet girl jocks. Girls don't belong on the racetrack."

She was used to blocking out hecklers, but Liv recognized the voices, and looked, breaking her other rule by responding. "Well, if it isn't Triple Stripe's dynamic duo."

"Your horse have a shot in here, Lachance?" Nate said behind sunglasses, sun-bleached hair falling over his forehead, grin reliably in place.

"Sure, she's got a shot. A 50-1 shot!" Michel elbowed him and started laughing as they followed along behind the spectators lining the rail.

"Good luck," Nate called after her.

She was afraid there would be nothing left of Blush by the time they made it to the gate. The starter's assistant loaded her, and Liv pushed aside the flashback of that moment at Belmont last fall, channeling confidence to counter the filly's nerves. The doors crashed open, and Blush fired away like she was being chased by zombies.

Blush started to relax once they were away from the scary metal barrier, letting Liv park her behind the leaders and on the outside where the claustrophobic filly wouldn't stress. She pulled around the turn, passing one of the fading pacesetters, and Liv started to think they might get a piece.

Okay...let's see what you've got. She picked Blush up and chirped, keeping her stick quiet because she remembered all too well what the filly thought of the whip. Ears flickering forward as she changed leads in the lane, Blush romped past the field, and galloped home in front by two lengths—much to Liv's own shock, not to mention that of most of the grandstand, she was sure.

The groom was all smiles when he met them, chattering excitedly in Spanish. Liv heard Nate's whoop, and found the guys in the crowd just as Michel let the torn pieces of a losing ticket fall from his hand.

"Those your friends?" Rod waved them into the winner's circle before Liv could answer.

She dismounted after the photo was taken, Rod patting her on the back as she scrubbed Blush on the neck. Her valet took her tack, and she overheard Rod talking to the guys.

"Maybe you'd better come next time she runs. You're good luck."

"Naw, you just had a good rider," Nate said. "Here, take our picture." He passed the phone to Rod and pulled Liv over.

"Oh come on, Miller," she protested.

"Just be a sport and smile." He wedged her between himself and Michel. "I'll send it to you so you can share it with your followers."

"I'll get right on that."

"You've been a little slack since you started trying to be three places at the same time. Sign this for me?" He just laughed when she made a face. "I don't want your autograph, it's a model release."

That earned him a smirk and a shove. "Why are you guys bothering me? You should be trying to pick up paddock girls."

"She has a point, Miller," Michel said.

"We're paddock guys," Nate said. "It's new."

She shook her head and headed for the scales.

"Are you done for the day?" Nate asked after she'd weighed in. "We should grab a bite before heading back."

Liv stopped, frowning as she looked from Nate to Michel. They had come all the way from Payson for her return to the races. "Maybe something quick."

She suggested somewhere off the track complex, quiet and casual, where they could be in and out in a reasonable time. The guys beat her there, securing a booth, and she looked from Nate to Michel, deciding sitting next to Nate was the better option.

Michel scanned the menu. "Nate's buying. He cashed a ticket on that."

"Did you really?" She wished there was just a little more room, feeling a swell of awareness faced with sitting so close. "I'm not sure I would have bet her."

"Fifty to one? That was worth a couple of bucks." Nate glanced up as the server placed glasses of water on the table. "Thanks."

The server's expression transformed from boredom to attentiveness as she looked from Nate to Michel. *Yes, they're both good-looking, you're right. Careful, you're drooling.*

"Are you ready to order?" Her fresh smile bypassed Liv.

Nate lifted his arm from the table and dropped it on Liv's shoulders like it was the most natural thing in the world, leaning in. "Know what you want, hon?"

She sat straighter and shot him a look—if she thought he'd been close before, well, this was a definite invasion of personal space. The server's eyebrows all but knitted together as she sized Liv up. It was worth going along with it just for that, except that the bump in her pulse was sending blood rushing to places she didn't care to acknowledge, and every last one of her nerve endings was on fire.

"I'll have the garden salad, thanks. Dressing on the side?" She handed over her menu with her sweetest fake smile, and got an eye roll so hard back she thought the girl's head would fall off her shoulders. It didn't, her perkiness rebooted as she turned to Michel.

When she sashayed away, Nate started laughing, his arm falling back to his side where it belonged. "Don't think she's one of your fans."

"Hon?" Liv glared.

"Too much? I was just helping Mike out. Removing myself from her options."

"And here all I ordered was a salad," she said dryly.

"You think I need your help, Miller?" Michel glowered at him, putting down his phone. Michel would probably be trying to get the server's number before they were done.

Nate grabbed for the cheque as soon as it came, Liv poking him. "You don't really have to pay."

He kept it out of her reach. "I don't mind. I probably made more than you did for riding her."

"How much did you bet?"

Nate smirked, throwing some bills on the table and crowding her so she'd get up. "Let's go."

She waved as they parted ways in the parking lot, then checked her messages before starting the car, the screen of her phone littered with congratulatory texts for the win. The last one was from Faye.

Nice win. Cute date.

Liv: *??*

Faye: *Check IG.*

Liv opened the app—Michel had tagged her in a post. Three photos: coming into the winner's circle on Blush, the one Rod had taken of the three of them, and another Michel had snapped in the restaurant, of course at that exact moment Nate had put his arm around her.

It was like looking at someone else, a little bit of fiction; the looks on their faces easily misconstrued, if someone didn't know better. Because he was cute, and she'd had fun, and if she'd thought any of it had been real, that never would have happened. As fictional dates went though...she could do worse.

You know you're jealous, she typed back, wondering what it would be like to be that girl.

12

MARCH

"Nate! You're breezing Claire this morning."

He stopped in his tracks, looking up the shed to where Roger appeared from the murky darkness outside the barn.

"What happened to Liv?"

"There's one Kenny says she has to work at Gulfstream this morning. She was gone before I got up."

*Kenny says jump...*but that was the life of a bug rider. She knew she'd be on Claire no matter what when the filly made it back to the races, so it was a no-brainer to skip out and leave Nate to get on her… even if it would kill her control-freak self. She'd never missed a breeze on the filly down here, always taking that one day a week to be at Payson.

"We'll get a couple of sets out first, let it get light. She'll go at seven. Maybe the bloody fog will have lifted by then," Roger said. Not that the horses really went out in sets when Liv wasn't here. Nate got on all ten of them, one by one.

It wasn't like getting on Claire made him feel exceptionally skilled. Claire was easy. Claire could go alone, or in company. She could hack out by herself without drama. Hell, he was pretty sure he could do mounted archery on her and shoot some of those wild boar out in Payson's back forty, if that legend was true. It was Geai's words getting in his head that complicated it all. *Don't take her loyalty lightly.*

Jo had Claire ready to go when he got back on the second horse. She took the filly a turn, and legged him up.

Even at the walk Claire had a smooth, fluid swing to her step. Saying she was the best horse he'd ever been on wasn't a stretch—while Roger had some nice ones, none of them were Grade One stake winners. He pulled his phone from his pocket, shooting a few seconds of the steady pulse of her head, the relaxed flop of her ears. He was more of a lurker when it came to social media, but this was noteworthy.

Up where the air is rarefied. #movingup #bigfilly #leclaircie #oakscontender

"Head out next turn," Roger called.

Horses appeared eerily from the mist like wraiths as they walked to the track, the usual sounds of the comings and goings dampened and distorted. It almost had a sedative effect—or maybe it was the rhythm of Claire's walk lulling him.

"I don't even know why I'm coming out," Roger muttered. "I'm not going to be able to see a damn thing."

"Because you'd drive them crazy back at the barn?" Nate suggested as they reached the on-gap.

"Don't get lost out there."

He backed up, Claire jogging smoothly until he turned her in on the backstretch, pausing to pull down his goggles before setting off counter-clockwise. She galloped like a pony, all the way around, but when he dropped her to the rail, the switch flipped.

He crouched over the lick of her black mane, content to be a passenger as she made the turn perfectly and switched leads automatically at the head of the lane. Cutting through the mist just made it more exhilarating, adding an element of danger because of the near-zero visibility—whizzing past the gallopers in the middle of the track, not knowing if there was a worker on the flight path in front of them. They swept under the wire, and he let her roll around the clubhouse turn galloping out, finally easing her on the backside.

Roger waited near the off-gap. "How'd she go? No surprise, I didn't see a damn thing."

"Wow."

"I'll take that as good."

"When does she run?"

"Florida Derby Day. First Saturday in April. She'll ship to Gulfstream for the next couple of works so she can go over the track."

Liv wouldn't have to worry about anything getting in the way of her being aboard for those final trials.

"Then it's back to Don at Belmont." Roger looked a little rueful.

"So unfair," Nate said, sharing the sentiment.

Once he finished cleaning and putting away the tack at the end of the morning, he stood in the doorway looking out as he dialed Liv. The fog had finally burned away, leaving behind steamy humidity.

She picked up immediately. "Is everything all right?"

He always texted, so he could see how a call might spook her. "Sorry, just thought you'd want to know how she went."

"Of course." The breath she released was audible. "I hear it was so foggy they didn't get a time."

"Well the clock in my head," he paused for effect, "caught her in fifty-nine and two."

She laughed quietly. "She's something, isn't she?"

"She's perfection."

"Thanks, Miller."

"Again, it was no hardship."

He disconnected and jammed the phone in his back pocket. The burn of his ambition amped up a few degrees. What was he doing, playing understudy when he could be out there riding races too? He'd told himself he was just buying time while he silenced the doubt in his head, but now it felt like he was just wasting it.

That envelope from his brother and sister-in-law was still jammed on the shelf where he'd left it two months ago, addressed in his brother's handwriting, no less. Like a stupid Christmas card could make everything right, when nothing could erase what Phil had done. He grabbed it, ripped it in half, and stuffed the pieces in the garbage. Moving up? *Moving on.*

13

APRIL

Paz gawked at the horrendous Pegasus statue as they jogged around the turn at Gulfstream Park. It wasn't anywhere close to them, but its sheer size made its presence inescapable, even though Liv had learned to block it out. Paz seemed convinced it was a Trojan horse, housing an army of goblins about to be set loose on the field of unsuspecting Thoroughbreds. Said Thoroughbreds, with the exception of Paz, remained unsuspecting.

"Stop being an embarrassment and do your job, old man." Nate dug his heel into the gelding to keep him from bumping into Claire. "I wonder who thought that was a good idea."

"I have no clue." Liv sat quietly, Claire snorting her disgust at the pony's performance—or maybe at the fact anyone deemed it necessary for her to have an escort postward in the first place. "Not that I've seen anyone but Paz react like that."

"He's just expressing what the rest of us wish we could."

Paz regained his composure once they were behind the gate, set in front of the grandstand for the Gulfstream Park Oaks. Liv pulled her goggles down as they milled with the other eight starters, waiting to be loaded.

"She's favourite," Nate noted.

Liv averted her eyes from the odds board. She didn't want to know; didn't want the pressure.

"Good luck. You got this." Nate waited for a fist bump before he relinquished them to the starter's assistant.

The bell ringing in her ears as the doors crashed open, the roar rising from the Florida Derby Day crowd—none of it rattled Claire. Liv asked her to relax, conserve, and Claire complied. Let the speed horses do their job, and set things up for the big filly's usual move in the stretch.

The leader was trying to run away with it as they turned for home, and Claire took aim, wearing the other filly down steadily with each stride. Liv unpacked her stick, putting it to work. One, two, smacks on her quarters, then back to the hands, pushing, imploring, but not getting the explosive kick she'd expected. Another burst with her stick—*just a little more, and we'll have her.*

Only just. *Would it kill you to win by more than a whisker?* But she slapped Claire's neck heartily, blowing out a big exhale of relief.

Nate should have been in the picture with them. He probably deserved more credit for this win than she did—galloping Claire day in, day out at Payson. There was that familiar guilt. She was just the rider, the one who worked the horse a time or two, then got all the glory on race day.

"See you back at the barn," Roger said after she'd weighed in, abandoning her to the little following of girls collected on the apron pushing programs and pens at her.

She scribbled her name, one program after another, the other riders back in the room by now. At least she was done for the day.

"Can we get a picture with you?" one girl asked, a woman—probably her mother—at the ready with phone poised.

Liv nodded, mustering a smile as they clustered around her—the up-and-coming, good-for-racing girl jockey—even if that role grated on her, and she just wanted to get back to check on Claire.

"How is she?" Liv ducked into the barn and cut to the inside, looking all cooled out herself in a sleeveless sundress, her hair pulled neatly back, a chain with a small pendant drawing Nate's eyes to her neck. "Great." He pulled Claire away from the haynet hanging from the rail and raised his free hand. "First stake win!"

She slapped it, though it seemed a little half-hearted. "For me, anyway. Couldn't have done it without you."

"I'll come to New York and gallop her for you if you want."

"Tempting."

She needed to not give him that kind of smile, saying something like that. It might make him forget they were just talking about Claire.

"Put her in, Nate," Jo said. "If we head back as soon as she's done up, we might beat the traffic out of here."

"I'll give you a hand." He snapped the stall guard in place and tied Claire in the doorway. She attacked the haynet as soon as he looped the rope through an eye hook, burrowing her muzzle into the nest and fiercely pulling out a mouthful before he even tied it off.

"No, I will," Liv intercepted.

He glanced at her dress and shoes. "I don't mind."

"Once I get back to Belmont, Jeanne won't let me touch her, so I'm going to do this while I can. I owe it to her after a landmark win like that, don't you think? Especially the way I've passed her off on you all winter."

"Here I thought I was helping you out, when really all this time you felt bad for Claire."

She smirked before ducking into the stall.

Roger pulled the truck and trailer up, and Nate helped him load Paz and the traps while Jo and Liv finished with Claire. At least Liv deferred to Jo when it came time to put Claire on the van.

Roger checked the doors were secure, and turned to Nate. "Jo and I can take them home if you want to stick around and watch the Florida Derby."

"You're assuming Liv will drive me back."

"You're not the worst company." She looked at him sideways with traces of that smile. She needed to stop.

He felt awkward for a moment after the rig eased out of the backstretch. "Guess we should get over there, then."

Liv hesitated, checking the time. "Do you really have your heart set on it? I think I'd rather beat the traffic out of here myself."

"So you were just trying to get me alone in your car, weren't you?"

She rolled her eyes and started walking to the little black Nissan. "My exact plan."

"I can drive if you're tired."

"I'm okay."

Of course she was. He let himself in when she unlocked the doors.

She started the engine, and Poe's *Control* blasted from the speakers before her hand snapped out to kill the volume.

He had to chuckle. "Your theme song?"

"Don't judge."

"I'm not. It's perfect. I sure as hell wouldn't mess with you."

She parried his grin with a smirk and a subtle shake of her head.

He kept watching her while she navigated out of Gulfstream's backside. "You should be happy with today. Why aren't you happier?"

Her lips pressed into a line, and she gripped the steering wheel a little tighter as they headed for the interstate. "I am happy. It's just...she didn't do it easily, you know?"

"She's been off since October. Sure she's been training great, but maybe she needed the race. She still got there. They don't give you extra money if you win by open lengths."

"I sound ungrateful, don't I?"

"You're just worried about her, I get it."

Her eyes darted over, and she sighed. "I wish she had another race before the Oaks. I'd feel a lot better."

"You're not one of those people who can just enjoy the moment, are you? She needed the time; you gave her the time."

"And Don is good at training horses up to races."

"See?" He reached for the stereo and started advancing tracks, laughing when he heard the opening of Panic! At the Disco's *Victorious*. "There's the song you need."

Her eyes flickered from the road, to him, and back again, probably totally regretting agreeing to drive him home as he sang along, right to the end—but she didn't interrupt him.

"I admit I'm jealous." He turned down the volume as the next song started. "You're going to ride in the freaking Kentucky Oaks."

"No one's stopping you from getting your license."

He stared out the window, the ocean-side sky a deep indigo as the sun went down in the west, figuring out how to answer that.

"Me coming out here created a big stink. Like my dad and I? We don't talk anymore. That kind of stink. So I have to do this right. I have to do well. I can't go back. The thought of him saying I told you so…I'd rather live in a dorm room and walk hots for the rest of my life." If only it were that simple. Like why was it that the thought of actually succeeding held him back more than the prospect of failure?

"So you want to skip the part where it took me two months to lose my triple bug?"

"Do you regret it? Wish you were back at school stressing over exams instead of stressing over riding Claire in the Oaks?"

"Not a chance. Just do it, Miller. Though barring any broken bones or tragedies, I don't expect to be back this fall, so someone's going to have to start Chique."

"Oh sure, I'll put my career on hold to break her, then you can come back and win the Plate with her."

"I didn't mean—"

"That's okay, I'd do that for you." He cut her off, letting her feel bad for a moment. "You think I'd let anyone else do that job?"

"It is only fair." Liv looked relieved, grinning back. "She is what she is because of you, after all."

Emilie's head popped around the corner of the tack room at Woodbine and she beamed, scurrying over and swinging up on the counter beside him. Her Blundstones knocked the cupboard doors and she pushed a piece of her dark hair behind an ear, leaning into him as she glanced over his shoulder at *The Form* spread on his lap.

"Have I told you what a great tan you have?"

Nate lifted his head. "I'm pretty sure it's faded since the last time you did."

"And you really didn't find yourself a girlfriend down there?"

"You know I'm waiting for you, Em."

Emilie patted his leg. "Sure you are."

Em was just as bright as her sister, just more emotionally balanced. He couldn't remember exactly what she was taking. Environmental Toxicology; something relevant and virtuous like that.

Roger strode past the doorway. "Okay, Nate, let's go. Dave's here."

Dave Johnson was the perennial leading rider at Woodbine, and rode the majority of the Triple Stripe horses when they ran in Ontario. He could ride, no question, but the guy rubbed Nate the wrong way—too arrogant, too entitled. Maybe that wasn't a good enough reason not to like him, but it added fuel to Nate's building fire of determination. He'd knock Johnson off his pedestal. *One day.*

Nate grabbed Emilie's arm. "Toss me up?"

"Of course." She followed him out and legged him up on a maiden three-year-old named Sans Défaut.

The sun fought to get through a filter of clouds on the walk to the main track, and he shivered, willing it to break free. It was a morning-long cycle. Work up a sweat on the track, come back to the barn and get chilled waiting for his next horse. He blew on one of his black-gloved hands to test if he could still see his breath.

"It's a lot warmer now the sun's up," Roger said.

"What sun?" Nate grumbled. "Next year, we don't come back so early, all right?"

"It's the middle of April, Nate."

"What's the matter, Miller? Not as cozy here as it was at Payson?" Dave Johnson leaned forward, so Nate couldn't miss his sly grin from the other side of Roger.

"You heard I got to spend some quality time with the Oaks filly, did you?" Claire, who was on her way to Louisville soon, while he waited for spring to decide to show up in Southern Ontario.

"Pretty sure if Liv got hurt again, you wouldn't be the one getting the call."

Nate didn't allow himself as much as a foul look—he wasn't giving Johnson the satisfaction. Besides, he deserved the digs, him and his so-called patience, telling Liv he'd break Chique, like the brownie points it might earn him would ever mean anything. It helped, though, when his colt out-worked Johnson's—Claude's Plate hopeful, Excursion. He contained the rush he felt and kept his mouth shut as they galloped out.

"You're gonna have to learn not to take life so seriously, Miller," Johnson called over as they pulled the colts up.

"I was just having fun out there, Dave. What the hell were you doing?"

Back at the barn, Nate pulled off the tack, leaving Sans Défaut to Michel and the hotwalker with a pat. "He'll be all right, this colt, you watch."

He ducked into the tack room to grab one of the coffees Claude had brought—lukewarm now, but he sucked it back anyway. Emilie popped in behind him.

"Nice move, Nate. Kicked Johnson's ass, didn't you?"

"I keep telling everyone what a nice colt that is."

"Well, *cher Papa* was a little shook up his Plate horse got beat, but he was still impressed. That might convince him to keep Sans Défaut eligible. Maybe if you got your butt in gear you'd get to ride him."

"Next year, Em. Going to start doing some freelancing once you're here every day to pick up the slack." Made sense, right?

"I see." Emilie peeked around the doorframe, looking down the shedrow. "Guess I have to go. Can't miss my first class now, can I?"

"One of you girls better stay in school." Nate grinned, and watched her go.

It wouldn't happen, even if he pulled himself together and got his license in time. If both colts ended up in the Plate this year, Johnson would be on one, and Liv would come back and ride the other. Liv would jump on the chance to ride in the big race if one came before Chique—while he found yet another excuse to stagnate.

14

MAY

Thurby, they called it, all part of the insanity that was Derby Week in Louisville. For Liv, it was the day before the biggest race of her not-yet-year-old career. Claire would school in the paddock with the Derby and Oaks contenders, and Liv would ride a couple of races at Churchill Downs to get a feel for the track. She didn't expect much from either of the mounts Kenny had found her, but maybe it would help settle her nerves. They weren't here for the Derby, but the twin spires still presided, passing judgement with the ghosts that haunted them.

It felt odd to have just one horse to get on in the morning—after galloping Claire under those spires as the sun came up, she had nowhere to be until she checked into the jock's room. So she got there early, changed into running gear, jammed in her ear buds, and found a treadmill.

And ran, maxing out the volume for some Poe to chase away the stress, going harder and faster until calm overtook her. When she finally slowed, saturated with sweat, she laughed at the looks she'd been blocking out…taking control. Nate was right. It was the perfect theme song.

Her first mount lived up to expectations, finishing nowhere, but the next one surprised her with some grit. Tucked behind the front-runners on the rail, a hole opened up. Liv went to the whip, but instead of the strike propelling the filly forward, she ducked in, bouncing off the rail and slamming into their neighbor, legs entangling. Liv grabbed mane as her filly scrambled, but the momentum was too much. She let go and tucked her arms in, tumbling, and the smack of her helmet sent her to blackness.

When she came to, the ambulance was just pulling up, and her horse was nowhere to be seen. She clutched the rail while her head cleared, and assessed body parts. All in working order.

The ambulance gave her a ride back, and she walked through the room with a silly smile. No one was blaming her for her mount's overreaction, and no one else had suffered as a result of it. The outrider had caught the loose filly, unscathed. Relief on all counts. The doctor checked her over but let her go. She didn't mention she'd hit her head and blacked out, not wanting to be on his radar for possible concussion. Her helmet was going in the trash, though.

First spill? *Check.* The medallion around her neck was cool as she fingered it. Protector of riders? Protector from storms? Maybe Ste-Anne was doing her job.

Even though she was only going to the backstretch, she put on the dress she'd brought, Geai in her head, insisting she keep this professional presentation when she left the room. It was crazy out on the front side. How could they pack any more people into this place? But they would, tomorrow for Oaks Day, and more yet for Saturday's Derby.

Claire dozed with her quarters to the door, one hind leg resting. Liv stole into the stall, apologetically offering empty hands to the seeking muzzle. She laced her fingers over the bridge of the filly's nose and pressed her cheek to Claire's. Her pulse slowed, her breathing synched.

The buzz of her phone jolted her. A text from Jeanne, Don's assistant, who had travelled to Louisville with Claire.

Where are you?

Um. *Claire's stall.*

Jeanne appeared at the door, her face looking like she wanted to tell Liv off, but she didn't. "You're okay?"

"I'm fine." Liv kissed Claire's muzzle, and slipped out.

Jeanne gave her a hard look, but seemed satisfied Liv was telling the truth. "I have tickets for one of the events around town. Do you want to go?"

"Oh—no. I'm looking forward to going back to the hotel to start psyching myself out about tomorrow."

Jeanne laughed. "Come on, you're already dressed for it. You're in Louisville two days before the Derby. It's part of the experience. Besides, it's pretty tame. Just cocktails downtown, and the Derby artist signing posters. You'll be in bed by nine."

"I don't know, Jeanne."

"Let's go. We'll take a cab."

Maybe it wouldn't kill her.

The lobby of the downtown Louisville Galt House was already packed when they got there. These were partygoers, not track connections, so at least she should go unrecognized—not that anyone knew who she was anyway. She evaded curious looks from some of the men as Jeanne scooped two flutes from a passing tray, and handed her one.

"It seems wrong to be having champagne before the Oaks." Liv held up the glass and peered through the golden liquid.

"Afraid you'll jinx yourself? You did survive your first spill unscathed."

Liv nodded, and touched the rim of her glass to Jeanne's. "I can drink to that."

GEAI PLACED a bowl on the coffee table, and handed Nate a beer before sitting in front of the television for the Kentucky Oaks. Napoleon planted himself squarely in front of Nate, soft brown eyes locked hopefully on his handful of chips.

It was strange, waiting to see Liv and Claire on television. An odd sensation came over him as he watched; a mix of unrest and anticipation. There was satisfaction for the part he'd played, however minor, but the envy stuck, gnawing inside him.

"Ah, there's my girl."

Geai's pride wouldn't have been greater had Liv been the old man's own daughter. She walked out with the other jockeys, adjusting the elastics around her wrists, whip tucked under her arm, eyes downcast in aloof concentration. The image she successfully put forward, anyway, though Nate thought he could detect a faint injection of nerves in her body. She released a tight smile as she greeted Don with a handshake, then chatted briefly with Jeanne—no doubt inquiring about the well-being of her beloved filly.

"Claire looks good, eh?" Geai commented once the fillies were on the track for the post parade. Claire was more on the muscle than usual, maybe picking up on that tense undercurrent from Liv. Eight minutes to post.

"Why are we not there, Geai? We should be there."

"Because we both have jobs?"

"Like you couldn't get a couple of days off to see your girl ride in the Kentucky Oaks. Now I know where Liv gets her hard-assery from when it comes to letting others do things for her. I'm pretty sure someone could have covered breedings for you. And Roger could have fended for himself. He owes me big-time for getting on everything for most of the winter."

"You wouldn't do that to him."

Nate sighed. "Yeah, you're right. Damn it."

"You like her, don't you?"

Nate looked over sharply. "Liv? She's all right, when she forgets to be so bloody guarded."

"You get along well."

"You really have to stop with the crazy matchmaking."

"I could see it."

"Of course you could, because you're a sentimental old man and we're your two favourite people. I hate to disappoint you, but I'm pretty sure Liv's thoughts on men are of the 'like a fish needs a bicycle' variety. And getting involved with the owner's daughter, if there were any chance of it even happening, is pretty high on my list of bad ideas."

"Ah, you're already like family. Chique's guardian, Claire's gallop boy."

Not to mention Geai's companion, while Liv was making a name for herself—though Geai had managed just fine without either of them for four months. None of it meant a thing. He was a glorified lackey. "It's my job. She's focused on her career, and I should follow her example." The texting back and forth around the pics he sent of Chique was fun, but it wasn't exactly the makings of a relationship.

"Never mind. It would just make me happy to know you were looking out for each other. I'm not going to be around forever, you know."

"Sure you are," Nate scolded. "Stop being so melodramatic. Can we watch the race now? They're coming up to the gate."

Claire balked uncharacteristically as the assistant starter led her forward—just a brief hesitation, really, but she'd never done anything but walk right in. *Breathe, Liv.* The camera view shifted to the front of the metal barrier, waiting for the break. *Breathe*. That one was for him.

Claire came out like a shot, getting first call, and Liv wrapped up on her right away. The big bay filly's head flew up, resisting as Liv tried to negotiate with her when Claire clearly wanted no part. That wasn't like Claire either. Nate glanced at Geai, concern mirrored in the old man's face.

"Easy, filly."

They murmured in unison at the television, like they had any influence.

Liv managed to get her tucked behind horses, saving ground around the clubhouse turn, but the filly still looked fired up, her head cranked to the inside against Liv's hold. *Breathe*. It wasn't a good feeling, to be in tight quarters with a horse running rank.

Along the backstretch, her stride evened out into a smoother rhythm, Liv balanced motionlessly on her back, both of them starting to look more composed. Around the turn Liv found enough room to let Claire move up steadily on the rail, still quiet in the irons. The field turned into the stretch.

In front of Claire, everything was breaking loose—the pacesetter was making a last-ditch effort to hold on, the stalking favourite giving chase and eating up ground. Liv pulled Claire off the rail in pursuit.

But Claire was struggling, looking like a horse Nate didn't recognize as the kickback pelted her in the face. Liv kept after her, a couple more hits with the stick, imploring with her hands, but there was no response. Liv eased her, and Claire galloped under the wire at the back of the pack.

Her face stung from the clods of dirt that had assaulted her on the track. At least her eyes had been protected by goggles—Claire's, rimmed red, had taken the full brunt. Jeanne had blown out the gritty residue, but they remained weepy and sore.

She'd watched the replay, beating herself up for getting into a battle, for not having enough faith to trust the filly—and her own instincts. It's not like Don had specifically told her to take the filly back, it's just what Claire did, came from off the pace. For some reason today, Claire hadn't been happy with that plan, and all Liv had done was frustrate her. Her own nerves had interfered despite her best intentions, and she'd made a mess of it, like some kind of amateur, for half the world to see.

Don stood outside with Jeanne as the hotwalker finished cooling Claire out. Letdown hung in the air, Liv contrite, waiting for Don to tear her apart. She deserved it, and maybe that would make her feel better, in some warped way—if she could explain away Claire's poor performance by assuming the blame. Claire had never *not* shown up.

Don looked down at her. "She bled."

Liv's mouth fell open and her brain rewound. "How bad?" Not that that let her off the hook. All that fighting could have compromised Claire's breathing, putting unnecessary strain on her lungs, inducing the hemorrhage.

"We'll take her back to Belmont, back off on her a bit, come up with a plan."

"She was so sharp today. That's just not like her."

"At least she has a good excuse, and we don't have to try and figure out what the hell we did wrong."

Liv caught the set of his jaw as he said the last part. She was still expecting some commentary on the way the race had played out, but it didn't come. Maybe he was content to let her beat herself up. She should have known better. She should have picked up on it. She knew Claire best, didn't she? But Claire seemed to make out much better without her. The Frizette last fall. All winter with Nate galloping her.

"Go back to the hotel, Liv. Get some sleep. And not a word about this to anyone."

She wanted to stay with Claire, but Don still scared her, more than a little.

The hotel was busy, revelry in the air—Oaks Day was Derby Eve—and it only added to her desperation to get to her room, away from all the happy flowing around her. She jabbed at the elevator button. Her gaze flew up in relief when the lift chimed promptly and the doors parted, then fell on Ricky Acosta as he stepped out.

He threw a black-clad arm around her waist and spun her away from the elevator before she could react. It chimed again as it closed, ascending without her.

"Thank you for that, princess. I should have the mount back on that filly soon."

Her flats slipped along the tile floor as she resisted, but he didn't let go, his lips so close to her ear as he continued that she could feel his breath.

"Such an ugly ride from such a pretty girl. I would run and hide, too, if I were you. Shame, though, when you look so nice. Come party with me. You'll look much better on my arm than you did out on the track this afternoon."

He wasn't any more appealing in a tux, his cologne making her gag as he pulled her against him. She pushed him away, trying to muster a smile to make it look like a joke instead of a struggle to assuage the turning heads in the lobby. "I think I'll pass. I'm not scraping the bottom of the barrel yet."

"Suit yourself, princess."

She dove for the stairwell; pounding her way up the steps because it forced her to breathe. Sometimes all that cardio came in handy. It didn't block out the truth, though. Acosta probably would get the mount on Claire now. Probably should. It was only fair.

There was a bottle of wine on the table in her room with a note from room service—courtesy of Kenny, who apparently agreed she had sorrows to drown. Too bad she didn't like the stuff enough to do that.

She turned her phone over in her hand—how had she missed a call from Geai? But she didn't call him back. The letdown she felt…not even Geai could help.

15

JUNE

Don picked an easy spot for Claire's first race back—one she could win going backwards over hurdles. He'd given Liv the mount. There was only one explanation for that—privilege. It was her chance to set things right again. Claire had been treated, and was training great. Had scoped clean every work since. But that only served to reinforce Liv's conviction that it had been her that screwed up the Oaks.

Liv stayed with the pony to keep Claire as calm as possible, fretting that the filly wasn't sweating enough in the scorching afternoon heat. Claire seemed to be back to her usual unflappable self, but Liv kept second-guessing—was she too quiet? *It's just the medication.* The race was only three-quarters, a glorified workout, really. Claire was picked across the board in *The Form. Much the best in here,* they said. Morning line favourite. Odds-on at post time. So much pressure.

Claire broke just right, and came back to her perfectly; running easily, coasting at the back of the pack. *Just believe.* They picked up a couple of horses on the turn, staying wide. *Don't ask too much too soon.* She waited for signs the filly was having trouble breathing; waited for her to fall apart at the quarter pole like she had in the Oaks. Claire hung as they straightened into the stretch and Liv froze, a sick feeling lurching inside her.

They were practically in the middle of the track, steering clear of any kickback that could impair the filly's respiration. But—there! A shift of gears as Claire realized she wasn't going to be stopped by an asphyxiating sensation in her lungs. Liv threw herself into supporting the drive, the filly zoning in on the leader, taking aim.

It was a big move, but a late move. Liv had spent so much time worrying if Claire was all right, she was going to pay for it. No amount of scrubbing and pleading was going to get them there on time.

A scattering of boos met her as they came back to the grandstand, and she deserved every one of them. She didn't make eye contact, didn't say a word to Jeanne as she pulled off the tack and went to weigh in.

There was really no point in putting on that post-race outfit today, was there? She wasn't a professional. She didn't even shower, sliding into her jeans, leaving on the t-shirt she'd worn under her silks. She dreaded going back to the barn. But she had to see Claire, just long enough to make sure the filly cooled out okay.

Don wasn't there, small mercies. Jeanne just shrugged.

"There's good news. She scoped clean. She ran a good race, Liv. She's not a sprinter. Six furlongs is just too short for her."

"She should have won. I got her beat."

She was losing it. Losing her timing, losing her confidence, losing her dream of Chique, and the Queen's Plate.

THE MAPLES WERE HITTING their stride, in full plumage shading the farm's long lane. Nate stretched his arm out the window of the Mustang as it crept along, breathing in the warm breeze like a tonic. He was looking forward to a run, though the mosquitoes were going to be vicious through the woods. Maybe he'd stick to the access road that connected the barns. He turned the corner by the main house towards his apartment, admiring the riot of colour spilling through the flowerbeds by the main house.

A form appearing from the driveway to the house startled him—Claude Lachance flagging him down, like he'd been watching for Nate's return. Nate braked abruptly, instantly conscious of his pulse. He was on good terms with Triple Stripe's owner, but their relationship was nonetheless formal; he saw Claude more often at the track than around the farm. The man's face looked much too serious.

"Could you come in for a moment, Nate?"

Nate swallowed and nodded, turning the Mustang into the driveway. He couldn't come up with an explanation for this. No one had tried to get hold of him on his phone. If something were wrong back in Calgary, someone would have called him. He waited until Claude caught up, following him up the steps.

Claude led him through the front foyer to a large main room decorated with neutral tones, racing-themed originals and reproductions on the walls. Only real horse people decorated their homes with equine art, the work distracting him temporarily as they walked down into a sunken living room. Cathedral ceilings towered above, sloping to sliding doors that opened onto a backyard patio. The midday sun reflected off a narrow pool. Claude motioned towards a large, soft, chair before seating himself on the chesterfield.

"Can I get you a drink?"

Nate's chair wasn't feeling so soft. "I'm fine, thanks."

Claude leaned forward, clasping and unclasping his hands between his knees. "Geai collapsed in the breeding shed this morning when he was bringing Just Lucky in to cover a mare. They called an ambulance..." Claude hesitated, gesturing helplessly. "He died on the way to the hospital. Cardiac arrest."

Nate stared at him blankly, the buzzing filling his ears making him think he'd heard it wrong. *This morning*…they bred the first mare at eight. In the last four hours, he'd carried on at the track unaware; getting on horses, joking with the rest of the crew, singing along with the stupid radio.

"Does Liv know?" It would tear her world apart.

Claude shook his head, looking down at his clenched hands. "I don't know how I'm going to tell her."

He needed to get out of there, before he suffocated, or screamed, or just broke down. "Let me know if there's anything I can do," he forced through strangled vocal cords, staggering to his feet.

"I'm sorry, Nate. I know you were close."

The fresh air outside did nothing to open his airway, his chest imploding, head spinning. There had been no final words—no chance to say goodbye. *I'm not going to be around forever.* He'd dismissed Geai's comment, joking it away. *Sure you will.*

How wrong he'd been.

THE PICTURESQUE COUNTRY church was probably a popular choice for June weddings, beautifully ornate with its heavy wooden pews, colourful stained glass filtering sparkling sunlight. A cascade of flowers filled the front, the sickening smell of lilies one he would forever associate with death.

All Nate saw of Liv was the long French braid trailing down her back, three rows up from him and on the other side of the centre aisle. The simple black dress she wore seemed particularly dramatic, almost severe, her neck and shoulders rigid, like a mannequin had been set between Emilie and her mother in her stead.

Geai's death brought up a lot of questions, questions he wouldn't get answers to in this lifetime. *For now we see through a glass darkly…now I know in part; but then shall I know, even as also I am known…*words he had memorized as a child. They weren't sitting too well at the moment. It wasn't the first time he'd struggled with admitting things were beyond his comprehension, but so far, it was the hardest.

After the service Liv blew by him without so much as a glance. He didn't know if he should feel sorry for her, or be angry she could close herself off so neatly.

Emilie trailed, but stopped when she noticed him, throwing herself at him. He held her tightly, and left his arm draped over her shoulders as they walked out into the inappropriately pleasant afternoon.

"How are you doing, Nate?" Her eyes were red, the bit of makeup she wore smearing even more as she rubbed away fresh tears.

"I'll be all right. Thanks for asking, though. How about you? Are you going to be okay?"

Her nod was slow, a controlled chin-drop. "It's not me you have to worry about."

Liv disappeared into the back of her father's Jaguar while her family lingered with the other guests among the trees.

"Any idea how she is?"

"Not a chance. She flew in late morning, and she's leaving tonight. I guess the plan is not to stay long enough for anyone to find out."

He should go over, drag her out of the car; shake her, or hold her. But who was he to tell her how to deal with this? Instead he went back to the apartment, skipping the gathering back at the Lachance house. He changed into running gear, because running away was what he did.

The trails were fully shaded and cool, and he forced himself to think only about his breathing, making the autonomic extending and contracting of his muscles a conscious thing—feeling the burn as they went anaerobic, pushing through. By the time he came to the clearing, he'd exerted himself enough to be drenched in sweat, endorphins flooding him, dulling the ache. He ended up where he always did—at Chique's paddock, where the yearling fillies that weren't being prepped for the sales spent their days.

The red Honda parked by the barn was Emilie's, but it was Liv's slender figure, still in the smooth black dress, leaning against the white stud rails as the fillies swarmed the fenceline.

He had to do this, whatever this ended up being. For Geai.

Chique had inserted herself squarely in the middle of the group, but her head shot up, ears forward, giving away his arrival. She gave a low, throaty nicker and unceremoniously butted the others out of the way, poking her nose through the rails and nibbling on his shorts until he produced a peppermint. He stole a glimpse at Liv, but couldn't read her eyes, see any softening there.

Her arms rested on the top rail, and she made no attempt to fix the strand of dark hair escaping from her braid. "Napoleon died last night, did *Émilie* tell you?" Her voice was flat, traces of a lost accent surfacing. "He had no reason to go on without his friend."

"Liv—don't..."

The thought of the poor old Lab was enough to pull him apart, break him out of his paralysis, but she recoiled when he stepped towards her.

"And this one, my little Chique, *p'tite Chique...c'est du chiqué.* It changes the meaning entirely, *avec l'accent, n'est-ce pas?* It's all just make-believe."

She stared at him now, all that icy grey in her eyes concentrated on him. "How could you not have known something was wrong?"

The accusation froze him on the spot, arresting any kind of response, slamming him because it was so totally justified, wasn't it? *I seem to be entrusting you with the things that matter most to me. Don't screw up, Miller.* But he had, completely. He should have known.

The yearlings startled at some imaginary predator, setting off across the field. Chique wheeled and raced after them, throwing in a few bucks as she caught up, cavorting with head tossing when they slowed. Nate looked back for Liv, but she disappeared into the car, driving away.

The sun glinted off something in the grass by the fenceline. He leaned over, picking it up—a small hand-painted medallion on a fine silver chain, with the image of a woman, and a horse that looked remarkably like Claire.

LIV STARED AT THE WINDOW, the dim glow from the streetlights creating obscure shadows on the walls. A bottle Kenny had given her—sedatives or sleeping pills, she wasn't sure which—taunted from her bedside table, unopened but not forgotten.

Her resolve faltered as the hours went by. Sleep deprivation would affect her ability to ride proficiently—not that she was doing anything close to that at the moment, wallowing in the boggiest of slumps. She had to keep riding. It held her world together, if only by delicate filaments. Riding, and Claire. Riding Claire, whose own status was in question.

Another unopened bottle beckoned on her dresser, thanks to Kenny again—the wine he'd sent to her hotel room after the Oaks. If she were to resort to mood-altering substances, that was a safer option. It was time to develop a taste for the stuff. It went down easily enough, once she got past the initial burn. It didn't take much to numb her into an unsettled slumber.

Geai's living room. He was saying something, his words reassuring, even if she couldn't make them out. It didn't matter. Just being in his presence calmed her. The call from her father, the trip home for the memorial; it had all just been a bad dream.

The vision faded, receding like wisps through her fingers no matter how desperately she clung to it. The sadness that came with consciousness burrowed deep, the visceral agony of it jarring her awake, forcing her upright.

Her phone vibrated, startling her, the screen lighting up briefly with a banner before dimming. She'd forgotten to turn the damn thing off.

Missed call. Nate.

The sight of his name added another layer to her pain. She'd trusted him. He noticed things. If there was a hair out of place on a horse, he saw. He should have picked up on something—anything—that might have saved Geai's life.

But—she was the one who'd run off with the big dreams, accepting Geai's support like an endorsement. She was the one who'd made a mess of everything. She was the one who'd failed to call him in her shame since the Oaks. *Guilty, guilty, guilty.*

What was Nate doing up this time of night, anyway? It was probably a mistake, some random middle-of-the-night fumble. Then the phone pinged. *Voicemail.*

The only reason she kept her mailbox clear was to be sure she could be contacted if something happened to Claire. She had to listen to the message to delete it. She held the phone just close enough to hear, to keep him from getting too far into her head.

"Listen...I'm sorry...just...call me. Please? Anytime you want to talk...I'm here, okay?"

Her throat constricted, her next breath a gulp. She'd been so unfair to him. Maybe even cruel. All those afternoons last fall. He would understand this...what? Despair? Desolation? She should call. She couldn't, though.

She'd always relied on Geai. She'd been relying on Nate, for too much. She needed to be stronger. She deleted the message, then held down the button on the side, suffocating the device until it powered off.

She grasped at the medallion like she hadn't cast it aside so carelessly back at the farm, a phantom at her throat. *Silly religious trinket.* Now Ste-Anne mocked her.

How's that storm going? Because you are, so very, alone.

16

JULY

His first time coming to Canada's most prestigious race, the Queen's Plate, and Nate wasn't feeling it. Em, social convenor that she was, wouldn't take no for an answer, but where the hell in this insanity was she?

Nate leaned against the rail of the walking ring, taking in the spectacle of food trucks and overpriced alcohol, and finally picked her out, though she blended in with this crowd—cobalt blue dress, hair coiffed and topped with a fascinator. She sidled up to him and looped her arm through his, her heels making her as tall as he was. Not that that was saying much.

"Looking pretty classy there, Em."

"What about you? You could have made a little effort." She grinned as she dropped her eyes to the polo and jeans he'd galloped horses in this morning. At least they were black jeans. That had to count for something, didn't it? "I'm glad you came."

"Had to at least check it out."

The crowd was inflated with people who'd probably never been to a horse race—people who bought into the advertising that the Plate was a fun fashion fest, and probably couldn't care less about the horses running in the actual event, let alone its history. People Nate's age, but worlds apart.

"Do you think Liv would have come home if we'd had one make it?"

He hadn't meant to ask, or even think about her, but she kept popping into his mind, every time he thought of Geai—which was all the time. Last year, the whole reason he hadn't come was because he'd stayed home to watch it with the old man. That as much as anything had convinced him to show up. At home Geai's absence would have been way too obvious.

Emilie didn't answer right away, and he put an arm around her as she leaned into him.

"My dad went down for a few days, hoping maybe she'd come back with him. My mom is freaking out, but there's no point in her going, because she's never even gone to see Liv ride. Liv comes by her stubbornness naturally." She paused as the paddock judge called riders up for the current race. "Want to stay down here so we have a good spot to watch them come in for the Plate?"

"Sure."

"Faye is pissed." Emilie curled her program in her hands, returning to the topic Nate hadn't really wanted to get into at all, even though he'd introduced it. "Liv should know better than to shut out Faye. They met a few months after Faye and Dean lost their mom and dad and brother in a car accident."

At least he wasn't the only one being frosted, and of all of them, he had the least right to be hurt. He was, though. He really had thought that, like Geai's wish, they'd be there for each other. Instead, he was left struggling with the blame.

"That's quite the hat." Desperate to get his mind off of Liv, he pointed out a particularly flamboyant one that looked like a pink shrub.

Emilie laughed behind her program. "I'm going to have to up my game next year."

The walking ring was filling with the connections of the Plate horses, a more civilized display of traditional Plate pageantry: men in morning coats and top hats, women in tailored suits and chic headwear. Even some of the horses were dressed up, with quarter markers and braids, trickling up the walkway to the saddling enclosure.

When the field left for the track, outriders brought up the rear of the procession in red jackets, their ponies decorated with intricate plaiting jobs, colourful pom-poms bouncing on top of their tails. The anticipation in the air did get to him then, a little; a buzz he'd noticed even on the backstretch that morning.

"Come up to the box and watch the race with us. You need to meet Faye."

"I'm pretty sure I'm not dressed for it, Em. I'll just stay down here with the other riffraff." He smirked as she rolled her eyes. "But thanks. Say hi to your parents."

"Catch up with you after?" She didn't wait for him to answer, swallowed up by the throng.

He headed trackside and found a spot on a raised part of the apron—it gave him a clear view, the start way down the mile and a quarter chute.

The favourite came through, emerging mid-stretch to win going away. He lingered long enough to see an outrider bring the victorious team back on the turf course, the jock leaning down to kiss the bubbling groom's cheek before they draped the purple and gold blanket of flowers over his knees.

See you at the winner's barn!

He replied to Em's message with his regrets, and made a dash for his car, hoping to beat the worst of the traffic.

When he got to the farm, he drove to the yearling fillies' paddock. Chique, ever curious, ambled over with tail swishing lazily at the flies, coat bleached and mosquito-bitten; far removed from the racehorse she was supposed to become. She lifted her nose and snuffled softly on his face, then began to lip at his hair before he offered up a peppermint.

Chique was still the smallest in the bunch, but had the biggest personality—that was all on Nate, good or bad. He tried to offer a mint to one of the other fillies who had wandered over, muzzle stretched inquisitively next to Chique, but Chique pinned her ears and snaked her neck, the other filly backing out rapidly and thereafter keeping her distance.

"Ever the cheeky little bitch. Maybe that'll be you at Woodbine in two years."

Not all that long ago, he would have snapped a photo for Liv, but what was the point? She hated him. He took the long way back to his apartment, past the paddocks with this year's mares and foals, behind the woods, to the stallion barn. One of the farm staff had stepped in to handle things for the final weeks of the breeding season.

See, Geai, we could have gone to Kentucky for the Oaks. They're managing without you. It goes on. We go on. What choice do we have?

17

AUGUST

The alarm droned through Liv's throbbing skull. A shower didn't clear the fuzz in her brain, and the ball cap she tugged on probably did more to deepen the shadows under her eyes than hide them. She blocked out Jeanne's concerned looks when she walked into the barn at Saratoga. Don left her alone, no doubt trusting she would take care of herself. He didn't know she shouldn't be trusted.

Just get through the next four hours...only to spend another afternoon sequestered in her changeroom, on standby, in case one of the other jocks booked off or got hurt, and some desperate trainer plucked her out of the barrel she'd bottomed out in. No one wanted to ride a stone-cold bug.

The morning was a blur. Caffeine made the headache from the wine worse. She popped a couple of NSAIDs, and the way they inflamed her empty stomach did nothing for her already non-existent appetite.

"You gotta eat something, darling'," Kenny said after her last horse, not even his now-rare use of the endearment getting a rise out of her.

She turned away from the hand he'd rested on her back, but gave in, selecting a yogurt cup from the track kitchen, and choked it down. It did settle her stomach, and the painkillers started to kick in to relieve her pounding skull.

"C'mon. We need to go see Don."

It was entry day for the Saratoga Dew Stakes, a restricted race for New York-breds; a softer spot for Claire after running in open company. Claire was her chance at redemption; the different venue was sure to change her luck. Don pushed back his chair from the desk when they walked in the office, his hard gaze levelling on her.

"I'm naming Ricky on Claire. You need to go home and get yourself sorted out. You won't be riding anything in this barn until you do."

NATE FELT the sting of the whip like it was flaying his own hide, but it didn't keep Claire from stopping like she'd been hit by a Mack truck. *Beat the ambulance.* That's what they said about horses that finished that far back.

He watched Acosta bring the filly back to the grandstand, her bold blaze mired by dirt, then turned and scanned the crowd. Still no sign of Liv.

"Jeanne!" he called, seeing the assistant trainer walking back behind Claire.

She turned and stopped, eyebrows arching. "Nate, isn't it?"

"Where's Liv?"

Jeanne's face fell into a frown. "She's been scarce since…"

Since Don fired her.

"You might find her at the house. She won't talk to any of us."

He wasn't sure he'd have any better luck, but he'd just spent six hours in the car because he had to try.

The split-level was on the outskirts of town. Liv's little Nissan sat in the open garage, the hood still warm. His gut had been right—she must have been at the races. The door from the garage to the house was unlocked, and he pushed it open.

A row of empty wine bottles lined the kitchen counter. He caught Liv in his peripheral vision, in the living area to the right, a glass of wine balanced on her thigh, legs tucked underneath her.

She looked translucent, as if something had eaten away at her. Her loose t-shirt draped her rigid shoulders, the muscles in her arms too sinewy. When she tucked a piece of hair that had fallen from her messy ponytail behind her ear, his eyes got stuck on the tension in her neck, the severe hollow of her cheek.

"So what, did you lose the coin toss? Draw the short straw and get suckered into coming down here to check up on me?"

This had to be an alternate universe. She seemed as unconcerned about his arrival as he was stunned by the state of her. She was drunk, when he couldn't remember ever seeing her touch alcohol.

"You could have picked up the fucking phone and saved me the trip."

He wanted her to flinch, like the anger, and fear, and frustration in his words would be a slap in the face, but she choked back a bitter laugh.

"You're the last person I want to talk to. It's not my fault you made a stupid decision. Seriously, why are you here?"

What had he been thinking, driving all this way just to confirm she did, in fact, despise him? He should leave. Hop right back in the Mustang and head home. But this wasn't about him. He inched into the room, but her glare stopped him, the contempt in it demanding an explanation.

"I came because…if I did somehow let you down with Geai...I don't want to make the same mistake letting Geai down, with you."

"That's very noble, Miller." Her tone mocked him. "What ever gave you the idea you were responsible for me?"

How did he explain that, without sounding like he thought he was here to rescue her? Liv, who didn't need anything but her career and a fast horse to carry it. No wonder she looked lost.

"I can take care of myself." She raised the wine to her lips.

It was his turn to stifle a laugh. "Sure. You're doing a stellar job." He reached for the half-empty bottle on the coffee table, and swept it up. It burned in his hand, igniting memories, his lips falling to a frown. "I tried this, you know. Drinking to forget."

Her eyes flashed to his, fingers tightening on the stem of her glass. "Recently?"

"Two years ago. After my ex announced her engagement, actually—all of a few months after we broke up."

"Ouch." It was so soft he barely heard it.

"Yeah. Her wedding anniversary is next week, so I hit my peak right about this time. No two-year engagement for her."

"Help yourself." She inclined her head to the bottle.

It was tempting. While that time was far enough away he was supposed to be putting it behind him, layering Geai's death on top of it disrupted what little progress he'd made. Selfishly he'd hoped they could share their grief—but not by plunging to the depths of her misery. He set the bottle back down. "That's why I came to Ontario. To get away. You giving me that job probably saved my ass."

She snorted, reaching for the bottle and topping up her glass. "We needed someone to break yearlings because I was going to school. You were qualified. Don't make it sound heroic."

"But still."

Her face lost its edge, her shoulders sinking. She looked bereft, and all he wanted to do was peel her fingers off that glass and wrap himself around her to absorb some of the pain—but she wasn't letting down her force field.

"You've fulfilled your obligation, Miller. You can go back and tell them I'm not going to kill myself. You can't help me. Just like I can't help Claire."

"You saw the race?"

She stared into the wine, fingers clenching and releasing around the stem. "Maybe I should feel vindicated she ran so bad…but I can't."

"Of course you can't." He stared out at the treed backyard on the other side of some sliding doors, then looked back to her, pleading, "Come back with me."

A beat of silence gave him hope, but she shook her head. "Please just go. You only remind me he's gone. I need to get away, just like you did. Get away from this whole soul-sucking business. If I'm not back by the time you start breaking Chique, go ahead without me."

I can't fix this. How do I fix this? He stood there, hoping the answer would come. It didn't, though. All he could do was leave, and pray she'd make it through.

THE COTTAGE WASN'T what would come to mind for most at the mention of a chalet in the Laurentians. Calling it modest was generous. It did have indoor plumbing—that was something—and a charming wood stove, which she very well might need. Beggars couldn't be choosers, looking for a summer rental in August.

It was secluded, and after that, Liv didn't care. Just like those posts on social media, with a photo of a rustic cabin in the wild, asking *for a million dollars, would you live here with no TV and no internet for a month?*

A month? Piece of cake. How about forever?

She slipped her bare feet into running shoes and stepped outside, skipping over a path of roots and stones, coming out at a lee in the river.

This was the only spot she had a hope of getting reception, and she waited while her phone found a signal. The texts and call notifications were fewer and farther between now, but she responded to one, as if to acknowledge her existence. Something kept her from throwing the device into the river.

Maybe here she'd find peace, with the birds and chipmunks, among the trees. There was nothing she could do for Claire anymore; it was childish to think she shared some special bond with the filly. Even the owner's daughter could get fired.

She'd let Claire down. She'd let Geai down. And Chique deserved better than a has-been if she was going to make it to the Plate. But could she even call herself a has-been? Because what had she even been?

18

SEPTEMBER

Chique rumbled, crowding the door as Nate opened it. He waited until he'd led her to the back wall before slipping her a peppermint, and snapped her to the rubber tie.

"Life as you know it is about to change, my dear," he said, plucking a hoof pick from his back pocket and running his hand down her left foreleg. Her foot popped up, but she pulled away, then leaned on him, testing the limits of the stretchy tie as she tried to reach his back with her lips.

"Hey, Miller."

He straightened abruptly, dropping Chique's foot without meaning to. *Wow.* Liv. She was back, liked she'd just teleported here—from wherever the hell she'd been.

"Hey." He tried to sound nonchalant, but it came out strangled. *Recover, damn it.*

Her steps were tentative as she walked past him to Chique's head. He stayed glued at the filly's shoulder, watching her stroke Chique's smooth, shiny neck before letting the filly nuzzle her empty hands. Chique threw her head impatiently when her investigation extracted no treats, and Nate was still too stunned to pull one of the mints out of his own pocket to give Liv to make up for it.

"How's she doing?"

Liv avoided his gaze, one hand on Chique's halter as the other straightened the unruly black forelock. Chique was still unconvinced there weren't treats somewhere, and grabbed the corner of Liv's t-shirt between deft teeth, flipping it up and down until Liv slipped a finger into her mouth to make her release it. The filly pawed and tossed her forelock, leaving it a chaotic mess around her ears again.

He couldn't even find his voice to answer—not that Chique hadn't adequately done so herself. Catching a glimpse of Liv's concave abdomen above her tightly cinched belt had reinforced his first impression—she didn't look a whole hell of a lot better than the last time he'd seen her. At least she was sober. He finished picking Chique's feet and grabbed the curry comb.

"Just pretend I'm not here." She slipped back into the aisle.

Like he could do that. She had, at least, checked in from time to time when she'd been AWOL, Emilie being her contact of choice. Logical, really, because Em was the hub of the network of people who needed to know. Not him.

Chique's tail lashed, hind foot cocked, and he realized he was currying too hard. He flashed an apologetic glance at the filly, then back to Liv, leaning silently against the doorframe. He finished currying more kindly, and knocked the dust off hastily with a soft brush.

"So just to clarify, you're not here, but you're here?"

Liv evaded his eyes, and passed him the navy surcingle and pad he'd left outside the stall, exchanging them for the brushes. She went to Chique's head and unsnapped her from the wall, attaching a long cotton lead.

It unnerved him they could go through these motions instinctively, without speaking, working in sync as if they'd been doing this together for years. Geai haunted his mind. How could he not? Liv had to feel it. Geai had been the one to show her how it was done in the first place. Did she find solace in the September ritual, or was it agonizing? He had no idea which, because her expression never changed. She just scratched Chique's forehead and carried on an unintelligible one-sided conversation in her soft voice.

He slid the surcingle off his shoulder and rested it on top of the pad, allowing the length to drop off Chique's right side as he held the roller at the top. Chique shifted her weight away from the strap as it hit her belly.

"Good girl," for caring less about that and enough about him not to step over. He rubbed her belly and reached for the dangling strap, drawing it up against her rounded barrel to buckle it first loosely, then up a hole—securing it just enough that it wouldn't move. Liv passed him the rope, and retreated.

With a flick he urged Chique forward, rewarding her first hesitant steps with lavish vocal praise, until she was circling around him.

"Ho-oh," he crooned, stepping in and rubbing her neck when she stopped. "What a good baby girl."

Snug up the surcingle, walk on again. Another halt, change direction, then repeat the process to the right. He'd expected more attitude, Chique being strangely good—not that he believed for a minute it wouldn't surface at some point.

Liv handed him the headstall, and he slipped the light bit into the filly's mouth, sliding the crown piece behind her ears and adjusting the cheek piece. He turned her loose, leaving her to get used to the feel of the equipment as she moved about the stall on her own.

"Who's next?"

Nate looked at Liv sideways, and moved to the adjacent box. "I don't know if this one ties—maybe you could hold her for me."

"Claire's coming back." Her comment dropped out of nowhere, just like she had. There was no discernible emotion attached to it.

He ducked away to hide his reaction. "Let me grab the surcingle from Chique." So was it the combined power of Claire and Chique that had pulled her out of hiding?

Chique stood in the middle of her stall, mouthing the bit, processing her first lesson. When he relieved her of the equipment, she shook her head, then shuddered, and followed him to the door like she was disappointed that was it.

"Real tack tomorrow, Cheeky." He scratched her forehead before backing out.

Liv was in with the next student, absently stroking her fingers along the bridge of the chestnut filly's nose.

"What's the plan?" That seemed a safe question.

"She could run at Woodbine, but I'm hoping she's done for the year."

"Why the hell isn't she?" So much for safe. His frustration seemed determined to surface.

"It's not up to me."

"Sure it is. Your father owns her. You gotta stand up for her. Do the right bloody thing and speak up."

He hadn't meant to let into her like that. He thought he'd dealt with his anger, for her checking out. For his own hurt, thinking *how bloody selfish of you, to withdraw, thinking you're the only one affected by Geai's death.*

"Sorry," he said quickly, but wished she'd throw the shank in his face for overstepping, and slink off. Anything to indicate she felt something.

"No, you're right." The filly was falling asleep under her repetitive touch, and it seemed to be bringing words out. "You still want to ride, right?"

He quirked an eyebrow at her as he lightly curried the chestnut. "Yeah." *Once more with feeling, Miller. Say it like you mean it.* The conviction he'd felt in the spring had gone missing, somewhere around the time they'd lost Geai, or maybe when she'd decided it was his fault.

"I've been doing a lot of thinking. You should ride Chique. It's obvious you've spent a lot of time with her already."

"Wait a minute—" He was pretty sure he knew what she meant, and it was delusional. This wasn't her letting him off the hook. It wasn't a peace offering. It was a business transaction, based on the lies she was telling herself.

"It'll be next summer, at least, before she runs," Liv continued.

"Hold on—"

"But I guess I'm looking for a commitment."

Last winter, he would have cracked a grin at that, wondering how it would sound to someone walking in on this conversation, but whatever they'd been then, they were miles away from now.

"No, Liv. I'm not—you can't—"

"Can't what?"

There was something there, finally. A challenge. But it wasn't one he liked. Maybe he should just take what she'd just offered him and run with it, but he couldn't. It felt like stealing her dream.

"You can't give up."

She went back to the methodical stroking of the filly's nose. "I just, can't, right now, Miller. So indulge me. Please."

He sighed. What was he supposed to say? "This isn't a permanent arrangement."

Liv didn't debate that, just offered her hand, the gesture awkward and formal. Her grasp was still as strong as he remembered last summer in Saratoga.

"I have one condition, though," he said, letting his hand fall. "You're helping me. Here."

Her eyes shifted, her despondent expression deepening to a frown. "Haven't you hired someone?"

"I'd rather have you."

He could see his declaration firing around her brain, inciting all sorts of conflict. *Good.* Let her figure that out.

Claire whinnied, like whoever was coming through the door had something better on offer than she did. Which was probably true; she didn't have anything good to offer anyone right now. She crouched next to the filly's foreleg to remove the flannel bandage and thick cotton, rising to stuff both in the feed tub before switching to the off side.

It wasn't hard to figure out her father had used Claire to lure her home. It had worked, as much as she hated to admit it. Her parents were being so perfectly careful with her. Not trying to talk. Not pushing anything. *Good parents.*

"Welcome back, Amazon filly."

Nate's voice set her on edge like playing piano wire, his jean-clad legs pausing at the stall door before going to Claire's head. Claire's weight shifted as her head swung towards him, and she crunched his offering, the mintiness of it filling Liv's nose. He reached for the bundle of cotton and bandage Liv had just removed, and she relinquished it under the filly's neck.

Nate, though. Not so well-behaved. She didn't trust him not to push—but she'd opened the door. After deciding she relied on him too much, she'd gone and invited him back in. Just for Chique mind you. The filly needed more than she was capable of right now, when it was so hard just being here, where she saw Geai everywhere.

"I assumed she was going to Woodbine." He crouched opposite her at Claire's quarters.

"I asked if she could come here."

"Good for you."

She flinched at the praise, and her hands wavered as she made sure they didn't collide with his while they unwound the hind bandages.

"Why don't you throw the tack on her, and she can play escort for Chique's first adventure in the real world?"

"She just spent ten hours on a van."

"She'll be quiet then. C'mon, it'll be good for her to stretch her legs. She can tell Chique all about being a racehorse."

Like those would be good stories. "I don't have any tack here."

"That's okay, I brought an extra set from the track. Because you're getting on some yearlings, right? Come with me."

His rusty Mustang was parked beside her Nissan, and he strode between the two cars, extracting an exercise saddle, bridle and martingale.

"Shit…I don't think I brought an Amazon filly-sized girth."

"Why would you have? Yearlings don't wear fifty-four inch girths." She might get out of this yet. It's not as if he could've been expecting to outfit Claire. But he deposited his armful into hers, and kept rifling through the front seat.

He emerged victorious and added the long girth to her collection. "Apparently I grabbed one by mistake. Must be fate. Bring her over to the training barn when you're ready." He walked around to the driver's side, flashing her his annoying grin, and ducked into the car before she came up with another excuse.

This was crazy.

Claire pinned her ears and swung her head as Liv started grooming. "I know. Stupid idea, right? I'm sure you'd be happier if I just left you alone." But the desperate void she'd felt through the six weeks she'd been separated from Claire was enough to make her long to be on the filly again, if only for a short hack around the farm. Claire began leaning into the pressure of the curry comb when Liv reached her withers, head torquing, lip contorted, and actually gave a happy snort when Liv tacked her up.

Her boots and helmet were in the car, where they'd stayed since the last time she'd been on a horse, in Saratoga—an unwanted reminder of her abject failure. The kerchief jammed under the helmet's harness was still knotted, stiff from dried sweat, but she tugged it over her head without bothering to untie it, smoothing it back over her hair before pushing her helmet on. The worn galloping boots were harder. Geai had given them to her years ago, her first summer getting on horses at Woodbine. Her feet had hurt for days from blisters on her heels before she'd broken them in.

Claire was dozing on the tie when she returned with bridle in hand. The filly was happy enough to accept the bit, her head curling into Liv as she did up the throat latch. Getting on would be the challenge—she should probably just lead Claire to the training barn and get a leg up there. But Claire was levelheaded, if a little too tall to just hop on.

Claire looked at her like she'd lost it—with good reason—but stood quietly as Liv climbed on a fence rail, draping herself over the tack before pushing her arms straight and throwing her leg over. She leaned down and threw both arms around Claire's neck like a kid on her favourite pony, burying her face in the filly's mane and breathing deep.

Nate was jogging Chique in the sand ring when they sauntered around the corner to the training barn. Chique's head flew up, and she propped and wheeled so fast Nate had no shot, dropping him unceremoniously in the dirt and whipping away with tail flagged. She did a neat one-eighty, landing with a stiff-legged thump and an emphatic snort.

"Well, that's a first, Miller. I don't think I've ever seen you come off before. You okay?"

Nate climbed to his feet and looked over his shoulder with a smirk, dusting himself off. Chique dropped her head, her nostrils fluttering with a big sigh as he approached. He grabbed the dangling reins and led her to the fence to get a better view of the big bay alien.

"I knew the Cheeky little bitch would show up sooner or later. See? Not a yearling-eating monster." Chique snuffled a greeting, admitting the intruder was equine, then Nate walked her over to open the gate.

Liv's eyebrows peaked. "You sure you want to do that?"

"Just stand over here and block the opening. We'll be fine."

With an effortless bounce he swung on, and to Liv's surprise, Chique didn't budge. He spent five minutes re-establishing *forward* before walking Chique over to where Claire remained posted by the gate.

"Lead on," he said. "Brave new world, baby girl."

Soon Chique was walking beside the older filly like she thought she knew where she was going, feeding off Claire's responsible presence.

"She's a bold little thing." Liv glanced down, Claire dwarfing the yearling.

"Bold and quick and smart. A lethal combination." Nate ran a hand down Chique's neck with an affectionate smile, his legs solidly hugging her barrel.

This crazy idea might have merit—the sun warming her back, the roll of Claire's walk soothing her. Chique shied and side-stepped at the dancing shadows from the overhanging branches, bumping into Claire for security. Nate's knee brushed Liv's calf before he nudged Chique away, and it sent a current up her leg. *Damn it.*

His eyes followed the steady pulse of Claire's head. "She looks happy, at least. Are you back on her, if she runs?"

Liv glanced away when his eyes shifted to her. "I'm not sure. Maybe we're both finished."

"What are you talking about?"

"She bled through Lasix in Saratoga, Miller. What if we can't get her right?" It was bad when the anti-bleeding meds most Thoroughbreds were treated with didn't work—and Claire had been on more than just that.

"You convince them to give her the time off, I'll help you get her right."

Liv snorted. "So what's your magical plan? What do you know that Don and his vet don't?"

"She needs to be rebuilt." His eyes narrowed on her. "Kind of like you."

"We're not talking about me," she snapped.

His words were measured. "There's a school of thought out there, that if you build them up, long and slow, you make the capillaries stronger. Give her the time to let her lungs heal; support her with good nutrition. Maybe some interval training. A few equipment adjustments when she runs again."

"She's probably got scarring in those lungs, thanks to that virus she had last fall. She might well be a lost cause."

"What have you got to lose?"

That much was true. She looked at him sideways. "So much more than just a pretty face, aren't you, Miller?"

His eyebrow twitched, and he pulled at Chique's mane with one hand, swallowing a broken laugh. *Loss for words?* For once she'd caught him off guard.

A circuit around the farm and they were back in front of the training barn. Nate dropped lightly to the ground, scrubbing Chique's neck, and Chique wiped the side of her face on his shoulder, leaving a frothy streak. The two of them were soulmates. Hashtag *relationshipgoals.*

"See you back here with the tack." He led Chique away.

Liv kicked her feet out of the irons and let her legs hang, sorry when they reached the barn. Claire stopped automatically. When she hopped off, the big filly curled her head around and gave Liv a nudge.

"Careful, I might think you liked that."

It hit her, at that moment—for the first time in what seemed like forever—she felt content. Back in the stall, she laced her fingers over the bridge of Claire's pink nose, kissing the softness of her muzzle.

"She's alive!"

Claire swung her head towards the stall door, knocking Liv sideways. Faye leaned on the doorframe, hand propped on one hip.

"You've been back for a week and haven't asked me over. What the hell is your problem?" Faye hugged her tightly.

"I'm sorry. I didn't realize you needed an invitation."

"Because you've been so open and welcoming lately."

Liv curried away Claire's saddle mark and braced herself, her wisp of tranquility evaporating.

"You've got to talk, sweetie. You can't drop off the face of the earth and expect anyone to believe you're okay."

"Will it make it go away?"

"No."

"Then I'll just stick to what I'm doing."

"Which is…?"

"I don't know."

"Obviously it's working, then."

Liv pushed past her and pulled the door shut. "I have to go help with the yearlings."

Faye placed a hand on Liv's arm, her eyes lighting up. "Is that exercise rider still working for you?"

Liv pressed her lips together. "Nate? Yes."

"Then I'm definitely coming along."

"I can't believe you haven't met him yet."

"I know, it's tragic."

Liv sighed. "Let's go, then."

Nate was getting the next yearling ready when they walked in the training barn. Liv stopped in the doorway with her tack.

"There she is," he said. "You want to get Jay?"

Liv inhaled, and tried to be casual. "Hey, Miller. This is my friend Faye Taylor, Dean's sister. Faye…Nate Miller."

Faye stepped forward, recognition flashing over Nate's face as he wiped his hand on his dusty jeans.

"I've heard so much about you." Faye tucked her dark hair behind an ear, her hand lingering in his.

Nate eyed her with mock suspicion. "Uh-oh. From whom?"

"Oh, Dean, mostly."

"It can't be all bad, then. I was worried you'd been talking to Emilie."

"Well *that* goes without saying."

Liv was used to seeing men react to Faye, but this was different. This was Nate. He was handling Faye Taylor like he handled a horse that was testing him—with patient humour. She felt some satisfaction—Faye was definitely not used to meeting her match. The chemistry, however, was undeniable, and for some reason, it made Liv feel very small, and very unworldly.

"So what do you do, Faye?"

"I'm still working on my degree at Guelph—unlike a certain drop out." Faye cast a sideways glance at Liv, looking for a reaction, but Liv wasn't about to be drawn into the conversation. "Just started my final year."

"Didn't the two of you go to school together?"

"I took her in on her first day of high school here and looked after her.

She could barely speak English then," Faye joked, then sobered. "Truth be told, that wasn't long after I lost my parents and brother, so she probably helped me a lot more than I helped her—as ironic as that seems at the moment."

Liv avoided Faye's pointed look before her friend turned back to Nate.

"I try to keep out of the horse thing—it seems to affect one's common sense. I just help Dean with the books. But enough about me. They tell me one of these days you're going to be challenging Dave Johnson for the title of leading rider at Woodbine."

Nate shifted his weight, the amusement falling from his features. "I don't know about that."

"Look, he's modest too. There's obviously a lot about you they haven't told me." Faye smirked, her eyes flashing to Liv.

Nate glanced over his shoulder as the colt he'd left on the wall stomped. "On that note—I'd better get back to work. Nice to meet you, Faye."

Faye's head tilted ever-so-slightly. "Likewise."

"Are you going to stand there and gawk, or are you here to see me?" Liv hissed in Faye's ear before she spun on her heel to tack up Jay. She swore Faye giggled before scurrying after her.

"We need to talk about your friend Mr. Miller. Now I know there's something seriously wrong with you."

Liv tied Jay to the wall, thankful they were far enough away she was sure Nate couldn't hear. "Thanks. My self-esteem is shaky enough right now without your help."

"I'll bet he could help you get over it."

"Why does everyone think sex is the answer to everything?"

Faye looked at her sideways, her lips twisting wickedly. "Don't knock it till you've tried it, sweetie."

Liv glared, blood rushing to her cheeks. "He's not interested in me, Faye."

"You wouldn't know someone was interested in you if they fell on their knees in front of you professing undying love for all eternity."

"He's all yours."

"Just remember you said that."

Liv put on the bridle and turned the chestnut colt towards the door.

"Are you sticking around to watch?"

Faye laughed low in her throat. "Absolutely."

Liv followed with Jay as Nate led his colt out into the ring, Faye trailing behind.

"You know how to give a leg up?" Nate's gaze leveled on Faye with a smirk.

If that wasn't flirting, Liv didn't know what was. Faye scuttled over. To her credit, she stopped to help Liv before breezing over to Nate, then retreated to the other side of the fence.

"That's the legend that is Faye Taylor, eh?" He gathered the lines and edged his colt forward.

"I didn't realize she was a legend," Liv grumbled as they walked the perimeter.

She forgot Faye was watching as she rode, letting the simple exercises absorb her attention. Jay was the best of the bunch, gentlemanly and quick to learn. He was also the most fashionably bred of the ones her father owned, a half-brother to Just Lucky, by a Kentucky stallion. The colt's barn name reflected Claude's intent to name him after Geai. She didn't know how she felt about that.

"Ready for a little hack?" Nate asked once they fell back into a walk.

Faye opened the gate for them. "I'll be going, then. Promise we'll get together soon, okay sweetie?"

"Wait—you're not going to stick around to call 911 when this colt sends me into a tree?" Nate called.

Faye fluttered her fingers in a wave.

"Guess we're on our own." He grinned at Liv. Always that grin.

Liv eyed him suspiciously as she bumped her heel into Jay's side to keep him from running into Nate's colt. Faye was wrong, of course. About Nate. He had some misguided hero complex because of Geai, but that was it.

But maybe it was best to be careful. She'd seen how things played out around the track. People worked together, then got together. Things went wrong, then blew up, leaving a big ugly mess. Innocent bystanders—like the horses—suffered. She needed him for Chique, period. She had to make sure that line between personal and professional remained precisely defined.

19

OCTOBER

Faye handed Liv the coffee cup, still looking skeptical she drank the stuff. She'd curtailed the wine on her little retreat in the Laurentians, but caffeine had stuck.

"How's school?" *Mmmmm, cappuccino...*the frothy warm milk was therapeutic.

"Midterms. Final year. You know. Oh wait, no, you don't." Faye set the cardboard tray on the kitchen table in front of Liv with a smirk.

"I'm thinking of going back. School is something I'm actually good at."

"What's that?" Anne Lachance swept into the kitchen, and Liv shriveled. "Hello, Faye. Where did you get that adorable sweater?"

Faye popped up. With her sensible educational path and fashion-conscious wardrobe, she would have been the perfect daughter for Anne. Anne accepted the coffee Faye offered with an air kiss, and magically extracted some croissants from the cupboard.

"That's not like you to give up so easily," Anne said, setting a plate of pastries on the table as Faye sat across from Liv. "And your father just bought a condo in the same complex as Roger and Hélène in Florida, thinking it would be there for you."

"He what?"

"It seemed to make sense, when he was assuming you'd be spending your winters there. It gives us a place to stay when we come down. I suppose the staff can use it instead." Anne picked one of the pastries for herself. "So nice to see you Faye. Have a good visit, girls."

"Well." Faye eyed Liv, tearing off the end of a croissant after Anne was gone.

"Was my mother actually just encouraging me to keep at a profession she made pretty clear she was dead set against?"

"Almost sounded that way, didn't it? Seriously though—she's right. It's not like you. I'm the last one who's going to tell you how to grieve, but at some point you have to accept you're the only one who can make things better."

"That's what I'm doing. Going to Florida isn't going to make things better."

"What's happening with Claire?"

"My father and Roger agreed she should have some time off while we figure out what to do with her. She's been playing pony for the yearling fillies."

"That's kind of below her pay grade, isn't it?"

Liv shook away the disappointment Faye's statement conjured up. *We were meant to be so much more.*

"She might just be retired." The two of them could slip away into oblivion. They could find something different. Something involving jumps, and dressage, and tearing around a cross-country course.

"I didn't realize it was that serious."

"It is."

Nate's idea was far-fetched, but it niggled at her. It wasn't a new concept to her, but she'd been scouring the internet for whatever information she could find, and had dug out and devoured Tom Ivers' *The Fit Racehorse* —the interval training bible, pretty much—from Geai's collection of books. It would be a longshot, a lot of work that might not pan out. She'd have to talk her father and Roger into that, too.

But it seemed she could have whatever she wanted right now, like they were catering to her every whim because they were worried she'd fall apart. It was embarrassing, and almost reason enough to reject their ploys. Except she owed it to Claire. And she owed it to Geai. Even if Nate's involvement complicated it all.

20

NOVEMBER

The weather sucked, the best racing of the season over, and the yearlings were off after their sixty-day start: it was officially the worst time of the year. Sure the horses were leaving for Florida in a couple of weeks, but Nate still hadn't heard if Chique was accompanying them...and he'd made a commitment, so if she was staying behind, so was he. This is what he got for making irrational promises. Limbo.

Instead of doing something productive like going to the gym, he was here in his apartment scrolling through his feed, scanning status updates—half from people he knew now, half from back in Calgary. Clicking on Cindy's profile, because he couldn't help himself.

Her cover photo was still from the wedding—so perfect in the white dress, the familiar smile next to her the one she'd deemed worthy, when he hadn't been good enough. Honestly, was there nothing else she could use from the last two years? More likely it meant she had better things to do than post something more current. Like he had better things to do than creep. Though, what, exactly? He was supposed to be moving on, but another year had gone by, and he wasn't really any farther ahead; stuck on whether this thing with Chique was because he was trying to make things right with Liv because of Geai, or because of Liv herself, or just because he was content to tread water. Because Cindy being right about *him* meant he'd been wrong about *them.*

A text notification interrupted his wallowing, but only for a second—because it was Liv.

Got a minute? I'm in the office.

Instead of answering, he put on his jacket and headed downstairs. Hopefully she had news. Good news.

It always felt like he was entering a shrine when he walked into that room: glass cabinets showcasing a scattering of trophies, the large oil of Just Lucky and Sotisse with Geai, hanging behind the desk. The sight of the painting stirred up his grief like sediment at the bottom of a pond, and he wondered what Liv had to do to be able to sit there beneath it.

She glanced up and held out a piece of paper. "We have names."

This better not be all she wanted to share. He scanned the list. *"Chiquenaude?"*

"It's a flick, like with your fingers." She demonstrated.

Geai'd done just that to his head on more than one occasion, but he couldn't bring himself to mention it. "I can see that from Sotisse. A little more civilized than *Cheekylittlebitch*, I guess."

Further down was Jay—now officially registered as Just Jay, which was just perfect.

Liv stapled name tags to foal papers and placed them in a file folder. "Chique's going to Payson. You still in?"

Hallelujah. "Absolutely. *'Love, honour and obey',* isn't that it? *'Till death do us part?'"*

"You have an odd sense of humour, Miller."

At least I still have one. "Have you made a decision about Claire?"

"She'll go too. If you're still willing to help with her."

This was encouraging. Maybe she was coming around. This winter was looking decidedly better than it had five minutes ago. "Definitely."

"I realize I've kept you hanging with this, so you might not've made arrangements for a place to stay, but the room at Roger's is available if you want it."

Hmm, it was almost as if she was thinking about him. "Wait—you're not coming?"

There was a beat, an unsure flash of her eyes, before she answered.

"I'm coming. My father bought a condo so I'll stay there."

It wasn't exactly relief he felt—in many ways it might be easier, for him, if she wasn't around this winter. But it wouldn't be better for her, he was convinced of that.

"That's good, because I signed up for Chique—even if I don't really buy into your why—and I'll help whatever way I can with Claire, but she's your project. She needs you."

"I'm not sure I believe in that sort of sentimentality anymore."

"Then you need her."

She pressed her lips together but didn't push back, just swept it aside, probably before it had a chance to settle. "Roger and Jo are staying till the end of the meet—Sans Défaut's going to run in the Valedictory. Michel and Sue will go down a couple of days early to get the stalls ready. The horses are leaving on the twenty-sixth, so as long as you're there the morning of the twenty-eighth it should be good. I'll follow the van."

"You have someone to share the driving with you?"

She shook her head. "I'll be all right."

"It's twenty-eight hours with the van." With nothing more than brief stops every four hours to hay and water the horses.

"I know how long it is. I did it last winter. Alone."

Yeah, when you were in a lot better state than you are now. "The drivers are pros; the horses will be fine. Why don't you come with me down I-79? It saves you eight hours. You can stop for the night and still be there to meet them."

She tidied the desk and stood, putting on her coat and zipping it. "I don't need you to take care of me, Miller. If you're feeling guilty because of Geai...I absolve you, or whatever." She made a vague gesture with her hands.

"Maybe you don't get to do that."

She brushed past him. "You can't replace him. You can't fill that void. I don't need you to, okay? Let it go. Lock the door behind you."

"Fine," he muttered, when it wasn't fine at all.

He could ask the drivers to keep an eye on her. It wasn't his job, trying to help someone who didn't want to be helped. He had to stop setting himself up. Like she said, let it go, Miller.

Sorry, Geai.

Nate's absence was obvious. He wasn't required to be there, but somehow she'd expected him to show up, to lead Chique off the van at Payson, laugh softly at the filly's fatigue. He was probably fast asleep, relishing his wiser choice.

"You okay?" Michel asked after settling the last of the horses.

Liv nodded, because words would make the lie more obvious. "See you guys in the morning. Eight is early enough."

She sat in the car for a moment, looking back at the shedrow, now in darkness. Would anyone really notice if she just slept in the car? The van had made an unexpected stop in the middle of the night in Tennessee, the drivers claiming the fog was bad in the mountains—but more likely they'd noticed her drifting. She'd slept like a rock until they'd come tapping on her window. It had put them two hours behind schedule.

She didn't remember the drive to the condo, unlocking the door, or falling asleep. Sitting up slowly, she waited for the haze to clear, glancing around at unfamiliar surroundings. Apparently she hadn't made it any further than the couch. Four AM. That gave her what, three hours' rest? Her internal alarm had decided that was it, so she groped for her bag, and dragged it upstairs to the shower.

The icy water was a shock, but couldn't make up for what she really needed—another five hours passed out in bed. She braided her hair back wet, pulled on a clean t-shirt and yesterday's jeans, and popped a couple of caffeine pills with the last swallow of water in her bottle.

Payson Park was already alive at five o'clock—shedrows illuminated, grooms mucking out, some horses already tacking the shed in the surrounding barns. Turning on the lights triggered expectant nickers, heads poking over the screens, feet tapping in anticipation as she lugged the bucket of grain from the feed room. Claire pinned her ears and backed up, rumbling from her throat as Liv dumped a scoop in her tub. Chique was next, looking uncharacteristically meek.

She continued down the row until everyone was fed, returned the empty bucket to the feed room, and unlocked the tack room. Where in this mess were the thermometers? Stepping precariously through the crammed equipment, she planted herself on a foot locker to stare at the disaster before her. The day ahead was going to be a long one.

"Morning."

Liv jumped. Nate stood in the doorway with a box of doughnuts and tray of coffees.

"Sorry." He looked nothing close to apologetic with that grin. "Caffeine?"

"Thanks." She resignedly accepted one of the paper cups. Maybe she'd feel better after the liquid top-up.

Nate appeared decidedly cooler and more together than she felt, neat polo tucked into clean jeans. He found a place to set the tray and turned over a bucket to sit. "Doughnut?"

Still smiling—how did a guy who had grown up playing hockey get away with those perfect teeth? She scowled, but took one—chocolate, for good measure. He chose one for himself before putting the box down.

"Cheers." He lifted his coffee, taking a sip. "How was the drive?"

"It's over."

"When's everyone supposed to get here?"

"Eight."

"What the hell are you doing here, then?"

She shrugged. "Couldn't sleep."

"What, you weren't tired enough?"

She didn't know if he was being intentionally annoying, or she was just totally exhausted, but whatever this was was getting old. "Find a shank. You can start walking while I muck."

"Yes, boss. No rest for the wicked, eh?"

Liv ignored him and started looking for a muck sack, rake and fork, finally finding a thermometer in one of the wallboxes in the process.

"Take everyone's temp. Start with Chique. I think she's a little under the weather."

He nodded and accepted the thermometer from her, and she followed him to the stall, removing the feed tub and water bucket while he tied Chique to the back wall.

"Oh yeah." He held out the thermometer for her, confirming her suspicion.

"All right. We'll see if we've got anyone else to worry about before calling the vet. Take her a couple of turns, and I'll get the stall done quick."

By the time the others arrived, they were almost finished with the horses. It had been easy to fall into a steady rhythm of routine. They worked well together, she couldn't deny that.

Liv called the vet to treat Jay and Chique for shipping fever while the others started to set up the shed. The tack room gradually emptied out as the barn took order: stall plaques up, gates and bars and webbings in place, wall boxes and foot lockers positioned.

"You want to go to the kitchen and grab some cold drinks, Michel?" They were almost done. All she needed to do was organize the tack room.

Michel nodded, taking the bills she offered, and dragged Sue with him.

"Get some ice, buddy," Nate called, halfway down the shed, methodically levelling the surface with a landscape rake.

It was mesmerizing, something undeniably appealing about him leaning over, reaching, then drawing back the sand. She shook her head and grabbed the fan rake. Definitely overtired, letting things like that sneak into her thoughts. She started raking, the herringbone pattern she created setting her mind straight, like meditation—back and forth, breathe in, exhale slowly; the horses snuffling happily in the background behind full haynets better than New Age music. It gave her something to focus on other than his ass.

Michel and Sue returned triumphantly with a six-pack of beer. Liv took one, even though she didn't like the stuff. It was cold, the bitterness refreshing.

"Everything looks great," she said. "We can start clipping tomorrow."

"You're actually giving us the rest of the day off?" Nate eyed her.

"Hey Miller, there's a pool in the complex at Rog's place, isn't there?" Michel said. "How about inviting us over?"

"Oh no, forget that. I'm not going to screw up my invitation to stay there by having a party when they're not around."

"You're so responsible, Nate." Sue laughed behind her can.

"Remember Liv has her own place now. We can just invite ourselves over there." Nate's grin taunted her.

Liv shot him a black look. "Sure, come and raise hell at my place instead. I haven't even unpacked."

"Oh come on, Liv," Sue said. "We'll behave. And we'll take care of everything. You don't have to worry about a thing."

Liv sighed. "Okay. But just you guys, all right? I don't want half of Payson showing up at my door asking where the party is." They were probably all leery enough of her not to overstay their welcome. "I'm going to feed lunch. Just tell me when you plan to show up."

Back at the condo, she took a stab at unloading everything jammed in the back of her car, but after two trips curled up on the couch, fatigue sucking her in like quicksand.

A knock at the door dragged her back to consciousness. She stumbled over, rubbing grit from her eyes, fumbling for her phone. Four o'clock! Michel and Sue waited on the front step, arms full of snacks and drinks.

"Come in. I still need to change." Her attempt to muster some enthusiasm was failing. All she really wanted to do was go back to sleep.

Somewhere she had a one-piece bathing suit—but not in the overnight bag she'd packed for easy access. Obviously back in the cold of Ontario, maximizing her exposure to the Florida sun had been more of a priority than modesty. The cover up she draped over the white two-piece disguised the most obvious of her angles—not that she thought she was fooling anyone.

When she rejoined them, Sue and Michel were looking quite at home in the kitchen with more beer, a bag of chips open between them.

"Sorry about that."

"Where's Nate?" Sue asked.

"Oh, I'm sure he knows where the pool is," Liv responded dryly.

The pool area was deserted. Liv spread her towel on a deck chair, tossing her cover up over the arm and stretching out. She opened a magazine on her lap, but the sun's warmth lulled her, and she leaned back and closed her eyes. The splash of someone diving into the water seemed distant as sleep beckoned again.

"Not going in?"

She pried one eye open to see Nate settle into the chair beside her—

with no shirt, looking ridiculously fit. Her nicely relaxing muscles tensed back up. At least he was as pale as she was.

"Not really my idea of a pool," she replied coolly. "Something about twenty metres would do, for a good sixty lengths or so."

"Snob."

He reached over and boldly took the magazine from her lap, leaving her feeling exposed as his eyes lingered a bit too long. She was sure he did it on purpose, and not because he was admiring her. She tucked her knees to her chest, wrapping her arms around them.

"What's going on with those two?" Nate nodded towards Michel, who beckoned Sue to join him in the water.

It hadn't really clicked earlier, but it was true—there was infatuation all over their faces, in every nuance of their body language. "I guess spending two days in a car can bring people together."

"That's the track for you—sooner or later everyone sleeps with everyone else." The smirk fell from his face as he glanced at her. "Present company excepted."

A flush crept from her neck to her cheeks as he continued flipping through the *Blood-Horse* he'd appropriated. Was her nonstarter status that obvious, or was it just a good guess on his part?

Nate stopped and looked at her sideways. "Sorry I've been such a jerk today."

His directness caught her off guard. "So that's what that was?" She made herself breathe. He was trying to be nice. "I probably deserved it. It was stupid to make that drive on my own."

"Yeah, it was. I'm just glad you got here safe."

Why did he keep trying to *care?* That she didn't deserve, with the way she'd treated him since Geai died. She wound a loose thread from her towel around her fingertip, fixating on it to avoid his eyes, leaving him to keep talking to the side of her head.

"Listen. I know you hate me, and I appreciate you gave me this chance with Chique anyway. I hope I don't let you down. I know you've had a rough year. It hasn't exactly been a cakewalk for me either. I just want us to get along, at least for the sake of Chique and Claire. Truce?"

They did have to get along for the sake of Chique and Claire. She needed to learn to be cordial while regaining her professionalism, which wasn't happening lying in a lounge chair in her bikini admiring his abs.

He shook his head almost imperceptibly, then stood, returning the *Blood-Horse* silently and tossing his shades on the chair.

"Wait—"

He stopped, eyebrow quirked.

"I don't hate you, Miller. Truce."

The corner of his mouth turned up every so slightly, and he nodded. "All right then."

21

DECEMBER

Mouthwatering aromas wafted from the kitchen, making Nate's stomach grumble. Roger's wife Hélène flitted from the stovetop, to the oven, to the counter. A decadent-looking cake stood out amid a fleet of savoury dishes.

"What's that for?" he asked.

"It's Olivia's birthday. I know she wouldn't want anyone to make a fuss, but I had to do something."

Great. That should be extra-awkward. "What can I do to help?"

"Find Roger for me? I think he's in the office. Olivia should be here any time."

Hélène had put a kink in his original plan for the evening—an early night so he'd be functional to work the next morning—but refusing hadn't seemed to be an option, seeing as he lived here. Maybe the birthday celebration would balance out his bad association with New Year's Eve. Just like maybe Liv would be happy about the cake. *Not likely.*

He dragged Roger away from watching the races at Santa Anita on his computer, and Hélène put her husband to work with a bottle of wine and a corkscrew. When the doorbell rang, Hélène swept over and ushered Liv in, greeting her with air kisses on either cheek.

Liv's eyes darted to Nate, her gaze reverting to the floor as she padded behind Hélène in bare feet, tucking her dark hair behind an ear. He was so used to seeing it pulled into a ponytail, or braided, or hidden under a helmet and kerchief, not all long and shiny and perfectly straight. With the simple pale blue dress she wore, she looked like someone he barely recognized—pretty, petite, and these days, just a little bit lost—instead of a rider, or his boss, or whatever she was at work.

They took their places at the table, and Roger glanced from Nate to Liv. "Wine?"

Nate almost laughed when they both pushed their glasses towards him simultaneously. Alcohol was going to be a requirement for getting through this night. He imagined Liv didn't want to be here any more than he did, but her sense of propriety demanded it. Roger and Hélène had entertained the crew on Christmas Day with a traditional meal, DVDs of corny movies, and the inevitable American football—in true Canadians-wintering-down-south fashion—and Liv had made merely a token appearance before ghosting. Not into larger social gatherings, apparently.

Hélène raised her glass and smiled at her husband expectantly.

"Santé." Roger reached forward to clink his to hers, and Nate couldn't help but wonder what it was like to have a love like that, one that endured. Did that ever happen anymore?

Roger turned next to Liv, and as Hélène looked at Nate with her glass aloft, he sensed there was custom to this, distinctly aware of being the only anglophone. He reflected her smile as he returned her gaze, clinked, then shifted uneasily to Liv.

Her eyes locked on his with their icy grey before she proffered her glass.

She wasn't wearing makeup—not that she needed it, with her dark brows and lashes, her face with some colour now from the Florida sun. Their glasses touched, and he stared right back until she pulled hers away and tipped the wine to her lips. He stopped himself from sucking back half of his.

"Bon appétit," Hélène said, lifting a bowl of root veggies and passing it to Nate.

"This is great, as always." He scooped some onto his plate.

Liv certainly didn't have to worry about her weight right now—and not because she wasn't back riding—but there was conscious control in the portions she served herself. He was the one who should be doing that. *New Year's resolution number one.* In three and a half months he was supposed to be riding at Woodbine. No more excuses.

After the meal, he jumped up to help clear the table, beating Liv—he needed to move, his muscles seizing from the tension. Hélène handed him dessert plates and forks and followed him back out with the cake. Liv looked like she wanted to crawl under the table when Hélène set it in front of her, Nate placing the plates and forks next to it.

"Hélène said no candles," he quipped. "I was looking forward to singing."

That got at least one corner of her mouth to turn up as Hélène passed her the knife. Liv looked at Nate pointedly when she passed him a generous slice.

"I'm going to have to move out soon if I want to be able to make weight in April," he said, smiling at Hélène, then quirking an eyebrow at Liv.

She took a careful mouthful of her own piece, drawing her fork out slowly, holding his gaze. With anyone else he would have thought that was flirting, but with Liv? He was sure it wasn't. Taunting, maybe. Kind of hot, just the same. He looked away.

Hélène gave him a strange look when he escaped to the kitchen again, blowing out a long breath, his jaw aching from too many forced smiles. She had to know things were weird with Liv right now. Instead of serving coffee, she handed him another bottle of wine. He looked at her sideways, and she patted his arm with what he took to be consolation.

"I'll leave the three of you to talk horses," she said once Roger refilled her glass. "I hope you'll come for dinner again soon, Olivia."

Liv rose, reciprocating a hug. *"Merci, Hélène. Bonne Année."*

"Why don't we go sit on the patio?" Roger stood, reaching for the bottle.

Liv hesitated, reluctance seeping from her pores, but she followed Roger out the sliding doors off the dining area. Nate filed out after them, parking himself on one of the metal chairs under the awning. Why hadn't she taken that perfect opportunity to bolt? He glanced at his watch. His early evening was floating away.

"What are we doing with Claire? Are we going to run her this winter?"

Roger placed the bottle on the round metal table between him and Liv, and sat back.

Nate laughed. "Aren't you the trainer?"

"I used to be. You two have been on your own project since September. I'm assuming you have a plan."

Nate exchanged a look with Liv. "You make it sound like some kind of conspiracy."

"Isn't it?" Roger smirked

Liv crossed her legs as she balanced her glass on a bare knee. "If I'm going to ride at Gulfstream, Nate's going to have to carry on without me."

It was the first she'd mentioned riding again. "Happy to," Nate said. "Is that happening?"

She shrugged him off.

"I'd like you on Sans Défaut in the Mac Diarmida, at least," Roger said. "Fountain of Youth Day, beginning of March."

Liv shifted. "Noted."

"We'll jog Claire and Chique tomorrow?" Nate looked over at her. She gave a short nod in response.

Roger watched with a wry expression. "Let me know if you need me to enter Claire or anything. Though you'd better have some breezes planned before that." He checked the time and rose abruptly, glass in hand. "I'm going to see in the New Year with my wife. No leaving before midnight, Liv." He pointed a finger at her. "I trust Nate can see you out."

Nate sat up quickly. *You're kidding, right?* He was pretty sure he read the same look of dismay on Liv's face as the trainer disappeared into the house.

He reached for the bottle, tilting it to gauge how much was left. "Guess we shouldn't let this go to waste."

Liv hesitated, her eyes shifting from the bottle, to Nate, to the door… but she held out her glass. Nate poured.

She took a demure sip. "Why aren't you at that party with the others, Miller?"

He grunted. "New Year's Eve is only enjoyable if you're drunk or in love." He slouched back into Roger's chair. He was halfway to the former, anyway. Maybe he should take a run at it. He'd seen another bottle in the kitchen.

"Well that's touching." She re-crossed her legs and brushed something imaginary off her knee. "You don't go home over the holidays." It was a statement, not a question.

"You didn't."

She turned her hand palm up in a gesture of concession. "Just making an observation."

Nate raised his glass. "Here's to avoidance. Who knew we had so much in common."

"So what are you avoiding, Miller?"

Bold question. "I'll tell you if you'll tell me."

She took another sip of wine. "You first."

Well...all right then.

"My ex, back in Calgary. I got dumped on New Year's Eve, two years ago. Thought she was the love of my life. Guess not." That wasn't the whole story, not by half, but he wasn't about to bare his soul tonight, no matter how much wine he'd had.

"The same ex that turned around and got engaged?" Her face softened slightly into what he could almost call sympathy.

"There's only one. Your turn."

"Now it's going to seem like I'm just feeling sorry for myself," she said. "This is part of it. I hate birthdays. And this year? My mother would be in full-blown overcompensation mode, trying to make up for Geai not being there. I don't want to be around during the holidays when everyone's supposed to be happy. All of them looking at me like I'm broken."

"Aren't you?"

He expected something for that—a scowl, a snarky remark—but she just looked down into her glass.

"It would be tough," he said, his voice softer. "Aren't you glad you're spending it with me?" He tried a grin, and she tried a smile back, but it didn't hold.

Five minutes to go, then he could go to bed. Time to queue up *Same Old Lang Syne*—his mom's favourite song, though playing it right before midnight was his New Year's ritual now. It fed his self-pity, and he wasn't alone in that department tonight. The first melancholy piano notes drifted from the tinny speakers on his phone, into the night, and he planted his glass on the table and rose.

"Dance with me."

Liv glanced up warily. "I don't dance, Miller."

"It's not hard. I'll teach you." He held out his hand.

"Forget it. I'm hopeless."

"Defies death daily on the backs of racehorses; can't move her feet worth shit on the ground," he cracked. "Make you a deal. I'll feel sorry for you, if you feel sorry for me."

He was about to give up when she set her glass next to his and reached out.

He could feel his pulse as his fingers closed around hers, her body tensing when he rested his hand on her ribcage. *This was a bad idea.* The fabric of her dress seemed far too flimsy a barrier to her skin.

"Dan Fogelberg?" She'd squared her shoulders, like she was making sure he knew she wasn't getting any closer. It pulled the corner of his lips up, just a bit, making him think of his mother again—dancing in the kitchen, her teaching him a proper ballroom stance.

That's it; keep thinking about your mother, Miller. "Don't judge."

A small smile from her, then. He inched closer, a little sway, his hand slipping to her waist. Liv braced, but didn't back away. Then relaxed, just a little. *A really, really, bad idea.* He should let her go. But he didn't.

The sound of fireworks obscured the soprano sax at the end of the song. Liv's head turned, searching the sky above the privacy fence that enclosed the little yard.

Midnight.

His eyes traced her delicate profile, the sweep of her hair, aware of the warmth of her hand in his, the way she moved when he inched his fingers to the small of her back, how very near she was. When she looked back to him, her mouth was a breath away. A tilt of his head, the softest brush, longing for just a taste.…a taste that sent tremors through him, his blood running simultaneously hot and cold as their lips touched. Inching back, he found her eyes, wide and dark.

"You should go." It came out wheezing, his vocal chords not cooperating with his lungs, and he dropped his arms, stepping away, when he wanted to dive back in. He grappled for his phone before the next song began.

She stood frozen, then shoved past him, darting for the sliding doors.

He stumbled after her, finding her toeing into her flats before diving through the entrance. By the time he reached it, she was halfway down the driveway.

"Happy New Year, Liv," he called, his voice gravel.

She glanced over her shoulder, closed expression blocking him out.

22

JANUARY

The lights of Nate's beat up Mustang cut through the darkness between barns, then extinguished next to her Nissan. Liv bent over the bucket, scrubbing furiously, as if she could rub out last night.

Why couldn't he be a typical racetracker and be a no-show after a night of drinking? Why did he have to be so *reliable?* She wanted to disappear. *I take it back. I do hate you.*

She was complaining about reliable help—in this business. But—that's all he was, right? The help. It was cold, but if she thought of him that way, maybe she could get through this. Everyone made mistakes. She'd made more than her fair share of them in the past year. Staying till midnight, letting him…*gah*…had been just one of them. Or was that two? Whatever. *Suck it up.*

He walked in the barn at the other end of the shed, hood pulled up over a Calgary Flames ball cap; one hand curled around a travel mug. The temperature had dropped drastically since midnight, a cruel joke at the expense of Canadians here to duck the cold.

"Happy New Year, Nate," Jo said, coming out of Claire's stall with a feed tub and water bucket.

He grunted. "You too, Jo. What do you want me to do?"

"Fill up the waters, then you and Liv can start putting horses out."

He dragged out the hose, pulling it to the bucket Liv had just cleaned, and threw her a sideways glance.

"Red wine is the devil. Whose idea was that?"

She let out a shallow breath. "What did you do, open another bottle after I left?"

"Clearly you have a much greater tolerance for the stuff than I do."

Or an agent who'd shared a great hangover remedy with her. Whatever.

"I don't know if there's enough ibuprofen in the state of Florida for the headache I have," he added.

"Sucks to be you."

He smirked and moved to the next bucket. They finished the row in silence.

Liv handed him a shank after he rolled up the hose. "Grab Paz. He can go out with Jay."

They walked the horses the wrong way down the shed, outside over the sandy path that led to the track, on through the crabgrass to the paddocks beyond.

Liv closed the gate, Paz going straight to his knees in the sand and flopping down flat, rubbing the side of his neck up and down before righting himself. He climbed to his feet, then dropped right back down on the other side. Jay stood at a distance and snorted, lowering his nose and pawing twice before nibbling at the scrubby grass, one eye locked suspiciously on the pony gelding.

"Watch and learn, buddy." Nate turned away from the paddock. "Who's next?"

"Gemma and Miracle. Then Excursion and Sans Défaut can go individual. We're getting on Claire and Chique, right?"

Nate grimaced. "I said that, didn't I?"

"You most certainly did."

She could overhear him singing *Happy Birthday* to Chique in the next stall while they got the fillies ready, and while it replaced the Fogelberg song that had been running through her head non-stop, the softness of his voice just reminded her she'd fallen for that last night. The kiss...the kiss had just been him feeling sorry for her. He'd said that up front. Stupid girl.

She slipped the bit into Claire's mouth, snapped on the martingale, and pulled the filly into the aisle.

"Throw me up, Jo?" She sounded like she was pleading. *Get me on Claire so I can think straight.*

Nate joined her outside, Chique strutting next to Claire, the sun sparkling at the horizon of a postcard-blue sky. "Turf course?"

Liv nodded, Claire strolling on the knot. Nate had his usual ready-for-anything grasp, one hand holding a long cross, the other floating on the right line. Chique's head bobbed a steady rhythm, ears alert, scanning. Liv wished Claire were more of a handful, so she had something to distract her muddled brain.

"She's wondering where the other horses are," Nate said.

"Who trains on New Year's Day?"

"Us, apparently."

Payson's turf course wasn't a typical racetrack oval—more of a European-inspired, random shape. Liv posted quietly to Claire's daisy-cutter trot, the big bay filly stretching her neck down with a happy snort. She'd never actually said it to Nate, but she loved this approach they were taking with Claire, the science behind it feeding her need to feel in control.

"Jog, jog, jog. Nice and slow, Cheeky," he dictated to the now-two-year-old filly. Chique pushed against his cross—jaw clamped, nose wrinkled, toes flicking out in front of her in a clear display of what she thought of *slow*.

He stood loosely in the irons, knees absorbing the bounce, his lean frame angled over the filly in perfect balance. No one could blame her for being drawn to that: his uncomplicated smile, clear blue eyes glancing from Chique's swivelling ears to the way Claire's flopped on either side of her head, relaxed. Or his laugh when Chique popped into a rocking canter before he brought her back; the way he reached forward to stroke the length of her bunched neck, encouraging her to unwind. That voice again, gently singing *I Got Spurs* in the filly's listening ear as they jogged along. It seemed to settle Chique, but it was having the opposite effect on Liv.

Wine or no wine, she'd let her guard down last night. She'd let herself think she wasn't the only broken one, when she was just that awkward, shy girl, dancing with the hottest guy in school at the high school formal.

There was a reason she'd never gone to those things. She needed to get herself back; get Claire back. New year, fresh start. No sympathy required.

"So where do we go with Claire from here?" She forced her mind to things she understood. Six weeks of building miles, long slow distance; it was time to move on.

"Assuming the goal is to get her back to the races, I guess it's time to start throwing some speed at her. Just not the way we're used to. Starting longer. Intervals. Stuff like that."

"Okay, Tom Ivers. But you get to sell that to Rog."

By the third circuit Chique had given up hope there would be galloping involved today, resigning herself to a slow jog without Nate having to constantly remind her. They turned in near the gap.

"How's the headache?" Liv asked.

"I think between the drugs and the caffeine and the company…" he drawled, grin surfacing, "…it might actually be gone." Chique pawed, but he stopped her when she tried to take a step forward, his eyes settling steadily on Liv. "Sorry about last night."

Her stomach flipped, and she nudged Claire away. "Already forgotten," she lied.

LIV WAS GONE, and that was just fine with him. Off to Gulfstream, or Palm Meadows, while he put in miles on Claire. Doing the grunt work. Though that was kind of what Liv was doing too—getting on whatever horses Kenny scraped up for her to work, hoping some of those trainers would put her up in a race.

It was okay. Putting in miles on Claire was good for thinking. Time to ponder life's great mysteries. Like what the hell had possessed him to do what he'd done New Year's Eve.

It was fine. It was too cold for the beach, so not too hot to train later in the morning. They had the track to themselves. Hotwalkers were probably already back in their dorm rooms, or drinking in the kitchen. Grooms doing up the last of their charges. Vets making their rounds.

It was great. Just him and Claire out here, round and round, doing a crazy long jog warmup. No one even looked at him strange anymore.

Why had he done it?

It wasn't because that's what you did New Year's Eve at the stroke of midnight. It wasn't that he'd drunk too much wine. It wasn't because, for once, she'd made herself vulnerable. Maybe it had been his own self-pity, trying to erase the bad association that night had. Was there more to it than that?

He thought *gallop* and Claire transitioned into her easy, ground-covering stride. He eyed the heart rate monitor on his wrist. Each day he had to let her go a little stronger to maintain the same numbers. Round and round.

Tomorrow was interval day. Liv would be back, and he'd pretend he wasn't aware. Aware of her presence, of the pull, of that memory of her being right there, his lips on hers.

He didn't know why he'd done it. But given half the chance and a bottle of Merlot, he'd do it again.

23

FEBRUARY

Chique stomped a foot impatiently.

"All right." Nate slid his free hand up her neck, under her crazy mane. The filly responded with a snaky toss of her head and a step to the side, and he let her start off.

"You let her get away with too much," Liv chided as she jogged Claire up next to them, the pair breaking into an easy gallop. The air current sent ripples through the quarter sheets covering their haunches.

"It's too cold to stand still for long." Not that they didn't already have windburn from galloping the earlier sets. Liv's presence made it an easy day from a work perspective, at least. She'd do Claire's intervals later; babysitting was just part of the older filly's warmup.

Chique grunted, rocking against his hold, her hind end swinging sideways and bumping Claire. Claire pinned her ears in warning, but Chique didn't look the least bit chastised.

"Try and keep her going straight, will you?"

That was a pointless request—only going faster would make that happen. It seemed to take every ounce of Chique's self-control to comply with his request to go this slow. She was just putting up with him, humouring him. *More, give me more,* she begged with each bouncy stride. Claire's wary wall eye watched her the whole way around.

When they came into the lane the second time, Liv let the lines slip through her fingers, Claire eating up the freedom. Chique eagerly lengthened her stride to keep pace as they flashed past the eighth pole, ears laced against her head. *You think you're so tough.*

Just past the wire, Liv stood in the irons, the big filly responding to the shift in her posture, and Nate talked Chique into easing, managing not to inspire a fight. They pulled up on the backside, Roger cantering Paz up to join them as they turned to face the infield.

"Just like that." Nate slapped the filly's neck, and Chique tossed her head with a happy snort, for once standing still.

"Did you catch a time?" Liv asked.

"You knew about this?" Nate stared at Roger.

Roger nodded, waving the stopwatch cupped in his hand. "But I don't think you need me to tell you, do you?"

"Twelve. Pretty damn close to flat, I should think," Nate snapped, then glared at Liv. "And here I thought you'd finally done something spontaneous." Maybe agreeing to that dance New Year's Eve had been spontaneous, but that was forgotten, right?

Chique bounced through the off-gap, proud of herself after that first taste of speed. She skittered across the pathway, Nate dropping his irons as she tried to pitch her head, shaking it back and forth as a squeal built inside her, humming just under the surface.

Roger sidled up with Paz, grabbing a line, and she sighed in resignation, not quite flat-footed the rest of the way back to the barn.

"Take her a turn for me while I get my boots off, Jo, and I'll walk her," Nate said, depositing the tack on the rail. None of the horses had been bathed since before the cold snap. He was done for the day, so he was in no hurry. This wasn't exactly beach weather.

He took the bridle with him and hung it on the tack hook, then pulled off his helmet, running a hand through his hair.

Liv came through the door. "That was easy for her."

He tugged his boots off and kicked the jack aside. "Ridiculously. She's going to be impossible to live with now."

"Maybe she'd better not walk tomorrow."

"Agreed. Otherwise I might not live to see her breeze a quarter." Chique's head bobbed past outside the door, but he had Liv captive for a rare moment. Jo could take her a few more turns. "So do I just wait and see when you decide to spring the next one on me? Guess I had to know one of these days we'd get to gallop along a bit after you x-rayed her knees."

Liv returned his look carefully. "She reads you too easily. You wanted that as much as she did. I don't think we could have slipped it in if you'd known."

"Obviously you either think I'm incompetent or don't trust me."

Liv sighed, sweeping a loose strand of hair out of her eyes and tucking it behind her ear. "You know we have to be careful with her. It's not just me being paranoid, saying that."

"Yes, it is. So like what, we might get her to the races by the time she's four? That rules out the Plate, doesn't it?" He smirked. "I'm thinking more like June."

"That sounds an awful lot like counting chickens, Miller."

"Gotta have goals, right?" Even if it was a little soon to be getting excited. It just felt good to have something to be excited about.

24

MARCH

Sans Défaut had run huge, beaten less than a length his first time on the turf. On a more selfish level…Liv had ridden a good race. She'd dragged her heels about riding at Gulfstream—she would have been perfectly happy spending the winter hiding at Payson, except for the whole weirdness with Nate she couldn't entirely put behind her—but she'd had to dive back in before Belmont, for Claire.

"Would you like one of our cheap, virtually tasteless American beers?" Jo stood, pushing Nate off the cooler they were parked on so she could open it. The colt was back from the test barn, tearing at his haynet in the receiving barn behind them.

"With that glowing endorsement...I think I'll pass." She'd made herself a rule. No more drinking with Nate Miller.

Nate took a swig, then looked deep into the can. "This is pretty sad."

"You bought the beer Nate." Jo sat back down. "You had choices."

They looked at each other and laughed.

"Roger been back?" Liv pulled her coat more tightly around herself. Would it be wrong to just head home and leave those two to their party?

"He's staying over there to watch the rest of the races."

"You wanna sit down?" Nate asked, popping up again to offer his spot on the cooler.

"I'm fine thanks."

"You guys should go over. I'll get the colt done up." Jo rose and drained the last of the beer onto the pavement.

"You sure?" Nate said.

"Go. This is my job. That's going to be yours soon."

Nate glanced warily at Liv. "Drive, or walk?"

Was she doing this? Really? She should have bolted when she'd had the chance.

"Walk," she said, turning on her heel and flipping up her collar to protect the back of her neck from the cool breeze. "Parking is a nightmare."

The frontside was packed, nine stake races on the card, highlighted by the Derby-prep Fountain of Youth. Liv didn't know where to go, feeling exposed out here. She fished the phone out of her pocket and stopped in her tracks, Nate wheeling to a standstill beside her with a question mark on his face. Thank goodness Kenny was quick to return texts, at least from his rider.

"This way." She set off again, needing to keep moving.

"Hold up a second." Nate grabbed her arm and dragged her to a halt.

Liv pursed her lips, shooting him a dark glance. He laughed, no apology in his grin, lifting his hand and tilting his head to the side.

The girl standing there was tiny, maybe twelve, bright eyes fixed on Liv with a hopeful expression. Those devoted few who still sought her out confused her. She didn't understand why anyone would look up to her, and was more than a little surprised to be recognized in street clothes.

"C'mon," Nate said quietly, nudging her with his elbow. "You'll make the kid's day."

Why did he have to be so *nice?* But he was right. Liv forced a smile, and stepped forward to take the offered pen.

"You going to be a rider one day?" Nate asked, and the girl nodded with a smile bigger than she was.

They had no idea—this wasn't a life to be lauded. It was hardness, and pain, and constant scrutiny—by the trainers, the owners, the horseplayers in the grandstand, the deadbeat hotwalkers in the track kitchen—all of them sure they could ride a horse better than her.

"Good luck," she said, returning pen and program, hoping it didn't sound ironic.

Kenny was in one of the bars. Liv weaved her way through the bodies, muttering *excuse me* and *sorry* until she spotted him. He chased away his neighbour to free up a seat, and Nate deferred to her.

"Kenny, this is Nate Miller. He's been galloping for us the last couple of years. He's going to start riding at Woodbine this spring."

Kenny reached for Nate's hand. He didn't give Nate any feedback on his grip.

"You kids want something?"

Liv balanced on the edge of the chair, Nate close enough behind her to push a current of awareness through her. *Damn it.* "Water, please."

"The same." When Kenny looked disappointed, Nate added, "She doesn't like me any better when I'm drunk."

Kenny roared and waved over the bartender. "Glad it's not just me."

Of course Nate hit it off right away with Kenny. Everything that was hard for her was easy for him. At least it meant she didn't have to talk to either of them. She focused on the television monitors, hands clutching her coat, once again feeling very much the odd one out.

Kenny tapped the side of her knee. "See darlin', you could learn a thing or two from your friend Nate here."

Nate's face contorted. "You let him get away with that?"

"I've given up." She turned back to Kenny "And I have. Learned a thing or two."

Pulling out her phone, she snapped a photo of the two of them, opening up a long-unused app, and posting, *I think Miller might be trying to steal my agent.* She showed them the screen, and went back to watching races.

"Are you any good?"

Liv peeked over as Kenny spoke. Questions like that seemed to always make Nate squirm.

"Guess that remains to be seen."

Kenny leaned forward and swatted at Liv's knee again. "Is he?"

Liv shrugged. "Probably. Looks good on a horse, anyway." She glanced over her shoulder at Nate with a smirk.

"Maybe you should come to New York."

"Sorry, Kenny," Nate said. "My girl's going back to Toronto, and I think it might be serious, so I'm going with her."

Kenny's eyebrows twitched, and Liv melted. That, there, was both the solution and the problem. The reason she had no doubt she'd been right to give Nate Chique; what made all the awkward worth it. The reason it needed to stay that way, so she didn't screw it up. His devotion was straightforward; she and Nate were anything but.

25

APRIL

Nate tried not to breathe, half-standing in the irons in an attempt to convince Chique they weren't really doing anything. Liv crouched low over Jay's neck. *An easy half.* Those were Roger's instructions.

The wind droned past his ears as they rounded the turn, and he focused on keeping still—not on the problem he was going to have when they hit the quarter pole. It flashed by, Chique's ears pricking forward, and she might as well have been speaking English—very clearly telling him to go screw himself.

"What the hell are you doing?" Liv yelled across at him.

The filly eyeballed Jay, and the colt faltered, Chique pushing her nose in front. Liv reached back with her stick, left-handed, and Jay jumped back up beside the filly. That just drove Chique on again.

Nate cursed. So much for an easy half. He was going to hear about this.

Chique still fought him, dragging him to gain half a length on Jay before she decided that was enough—just in time to pass under the wire. The challenge off, she came right back to him, and galloped out fluidly beside the colt.

Jay was blowing when they pulled up and turned in halfway down the backstretch. Chique snorted triumphantly, and Nate glared at the back of her head. He tried to read Roger's face. He didn't dare look at Liv.

"Who's *that* one, Rog?" somebody called as they started towards the gap. "Forty-five and two!"

"Holy shit," Nate muttered, and felt like he was going to be sick.

Roger glanced at him. "You okay?"

He made a face in Liv's direction. She still hadn't spoken. Her face was grim as she stared him down.

"Well Miller, I guess we've got ourselves a racehorse."

HE STOOD SILENTLY at the end of the shank, Liv hosing the remains of poultice off the filly's forelegs. Chique didn't like the cold running water, her hind legs alternating kicks as it splashed. She lipped at Nate's arm, weight shifting from side to side.

Liv kinked the hose to stop the flow and squeezed the water from each foreleg. She ran her hand more carefully down the left one, probing the ankle before standing.

"Hose her when she's done walking. We'll take pictures of it later."

Chique wasn't sore on the ankle, but there was pressure in the fetlock joint…and none of her usual squealing and bouncing as they rounded the shed. He pulled his hat low over his eyes and started turning left. Liv set him up with the hose when they were done walking, then disappeared back into the barn.

Michel walked up to his elbow, cleaning a halter.

"You look good on the end of a hose, Miller. Nice to know you have the whole hotwalker thing to fall back on, if the pinhead thing doesn't work, eh? Though I think you've got the pinhead thing nailed. Just sit there and hang on."

"Shut up, Mike."

"Breaking down the star two-year-old, I don't know. You and Liv haven't been getting along so great lately. I hate to tell you, but this ain't gonna help."

It was a good thing his hands were occupied. He really, really, wanted to smack the guy.

"It gets even better. Jay's tendon ain't looking so good. Great work. Looks like maybe you took them both out. Maybe singing hotwalkers make more money than normal ones. What do you think?" Michel finally walked away, and Nate resisted the temptation to turn the hose on him.

He kept the stream on the middle of the filly's left shin so it flowed around the ankle. He knew they'd gone too fast—the filly had just done it way too easily. It hadn't helped when Liv had sent Jay after them—that had only fired Chique up more—but what was Liv supposed to do, let Chique dust the colt?

The alarm on his phone let him know when he was done, and he dropped the hose in the grass, leading Chique over to turn off the water. He put the filly in, hanging her bucket and haynet, and went to do his tack. And wait.

Liv held Chique when Doc Benson came, the filly standing like a champ while the assistant positioned the plate this way and that. The vet captured a series of angles, peering at the images as they popped up in succession on the laptop.

"Right there." Benson pointed out a chip on the front of the fetlock joint.

Nate skulked back to the tack room. He heard the vet's SUV rumble off, then Roger's voice outside the door.

"Some time off will let her grow a bit."

"I'll let you make the arrangements for the surgery when you get back."

Liv. She walked in, Roger behind her, and glanced at Nate as she went to the back of the room to pick up her keys.

"Guess you'll have your girl back at the farm for a bit, Miller. I'm going to the beach."

THE OCEAN WAS COMMANDING, rhythmic as it crashed up on the shore, leaving abandoned shells and glittering stones in its wake. Distant clouds stretched across the horizon of an otherwise perfect blue sky, a hot breeze carrying the salty smell of the surf across the sandy beach.

Liv gazed beyond the waves to the faraway point where the never-ending blue-green of water dropped off to meet the heavens. She loved the ocean, the mesmerizing roar, and the sound of the seagulls calling and sweeping overhead.

She didn't know if she believed in God, but here she felt a presence that made her feel foolish for doubting. *Everything happened for a reason* Nate had said after she'd broken her arm, and with things like Chique's injury, she could agree. The filly scared her a little, she was so precocious. That word was thrown around liberally with young Thoroughbreds, but it seemed particularly appropriate in Chique's case. A few months off would be good for her.

It was losing Geai she couldn't figure out. Life had gone on, despite her pain and confusion. She didn't think Geai was up there somewhere, beyond the expanse of endless sky, watching her as she struggled—but she knew if he was, he'd be telling her to get on with it. Life was too short. She had no real concept of that, still believing she was invincible. She tested it every day she got on a horse. But life had certainly been too short for Geai, even though he'd lived his years fully, so his death brought the idea a little closer to home.

Claire was her constant, but whether this winter's methodical program would get her successfully back to the races remained to be seen. If it didn't, it was something else she had to figure out how to accept. Claire would be retired. Would her conscience let her take the mount on Chique back from Nate, after all the work he'd put into her? For now, Chique was his.

She pulled her eyes away from the hypnotic waves and scanned the stretch of sand extending north. Something about the figure walking in her direction attracted her attention, then the casual walk became familiar, the understated confidence and athleticism Nate's.

She boldly watched him, knowing he wasn't aware of her yet. The wind tousled his blond hair, his t-shirt in his hand, the sun deepening the tan on his bare back. He was the skinny one now—reducing evidently in progress in preparation for riding back at Woodbine.

He hesitated, spotting her. But he came over, spreading his t-shirt on the sand next to her and sitting cross-legged.

"What a disaster of a winter," he said.

She had to laugh. "Well it's over now."

"You seem nicely back on track."

He glanced at her, his eyes sweeping from her face to her arms, wrapped around her shins. She pulled her knees closer to her chest and looked away.

"But now it's back to New York," she said. "I got chased out of there."

"You'll fight back. With your dragon." One corner of his mouth twisted up.

Claire was training like a monster, but Nate had done most of the work, so the question of her own competence still lingered in her head.

"Rog says he's going to put you on Gemma for your first mount."

"Guess I can't put it off any longer, eh? Too bad I broke my secret weapon."

"You'll be fine. You're way better prepared than I was." She watched him as he stared out over the water. "You know I don't blame you for Chique's injury, right? She's hard on herself. It was probably in the cards."

"It was too fast."

"Just the proverbial straw."

He shrugged her off.

"I don't blame you for Geai, either. It wasn't fair, to suggest that."

He was silent a beat, still staring at the waves. "I wracked my brain, trying to think what I missed. Maybe he didn't know. Typical horseman, neglecting his own health when the horses get the best care. Did he ever even go to the doctor?"

"I should have been around. It's not like I've been setting the world on fire down here."

"But that's just it. He never would have let on. He wouldn't want to worry us. He wouldn't want to hold you back."

"You're right, he never would have let on, if he even knew anything was wrong." She looked down at her toes, pushing them into the sand, her voice faltering. "I still can't believe he's gone."

"Stubborn old man." Nate picked up a handful of beach; let it fall through his fingers.

"I do blame you for getting me drunk on New Year's Eve, though."

She'd said it to lighten the tone, expecting his default grin, proving to herself she was past it. Instead, the look he gave her was like throwing kerosene on embers, her intent blowing up in her face.

"I apologized for that."

"I realize you were just feeling sorry for me."

"What if I wasn't?"

She searched the ocean desperately, calling on the waves to calm her, without success. Then she forced herself to meet his eyes again, beating back the flames the only way she knew how.

"It's never going to happen, Miller. You and me? I'm not your rebound girl."

AFTER THREE YEARS of killing time, buying time, *wasting* time...it was time. Nate almost felt guilty, it came together so easily.

With Chique on the farm and Liv in New York—out of sight, out of mind, her point driven home—he had no excuses not to be laser-focused. At least she'd been honest. Saved him the embarrassment of pining over someone who didn't want him—again. Been there, done that, wrote the song about it.

He didn't intend to have the ten-pound bug for long. He'd worked hard to lay the groundwork, and it was going to pay off.

And it did.

26

MAY

Nate parked his tired Mustang behind Johnson's shiny BMW. It would take several hundred more winners before he'd be driving a car like that. Johnson surprised him by waiting, and they walked into the barn together.

"Excursion ran huge, eh Dave? He looks good for the Achievement Stakes."

"Sounds like you're trying to take the credit there, Miller," Johnson replied.

"You rode him all right." Even though Nate had galloped the colt all winter, and breezed him more than once leading up to the race when Johnson was busy elsewhere.

Liv stood halfway down the shed with Emilie and Faye, looking like she'd stepped out of an office in a black pencil skirt and white blouse. She'd flown up to guide Sans Défaut to an easy win in the Eclipse Stakes. Just in case Nate had forgotten: he might be the hot bug at Woodbine, but he was still second—or maybe third—string at Triple Stripe.

"Gentlemen." Liv looked from Johnson to Nate, eyebrows slightly raised in amusement.

She looked good. Healthy. Dare he say content? Definitely good. *Nope. Not your rebound girl.*

"Isn't that nice, Woodbine's top two riders gracing us with their presence," Faye interjected.

"What's the occasion, boys?" Trust Em to come right out with it. "Christmas isn't for another seven months yet."

Johnson kept a straight face, enduring the wisecracks, but Nate didn't imagine he'd joined this group to be made fun of by three smart-assed women, regardless of how attractive they were.

"Everything going well in New York?" Johnson homed right in on Liv.

"Yes, thanks."

"How's that two-year-old doing on the farm?"

There it was. Cut to the chase.

"Which two-year-old is that?"

"You didn't have to be at Payson this winter to hear about the Just Lucky filly. Sounds like she's going to be a runner. She outworked Just Lucky's half-brother, didn't she?"

"Something like that."

"When's she coming back in?"

"I don't know. You'll have to ask Nate. She's his project."

Nate smothered a grin. He could've—no, thinking about kissing Liv just got him in trouble.

The clench of Johnson's jaw was brief but unmistakable. "I'm sure I'm not the only one looking forward to seeing if she lives up to everyone's expectations. Nice seeing you, Liv."

He shook her hand and stepped away, stopping at the office to check in with Roger.

"I don't think he much liked our company," Faye said, a smile toying with her lips.

Nate glanced at Liv. "Thanks."

"Just stating the facts. How is our filly?"

"She's good. Even if she doesn't think so. I can't wait till she can start jogging, though I fear for my life, getting on her after her little vacation."

"You have the time?"

"I'll make the time."

Between not trusting anyone else to do it and considering it his penance, he'd taken it upon himself to walk Chique every day, as per the post-op instructions. On dark days he walked her in the afternoon, on race days—every one but Wednesday, when they had night racing—in the evening. The staff at the farm thought he was crazy, but no one complained about not having to deal with the cheeky little bitch.

"You're off to a quick start." Liv crossed her arms, her manner as professional as her outfit. "Good things come to those who wait?"

"Where have I heard that before?" He matched her pose, but the corner of his mouth tipped up. "I can't complain. Claire still on track for the big comeback?"

There was a little shift to her eyes, her posture, as she nodded. "Guess we'll find out if the same holds true for her."

Faye was following the conversation with more interest than Nate would have expected for someone who claimed not to care about the horses. Emilie looked like she'd pulled up a chair and a bowl of popcorn. He felt like he'd missed a memo somewhere.

Johnson left the office, and Nate saw his chance to escape whatever was going on here. "My turn to check in with the boss. Catch you all later."

Roger was preoccupied with the condition book, like every other trainer who'd run a horse today, when Nate opened the door.

"Looks like you had your work cut out for you out there, Miller." Michel eyeballed him, sprawled on the couch. "Faye Taylor, Liv Lachance, and Emilie. That's my idea of pain."

"Shut up, Mike."

"I'm really surprised Faye hasn't taken a run at you yet. Hot bug riders are her thing, you know."

Was that what that had been about out there? He kicked Michel's legs out of the way, and parked himself on the other end of the sofa.

"I'm thinking the Steady Growth next time out for Sans Défaut," Roger said. He hadn't lifted his eyes from the book. "What do you think?"

"Sounds like a no-brainer. Do I get to ride him?"

"Not likely."

No surprise. "Johnson was sniffing around. He say anything to you about Chique?"

Roger shook his head.

"I'd still put money on Liv coming back to ride her when the time comes," Michel goaded.

"Probably." He couldn't disagree, because the thought crossed his mind every day. "I'll cling to the fantasy in the meantime."

"Of course, she may turn out to be no good."

Nate laughed. "There's always that. They're all champions until they get a chance to prove otherwise, right?"

27

JUNE

It had been almost a year now, Geai had been gone. She could still feel the pain like stitches pulling at the edge of a wound, but it finally felt like she was coming to terms with her loss—both of Geai, and her sense of self. It wasn't on Claire to restore her, but an encouraging performance in today's comeback sure wouldn't hurt.

As she walked into Belmont's paddock, Liv's eyes went automatically to the tall filly—that flash of blaze, the three white legs, the glint of gold in her coat—before she located Don, and the cluster around him. Jeanne, her father, Emilie, and…her mouth fell open.

"Maman? You came!" She choked up, blinking hard as she gave her mother a hug. "Thank you."

"She's here, but no guarantee she'll actually be able to watch." Emilie grinned.

"True," her mother said, squeezing back. *"Bonne chance.* Come back safe."

This was the Belmont Gold Cup Invitational, two miles on the turf—which seemed an insane choice for the filly's first race in nearly ten months. Some thought running on the grass was easier on bleeders, but the air quality worried Liv—the mugginess suffocating, like breathing pure New York smog.

After the post parade Liv broke Claire away from the pony, the breeze cooling her face as they zipped through their new pre-race routine, leaving the others behind. None of them probably broke out of a trot—it seemed common sense to conserve every ounce of energy, and she fought the doubts that crept up. She had to believe—all or nothing, right down to the aggressive warmup.

Claire had a healthy sheen of sweat on her neck as they loaded into the gate. *Check*—internal cooling systems functioning as they should. The doors sprang open, bell rattling Liv's ears, and she let Claire fall out and settle into her stride, the filly relaxing in her favourite spot, at the back of the pack.

It wasn't until they came into the backstretch for the second time that Claire started picking up horses along the rail, the distance weeding out the pretenders. She snuck up the inside, Ricky Acosta's mount, a big grey named Eureka Moment, rolling now on the outside. They wheeled around the turf course's tighter turn, the leader tiring. Liv pulled Claire out and into Eureka Moment's slipstream.

Claire's ears flipped forward as they turned for home, and she started closing the gap between her and Eureka Moment before Liv even started to ask. The filly inched her nose to the edge of his saddle cloth. Acosta looked back, going to the whip, left-handed, and Eureka Moment began to drift out.

Not that she'd expected anything different from Acosta—it wasn't a surprise he'd float her to the middle of the course if she let him. She gauged Claire's reserves, and took a chance. Asked the big filly to back off, getting an ear flick in response. Eureka Moment jumped ahead.

Liv glanced over her shoulder to make sure no one had moved up the rail, and fired Claire back up—on the inside. The filly dragged her to Eureka Moment, ears laced against her head. Acosta let the grey horse drift back in, and Liv reached back left-handed, hitting Claire for three strides…then drove with her hands, pushing with each thrust of the filly's neck. Claire's ears snapped forward, bounding past her rival, drawing clear.

Galloping out, Claire powered on, and Liv laughed as she tried to pull the filly up. All those crazy long miles of jogging and galloping, the methodical reintroduction of speed, the intervals—just old school training, no drugs. It was madness, impractical, but it had worked.

Jeanne met her with a bucket of ice water, sluicing it over Claire's neck, then passed the sponge to Liv so she could douse the filly between the ears while Jeanne undid the tongue tie, peeled off the nasal strip, loosened the noseband—all little pieces of the puzzle. A cooling spray with the hose, then on to the winner's circle, the coveted space that had eluded them far too long.

Back in the room she sat in front of her locker; let it sink in, let herself feel all of it. There was a tightness around her heart, knowing she couldn't call Geai. The wound prickled, and wept a little.

Her phone buzzed, the screen coming to life, the message from Nate just the most recent in a stack of congratulations.

Annnnnnd...she's back. Mother of dragons.

She wished he were here. Then again, it was probably a good thing he wasn't, because her resistance to him—to them—might've gone out the window.

"*Hi Nate, it's your mother...*"

Like he wouldn't recognize her voice, always and forever; like it didn't always make him smile, the only thing about Calgary that could do that.

"I just wanted you to hear before you saw it on Facebook...Cindy and Phil are expecting. Call me okay?"

He blew out a long breath, and disconnected.

It didn't sting as much as he'd thought it would. Time and space. He was living the dream now, right? Battling Johnson at the top of the standings. And in the shadow of Geai's death, it seemed almost benign.

He fired off a quick text. *Thanks for the heads up. I'm good. Going upstairs for a drink—had an especially nice winner today. Call you later.*

He didn't make a habit of it, but it felt justified after piloting Dean's promising two-year-old colt, Touch and Go, to an impressive maiden win this afternoon. Dean waved him over from a table off to the side, sitting across from his sister, Faye. Dean had already ordered.

"If we can keep his shins under control, what do you think of the Victoria Stakes?"

"Sounds like you read my mind," Nate replied, taking a careful sip of his beer and stealing a look around. "I say go for it."

One sure bet at the racetrack was someone was always watching. There were no corners here in the grandstand's fourth floor lounge, and Nate was aware his every move was likely being monitored for bad behaviour.

"Would you be free to ride him?"

"Absolutely."

"Have to take advantage of Triple Stripe's bad luck this spring, because if those two of Roger's make it to the races this fall, we might not have it so easy. Is that going to happen?"

"Hopefully. We brought them both in from the farm this week, but it's kind of early to be making predictions."

"Right. From what Emilie says, you're pretty high on that filly." Faye used the leafy stalk of celery in her Caesar to stir, the bracelets on her wrist jangling softly.

Nate ran his eyes from the bangles to her tanned, bare shoulder before reaching her eyes. "She's a long way from running yet."

"So cautious" Faye peered at him slyly over her drink.

"I've already been accused of counting chickens," he countered, with another swallow from his glass.

Conversation centred around the afternoon's races, he and Dean running through the standouts and disappointments while Faye looked bored, until Dean glanced at his watch and drained the last of his ale. "I'm beat, kids. You ready to go, Faye?"

Well that was good. Dean didn't seem to be a big drinker either.

"Already?" Faye flipped her dark hair off her shoulder and locked on Nate. "Maybe if I offer to buy Mr. Miller another drink, he'll agree to give me a ride home."

He gulped the mouthful he'd just taken, Faye's perfect eyebrows arching at his hesitation. She'd made it awkward for him to refuse. "Sure. But just water for me."

"So responsible." She plucked out the celery stalk and crunched off the bottom.

Dean left some bills on the table, apparently unfazed by his sister's forwardness. "We'll see how the colt is in the next few days and talk about the Victoria again."

Nate nodded. "Thanks Dean."

Faye used her smile to summon their server. "Another Caesar for me. And a glass of water for my driver." She tipped her chin towards Nate, and picked up the bills. "My big brother. Guess he's paying for that drink."

"He's a good guy."

"Yes, he is. He's taken care of me for a long time."

"I kind of doubt you need much taking care of anymore."

Her eyes lingered on him until the arrival of the drinks interrupted her perusal. Nate took a deep breath, and almost wished he'd opted for another beer.

"So what's your story?" Faye picked up the fresh Caesar and pushed the celery stalk out of the way, closing her lips over the peppery rim.

"My life isn't that interesting."

"You didn't leave Calgary because you were running from the law or got some girl in trouble?"

"Nothing that exciting, trust me. Dean's a bit older than you, isn't he?"

Her eyes flashed suspiciously as she registered the subject change. "Eight years. There were only three between my brother Shawn and I, so we were a lot closer." She fingered the coaster under her drink. "I didn't really get to know Dean till he came back to help settle things after the accident. He gave up finishing his masters to take over training my dad's horses. I was only fifteen."

"That must've been tough."

"It's hard to believe it's already been ten years." She shrugged. "Life does go on."

"But no boyfriend?" Her boldness was catching.

"Not currently. I haven't found anyone who holds my interest." She smiled coyly. "What about you? How have you managed to keep your nose clean all this time? You're Woodbine's mystery man."

"Please." He rolled his eyes, then frowned. "There was someone back home. It didn't work out."

"Oh, he's *wounded.* I like that in a man. Sounds like it's time to get over it." She placed her elbows on the table and rested her chin on the backs of long, intertwined fingers. "Don't worry, I don't need your relationship CV. I certainly don't intend to give you mine."

Well. No need to wonder what was on Faye's mind. He sucked in some water and checked the time. "We should get going. Some of us have to be up at four in the morning. You can finish your cross-examination in the car."

She didn't look nearly as disappointed by that suggestion as she had the similar one from her brother, promptly shouldering into her cardigan. Her dark lashes swept at him sideways as they walked to the escalator.

Faye watched him carefully after he opened the Mustang's passenger door and made sure she was settled before walking around and slipping behind the wheel. He turned the key in the ignition. "Don't look at me like that. What can I say, my mother taught me right."

One thing was certain, there would be some new rumours flying in the morning. He'd bet the moment they'd left Champions the first text had been fired off.

"Emilie says you're musically inclined as well," Faye resumed, shifting in her seat so she was angled towards him. "Not your average bug boy, are you?"

"What all has Emilie told you?"

"Everything she knows. Which isn't nearly enough."

She obviously liked this game, and played it effectively. By the time they reached the Taylor's Northwest Stud—down the road and on the opposite side from Triple Stripe—he felt as if he'd been vetted and deemed worthy of acquisition.

A short lane led to an old Victorian red brick farmhouse, and Nate pulled in beside the two vehicles already there. Faye made no attempt to let herself out.

"You're going to make me do this, aren't you?" he said, one hand resting on the wheel.

"I am." She smiled at him unrelentingly. "You've given me expectations."

He started to sweat as he walked around the car. *No one's watching you now, Miller.* Assumptions have already been made. *So?* Maybe she was right. *Time to get over it.* It was a short walk to the back door, and she turned to face him.

"Thanks for the ride home."

Before he could reply, she laced her fingers behind his neck, drawing him closer. It was easy to yield, their lips meeting as he caught the subtle scent of her perfume; his hands slipping around the curve of her waist, the way the warmth of her moulded to him messing with his self-control.

She broke off slowly, her mouth still close, dark eyes luring under those lashes.

"Well?" she murmured, tracing fingers from his neck to his chest. "Perhaps we should continue this discussion inside."

Cindy was having babies. Liv just made him crazy. Faye had been clocking him since the day they'd met, and might as well have been holding up a sign in bold letters: *REBOUND GIRL HERE*. Would it be such a bad thing, to go for that? But he wavered, his heart pounding against her palm.

"I'd better get home. That four AM thing."

Her head tilted slightly, then she kissed him again, soft but brief, and backed out of his hold with a meandering smile. "Some other time, maybe."

He'd sleep on that. In his own bed.

"MONSTERS!"

Nate laughed as Chique leapt into a canter, skittering to the side when a car drove past them beyond the tall chain link fence to the left. He eased her back to a jog, reaching forward to stroke her neck with one hand.

Taking a two-year-old to The Field without company wasn't necessarily sensible, but it got her out before the main track opened; one horse taken care of before his day took off at its usual torrid pace.

Chique was used to galloping in the dark. They'd done it at the farm until she shipped in—early enough none of the staff were working so he'd have been SOL if they'd parted company—but at least the training track at Triple Stripe had proper rails. There were none out here. Every day he expected her to take a shortcut through the infield, deposit him in a heap, and head home without him.

Next time around he let her pick up a slow gallop, still travelling the wrong way. Chique's ears swept forward when headlights came towards them, her head flying up with a snort that bounced off the trees.

"Goblins!" He chased her forward until the car went past. "We do this every single day, Cheeky." But every day was a new day, when you were an opinionated two-year-old filly.

They went a couple more times around, finishing with a jog past the gap. He turned her in. Both of them exhaled. *Lived to tell.* Except, sometimes the walk home was the scariest part.

So far the sun was just making the clouds pretty colours over the city to the east. Chique did her fire-breathing dragon impersonation when the silhouette of a horse grazing on the lawn outside one of the barns lifted its head. The horse whinnied. Chique whinnied back. Nate smiled. This was the best part of his morning.

"One of these times you're just not gonna come back," Jo said, ready for him when he steered Chique into her stall.

"It's all part of the adventure."

Safely back on the ground, he ducked out of the stall and set the saddle in front of Jay, pulling out the saddle cloth and girth cover to add to the laundry and leaving Michel to tack up the colt. Gallop Jay at six, then off to Barn Twenty-five to work one. And so on, all morning long.

Emilie's head popped up from pulling on her boots as he walked into the tack room.

"Hey Nate." Oh, that grin. She knew.

"Hey Em. What's up?" Might as well at least try to feign innocence.

"You'll never believe what I heard in the kitchen this morning. Apparently you were seen leaving Champions with Faye Taylor last night."

Yep. He'd called that right.

Emilie straightened and leaned back against the cupboards, crossing her arms. "So?"

"So nothing."

"Ha! Why do I not believe that?"

"Okay. Maybe I drove her home after Dean left early."

"And?"

"Maybe she kissed me, and I didn't see any reason to fight her off. But that's all."

"Really."

"Come on, Em, I've been good to the point of monkish since I came out here."

"Fools rush in, Nate."

"Yeah, yeah. I didn't get her number or anything."

"What does that mean?"

"That I need her number? I could just show up and throw stones at her window, but…"

Emilie pressed her lips into a hard line. "Are you sure about this? She has a pattern."

"That's cute, you looking out for me. I'm making an informed decision. I understand Faye doesn't like to get attached. Sounds perfect."

Emilie's frown poked at his conscience. "I didn't think you were like that."

"You don't know everything about me, Em."

She scowled as she picked up her phone, and seconds later he heard his chime with Faye's contact info.

"Promise not to hold you responsible." He tapped her on the shoulder and went to get on Jay.

28

JULY

The hardest part of coming back to New York was returning to Saratoga. Her demons lurked here, in the eaves of the old barns and seats of the fabled grandstand. The association was strong—a dark time she never wanted to go back to—so it made Claire's win in the Bowling Green Handicap that much sweeter.

Two for two.

Nate's text had a thumbs-up tacked on the end; the congratulatory message less personal, his influence on the result more remote. She was the one carrying out Claire's unconventional training regime now, day in, day out. He was busy with his own career, and his shiny new relationship.

Hot bug riders were Faye's go-to—but for some reason Liv had thought Nate would be immune. Which was silly, because Faye was beautiful, and confident, and experienced. And he was just a man, after all. It was a relief, really. It let her off the hook. She was happy for them. Really.

Never mind. She had Claire—Claire, back on track.

Faye's expression said what she didn't verbalize. *A picnic? Are you serious?* Yet she followed him along the path, negotiating rocks and glancing up at the overhanging trees.

"I must trust you," she said wryly.

"What, you think I'm going to take you captive?"

"Obviously not. You are quite captivating, however."

He glanced over his shoulder, catching the mischievous look in her eyes.

He slid the backpack to the ground when they reached the clearing, and pulled out a blanket. Faye helped him spread it, then sunk to her knees —digging into the bag for the bottle of wine, nodding as she appraised the label.

"Plastic cups, though?"

"The bottle's already too much glass out here."

"Were you a boy scout too?"

He smirked, sitting next to her to pour the wine, and she leaned in, kissing him.

"Is this where you propose? Because I'm starting to think that's what it's going to take to get you in bed."

Of course she didn't mean to be cruel, but it was as if her nails had dug into his old wound, making it bleed all over again. He stared at his chest, expecting to see it oozing through his shirt.

Faye frowned, her brow wrinkling. "I'm sorry, I was kidding."

He set his wine down, biting his lip and focusing on the clouds drifting overhead. "Listen, Faye...this really isn't how I thought this would go, either. It turns out I'm not that guy. That girl back home...she really did a number on my head. I don't want to make that your problem." He shifted his gaze back to her. "I get you didn't sign up for this, so I won't take it personally if you want to move on."

Instead of the sassy comeback he expected, her head tilted to the side, eyes mellowing. She rested a hand over his heart, her lips gently touching his. "This is unfamiliar territory for me. I've never had a guy not be up for sex, let alone take me on a...picnic."

"I didn't say I wasn't up for it." He was still fixed on the curve of those lips, and dragged his eyes back to hers. "But sex is easy, Faye. It's the other stuff that's hard. If we can halfway figure that out, it'll be the icing on the cake, right?"

"There might have to be real cake to get me through this, but okay."

There she was, the Faye he was used to, but the hand still on his heart somehow slowed the bleeding.

29

SEPTEMBER

Chique danced, outfitted in a bright white shadow roll and matching polo bandages. Jo had a death-grip on the shank, and despite Sue on the other side, both women were red-faced as the filly dragged them into the saddling enclosure. When Jo stopped in front of the identifier and lifted Chique's upper lip—exposing the new tattoo, imprinted just last week—the filly tossed her head and swung her hindquarters sideways, her compact body vibrating.

"Put them in, please!"

The paddock judge's voice rang out, and Liv ducked through the gap in the middle of the saddling stalls. She slipped into the number one slot, rubbing sweaty palms on her black slacks as the two-year-old fillies gradually filed into their assigned spots.

Jo spun Chique to face out, Chique gawking at her surroundings. It was as if she could tell the people were studying her, glancing at their programs and *Forms* and trying to figure out where she fit in this group of maidens.

"How is she?" Liv asked as she crouched opposite Sue, the two of them quickly unwrapping the polos.

"How does she look?" Jo snapped, holding the filly steady and monitoring all four feet. "You'd think we'd never schooled her over here. Watch yourself!"

Liv skipped out of the way as Chique kicked, skittering over the rubber bricks. "If she hadn't given you a hard time, I'd be wondering what was wrong with her."

"Everybody still alive?" Roger slipped into the stall and ran a hand over the network of exposed veins on Chique's neck.

Chique was rigid from her poll to the tip of her tailbone, Liv holding her breath as Roger and the valet worked. Before Roger managed to buckle the elastic girth to the billet of the saddle, the filly erupted, scattering the tack in a heap behind her and launching away from it, taking Jo with her.

"I'm going a turn!" Jo growled over her shoulder.

It seemed, more accurately, Chique was taking her a turn.

"We'll do her on the walk," Roger said when she came back around, handing his jacket to Liv.

Sue quaked next to her, face pale. "Okay! Breathing! You?"

Liv dipped her chin with a jerk and peeled herself off the wall of the stall, trying to catch a glimpse of Roger and the valet putting on the tack as Jo led the filly around. Roger waved away his jacket when Liv offered it back as he rejoined her, pulling the collar of his shirt from his flushed neck.

Someone grabbed her elbow, and she dragged her gaze from the filly. Nate, oblivious to the shenanigans.

He reached across and shook Roger's hand, then turned to Liv. "Are you allowed to be here? How's our girl handling everything?"

"She's sharp," Roger answered flatly.

Sue started to laugh, a little shrilly, and Nate quirked an eyebrow. "What did she do?"

"A very impressive kite demonstration?" Sue quipped.

"It was ridiculously athletic," Liv agreed.

"So, nothing I haven't seen before?"

"Hold up, Jo." Roger motioned her into the stall when she came back around. "Let's get the halter off and put her blinkers on."

Liv stepped around the corner to be safe, Nate following her lead.

"Any instructions?" he asked.

"Ask the trainer."

"Don't let her run off with you." Roger's voice reached them from the other side of the wall, and Liv didn't think he was kidding.

"Bonne chance, Miller," she said as the paddock judge called for riders up. "Don't fall off."

She caught the grin he flashed as he hopped up from Roger's leg up, Chique jigging away. They disappeared behind the outrider, her sense of helplessness growing the further they were away.

Emilie—who had stayed outside of the saddling enclosure—caught up with her as she weaved through the crowd to the escalator, Roger trailing with less urgency. The horses were on the track by the time they reached the seats.

Liv fumbled for her binoculars. "Is he still on?"

Nate looked perfectly relaxed, standing in the irons as they jogged to the front of the grandstand for the post parade. He chatted to their new exercise girl, Nicole, who had also taken on afternoon pony duties with Paz. Chique's neck glistened, lather forming between her hind legs, but she was moving forward, not sideways, or backwards, or up. That was a win in itself.

Liv didn't even hear the announcer as he rattled off the names and connections of the six fillies, the lack of control eating at her, nausea rising in the pit of her stomach. Chique jumped into the warmup—bumping Paz, nose flipping up—but she gradually settled into a rhythm, galloping around the clubhouse turn in stride with the pony.

The view of the gate was obstructed, set down the seven-furlong chute, and Liv dropped her binoculars and focused on the infield screen once the horses disappeared from sight. They were leaving Chique for last, despite her inside post position. *Problem child?* When the assistant starter took the filly from Nicole—leading her towards the metal barrier, away from the security of Paz—Chique froze, her legs braced. *Yep.*

"Did you forget to gate school her?" Liv muttered, tension gripping the back of her skull.

"She's been there practically every day." Roger gave Liv a long-suffering look.

Two more of the gate crew joined the effort, locking arms around the filly's quarters, and Chique fired out, scattering them, then reared and spun away from the man at her head. Nate stuck like it was an afterthought, calmly steering her around to face the gate again, but the camera shifted away.

"Oh, come on!" Liv stared at the screen, then futilely across to the chute, cursing the massive, inappropriately placed building that blocked the view. Her eyes flashed back to the screen to see a head-on of the gate as Chique's head finally bobbed in.

"She comes out like a bullet," Roger said.

But the starter wasn't releasing them. "What's the hold up?" Then, "Where'd she go?"

Muffled words she was sure weren't kind came out of Roger's mouth before the intelligible ones. "Nate's off her. He's on the frame."

Blood rushed in Liv's ears, seconds dragging with no way of knowing what was going on before she caught movement. "I see her. I think he's back on."

With a jolt they were off, Chique catapulting from the barrier like she'd been fired from a cannon.

"You weren't kidding," Liv mumbled.

Nate let her fly, and Liv clenched her jaw, knuckles white as she gripped the binoculars. This was not the good experience she'd had in mind. She glanced at the tote board to catch the first quarter fraction and quelled a moan.

"Make it stop, Rog. There's no way she can keep this up."

"Try telling her that," Emilie cracked, and Liv shot a dark glance in her direction before turning back to the spectacle unfolding on the track.

Chique opened up a lead with her little game of catch me if you can, still showing no sign of letting up. Nate wasn't trying to rate her, but he wasn't working on her either. Chique just kept rolling, and he really didn't have much say in the matter. At the head of the stretch, she had to have five lengths on the others.

"Now we'll see if she's got any stamina to go with that speed," Roger said.

"She should," Emilie interjected. "With the three miles Nate gallops her every day."

"What?" Liv gasped, the binoculars falling as she stared at Emilie.

"I'm kidding. But look. He's riding her now. If you can call it that."

Mid-stretch Nate picked her up, throwing the lines at her–and Chique responded by drifting right, then left, running like she was drunk, so he resorted to pushing with hands only, his body still. She was tiring, and now the other fillies were coming at her. That zippy pace she'd laid down set it up perfectly for the closers.

"C'mon Chique, hang in there. Come on, Miller!" Liv screamed.

Emilie joined in, even Roger, the three of them on their feet hollering at the staggering filly, as if they could help Nate carry her to the wire. Someone was charging up the rail, into all that room Chique had left in her erratic drive.

"Don't fall over, Chique!" Emily dissolved into laughter, and Chique held on by half a length before letting the field eclipse her as they galloped out.

Jo and Sue were already waiting on the turf course when they got down there, mirroring expressions of disbelief.

"Maybe she's going to be worth all the aggravation," Jo said.

"Show's not over yet!" Sue pointed towards the clubhouse turn. Chique balked as Nate pointed her at the gap from the main track onto the grass.

"It's ironic an outrider escorts the stake winners back, but not lost maiden winners, don't you think?"

Emilie made a good point.

Nate finally threaded Chique through, and she travelled in an irregular serpentine towards them: head up, ears fixed forward, questioning every step of the route. Nate dropped his irons for better control, and Jo intercepted to lead them the rest of the way.

The smile Nate turned on Liv as Jo walked them into the winner's circle looked a little unhinged. "I don't even know what to say."

"I didn't think I was going to live through that," Liv said once he was safely back on the ground, Jo and Sue leading Chique away.

"What about me?" Nate chortled. "I didn't dare get in her way."

"I kind of got that."

"If the race was any longer, they would have caught her," Roger said.

"It's her first start." Nate was ever Chique's champion. "She's got a lot to learn."

He weighed in, and Liv walked with him down the stairs and through the tunnel under the grandstand.

"What happened in the gate?" Though it crossed her mind maybe she didn't want to know.

"She laid down! I thought she was going to crawl out of there. The bridle broke when they were trying to hold her, then she popped up and stood like nothing happened, so they just put another bridle on. I never knew they kept one back there, did you?"

Liv rubbed her forehead, trying to smooth out the wrinkles. "Never had reason to know. Why didn't you have her scratched?"

"She wasn't even fazed. All we need is for her to think she can get away with that."

"Still a little risky, don't you think?"

They came out the door by the paddock, Nate waving at someone. "See you back at the barn."

Liv turned, and the sight of Faye next to Emilie made her pause. She put on a smile, strolling over and giving Faye a squeeze.

"Congratulations! That was...ah..." Faye gave up. "How are you?"

"More importantly, how are you? Three months with the same guy?" Liv gave her an exaggerated eyebrow arch. If she stayed detached, she could joke about it. "You coming with us? You know he'll be going back to the barn when he's done."

"When are you heading back to New York?"

"Tonight—but we're coming back soon. Me and Claire."

Claire stepped off the van and stopped, Liv holding the shank loosely while the tall filly stood, statuesque, taking in the Woodbine backstretch. Chique's whinny reverberated from the first stall, head bobbing, forelock flying. She disappeared, squealing, the solid thud of aluminum shoes on rubber-matted wall making Nate wince.

"Easy, filly."

He stepped back next to the door as Liv led Claire by, the leggy filly outfitted in bell boots and white flannel shipping bandages, the top of her hindquarters decorated with fancy red and blue kinesiology tape. Chique charged the webbing and Nate ducked.

"She all right?" Liv called.

"Reunited and it feels so good..." he crooned, giving Chique a wary eye before he looked in on Liv and Claire. "She's a little excited."

Liv crouched in the straw, taking off the bandages, Claire tied to the back wall. "Hang that haynet for me, would you?"

He picked up the rope net, shaken and stuffed into a perfect nest of timothy and alfalfa, and hauled it over. Chique reached for it as if Claire's was better than her own as he secured it and gave it a flip.

Liv was removing the last bandage when he peered in again. "Good to have you back."

She looked at him sideways. "Let's see if you feel that way when I start stealing wins from you."

He scooped up the bandages she'd left on the mat and shook them out, draping them over the rail while Liv turned Claire loose. Claire followed her to the door, diving into her hay as Liv snapped the webbing in place.

"So how is our little freak show?" she asked.

Nate scowled and reached up to cover Chique's ears, drawing her head into his torso. "Don't listen to her, Cheeky." The filly grabbed the edge of his polo shirt, and he extracted it from her mouth.

Liv watched, arms crossed. "Rog nominated her for the Mazarine Stakes. Ambitious maybe?"

"If she runs like she did first time out, nothing can touch her."

"Don't hold back on the confidence, Miller. It's two turns, a stake race, against open company. If she runs like she did first time out, she'll get beat."

"She'll get a lot out of that first race."

"You mean more than just a sense of entitlement?"

"Come on, Liv, a little faith." He cradled Chique's head again until she latched on to the end of his belt and started tugging.

She was right, of course. A furlong and a half farther, a Grade Three stake with no protection for being Ontario-sired, or Canadian-bred. Liv always had to be so damned practical. "Rog promises she'll be better behaved, so she should have some energy left for the extra distance."

"Like maybe you'll be able to rate her a little?"

"It could happen." He grinned. "The gate crew is sick of seeing us, so she might even load this time."

Liv turned to Claire's bold-blazed face, and Claire shifted her focus from the haynet, ears swivelling forward and head tilting as she stretched out her neck. Liv pulled a peppermint from her pocket, and it disappeared from her palm.

"The E.P. Taylor Stakes for this girl." She drew the hairs of Claire's black forelock together, her lips set in a line. "Time to move up."

"Not tempted to go for the International? Turf plus distance, Claire's favourite thing." The Canadian International was a quarter mile longer—but it wasn't restricted to fillies and mares like the E.P. Taylor. Both races were often stepping-stones to the Breeders' Cup, but he wasn't bringing that up. Yet.

"Tempted, yes. But even the E.P. Taylor will be a tough race for her, after the company she's been keeping."

"The company she's been toying with, you mean."

Liv dropped her hands and stuffed them into the pockets of her jeans. Claire kept one white-rimmed eye on her, in case another mint appeared.

"I really wasn't sure we'd get her back. But your little one-rat study worked, Miller." She met his eyes. "Honestly, a year ago?" She shook her head slightly and fell silent, her gaze turning back to Claire.

"Well, you know what they say about time…"

He wasn't sure he'd meant it to be deep, but it was out there now. Her expression suggested the significance wasn't lost on her.

"Thank you."

It wasn't a sarcastic comment to deflect his sentiment like he might have expected. He tried to laugh it off anyway. "For what?"

"For pushing, when everyone else backed off. Which is exactly what I wanted, of course—for everyone to just leave me alone. But you didn't. I may have considered it insensitive at times. But someone needed to do it. So thank you."

The word dumbstruck was meant for moments like these, his mouth falling open for words he couldn't find.

"Life goes on," she said, eyes still steadily holding his.

"It certainly does."

Not that he could ever get a read on Liv—most times it was like there was so much conflict bouncing around in her brain, it was no wonder wires got crossed—but he would have put money on that being about Faye, and the last time he'd been alone with Liv, on a beach in Florida.

30

OCTOBER

The second start of a young horse's life usually went one of two ways: either they were better behaved, because they'd adapted to the routine, or the exact opposite, because of the anticipation.

"She is being better so far." Liv watched Jo circle Chique beneath the huge old willow in Woodbine's walking ring.

"She thinks she's got it all figured out." Nate smirked, his arms crossed.

"Let's hope she's right."

"Oh, I don't know. Chique thinking she's in charge is a dangerous thing."

Liv touched his arm as the paddock judge gave the call. *"Bonne* chance, Miller. Come home safe."

She stayed next to Emilie as Roger tossed Nate up, Chique dancing along with calm focus. A little calcium, a little ACTH—both legal pre-race treatments that had a settling effect—*better living through chemistry.*

"There's Faye," Emilie said, following Liv through the crowd. "Faye! Come watch the race with us."

Liv had been too intent on getting upstairs to notice. She managed to slow down enough to give Faye a quick hug. "You'd better keep up."

"I don't know if I can deal with the tension."

Emilie grabbed Faye's arm and steered her forward. "If we don't keep moving, my sister will self-destruct."

They rode the elevator to the fifth floor, and Liv went straight outside to stand next to Roger. The view was panoramic, the sky so clear she could see downtown Toronto, but she focused her binoculars on Chique and Nate as they went through the post parade. Chique was perfectly composed.

Liv glanced at Roger. "She's actually behaving like a grown-up."

"You're welcome," he responded.

They broke into their warm-ups, Chique galloping next to Paz the wrong way around the turn. "I hope you didn't give her too much."

Roger peered at her sideways with that long-suffering look she'd accepted as part of every discussion about Chique.

Emilie and Faye rushed out and joined them with the tote board reading zero minutes to post, and Liv felt Faye's fingers wrap tightly around her arm as she kept the binoculars locked on the gate, backed into place at the sixteenth pole. The schooling paid off—the crew still left Chique till last, but she filed in quietly, and stood until the latch was sprung. She popped out perfectly, with none of the frenzy from three weeks ago. She even let Nate take her back, running mid-pack on the outside as the field raced into the clubhouse turn.

"You sure that's the same filly?" Emilie quipped. "Look at her, being all professional."

Chique maintained her position, through the backstretch, and past the half-mile pole. Liv glanced at the time, waiting for Nate to set her loose. Turning for home, she saw him pick her up, imagined him chirping to her…but Chique's stride didn't change. A filly flew by them on the outside, but Chique didn't take up the challenge. Finally he hit her, once—then when she didn't react adversely, he smacked her a second, then a third time. But Chique showed no interest in going on no matter what Nate did to rouse her. The pace-setters faded behind her, but Liv didn't try to count the lengths Chique finished behind the winner, watching her gallop out like a pony.

"I hope she's okay," Faye said carefully, like she was afraid things were about to blow up.

Liv glanced at Roger. His face was blank. "I'll go talk to Nate," he said.

Liv was right on his heels. She frowned at Faye and Emilie.

"We'll catch up," Emilie said.

Chique was on her way back to the barn next to Jo when they made it down to the apron, Nate walking across the turf. He stopped in front of them, threw his hands up, and flopped them back to his sides.

"Do you think she bled?" Liv asked.

"I guess it's possible." He looked Liv in the eye. "I'll talk to you back at the barn."

Liv turned to Roger. "You'll scope her, right?"

Roger nodded and took out his phone, calling the vet as he walked away.

Emilie inched up, Faye beside her. "What did Nate say?"

"Not much. You want to come back with us, Faye, or are you waiting for him here?"

"I'll come."

There was no flare to Chique's nostrils as she toured the shed back at the barn, walking with a casual sway, stopping the hotwalker to gaze out the end of the barn before carrying on. The vet pulled up, and Roger waved the hotwalker into the stall.

The vet handed Liv the twitch, and Chique did her best to evade her fingers as she grasped the filly's upper lip and twisted the rope snug. She passed the handle to the hotwalker and stepped out of the way. Chique shoved her head sideways, knocking the hotwalker off balance, but he held tight. She huffed, dropping her head in resignation. The filly's eyes shifted as if she thought they were the only things safe to move in her current state of restraint, the vet slowly guiding the scope through one nostril. She inched it along the filly's airway, then offered the eyepiece for Liv to see.

Removing the tube carefully, the vet nodded at the hotwalker to release the twitch. "Not a speck," she said. "She's got a beautiful throat. Sorry?"

"Take her out for some grass, Marc," Jo said as Roger followed the vet to her SUV.

Liv wandered out to the picnic table where Emilie and Faye waited, both of them watching her expectantly. She sat next to Emilie and shook her head. "No excuses."

"Don't you just love horses?" Emilie said.

Chique dragged the hotwalker over the lawn like a dog taking a kid for a walk as she searched for the best spot, settling on a patch of dirt. When Nate's Mustang pulled up, her head popped up, dark eyes drawing him like a magnet.

Faye rested her chin on the heel of her hand and drummed her fingers against the wooden table, and Emilie laughed. Liv swung her legs away from the table.

"I'll spare you the pain of having to listen to us, Faye. You can have him in a minute." She patted Faye lightly on the shoulder, and met Nate in front of Chique.

Chique gobbled up a peppermint, then smeared her muddy lips against the arm of Nate's suit jacket. "Good thing I love her more than this suit, isn't it?" He took a step away, and Chique went back to licking her patch of dirt. "You scoped her, didn't you?"

Liv nodded. "If we'd been betting, you would have won."

He smirked. "Now what?"

"She's your project, Miller. You figure it out."

His eyes levelled on her. "You want to know what I really think?"

She choked back a laugh. "Of course."

"I think the pre-race took away her crazy. She needs her crazy. We just have to find a way to work with it."

Liv sighed, glancing at Chique, who'd finally settled on some grass. "As ridiculous as that sounds…I think you're probably right." She looked back to him. "So what are you going to do?"

He gave her a twisty grin. "Leave it with me."

"Can the four of us maybe go somewhere, so at least Em and I can eat?" Faye called, interrupting.

Liv walked more slowly as Nate strode over, sitting next to Faye. His arm went easily around her shoulders as he turned her face to his and kissed her.

"Come on, Faye, you know better than that. We're not going anywhere till the filly's back in her stall and done up."

Faye rolled her eyes, but her lips melted into a smile. "Here I thought Roger paid people for that. Maybe Em and I should go, and you two can join us when you've got the little princess all tucked in."

Emilie reached over from the other side of the picnic table and patted the back of Faye's hand. "Better get used to being second to a horse, sweetie."

NATE PLUNKED himself next to Liv, putting his feet up and stretching with his hands locked behind his neck. Though he was pretty modest most of the time, he did, on occasion, act as if he owned the place. Which wasn't entirely inaccurate.

"It's beautiful out there today, isn't it?"

"Enjoy it while it lasts," Liv responded, refocusing on the novel in her lap.

"You're such a pessimist."

"I prefer to see myself as a realist."

"Oh yeah?"

"Yeah. And you will too, when the cold and snow settles in for the last part of the meet."

He laughed, his current expression making it obvious those days were far from his mind. "You could stay and make it interesting."

"No thanks. I'd hate to take any more wins away from you." Not that she was putting any kind of a dent in his hot bug rider lead. "The girls and I will be heading to Florida end of November, as planned."

"Rub it in."

"If you keep winning races at the rate you're going, you'll be in the running for the Eclipse Award for top apprentice. That would be a big deal."

He sobered, sitting up and dropping his arms to his thighs. "It would. It's only October, though. It could all fall apart any day now."

Liv tipped the book down. "Who's the pessimist now?"

"Realist, you mean." The grin came back.

Would she trade places with him, for the kind of success that had eluded her that first year? It wasn't as easy as it looked. Part of it was luck; most of it was hard work. Nate just happened to have a magic balance of both.

"Speaking of reality…" Liv placed her bookmark in the pages, closing the paperback. "I'm assuming Dean is planning to run Touch and Go in the Coronation."

"Last I heard."

"Roger's nominating Chique."

He straightened. "Why would he do that?"

"Just keeping Chique's options open."

"Isn't the Princess Elizabeth more appropriate?"

"Or maybe a non-winners of two?"

"Really. Well, it's nice he thinks that much of her."

"Or whatever your plan is to deal with the crazy." The corners of her lips drifted up, then settled back into a line. "Unless you choose to ride Touch and Go."

He met her eyes, shifting uncomfortably. "Is this where you step in and ride Chique?"

"I will, if that's what you decide. But you have to pick."

His gaze was unwavering. "I made you a promise last year."

It was more than his word; it was the kind of commitment he joked about, when Liv had no doubt he was utterly serious. Loyalty that touched her in a way she still couldn't let herself feel, stirring an attraction she wouldn't allow.

Dave Johnson sauntered out dressed in the Triple Stripe silks, a curious smirk on his face, like he knew he was walking in on something.

"Excursion has a good shot, Dave." Liv commented pleasantly, forcing herself to switch off. The Triple Stripe colt was one of the favourites for the next race, an undercard stake.

"Yeah, I think he does." Johnson turned to Nate. "Quiet day today, Miller?"

Nate looked up, and Liv could tell he really wanted to snap back at that dig.

"Yeah, Dave," he said. "Pretty quiet. Good luck. The colt's training great."

Liv suppressed a smile. *Very good, Miller. Very controlled.*

She could see him simmering, pondering the reality behind Johnson's taunt. It was Canadian International Day, second only to the Plate in hype at Woodbine. Riders had flown in from France, England, California and

New York; it was easy to feel insignificant in a place he ruled the rest of the time.

Claire made up for any insignificance she might feel herself. When it was time for her to head to the walking ring for the E.P. Taylor, she tucked her whip under her arm, leaving her nerves behind.

The fitness and power Claire radiated bolstered her confidence. Claire was impeccably turned out, black mane falling in a neat line over her almost-metallic bay coat, a perfect quarter marker pattern accentuating her hindquarters. Once Liv was up, she concentrated on each step; heard each footfall on the rubberized walkway until they met the pony at the tunnel and headed to the track. Claire's extensive warm up routine wouldn't look so out of place amid the European contenders.

The gate was positioned out of sight of the grandstand. Claire broke sharply, but Liv convinced her to settle and drop back, ready for the sharp left-hand turn ahead. From there it was a long straightaway, the whole field travelling like a cohesive unit, the drumming of their hooves and rhythm of their breathing filling her ears. She imagined this was what it must be like on the gallops overseas, except for the layers of white rails separating three different track surfaces here, the stable area to the right, and the jet overhead, taking off from the International airport next door. Claire loved it too, loping along with her ears flopping like she could do it all day.

The next turn was huge and sweeping and carried them downhill, momentum building with it. The action started to unfold, Claire's ears sweeping forward, then swivelling back, waiting for her cue. With the final turn still seeming forever away from the finish, Liv remained motionless, weighing the distance remaining against the stored energy beneath her. Then she pulled Claire off the rail and sent her on.

Claire joined the charge, four-wide, ears laced as she flattened into an all-out drive. Liv pushed with each extension of the filly's neck, the spring of the turf sending power back up Claire's limbs. She reached back with her whip, one, two, three, then pumped again with her arms as they hurtled to the wire in a blanket of horses. The stewards would need a photo to separate them.

She pulled Claire up, scanning for the outrider's red coat, but he picked up the dark bay favourite from France. Liv reached forward and stroked Claire's neck, still thrilled. These were some of the toughest turf distaffers in the world.

Nate was waiting to go out for the next race when she got back to the room.

"So freaking close. The way she galloped out … you should have gone in the International. She wanted that extra quarter-mile."

"Maybe." She gave him a wistful smile.

"Gotta go. Some of us have to stick around and ride the in-between races." He tapped her arm as he turned away.

Liv showered and changed, then stole past the crowd waiting for the International horses to arrive. She stopped at a monitor to watch the ninth race—another winner for Nate. Of course he wanted to ride in these big races, but he was doing a good job of paying his dues in the meantime. As the horses galloped out on the screen, she ducked away against the flow of traffic.

It was quiet back at the barn, Claire already cooled out and tearing at the grass on the lawn with the hotwalker. The filly lifted her head in aloof acknowledgement before returning to her mowing.

"I'm going to watch the International from the bleachers, Jo," she called, and walked across the road towards the bank.

"Wait up!"

Faye flagged her down, climbing out of her car and skittering across the road in her heels. She followed Liv up the steps.

The bleachers overlooked the lengthy backstretch of the turf course, the faint hum of the buzzing crowd drifting across the infield. Faye kept silent, and Liv could hear the track announcer giving the play-by-play as the starters entered the gate. *They're locked up*...but not for long. The horses were off before the sound of the starter's bell reached them.

It wasn't the best vantage point until the field entered that long straightaway and came thundering past, forty hooves thrumming along the green. They swept by and around the turn, rolling down the incline to the homestretch. The finish was obscured, the announcer's call drowned out by the roar of the crowd, the result a mystery.

"Why'd you come here to watch?" Faye asked.

"Probably so I couldn't see the time, compare it to the E.P. Taylor and go through all the coulda-shoulda-wouldas." She'd hear about it either way, eventually. "What are you doing here?"

"I came to see you. We haven't really talked in ages."

"You can't blame it on me this time." Liv looked at her sideways. "You're distracted."

"Guilty."

Faye beamed with genuine happiness Liv had rarely seen, and definitely never relating to a man. It irked her, then irked her more that she was bothered.

"I'm sure you don't want to hear it, but he just doesn't stop being amazing."

Faye was right, she didn't want to hear it. She knew it already. And she had, like some kind of mutant girl, pushed him away. But she rolled her eyes and smirked. "You're making me nauseous."

"Sorry. So not me, is it?" Faye laughed lightly.

Liv eyed her. "It's concerning. Have you considered asking for an MRI?"

That earned her a swat. "You don't mind, right? I warned you, remember."

"Of course I don't mind. As long as you don't distract him from riding Chique." She paused, telling herself it was true.

"It's so weird. He's so old-fashioned, but…it's kind of nice. Not that I won't jump his bones the second I get an opening, but, it's sweet, you know?"

Liv's eyebrows shot up. "You mean you're not—?"

"I know, right? So not me."

That just churned her gut more. How did Faye, who made no secret of her fondness for sex, land, then fall head over heels, for the one remaining guy on earth who didn't single-mindedly want to get a girl in bed?

You had your chance.

She ploughed ahead. "Seriously, Faye, it's a good thing. You never let anyone get to know you. It's about time you found a nice guy, one who's more than a passing amusement. You both deserve to be happy. He's been through a hard time too."

Faye tilted her head. "How do you know about that?"

"It was New Year's Eve, there was wine." She waved her hand through the air. "He didn't give me details."

"Why are you just telling me this now?"

"Because it was nothing." Even if it wasn't. "Nothing happened." Even if something did. It didn't matter anymore.

Faye sighed. "I didn't mean to suggest anything had. You two barely even tolerate each other most of the time. How have things been since you got back?"

Liv rose, glancing at Faye. "We're managing to be civil. We have Chique as our mediator."

31

NOVEMBER

Chique flipped her head, froth flying. *That was close.* It'd be embarrassing to blow the chance to prove his theory by getting knocked out in the post parade of the Coronation. Roger was going with it, but Nate was sure he'd only get one shot.

"Let us go."

Nicole gave him a look he was well familiar with—that *you're crazy* one—but she turned the filly loose.

Chique sprang forward, the horses warming up around the turn in her sights. The only thing that stopped her from running off with him was probably the direction—she was unsure enough galloping the wrong way to display a modicum of caution. It was still quicker than anyone else was going, and she caught up with them, passing them and dragging Nate into the backstretch. If she decided to head back to the barn he was sunk. But though her attention narrowed at the wide straight in front of her, she let him pull her up and turn her to face the infield, the grandstand in the distance. She even stood a moment, frozen to a statue as the faint hum from the crowd reached her. Nate stroked her neck, and they shared a deep breath before they set off, back towards the gate waiting for them at the eighth pole.

"That probably put the final nail in the coffin for anyone thinking of betting her, eh?" Nate said when Paz met them, Nicole looping the leather latigo through the bit. Chique snorted and dropped her head, trying to rub it against Paz.

His eyes settled on Touch and Go, disappearing into the metal barrier. Johnson had picked up the mount. No regrets. Even if the colt was the better option on paper, his heart was with his little wild child.

They were the last ones in, the doors slamming shut behind them, and before Chique had time to think about doing anything bad, the starter released them.

Nate almost laughed, because she was caught off guard, breaking at less than her normal mach 10—though it only fed her determination to make the lead. Trying to rate her might have seemed a reasonable choice, but when she'd won, she'd been in front, so he let her go on. Chique threw herself into the plan, her strides coming short and quick as she built up to cruising speed. When they were clear, he let her drop to the rail, and they led the field past the grandstand and into the clubhouse turn.

No one challenged, perhaps lulled into the reasonable assumption that Chique was only a speed horse, even though they weren't going that fast. *Perfect.* Chique wasn't running like it was the zombie apocalypse this time. Maybe that warm up had taken the edge off, though it might come back to bite him. He'd see if the longer morning gallops had done enough to build the stamina she'd need for the extra distance. Along the backstretch, she stayed a length up.

At the head of the stretch, he chirped, and Chique's ears flicked forward as the next gear kicked in. Nate grinned when he felt it. She might be more than a sprinter after all.

They were alone in front, and he resisted the temptation to look back to see if anyone was coming. Finally, he could feel Touch and Go closing ground; isolate the sound of the colt's hoofbeats behind them. Chique didn't need any encouragement to hold the colt at bay, Nate simply cocking his whip and flashing it before going to his hands. They still had a length and a half advantage when they hit the wire, and she had no intention of letting the colt pass her as they galloped out.

He was still laughing when the outrider picked them up. Chique tried to bite the pony, her attempt cut short as the outrider popped her head straight and growled at her.

"Stop that, we may need him one day," Nate said, but the rub on the neck he gave her was all affection.

Touch and Go galloped past, on the way back to be unsaddled. He didn't feel the triumph he thought he would, besting Johnson. He had nothing but respect for that colt, and in a rematch Johnson wouldn't let him get away with another steal. That rematch might not come until the Queen's Plate. *Chickens, Miller. Stop counting them.* It was a long way off.

Liv met them before Jo, lips twisted into not quite a smile, apparently lost for words as she reached up to grasp his hand.

"What did I tell you?" He grinned, squeezing so hard she should have flinched. "Just relax and embrace the crazy."

THE SUN SLIPPED below the horizon in the west, reminding Liv in just a couple of weeks, they'd be packing up the shed and heading to Florida. Roger had organized a little stake party, as much to commemorate the approaching end of the season as the unlikely event that Chique would win. Liv had declined the sparkling wine, even though the post-race buzz that had kept her warm on the frontside had worn off.

She saw Chique's head pop up, then noticed Nate's Mustang rolling to a halt. The filly watched every step as he approached across the lawn. He offered her peppermints, said a word to the hotwalker, then rubbed her face before heading towards the barn. Chique continued to track him.

He squeezed in through the door, pulling it shut—not that it was a whole lot warmer inside than out—and sidled up to Faye, slipping an arm around her and kissing her quickly. Liv glanced away.

"Where's mine?" he said, eyes running over Faye's and Emilie's drinks, then quirking an eyebrow at Liv's lack.

"Go see Rog," Emilie said.

Nodding, he left them, walking down to the office and coming back with two glasses. He held one out to Liv.

"Oh come on. Drink up. To the big filly! An appropriate coronation, don't you think?"

She met his eyes and shook her head, still convinced it wasn't safe to consume alcohol when he was around, despite his thing with Faye. She still didn't know what to say about Chique. When the filly was good, she showed so much talent it was scary, but her performance in the Mazarine Stakes still lurked in Liv's mind, feeding her doubts.

"It wouldn't kill you to believe a little," he said.

Liv laughed then—it was impossible not to be just a little bit affected by his conviction.

"So it's true, eh?" His mouth leveled into a line. "They're switching back to dirt at the end of the season."

"I guess there was too much pressure." Nearly all the tracks in North America that had invested in synthetic all-weather surfaces had reverted to dirt.

"What do you think?"

Liv shrugged. "I think it doesn't matter what I think. They're going to do it anyway. We'll find out what she thinks this winter, I guess."

Hopefully her opinion was favourable.

32

DECEMBER

Nate drove up to the farmhouse at Northwest and parked the Mustang, stepping out onto the packed snow. There were about six inches of the stuff on the ground, King Township's rolling hills a bloody winter wonderland, but he didn't mind. For the first time in three years, he was getting Christmas the way Christmas was supposed to be.

Faye met him at the door and he wrapped himself around her. She pressed against him and kissed him, sliding the coat off his shoulders.

The Woodbine meet had passed tolerably, despite several cold and miserable days, but he'd made it worthwhile by beating Johnson in the standings to finish on top. Spending time here at Northwest had gotten him through it. Faye—he'd never expected her to stick with him, to be that understanding. This was more than he thought it would ever be—even without the icing.

She had wine poured, and handed him a glass. The iron wood stove warmed the small kitchen, filled with the incredible smells of a holiday feast that had never felt right in Florida.

"Merry Christmas," she said, holding his gaze over her glass.

"Merry Christmas." He slipped his arm around her and kissed her again before they sipped. "Where're Dean and Gus?"

"Watering off. They'll be back soon."

She curled her hand into his and led him to the living room. He felt a tiny bit homesick for Calgary as he sat on the couch next to her, taking in the tree, sparkling with lights and tinsel, the fresh scent of spruce and citrus reaching him. It was the first time since he'd left home he'd felt part of something, these past few weeks—something like family—though the thought of family still brought traces of pain.

He set his glass on the coffee table, and dug out the envelope stuffed in the shirt pocket under his sweater. "Here. While we're waiting for Dean."

Faye's eyebrows arched as she took it. "What's this?"

"Your Christmas present."

She ripped it open with her thumb, and unfolded the paper. "A plane ticket? To Fort Lauderdale. At the end of January."

"It's a pretty safe bet I'll be nominated for the Eclipse Award for top apprentice. I thought maybe you could come down. Break up the winter at least a little."

Four months he'd be gone. While he was excited about Chique, and what lay ahead there, the separation would be hard. On him. On the relationship. One that was still in its infancy, thanks to the turtle-slow pace. Faye wouldn't go along with it forever. He'd have to figure out what was next. This winter would be a test.

"That would be incredible."

She leaned into him, pulling him close as she kissed him, and he reached around her and kept her there. He heard the door open, the click of nails over kitchen tile, but Faye didn't stop, so he saw no reason to either—until a wet Golden Retriever nose inserted itself between them.

"Gus the chaperone." He laughed, breaking away and slapping the Golden's ribcage.

It was all just right—the food, the wine, the crackling fireplace and candlelight, the festive music playing softly in the background, Faye at his side. He almost felt whole. Like this could be his life, if this was who he chose to be.

33

JANUARY

Paz's strides quickened to match Claire's, and Nate loosened his hold, releasing her. He zeroed in on the mare as she set down to work—the early morning sun hitting her gleaming coat, Liv's slender form poised low and motionless over her withers.

Mopping the sweat from his eyes with the sleeve of his t-shirt, he glanced at the stopwatch clutched in his hand. Claire approached the sixteenth pole of Gulfstream's main track, Liv still unmoving as they flew down the lane.

The siren wailed, and every muscle in his body tensed.

Loose horse.

Paz's head flew up, feet dancing as they both went on high alert. Then he saw it, on the far side of the track, barreling wildly in the wrong direction.

The warning cry that escaped his throat was futile—there was no way Liv could possibly hear—but he couldn't stop it, any more than he could stop the danger coming at her. He spun Paz into action, the old sprinter taking off, flat out.

The wind rushing past his ears didn't mask the deadening thud—a head-on collision, flesh on flesh; the force of a thousand pounds from each direction crashing, then crumbling into a treacherous heap of thrashing legs. Nate drove with hands and voice, pushing Paz still faster. The stretch seemed endless, like a nightmare where he'd never reach the disaster waiting just beyond the wire.

Paz's hocks dropped as Nate sat back, hind feet leaving a trail in the sandy surface that would have made any of the rodeo horses back in Calgary proud. Nate was out of the saddle and running in a single motion, leaving the pony like he knew how to ground tie; nostrils flared, ribcage heaving.

Both racehorses were on their feet. Claire stood by the rail, left hind held gingerly off the ground. Someone held her bridle, though the mare didn't look as if she intended to move. A murmuring group gathered around Liv's unconscious form.

"The ambulance is on the way."

He barely heard the words, pushing in and dropping to his knees beside her; hesitating. He wanted to take off her helmet and straighten her body, somehow make her crumpled form seem more comfortable. Reaching out, he touched her face lightly with the back of his hand. Her cheek was cool and clammy despite the heat, shock taking over with uncompromising stealth.

"Where the hell are they?" He stilled his fingers enough to find her pulse, rapid but weak, just below her jawline.

The ambulance was parked trackside during training hours so it wasn't long before it arrived, but it felt like hours. Nate answered questions and gave information as best he could while the paramedics worked, but jerked away when the vet arrived. Someone had stripped the saddle from Claire; another man had rescued Paz from where Nate had abandoned the blowing stable pony and walked the gelding in an irregular circle. The vet filled a syringe. Nate felt like he was the only one not doing anything.

Liv was on a backboard now, and the medics carried her to the ambulance. Nate took a step after it as it departed, lights flashing but silent. The emergency horse trailer pulled up, and his head snapped back to Claire. He pushed himself towards her, feeling like he was moving through deep sludge, and took over at the mare's head.

Claire followed him slowly up the low ramp. Her breath blew warm on his arm, eyes distant with sedation, and he placed a hand at the origin of the long white marking on her face as they were closed in, feeling as numb as she looked. He wanted to follow the ambulance, but Liv would never forgive him if he didn't wait to hear the status of her beloved Claire. She might be unconscious, but when she came to—assuming she did—Claire would be the first thing she asked about.

The trailer stopped moving, the doors opened, and the team at the backstretch surgical clinic took over. Now, at least, everything happened quickly, radiographs taken immediately to assess the damage. Nate hung over the surgeon's shoulder, focused on the images.

"It's good news, all things considered." The vet indicated a line, just above the fetlock joint. "Incomplete lateral condylar fracture of the third metatarsal. We'll realign it surgically, do an internal fixation—just screws. We can do it standing up. If everything goes right, she should be okay."

At the hospital, news took longer. He perched on the edge of a chair in the waiting room, alone amid the others there. Scrubs and a lab coat appeared, scanning the room. Nate rose, straightening his shoulders. That had to be the doctor. The man offered his hand; grasped Nate's.

"You the boyfriend?"

Nate laughed abruptly. "Ah, no," though that might have been what he'd led the nurses to believe in order to get this far. "We work together. We came down from the training centre in Indiantown to work a horse at Gulfstream this morning. Her family's in Canada. I'm as close to next of kin you're going to get at the moment."

The doctor waited out his rapid explanation. "She's stable. She's conscious. No head trauma, no internal injuries, no spinal injuries as far as we can tell. She's broken a couple of ribs but her lungs are okay. The worst of it is a fractured left femur. She'll need surgery, but because the femoral artery is involved, she's lost a lot of blood. She'll need a transfusion first."

Nate exhaled. It was a miracle she'd gotten off that easily. "So when will you do the surgery?"

"Once we have her blood back to where it needs to be, which is what the transfusion and fluids will accomplish."

"Can I see her?"

A nod. "Come with me."

The doctor pushed a door open and held it, waiting for him to go through. Nate walked in hesitantly, the door swinging shut behind him.

Her consciousness was relative. He didn't want to disturb her, and stood rooted, observing silently. Fluids hung from the drip feeding into her left hand. Her eyes were closed, her face ashen, and he assumed the medication coursing through her system did more to dull her reactions than to deaden the pain.

She must have sensed someone there, because she turned her head and opened her eyes, so he walked forward to the edge of the bed. He found himself reaching for her hand but stopped himself because of the intravenous needle, lightly touching her elbow instead.

"Hey." He tried to smile.

"Miller," she said, faintly. "What happened? Is Claire okay? I don't remember anything."

His answer came out slowly. "A loose horse ran into you."

"What about Claire?" The crease in her brow deepened, worry building on top of the pain.

He told her, watching her concern recede.

"I guess we should be thankful."

"Absolutely." He'd feared it was so much worse, when she'd been lying there on the racetrack. People died in wrecks like that. "Just so you know, I had to tell them we were married to get in here."

Her face contorted as she feebly tried to lift her free arm towards her torso. "Don't make me laugh, please."

"Oh, shit, Liv, sorry. The ribs, right?"

She was weak, and fatigued, and had to be in agony, but relief rushed to the tips of his limbs and back to his heart.

"What?"

Her tiny smile sent a surge of something he was afraid to identify through him. "It's just really good to see you. You had me pretty scared."

"Sorry about that." The way her eyes crimped threatened to pull them closed, her lids heavy. "Will you stay?"

How could he leave?

THE HAZE of the anesthetic cleared, leaving a monumental headache, aching ribs, and a fierce pain in her left leg, pinning her to the mattress.

Liv pulled her eyes from the ceiling, registering a regular hospital room—curtain drawn on her left side, a wall on her right—and Nate dozing in the chair beside the bed. He stirred and sat up, rubbing his eyes.

"How long have you been here?" Her throat was so dry and sore, it came out somewhere between a whisper and a croak.

"I told you I wasn't going anywhere."

"You did? That wasn't real bright, was it Miller?"

His blond hair was mussed and his t-shirt rumpled, a smear of dirt on the sleeve, and beyond the antiseptic hospital smell, she caught the faint scent of leather and horses. She had no right to want him here, but wished she could put into words how much it meant that he'd stayed.

"Thanks would do, you know."

Such a simple response seemed wildly inadequate for so many of the things he'd done for her.

The door clicked and Nate looked over, Roger shuffling in next to him. "What did you do, stand in front of a train?"

"Just about." Nate leveled his gaze on her.

She glanced away, the warm blue of his eyes feeding too much emotion, and forced hers to Roger. "How is Claire? Have they done the surgery?"

"Everything went smoothly. She came out of recovery with flying colours. She'll be fine. We're going to have to miss that race though."

The comment was meant to be light-hearted, no doubt, but an empty hollow formed in her gut as the reality struck her. That was it—Claire's career was over. A flicker crossed Nate's face—like he'd noticed, when she thought she'd kept the sadness inside.

"You should probably send Nate home, or you're going to have to gallop the barn yourself tomorrow." More reality. He'd done beyond enough, staying this long.

Roger rested a hand on Nate's shoulder. "You heard what she said. I don't think it's safe to give Chique another day off. She'll tear the place apart."

Nate pushed himself to his feet, touching her arm gently. "I'll see you tomorrow, all right?"

"Thank you." It wasn't enough. It was never enough. But it would have to do.

Roger didn't stay long, leaving her to drift back to sleep. She was plagued by broken visions of a scene she couldn't actually remember—the flashy bay mare's brilliant turn of foot in the lane, the dark form of the colt bearing down on her in the wrong direction, a collision, the clash of tangled legs. Then Claire was gone, Liv couldn't find her, the anguish waking her. In the darkness it became merely physical, and she embraced the pain, reminding herself Claire was fine, injured but recovering, just like her.

It was some sort of sick joke on Jo's part that she left Chique for last, the filly as fresh as Nate was tired by the end of the next morning. Chique was too close to running for any lapses, so he mustered his last bit of strength to hold her, much to the filly's disappointment.

"I'll get one of the hotwalkers to do the tack if you want to get going," Jo offered when he came back.

"Thanks." He slapped the filly on the neck, grateful to be back on the ground unscathed. "You're exhausting me, Cheeky."

He grabbed the keys for the farm truck, and for the second day in a row, made the trek to Fort Lauderdale. Roger was picking up Liv's parents, so someone had to bring Paz back. Of course he was going to stop by to see Liv while he was there. It was just the right thing to do.

He picked up yesterday's work sheet and the *Form* for Wednesday's races when he was at the track. At the hospital, Liv was sitting up, the bed cranked as far as it would go. She looked brighter and happier to see him than he'd expected. He presented the papers and dropped into the same chair he'd fallen asleep in last evening.

"Claire got the bullet yesterday." He hadn't known himself until he'd picked up the work sheet, the mare's final breeze the fastest of the day for the distance. "Not that you probably want to hear that."

"At least she went out with a flourish," Liv responded quietly. "How is she? You went to see her, right?"

"Yes, I did. She's doing great. I guess they'll keep her there for a while."

"At least until she's able to travel." Liv bit her lip, turning the work sheet face down and smoothing it with her hand, her face clouding. Nate could almost see her pushing through the darkness before she forced a smile and looked back to him. “How was Chique today?”

“No surprises—she hauled my ass around. Took everything I had to hold her.”

“Still going to breeze her tomorrow?”

“I’d better. I don’t think she’s going to put up with me much longer.”

“I hope I’m out of here and recovered enough to see her run.” Dejection surfaced again as she glanced down at her leg.

“Sure you will be. Might not feel like it today, though.”

“You have no idea.”

He was sure he didn’t, but avoided dwelling on it. “Faye says she wishes she could be here, and made me promise to talk you into FaceTiming her when you feel up to it. And Rog should be here any time with your parents.”

Before the words were out of his mouth, there they were, huddling into the room. He pressed his hand to Claude’s, then was caught totally off guard when Anne Lachance wrapped him in a tight embrace. She pushed him back, still clutching his shoulders, and mouthed *thank you* before sidling past him to Liv.

Geai might as well have been whispering in his ear, *you’re already like family.*

Like a brother, right?

34

JANUARY, CONTINUED

Nate sat on the other side of the living room, guitar in his lap—playing absently, sometimes singing—undisturbed by her scrutiny. She tucked the blanket around her legs, propped against a series of cushions, book abandoned in her lap.

He'd come to see her faithfully each day in the hospital, an hour and a half away, after galloping in the mornings—which she hadn't expected any more than she'd expected his visits to continue after she'd been released yesterday. Yet here he was.

If his intent was to distract her from the inevitable—the crutches lying on the floor beside her which would be her primary mode of transport for at least two months, and the orthopaedic surgeon's instructions to keep off the back of a horse for longer than that—then his mission was futile. She had enough time left to herself to dwell on it, lying awake at night when the discomfort still kept her from sleeping. The medication they'd sent her home with, when she actually took it, only did so much. But he was easy company, and the fact that she'd become so comfortable with him was the very thing that troubled her.

"You're very talented."

He glanced at her, but kept playing. "Thanks. Just another one of those things I've been blessed with that it's hard to make a go of."

The songs sounded vaguely familiar, and he played the notes like old friends, telling stories hardly unique in their tales of love that didn't work out, and freedom that remained elusive. The words obviously held meaning, like he was exposing his soul, but he didn't seem the least bit self-conscious—while the sound of his voice made her skin burn, blood roaring through her veins, pulling her back to New Year's Eve a year ago. He'd been down by then this winter, after staying in Ontario to spend Christmas with Faye, but it was no coincidence—on her part, at least—that they weren't in the same place this time around.

She batted those thoughts back where they belonged. "You thought about it?"

"Sure. Another cliché, group of teenage guys forming a band in a garage. Kind of fell apart after my dad kicked me out for quitting school." He stopped and set the guitar flat on the floor beside him. "Can I get you anything? Water?"

"That would be good, thanks."

He came back with two glasses, handing her one before returning to his seat. Liv wrapped her arms around her good leg, vision narrowing.

"What?"

"You quit school to start a band?" More stuff she didn't know about him, and didn't need to know, but he was here, so…

"No, I quit school because my girlfriend turned me down when I proposed, and I kind of fell apart."

"You *what?"*

She hadn't meant to spit out the words with such force, but there they were. He ducked her stare, placing the guitar back in his lap, though his fingers stayed flat and still on the strings.

"New Year's Eve Girl? You'd proposed? What were you thinking?"

He shrugged. "She was older—"

"Like Mrs. Robinson older?"

He shot her a look. "She wanted all that. To get married, have kids. So did I."

"Like normal people."

"We already know where you stand."

She didn't correct him; it was a fair assumption, but she didn't know herself.

He grabbed his glass of water, looking at it like it was inadequate, and set it down again. "It was a bit of a blow to realize she just didn't want it with me. She said she was holding me back, that I needed to leave Calgary if I wanted to be a rider."

"Obviously she was right."

"You suck as a friend."

"Is that what I am?"

"I'm still trying to figure that out."

The way his eyes leveled on her knocked her off stride, like he'd invited a massive mammal with a long trunk into her living room, and it was sucking up all her oxygen. She glanced down, pulling at the edge of the blanket, wishing she could hide underneath it.

"You don't have to be here, you know. I may be an invalid, but I don't require twenty-four-hour supervision."

He smirked, recognizing her retreat. "You could be a flight risk. You do have a history."

"I'm not highly mobile at the moment."

"Still wouldn't put it past you."

Not a time she cared to remember…but it did remind her she'd managed to find her way back. And, reluctantly, that he'd been part of it.

"Maybe I just feel sorry for you." He strummed a random chord.

"Bastard," she retorted, one corner of her mouth curving up. "I definitely feel sorry for you."

"Do you want me to stop coming?"

She should say yes. This terrified her. She'd only ever had this kind of connection with Geai—mentor, practically a grandfather figure, safe. For it to come wrapped in the guise of a guy her own age—serenading, good-looking, *nice,* and quite possibly just as broken as her—was dangerous. Then there was Faye, and that niggling sense that such feelings, no matter how hard she kept trying to deny them, betrayed her only real friend. *Not a threat,* she told herself. She would never be a threat.

She met his eyes, pursing her lips. "No…but if this is about job security, I don't think you have anything to worry about. If we get Chique to the Plate, you'll be on her." Maybe it wasn't entirely impossible that she'd be sound enough again to ride, but she could never take the filly away from him now.

His fingers clenched the guitar's neck as he stared her down. "That crash scared the hell out of me, Liv. I know this sort of thing happens around us all the time, and it's bound to hit closer to home eventually—and I know one day it'll be my turn. But it has to make you take a step back and think about what's important."

"Do I want to know what that means?" It came out slowly, because she wasn't sure she did.

"I'm here because I want to find out. Because all that shit I left behind in Calgary was about more than me coming east to ride, and being here feels like it's about more than just riding horses."

She reached for her phone, a way out, fumbling. "When does Faye get in?"

His eyes shifted. Was that guilt, or was she just transferring her own?

Her mother burst in the front door, bearing groceries and calling a cheery salutation. Nate sprang over to help, disappearing into the kitchen. When he came back, he put the guitar away in its case.

"I'll see you later. Take it easy."

Then he was gone. Liv blinked. She jammed in her earbuds, blindly hitting play on the phone.

Damn Nate Miller, threatening to topple walls she'd so carefully constructed. He had some nerve, coming here, saying things.

Not saying things.

Oh, shit...

The lights flashed in his rearview mirror, but he didn't hear the siren until he turned down the music, pulling over to the shoulder of the highway. There was no debate. He'd been flying.

No, I actually don't know how fast I was going.

He mumbled thanks to the officer as he took the ticket, even if he was going to have to start back riding to pay the damn thing. Not that it didn't serve him so, so right.

His eyes stayed on his side mirror as the officer climbed back into the cruiser, and he made himself take a deep lungful of air, pushing it out slowly. How about some calming tunes for the rest of the drive, Miller?

Something to ease the frenzy. There—the playlist he'd made up of his mother's favourites; one he called on when he missed her most. Thinking of her would keep him sensible.

Or not. Even those lyrics chased him, called him out. *Living in a house of cards...*

It was getting to him, that was all—the driving back and forth; galloping the barn until Rog got things organized for Nicole to come down and help. He was on overload, his brain conjuring warped things about Liv that weren't there. Faye would set his mind straight.

At the Fort Lauderdale airport travellers emerged from the gate, and he saw her before she spotted him—her hair loose around her shoulders, wearing a flowy skirt and white blouse, a sweater over her arm. She glanced from side to side trying to locate him in the crowd, her face lighting up as her gaze finally reached him.

He enveloped her, his lips searching for reassurance as his mouth closed over hers, breathing her in until she pushed him back.

"It's almost like you missed me."

"You have no idea. I got a ticket driving down." He cracked a grin, letting go and grabbing her bag, and took her hand to lead her through the surrounding crush.

"How's Liv doing?"

His chest tightened. *Stop that.* State the facts. "She seems to be handling it all right so far."

"How are you holding up?"

"My blood pressure has dropped ten points in the last five minutes." He squeezed her hand. That was all that mattered.

At the condo, Anne welcomed Faye with a hug and air kisses before Faye caught sight of Liv, still on the couch like she hadn't moved since he'd left. Faye leaned over and gave her a gentle squeeze, then carefully sat on the end. Nate shoved his hands in his pockets, eyes drifting from one to the other. It wasn't supposed to feel like a mess, but it did.

"I guess you're not coming with us to the Eclipse Awards."

That was relief, not disappointment in the smile Liv gave Faye. "I'm heartbroken."

"The lengths you'll go to, to get out of an awards dinner." Nate tossed a smirk more or less in her direction.

"I'm looking forward to seeing you in a tux." Faye peered at him, then swiveled back to Liv. "I'll send pictures. And you can watch online."

Anne poked her head from the kitchen. "Can I bring you kids anything?"

"I should probably get going, but thanks." Nate sauntered to the couch, pulling Faye to her feet and slipping an arm around her as he kissed her. "I'll give you a heads up in the morning to let you know when I'll pick you up."

Liv glanced up at him before pasting on a fresh smile for Faye. "I'm counting on you both to make sure I get to the races next Saturday."

"You'll be there," Nate said. "What are friends for?"

Congratulations, Miller. Well deserved.

The message from Liv pinged onto the screen. Nate let it fade to black, and started the Mustang.

"Which one of your fans is congratulating you now?" Faye's smile teased, bronze statue cradled in her lap.

"Liv." He caught himself before he frowned, and held up the phone to snap a shot of Faye, writing *Thanks* and sending the photo in response. "I'm sure she's sick of you sending her pics of me in a tux."

"I agree. She'll appreciate this shiny trinket more." Faye stroked the trophy.

"Right you are." He powered off the phone.

None of it felt real. Not the perfect girlfriend in his passenger seat, not the fancy award. Not the feelings beyond simple gratitude for the opportunity that had led to it, aroused by that last text. Feelings that had to stop.

"Where are you going?"

"It's a surprise." He headed north, but not via the highway.

Faye's eyebrows peaked when he pulled into the hotel parking lot, and again when he mentioned *reservation* at reception.

"Well. Quite the surprise."

As she walked into the room, she dragged the shimmery shawl from her shoulders, dropping it on the bed. He set the trophy next to the television, eyes following as she kicked off her shoes and wandered to the window to peek out at the dark ocean beyond.

She turned, eyes meandering over him with a look that offered to give him what he'd brought her here for. What he'd made her wait for. "I hope I'm not making assumptions here."

His life had become a heap of self-restraint. Controlling what he ate, controlling what he said, controlling how he felt. This one thing, right now, he could run with.

The cool evening hadn't taken away the lingering flush in her cheeks from the wine—wine he'd skipped, in keeping with the image of straight-laced apprentice for his fifteen-minutes-or-less in the spotlight. He met her halfway, catching her lips as she laced her fingers behind his neck. Her hands roamed, knocking the jacket off his shoulders, tugging his bow tie free, her other palm resting on his pounding chest.

He hooked his hands around her waist and pulled her against him, pushing into her mouth.

"If you're sure about this, get me out of this dress."

Reaching behind her, he found the tiny metal pull of the zipper, and edged it down.

Faye waltzed in the door with fresh bagels Liv could smell from where she was sitting, and disappeared into the kitchen. Resurfacing, she marched over and pulled the cushions out from behind Liv.

"It's a gorgeous day. The sun is shining. I didn't come to Florida to sit inside."

"You already look like you have some colour."

An impish look transformed Faye's face. "So maybe we went to the beach this morning."

"Wasn't it kind of cold?"

"Not when you've just come from Ontario, let me tell you. Come on. You could use some colour yourself."

She helped Liv get settled on the patio, retreated into the house to retrieve the bagels, then stretched out on her own chair.

"Where's Nate?" Liv huddled in her sweatshirt, winding the blanket around the bottom half of her body.

Faye sloughed off her cardigan to bare her shoulders, her legs already exposed mid-thigh below her sundress. "Your mom invited us for dinner. He's going to pick something up so she doesn't have to cook."

"So? How was it?"

Faye's smile was far too self-satisfied as she dropped the sunglasses over her eyes from where they'd been propped on her head. "Oh, you mean the awards dinner. Silly me."

The heat crept up Liv's neck, a knot settling in her stomach. Even she, naïve as she was, could put the pieces together. She'd known they were staying in Fort Lauderdale overnight after the awards, but she could be forgiven for assuming it was a foregone conclusion, couldn't she? It had taken them long enough to get to that point.

So that was it, then. So foolish, to think the conversation with Nate the other day had meant more than it really had.

"You can spare me those details, thanks," she said, grabbing the bagels, and shoving too large a piece into her mouth.

"You're no fun. Sweet twenty-*six?* And never been kissed."

Not never. Not forgotten, as hard as she'd tried. It felt like it was yesterday. She clamped her lips shut and let Faye believe the flush persisting on her face was because of just that.

Liv felt him before she saw him—it unnerved her as she realized it, glancing over her shoulder, catching him wavering at the door. How long had he been there?

He slid open the screen, fingers gripping a coffee cup, his gaze shifting like he knew he'd been caught. "Why didn't I think of this? Much better than sitting inside."

"Apparently I had to come all the way from Toronto to sort things out around here." Faye bent her legs enough to make room as he sat on the end of her lounger, and poked him with a bare toe. "Where's mine?"

"Your ability to sleep till ten AM means I need it more than you." He looked at Faye sideways, smirking, shoulders slouched as he rested the cup on his knee.

"Sorry to have messed up your sleep schedule." She reached for the coffee, took a sip, and handed it back. "What's for dinner? Are you going to cook for us?"

It was like watching a foreign film, a story Liv could never imagine starring in. She would always be on the outside, trying to understand the players, passing silent judgement as she attempted to interpret the scene.

Nate's eyes isolated her, making her gut clench again. "You look tired. Maybe I should have brought a coffee for you."

She adjusted the blanket, forcing herself to return his gaze while she pushed away the thought of him and Faye in a hotel room. "I'm always tired these days, Miller."

His expression morphed from self-pity to concern. They all still looked at her like that—like she had a torn "handle with care" sticker on her forehead. Claire, her big mare, came flooding back to her mind, both of them brought to a standstill.

"You'll get to see her next Saturday."

She didn't know how he'd understood exactly what she'd been thinking. She had to push through the darkness when it seeped in; prove to everyone, including herself, she wasn't going to succumb to the despair lurking at every corner. It got old, feeling as if her mental health was at risk.

Nate dropped his eyes back to his coffee, lifting the cup to his lips. "Dean's sending Wampum down—that three-year-old of his. He's going to run down here."

Liv rejoiced silently, grateful to him for getting the conversation to more neutral ground. "He broke his maiden at the end of the Woodbine meet, didn't he?"

Faye nodded. "Nate rode him."

"Nice colt." Nate pulled his phone from his back pocket and checked the time. "I'm going to go help your mom get things ready."

He shook his cup, looking disappointed it was almost empty, and tipped it back. When he walked by, he touched Liv's shoulder, hesitating when she looked up at him and smiled with determination. She was sure now he was struggling with some crisis of conscience, and hated that he felt that way. Even more, she hated she could see it.

35

FEBRUARY

Ouf.

Liv caught her breath, jabbed in the ribs as she raised her arms to shimmy into the slip-on dress. She tugged it to her midriff with merely a twinge, and pushed herself up, balancing on her good leg to ease it the rest of the way down. The skirt was long enough to cover her scar without being annoying with crutches.

She stared into the mirror, and reached carefully for her brush. Gingerly, she pulled it through the wet tangles with her right arm. That wasn't going to work.

"You need any help?" Faye's voice came from outside the room.

"No!"

Faye laughed, and opened the door. "That was mildly snappish. Here, if you let me do it, we might actually make it to the race on time." She extracted the brush from Liv's grip.

Faye was right. Liv sat on the end of the bed with a sigh, Faye tucking behind her and pulling strands of damp hair into a braid. She was done in probably the same time it would have taken Liv to do a simple ponytail.

"Elastic?"

She rolled it off her wrist, and placed it in Faye's waiting palm.

"There. Ready to get your picture taken."

"Might be best not to jinx us by saying that." She gave Faye a sheepish grin. "Thank you."

Her mother locked the condo behind them, and Liv stepped and swung herself to the car. The sky was clear and blue—the track would be fast for their little speed freak. Liv lowered the window and pushed out her arm, letting the rush of air against her fingers distract her from thoughts of this afternoon's race. She felt so out of touch, despite regular updates from Nate and Roger. It wasn't the same as being in the barn every day.

Decelerating off the interstate ninety miles later, her mother pointed the Nissan towards the massive complex of Gulfstream Park. "I'll drop you two off. Straight up to the seats." She looked pointedly from Faye to Liv.

An order, not a suggestion. Liv smiled her most agreeable smile. "Thanks, Maman." She'd pick her battles today.

The Forward Gal Stakes was in the middle of the card, so at least there wouldn't be too long a wait. Liv tuned out the conversation between Faye and her mother and went from reading the *Daily Racing Form* Nate had brought her yesterday, to checking the minutes to post for the next race, at which point the fillies in the Forward Gal would head over to be saddled. She didn't even watch that race when it went off, turning instead to Faye.

"Go down to the paddock, Faye. I promise not to hate you for it."

Faye wavered. Had her mother not been there, Liv would have gone too, regardless of how tired she was already.

"Tell Nate *bonne chance* for me. Tell him not to fall off and to not get run off with." She hoped she didn't look too miserable.

"Got it." Faye gave her an apologetic pat before dashing off.

Liv turned back to the *Form*, glancing over the picks and comments. They didn't discount Chique—her runaway maiden victory last September boded well for her here, the Forward Gal the same distance at seven furlongs. *If regular rider, apprentice Nate Miller, can rate her here, she deserves a look.*

"Who does she have to beat?" Anne asked.

"All of them." Liv's laugh was as automatic as the thought. "The favourite is Longstreet. She was second in the Eclipse Award balloting for last year's two-year-old filly. This is her first race since the Breeders' Cup. She prefers to go long, so we have that in our favour. Nothing in here has Chique's speed. If Nate can control the pace…" What a big if that was.

A brief view of Chique in the paddock on the tote board jumbotron grabbed her attention—there was no mistaking the big white shadow roll against her smudgy-dark face; the curl of her neck as she pushed into Jo's hold. Why hadn't she thought to ask Faye to FaceTime her, to give her a private video feed? Gulfstream's cameras seemed to feel the need to show the other starters, damn it.

There, at last—riders up—and one more quick shot on the screen of Nate on Chique, legs dangling at her sides as he knotted his lines. Liv twirled the neck strap of her binoculars around her fingers, toe on her good leg bouncing as she waited.

Chique danced onto the track, a sheen of sweat darkening her neck to black, Nate resting a hand on her crest where her unruly mane spiraled. Faye squeezed Liv's arm when she slipped back into her seat, and Liv gave her a tense smile in acknowledgement before turning to Roger, settling on the other side of her mother.

"How was she?"

"She didn't take anyone out in the walking ring."

"So far, so good," Faye agreed.

Nate took Chique off on his own to warm up, the filly free-wheeling around the clubhouse turn, leaving the others jogging and hobby-horsing with their ponies. He insisted it kept her better settled—and their performance in the Coronation backed up that assertion—but Liv still had visions of Chique going for a joy-ride down the backstretch. She didn't breathe again until he had her pulled up and turned around, Chique jogging to the gate with head down, toes flicking.

"She seems to have her gate issue sorted out," Roger commented when the filly filed into her position without complaint.

"A two minute-lick for a warm-up probably took the wind out of her sails." Liv bit her lower lip so hard she tasted blood.

The doors flew open, and Chique catapulted out a jump ahead of the rest, Nate with plenty of room to capture the rail. It was where the filly wanted to be, and there was no sense arguing with her in a sprint. Liv glanced at the time when the first fraction popped up. Surprisingly reasonable.

Chique was four lengths clear at the half-mile pole, Nate like a statue on her back as he held her. Her ears went straight up midway around the turn, and it was like centrifugal force took over.

"What the hell—" Roger leapt to his feet, binoculars locked on the filly as Chique blew the turn, heading to the outside fence. Longstreet, stalking tight to the rail, dragged her rider to the lead.

"Oh come on, filly!" Liv couldn't take it, hopping up on her good leg. Faye's arm threaded around her waist to steady her, watching just as keenly, while on the other side her mother tried to pull her back down.

Nate got Chique back on course, more or less—she was in the middle of the track, but at least headed in the right direction—but his attempts to re-engage her were coming up short. Then her ears flattened and she made a beeline for the other filly, swooping in with such single-mindedness Nate had to wave his whip alongside her to keep her from barreling into Longstreet. Finally straight, Chique locked on and fought back as they yelled themselves hoarse. When the two fillies hit the wire, Liv couldn't tell who'd won.

She slumped into her chair, eying Roger. "What do you think?"

"No idea. I'll go see what the rider has to say."

"I'm coming down."

"Don't be ridiculous," her mother snapped.

"It'll be all right." Faye smiled sympathetically at Anne, and set Liv up with the crutches.

Once trackside, they waited on the apron while Roger strode out with Jo to meet the returning filly, just as the tote board broadcast the result.

"Yes!" Faye bounced and threw her arms around Liv, threatening to knock her off balance. "Come on, Anne! Picture time!" Faye looped her arm through Anne's and left Liv to swing herself to the winner's circle.

Liv edged forward when Nate dismounted after the photo, and the strength with which he grasped her upraised hand reminded her how weak she was. Her thigh throbbed, her ribs ached, but she was determined to ignore both, waiting for him to weigh in.

"You look wiped." He passed his tack to the valet, rubbing sweat from his eyes, though Chique's front-running trip had kept him clean.

Liv waved it off. "That was…what was that, Miller?"

"That was Chique taking offence to the Pegasus monster. Or wanting to commune with it, I'm not sure which."

She raised her eyebrows, not buying the excuse, but Chique didn't miss much. "She's been here before. She worked here. She schooled here."

"Maybe she was lonely, up there all by herself. At least once the other filly went by, she decided to run again. We just have to have it figured out by June, right?"

His offhanded confidence managed to disarm her, the corners of her mouth creeping up. "Before that would be nice."

Nate turned to Anne. "I know you're wanting to get her home, but you'll make a quick visit to see Claire at the clinic, right?"

Anne nodded wearily, and Liv's smile grew, for a moment forgetting her fatigue. If Nate's charm worked on her mother, she was all for it—though her appreciation was tempered when Faye wrapped herself around him for a lengthy congratulatory kiss before coming along to assist.

Claire's whicker of recognition reached her before she even saw the mare, melting Liv's heart, and she shuffled to the stall.

"Be careful, Liv," Anne sighed.

"It's Claire, Maman. We'll be fine. Poor Claire," she murmured, letting the soft muzzle explore her hands, apologetic for the lack of tidbit. "What's going to happen to us?"

NATE DROPPED down on one elbow, running a hand from Faye's shoulder, down her back to the curve of her waist. She rolled over, and he kissed away her sultry smile.

"What would it take to convince you to stay?"

"For you to be making enough money I wouldn't have to go back to my job? I've never been a kept woman, but I bet I'd be just darling at it."

"I see." He grinned. "You could get a job walking hots or something in the meantime."

"Oh no. I'm happy to leave those crazy horses to you."

Faye pushed herself up, eyes hidden behind her sunglasses. "It'll be at least April before you're home, won't it?"

He sighed, and sat up next to her. "At least. I don't know what will happen with Chique, but I have to go wherever she goes."

"Here I'm thinking I'd follow you anywhere, and you're following a bloody horse."

"Easy now, don't be using that horse's name in vain." He tried a grin, pulling her against his shoulder. "She's crazy and erratic, but she just might be my ticket to the Queen's Plate."

As, more or less, was Liv.

He could do this friends thing with Liv. He could balance that, and Faye, and Chique. This was him, having it all.

Liv stuffed her water bottle in the tote along with her book—catching up on her reading was the only good thing about all this. With the bag slung over her shoulder, she set off with the plant-swing stride that was second nature now, the soreness from overdoing it on Saturday just starting to ease. She reached for the handle on the screen door, pushing it the rest of the way open with the end of one crutch, and eased out onto the patio.

Solitude was like an old friend; it was the loneliness that was strange, even if the letdown after the last week was inevitable. Faye was back in Ontario. Chique was oblivious to the ruckus surrounding another unorthodox victory. She hadn't seen Nate since he'd come to take Faye to the airport. Their lives went on without her, while she was left trying to sort it all out in her head.

Did Nate's absence mean he'd decided his visits were a problem, especially now that he'd gone the next step with Faye? He had to do what he thought was right to preserve that. But it didn't make it better. It meant there was something to be avoided.

So, she was back to this, striving to keep it all professional, which she never should have let go in the first place. The anesthetic from the surgery had obviously messed with her brain chemistry, left her vulnerable, flooded with angst like some woebegone teenager.

She heard a light tap, the screen door scraping open, and there he was, like her brain had conjured him. The little surge in her chest was temporary, quickly fading to sadness, leaving her frustrated she couldn't control either the rise or fall of her fickle emotions.

"Sorry I haven't been by." He held a booklet in his hand, but didn't offer it to her.

"That's okay. How's the freak show?" A problem she could tackle head on.

He smirked. "Great. Got on her this morning, because she was starting to wreck the barn."

"Well you're here, so she didn't kill you. That's good. What's next?"

"You're the boss."

"You're the custodian of the crazy. Besides, no one's given me a stakes schedule."

He tossed over the booklet. "Though I'm pretty sure you know what the options are."

"So what do you think?" She flipped through the pages until she reached the first weekend in March.

"Rog wants to run her in the Fountain of Youth."

"I'm sorry, what? Clearly the crazy is contagious."

"The Davona Dale is only a mile. The Fountain of Youth is a mile and a sixteenth. We want to run a mile and a quarter at the end of June, right? Chique can sprint a mile; she needs the practice going longer." His grin finally showed up.

"Or you need the practice rating her?"

"That too." He swung his legs onto the lounge chair, and leaned back. "Your mother out right now?"

"Yes. Apparently I don't need constant supervision anymore. What does that have to do with figuring out where to run Chique next?"

"How do you feel about the beach?"

"What?"

"You know, that sandy bit by the ocean? You plan on staying cooped up here for the next two months?"

"You saw me Saturday. I'm not exactly strong yet." The excursion had made her aware just how weak she'd become…though she was determined to turn that around. One thing she knew—she needed to get back to the barn, just to be there, or her long-term sanity was in jeopardy.

"It's not hard," he insisted. "You lie there, catch a few rays, plan the path that gets Chique to the Plate. I'll make it even more attractive by taking you to see the horses first."

He knew her weak spot. "My mom's going to kill you."

"Aw, she loves me. I can do no wrong."

"That's what you think. Just when she's decided it's safe to leave me alone."

"I'm just going to run home and have a shower. Be back in twenty."

When he returned he looked like the shower had washed away the tension he'd carried earlier, his hair damp, the bright blue Gulfstream t-shirt he wore making the colour of his eyes that much more vivid. He picked up her bag and held the door open.

"Trying to escape, are you?"

Her mother. Thank goodness. Just in time to get her out of this ridiculousness.

Anne smiled, too suspiciously for Liv's liking. "Have a nice time!"

Liv glanced at Nate. "Conspiring with my mother now?"

He shrugged. "Like I said, she loves me."

What's not to love? she thought wryly, but wasn't about to say it out loud.

She didn't know exactly what was happening; wasn't sure it was right, but couldn't seem to stop it. For once she decided to relax and go with it—not that she was particularly good at that.

Chique's head popped out when he pulled up to the barn—Liv swore the filly recognized the sound of the Mustang's tired engine. Nate helped her out, and she swung to the first stall and blew into a nostril when Chique lifted her soft nose.

"You have no idea the stress you cause me."

Nate leaned on the rail, watching. *And you, too.*

"Beach?" he said.

She nodded. "Beach."

The weather was perfect, which wasn't necessarily a given for Florida in February. He'd brought one of those little chairs, and set it up on the sand for her, standing by while she got organized.

"So...friends, then." She peered up at him over her sunglasses. "Just so we're clear."

He chuckled. “Yeah. Crystal.”

He left her there, pulling off his t-shirt and wandering down to the surging water. Part of her yearned to follow him, and she pretended the draw she felt was nothing more than the pull of the waves and a longing to taste the salt on her tongue.

36

MARCH

Just over five weeks since the accident, and Liv still woke well before dawn, her internal alarm prodding her to consciousness. This time, she pulled on jeans, zipped a hoodie over a long-sleeved t-shirt, and parked herself on the bed with her book to wait.

Stairs creaked around seven—her mother up now—and she thought about where they would be in the routine at Payson. Nate liked to take Chique out first, so the filly would be back in her stall enjoying her haynet—six days away from her next test.

Emilie stirred, peeking around the door.

"There you are." Liv shuffled her hips over to make room. "Sorry I didn't wait up."

"I wasn't expecting you to." Emilie crawled onto the bed beside her and looked down at Liv's book. "I forget what it's like to read a novel."

"I remember that world. Research papers and textbooks. Hope you left all of them at home."

"Much too heavy for travel." Emilie nodded. "I'm mostly caught up, so semester break can actually be a break."

"Did you see *Maman?*"

"Not yet. She told me last night I'm supposed to take you to Payson this morning though."

"Good." Liv gave her a shove. "Go get dressed. We can catch the last set."

The training centre was still busy, the grooms on the Triple Stripe shed ready for the current pair to return from the track while preparing the last two horses. Liv negotiated past the first stall, ignoring Chique's tap-tap-tap, and stopped to meet the bold blaze pushing out over the webbing. Claire pressed into her chest.

"Would someone please give that woman a peppermint?"

Nate's voice reached her at the exact moment Claire shoved her with her nose.

He pulled his horse to a halt and dropped his feet from the irons. "You're late, Em! We're almost all out. Grab this horse's halter, will you?"

Emilie scowled, picking the halter up from the rail. "Where's Michel? I'm supposed to be on vacation, you know."

"You're cuter. Get out here."

Liv backed into Claire, letting the mare nuzzle her neck from behind, and inhaled, drinking in the surroundings as she listened to their banter. *This is home.*

Roger tucked Paz away in the end stall and strode down the shed. "I thought you might show up this morning."

"I'm so glad she's back." She kissed Claire's pink muzzle and moved to let the mare go to her haynet.

"If this is going to be a regular thing, just do me a favour and stay off the horses for a while yet." Roger patted her lightly on the shoulder. "I have to go find Doc Benson."

When Liv was sure he was gone, she swung down to the end of the shed. Nate was setting his saddle in front of his final horse after sending Emilie walking with the one he'd just returned on.

"Come with me, Miller."

She ducked into the last stall where Paz stood, still tacked up.

"What are you doing?" Nate asked, his tone matching his suspicious expression.

"Get in here."

His eyebrows rose when she dropped the halter from the gelding's head. "Oh come on. Forget it."

"Throw me up."

"No way."

"It's Paz, Miller. Come on. Rog is gone. Throw me up." She leaned the crutches in the corner and hopped back over, gathering the reins. Nate shook his head, but stepped in behind her, Liv looking over her shoulder at him. "Okay, just easy now."

She couldn't completely mask her grimace as pain shot up her leg, but as soon as she transferred her weight to her arms, all she felt were pokes from her healing ribs. She quickly swung her good leg over and eased into the tack, taking a deep breath, then reached down and patted Paz's neck, grinning like she was four again.

"I'll get your helmet," Nate grumbled, turning to drop the bar.

"Thanks, Miller."

"Yeah well, if I get fired, it's your fault."

"No one's getting fired," she said, still beaming as she neck-reined Paz to the door. "Besides, if you haven't been fired by now, I don't think you have to worry."

Paz took her to the tack room, where Jo already waited with her helmet, then held up her safety vest. "Better put this on, too."

Nate met her outside on a plain bay horse she didn't recognize. "Is that Dean's colt? Wampum?"

He nodded. "Guess he's our competition on Saturday. The downside to Chique going in the Fountain of Youth instead of the Davona Dale is I don't get to ride them both."

Liv could think of other downsides, like the possibility Chique would get dusted by a bunch of colts, but she kept her mouth shut.

She parked Paz by the clocker's stand until Nate disappeared the wrong way around the turn, backing up, then nudged Paz to the right, restraining her impulse to canter him to the off-gap. Wampum zoomed past, galloping strongly.

"You look good on the pony," Nate said when they met up again. "You should get your trainer's license."

His expression was totally serious. It hadn't even crossed her mind. Why not? She needed something to occupy her mind—not that the object of the prospective job title wasn't already doing that. All the license would do was make it her official responsibility.

"Rog and I have already talked about it. We're a team, right?" Nate said, eyes steady on her as they walked off the track. "Maybe you won't be riding her in the Plate, but your name needs to be in the program. You deserve credit for your part."

"A one-horse stable?"

"But what a horse, right?"

"Temperamental, wildly unpredictable? Yeah, what a horse." But she matched his grin.

Emilie took over Paz when she got back, bathing him and letting him graze the coarse grass outside the barn. Roger was in the tack room, and Liv sheepishly rested the crutches against the wall, and settled into a chair.

He didn't look up, completing the morning's training record. "Someone said they saw you on my pony. I said that was impossible."

Liv grinned. "Really. They'll say anything around here, won't they?"

CHIQUE'S EARS FLATTENED, sticking out from her head like handlebars, and she pressed her face into the pony rider's lap as if hoping it would shield her from the driving rain. Nate hunched his shoulders, but otherwise tried to ignore the unrelenting downpour quickly threatening to turn Gulfstream's dirt track into part of the Everglades. Chique made no such effort, the look on her face almost comical—except that he feared for their chances of success with her display of disdain.

The veteran pony wrinkled his nose and glared at the filly, but said no more. Paz had stayed at home because they needed the stall on the Triple Stripe van for Wampum, who was looking far less concerned about the weather a couple of spots up in the post parade.

He sent Chique away from her new best friend to warm up, but the filly lacked her usual zeal, her gallop mincy as she picked through the swamp. They wouldn't prolong the start with this deluge, so Nate didn't take her far, turning back towards the gate with the others and finding the solace of her pony pal to wait for their turn to load. Good thing it was a mile and a sixteenth today; maybe she'd get over herself in time to make a respectable showing. Chique butted the pony with her head, velcroed to the grumpy gelding's side.

"Sorry," Nate muttered at the pony rider, nodding thanks to her before she transferred him to the starter's assistant.

The filly walked into the outside stall and sighed, relieved to finally have shelter. Nate weaved his fingers through her mane, looking out at the murky stretch of soup in front of them, trying not to let her contempt for the conditions wear off on him.

She broke flat, a beat behind her rivals, popping out with the same caution she'd shown in her warmup, then veered for the outside rail as the rest of her opponents battled for position. Nate scrambled to refocus her, grateful they'd had no one to their right to interfere with. She'd sacrificed lengths with that move, and Nate had to hustle her to make up ground. It was such a short run to the clubhouse turn they got stuck three-wide, but he was pretty sure getting mud slung in her face on the inside wouldn't have gone over well anyway.

She tried to climb over her own splash, her head too high and her stride horribly inefficient, burning valuable energy. The splatter and slap of hooves ahead of them was unrelenting, and did nothing to invite her to join in. She drifted even wider before they straightened into the backstretch, just to be sure she was clear of the assault, and swapped leads so dramatically Nate almost laughed.

On the far turn, a couple of horses started moves, and he glanced to his left and saw Wampum. The colt looked like a clay sculpture, bay coat covered in a layer of uniform slate grey, and Chique matched strides with him like she'd found a familiar face in a foreign country. Maybe there was hope, because Nate was sure Wampum would fire, and perhaps that would rouse the filly out of her wallowing.

They turned for home, and Wampum jumped into action, the mess of kickback breaking over him like a wave. Nate asked Chique to go with him—but Chique just let him go.

Liv didn't look surprised to see him, or concerned he'd let himself in. He'd brought pizza—with two dark days ahead, he could manage the indulgence, and knowing Liv, she hadn't eaten and wouldn't have any food, since her mother had returned to Ontario. He set the box on the kitchen table, and called towards the living room.

"Get in here, trainer, and tell me what's going on in that head of yours."

He opened cupboards until he found a couple of wine glasses, and poured from the bottle of red he'd brought.

She appeared in the doorway in an oversized sweatshirt and shorts, her hair pulled loosely back. The way she leaned on the doorframe, that slight curve of her lips accompanying her raised eyebrows…none of it intended to be alluring, but totally…*no.* He shook it off, and set out plates.

Awkwardly, without crutches, she came over, which probably wasn't surgeon-approved—not that hopping on the pony a week ago had been either. He pushed a glass across the table. She pushed it back.

"I'm not drinking wine with you."

"I think we can put that drunken pity party behind us, can't we? We're good. We're friends. We've established that. Declarations have been made." He pushed the glass towards her again. "One glass. To friends."

She sighed, lifting it, then held his eyes as she accepted the toast.

Right. Friends.

"How was your afternoon? You obviously got Em to the airport in plenty of time—she's already home and whining about the cold."

"It was uninspiring." He joined her at the table. "So have we recovered enough from yesterday's embarrassment to talk about it?"

"I don't think she liked the slop," Liv said out of the corner of her mouth as she bit into a piece of pizza. When her look shifted to him, they both cracked up.

"So we can agree to throw that one out?" he said.

"And pray it doesn't ever rain again when she runs?" She took a careful sip of the wine. "I'm thinking Keeneland next. How does that sound?"

"Keeneland in April…sounds amazing."

"Assuming she comes out of this okay. Dean's sending Wampum, too."

"He ran huge yesterday. I'm proud of him." Wampum's big move on the turn, leaving Chique literally in his wake, had got the colt up for third.

"Dean was thrilled, but I'm sure you know that. Any regrets about picking the wrong horse?"

"Chique will never be the wrong horse. She'll always be my girl."

Her face softened into what he wanted to think was affection, but just as quickly bounced back to business. "I think we'll opt for fillies in the Ashland this time. If Wampum goes in the Blue Grass, maybe you'll get the mount back."

"So…any chance you're thinking Churchill for the next stop? Kentucky Oaks?" A guy could dream, right?

"Let's see how she handles the Ashland. If she runs back to yesterday's performance, we'll be packing our bags and going home."

"So little faith."

"I thought picking a Grade One instead of just waiting for Woodbine was showing faith. Are you in?"

"You keep asking me that, like you're afraid I'm going to disappear. Have I ever let you down?"

Her eyes dropped to her glass. *Oh.* Not a good sign.

"No," she finally responded.

"But you had to think about it."

"It's not like that."

He wanted to ask what she meant, but was afraid he was reading too much into it. *Because you want to. Reel it back, Miller.*

"You'll get your trainer's license there?" Back to safer ground.

"It might be simpler to just let her run in Roger's name and get Dean to saddle her. Wait till we get back to Woodbine."

"Just do it."

"Boldly go?"

He wished she'd stop looking at him like that. Did she really have no clue? "That's more like it."

She left the crust of her slice on the plate, and took another measured sip of the barely-touched wine, slipping into silence. If he'd let her down, he needed to know, didn't he? *Leave it alone*. But he couldn't.

"What did you mean, just then? *'It's not like that.'*"

A crease formed between her brows, her lips pressing into a line. She glanced somewhere over his shoulder before her eyes fell back to his, and her words unfolded slowly, like she was having a hard time working them free. “You haven’t let me down, Miller. Ever. You go above and beyond, with everything. And I worry it might be too much. I worry now it might...become a problem.”

Faye.

“Right.” He pushed back his chair. “I’d better go. I’m leaving the rest of the pizza with you. And the wine. You need the calories; I don’t.”

He ducked away from her perplexed expression, out of the kitchen, out the front door, out where he could breathe.

The phone buzzed a text notification in his back pocket, and he extracted it, willing it to be Faye just in time to help him settle his pulse, bring him perspective, but he went cold at the name he saw instead.

He’d never taken Cindy out of his contacts, though at least he’d had enough self-respect never to drunk-text her on the holidays—even if he’d come close a couple of times. And since Faye, he’d almost, but not quite, forgotten she was even in there.

I thought you might want to meet your new niece and nephew.

But oh, she was there, cutting off his airwaves, draining the blood from his veins.

He unlocked the screen, finding a photo of her holding a carefully placed bundle in the crook of each arm. Their tiny faces were pink and squinty-eyed, not terribly attractive...and perfect. And she was perfect. Radiant. It left a fresh bruise on his scarred heart.

Too many worlds colliding, here and now. Liv calling him out on Faye, who had helped him see the possibility of a future different from the one he’d thought he wanted with Cindy. Cindy, who had maybe been right to break it off. And maybe Liv had been right when she did, however bluntly, point that out. But Liv had never given him a single, tangible reason to think there was any chance of them ever being more than they were right now. Cohorts. Uneasy friends.

He fired off a text to Faye.

You’re coming to Keeneland, right?

Going back to the photo, his thumb hovered over the keypad. In the name of resolving at least one thing in his head, he typed *Congratulations* and hit send.

37

APRIL

Chique emerged from the shadow, the brilliant morning sun at the head of the stretch spotlighting her against the dark wash of green behind her. Liv propped her binoculars in her right hand while her left held the reins on Paz, who had taken to Keeneland the same way the rest of them had—like he'd been meant to be here all his life. She hadn't expected Rog to offer up his pony for this side trip, but she was grateful for the veteran's steady influence on her own nerves as much as Chique's.

The filly's ears flickered forward as they got closer, but Nate's focus remained unwavering as they galloped by around the clubhouse turn. Chique's final breeze had been perfect; entries were in; post positions drawn. Now they were just counting hours, and praying for a fast track.

Nate didn't try to jar her out of her preoccupation on the walk back—he seemed absorbed in his own, like he had been more often than not in the last few weeks. No more visits with wine and pizza, an appropriate withdrawal after that evening that told her all she needed to know—he was, rightly, committed to Faye. She tried to counter her scattered thoughts by drinking in a breath of the cool, crisp air, focusing on the beauty around them—the immaculate grounds, the cherry blossom-laden trees; the sense of serenity on Keeneland's backstretch that seemed so at odds with her underlying anxiety.

He glanced at her with a smile several watts below his normal grin, then dialed it up at the sight of Faye and Dean, waiting at the barn. "Hey, you made it!"

Liv swung off Paz. "What time did you guys leave?"

"We flew to Cinci last night, rented a car, and drove the rest of the way this morning." Dean came up and gave Liv a peck on the cheek, squeezing her shoulder. "Can I take your trusty steed for you so you can look after the big filly?"

"Thanks." Maybe she could relax a little now that it felt like a grown-up trainer was here. She pulled off her helmet and hugged Faye.

"Don't expect me to do anything." Faye smiled with mock sweetness.

"Wouldn't dream of it." Liv grinned back, grabbing Chique's halter.

"You're in time to see your boy go." Nate dragged the saddle off and pulled the bridle over Chique's ears, then left the tack on the rail.

Liv wound the chain around the halter's noseband, following with her eyes as Nate drew Faye in and kissed her, then wordlessly came back to hold Chique for a steamy bath.

"Grab that cooler, Faye?" Liv asked as she scraped away the rinse water.

"I can do that much." Faye handed it to Nate, and Chique's neck snaked with a snap of teeth, sending her jumping out of the way. "Jealous?"

Liv looked sideways at Nate, but his eyes stayed on the filly.

"I'll walk her," he said while Liv threw on the cooler.

"No hotwalker?" Dean asked when she returned to the barn, finding he had Wampum already tacked up.

"Didn't think we really needed one, with just two horses. You're not in a hurry, are you?"

"Hardly." He tilted his head to the colt. "He looks phenomenal. I'm excited about tomorrow."

"I'm terrified. It's all Nate's fault. I was more than willing to let you do the saddling honours for Chique."

"Where's the fun in that? Good job, Miller."

Nate stopped to let Chique have a drink. "You making fun of my hotwalking skills?"

"Just singing your praises. The colt's in good order, and you successfully prompted our girl here to get her trainer's license."

Liv tried and failed to read Nate's expression as Chique pulled him past.

Faye and Dean walked out with them when they took Wampum to the track, and Liv tried to pretend the new, weird tension she felt wasn't there. Putting on a cheery front wasn't exactly her forte. It exhausted her, when she was stressed enough already.

"He's going great, Liv," Dean said as Wampum galloped past. "If Touch and Go comes back good, I might have two Plate horses this year. How incredible would that be?"

His face was uncomplicated by the strain that added a beat to her own heart rate hearing *Plate*, her mind automatically calculating *twelve weeks*. She kept her own raging doubts about whether or not Chique was going to make it to herself. Three months was so close, yet forever away.

Dean stepped in to hold Wampum for his bath once they were back at the barn. "I'll buy you guys breakfast once we're done."

"I've gotta check into the room, got a couple mounts this aft, so I'm out." Nate looked lost for a moment, watching Dean take over his usual position. He turned on his heel and went to clean the tack, then left with half a wave.

There was definitely weird in the air, and it wasn't just her. Liv pulled her eyes back to Wampum. "The kitchen food is pretty good here."

When she tried to take the shank after the colt's bath, Dean shooed her away. "The least I can do is walk my big horse. Catch up with Faye while you get your filly done up."

Faye was strangely silent as Liv gathered brushes and bandages for Chique.

"Everything okay?" Liv eyed her.

Faye waved her hand around in a non-answer.

"I thought things were good in Florida," Liv ventured.

Faye sighed. "It was. Florida was amazing. I'm just not sure it was real."

"That makes no sense at all."

"You don't see it, do you?"

"What, Faye? I'm trying to get this filly ready for a race, not monitor the state of your relationship."

"The writing," Faye said, looking overly dramatic, even for Faye, as she swept her arm through the air. "It's all over the wall."

A HINT of white showed in the corner of Chique's eye as she rolled it at the real umbrellas and the makeshift ones, programmes perched over horseplayers' heads like little paper rooftops. Her feet lifted off the path in an ultra-slow jog, and she curled into the groom with her teeth squeaking as she mouthed the bit. She looked ready…but whether or not she was going to play today was anyone's guess.

"She's not the only speed, so if she does end up on the front end, well…do what you can to keep her happy without burning her up."

It wasn't as if they hadn't discussed the race already, but there needed to be words to fill the air, so Nate didn't care that Liv was repeating what had already been said. He had to ignore his doubts, doubts justifiably inspired by a filly who had a penchant for making things up as she went along. It was only her sixth start, they'd reminded each other. She was still learning, and they were still learning how she operated. It was an ongoing odyssey.

"Riders up!"

He grasped the lines at Chique's withers, bouncing as Liv lifted him into the tack.

"Bonne chance." She glanced up. "Stay safe."

He met her eyes. "Thanks."

The drizzle wasn't enough to alter the track condition, so it remained fast. Nate nodded at the pony rider when it was acceptable to break out of the line of the post parade—like the groom, the woman on Paz was a hire for the day. Chique leapt into a gallop, leaving Paz behind without hesitation and powering the wrong way around the turn.

He tried to time it so they weren't left milling with the others behind the gate too long before they were loaded. Their reunion with Paz was short before the starter's assistant came for them, leading them into the fourth stall. He felt Chique's muscles tense.

"Easy, there," he murmured. "We have to wait for everyone else."

Chique shifted her weight beneath him, but she stood, ears swiveling as the activity carried on around her. The filly next to them started pawing and popped, prompting some pointed words from her handler and the jock. Chique tilted her head at the commotion, rocking her left shoulder to the side of the frame.

"C'mon, let's keep her straight," Nate grumbled at the assistant. Their neighbour stilled, and the starter sprang them from the barrier.

That second of distraction before the bell cost Chique the break, and Nate cursed as she jumped out a beat behind. He took a careful hold, leaving the other speed horse to assume the lead—praying the filly bought into the plan. She was quick enough to regain the ground she'd lost and let him park her out from the rail where she had a clear path, and couldn't complain about kickback.

He didn't like being three-wide around the clubhouse turn, but it was a matter of compromise—better than being buried on the inside. When they straightened into the backstretch, Chique neatly swapped leads and zeroed in on the frontrunner. He let her close the gap until she had her nose at that filly's saddle cloth, pressing the pace with her ears laced back, but wonder of wonders, she was waiting for him to tell her the next move.

Inching closer around the turn, the leader pressed into Chique, floating her wide—completely intentional on the rider's part. *Sure, let's give the new kid a hard time.* There was nothing he could do about it. Someone crept up on his right, drawing even, wedging Chique in the middle. Chique pinned her ears, but Nate was happy to let them go by…until that filly dropped in before she was clear, leaving him scrambling to check Chique —too late. She stumbled, staggering, tossing him forward as he grappled for her mane. Clambering to her feet—freaky athletic thing that she was—she threw him back into the tack, and he groped for the lines so he could help her out.

Shuffled to the inside now, the kickback came full force. *And here's where she packs it in.* But instead, Chique was mad, her adrenaline pumping as much as his. She was eyeballing the rail, which was a ridiculous option—there wasn't enough room. But who was he to tell this filly what to do? She thought she could fit. He picked her up and chirped, sending her.

It was so tight his boot scraped the fence, and he all but closed his eyes. Chique crept up, fighting even though she was tiring. He was afraid to hit her—it was crowded enough that an over-reaction would have a dangerous domino effect. So he pushed and pleaded with each stride, hollering in her ear until the mirror flashed past on his left. She let up as soon as he did, the blow from her nostrils sounding like a freight train.

The grandstand was shrouded in a fine mist as they came back, his anger smouldering. Liv approached with the groom—he couldn't remember if he'd seen the crutches since they'd arrived in Lexington.

"Is she all right?" Liv tore off the dirty blinkers, scanning Chique with concern.

"I think so. She got bounced around out there pretty good though—she'll be sore tomorrow. So will that bastard, if I have anything to say about it." He fired his whip at his valet.

"Forget it, Miller. You don't want any trouble. Especially with Ricky Acosta."

"Is that who it was?" He dismounted, face set as he reached down to release the overgirth. "Where'd she finish?"

"Third. She ran huge, Nate."

Liv's face made him pause—here he was getting all riled up, when Chique had saved his ass, and still run her guts out. "She grew up a little out there." He planted a kiss on the clean spot the blinkers had left on the filly's cheek and went to weigh in.

Liv fell into step beside him. "That was a risky move, taking her up the rail."

"What was I supposed to do? Go down the middle of the racetrack?"

"Anything would have been better than putting yourself in that position."

"I didn't know if she was going to run at all. If I'd told her not to go, you know exactly what she would have said back. Anyway, what does it matter, as long as she's all right?"

"Let's just hope she is."

"We'll talk after the Blue Grass, okay?"

She nodded, and he started jogging back to the room. And headed straight for Ricky Acosta, shoving him against the wall, pressing into him.

"What the hell was that?"

"It's called race-riding, kid."

"My ass."

Acosta's laugh taunted him. "Get out of my way, or it will be. Maybe you'd better run along back to Canada where they play nice."

"So help me, if there's anything wrong with that filly—" He was trembling now, he wanted to hit Acosta so bad.

"C'mon, pretty boy, take a swing. Give me an excuse to mess up that face of yours. He's not as pretty as our princess, though, is he boys? She don't seem so sad anymore. You have something to do with that?"

Acosta stepped closer with a smirk and Nate shifted his weight and snapped his fist back. A vise-like grip seized his wrist before he could follow through and dragged him away. He spun and twisted out of the hold, ready to strike…and stopped dead.

"I told you to forget it," Liv hissed, grabbing his arms and pushing him back. "I'd throw you under a cold shower if it was in any way appropriate."

"Like this was?" he snapped, glaring at her. He could feel eyes on them as she glared back.

"Put this behind you and get ready to ride Wampum. Who knows, if he runs well enough, you might get to ride in the Derby. You wouldn't want to screw that up, would you?"

His gaze dropped to the floor.

"Good luck." She stepped away. "I'm going back to check on Chique. Stay out of trouble."

The looks and whistles as she retreated seemed to have no effect on her, but Nate kept his eyes averted, sure the smirk was still on Acosta's face.

He washed away the dirt and dressed in fresh breeches, pulling on Northwest's red and white silks. Boots wiped clean, his helmet ready with a red cover and new goggles, courtesy of his valet. Nate grabbed his whip and took a moment to breathe before riders were called outside.

Faye and Dean were waiting—Dean watching Wampum, Faye watching Nate. He had to keep her out of his head until after the race.

"How's the filly?" Dean asked.

"Appears to be fine." He couldn't let himself think about Chique, either, or his anger flared again. "This guy's been loving the track, so here's hoping."

"Maybe we'll get a piece of it."

And the Derby points that went with that.

The same pony rider, using Paz, accompanied them to the post. Added to the list of things Nate didn't want to think about was his post position: Ricky Acosta, on the favoured Buck Ruler, set to start next to him.

Wampum got away clean, and Nate took him back, letting the speed horses go. Everything was going according to plan, around the clubhouse turn and into the straightaway. Nate sat like a stone, aware of Acosta on Buck Ruler, right beside them. He relaxed slightly. Really, what was Acosta going to do? Certainly not ruin his own chances to mess up Nate's trip. But right now Buck Ruler had Wampum boxed in, and as they travelled around the turn, the two colts bumped. Wampum faltered, backing off, and Nate getting after him didn't help. Acosta picked up Buck Ruler as they hit the head of the stretch, and the big colt went into overdrive.

And then it was déjà vu.

Acosta cut in front of Wampum. Wampum clipped Buck Ruler's heels. Hard and fast, with no hope of a save.

Nate hit the dirt, air rushing from his lungs as the momentum rolled him under the rail. Gulping in a breath, he dragged himself to all fours on the turf, catching glimpses of horses flying around Wampum. He pulled himself to his feet, grasping the rail to get his bearings, then ducked under, grabbing Wampum as the colt lurched up. Wampum hopped around him, eyes wild, but he used all four legs equally. Nate exhaled, talking the colt down. Talking himself down.

In no time he was surrounded—track ambulance, horse ambulance, state veterinarian…random maintenance person taking over at Wampum's head so he could slide off the saddle. Then Dean was there, resting a hand on his shoulder.

Nate shrugged him off. "I'm fine. I think he's okay."

"We'll take that ride." Dean nodded at the van. "You should do the same, Nate. Come back when you can."

Wampum marched up the ramp, still not favouring anything, but adrenaline could cover up pain. It was best to take precautions. The ambulance attendants were battering Nate with questions as he climbed into the back. He brushed them away. His ankle was starting to hurt, that was all. Back in the room he collapsed in a heap on the bench, trying to regroup, then changed without showering, and skulked out.

Fog hung over the backstretch, masking the barns and bringing dusk prematurely. All he wanted to do was go back to his room, with or without Faye; put this wretched day behind him and figure out his head in the morning. He didn't trust it right now. He might have done just that, except for the shit he'd find himself in if he didn't check in.

"You okay?" Liv scanned him, half scrutinizing, half worried.

Faye rushed over, her arms folding around his shoulders, face pushed into his neck. He should have probably felt something, but he didn't.

He ducked away from her and went to Chique, then Wampum, both of them done up to their eyeballs—poultice to their knees, sweated to their hocks. Chique bumped him with her nose.

"How are they?" He didn't look at Liv, but could feel her hovering just behind him.

"Seem to be all right. We'll see how they are in the morning."

"Guess none of us are going to Churchill this year. Should we grab something to eat?" Trust Dean to be practical.

"As long as there's wine." Faye shivered, shoulders hunched in her coat, even though it wasn't that cold.

Liv glanced from Faye to Nate. "Meet you guys there?"

His stomach gnawed at him even though he wasn't hungry, and he led the way to the Mustang, Faye's silence as unnatural as the murky atmosphere. The twinge in his ankle was getting worse.

"Are you okay? Really?" She frowned, twisting in her seat once he was behind the wheel.

He grimaced, depressing the clutch and popping the car into gear. "Fine."

"How can you be fine? I'm certainly not. That was terrifying."

"I get it. It's scarier when it's someone else."

"Apparently."

The traffic leaving the parking area was heavy now that the big races were done, and his ankle screamed each time he rolled the car to a halt. They would have been better off waiting, because no one was going anywhere fast at the moment. He just wanted to get out of there.

"It was a spill, Faye. They happen. If you can't deal with it, maybe you're dating the wrong guy." *Shit.* That wasn't the right thing to say.

"Maybe you're right."

He'd handed her the knife she'd just pushed between his ribs, sending this conversation in an unintended direction. He wasn't up for this, not now.

"Are you going to tell me what's going on?"

He could throw that one right back at her—but he'd already dug himself a hole. "It's just been a shitty day, all right?"

"What about yesterday?"

"You were the one who opted out of staying with me."

"I told you, I didn't want any trainers mad at me because I kept you up."

"Well it's not like I slept very well anyway."

"Why would that be? Your conscience getting to you?"

"What the hell are you talking about?"

"What's going on with Liv?"

She blindsided him with that one, and he choked back a laugh. "She's your best friend, so I'm pretty sure you know the answer to that is a big fat nothing."

Her exhale was audible. "We really need to talk."

"Can't it wait? We could skip dinner, grab a bottle, go back to my room. I don't think either of us is particularly rational at the moment."

"I'm quite rational, thank you. This is as good a time as any, don't you think? Seeing as we're stuck here, and you're already having a shitty day."

He dislodged a hand gripping the wheel to rub his eyes, trying to ease the throb behind them.

"Tell me if I'm wrong," Faye began. "The only reason you decided to sleep with me in Florida is because you were feeling guilty about spending so much time with Liv after her accident. And, lo and behold, you were starting to have feelings for her. What no one seems to want to admit, though, is she has feelings for you."

"Liv? Feelings?" If only he were that convinced. "See what I mean? That's totally irrational."

"Is it, really? What happened New Year's Eve?"

"What? I was in bed by eight. Slept through it." Made sure of it, this time.

"Not this year. Last year."

"She told you about that?" That just reinforced Liv had laid it to rest, because he was sure she wouldn't have said anything to Faye about that night had it actually meant something to her.

"For one, you and I weren't even seeing each other then. And for another, it was nothing. We finished off a bottle of wine after dinner at Roger and Hélène's. At midnight I kissed her. It was just a kiss, Faye. A stupid Happy New Year kiss." Which hadn't made either of them happy.

"It's never just a kiss." She looked out the passenger window, hiding her face from him. "I can't deal with it anymore. I can't compete with a horse, let alone whatever this thing is you two have going on. It's not going to disappear."

"Why can't you see all she and I will ever be are friends?"

"Because I don't believe it anymore. It's just a matter of time."

It made no difference that she was wrong—she'd clearly made up her mind. The pounding in his head crept to his neck, shooting into his shoulders. "So this is it, then." His voice sounded as flat as he felt.

Faye's fingers flew over the keypad on her phone. "Just take me back to the hotel, please."

He didn't argue.

Liv rapped on the door, then crossed her arms, shaking from a chill she couldn't keep at bay. The damp weather, the sequence of events...it came from one of them, or all of it.

Maybe he'd gone to get something to eat on his own. Maybe she should leave well enough alone. She turned away, then the door clicked.

Nate left it open as he retreated.

"You're hurt." The crease between her brows deepened as she caught it, hovering on the threshold.

"It's nothing." He hobbled a step, his face screwing up.

Her shoulders dropped with a sigh, and she stepped in, the door shutting behind her. "Let me look at that. Get on the bed."

"Never thought you'd be the kind of girl to take charge in the bedroom." He took another bad step, his smirk falling away as his jaw tightened. "Guess I shouldn't be surprised. You're a control freak with everything else."

"Grow up," she snapped, heat flushing her cheeks as he perched on the edge of the mattress and carefully rolled off his sock.

His foot felt cold and bony between her hands, but the ankle was hot and starting to swell. She rotated it like she would have a horse, checking mobility, and he winced, pulling away.

"Easy!"

"Well you didn't want to let a professional check it out." She straightened, squaring her shoulders, hands on her hips. "You need to get that x-rayed."

"It's just bruised."

"Don't be an idiot. Or am I too late for that?" Could she just smack him? She'd feel so much better. She grabbed his key card from the end table. "Stay here."

"Got nowhere else to be."

She should just leave him to suffer. But she came back with her crutches, a six-pack of beer from the gas station downstairs, and a bucket of ice.

First she twisted a can free and handed it to him, then made an ice pack with a damp hotel towel. "Put this on it. And stay off it."

"You going to give me a lesson on how to use those?"

"Google it. Here."

He closed his hand on the two capsules of Advil she dropped into his palm, cracked open the beer with a tight smile and washed them down. "Not joining me?"

Just one good cuff? He totally deserved it. Instead she reached for a can, and walked around the bed to the chair on the other side, letting the first sip sting her tongue. "This stuff is disgusting."

"You bought it."

"Forgive me, I'm not a connoisseur." The second swig didn't taste as bad as the first.

He propped the pillows against the headboard and swung his legs up onto the bed. "I know why Faye's mad at me, but what's your problem?"

"Faye is my friend. She was my friend long before you. You put me in the middle of this."

"So why are you here?"

"She didn't want to talk to me." Liv tried another mouthful before abandoning the can to the small table next to her. "I'm guessing it's over."

"So it is."

And with that went her safety net. Why was she here, really?

"Listen, you don't have to stay. Thanks for checking in. Go find Dean and have some dinner." He adjusted the ice pack, focusing on it like it required his full attention.

Dean would still be in the hotel restaurant. Not that she felt like eating, or needed company, but it would be a much more logical option than this. This though...something kept her here. "You hung out with me in Florida when I'm sure you had better things to do. I think I can return the favour." That was it, right?

His eyes flitted over. The defensiveness faded from his expression. "You haven't got it all wrong, you know."

She frowned. "Well, thanks, Miller, but what?"

"Your philosophy on relationships."

"Which would be?"

"That they're best avoided. Am I wrong?"

She leaned forward, resting her arms on her knees, her gaze drawn to him. "Not entirely. I'd think you of all people would have figured that out before this."

"Just because I got burned once doesn't mean I want to be alone for the rest of my life. I couldn't know Faye wasn't the one."

"Oh come on."

He shot her a dark look. "You say that like I deserved to be dumped."

"Faye's MO is to sleep with a guy without getting invested. You made her get invested, then you slept with her. That was significant."

"I didn't make her do anything." He dropped the ice pack on the floor, and grabbed the beer. With the way he threw his head back as he tipped it to his lips, he must have downed half of it. "You know Faye called it off because of you, right?"

The hairs on the back of her neck tingled, and she reached up like she could smooth them into submission. "What?"

"I told her about New Year's Eve."

Her chest spasmed as his words conjured up the forbidden memory. *Control, Liv. Get it back.* "Great. So now she hates me, too."

"She's decided we have a thing for each other." His eyes, which had mostly been avoiding her, settled on her now, challenging.

"Do we?" She felt strangely calm, then her heart gave a deliberate thud, balanced on a precipice. One nudge would send it from safety into danger.

"I can only speak for myself."

"And?" Another thump, waiting for his answer, when she didn't think it would be a surprise.

"I've been talking myself out of it for three years." He crushed the can in his hand. "If I thought there was any chance in hell you felt the same, I'd say what are we waiting for? In the last three months we've both seen our lives flash before our eyes. Life's too short not to run with it."

It was the way he said it, like it was their destiny, curled her fingers into fists; drew her back from the edge.

"That's not how this goes, Miller. Faye dumped you because you were an asshole. You want me to step up to the line and say sign me up? No thank you." She strode around the bed, crouching to pick up the pieces of ice that had scattered from the pack, and handed it back to him. "I don't mean to kick you when you're down. I'm sorry about you and Faye. But I'm not going along with your little plan."

She didn't look back, desperate to tidy the messiness of it all in her head, and didn't breathe until the door clicked shut behind her.

38

MAY

The mosquitoes were brutal in the woods, and Nate ran faster, Switchfoot in his ears spurring him on. He burst out to the clearing by the stallion barn, leaving most of them behind, slowing to swat the last one off the back of his neck—but not before it left a fresh welt. Then *We're Gonna Be Alright* started playing, trumping his aggravation. There was really no proper response but to take a dance-like-no-one's-watching moment. Because who would be, out here? And why would he care, anyway? Sing it out, believe it.

He opened his eyes with the last beat, and folded over, laughing. *Of course.*

"Don't let me interrupt you." The corners of Liv's mouth curved up as she pulled the elastic from her hair, resetting her ponytail. "Seriously, carry on."

She left him standing there, running towards the path he'd just left. He turned and sprinted after her, because he had nothing to lose but more blood.

Her eyes flashed over when he caught up, and he waited for her to tell him to get lost.

"Try to keep up, Miller," she said, picking up the pace, skipping over a root onto the narrow trail.

The sky had an eerie green cast when they broke out on the other side, trees coming to life like Ents as the wind whipped through them. Liv kicked it up another notch, and Nate wiped his mouth and matched her stride.

"Come on, girls!"

Mares and foals in the adjacent paddock took off, summoned by the farm worker's call and the rattle of chain on metal. Nate and Liv raced past the gate, the rain starting with cold, heavy, drops that soon turned to a downpour, drenching them.

Chique and Claire huddled in the corner of their paddock next to the barn, Chique's shrill whinny a clear indication the current situation was unacceptable, if not outright abusive. Nate grabbed a shank from Liv, and Claire shuffled over, but Chique stayed put—quarters spun resolutely to the wind, head at knee level, tail streaming between her hocks.

Water gushed into his runners as he sloshed through the stream that coursed through the paddock. He snapped on the lead and dragged her in. As soon as he pried off her sodden halter, Chique dropped to her knees and rolled with a grunt. She rose, snorting as she shook off the loose straw, then buried her nose in the pile of hay in the corner, too disgusted to even search for peppermints.

"It doesn't look like it's going to let up anytime soon, does it?" Liv stared at the sheets of rain, wincing at the crack of thunder that followed a particularly brilliant shard of lightning.

"You can come upstairs for a bit and wait it out if you want."

She caught a drip on her forehead with the back of her hand. "Okay."

He'd expected her to say no, to come up with the excuse of some paperwork in the office and wait out the storm there. Things hadn't exactly been awkward since Kentucky—Liv was, if nothing else, professional to a fault at work—but they'd reverted to just that. Friends, like Jo or Michel were friends, because they'd been working together for three years and didn't hate each other. Nothing more. Maybe all they would ever be.

This, like the run that had led to it, crossed a line she'd redrawn in black in his hotel room in Lexington. The sting of truth from her little tough love speech had eased, both his bruised ego and ankle recovering, but the line had remained. Until now. He led the way up the stairs, almost tripping as his legs shook—and not from fatigue.

She left her waterlogged shoes and socks in a puddle by the door and gravitated to the picture window framing a still-angry sky. Rain pattered steadily against the pane.

"I'm surprised you're still here. I would have thought you'd want to live closer to the track."

He probably should have moved, considering he wasn't even a farm employee anymore, but they'd never asked him to leave, and he'd never wanted to. "It'd be hard going back to living in the city after this. Besides, right now it means I can get on Chique before I head in."

"You couldn't possibly leave that to me." There was a hint of affection in her expression, and he bathed in it for a moment before it drifted away. "Still planning to ship her in tomorrow?"

Liv nodded, dragging a hand over her wet hair. The Ashland had left Chique battered enough Liv had brought her to the farm when they'd come home, and a couple of weeks of turnout had turned into five. She'd been galloping for three of them, and had started pulling out his arms again, so it was time. Time to get serious, and see if the Plate, just seven weeks away, was still possible. Chique had fared better than Wampum, at least. The Northwest colt was on stall rest with a stress fracture in his shoulder and was out of the Plate for sure.

"I should get you a towel." He dragged himself away and went to the bedroom, peeling off his t-shirt, fantasizing he'd brought her with him. *Dream on, Miller.*

She was looking down at the picture frame on the piano when he returned, and it chased off the fantasy as he cursed himself once more for never putting it away. Then again, what was he worried about? She knew most of the story already.

"I'd forgotten this was up here." She looked away from the photo quickly, and fingered the piano keys.

"Do you play?" He kept himself from staring at the way her t-shirt clung, handing her the towel on his way to the kitchen.

"I took lessons for a bit as a kid. One of my mother's failed attempts to instill something other than horses. You?"

"It's what sold me on the job." That and the fact he'd needed to get his head out of his ass. "Want something to drink?"

"Water?"

She accepted a glass, her eyes lingering on his face before wandering back to the piano, and the frame. "Is that New Year's Eve girl? She's beautiful."

There was no jealousy in her voice; she was merely making an observation, appreciating an aesthetic. He stood behind her, looking over her shoulder and inhaling, the scent of her a mixture of rain and sweat and something tropical, and he had to step back. Forget lines. He needed a force field.

"Yeah. Cindy."

It was after one of those adventure races. He had an arm around Phil on his left, Cin on his right, little brother Tim next to Phil. All of them wearing huge smiles, and a whole lot of mud. Good times. *One big lie.*

"She came home from school with Phil one day. They were supposed to be studying. We hit it off right away."

Liv set the picture back on the piano, her gaze landing on him as she turned. If he'd stayed where he'd been, she would have been close enough to…*damn it.* She moved away like she could read his thoughts—though talking about the past was a good antidote for that.

"She was supportive of everything my dad hated—my music, the horses. Drove him nuts. He had a big problem with us being together. My mother loved her, though." *Still does.* "I really just went to U of Calgary because of her. I thought if I was the guy with the degree that got the steady job that she'd want to be with me." He shrugged. "You know how that went."

"How long were you together?"

"Three years, four months." He could have told her right down to the number of minutes.

"Four years ago. So why is it still with you? What are you leaving out?"

It was eerie that she'd figure out he was withholding details. Or maybe he just wanted to believe they had a special connection, that she could read into his soul and see the holes there.

"She had twins in February."

There was a question mark etched on her face when he handed her his phone, open to a photo of those twins—fair, what did she care about babies? It did seem a strange way to explain. The creases in her brow deepened in confusion.

"This is crazy, but I want to say...they look like you." She stared at it again. "That's impossible, right? Or..."

"I didn't go back for a random fling last year, if that's what you're thinking. She married my brother."

"Holy shit, Miller."

He almost laughed—he didn't think he'd ever heard her swear before.

"I should have known I was just a passing amusement." He backed up to the piano, dropping to the bench. "Phil was going to law school. He really was the guy I was trying to be. All kinds of ironic, really. I only started flirting with her that day he brought her home to piss him off. Guess he got the last laugh."

He swung to face the keys, resting his fingers on them, another of his mother's favourite songs coming to him when he thought of how blindsided he'd been when he'd found out they were together. *Why is love always the last to know?*

Liv pulled up a chair from the kitchen, tucking her knees to her chest as she rested her bare toes on the edge of the bench.

"So what did you do for...eight months? You quit school after she turned you down. You could have been here for the start of the season. Everyone's looking for good exercise riders in the spring."

"You make it sound like I should have been thinking straight. She dumped me, I quit school, my dad kicked me out. I spent the rest of the winter working on the farm and nightwatching mares for Al, the trainer I worked for, and he gave me a place to crash. Seemed a good place to hide. I stayed till the wedding, because I thought I should. Because I thought it would make my mother happy. Which was stupid. She of all people would have understood I never should have been there."

There was a strange stillness to her voice when she finally spoke. "How do you get over something like that?"

"I'm not sure I'm qualified to answer that. I haven't been very successful."

"I fell apart over much less. You seem to have handled it pretty well."

"Hardly. I got drunk and bolted in the middle of the reception, and I've never been back."

"You started fresh. Successfully."

"How long did it take me to get to that point? Sure you went through a dark patch, but you put things back together."

"Only because you kept after me. You had no one."

"I had Geai. I had Em. But I still kept running away. Until you gave me Chique."

"Because I was so totally incapable of dealing with her myself."

"Like this is some kind of competition."

She smiled, but there was sadness in her eyes. "So why tell me all this?"

"Because even though you might be completely baffled by it, you still hear it, and feel it. Sometimes I think we're opposite sides of the same coin."

Her eyes flashed and she rose, hands wringing as she walked away. "That doesn't mean we should be together."

Nate spun around on the piano bench, silently begging her not to leave. Not now, when they'd come so far. "Isn't it worth a shot?"

She stopped, turning but avoiding his gaze. "It took me a long time to make it here. I don't want to ruin what we already have. We work well together. Why isn't that good enough?"

"There's got to be more to it than that, doesn't there? Or do you really think you're better off alone?"

"You said my philosophy had merit. Relationships are best avoided. Doomed to fail, especially in this business. What makes you think it would be any different with us?"

"Hope, I guess." Some crazy belief that some things are meant to be. "What if we don't fail?"

"Is that resilience, or stupidity?"

It was blunt, but it triggered a smile, because he'd spent a lot of time pondering the same thing.

"It's not that easy, though, is it?" she continued. "What about Faye? I couldn't do that to her. How could you? And please don't tell me life's too short. I can't live like that."

It was, though, couldn't she see? But he kept quiet, letting her work it through.

"I don't want things to be awkward. I don't want anything distracting either of us before the Plate. I have enough going on in my head right now. You don't even know what you'd be signing up for, Miller."

Maybe he didn't. Maybe that's all this was, the thrill of the unknown, the risk of it all. That's what they did—put their necks out there, throwing a leg over the crazy. But who wanted to stay on the ground?

"Just tell me we won't go backwards from here." It was a plea, but he didn't care.

"Are you looking for a promise?"

He threw his eyes at the ceiling, wanting badly to go to her and pull her into his arms, to kiss her speechless. "You sure like to overthink everything, don't you?"

"You think you have me figured out."

Her smile toyed with him, driving him a little nuts. "Not even close."

She glanced past him, and he looked over his shoulder to the window. The storm had moved on, patches of rich cobalt growing through wispy clouds.

"I should get going."

He wanted to cling to this, afraid they would never recover it, but short of holding her hostage, it wasn't going to happen. "I'll come downstairs with you."

Everything glistened from the rain, the air earthy and cool as a light breeze offered to dry up the puddles.

"À demain, Miller."

It wouldn't be dinner and movies; a two-year engagement; one-point-five kids—or twins. But how could they know what it could be, if they didn't try?

They'd win the Plate, then continue this discussion. He had to believe that, the Switchfoot song playing in his mind feeding his conviction.

39

JUNE

Chique quivered, transfixed by the buzz on the other side of Woodbine's main track. Nate matched her stare with the same focus.

Liv gave a gentle tug on the bit. "Okay?"

The filly's ear flicked, and Nate nodded. Liv nudged Paz forward. A few jog steps, and they popped into a gallop.

This was the day that would define the Queen's Plate, three weeks away. They'd had options: both the Canadian Oaks and the Plate Trial Stakes went this afternoon at a mile and an eighth. Instead, she'd sought and received permission from the stewards to work Chique a mile in between races—her idea of a compromise.

She could deal with the haters saying she was just ducking Touch and Go in the Trial, and Penny Postcard in the Oaks, both of them last year's divisional champions. Her own doubts, the ones that questioned her gut—a gut that insisted Chique wasn't ready for a race yet after her roller derby experience at Keeneland—were harder to dismiss.

Paz matched Chique's strides until Liv let go inside the sixteenth pole. She steered him to the middle of the track to avoid the flying clods of dirt as Chique swept away, Nate crouched flush to her back as the filly sailed around the clubhouse turn.

She tried to track their progress as best she could, but it was mostly futile. Why she'd turned down Nicole's offer to take Chique to the pole, she wasn't sure, except maybe watching was harder than not, when she wasn't up herself.

Nate's smile was the first thing she noticed through the shimmer of heat radiating off the new dirt track when Chique glided into the backstretch, galloping out. He pulled her up, slowing to a jog and turning in beside Paz. Liv reached over and removed the blinkers, and Chique resumed her stare: nostrils flaring, a sheen of sweat on her neck, a heightened look in her eye as she gazed into the distance over her big white shadow roll.

"Time?" They'd announce it, but Nate would know.

"Thirty-nine and change, last quarter in twenty-four, galloped out a mile and a quarter in two-o-six. Or thereabouts."

There was no dodging the emotions that slammed her when he flashed that grin, totally prepared to admit she wasn't immune to it anymore. *Never say never.* Each time he looked at her like that, it seemed just a little less crazy.

Back at the barn, she stuck her head under the hose, cold water shocking the warm fuzzies back into hiding. It was the closest she'd get to a shower on the backstretch. There were races to be watched and competition to assess on the front side.

Emilie was waiting for her by the walking ring as the horses for the Plate Trial started coming up the path. "Cheeky looked great!"

"What did they catch her in?"

"One thirty-nine and three; out in two-o-six flat."

Or thereabouts. Emilie gave her a strange look as she laughed.

They watched the Trial from the box, Touch and Go emerging as the leader mid-stretch, drawing away from the field under Dave Johnson.

"He won't have any trouble getting the mile and a quarter," Liv commented dryly.

No surprises in the Oaks, either—Penny Postcard equalled Touch and Go's time for the mile and an eighth. Someone would note how fast Chique had completed the same distance in her gallop-out for comparison. For what any of it was worth, because anything could happen on Plate Day.

Faye had been scarce since they'd got back from Keeneland, but Liv found her at Dean's barn after the races, sitting on a bench outside looking bored as a couple of exercise boys tried to chat her up. In her current state, she was probably particularly fierce. Definitely not looking very celebratory after a win that would likely send Touch and Go off as favourite for the big race.

"Filly breezed good," one of the guys said to Liv.

She nodded with a curt, "Thanks." That seemed enough of a hint to chase them away, and she sat cautiously next to Faye. "How long does this go on for, then?"

Faye tucked one side of her hair behind an ear. "I don't know. It's all new to me." She gazed across the lawn, zeroing in on Nate as he congratulated Dean. "I don't know if I'd feel better or worse if you told me I was right."

"Right about what?"

"Right to break it off with him." Faye hesitated. "Right about you. It's pretty ironic the only guy to ever get to me is the one who's perfect for you, isn't it?" Her eyes shifted to Liv, her smile wan. "Don't use me as an excuse, sweetie. I'll get over it."

DAYLIGHT WAS SLOW IN COMING, a dense haze hanging over the track, the smog of the big city burning Nate's throat as he inhaled. Chique, on the other hand, seemed oblivious to the humidity that was making human tempers short and working uncomfortable. She was everything she should be coming up to tomorrow's Plate: both her body—so carefully sculpted by the meticulous conditioning—and her mind, always the wildcard.

They detoured through the walking ring so she could see the ensuing mayhem of the Queen's Plate Festival—the huge mechanical arm for the television camera, the tents, the concert stages, the temporary fencing.

"No giant Pegasus. No fire-breathing dragon." Nate stroked Chique's neck, dark with sweat from air that was practically at the point of saturation. It had to rain soon. This humidity had to break.

Paz snorted his approval, while Liv eyed Chique protectively from the pony's back, preoccupation all but seeping from her pores like the perspiration on her skin.

Back at the barn Nate held Chique for her bath, catching a glimpse of a photographer stopping to take a shot with a telephoto lens. Chique noticed too, ever the diva, striking a pose, suds shimmering in a slick film over her inky coat. There was no mistaking her awareness of the electricity in the air, the undercurrent humming through Woodbine's backstretch as obvious as the plunging barometric pressure.

He passed Chique to Liv once the filly was bathed and sponged, giving her arm a squeeze. "I'll see you at the end of the morning."

When he returned, there was a cluster in front of Chique's stall, and he kept his distance. The week had been full of press engagements, starting with the media barbeque on Monday, and Wednesday's Plate Breakfast and post position draw.

The filly embraced the role of Queen's Plate darling: head poked over the webbing, bumping Liv with her nose like she was trying to encourage her trainer to do the same. Liv remained straight-faced, answering questions, while Chique butted her haynet, twirling it over her head and scattering blades of timothy and alfalfa leaves through Liv's hair. The filly finished the performance with a big green snort that finally did Liv in, the tension temporarily washed away.

It was good to see her laugh. It made him laugh. Maybe she was right. Maybe this was enough. He might have to accept that it was and make the best of it. He waited till the crew cleared before sneaking in.

"She'll teach you not to be so serious." He pulled out a peppermint, and Chique dove for it, then tossed her forelock around, hoping for more. "They're predicting rain tonight."

Liv set her jaw, staring out into the gloom. "I can't believe it hasn't started yet. Can't you do something about this, Miller?"

"I'll get right on that." He smiled. "That's just the point. We can't do a thing. Maybe it'll pour all night, and stop in time for everything to dry up. Or seeing as it's held off this long, maybe it'll just wait and rain on the amazing Plate Party we're going to have."

"Do you ever get tired of being so reassuring?"

"It's work. But someone has to hold you together, right?"

40

PLATE DAY

The resounding boom startled Liv out of a restless slumber, her spirits sinking with the torrential downpour that followed. She rolled out of bed, her thin tank top sticking to her, and stumbled to the open window.

Leaves battered the pane, rain blowing in through the screen. Sliding it shut felt like cutting off her supply of oxygen—of course the central air had decided to conk out during a heat wave on a long weekend. She dozed, lightning brightening the room at regular intervals, shattering cracks of thunder at times so close the windows trembled, jolting her back awake.

It was like the universe was laughing at her, years building to this day; all of it potentially obliterated by a force of nature. Did it really come down to this? But if Chique truly were the best horse out there this afternoon, she would overcome. That's what Nate would say. They would still need a good dose of luck, when it felt like luck had abandoned them.

At four AM she gave up on sleep. The heart of the storm seemed to have passed, but the heavy rain persisted, settling in all too comfortably. She wandered to the bathroom she shared with Emilie to shower, envying her sister's ability to sleep through anything.

It was too early to head to the track, so she drove to the office barn.

Claire and her new companion were happy to eat an early breakfast and she left them with grain in their tubs and a flake of hay in the corner.

The strip of track lighting in the office highlighted the pictures on the walls—the large framed images of Just Lucky winning his Plate, Sotisse's Oaks, and the oil painting of the two together, posed on the lawn outside the Triple Stripe stallion barn. Geai, standing between them, smiled at her from the canvas.

"Do you think he knew? You, me, the filly…"

She didn't startle at the voice. Who but Nate would be up at this hour, with a brain so in tune to her own?

She turned slowly, facing him. "It would be nice to think that. I just wish he were here to see it."

"Me too."

"It's still raining."

"It doesn't matter. I'll take care of her."

How did he do that? He had this knack for somehow addressing her fears—ones that worried about more than a poor performance this afternoon, because the track condition raised the issue of safety. He couldn't be sure Chique would handle the slop, but stood by her, ever confident. Nate had believed in this filly every step of the way.

"I thought you might want this today."

He held out a fist, and she stepped towards him, raising her eyebrows.

When she recognized the lightweight chain and tiny medallion he placed in her open palm her eyes blurred, blinking back tears she'd never shed. She turned the pendant over, trying to focus on the exquisite miniature painting of Ste-Anne and her Claire lookalike, no words coming.

Fingers closed around her wrist and Nate gently pulled her forward, directing her towards the door. "Come on. Time to go face it."

Liv detoured to Claire's stall, medallion clenched in her hand, and pushed it to the grill to meet the pink nose.

"Wish us luck, mare."

Claire blew softly in response.

Nate's headlights stayed in her rearview mirror the whole drive in, her wiper blades beating a monotonous rhythm. Jo, Michel, and Sue were already on the shed, carrying out a routine that was so familiar, but today surreal. Liv went through the motions, sweat pouring freely from her brow, stinging her eyes.

Chique pushed against the webbing after Liv turned her loose, her *tap, tap, tap,* demanding hay that wasn't coming. When a drowsy hotwalker from the other side of the barn came around the corner, the filly's neck snaked out. The kid ducked, which probably saved him from tripping over the fan Liv had left in place to keep the air circulating in the stifling stall.

"Sorry," she said sheepishly as the kid walked by. She was going to earn herself a fine if security came by to find Chique's screen still open and the fan in the way.

The kid waved it off with a sleepy grin. "Good luck today!"

Liv forgot for just a moment the feeling that everything was against them.

"Nothing wrong with her." Roger stopped at a healthy distance. "Let's get some horses out there so we have an idea of what the track's like. Are Nicole and Emilie here yet?"

Liv's face fell. "I forgot all about Emilie."

"It's going to be a long day." Jo patted her on the back. "There they are."

"Sure, thanks, sis," Emilie chided. "Good thing I called Nic last night as backup. Now will someone please put her on a horse?"

Liv scuttled to the tack room, but stopped short in front of the door. Someone had written on the whiteboard, in a neat, flowing, script.

Good things come.

It could only have been Nate. He must have stopped by after the races last night to check on Chique. Her face crinkled into a smile. *That guy.* He even had nice handwriting.

The gallopers were a moderate distraction, but after the last set, it was time to get Chique out for a bath. Emilie held her, Chique's head bobbing and teeth gnashing as Liv scraped off the excess water.

"Thanks, Em. I'll take her."

She glanced at the time every pass of the tack room. Nine o'clock. In just over seven hours, the Plate horses would start the walk over to the front side. Each time Chique acted out, squealing and bouncing her way around the shed, Liv winced. *Just hold it together for seven more hours.*

They were still walking—now that Chique had settled, Liv could call it that—when the commission vet arrived. Liv broke into a controlled jog, but the filly sprang into a canter-in-hand. Once she managed to get enough of an even trot both ways to satisfy the vet, she held Chique still, fixing her with a stern look as he examined her legs.

He straightened, and stroked Chique's neck, smiling. "Good luck."

Liv nodded thanks, collecting all the *good lucks* and tucking them away like she might amass enough of them to ensure success.

One more turn, and she'd put the filly in…to wait some more.

"Short on hotwalkers?"

Nate waited just beyond Chique's stall, his grin distracting Liv from her nerves for a moment.

"You think I was going to let someone else walk her? I'm not putting that kind of pressure on anyone today."

"Just me, right?"

"You signed up, remember." She turned Chique loose in the stall, snapping the screen shut and hanging the shank on the door.

"You seem almost cheerful."

"It's the calm before the storm—forgive my choice of clichés."

"Maybe the calm between storms."

She leaned on her hands, the cold cinder block wall cooling her palms as the tension crept back. "What did you think of the track?"

"It's a lot better than I thought it would be. They closed it early, but there're nine races to run over it before they get to the Plate. And if it stops raining, it's gonna get real slow."

"I can't believe we're hoping it doesn't stop."

He stepped forward, holding an empty hand out to a disappointed Chique. "I'd better go. Try not to self-destruct, all right? I'd hate for you to miss it if we win." He left with another of his grins, Liv wondering if he was really that calm, or just did a better job at keeping his nerves under wraps.

Ten o'clock.

She fed Chique a reduced portion of grain for lunch and started checking tasks off her list. Halter and shank cleaned; brass polished. Bridle and bit immaculate. Shadow roll pristine—maybe Chique would keep it that way, running on the front end. Blinkers too. Busy work, all of it.

Next, something she'd only do for the Plate. The traditional hunter braids in the top half of the filly's mane fed her need to control whatever minutiae she could, tiny even plaits tied with yarn and bumped with a crochet hook. It was a shame to have to switch to elastics for the bottom, but they needed to be easily removed. Something for Nate to do as they walked out for the post parade, leaving him mane to grab in the gate.

Chique shook her head as water dribbled down her neck, and Liv dabbed the drops away with her sponge. "You have my sincerest apologies, miss." The filly was no more comfortable getting dressed for the occasion than she would be herself.

Now there was really nothing left to do. Emilie napped on the couch in the office. Liv gave her a nudge.

"Let's go."

"You sure?" Emilie grinned through her yawn.

The rain backed off to a steady drizzle on the drive home, Liv distractedly punching at the stereo, advancing through the tracks searching for just the right music to match her mood. It wasn't happening. That song wasn't written yet.

A shower to wash away the stickiness, a French braid in her damp hair, a simple sleeveless navy linen dress. She smoothed the skirt with her hands, and dug the little medallion from the pocket of her jeans, fumbling with the clasp. When she placed the ivory hat on her head to check her reflection, fingering the pendant unconsciously, she saw someone, pretty enough, in an outfit befitting Woodbine's most prestigious day. Funny it was her.

"You look great," Emilie said, inching open the door. "Might be a little too distracting for Nate."

Liv rolled her eyes to keep the smile from her lips. "Better not be. Let's get back there."

Once she dropped Emilie off on the west side of the grandstand, she headed to the barn, the humidity assaulting her as soon as she left the air-conditioned car. Chique dozed in the corner of her stall. Probably a good thing, but maybe she should check the filly's temperature to be safe. Nate would laugh at her. *Breathe.*

If only there was a fast-forward button to skip through the next few hours. All she really had left to do was put on the rundown bandages, and it was too early for that.

The PA system crackled. "*Bring them over for the fifth...*"

A squeal and a thud sent her flying back onto the shed. Chique pressed to her screen, vibrating, fixed on the procession assembling not far from the barn. So she was fine, unless she'd sprung a shoe or cracked a bone with that kick.

Possibly more terrifying than Gulfstream's Pegasus and the fire-breathing dragon—the Horse Guards. They gathered with the open landau, preparing to pick up the Lieutenant-Governor General, this year's Royal delegate. Liv touched Chique's neck, warm and damp beneath her hand. *Just a few more hours, filly. Please?*

"We'll give her a quick hose-off once they're gone." Jo hovered behind Liv. "At least she hasn't rubbed her braids out."

"Yet. Better check her shoes, too."

Chique huffed and dropped her head, letting the fan blow in her face.

The calls came at half-hour intervals, counting them down. Each time Liv recalculated, obsessively—*the seventh was coming back, the eighth over there, they're calling for the ninth...the next call will be ours.*

One and a half hours until the Plate went off.

"I can do that, you know." Jo stood, hands on hips as Liv gathered what she'd need when it was finally time to put on the rundowns.

Liv just shook her head.

She wasn't taking any chances today with that track—bandages all round. She wound the white vetraps with fanatical precision, the perfect V in front, rundown patches just so, smoothing everything and finishing with two strips of white electrical tape around the top for added insurance.

"Get them ready for the tenth..."

Jo would take care of the rest. Liv left Chique with a kiss on the nose, and the sense of helplessness began, clinging to her more than the sticky air.

So many people on the front side, getting in her way as she skipped around puddles. At least the rain had finally let up. *Relax.* The horses hadn't even begun to arrive yet. But that made her twitchy, wondering why they weren't here already as she waited in the saddling stall.

One by one they appeared, and at last there was Chique's dark face with the big white shadow roll, eyes bugging out of her pretty little head.

"Give me your hat." Emilie elbowed her as the valet showed up with the tack.

She froze, wishing it were Roger putting it on. She'd only done it that one time in Keeneland—what if she screwed up, today, the most important of days? Her hands shook as she pulled the elastic girth up and found the last hole.

"Right to the top here." Her voice quavered.

The valet's helmet bobbed, and her nerves dissipated slightly as they secured the overgirth.

"Good luck." He scurried off as she thanked him, and she stashed that one with the others before stretching out Chique's forelegs.

Halter off, blinkers on, double-check the tack. "Okay Jo. See you outside."

"Hang on." Emilie grabbed her arm. She set the hat back on Liv's head and adjusted it, then nodded in approval. "Okay."

Outside, Emilie squeezed between Nate and her father, standing by their number. Em bounced on her toes, and Liv wanted so much to do the same, to disperse some of her anxiety, but it didn't seem befitting the trainer of a Plate horse.

Her mother's arm weaved around her waist. "I know your original plan was to be the one riding today."

"At least this means you can watch." Liv smiled. "Chique picked him. Who am I to get in the way of that?"

"You're quite the team, the three of you."

"So we are." Her composure faltered for a second when she saw her mother's glistening eyes. "Thank you." She wrapped her arms around Anne's shoulders, then Nate's gaze drew her away.

She grasped his outstretched hand, unflinching.

"So formal," he said.

His grin launched her pulse into a whole different tempo, but she didn't let go. "It is the Queen's Plate."

"Looks like we made it..." He sang it softly, and she laughed.

That guy. Singing Barry Manilow in the paddock before the biggest moment of their lives, just to ease the tension enough that she didn't explode under the pressure.

She compressed all her emotions into a compartment, and pulled her pragmatism back out. "This far. It's not over yet. Safe trip. *Bonne chance.*"

Sending her collection of *good lucks* along with him, they walked up to Chique.

THERE WAS no room for emotion back here.

Besides, there was enough of it flowing, the gate crew in a struggle that had already been going on too long with a behemoth of a colt. They squeezed him in. He banged against the sides, the jock scrambling onto the frame. The colt settled. The jock got back on.

Chique flicked an ear back at Nate as the assistant starter inched her forward.

You want me to go in beside that?

Yeah. Sorry. Gotta trust me, Cheek. We won't be there long.

He pulled out the last elastic, his thoughts shooting briefly to Liv—she'd be riding this with him every step of the way. He was barely aware as the last horse filed in beside them.

The doors crashed open, and a jarring impact from the left slammed Chique mid-leap, sending her nose-diving sideways into the quagmire. Nate pitched forward, swallowing a string of offensive phrases, sure he was headed for the bog below, but she scrambled, somehow finding her feet.

Chique fought him, climbing in the slop but showing no sign of pain—as if he could trust that. He eased his hold enough to let her settle, and the lengthening of her stride convinced him she was okay, but now there was a lot more than a bad track to overcome. She would use up everything in her heart trying to catch up if he asked, and he wasn't sure he had that right.

She channeled her fury into the chase, zeroing in on the trailers as they raced past the grandstand for the first time. The behemoth was at the back of the pack, and the last thing Nate wanted to do was take Chique wide around the turn, but it was that or keep her behind the unpredictable colt who had assaulted them. After recovering from such a major setback, he hated to ask her to wait, so he let her go.

Picking up more horses as they reached the backstretch, one thing was clear: she wanted the lead, though she was still nowhere near it. Nate closed his hands on the lines, asking her to take a breather. Her ears swivelled, acknowledging. *Okay, maybe just a little one.*

Touch and Go sat behind the front-runners and just wide, staying out of the messy kickback, inching stealthily up as the field rounded the next turn. Nate tucked Chique neatly in behind the favoured colt, letting her cruise in his slipstream. Chique went with Nate's decision, putting up with the mud pelting her face. Maybe they would have a say in the result of this Plate after all—there was still something there, though where it was coming from, he had no idea. Just over a quarter of a mile to go, and the real running had yet to begin.

Touch and Go shifted into gear and surged to the front, eclipsing the leaders. Nate swung Chique out to avoid the tired pacesetters and sent her after him. She lined the colt up, pounding through the slop, steadily wearing him down.

Nate didn't bother cocking his stick, Chique digging deep to access assets she possessed that he could never truly understand. She drew even with Touch and Go. With each thrust of her neck, each reeling stride, the finish loomed. He gathered her and threw everything at the wire with one last ask.

Chique pulled herself up, exhausted, and Nate dropped his eyes to her neck, reaching up to stroke her reverently. All that fearlessness and grit in such a small package. Then he finally dared to look around. The outrider headed toward them.

Who cared if the sun didn't shine? Nate beamed as the outrider escorted them onto the turf course. Everyone in the packed grandstand was on their feet, cheering, and he waved a salute before dropping the lines. Throwing his arms wide, he grinned down at Chique as if presenting them with their new Queen's Plate champion, then leaned forward and wrapped himself around her neck.

Liv pushed through the throng of photographers, reaching up and grasping his hand, pressing it against Chique's shoulder. She didn't let go until the blanket of purple daisies with its yellow crown was draped over the filly's withers, taking the shank from Jo to lead them across the muddy track to the winner's circle—with a detour to the hose to give Chique a cool shower and a drink.

Head high, nostrils flared, eyes rimmed red from the assault of the track, Chique posed with her people gathered. Nate didn't even look at the camera, he just looked at her.

Stepping on the scales made it official: winner of the Queen's Plate, *Chiquenaude, dark bay or brown three-year-old filly by Just Lucky, out of Sotisse.* Jo and Sue led her away to a fresh ovation, and Nate passed the tack and his helmet to his valet and clapped with them. Then he raced to the base of the podium, throwing his arms around Liv and spinning her.

"Oh, sorry." Remembering he was soaked through and wearing half the racetrack, he set her down, grinning. He brushed some of the sand off her bare shoulder before he could stop himself.

"Sure you are." She laughed, and they joined the presentation.

MAYBE SHE STAYED at the test barn too long, but it wasn't until Chique's breathing normalized—her thirst lessening, her walk becoming less agitated—that Liv felt she could leave. Besides, it was peaceful here, the routine the same as after any race, from a cheap claimer to this. Barn Five would be anything but.

A breeze chased off the humidity, snatches of blue sky widening as the clouds broke apart. The lawn was alive. Liv waved away the glass of champagne Roger tried to press into her hand. There would be champagne, but it wasn't happening without Nate.

"What's all this?" Three men checked equipment and tuned guitars beneath the tent her father had rented.

Emilie sipped bubbles from a plastic glass. "What's it look like? Nate asked his buddies to come play at the party."

Faye put an arm around Liv's shoulders and pressed her lips to her cheek. "Way to go, sweetie."

"Sorry we had to beat Touch and Go. He ran a gutsy race."

"If anyone was going to beat us, I'm glad it was you."

Liv returned her attention to the musicians. "How come I didn't know about this?"

"Oh please." Emilie rolled her eyes. "You've been in your own little world."

"Who's that, Em?" Faye sized up the strangers. "The guy with the guitar there, do you know?"

"Kinda tall for you, isn't he?" Emilie quipped.

"Maybe that's where I've been going wrong."

"You're gonna have to wait for Nate to make introductions. Nice to have you back though." Emilie nudged Liv. "You should grab some food while there's still some left. I bet you haven't eaten all day."

Liv managed to fill a plate, and nibbled at it between accepting kudos and keeping an eye on the shed, waiting for Chique to return. She saw Jo first, but the filly wasn't far behind. The hotwalker took her a few turns before coming out, and Chique's head dropped before she was even off the asphalt apron, tearing at the blades. The only time she came up for air was when Nate's old Mustang pulled up.

After checking in with Chique, he pushed his way gradually through the crowd, cleaned up and turned out in his navy suit and tie. Emilie launched herself at him before he could speak, and Faye commended him with an impressive show of congeniality as he waved over someone from the band.

"This is my friend Will. Liv Lachance, her sister Emilie, and Faye Taylor."

Will shook hands with each of them in turn, and Faye held on just a little bit longer. Emilie was right.

"I think this is going to be the best Plate Party ever." Faye peered after him when he excused himself with the promise of music.

Emilie looped her arm through Faye's. "Let's get it started, then. Looks like we've got some dancing to do."

They wandered towards the tent, and Liv turned to Nate. "Come on, Miller. Time for some real champagne." When they got to the shed, she disappeared into the office, emerging with a fat bottle and two crystal flutes.

"Don't be popping corks in this filly's face while I'm trying to put bandages on," Jo warned as the hotwalker brought Chique to her stall, "or

I'll just leave her for the two of you. You put rundowns on in that outfit, Liv. I'd like to see you do her up in it, too."

Nate removed his jacket and draped it over the rail. "Here." He plucked the hind cottons and two bandages from Jo's arms.

Jo added some sheet cotton, plastic, and a tub of furacin. Nate Miller, leading apprentice in North America, Plate-winning jockey, putting bandages on his Plate horse. *So much more than just a pretty face.* Liv snapped a photo with her phone. Because, really, that needed to be broadcast.

"Stay for champagne?" She peeled the foil from the bottle's neck as Jo dumped her bucket of poultice water.

"I think there's plenty out there. You two go ahead."

Liv threw a clean rub rag over it and held the cork, carefully twisting the body.

"Gah, are you kidding?" Nate grabbed it and popped the cork, slipping his thumb over the top and letting the towel fall as he shook it.

He released the spray between them, then handed it back, froth coursing messily over the neck. Liv held it at arm's length, laughing, then filled the flutes and passed him one. No toast could cover it, so she said nothing, silently holding out her glass. He clinked it, locking in her eyes, even as the bubbles hit the back of her throat.

Chique stretched her neck out, poking him. He poured some into his cupped hand and she pressed her muzzle to his palm, but withdrew, upper lip contorting.

"Fine, all the more for us. This better?" With a toss of her forelock she swept up the peppermint that appeared from his pocket.

Liv didn't stop him when he topped them both up, the band starting behind him. "This was your idea, obviously."

"I told you we were going to have a great Plate Party this year." He set his glass on the rail and held out his hand. "Dance?"

She looked from the hand, to his eyes, a slow smile spreading over her face. One more swallow of champagne, and she put the glass down and folded her fingers over his. His hand went easily to her hip, his shoulder firm against her palm. And then it was just the two of them, the music irrelevant as he drew her closer, a tremor in her fingers she couldn't tell was his or her own spreading through her with their gentle sway.

"Geai wanted us to be together."

The words were barely a whisper in her ear. She froze, ducking the intense blue of his focus, blocking out the timbre of his voice and pulling away. "That's not fair."

It was the perfect out; the last excuse. His face, though. He wouldn't say it if it wasn't true. She'd done it again, spooking more often than any horse she'd been on, always afraid a man would get in the way of her dream. Meanwhile, Nate had become its whole foundation.

She willed herself to stop shaking, slipping trembling hands to his chest, feeling his heartbeat as much as her own. The hurt on his face fell away as her mouth tasted the tang of champagne on his.

"Don't worry, I told him he was crazy," he murmured with a muted version of the grin that had always made her just a little bit insane. Easy solution this time. She just kissed him again.

He wrapped her in, her knees threatening to give way. If her arms hadn't been coiled around his shoulders, if his hadn't held her up, she'd have fallen. So what. Control was overrated.

"You do crazy so well, Miller."

His lips hovered. "It got us this far."

"What now?"

Chique's throaty rumble interrupted, and Liv felt his laugh.

"Now we feed the guest of honour her dinner, apparently. Then, I don't know, my memory's a little fuzzy at the moment, but I think there's a party going on out there."

"Parties are definitely overrated."

"It's for a good cause."

Chique *tap-tap-tapped.*

Liv took in the filly, and the guy, and the crazy they both sent through her.

"That it is."

THE END

ALL THE LITTLE THINGS

BOOK 2

For my Woodbine circle, Theresa, Lorna and Nathalie; and my Saratoga circle, Juliet, Kim, Sharon, Jen and Alecia. Miss you all. One day we'll visit Mrs London's again!

1

Everyone should set themselves on fire at least once in their life.

For Faye, that one time was Nate Miller. Oh, it had been exhilarating at first, dancing through the flames, assuming it wouldn't consume her – because she did not get attached. That was her rule. But somewhere along the way, something had gone wrong, and in the end, she'd been burnt. Crispy and black around the edges, with no one to blame but herself. Though she blamed Nate anyway, because hating him felt better than loathing herself.

And now, someone's hands covered her eyes from behind like blinker cups, to shield her from the scene on the shedrow.

Nate. Liv. A bottle of champagne, and...

"We're supposed to be dancing." Emilie, Liv's younger sister and perhaps, now, Faye's best friend, steered Faye away, and towards the band.

Faye's appearance was required at the Queen's Plate party. A whisker was the difference between that party being here, at Barn Five, home of Triple Stripe Racing Stables, instead of Barn Twelve where her brother's trainees were stalled. *A whisker.* But while she could hate Nate for being the cause of her pain, she couldn't hate Liv for her horse having the victorious whisker. Okay, she did want to hate Liv, just a little, but not for that. And Nate was on the horse with that whisker, so…

"I called it, didn't I?" She hated being right about them, and couldn't help but look over her shoulder like the witness to a train wreck as Em dragged her away. Except it wasn't going to be a train wreck. It would be sweet, Liv, like one of her beloved horses, some combo of curiosity and self-preservation as she so cautiously moved closer to him; Nate holding out his hand like he was asking her to dance, all handsome and chivalrous. If she'd been watching a Hallmark romance instead of her best friend and her ex, it wouldn't be stinging like the wasps that hid out in the galvanized gates at the farm, coming from nowhere to pierce you when you disturbed them.

Em gave her another tug, but not before sweet got a little bit closer to steamy. There was some repressed stuff in her friend Liv, apparently.

"Maybe so," Em concurred. "You also told Liv not to use you as an excuse."

She had. Otherwise, Liv would have suffered in silence, continued to deny her feelings for the one guy even Faye had to admit was perfect for her.

"And I saw you eyeballing his friend," Em continued.

"Hmmm, yes. Time to get back on the horse, right?" Had she really just used a horse-based cliché? *This is worse than I thought.*

What she really wanted to do was to keep drinking the free-flowing cheap champagne, to wash away the image of Liv and Nate looking so… inevitable. But, to give Nate just a tiny bit of credit, getting his buddies to come play at the party had been a brilliant idea.

Nate's buddy from Calgary was a nice surprise. Not her type; he was tall, and Faye didn't know why, but she'd always gone for short men. Probably because they were accessible. Maybe she liked to take on their big egos. She'd grown up in a horse racing family, and spent plenty of time on the Woodbine backstretch in her formative years. Her six-foot brother was a giant back here. Nate, at five-six, was tall for a jock. He also lacked some of that ego. That probably should have been a warning sign for Faye.

She and Em elbowed to the front of the group collecting as the music started. She had a good view of the friend here. Will, wasn't it? Time to work with that. Em started dancing, and Faye joined in, because bouncing to the beat was as good a way as any to get her mind off the scene on the shed.

Will, as it turned out, was proving to be an excellent distraction. His voice was a bit rough, the timbre of it making things in her hum. The rakish angle of the guitar, the broad shoulders, and the beautiful long fingers that moved smoothly over the frets amplified the effect.

She leaned into Em, mouth by her ear, and hissed, "I bet he'd sizzle if I kissed him. I bet I'd burn my tongue."

Em laughed. "That's more like it."

Faye knew now she was Nate's rebound, even if both of them had been in denial about that for most of the relationship. His brokenness had appealed to her; his attempt to pretend he was fine, when he was anything but. She'd never been the woman who felt the need to fix guys, and at the outset he'd just fit her usual, basic, criteria – single, hot (both physically and professionally) apprentice rider. She'd honestly just wanted her typical short-term gig. But despite thinking he'd go for that early on, he'd turned the tables on her when she hadn't been able to reel him in on the first cast. She'd been intrigued. The chase was going to be a little harder this time. She'd thought it might be fun. Maybe it was for a while.

Fake champagne and the music helped numb her. She didn't care at the moment how she was getting home. She'd come with Dean, assuming Liv would give her a ride. Dean had left ages ago – hadn't even waited to see the band. Her big brother kept an eye out for her, but he wasn't a party kind of guy. He knew someone would get her home safe, because she wasn't going to adhere to his old-man hours. Em was responsible; it would probably be her. But Faye saw a fresh challenge before her now. Will would be a fine chauffeur. She could think of several ways to thank him. She didn't even know the guy, and she already had plans for him tonight. Seemed like as good a way as any to break out of her slump.

They were playing covers, from oldies and 90s stuff all the way through to current tunes. *Oooh, that one's perfect.* The Flys' *Got You Where I Want You.* She snagged Will's eyes as the hum in her continued – or was it a coincidence that he'd looked at her just then? She gave him a smile anyway, like the song demanded, slow and sultry. Closing her eyes as she swayed, she let the distance between them vanish, in her mind, at least, trying the idea on.

When the song ended, her little fantasy blew up, because Nate was next to him now, grabbing the mic. It was annoying as hell that he'd messed up her escape. But him being there meant Liv was hiding out somewhere.

Faye didn't owe her anything.

But for eleven years, Liv had been her best friend. And Faye was *not* standing up here now that Nate was singing.

She turned her back on the band and weaved through the bodies amid whoops and whistles as Woodbine's freaking Golden Boy – Plate-winning jockey, last year's Sovereign and Eclipse award-winning apprentice…and breaker of her heart — started in with Panic! At the Disco's *Victorious*. Of course.

The kiss from her Prince Charming had not miraculously transformed Liv into an extroverted princess. She stood on the fringes, just enough apart from everyone to look her awkward self, too afraid of her own body to even step in time to the music's beat. She probably didn't even dance when there was no one around. Faye had given up trying to drag her into it, because it had just started to feel cruel.

Right this moment, Faye wished Liv wasn't her best friend. She wished she could either ignore her, or let fly with the barbs poking in her brain. But she probably shouldn't even acknowledge that she'd seen anything, because Liv would only be embarrassed. And Liv didn't mean to hurt. It wasn't her fault that she and Nate were better suited than Nate and Faye ever could have been. *Nice guys are wasted on me anyway.*

She hoped Will wasn't a nice guy.

She sidled up to Liv, looping arms. "They're good," she said. "I'm impressed. Too bad Nate had to join in." *Couldn't you have distracted him just a bit longer?* Just a bit of snark. She couldn't help it.

"Too bad security will probably shut them down any time."

You're probably looking forward to that. But Faye said, "Gotta make hay while the sun shines then, sweetie!" She started bopping around, even if it was to Nate's voice. Liv smirked as Faye jostled her, but none of it was rubbing off on her.

Wait — that wasn't another horse reference, was it? Making hay? *I need to watch that.*

Nate was on to *Finding Out True Love Is Blind* now, which was a little risqué for this venue, but damn, Faye loved that song, even if it was older. He liked older stuff, the Golden Boy did. And as Nate's taste went, this one wasn't actually that old.

"Where did Em go?" she yelled at Liv over the music.

"No idea."

"She'd better not have left." Faye had already growled at a couple of guys who'd thought they'd try their luck with her, so it was time to secure her ride before she got any drunker. She spotted Em. "Sorry, sweetie, you gotta excuse me."

At least it was the backside, and not a dance club, so Liv could always slink back to the shed if she wanted and commune with one of the horses. Faye wasn't worried about her fending for herself. Even without the Nate development, men had always backed off from Liv for the most part, between the anti-social veneer she'd perfected and her status. Liv would hate hearing it, but she was kind of racetrack royalty: daughter of the owner of a prominent stable. She worked hard, but it hadn't hurt her any to have that behind her.

Faye reached Em just in time to scream out the last lines of the song, and they collapsed into laughter. Faye grabbed the plastic glass out of Emilie's hand and downed what remained of the golden liquid in it. Then Nate was back to Panic! At The Disco, *Collar Full*, and he only had eyes for Liv, who had not, surprisingly, retreated. The song was kind of perfect for them. Faye would have loved it if she didn't hate it. Em probably didn't notice, whereas Faye felt like Nate might as well be serenading Liv under a window. She needed more fake champagne.

It was a relief when it was over and he relinquished the mic, giving Will a man-hug before leaving them. She and Em squished their way back to the front as Will started a new song, all gravelly voice and guitar. He was singing Blue October's *Soar*. That wasn't actually the name of the song, but it's how Faye always thought of it. Once again she obeyed the lyrics he sang, smiling at him, looking up, and there was no question this time that Will was returning the gaze, his eyes dark but soft and seeing her. It sent a warm rush through her, on top of the vibration of the deep-down hum, and in that instant she felt like this was her destiny. *He is my destiny.* Then her head went dizzy and pain shot up the side of her neck. She dropped her chin and jammed a thumb into the overstretched muscle.

This is why I don't date tall guys.

There was a buzz of activity behind them, and Faye turned sideways – because her neck hurt too much to just glance over her shoulder. Sure enough, a security guard stood talking to Roger and Nate and Liv. Nate made a gesture with a finger across his throat to Will, and the band stopped playing. Em pushed out her lower lip and headed towards Nate and Liv while Roger wandered to the food and drinks, where a couple of the grooms were starting to pack everything up. The Triple Stripe crew would eat well for a few days.

Faye followed Em slowly, concentrating hard on negotiating the lawn as her heels poked through the grass, in no hurry to join the lovebirds. In her advanced state of inebriation, she couldn't be trusted to maintain a filter.

"Oh well, we had a good run," Nate was saying with a shrug.

Faye grabbed Em's arm and pulled her to the side. "Can I catch a ride home with you?"

Em glanced at Liv, whose head was tilted into Nate, and Faye couldn't help watching them. They weren't touching, but there was an intimacy there, and it hurt. *I need the pain to go away.* Which meant either more alcohol, or getting out of there.

"Em?" she hissed.

"I came with Liv," Emilie said apologetically.

"Maybe she'll go with Nate, and you can take me with you in her car." Liv was still Liv, so Faye didn't imagine Nate driving her home would end with her in his bed, but wouldn't they want to prolong this disgustingly magical evening?

"This is my sister we're talking about. I'm sure we can give you a ride."

Which would be all sorts of awkward, even with Em there. Faye sighed. "Let me know when you're leaving." What choice did she have? She could just ride in the back seat and pray she passed out.

Em went to help with the food, Liv went to check on her horse, and Nate went over to the band where the guys were loading equipment into a van.

Was it too late to make a play for Will? It was desperation, not destiny.

Destiny was not a real thing. Even if Nate and Liv made a pretty good case for it.

Nate glanced her way, but she was beyond caring enough to try to read his expression. He said something in parting to Will, and headed for the shedrow. He and Liv had to tuck their precious baby in together, right?

Well. *Hello.* Will was headed in her direction. Maybe the night wasn't a complete failure. There was no more music, but the hum rose up again as he got closer. Okay, truth be told, it was probably the fake champagne.

"Will, wasn't it?" She was conscious of pronouncing her words, and hoped it wasn't obvious. She didn't offer her hand, because she at least remembered she'd done that earlier, and it would seem like she was trying too hard if she did it again. She wasn't the girl who fell over a guy, no matter how much she needed him to help her get over Nate Miller. "That was fun." *And that was lame.*

"You're–" He stumbled over his tongue before taming it. "–Liv's friend."

Nice recovery. Sort of. At least she wasn't the only one who was less than smooth tonight. If he and Nate were real friends, he would know exactly who she was. Would that be a problem? Was there a code? Would Will think it was wrong to sleep with his friend's ex? Did guys care about that? She couldn't worry about it. She'd never been Nate's property, and couldn't let her past with him dictate her possible future. Drive on.

"So what do you do when you're not, you know, rocking the backstretch?"

"You're assuming this isn't a full-time gig?"

"Well, I haven't heard you on the airwaves, so…"

"Maybe I don't normally play the kind of music you listen to."

"Do you know what kind of music I listen to?"

He looked like he was thinking hard, thumb and forefinger resting on his chin. "The poppy side of Alternative, I'm going to say. The Killers. Maybe City and Colour. Bastille."

"Not bad. Are you mocking my musical tastes?"

"No. Everyone has their own taste, and just because mine might be different, it doesn't mean that it's better than yours."

"That sounds very diplomatic. Do you mean it, or are you just saying it?"

He chuckled, the crimping of fine lines around his eyes and those tasty-looking lips as he smiled making him even more attractive. She wished she had something in her hands, because suddenly she didn't know what to do with them, because they wanted to grab his t-shirt and pull him down, press her mouth to his, and see if he really did sizzle. "I knew Nate had secrets, but how did I miss you?" It came out breezy and breathless. Maybe she was laying the sultry on too thick.

"He's a busy guy. And our schedules don't exactly mesh."

"So we're back to, what do you do, when you're not rocking –"

"The backstretch – is that what you called this? What does that even mean."

"Damned if I know."

"Want to grab a coffee?"

Faye's eyebrows shot up. The biggest party night of the year for the racing crowd and this guy wants coffee? But she smiled, coyly, she hoped. Considering she'd thought she'd gotten nowhere at all, she would not stick her nose up at this offer.

"Sure."

She'd found her ride home after all.

So, this was Nate's ex.

She was...lovely. That's the word Will had used when he'd seen pictures, instead of the more raw reaction her appearance inspired. Not that Nate had exactly shared them, but she was obviously a social media fan, and tagged him relentlessly. Nate did have his own accounts, though Will didn't really know what for. To torture himself about the past, mostly, was Will's bet.

Picnics. Dancing. Downtown. Hashtags galore. But Will had never met her. Nate had never brought her out to their jam sessions like the other guys sometimes brought their girlfriends. It wasn't as if she'd been a secret, but he'd kept her in a weird bubble – like the rest of this bizarre horse world.

Will had dated horse girls in Calgary. Ones that rode those jumping horses and had dreams of the big classes at Spruce; ones that rode barrel races and were determined to compete at the Stampede. Where did racetrack horse girls fit? Nate's ex was forward, that was for sure. She'd had her eye on him all night.

She was still Nate's ex.

Before she'd been Nate's ex she'd been his rebound, and Will knew one thing for certain: he wasn't going to be hers. He'd do this favour for Nate, and make sure she got home safe – even though it was wildly out of his way – so she didn't have to ride with his *new* girlfriend (as of the last minute, apparently). Even though the two women were supposed to be best friends. The whole thing was strange.

Nate had offered to let him crash at his place, but Will was used to late nights, and this one was not late. It was only just getting dark. He could do this little thing, for his oldest friend, and still be home earlier than he would have been on a work night.

She'd been looking all forlorn over there, now that things were winding up and she was left on her own. The look didn't quite fit her. She didn't look comfortable with it. And that made Will feel sorry for her. So, he'd walked over there like it wasn't planned; enjoyed her face as it brightened.

She was trying to play it cool, hide that she had an agenda, which Will was pretty sure was to use him to make herself feel better about the obvious fact that Nate was totally – though apologetically, because he was Nate – into someone new.

Her expression when he suggested coffee had been priceless. He saw a lot of drunk people in his line of work, and she'd had enough alcohol tonight. And while there was something about the whole damsel in distress thing, she was likely the type who would punch him if he called her that to her face because she'd be too proud to admit she'd found herself in such a position. This wasn't the real her. It caught Will off guard, but he found himself wanting to know the real her. The her that had drawn Nate in enough to stay with her for eight months.

"C'mon," he said, motioning to his Chevy as the other guys tucked the last cords into the van. She teetered on heels that looked dangerously unstable for a sober person, let alone one in her tipsy state. She slipped into the passenger seat, and he swung the door shut.

"Is there some pact that guys from Calgary have to drive beat up old vintage cars that are probably older than they are?" she asked, her eyes travelling over the Camaro's dash with one eyebrow quirked. Despite her level of impairment, she looked classy. Classy and smart. The alcohol was merely a coping mechanism.

"Is there a problem with that? What do you drive?"

"Let's see if you can guess that like you did the music."

Will pulled on his seatbelt and put his foot on the clutch. "You're going to have to tell me how to get out of here, because I'm pretty much lost."

She directed him to what he recognized to be Highway 27, but heading north, instead of south back into the city. He figured she was a Starbucks kinda girl, but wondered where the hell around there would be one of those. It seemed like solid Tim Horton's territory.

He shouldn't have worried. She probably had an app that told her the location of every last franchise.

Even under the dwindling influence of too much cheap champagne, she had a quick smile and a thank you for him as he held open the door and let her walk through. The rich smell of coffee overtook the subtlety of her perfume, and he breathed it in, the sharp blast of pressurized steam frothing milk punctuating the background buzz of seated patrons. It was one of his favourite things, the quiet atmosphere of a coffee shop – at least if they served proper espresso.

Faye ordered a cappuccino – double-shot Venti. Seemed a good choice.

"Same," Will said. "Want something to eat?" He looked down at her, but she shook her head. "I'll have one of those brownies." They'd cleared the food by the time the band had been done playing, and he was kind of hungry, but the savoury stuff wouldn't have dealt with being almost a day old as well as the sweets would have.

He reached for his wallet, but Faye waved her phone in front of him. "I'm buying. I collect rewards. And the least I can do is pay." She glanced up at him with one of those cute smiles she'd been giving him all night, then flashed the phone in front of the reader.

They lucked out with a table, someone leaving just as they picked up their order. The place looked to be populated predominantly by students, tucked behind laptops looking either intent, or bored, or in some cases, asleep.

Faye stood out, and it was more than because of the way she was dressed – the fancy outfit, the makeup that had withstood the day's events. She had an air, though it seemed a little deflated, a light that was running a few watts lower than it should be. Anger poked at him, catching him off guard. Nate had done this, to this beautiful person. Nate said she'd broken up with him, but that didn't mean she hadn't suffered for it.

"Is there a school close to here?" he said to make conversation before he lifted his cup.

"Humber College's main campus is just over there." Her chin lifted, indicating the direction.

She reached for the brownie, long fingers breaking off a chunk, and placed it languidly on her tongue. Didn't want something herself, but had no problem scavenging his. Her lips closed, savouring, in her own little world for a moment before she swallowed and chased it with the cappuccino.

"So why did you come to Toronto? Were you running from something too?"

She was talking about Nate, of course, but he hoped his flinch wasn't visible. It wasn't like Nate, the reason he'd left. Nate's impetus had been all angst and drama – not that it hadn't been warranted. "I came on a scholarship to U of T for music."

"Wow. So it's a serious thing for you. Did you finish your degree?"

"And started a masters."

"Wow." She was still a little drunk, he could tell; more impressed than she should be by that. "What do you plan to do with that?"

"Nothing. I mean, I could teach, but I'm not a teacher."

"How do you know?"

She had him there. Cue subject change. "So this Queen's Plate thing is a big deal?"

Her laugh came easily, a clear timbre behind her vocal chords that made him wonder if she could sing. "You don't know that? It's Canada's most famous horse race. It's the longest continuously-run sporting event in North America. During war time when the Derby wasn't run, the Queen's Plate went on." She could have done a commercial for the event. "The Plate is special. I love the Plate. It's when Woodbine dresses up and shines. I get to wear a hat." She put another piece of brownie on her tongue, and Will fixated on it until she pursed her lips and looked perplexed. "I have no idea where I left my hat."

He hadn't seen the hat, but she was ridiculously adorable. Her dark hair had probably been a bit tidier when she'd been wearing it. Definitely before the band started playing. The way she'd been swinging her head around as she danced had left those wavy tresses in sexy disarray. Not that he'd been watching her dance. No, not at all. He blinked it out of his mind.

"Your brother works on the farm?" Will was picturing a straw hat and suspenders; combines and hay rakes, maybe a few beef cattle. In other words, his childhood memories of his grandfather back in Alberta.

"He does some stuff, but he has a live-in manager to run things. Technically he's a trainer. He has a public stable here." She gestured in the general direction of the racetrack. "Well, there. About twelve horses, mostly for clients he inherited from my father, and a few of our own that he bred – again, the result of my father's breeding program. Some of them he's had to sell pieces of here and there to keep things going."

"Pieces? Like an ear? Or a tail?"

Faye smirked. "A comedian, I see. Do you really know nothing about racing? Like Nate doesn't tell you anything?"

"I think getting together with me and the guys to play some music is his escape from it, to be honest."

She looked slightly bewildered. "Huh. I never got the impression Nate felt it was anything he needed a break from."

Will shrugged. "Maybe when he was with you, you gave him that break." He thought of those social media posts, a picture record of their time together, and made a mental note to check to see if she'd deleted them, erased what she could when the biggest reminder was an unavoidable part of her life.

She looked completely sober now, her face impassive as she seemed to absorb that thought. The flicker in her eyes was a little nostalgic.

"Well if so, he's gone full immersion now." She straightened, stealing another morsel of brownie so that there was only a tiny piece left. "Let's not talk about my ex, all right? That's just bad manners on a date."

"This is a date?"

"It would be weird if we dated, wouldn't it?"

"I don't know. Because our friends are involved? That's just life."

"I suppose. Besides which, Nate and Liv are far too engrossed in their own lives to probably even notice, right?"

There was a touch of bitter there. A hint of resignation. He felt bad for her, that she'd happened to fall for someone who, plunked into different circumstances – a different time, a different place – might have really loved her. Will didn't understand the racehorse world or its people, but he'd been around enough horse girls to understand that their priorities were a little skewed. The racetrack seemed a level deeper, a place where you just ended up with someone you worked closely with because you were together all the time anyway.

"Sorry. I'm doing it again. I am so not that girl. I apologize for embarrassing myself."

Will waved her off, and tipped back his cup to catch the last drops. "Don't worry about it. I don't date horse girls anyway."

Her laugh this time was a spontaneous burst. "You think I'm a horse girl?"

Will narrowed his gaze. A fair assumption, wasn't it? "Ready to go?"

He hoped he said it in a matter-of-fact, *hey I'm just getting you home safe* way. She nodded and rose, picking up the empty cups and napkins and depositing them in the trash on the way out, leaving him to watch the sway of her hips under the fabric of her dress. She knew what she was doing. She might be down, but she was not out. She was probably never out. She was *that* girl.

Casual, impersonal, conversation about nothing carried them all the way to King City, Faye interrupting to give him directions when needed. They talked about last week's incessant humidity, and he answered her questions about Calgary's weather, where the higher altitude made that a non-issue. How did he like Toronto? Had she grown up out here? There's Triple Stripe, Liv's dad's farm, also where Nate lived; the farm where Faye lived a little further on. Up a short driveway between fences, to a century home. Her brother's truck next to the house. A little Corolla beside it. Hers, most likely.

He escorted her up three steps onto a deck. Outside the back door, she turned, gazing up under dark lashes with one of those smiles, standing bathed in yellow light. He caught his breath, gave her a quick kiss on the cheek, and left her there.

Back in the car, he waited, watching her. She waited a beat too, watching him, before opening the door and disappearing inside. She was still too much Nate's ex, and not enough whoever she'd been before him. He wanted to meet that Faye – because this suppressed, trying-not-to-feel-everything-she-was-still-feeling person, was not her. He wasn't going to be her rebound, he reminded himself. He wasn't going to think he could put back together what Nate had torn apart. And he didn't date horse girls.

2

This should have been the time she slept through the sounds of Dean getting up, but no. Her face was so imprinted on her pillow she was glad there was no need to lift her head, or open her eyes, which seemed to be stuck together. At least *she* didn't have to get up at dark o'clock and head into the racetrack. She wondered again where her hat had ended up. *I liked that hat.*

When she heard Dean's truck rumble out the driveway, she rolled over with a grunt, her mouth dry and vile, but sleep beckoned her back before she could reach for the water bottle on her bedside table.

It was the bathroom calling her that made her finally drag herself out of bed. The sun was aggravatingly all bright and cheery in a cloudless sky. Someone needed to turn it down. Where were her sunglasses? Probably wherever her hat was.

The face that met her in the mirror was not an attractive one. *Not a good look, Faye.* Crusted mascara, creases on her cheek from her pillow. That humming that had enchanted her last night had been replaced by an incessant pounding behind her temples. She should have just kept drinking, then she wouldn't have this headache. This – face it – hangover. Damn Mr Straight-Laced musician. How did that even make sense? Coffee and a chaste kiss on the cheek. That's what he'd left her with. At least she'd got her tongue down Nate's throat the first time she'd kissed him.

I have lost it. I've lost my touch.

Either that, or she needed to avoid these Calgary boys. They were too *good.* How boring. She shuffled back to her room, guzzled some water, and stared at her bed. This was not how it was supposed to go.

In the sobering light of the morning after, it probably hadn't been a good move, trying to land Nate's best friend. It irked her as much as it hurt, that Nate had landed squarely on his feet –winning the big race, getting the girl, living the dream – while she floundered. She wasn't the girl that did that. She'd dropped him. Why was it taking her so long to recover?

And how did she still know nothing about his friend? She knew music wasn't his full-time gig, that was it. He lived in Toronto. He was educated. He had to pay the rent somehow, didn't he?

He hadn't even asked for her number. Then again, neither had Nate, after her initial play. But Nate had known where she lived. Knew many ways of finding her. So there was that. This Will character could track her down, quite easily. By asking Nate. Now that was just…she didn't know how to feel about that.

She wasn't holding a torch for Nate, honestly she wasn't. Just a whole hell of a lot of resentment. Mostly that she'd let herself fall, for the first time in her life. Damn Mr. Straight-Laced, again, for not helping her get back on track. Well. She had to do something about that. Enough was enough. She needed to find another project and regain her form. One good thing about the racetrack, it wasn't a matter of finding someone to sleep with, it was just a matter of whom.

Thank goodness she didn't have much to do today. She always planned ahead, so the day after Queen's Plate was relaxed, in case she did run off a bit at the event itself.

It appeared she couldn't help the horse racing metaphors. Something else to get over. Maybe it was fair Will thought she was a horse girl. She hadn't had the chance to tell him he couldn't be more wrong.

There would have been many pages this morning at Woodbine from employees citing mysterious "car trouble." Not Nate and Liv though. They'd both be there, dedicated souls that they were, riding the high of a big win and shiny new feelings. A year ago, those kinds of feelings for Nate had been starting their drip of lies to her. *Maybe this time will be different. Maybe you can fall in love.*

Wrong.

She needed a shower, then, breakfast. Coffee and Advil would be about right. On second thought, drugs first, then shower, then coffee.

A couple of Liqui-gels and some scorching hot water later, her headache began to ease. The clatter of nails on hardwood met her when she reached the bottom of the stairs, and Gus scrambled over to greet her. She trusted her head enough to bend and take his big Golden Retriever head in both hands, and planted a kiss on top of it. Satisfied, he wandered back to his spot near the back door, tail wafting lazily back and forth, and collapsed into a fluffy lump of long, yellow hair.

The pot Dean had brewed hours before waited on the counter, a dreadful, dark concentrate of its former self. She drank it black, its harshness enough to kickstart her brain so she could generate a proper cup. That life-saving aroma of fresh grinds filtered by steaming water in her French press made her think of Will. He'd seemed relieved at her choice of coffee options, and hadn't said a word when she'd eaten most of his brownie. He might be a catch, if only he was looking to be caught. Which he obviously was not. At least not by her.

She reached for a bottle from a cupboard by the sink, and added a shot of Baileys to her mug – for medicinal purposes, of course. Now she could take on this day. A day for accepting reality – at least when it came to her non-existent love life.

Not a lot had changed in the farmhouse in the last eleven years. The office still displayed photos of her father's greatest training wins, and a framed image of the family old enough that Faye was scooped up in her father's arms. There were no recent photos save for in Dean's office at the track, where she'd been in some of the win pics of horses he'd trained. He didn't bring them here. Didn't think they were worthy of holding court alongside the accomplishments of Ed Taylor.

Gus joined her as she parked herself in front of the computer and went right to the spreadsheets, just in case Facebook showed her things she didn't want to see. Things she already couldn't unsee. It was the end of the month, so she started by invoicing Dean's owners. Touch and Go running second in yesterday's Plate to Liv's filly wasn't anything to be embarrassed about – a million dollar purse, second was worth twenty percent. Dean owned a third of him, and as trainer got ten percent of the other partners' pieces. Faye calculated in her head quickly. That would pay the bills for a bit. The numbers helped her, got her mind off less tangible things. Like how the two of them would probably grow old here, die here. Dean the quiet farmer bachelor, Faye his spinster sister. She'd be a hot cougar spinster though. There would be no bun and dowdy clothes for her.

Her mother had taught her how to do the bookwork, a way she could contribute to the family business when it became obvious she had no interest in the horses. She took after her mother. But at least her mother had been capable enough to pitch in when needed. Brave enough. So Faye learned the books, and learned how to cook, and to bake her father's favourite dessert, forever trying to make up for not being a horse girl.

When her phone rang at eleven, she'd accomplished enough to ease the annoying thoughts in her brain. She grabbed for it. Liv? Calling her? It kept ringing, and Faye sighed. She couldn't not answer.

"Hey, sweetie, what's up?"

"Everything's fine. Yes, I know, me on the phone. Do I need to come over with a defibrillator?" Liv typically only used the actual call function of her phone in dire circumstances.

"You might, actually. To what do I owe the honour?" She tried to keep her tone light, instead of tired. "Tell me again that everything's okay."

Though on some level, she was hoping it was not, that things had already gone south with Nate. Because with Liv, that was totally possible. She was an expert at removing herself, all with perfect justification. The animals would always come first; relationships could be collateral damage.

Stop that.

Besides, Nate would always adapt, because he was, Faye was quite sure, very much the same. He would gentle that resistance in Liv, with all the patience and compassion he showed the horses he partnered. And the boy had enough of his own hangups; the two of them were probably just as perfect together as Faye feared.

"Everything is fine," Liv repeated. "How are you?"

Faye didn't know how to answer that. Did she tell the truth? Instead, she redirected. "How is the filly this morning?"

Faye asked because she had to. It was proper etiquette, unforgivable not to, especially after a hard race like yesterday's. Even if she didn't have the same draw to the horses, they were the reason Faye had the things she did. They'd always been what fed and clothed and sheltered her. She would forever acknowledge and be grateful for them, for that reason. Plus, being best friends with a bona fide horse girl – or the daughter or sister of a trainer, or the girlfriend of a jock – one began to ask such things out of habit.

"Good. A little tired, no surprise."

There was an awkward silence between them. Because why was she calling? Liv had a history of avoiding Faye, and for once, she had an excuse Faye could go along with. But the small talk wouldn't last long. Liv wasn't one to talk for the sake of talking. She needed a purpose. Faye usually drew it out, but she wasn't sure she had it in her this time. Heaven forbid she was asking for advice about something delicate.

"Can we get together?" Liv said, finally.

Faye tried to sound casual, but was afraid just a little bit of frost crept in. "Are you coming over?"

"Am I still welcome?"

Faye sighed. "Of course. If you bring cappuccino, that is."

She thought she could feel Liv's slight smile.

"I can't today…if I don't go for a run this afternoon I'll explode–"

There had been a time when Faye would have mentioned glibly that there were better ways to relieve tension, but given what that would imply in the new state of things, she didn't want to think about it.

"–and I have some stuff to catch up on at the farm. Tomorrow though, for sure? We could meet at Lucy's at noon for lunch. On me."

"Of course on you. You just won the Plate."

"It's a date."

"See you tomorrow."

Liv hadn't said it, but that run she was so desperate for was a date too, of sorts, because Nate would be running with her. There were trails on the Triple Stripe farm, but one day last week, Faye had caught a glimpse of them on the road. One of the little clues that tipped her off that something was closer to happening, despite Liv's protestations. Liv ran alone. Period. Except now she did not.

Faye sighed, a heavy release from her too-tight chest. She had twenty-four hours to prepare for whatever Liv felt they needed to talk about. And Lucy's didn't serve alcohol. Or cappuccino, for that matter.

On that note, another coffee was in order. The mention of Lucy's made her crave something sweet to go with it. Gus followed her to the kitchen. She wanted to think it was loyalty, but it was really just because he hoped there was something in the trip for him.

The selection was a little sparse today – Dean usually picked up groceries after morning training on one of racing's dark days, so he'd be restocking soon. Then she heard his truck. Gus did too, leaving her feet to scramble to the back door.

Their reunion was joyous, like they'd been separated for weeks instead of hours. Dean cooed goofily at the dog, setting down grocery bags to give a proper hello. Faye wasn't jealous, because Gus lavished the same excitement on her. Or anyone, for that matter.

Dean picked up the cloth bags and set them on the counter, while Gus ran off to retrieve his ragged, once-plush, squirrel toy. The dog bounded back into the kitchen and dropped the drool-soaked mass proudly on Faye's toes. She shuddered, and edged it carefully away.

"You good for coffee?" Dean asked, picking up the rinsed-out carafe.

"I was just about to make some." Gus tossed the filthy squirrel at her, and Faye pushed it away again. "You left early last night."

"Well, you know. Too much hullabaloo."

Who said things like that anymore? Dean, that was who. All the time. It was so silly it was endearing. It reminded her of her mother.

"It was a tough one to swallow, losing like that." He leaned back against the counter as the coffee maker started gurgling, and Faye began to put away the groceries. "Though of course if we were going to get beat, I'm glad it was Liv. That's one gutsy filly."

Faye wondered if he'd stayed long enough to see what had transpired between Liv and Nate. Little known fact: her brother had a crush on Liv. He'd never outright admitted it, but Faye knew. It wasn't hard to figure out. He brightened in her company. Got even more awkward than his normal awkward.

"How's the colt this morning?" Faye asked. Duty, again.

"Tired. That track took a lot out of him."

"That's what Liv said about Chique."

"You talked to her?"

Faye nodded, and opened up a package of shortbread fingers.

"I'm proud of her," Dean said, like the big brother Liv saw him as – a perception he stoically accepted. The coffee maker made its final hiss and sputter, and he pulled out clean mugs.

Liv was oblivious to his suffering, of course. Look what it had taken for Nate to get through to her. Faye certainly didn't plan to tell her, especially not now. It would fry her already over-taxed mind. And if Dean did know about Liv and Nate, he wasn't saying. He probably wouldn't – he'd just quietly endure. He and Liv were a bit too much alike in a lot of ways.

"Should be able to cut more hay tomorrow. Looks like the weather's going to be good for the rest of the week," he said, taking a sip of the brew.

Faye didn't know how he could drink it that hot. "Don't forget about the concert tomorrow night."

"Right." He threw back the rest of the coffee like it was water, then rinsed out his cup. "I'm going for a bike ride."

She could tell he was pondering a way to bail, and haying would be a legitimate excuse, but who would she take? Not Liv, not right now. Em would probably be game.

"Figure out if you can still come with me while you're riding. Have fun." How she'd ended up with such a sporty group of friends, including her brother, was beyond her.

So, note to self, round up haying help. Because if she found enough of it, she wouldn't have to fight with the bales herself.

"I DIDN'T EXPECT to see you today."

Will opened the door wider to let Nate into his loft before wandering back to the kitchen and extracting a couple of beers from the fridge. He held one out.

Nate accepted. "Thanks. It was kind of a surreal night. I needed to come here to keep my feet on the ground."

"Didn't get to see much of you. Other than your little cameo. Man of the hour. And I can say I knew you when."

Nate's lips twisted, the bottle's cap gone with a quick flick of his wrist. "Think my dad will be impressed?"

"I'm betting he didn't call to congratulate you."

"You would win that bet." Nate gravitated to the keyboard, like he always did, sliding onto the bench and setting his bottle carefully on top. He started warming his fingers up with scales, traveling easily over the keys, head moving to the tempo he set.

"So, made some progress with the boss?"

Nate glanced sideways, missing a beat before carrying on, a smile of simple contentment on his lips. "Like I said, it was a little surreal. Speaking of –" He dropped his fingers from the keys, one hand closing around the bottle, and spun a hundred and eighty degrees. "How'd it go with Faye Taylor?"

"I made sure she got home safe. Rest assured I behaved like a perfect gentleman."

"Much to her disappointment, I bet. She's probably pissed as hell this morning that she went to bed alone. But thank you."

"Anything to help ease your conscience, buddy."

Nate was too wrapped up in his new happy to even take offence to that. Disappointing. People in love were so annoying.

"What if I told you it was nice?" Which was true, but Will was still hoping to get a rise out of him.

"Like visiting with your grandmother? I wouldn't believe it."

"Like I like her company. Like maybe I like her." *There.*

Nate took a slow pull from the bottle. "That would be interesting."

"Would you mind?"

"It has nothing to do with me anymore."

"But I'm getting a vibe, like you're still a little protective of her."

"Because I feel bad about what happened between us. She deserves better than that."

Thank you. Will didn't believe it had been intentional, whatever Nate thought he'd done to Faye. Nate was probably being harder on himself than he had to be, but he was like that. He held onto things. But he was obviously getting better about it, because after Cindy, his first girlfriend back in Calgary, he'd pined for four years, and whatever had happened with Faye hadn't kept him from starting something new with Liv a few months later. Maybe that's what he felt bad about – that he'd moved on while it was pretty obvious that Faye had not, despite what she might want everyone to think.

"So you really wouldn't want me to ask her out?" Will had no intention of doing so, but it was entertaining, watching Nate stew about it.

"I don't know. It's your call. But it might be in everyone's best interest if you don't."

"Why?"

"Because if things don't work out, then both of you are going to be mad at me. Right now it's only Faye. And well, if you do go out with her, you're bringing something pretty significant from that world into this world, and this is supposed to be my break from that."

"So this really is about you, then."

"Fine, all right? Do what you want. Just keep me out of it. And at least for a while, can you keep her out of here? Just let me have my little sanctuary, at least until the two of you figure out if it's more than just a passing thing."

"You've got a lot of demands, don't you?"

"Can we just play some music? Where are the others, anyway?"

"Who knows. Late, obviously. We can start without them."

Nate started pounding the keyboard with *A Song For the Dumped* like it was in any way relevant to his life. So Faye had dumped him, and there was some toxic residue. But he had this shiny new thing, and this fancy life, so he needed to get on with that and stop worrying about things that weren't his to worry about anymore.

"The real question is…" Nate turned away from the keyboard abruptly. "…do you really want to ask her out? Because I will tell you what I was told. Faye doesn't like to get attached. Though it didn't exactly play out that way, with me."

"Women get attached to you, Miller." Even if he hadn't intended it with Faye, it was just in his DNA. Will, on the other hand…

"Ha. Hardly. If Cin had been attached we'd be married right now."

"And Liv?"

"We'll see about that."

"She looked pretty attached to you last night. Physically."

"Funny guy."

Will moseyed over to his guitar, parking himself on a stool. "Last night was fun but that whole scene was a bizarre experience. It's a different world, isn't it?"

"Oh, definitely."

Which is why whatever impression Faye had made on Will didn't matter. Their paths crossed due to a series of events that wouldn't likely be repeated. The only reason he ever saw Nate was when they got together like this, which was pretty rare. Will had never been to the country where Nate lived – until last night, when he'd driven Faye home – and he lived an hour away in the city. So what were the chances of him ever seeing her again? And after he'd treated her like a sister last night, he didn't imagine she'd be all that warm towards him in the unlikely event he did decide it wasn't too strange to get her number from Nate. She obviously had a good dose of pride, however fragile it might be at the moment, and he'd injured it last night. Not that he'd do things differently. It had been an interesting encounter; that was it. He'd leave it at that.

"Do you think you'll make it down a little more consistently now?" Will started tuning the guitar. "Even if it seems kind of backward that being more famous might suddenly give you the inspiration to make time for it."

Will had thought they might pick up again as friends when Nate had made his own way east, but their worlds were opposites: early racetrack mornings versus Will's late nights at the restaurants. It would be good for Nate to make the effort, create a balance with the all-encompassing nature of his job. He didn't get to leave it behind like Will did. When Will left work – at whatever time he managed to get out at the end of the night – he didn't really think about it again until his next shift.

"I'm not famous. But, yeah. I want to make a point of it. And Liv's going to be her usual preoccupied self leading up to Chique's next race, so it's probably best if I give her space. Coming down here will distract me from the fact that we're always one step forward, two steps back, you know?"

"How long is that for?"

"Three weeks. And if she wins that, another three weeks till the last race of the series. I know it'll fly, but still."

"Not so good for you, good for the band." Will grinned.

"So we're a band now?"

"If you keep showing up, we will be."

"Can we be a Switchfoot cover band?"

"I don't know about that. But maybe we can have a show that's not at a horse barn."

"I'm still going to Florida for the winter."

"Then we'll have to practice by Zoom."

"Y'know," Nate said, a slow smile taking over his face, "that might actually work. Because this is going to be the winter where it all comes together."

He started playing that Blue October song Will had done last night, singing the bit about not being able to wait to see what was around the corner. The guy was really an optimist at heart; it had been hard to see him so squashed by what Cindy had done. This recommitment to music was probably as much about getting beyond that as needing a break from the pressures of his dangerous job. Not that Will was a psychologist or anything.

"Do you think you'll ever spend the winter up here again?" Will asked.

"When there's the option of going south? Are you kidding? Do you remember what it's like to work on a farm in the winter? It's bad enough I have to stay here till the middle of December. Especially when I'm betting Liv will be gone with the first load of horses in November."

"But do you really even work on the farm anymore?"

"If I didn't go south I would be. You think I'm going to sit on my ass all winter and still live there?"

"Florida's made you soft, buddy. Remember when we used to be on the slopes in Banff every chance we got?"

"When we weren't on the ice?"

"What happened to us?"

"Life, I guess. Though it's worked out all right."

"For you, maybe."

Nate looked at him carefully, cradling his bottle. "What's up?"

"What happened to me, then? I'm stuck in this job I hate, living in a city I hate." Will set the guitar down and wandered back to the kitchen, grabbing an apple from a bowl on the counter. "After I dropped Faye off last night, I drove past this 'For Rent' sign in front of one of those places in town there, on King Sideroad. A coffee shop, I think."

"Lucy's? It was probably one of the other places there. Lucy's an icon, albeit a crusty one. I can't imagine her leaving. King City would fall apart without her."

"I'm pretty sure it was for the coffee shop."

"That's crazy. Everyone within twenty-five kilometres of King knows Lucy's, there's no way she's giving it up. Unless she's found a better place, but I can't imagine where that would be. She's right on the main strip, and that big parking lot is great."

"It just made me wonder what it would be like to get out of the city, and start my own thing."

"It would be cool to have you out that way."

"Didn't you make enough money to buy a house yesterday? We could be housemates."

Nate laughed. "Oh, I'm not giving up my apartment now. The girl next door and all that."

"Next thing I know you're going to be married, and I'll still be stuck in a dead end, if I don't make a change."

Nate's brow was furrowed, watching him. "It scares me that Faye Taylor inspired all this."

"She didn't." Did she? "And just so you know I was having you on. I'm not asking her out. Remember I don't date horse girls."

Nate laughed, much the way Faye had at the same statement. "Well, Faye Taylor is no horse girl. The closest I've seen her to a horse is next to the groom in a win photo. She's terrified of them."

Will raised his eyebrows, and took a bite out of the apple. He still wasn't going to ask her out.

3

The memory of the day Faye had met Liv remained distinct, a solid stake in the survey of her life marking where the property line had changed.

She hadn't expected the school bus to slow, then stop, at the big farm just down from hers. Upgrades had been going on there since the sale had closed that spring – fences repaired and painted a classic white, evidence of a major reno happening at the house – but it wasn't until a slight, dark-haired girl around her own age climbed aboard that Faye realized a family had moved in. The bus was packed the first day of a new school year, when attendance by the rural kids seemed to be at its highest. Something about the new girl grabbed Faye, because Faye felt as much a stranger on this bus as that girl was. They stared at each other for a beat before the girl scanned front to back. Faye picked up her bag and moved it onto her lap. New Girl's gaze swept the seats again, but Faye was the only one making space.

The girl's eyes flashed sideways as she slipped onto the bench, hugging her backpack to herself.

"I'm Faye," she'd offered. "I live at the farm just down the road. We've got Thoroughbreds too."

New Girl ventured a small smile, and Faye felt bad that she'd be disappointed when she found out Faye was not really into horses.

"I'm Olivia. Liv."

There was a certain cadence to the syllables – French Canadian? Her loss might not have been as drastic as Faye's, but she was grieving something just the same. Her old home, and old friends, and lost confidence faced with all the new? Whatever it was, Faye found herself softening. She felt like they saw each other.

The admitted attraction of the prospect of a friendship with Liv was that she didn't know Faye before the accident. She just knew this Faye, unlike her former friends and classmates, all of whom had drifted away during Faye's lengthy absence from school. And behind Liv's reserve, those spooky grey eyes, was something unknown, like she carried around her own darkness, so she wouldn't be turned off by Faye's. Faye had suspicions now that something had happened in Liv's childhood that was buried deep in her subconscious, but it was only a theory. Faye hadn't made any attempt to extract it, because it might have meant exposing her own dysfunction. That was one of the best things about Liv; she didn't probe, because she didn't want to be probed. Okay, sometimes it was exasperating.

They were total opposites for the most part. Liv was as quiet as Faye could be outspoken; Liv dressed to blend into the background while Faye liked to stand out; tastefully, of course. Maybe it was a youngest child thing. She'd adored the brother she'd lost, Shawn, but he was the family's bright light, and even though he complained that Faye got away with too much because she was the cherished baby girl, Faye still had to do her bit to get attention. Especially as her father's was always shared in a lopsided fashion with the horses.

So, unlikely as it might've seemed from the outside, they became fast friends. But not in the usual, teenage girl way. They were always just left of popular, admired by those much lower in the pecking order, hated by the cool girls. Faye had been one of those cool girls before the accident, but death had taken that from her, too. But the best part? None of that mattered to either Liv or Faye, one bit.

This, today, was new territory for them, though. They'd never been in a place like this. Faye glanced at the clock on the kitchen wall. Time to get ready.

The farm landline sidelined her, ringing out from the office, and she rushed to grab the receiver and check the number. Her biggest client, a powerhouse on the Ontario circuit. And, it was the boss-man himself. She gulped her last swallow of coffee, wishing it was something stronger, and listened while he delivered one more thing to make her life just a bit more miserable. Her cell buzzed on the desk with a text from Liv as she hung up.

Running late. 1PM okay?

For once, she got how Liv felt about such get-togethers. *I don't want to go.* But she keyed in, *Sure. See you then.*

Faye showered; dried and styled her hair; put on makeup. This whole funk she was in would *not* keep her from looking good. Lucy's was a drab place, so she found some bright turquoise capris and her favourite cap-sleeved blouse, a cheerful pattern of flowers on a background of white. Now she felt prepared for whatever Liv had on her mind, a mystifying place at the best of times.

Liv was waiting outside. She was still in her barn clothes, her t-shirt mostly clean, faded jeans cinched at her tiny waist to keep them from sliding down practically non-existent hips. She was still feminine, even without curves, with perfect skin and dark hair and lashes. Her slate eyes were always so studious, and still her most startling feature. Faye had never been able to convince Liv to wear makeup, but the truth was, she didn't need it.

Faye put on a smile and clutched Liv's shoulders in a quick hug, catching the familiar whiff of racetrack: dust and leather and horse. "Shall we go in?"

Liv nodded, and swung open the door. It didn't matter how many times they'd been here, they both approached the café's counter with trepidation. Lucy burst out of the back, wiping her hands on her flour-dusted apron, five feet tall and half as wide, her hostility thinly veiled, from her dark, close-cropped curls to her sturdy feet. Dean called her the Angry Hobbit, and Faye couldn't see the woman now without thinking it. She bit her lower lip to keep control of her features.

"What can I get for you?" Lucy said brusquely.

Faye almost ducked, the words punching out into the air. "Coffees?" she said, like she was asking permission. They would not get cappuccino here, and Lucy wouldn't have let them in the door if Faye had asked Liv to pick some up on her way back from the track.

Liv nodded silently.

"And I'll have the chicken wrap," Faye said, gaining a little confidence.

"Me too." Liv quickly took the path of least resistance. "And a butter tart for each of us, of course."

"Only one left," Lucy barked.

"We can share," Faye said, sliding Liv a sideways look. Liv wouldn't look at her – Faye had the impression she was at risk of breaking out laughing too.

Lucy served up their coffees in ceramic mugs and presented the revered butter tart on a plate. "I'll bring your wraps out when they're ready."

They retreated to a table with thanks – to Lucy, and for the dismissal – after doctoring the coffee. Faye cut the butter tart neatly in half, and didn't ask about Chique again. She waited, cautiously taking a sip from her cup.

"I'm worried," Liv said, finally, staring intently at her own mug, clutched between her hands. She glanced quickly at Faye.

One of Faye's eyebrows crept up. "About what?" she asked, slowly, thinking her worst fears about a request for delicate advice was about to come to pass.

"About us. We're broken. This thing…is messy. With Nate."

Faye sighed, and stared at the butter tart, pondering if she should just eat it now. She could use the sugar high for this. "I told you not to use me as an excuse. I'll deal with it." Even if she hadn't been doing a very good job, something last night had made very clear.

"But I need to know…we need to, somehow…we can still be friends, can't we? Because this friendship is more important to me than whatever might happen with him."

Oh, don't say that, sweetie, Faye wanted to say. *You have to put him first now, if you want it to work.* But Liv had a point. It shouldn't have to be one or the other. Faye had always believed guys shouldn't get in the way of friendships between women. Romantic relationships came and went, but it was your female friends who were always there waiting to pick up the pieces. Or should be. There was nothing that irked her more than women who disappeared when they hooked up with a new guy, all in love. Worse yet when they crawled back heartbroken and lonely when it didn't work out. Until the next time; the next guy.

And now there was this. Liv hadn't done anything on purpose to hurt her. She'd tried very hard to spare Faye's feelings, at the expense of her own. And really, Nate hadn't broken Faye either. She'd been messed up for a long time before he came along. It was just more satisfying at the moment to ignore that fact.

"We can't let a guy get between us. Not even Nate." Liv stared Faye down, and Faye wanted to believe in that conviction. "We have to do better."

She's growing up, my backward little friend, talking to me like this.

"Okay. But first off, you don't get out of this Nate thing because of me. I won't let you. You suffered in silence to protect me for longer than I know, I would bet. I've had my pity party and I'm getting over it, as of this morning. Mostly because I hate hangovers like I had yesterday." She made a feeble attempt at a smile. "You deserve all the happy. The great career, the great guy. And, a great friend, so I will do better."

Lucy interrupted, bringing over two more plates with their wraps, then leaving wordlessly.

"So when does that start?" Liv asked.

"Now, I told you. I mean it."

"All right." Liv nodded resolutely. "So tell me what happened with Will."

"Sadly, nothing. We went for coffee. I didn't even really learn anything about him. He left me on the doorstep." She spared Liv her recollection of that similar scene with Nate which pushed its way immediately into her brain.

"Too much sad girl?"

"Apparently I'm not a very good actress."

"Are you supposed to be?"

"'Fake it till you make it?'"

Liv didn't debate the concept; in fact Faye felt she was quite familiar with it.

"I just badly need to break out of this funk," Faye continued. "I was hoping he could help with that. I guess I picked a bad spot." She was going to need a cattle prod to make the horse racing references stop.

"Maybe you're supposed to go forward instead of backward."

Because you're suddenly an expert on life? Faye bit the words back before they made it out. She didn't want advice from a friend who hadn't even kissed a guy before – oh, wait, like a year before Faye had learned about it? "I have to ask you something, then. Not to rehash old news, but I'd like to understand. That New Year's Eve, in Florida, when you guys kissed, why didn't you tell me?" If she'd shared that little event, maybe Faye would have spared herself the whole Nate Miller fiasco.

"Do you remember where my head was then, Faye? How screwed I was? I told you nothing happened, because it didn't count. I thought he was just feeling sorry for me. And sorry for himself. Trust me, even if I'd known then what I know now, it would not have been a good time to start something between us."

"I should probably agree with that. Like throwing myself at Will was a reasonable thing to do. Even though I'm still disappointed with how that ended. A sensational non-event." Faye shook her head slightly, then zeroed in on Liv, determined to play her part in this new friendship dynamic. "But your evening was not." The corners of her lips curled up, if only because she forced them.

Liv's eyes swept to hers, then back to her mug. "It's too weird to talk about that with you, Faye. I feel too bad about it."

"This feeling bad has to go out with my feeling sorry for myself. All that ends right here, okay? Tell me you're happy. You get it now, right? You're excited about what comes next, if a little terrified?"

"What comes next is I'm taking Chique to Fort Erie to train until the Prince of Wales."

"You're what?" Faye snapped. "Why the hell would you do that?"

"Because it's the right thing to do for the filly? To give her the best shot at success?"

The Queen's Plate-winning filly was, as Nate liked to call her, a bit of a wild child. She tended to be nervous and quirky. So, from that point of view, giving her plenty of time to get used to her surroundings, instead of shipping in on race day, made sense. But that would put almost two hours between Liv and Nate. Not such a good thing for a budding relationship. But this was, Faye had to keep reminding herself, Liv, the spooky, green, filly. It would give her time to process, and the ability to focus on what still mattered most in her world – Chique.

"Speaking of moving forward, that's not going to do it. Have you told Nate about this plan?"

"Of course."

"And he's okay with it?"

Faye thought she was going to say, *What choice does he have?* And it made Faye feel just a little sorry for the guy. He had his work cut out for him with this one. But he'd ride it out. He'd ridden out worse.

More horse references. Did they have a cattle prod at the farm? Her parents had kept a few Limousins for a while.

"He'll come down to work her," Liv said, like that answered the question. "It's only three weeks," she added, frowning when Faye kept silent. "And just because something has started between us, doesn't mean I'm going to let it get in the way of my job. I'm not going to change who I am."

"Oh, you don't need to explain. You forget I'm not new around here." Faye had been born into that kind of logic. Her mother had come to accept it. Faye wasn't sure she ever would. "But you have to stop avoiding my questions. You are happy, right?"

The look on Liv's face managed to both tug at her heart and frustrate her. It was soft, except for a little wrinkle of tension between her eyes, the upward turn of her lips faint and uncertain.

"It's still so new. I've gone twenty-six years without these kinds of feelings. I can explain it away however I like – like it's just the chemicals in my brain, but I can't control them. And yeah, that's scary."

"Only you would try and dismiss love as science."

The soft disappeared, Liv's lips pressing into a line, her eyes defaulting to a more familiar skepticism. "It's a little too soon to be using labels like that."

Faye laughed and wrapped up the rest of her lunch for later. "Whatever you say, sweetie." She reached for her half of the butter tart. "Just give it a chance, okay?"

"You too."

"Which means?"

"Maybe don't go falling back into old patterns quite yet."

"Why not? It was a winning formula, before Nate. It's hard to mess with that."

Liv scowled at her. Easy for her to say, wasn't it? Old habits died hard, especially when the one time you deviated from them it ended up a disaster.

The lingering taste of the tart made everything right with the world for a delicious moment, and Faye eyed the other half. "When do you leave?"

Liv scooped it up possessively and took a bite. "She'll ship down tomorrow. I'll see how she feels Wednesday morning, and maybe take her for a jog and let her see the sights." She sipped her coffee, then finished the butter tart. "Are you sure we're all right?"

"We're fine."

They left their dishes on Lucy's counter, Lucy herself nowhere in sight, and slipped out, standing in the middle of the parking lot. Faye's eyes wandered, the *For Lease* sign on the marquee out front catching her eye.

She turned back to Liv. "I got a bit of bad news today. McIntoshes are getting out of the industry."

Liv frowned. "I'd heard rumours, but hoped they were just that. It sucks, on so many levels."

"My biggest client. I did everything for them. Books, their website, social media." Faye sighed. "I might have to find a job if no one comes along to fill that void."

"I'm sorry, Faye. I'll keep my ears open if I hear of anyone looking."

"Thanks, sweetie." Faye gave her a hug in parting. It had been a good thing, this. No small thing, either.

"Oh!" Liv's eyes popped wide. "I almost forgot. I have your hat." She grinned.

"Thank goodness," Faye said, following Liv to her car. She'd take all the good news she could get right now.

DEAN HUNCHED behind the wheel of the Corolla, angles folded awkwardly, but it was a more economical choice for a trip into the city than his big truck. Faye had offered to drive, but in the end they'd agreed to split it – she'd drive home, because he'd be half asleep by then, long past his usual bedtime.

"We'll be okay, Faye. Maybe we can beat Liv's filly in the Prince of Wales. She's not invincible. But if I have to, I'll sell a piece of Ride The Wave."

She'd told him about MacIntoshes. His words pained Faye, knowing how much he was in love with that colt. And if Faye could have feelings for a horse, it would be for Ride The Wave. The two-year-old, as yet unraced, was one of the last foals sired by Catch The Joy, the horse their father had won the Canadian Triple Crown with. She was used to Dean taking on partners for the homebreds to keep things afloat, but selling a piece of that colt would feel like selling a slice of their hearts.

"Don't do it yet. You know he'll be worth more once he runs." Or not, but she had to at least pretend to have the same faith in the colt's potential that Dean did.

They were waved away from the lots nearest the concert venue, already packed, and parked on the other side of Lakeshore Boulevard, in the Canadian National Exhibition grounds. In another month the CNE would be its own kind of mayhem, but for now it was a concrete ghost town, so there was plenty of room.

A warm breeze blew off the lake, seagulls dive-bombing to snatch up bits of food discarded by the gentle flow of people drifting into the Amphitheatre. Faye was attached to Dean's elbow, mostly because she couldn't remember where their seats were, and he held the tickets. It didn't hurt to have him as a shield, either, to deflect the occasional cluster of rowdiness in the midst of the otherwise well-behaved crowd.

"Faye!"

There was something familiar about the voice that reached her over the drone of voices around them. She scanned, staying tight to Dean. A wave caught her eye. Oh, no way. It was Nate's friend. She looked around him nervously. Nate had given her the tickets for her birthday back in March – a couple of weeks before they'd split up – but it wasn't a stretch to think he'd still want to come, and would be with Will. And just because she didn't see him didn't mean he wasn't here, somewhere.

Dean gave her a strange look when she stopped in her tracks. Running didn't seem to be an option at the moment, so might as well face it.

"Oh, hi Will," she said, unenthusiastically, though the sight of him sent an involuntary shiver through her that seemed to ignite her nerve endings, leaving her with an embarrassing glow, that stupid humming sound starting up. So random to run into him down here, and she wondered fleetingly if the Dave Matthews Band qualified as "the poppy side of alternative." Then a blonde peeked around him – a relief, really because it made a Nate ambush seem less likely – except she was taller than Faye, and younger, too, a high ponytail swinging across her elegant neck. *So I was both too old and not blonde.* Whatever. Faye took a cleansing breath, and her heart rate tempered. One step closer to being the foxy spinster, hanging on the arm of her bachelor brother.

She dislodged one hand and swept it in front of Dean's torso, maybe a little too dramatically.

"This is Dean," she said, and left out the part about him being her sibling. Will didn't need to know that. Faye and Dean looked different enough that the fact they were closely related wouldn't be immediately apparent.

The men shook hands, and Faye hoped she didn't imagine Will's sudden stiffness. He and Dean were about the same height, both dark-haired, lanky, and handsome. If Will didn't already know the last guy she'd dated was short and blonde, he might be thinking this Dean character was her type, so Will could be, too, making him – hopefully? – a little bit jealous. Why was she bothering to think about it? He was here with the blonde.

Will introduced her as Monique, with no more detail than Faye had provided about her own companion. In order to pre-empt the possibility of that changing, Faye inconspicuously dug her nails into Dean's arm. Dean flinched, his head flipping down to her. Okay, not so inconspicuous. She'd left red marks on his skin.

She smiled up at him sweetly. "We'd better go find our seats. Nice to meet you, Monique!" *Not really!* "Enjoy the show!" She almost shoulder-checked Dean to catapult him into motion.

"What's got you all in a kerfuffle?" he asked, trying to rub his arm. "Who was that?"

"If you hadn't bolted the other night, you'd know. That's Nate's friend, from the band."

"So what's with the animosity? He seems like a nice guy."

"He's the one who drove me home."

"Which seems like a nice thing to do."

"Yep. He's an upstanding citizen. Forget it." Not that Dean didn't end up hearing her stories about men – he was remarkably unperturbed about her bringing them into her home, more like a platonic friend than a big brother – but she'd had enough reminders of her most recent failure to snare that particular one. "Where are the tickets? Give me mine."

Dean separated the laser printouts she'd entrusted to him for safekeeping and Faye plucked one from his fingers.

"I'll meet you there. I'm getting a drink. You want something?"

Dean shook his head, and Faye skulked off, her eyes constantly on the lookout for Will and his blonde. She really didn't need to run into them again. What she did need was to find a willing participant in her plan and clear her bad juju. She tapped a text to Em as she stood in line at the concession. *Please tell me I didn't make too much of a fool of myself the other night.*

Em: You didn't make too much of a fool of yourself the other night. Did Liv give you your hat? What happened with Will?

Faye: Will was a disgustingly perfect gentleman. Also, really, really not into me.

Em: Looked pretty interested to me.

Faye: Well, Dean and I are at the DMB concert, and guess who we ran into, complete with tall blonde? So, I think not.

Em: Sorry.

Faye: We need to go to the races this weekend. I'm clocking prospects. You in?

Em: (laughing emoji) Sounds like fun. Keep me posted.

She made it to the front of the line and ordered her overpriced beer. She and vodka coolers did not get along. Faye handed the plastic cup to Dean as she climbed over the back of her seat and settled into the chair. He took a sip before handing it back.

"Anyone running this weekend?" she asked.

"I'm entering She Brews for Saturday. She should win."

Of course she should. It wasn't often Dean thought his horse wouldn't win, regardless of how realistic it might or might not be. He got points for positive thinking. She made a mental note to ask Liv if the maiden filly actually had a shot. She didn't ask who was riding, guessing it was Nate, because he'd been on her the last time. She could handle him in that context better than any other. It would just be a pleasant surprise if he had another call, and it ended up being someone else.

By the time they were driving home, the buzz from the beer she'd had was a safely distant sensation, the music intoxicating enough to ease the shock of running into Will and his friend. Dean slept soundly in the passenger seat despite looking horribly uncomfortable.

He was a good sport, coming with her. Shawn had always been her go-to for concerts. Shawn was largely responsible for forming her taste in music, sparing her from adopting the pop or country so many of her high school classmates had loved. These were the times she missed him most. Eleven and a half years, but let her hear Dave Matthews singing *Where Are You Going,* and it was almost as if he was there, singing along with her.

WILL HADN'T SEEN HER – them – again, but not for lack of searching. Not really surprising, at a venue that held about sixteen thousand people when it was sold out like it had been for a popular band like tonight. It had been so unexpected, a beacon in the midst of the nameless faces he'd taught himself to glaze over, living in a city this size. When he'd realized she was with a guy, yes, all right, he admitted it: it was a blow. Good for her, though. She'd obviously found someone. She didn't waste time. And, it solved the whole *Nate's ex* dilemma. Not that he did like her, or want to ask her out. Okay so he liked her, but did not want to ask her out. Or would not. Which now, obviously, he didn't need to worry about.

Ontario Place emptied out, the crowd still energized from the show, which had been shut down before a proper encore, like his band had been shut down at the Queen's Plate, only a little bit later. Noise ordinances.

The new bane of concerts. Though being right on Lake Ontario, music playing at the Amphitheater could probably be heard all the way to St. Catharines.

Monique bumped him intentionally as they were swept towards the parking lot. “Who was that girl?”

Will didn’t look at her, just kept walking. “My buddy’s ex.”

“Uh-huh. That’s a problem.”

“Why?”

“You’re obviously into her.”

“Why would you say that?” He didn’t mean for it to come out like a growl, but it did.

“Because exactly that. You just snapped at me! And your head’s been bobbing all over the place hoping you’ll see her again.”

“It is not. And I am not.”

“You are such a liar. Does your buddy know?”

“I only just met her Sunday night. There’s nothing to know.” But, for some reason, when he’d seen Nate, he’d felt the need to test the waters. And received a wave of protest back. Not a tsunami or anything, but enough to remind him to back off. “Besides, you saw her. She was with someone.”

“That was nothing.”

“How can you be sure?”

“I can sense these things.”

Will wondered if she was right, and if so, if Faye could sense those things too – if it would be just as obvious to her that he and Monique weren’t together.

“She is really pretty. It’s too bad. You should have a proper girlfriend, a nice guy like you.”

It was slow getting out of the lot, cars inching out of spots and into lines that slowly flowed onto the Lakeshore. Monique turned up the radio, which was so permanently tuned into The Edge that the dial probably wouldn’t have let her switch it to anything else if she’d tried. She didn’t live far, and he pulled up in front of the house she shared with friends.

“Are you going to be at work tomorrow? You’ve been missing a lot of days lately.”

Just two, but still, for the guy who was everyone's old reliable, it attracted curiosity. Maybe it was a sign of his dissatisfaction.

"Yeah. You need a ride?"

She shook her head. "Not this time. Thanks though! See you then."

He waited until she disappeared inside before he drove off. The radio station started playing *The Coldest Night of the Year* which left him with an inappropriate earworm on a perfect summer night. It must have been the *you're not even here* part wriggling things free from his unconscious mind. So, who was it his brain thought should be here?

Not Monique. She was quick to accompany him when he asked if she wanted to come along to shows, waving a free ticket. He didn't plan these things, just always grabbed two when they went on sale for something he wanted to see, figuring out later who his company would be. Who it was depended on his mood. Sometimes he went alone. He wasn't adverse to that, selling the extra ticket to scalpers, or gifting it to a starving student, because he knew what that was like. And truth be told, he didn't feel all that removed from it, even now.

Faye, then? Seeing her with that guy, thinking she'd be more inspired company than Monique. As much as Monique was cute and sweet and funny, anything that occurred between them outside of work had always been superficial, which he was pretty sure both of them had no complaints about. Monique had her sights set higher than the likes of Will. Will didn't really know where his own sights were set.

Which led to, the ghost of missed opportunities past? It was still stuck there, wedged firmly in whatever part of his brain processed rational thought, refusing to budge. Childhood memories weren't to be trusted, especially emotions that harkened back to those early teenage years when hormones started doing their thing. But he still kept her propped on a pedestal, comparing everyone he met to her and gauging their worthiness. Even if he'd never told her how he'd really felt about her. If he had, though, he wasn't sure it would have changed the outcome.

Maybe that's why he'd come to Toronto: more for the noise than the music. He'd grown up on the outskirts of Calgary, where the mountains were only ever an hour away, beautiful and deadly. On the way to them were safer expanses, grassy ranches that he'd loved even more than the tremendous rock faces…not quite still, still changing. All of it – all the space, and the calm – had turned upside down on him, like he'd become agoraphobic. Toronto was a place he could get lost, and hide from the memories that were embedded in every crack in the pavement, every favourite bar, every shadow of those momentous peaks. This was a place where no one knew him.

But the comfort was wearing off. What was the answer, though? The café near Nate niggled at him, but it was really just a fantasy. He couldn't leave his job in the city; couldn't afford to. So the idea of not only trying to pay for, but run, such a place, wasn't realistic.

When he'd finally wound down enough to crawl into bed, he still lay awake, all of a sudden hyper aware of the noise. He supposed Toronto did sleep, but not quietly.

4

Faye scanned names and weights in the program, but not because she was any kind of handicapper. At least, not of horses. She was looking for numbers, little superscripts to the pounds each horse had to carry, because they indicated an apprentice rider, her prey of choice.

Emilie sidled up next to her, eyes going first to the horses. Em might not be as hard-core as her older sister Liv when it came to them, and claimed she was determined to make her career outside of the industry, but she still galloped for her father's trainer on weekends, and whenever she wasn't otherwise occupied with working towards becoming a physiotherapist.

She Brews was in this race, a legitimate excuse for Faye to be at the track besides clocking bug boys, though she stayed safely outside the rail with the public rather than in there with Dean as she probably should've been. It was a perfect summer afternoon, the unbearable hot spell having mercifully moved on, that big storm on Plate Day taking away the humidity and leaving temperatures that were just right. It was the kind of weather Canadians dreamed of when they were complaining about the cold in January. Somehow that cold was quickly forgotten during heat waves like they'd suffered last week.

"So, who do you like, Em?" she said, alternating between the program and the vibrant hues before her. She'd always found the traditional outfits jockeys wore on the silly side – baggy nylon pants and stockings that came up to their knees, slipped into paper-thin patent boots with slipper soles. The silks were nice, though – at least when they were tastefully done – but the helmets they wore were a reminder of the insane danger of the job. Those helmets and the dense safety vests hidden beneath the flimsy colours always seemed inadequate defence against the possibility of life-altering – and life-ending – injury. Small humans dressed up like lawn ornaments and sent out to risk their necks.

"So I asked Nate if Will has a girlfriend," Em said casually.

Faye pursed her lips, and tried to sound disinterested as she responded. "And?"

"Not that he knows of."

"So who was the blonde?"

Em shrugged. "I couldn't ask that, could I, because that would have brought your name into it, and you wouldn't want that, right?"

Faye groaned, and curled the edge of the program between her fingers. "None of it matters. We're here to scout new candidates. Will had his shot, and it was a hard no."

"Don't write him off yet. It might've just been that he and Nate are old friends, so he has to be careful."

"Did Nate say that to you? Because if he did, you need to tell him he doesn't get a say. He can stay the hell out of my life."

"Except, it does affect his life, if it involves Will. But I didn't bring your name into it, remember?"

"Stop making so much sense," Faye grumbled.

Faye doesn't like to get attached. That was her reputation. Was Nate afraid she'd compromise his friend, or something? Because he surely didn't think Faye was going to let herself fall for someone again, and be around enough to mess up his precious little bromance. He should know better than that. "How good a friend can Will be, anyway? I'd never heard of him."

"Because how much did Nate talk about Calgary with you?"

Faye rolled her eyes and gave her a gentle shove. "Didn't I just tell you to stop that?"

It was true, though, because the original intent of her getting together with Nate had been the same as every other time she'd hunted down a man – something he was supposed to be a willing party to. That had been the deal. They were day-to-day, living in the moment, until it became obvious they should be beyond that. By then they'd gotten way too good at not sharing the important stuff to start.

It had been foolish of her to think she could have a sustainable relationship. She'd always been the one to break hearts instead of waiting to have her heart be broken. Until Nate had made her think perhaps it was time to evolve. She hadn't figured Liv into the equation, though. That had come out of nowhere. Had it, though? Had she just refused to see it? There was probably a lot about Liv she failed to see.

And here she was, back to seeking out a non-relationship. So much for evolution. Well, evolution happened over millions of years, right? *Take it a little easy on yourself.*

She studied the riders for likely candidates. A few of them, of course, were in the lines of her past performance, journeymen now. It was this time last year that she'd connected with Nate. No, she definitely would not let something like that happen again. She would be on alert at every turn to nip any possibility in the bud.

The paddock judge's *riders up* call rose over the hum of conversation, interrupting the crowd's collective watchfulness. Groups inside the walking ring broke up as the horses formed a line with their grooms, and trainers lifted feather-light bodies onto bunched muscle. Even Faye couldn't watch impassively; it sent a little shiver through her each time, anticipation and apprehension all bundled together.

Nate was on She Brews as Faye had expected, and stuck his tongue out as they went by before firing off one of his dazzling smiles.

"This looks like trouble," he said.

Faye kept her face neutral and said, "Good luck," to keep herself from snarkier retorts, because Dean owned all of this filly, so Northwest would get the full sixty percent winner's share – less Nate's portion, and the stake money Dean would allocate to his crew for their hard work. Nate's mounts always went off at shorter odds than they might have with a less notable rider, but that wasn't always an indication of the kind of chance the runner had. So Faye turned to Em, who was actually quite a shrewd handicapper.

"Are we getting our picture taken today?"

"I think she has a decent shot, but Extra Blonde has run second, like, five times in a row, and Watanabe needs just one more win to go to lose his ten pound bug, so he's extra hungry right now."

Literally.

Faye had noticed Jiro Watanabe's name in the program, thanks to that number ten superscript, and eyeballed him from a distance, pinning him as a definite possibility for the *Faye Gets Her Groove Back* project. He was a recent import from Japan. Maybe she could learn a new language. She remotely heard Em cooing *she's pretty* as Extra Blonde danced past, and had her own appreciative thoughts about the rider.

Very cute. Yes, he would do nicely.

She had to play along as a tradeoff for Em's company, following as the horses left the walking ring on the way to the track. They took the escalator to the second floor, meeting Dean at the seats outside. He was in trainer mode, binoculars locked on She Brews instead of acknowledging their arrival.

The Northwest silks were the original ones, her father's simple design, Faye finding them easily. They could use an upgrade – old school checkers, a red and white version of the famous Meadow Stables colours Secretariat had carried – but Dean would never change. He'd feel it was dishonouring their father, even though their father and Dean hadn't exactly got along.

She let herself admire Nate, despite their history, his posture perfect without tension, his easy-going manner coming through even from this distance as he chatted with the pony rider. Then Faye moved on – because she was moving on – to peruse Jiro Watanabe. Even though Faye had never taken up riding, as much as her father had tried to inflict ponies upon her as a child, it was easy to see Jiro was comfortable on a horse. Her admiration effortlessly shifted from Nate to him as Extra Blonde's escort initiated an easy gallop around the clubhouse turn.

Her attention faded as the horses got farther away, and she scanned the apron below them instead, searching it for interesting people.

"Em – who's that with the baby?"

Emilie pulled her binoculars a few inches away from her eyes, and followed Faye's gaze. "You're not up on the gossip? Where have you been? That's Pat Simon's girlfriend."

"And baby?"

"Yep. She's one of MacIntosh's grooms."

"What happened to the wife?"

"I guess he fell madly for the groom last fall. I heard they were together all last winter in Florida. Though obviously the baby was in progress by then." Em gave her a sly grin.

"You're right, where have I been?"

Pat Simon. He'd been top apprentice what, five years ago? He'd been fun, then married his next love interest. And here he already had a failed marriage and baby with a new girlfriend, while she was still chasing bug riders. It was like he'd lived several different lifetimes, while she'd been looping through the same one. Same old, same old. Not that she wanted something else. Did she?

The horses were in the gate now, just in time to distract her from that depressing train of thought.

She Brews broke on top, keeping her head in front of Extra Blonde as the field raced along the backstretch. *You're helping Dean with the farm.* That's important.

They zipped around the turn, and Extra Blonde pushed her nose in front at the quarter pole. *Dean needs you. He came back to take over Dad's horses and abandoned a masters to do it, so he could take care of you. You owe him. And you owe Mom and Dad, to maintain their legacy. Besides, you were supposed to be in that car.*

The two fillies – and riders – were locked in a battle down the stretch. Faye leapt to her feet at the same time as Dean and Em, and started screaming.

"Come on Brew!" *Come on, Nate. Dean needs to win this one.*

That kid Watanabe was pushing insistently, the left-handed rhythm of his stick measured, coming every third stride. Extra Blonde was pouring out a huge effort, like she was done being a bridesmaid. It was just a nose at the wire, but that's all she needed to deny Nate and She Brews.

"Well. He can ride." Faye watched the two fillies gallop out, still side by side, Nate reaching over to congratulate Jiro. His fifth winner. Ten pound bug no more.

"Told you he was hungry," Em quipped.

"I'm sure that was delicious." Faye was kind of hungry too.

Her plan of attack came so easily it was laughable. She followed Dean down to the apron, Emilie behind her. "Maybe if you get him on She Brews next time, that five pounds will make the difference."

Dean glanced over his shoulder. "You're suggesting I fire Nate?"

"Not because it was his fault. It's just a business decision. He'll understand."

And she would have an innocent excuse to meet Jiro Watanabe.

THEY WEREN'T ALL that busy tonight, which was a good thing, because Will's head wasn't in the game. He kept getting stuck on seeing Faye with that guy, a bruise that should have faded by now. So he didn't want to take her out, but apparently he didn't want anyone else to take her out either. Like he had any right to feel that way. They'd seemed very comfortable with each other, Faye and that guy. He could ask Nate who it was. Except that would piss Nate off, because he'd think Will wanted to take her out. When he didn't.

Busy or not, the chef, Gerry, was in a mood, and Will was supposed to be the buffer between Gerry and the staff. He had to get his mind back where it belonged.

In the blink of an eye, the guy could go from inappropriately teasing the female servers to tearing them apart for the slightest transgression. For some unknown reason though, the women put up with it. Worse, they seemed to like it. And Gerry rotated through them after hours like the specials on his menu.

The chef's behaviour often meant Will was the shoulder some very pretty women cried on; shoulder being a figure of speech, of course. He'd been the beneficiary of Gerry's castoffs on more than one occasion, Monique being one of them. They were always temporary, which was probably just as well. *Don't play where you work.* Nate had dipped his toe in that pool, with his new relationship. The waters were perilous, but it was hard not to fall in when it was your most viable option.

Faye popped into his head again, like she stood for something important, something he was supposed to figure out; the answer to getting off this merry-go-round. It wasn't a job he'd felt worth sharing with her. She hadn't told him what she did for a living either, so they were even.

Maybe she didn't have to work. She lived on a farm in King City, after all. The land up there was worth a ton. The farmhouse hadn't been fancy from the outside, but her family owned racehorses. Racehorses – even pieces of them – cost a lot of money, he knew that much. Will couldn't even afford a cat, with the cost of small animal vet medicine these days. Goldfish might not even work with his budget right now. So why was he building café castles in the air?

Tonight, Brenda was having a bad time. One of her tables had a real jerk of a guest, and she never did well with that sort of thing. She was one of the newer servers, her bright face and cheery, chatty personality usually making up for her lack of experience, but not with this guy. The more her anxiety escalated, the more mistakes she made, and Gerry was going to blow soon. When that happened, they were all going to pay.

The answer? Dessert was Will's favourite thing. Because, really, what couldn't be solved with sugar?

"Here, take them this," he said, handing her slices of cheesecake and carrying out complimentary cappuccinos.

Brenda breezed back into the kitchen. "You saved me again." Her sweet face was starting to look a more normal colour than the extremes he'd seen in the last half hour – from flushed to pale and back again.

"All part of the job description," he responded.

"He told me I wasn't pretty enough to be that bad at my job." She was controlling the quiver in her voice, and Will would bet the time she'd come back on the verge of tears had been when the asshole had said it.

"Never mind him. I'm sorry we wasted that amazing cheesecake on him."

She smiled. "I hope you saved some for me, because I'm going to need a piece."

She was more than pretty, really, so the guy had to have been blind. She'd take dessert over alcohol to console herself, which wasn't a terrible thing. Faye Taylor, though…liked both, Will recalled.

At the end of the night, disaster averted, Gerry was chatting Brenda up. Will sat at the bar and watched her leave with him.

"Why do you all go for that?" he asked Monique, who was trying to hide the fact that she was disappointed Gerry had a new flavour of the week. Last week, it had been her.

She slid her long lashes sideways, and slapped a couple of shot glasses down. "It's called charisma, Will. It covers up a lot of stuff that really should revolt us."

This was such a toxic place. But he was stuck here, for now. Because Gerry was one of the top chefs in the city, and if Will could put up with him just a little longer, gleaning what knowledge he could, and leave on good enough terms to get a decent reference, he could find a job – out of the city somewhere. Or make the big move, and open his own place. The number for that spot for rent in King City was behind a magnet on his fridge. Maybe he could work on the farm Nate lived on. Will didn't know anything about horses, but he could shovel shit and drive a tractor. They needed guys like that, didn't they? Even if he didn't swing an apartment like Nate had, it had to be cheaper to rent something out there than it was in the city.

He tossed back the tequila Monique had served him up. He'd let Brenda have the last slice of cheesecake. His loft wasn't that far; he could walk home.

He should have slept like a log, after the tension and the tequila, but he only tossed and turned, and wondered how his escape east had become just a different kind of prison.

5

So much hay. A good thing for the farm, but horribly bad news for Faye. Her arms and back still ached from last night, and there were still three more wagons to be unloaded and stacked in the barn. It had to be done today, because there was a sixty percent chance of rain in the forecast. At least the way Dean was going on about the yield this year, they probably wouldn't have to supplement their supply with outside sources.

Haying was one of the best justifications for keeping the male of the species around – besides sex, of course. Manual labour. Unlike Liv's anything-you-can-do-I-can-do-better attitude, Faye was more than willing to concede men were stronger, and it was important to take advantage of that fact. At times like this, she needed more than a bug boy; she needed the entire jock's colony at Woodbine.

In the absence of finding a magical genie to conjure that up for her, Faye had shamelessly begged a favour, and Emilie had promised to steal some help from Triple Stripe. With enough people, it would go quickly, so she was hoping Em would bring a busload. That way Faye's job could be serving up pop and Gatorade for her hot, sweaty saviours. Unfortunately all the workers at Triple Stripe right now were young and female – other than the older guy who'd taken on the farm and stallion manager position, and Em wouldn't try to recruit him. So, no eye candy for Faye, though any guy who had ever helped stack hay knew better than to do it bare-chested like in some Facebook meme. Still, Faye had a pretty good imagination.

The fridge was full of cold drinks and there were stacks of ice cube trays in the freezer. She'd done the groceries this week, stocking up on all manner of snacks, from healthy to not and in-between. Apples and oranges, granola and protein bars, various kinds of chips and dips. Hot dogs and burgers to grill after, a thank-you bonus barbeque on top of the $20 an hour – cash – Dean would dole out.

Her phone pinged with a text from Emilie. *On our way.*

Thank heaven Em was going to come through. Maybe the farm girls had boyfriends who would see tossing hay bales around as the great workout it was, if you were into that sort of thing.

She dumped ice in the cooler and jammed it full with bottles of water and Gatorade, then hoisted it to her thighs, using her butt to push open the screen door.

"Perfect timing," she said as Dean tromped up the steps to the deck. "Drop your tailgate so we can drive this to the barn?"

Dean went one step better and relieved her of the weight, so Faye scooted around him and ran to the truck, just as a couple of cars pulled up. One of them she knew far too well. She threw her weight behind the tailgate to close it, then leaned back against the bumper, arms crossed.

"Well…this is a surprise. Em, you've outdone yourself."

Em climbed out of her red Honda, grinning. Yes, there were three girls from the farm, but she'd also recruited Nate…and, out the passenger side of that familiar, decrepit, Mustang, Will.

"What did you have to promise to get these two to come, Em? I will have to take a pic for Liv, because there is, apparently, no end to the niceness of Nate Miller."

"Now, don't be snide," Em said.

"Beggars can't be choosers." Nate threw Faye a crooked grin, and she gave him a withering look in return.

She forced herself to be civil. "I'm sorry if that sounded ungrateful." Her eyes fell on Will, who was even dressed appropriately. She wasn't going to complain about the way his jeans fit, or how his t-shirt fell from those shoulders of his. There would be eye candy after all. "It's nice to see you again, Will. You've met Dean…my brother," she said slyly.

Will's lips curved slowly into a smile, his eyes locking onto hers for a moment before he nodded and pulled them away to send a far less sexy expression to Dean. "Hey, Dean."

"Nate must be a really special kind of friend, to introduce you to the horrors of haying," Faye said, letting her gaze wander over Will again.

"Will's an old pro," Nate said. "I sat on my first pony at his grandfather's ranch. We were the child labour there for a lot of summers."

Will and Nate grinned at each other, and Faye recrossed her arms. Grandfather? So they'd grown up together. She wanted to sit both of them down and tear them apart with her questions, but it was too late to do that with Nate, and too soon to do it to Will.

"Could I maybe talk you both into taking your shirts off for the photo?" she tried instead, sweeping her phone from her back pocket.

"Liv would know that was fake." Nate smirked.

"True. But that doesn't mean she won't still appreciate it. No? Fine," she huffed when they refused to comply, and settled for a far less entertaining image.

The three girls behind Emilie silently watched Nate and Will with sparkly eyes, looking as if they were on the verge of giggling. Faye stopped herself from barking at them that they'd better keep their minds on the work, because a) they weren't her employees, and b) she still might be slugging bales alongside them, which would require her to follow the same order. It would be very easy to stand back and watch two gorgeous, muscly men at work.

Emilie slipped on her gloves, slapping her hands together. "Let's get this party started."

Dean tossed Faye his truck keys. "You want to drive it back? Conserve your energy." Even Dean was getting into the teasing. "Faye doesn't like to perspire."

"He's allowed to say that. I'm not." Nate's grin had lost its effect on her forever ago, and now Faye just wanted to smack him.

She flicked her hair over her shoulder and pulled it into a ponytail as she walked to the cab. She heard the tailgate come back down, and Nate and Will hopped up to sit on it. *Oh, brave, brave boys.* She resisted the urge to accelerate over potholes as she drove back to the barn, passing Em and her farm girls. It wouldn't be nice to break Liv's boyfriend. And other than her wounded pride from Plate night, she had nothing against Will. Unfortunately. She'd like to stretch against him, from lips to toes.The truck lurched, bouncing her up off the seat, Nate's curses reaching her ears as she heard cooler and men scrambling in the back. She glanced sheepishly in the rear view mirror.

"Sorry!" she called through the window in the back of the cab. It didn't look like either of them were any worse for her distracted driving.

The first wagon was already backed up to the hay barn, and Faye pulled in adjacent to it. She put the truck in park and sighed, tugging on her gloves, feeling the shift of weight on the tailgate as the guys hopped off. Nate gave her a sideways look, clearly thinking the rough trip was intentional. Will just grinned, like he might be enjoying their little squabble.

Dean began snagging bales with a hay hook, throwing them off the wagon until there was room for him to climb on. The minions set to work. Em grabbed the first bale; the guys, of course, took one in each hand because they had to be all manly and toss around as much testosterone as possible. Somehow they were back for more before Faye had managed to grab even one. Everyone was faster than she was. She dodged a wild throw off the wagon from Dean, and rammed right into Will's – quite solid – chest, his hands coming up to catch her by the arms.

"No offence, Faye, but you're kind of just getting in the way." Which, coming from Nate, was completely offensive.

Like, in the way of getting the job done, or in the way of your bromance?

She dragged the back of her hand over her brow, already dusty and sweaty without having really done anything, and stared him down as he stared back, lifting the corner of his shirt to wipe something out of his eye.

Will's hands were still on her shoulders. "There are plenty of us here. Why don't you grab the cooler?"

Faye twisted out of his grasp, pulling off a glove and brushing hay dust, and his touch, from her arm. "You just can't help coming to my rescue, can you?"

He looked back at her like he was doing a full appraisal. Was she flirting, or was she being snappish? She wasn't sure herself. She hated stacking hay, could barely lift the damn things, and half an hour ago would have jumped on getting out of it, but damsel in distress was not naturally in her repertoire. She certainly didn't appreciate being dismissed.

Dean hadn't stopped unloading the wagon, and Em and the farm girls cleared the accumulation. Nate held up a hand to keep Will from grabbing the next two, looking happy to escape.

"Seriously," Will said. "I'm pretty sure you're not getting paid to be here, like these guys are."

"Nate better not be getting paid for this," she grumbled. He owed her in more ways than she could count, in her not-so-humble opinion. *Fine.* She went back to the truck and lifted the cooler out, setting it nearby. They almost had the wagon empty, and everyone would be ready for a water break while Dean moved it out of the way and parked a new one.

She decided she couldn't stand there and watch them toil, so she went back to the house and cleaned, to feel like she was doing something almost equally abhorrent, but necessary. Emilie texted her when they were done, and she wandered back with Gus, finding the group of them draining bottles and cans and looking tired and grimy, but somehow still smiling.

Dean tossed his empty water bottle into the open cooler. "I'm going for a dip in the pond."

"Pond? How did I not know you have a pond?" Nate asked.

Oh, there is so much you don't know, and so much I don't know, because we never asked. But she kept those thoughts to herself.

"Wait up Dean," Nate called as her brother marched away, Will grinning and following. Em and the farm girls trailed, more out of curiosity than intent to join them, Faye guessed, because that was definitely what motivated her.

And there was her photo op. She whipped out her phone, and swiped it to video. Dean was already in, clothes dumped in a heap on the ground, Gus launching after him, like the self-respecting water dog he was. Gus loved a good pool party. The other two boys stripped down to their skivvies – such a disappointment they stopped there, but maybe a little modesty was appropriate in the company of the farm girls. They both leapt in like a couple of crazy adolescents. Faye shuddered at the thought of that water, but it was amusing nonetheless.

"C'mon Faye."

That was Will, taunting her. *Dream on, buddy.* She hadn't gone swimming in the pond since she was fourteen, that last summer, before the accident. It was fine, then. She and Shawn, laughing and tossing a ball around, or floating on old tractor inner tubes. Memories of her lost innocence, back when boys had only been friends or brothers. At her age, now, it wasn't fitting. She was too old for that. She didn't exactly consider herself demure, and let's face it, Nate had seen her naked, but Will was a stranger.

"I'll pass thanks. I was working inside in the air conditioning while you all got dirty and sweaty. I'll just watch." That prospect turned her on, just a little. Okay, a lot.

She kept videoing, then quickly edited it, and sent a clip off to Liv. *You're missing the fun.*

The reply came back quickly. Late afternoon, Liv had probably just finished feeding Chique, and had nothing better to do than check her phone. Her response was brief.

Damn. There was an ROTFL emoji attached.

Will climbed out, tilting his head like he had water in his ear. He walked over to Faye, and shook his wet hair on her like a dog. She jumped back, protecting her phone.

"I should go get you boys some towels," she said, taking in the way the water made his pale skin glisten. He needed to spend more time in the sun. Farm work would look good on him.

He grinned, then snatched the phone, tossed it at Em, and scooped Faye up.

"Hey! Put me down!"

Will just chuckled, heading for the water.

"Oh, no way. Don't you dare."

He wasn't stopping, even though she tried to twist out of his hold, and grab at his hair. It was too damn short. She kicked hard enough with her feet to send flying the sandals she'd slipped on at the house, but that was about it. Will waded in, then tossed her, fully dressed, into the water.

Her head went under, and she kicked herself to the surface, coming up sputtering. "You bastard!"

All of them were laughing at her now, Will looking pretty proud of his childishness. She shook her head, clawing her hair away from her face, and started treading water – keeping her knees high, which made her beating legs less effective at keeping her buoyant. The pond wasn't deep, but the silty, reedy bottom creeped her out. Things lurked down there. Things she didn't want to think about.

She scissored her legs, and with a few crawl strokes made it to the shore, shuddering at what she felt between her toes as she clambered out, dripping. Now she really wished she had some towels handy.

"Oh, you're kidding me," she said, scowling as Em waved her phone. Of course she'd captured the whole scene. "If that goes beyond Liv, you are so dead, my dear friend."

Em's smile was full of mischief. "You know Liv. She's discreet."

Some things one could count on in this life.

Em relinquished the phone, and there was already a response to a text Em had sent to Liv – extensive video evidence included – and added Faye on.

Liv: *I am so missing out.*

Faye texted back. *You are. See, this is what you get for going on a retreat to Fort Erie with a horse. And like I said to your sister, if that video ends up anywhere outside our circle, they won't find your bodies.*

Liv: *It won't be me.*

Faye glanced over to Em. It wouldn't be her, either. She texted Liv back. *Those boys can't be trusted, though.*

Liv: *Em didn't share it with them, did she?*

Faye: *I don't think so, but Nate's powers of persuasion are dangerous, as you know.*

Liv: *True.*

Faye felt Liv's coy smile in that single word, and it made her smile too as she pushed back a sodden dread of hair. The boys were clambering out now – one soaking wet Golden Retriever included – and for what Will had put her through, Faye figured she'd earned the right to freely check him out. He didn't have Nate's zero body fat, finely-tuned physique, but, well, she wouldn't kick him out of her bed. If she could just get him in it.

Shower. She really needed a shower. She didn't know Will well enough to invite him to join her, did she? She'd have to let her imagination run with the idea.

"Everybody back to the house. I've got a ton of food. Dean, you can get the barbeque started up."

She fully intended to have that shower to wash off the pond slime first, and left them to fend for themselves. Afterward she felt human again, piling her damp hair on top of her head, and she skipped downstairs in shorts and a tank top.

Bursting onto the deck with a salad in each hand, she felt Will's eyes land on her, drawing her own. He looked a little goofy with his hair sticking up in a couple of places, wet splotches on his t-shirt because he hadn't been completely dry when he'd pulled it back on, but that gaze was totally grown-up. A bit too much for this farm family gathering, if she was reading it right. The same humming she'd felt the night of the Plate vibrated through her, from her toes right through to her ears. But there was no champagne here, no music, so she couldn't blame either of those things.

She pivoted abruptly on her toes, and set the salads on the table. Dean had the grill fired up, and he'd passed around beers to the boys. Em and the farm girls had glasses of lemonade. Faye avoided Will, recalibrating, and poured a glass of lemonade for herself. Sipped, and sighed.

This is how farm work should be done. It made her a little homesick for her childhood.

WILL'S SHOULDERS ACHED; his arms, too. But it was a good ache, a satisfying ache, the kind born of old-fashioned physical labour. As a kid working on his grandfather's farm, he'd cursed haying season, but yesterday afternoon reset the memory, making him miss that kind of honest work, the camaraderie of sharing it. Those few hours had been as good as a vacation – and a trip to the gym. Funny that Nate's escape was to come to the city, and Will was being drawn back to the country. Was it just the country?

The whole experience might have been made all the more enjoyable due to his discovery that the guy he'd met at the concert was Faye's brother. That new knowledge had fed his actions, imbued him with a long-repressed feeling of being carefree and reckless. He might have taken it a bit too far, tossing Faye into the pond, going by the way she'd avoided him after that. But all of it had been about more than reliving his youth. He hadn't had that much fun in forever. It had made his day-to-day a bit more bearable; refreshed his sanity.

Which he was going to need for lunch. He'd taken another day off for this. Such a waste – if he was going to miss work, he'd much rather it be for more farm work – but it couldn't be avoided.

His father was late, of course. Refreshed sanity aside, the beer Will ordered while he waited was probably in everyone's best interest. It would take the edge off a meeting he wasn't convinced deserved his best behaviour, but he should probably strive for that anyway. One of them needed to be a grown-up.

By the time Will spotted dear old dad, he was striding over to the booth, his smile, no doubt intended to be warm, looking just as fake as ever. Will didn't stand to welcome him, even though his father hesitated, arms held out slightly from his sides, palms at forty-five degrees like he was hoping for a hug. Where he got that idea, Will had no idea.

The server scurried over, and Will gave her an affable smile, then looked at his dad. "What'll you have to drink?"

"What's on tap?" he asked, making the server ring off the list before settling on exactly the same thing Will was drinking. He turned back to Will. "Nice to see you, son."

The words grated on him. He was determined to be civil, though, and not say the things that came to mind. This meeting wasn't on the schedule. He saw Dad at Christmas when he went back to Calgary when they endured each other's company for a single meal out – in the name of being blood relations – and that was it. To what did he owe this honour? Flying across the country for lunch seemed suspect.

"It was a surprise to hear from you," Will responded, trying to keep out the irritation out of his voice. "What are you in town for?"

"I've…" His dad hesitated. "I've met someone. Here in Toronto."

The server came back with his father's beer just in time to distract Will from the immediate feeling of *here we go again*. As she set the glass down, Will caught her eye. "Uh, can you bring me another of these?"

She gave him a warm smile and nodded. "Sure thing."

"We met online," his father was saying, as if Will had asked. "I've been here a couple of times, and she's flown out to Calgary a couple of times."

So, great, how often had he been to town, and not once called Will? Just come for his trysts and slinked away. And why would he look so far afield for a new partner? Will finished the last of his drink and the server, who he'd decided was an angel, appeared with the other and removed the empty glass.

"We're getting married."

If Will had taken a sip from his pint, it would have been spewed all over the table. He set the glass back down and tried to loosen his jaw because his teeth were clenched so hard it hurt. "Does Mom know?"

"Not yet. Please don't say anything. I'll tell her, I promise."

When his parents had split, it had been the typical man having a mid-life crisis and leaving his wife for a sexy co-worker story. Which had seemed insane to Will, because his mom was the mom his buddies had to stop saying lewd things about, deflecting to *that's your mother? She looks amazing!* But Dad had gone all-in, abandoning them and moving to Vancouver with the woman. That first relationship had fizzled out after a couple of years, and Will had hoped his dad had got it out of his system. When he'd moved back to Calgary, he'd naïvely thought there was a chance his parents would get back together. Nope; his father had just started what had become a cycle of younger and younger girlfriends. Was it any wonder Will stayed single? If there was any possibility he'd inherited that tendency, he did not want to become that man.

Now, his mom was far too smart to take Dad back. But this?

"I'd like you to meet her, Will. Would that be okay?"

The edges of Will's eyes hurt, he was scrunching his brows together so hard. He sighed. "Yeah, sure."

His father half-rose in his chair, waving someone over. *She's here?* Unbelievable. Hiding at the bar, waiting to execute the surprise attack.

She was tall, slender, with shoulder-length strawberry-blonde hair. Almost a younger version of his mother, Will realized with horror. *How old is she?* He came way too close to blurting it out. Ratchet that cliché up a level, Dad. She looked like she was Will's age.

His father rose, and Will did too, his shock not enough to override basic manners. Dad kissed her and Will swore she purred.

"This is Ashley."

Her hand was small and damp – she was nervous about this, apparently. Her smile made Will think of an Invisalign commercial. Dad helped her with her chair, and the angel server magically appeared with a glass of white wine.

"So nice to finally meet you, Will."

Nice. Yeah, not the word he would use. He went along with the small talk, keeping his voice level, and resisted the temptation to check his watch or his phone. This would be a great time to get a call he had to take, any excuse to get out of here.

"Come to the wedding," his father said magnanimously, like Will would feel left out if he wasn't invited. "It's just going to be small. It's here in Toronto next month. Bring a friend."

Will's mouth opened, then closed.

"Are you seeing anyone?" Ashley asked.

Will shook his head. Maybe these two could give him dating advice.

"It would mean a lot if you'd come," his father said, seeming to realize Will was going to take some convincing.

"Please come," Ashley said, placing her hand over his father's. His father flipped his palm upwards and wrapped her fingers around hers. *Ugh.*

"I'll have to let you know. Friday nights are busy at work."

"Bring Nate. It'd be good to see him again. Each of you can bring a plus one, if you like."

Will wondered in passing which would be worse for Nate, coming to Will's father's wedding, or Nate seeing his own father. Beat-up vintage cars and fathers they liked to avoid: it was the little things that drew old friends together.

He prayed his father's brand of stupidity skipped a generation. His grandfather had been so solid and faithful, something lost in a bygone era, but that was what Will would hold out for. Not this.

6

It took a lot to get Faye up early enough to watch a horse train in the morning – like maybe Dean admitting he'd taken her advice. Jiro Watanabe was going to breeze She Brews, and his agent had told Dean to give them the call next time he entered the filly.

Not that she'd come in with Dean. Oh no. The work wasn't until eight, so there was no need.

The crew liked it when Faye came. She always stopped at Tim's to buy bad coffee and pasty doughnuts for them. Her travel mug contained something more palatable, and she couldn't eat before ten AM, so the doughnuts didn't tempt her.

She set them in Dean's office, because it was open season on the shed. Racetrackers could smell doughnuts as soon as they hit the east gate, but Dean's office was off limits. Hotwalkers and grooms – okay exercise riders, trainers – from other barns wouldn't go in uninvited. Leave them on a foot locker in the shed though, and word would travel. They'd be gone in no time, usually before Dean's own staff had had a chance to grab something themselves.

Faye hadn't seen Dean yet – he was probably out with a set – so she hid out in the office. His crew was okay, but it was too early for the kind of inane conversation that went on out there. The peace and quiet in here while she finished her coffee – brewed from a fresh roast from Java Works – would suit her just fine. What did people do before cell phones? She would have had to resort to reading one of the old *Daily Racing Forms* Dean had stacked on his desk. Instead she could use social media to avoid looking at the win photos that wallpapered the walls, many of them old enough her parents, and Shawn, were in them. Dean would never take them down, but they were an unwanted reminder for Faye. S*he was here, and they were not*. No amount of therapy would erase that.

She jumped out of those thoughts when the door popped open, and scowled a little too readily at the intruder. "What are *you* doing here?"

Nate grinned, heading straight for the box of doughnuts. "Good morning to you, too. Why do you think I'm here?"

"To eat the doughnuts I brought for the crew. Get out of there!"

He ignored her reprimand and selected a glazed sour cream, breaking off a piece and popping it in his mouth. "I know what *you're* doing here."

He was tall for a rider – taller than her by an inch – so how did he not have to watch his weight? He'd been an apprentice when they'd been together, and he'd needed to be more careful then – but that designation had run out in the spring, and apparently the extra five pounds it afforded him meant doughnuts – no doubt in moderation – were a reasonable choice, on occasion. The guys in the room who had to sweat off pounds – and far worse practices than that – must hate him. Faye still wanted to hate him, and sometimes she still did.

Graduating to journeyman status hadn't slowed him down at all in the local ranks. Still leading rider at Woodbine. Queen's Plate-winning jockey. A smooth transition. It was probably just as well she'd broken up with him. Journeymen didn't fit her M.O.

"So why do you think you know why I'm here?"

"Because I remember last year, you'd be here pretty much every time I worked a horse for Dean, and Nikki would tell me she hadn't seen you around that much since the last bug rider who'd caught your eye. It's a well-known fact you don't come to watch the horses go, Faye. And well, you're not here to see *me* now, are you?"

Faye heard the buzz of his phone, and was grateful when he unzipped a pocket to retrieve it instead of waiting for a response from her. Oh well. His words were true. Own it, girl.

The smile on his face made it pretty obvious the text was from Liv, and not something he felt the need to share with her. His finger swiped some more, his face returning to a more professional state of interest, and he tucked the phone back in his pocket.

"Let's go. Jiro's here. Maybe a leg up will be the start of your next great encounter." He smirked as he held the door open for her.

The morning was cool, the sky a uniform grey, and she was glad she'd been nursing her coffee so she still had some. "There're doughnuts in Dean's office, Nikki," she said to Dean's assistant after glancing around to make sure there weren't extra ears around.

"I'll have to take my chances, because I'm coming out to watch these two. You didn't tell anyone you put them there, did you?"

"I didn't, but you'd better make sure Nate keeps his mouth shut."

Jiro was waiting down the shed. He looked even better in jeans. Downright edible, in fact. He was probably the same height as Nate – though he looked small with Dean towering over him, of course. Similar build to Nate too, which was not a bad thing at all. He was just skinnier, if that was possible. Faye quite enjoyed this chance to study him as he exchanged words with Dean, and didn't mind that her brother was horrible about making introductions. Once Nate was on a horse, he ignored her, but she felt a small thrill of victory when Jiro gave her a quick smile as Dean led him past on his mount.

"Come on." Nikki set off after them, power-walking. "I'm not going to miss this."

"You seem pretty excited about going out to watch a couple of maiden claimers."

Nikki snorted. "I'm going to watch for the same reason you are. Nate Miller and Jiro Watanabe."

"If I'd known Nate was coming I might not have been so quick to make the trip," Faye said wryly.

"Ooh, yeah. Sorry."

"Don't be. I'm over it." She was just going to keep telling herself that, and before long, it would be true.

They followed the horses through the tunnel and up to the gap, Dean turning Jiro and She Brews loose, Nate, jogging the other filly up beside them to back up. Nikki and Faye shuffled along to find a spot on the rail.

"Have you talked to Dean yet this morning?"

Faye shook her head and glanced sideways. Faye knew better than to bother her brother when he had workers, so she'd left him alone. She'd done no more than hand him a coffee by way of good morning.

"No – what's up?"

"Touch and Go. We think it's just a stone bruise, but Dean's going to do x-rays later. I think he's out of the Prince of Wales either way."

"Ouch. That sucks." Could they have worse luck this year?

Faye saw an injured horse for how it affected their bottom line. A horse on the farm didn't bring in as much money as a horse at the track, where owners paid trainers a hefty day rate. Then there was the possible lost income from missed purses, especially with a nice horse like Touch and Go, last year's champion two-year-old in the country. Not that that part was in any way guaranteed. Dean, on the other hand, would feel the disappointment and heartache. Maybe it was how he paid the bills, but Dean was in the game for love.

"But Wampum's training great, so here's hoping it's not too long before he's back at the races."

Wampum.

That colt's name sent her mind hurtling back to April, in Kentucky. The terror she'd felt watching the accident, Nate and Wampum both going down, and Nate's confusing aloofness afterward. It had given her painful clarity about their relationship. Her reaction to Nate's brush with death made her realize she was in much, much too deep.

So yes, she'd been the one to end it. Yes, she'd used Liv as her scapegoat, not that the whole kindred spirit thing between those two hadn't been a growing issue. But if she were honest – as hard as that might be – it wasn't *the* issue. *The* issue was that she couldn't have feelings for someone who loved to do something that had the potential to put him in a morgue as a result of a simple misstep by one of those insane, if beautiful, beasts. It didn't make acceptance any easier. It didn't hurt any less. But it was why she'd have to let Nate off the hook eventually.

This wasn't really the best place to watch horses breeze – the bleachers would have been a better choice. Faye would act like she cared – okay she did care, just not with the same passion her brother did. Horses were horses, and her eye for them wasn't as keen as his. Her eye for good-looking men, however…and those two boys going past, poised just so with their acey-deucy irons? They provided quite a pleasant view. She tucked her now-empty travel mug under her elbow, keeping her arms pressed to her sides as she lifted her phone and snapped a pic, which, with the delay of the shutter, pretty much just caught their butts. Not that that was exactly disappointing.

When the workers disappeared behind the tote board in the stretch, Nikki waited just long enough to see them reappear on the other side near the wire before she nudged Faye's arm.

"I've got to beat them back to the barn. Catch you later."

There was bath water to be made ready, and stalls to be finished up, if the others hadn't stepped up in her absence. Sometimes they did, sometimes they didn't. Faye was in no hurry to get back though. She watched them gallop out, getting another good look at them while Dean shuffled by so he'd be there to meet them coming off the track after they pulled up.

Faye went in the other direction, a few vague *good mornings* and half-smiles coming her way as she went. She carefully negotiated the steps and made it through the tunnel before Dean and the horses.

It wasn't far to Barn Twelve where Dean's stalls were, and the walk back warmed her up again. Really, where was that heat from a couple of weeks ago? A little moderation would have been nice, instead of going from one extreme to the other. This was just a weird summer across the board.

With the bland look of disinterest she'd perfected, she waited for them to come back. Nate was on the shed first, steering the filly he was on into one of Nikki's stalls. Faye didn't know the horse's name, and felt guilty for not attempting to find out. She moved a little closer, deciding part of being over Nate meant carrying over the *do better* initiative to him.

He came out of the stall, tack draped over one arm, bridle in the other, and dunked the bit in the water bucket hanging on the rail before depositing the tack in an organized heap next to it.

"So I know you don't care how the horses looked; how did we look?" he said, cheeky grin and post-breeze adrenaline flowing.

"You're in fine form, Mr. Miller." She gave him a smirk.

Nate glanced a few stalls up where Jiro emerged from She Brew's stall. "Hey Jiro? Have you met Dean's sister?"

Faye controlled her expression, because why not? Jiro came up, Faye's appreciation growing the closer he got. She offered her hand, smiling just the right amount. *Enchanted, I'm sure.* She didn't say it out loud, because the nuance might be lost on him, but definitely not on Nate, who was looking a little smug. Faye didn't quite understand that, but she wasn't going to waste time trying to figure it out.

"Faye," she offered, because Nate had forgotten that part.

Jiro smiled and nodded and said, "Nice to meet you," with his adorable accent, then apologized for needing to leave. Both the riders had to keep moving, of course – in-demand enough their agents kept them hopping all morning long. Which suited Faye perfectly. All she'd wanted to do was plant a seed.

There was no need for her to stick around, so she walked to her car, parked in the lot by the kitchen, and sent Liv the photo. *Just in case you're missing him. I'm calling it, "Breezing Butts."* Then, on a whim, she dialed. And Liv, miraculously, picked up.

"It says a lot about our friendship that I'm answering, you know," Liv said.

"I'm so proud of you. You're learning to adult."

"So what are you doing at the track this morning? Nice picture, by the way."

"It's okay if I still admire his butt, isn't it? It's the other one I'm interested in now, though, so don't worry."

"I'm sorry, I don't recognize it," Liv said wryly.

"Well why would you? You've only got eyes for Nate, and it took three years for you to admit that. Jiro Watanabe worked She Brews for Dean this morning. Don't ask me who Nate was on."

"So that's who you're clocking these days, is it? All right."

"He fits the profile nicely, I must say." Faye paused. "Touch and Go's out of the Prince of Wales."

"Oh no, Faye. I'm sorry. Tell Dean too, okay?"

"I will."

"But you'll both still come down for it, right? Please?"

"Sure." Faye was always up for a party, and Fort Erie did a good job.

With any luck, Jiro would be riding down there that evening. She needed to build on the progress she'd made.

She stopped at Starbucks for a cappuccino on the way home, badly needing a cleanse from exposing herself to track coffee – not that she'd been drinking it.

"A brownie, too please," she said, and it made her think of Will, and that night after the Plate party. She'd eaten most of his brownie when they'd come here. She should probably make him a pan of them to apologize, and to thank him for helping with the hay. Though he had tossed her in the pond, which really should erase any debt she might feel she had.

THE CAPPUCCINO WAS SO HOT, she was almost home before she could safely sip it. Except for a few nibbles, she'd saved the brownie, so she pulled it from its brown bag and set it on a plate, then planted herself in front of the computer to catch up on some web work. The internet seemed to have other ideas about that plan.

Faye hit reload again, with the same result. Nothing but an inadequate apology from the browser. Rural Canadian internet was something even third-world countries couldn't comprehend. In this day and age, someone should have come up with a way to provide reliable service, even when you lived in a location where tall trees and rolling land made line of sight a challenge. She sighed, and gave up, putting the brownie back in its bag for later, and grabbed her coffee.

"Hey Gus! Wanna go for a walk?"

Like the answer was ever *no* to that question. The Golden was bouncing at the back door, tongue lolling, before Faye even got close to her shoes.

They wandered beyond the pastures where the mares and foals grazed to the hay fields, the new growth looking like a green brush cut. It needed to warm up again so they got a decent crop of second cut. She zipped her jacket up to her neck, grateful the cappuccino in her hand was still warm. It was ridiculous to need a fleece in the middle of July. No one would have been so quick to jump in the pond if they'd been putting up hay today.

Except Gus, of course. He launched right in as they got close, then swam happily back to the edge when she called him, bounding up to her and stopping to give himself a good shake.

"C'mon, goofball. Thanks to that shower, I'm going to need to change before I freeze out here."

Dean's truck was parked outside the barn where he kept the layups, and she followed Gus into the dark interior. Gus tracked him down. He was in a stall grooming a big colt, a task that was the farm manager Stacey's job, but this particular colt was Ride The Wave, who Dean loved with optimistic devotion. There had been no more talk of taking on a partner.

The fact that the colt was here and not at Woodbine was not a good thing. Two-year-olds. *Ugh.* Maybe if Dean would take him into the track, he'd get some more interest, as much as Faye struggled with the idea. But Dean was treating the colt with kid gloves, determined to do right by him. Ride The Wave was a big, growing thing, and Faye feared, left to his own devices, Dean wouldn't get him to the races until he was five.

"How's your baby?" she teased.

"You think I'm an old fuddy-duddy." Dean sneezed at the dust rising from Wave's muddy coat.

Faye choked on a laugh. "You are an old fuddy-duddy."

"This colt is the last of Dad's legacy, Faye. He's got to be good. I mean, look at him."

"Because I know what I'm looking at." It was a good way to deflect Dean's hopefulness.

He raised an eyebrow as he switched sides. "You do. You just don't want to admit it."

"Well, it doesn't matter. I lack credibility because if I get any closer than this, I start having a panic attack."

"Don't worry, I'm not suggesting you start helping with the hands-on stuff." He grinned. "I still think you could be a bloodstock agent or something like that."

"No thanks," she said. Just because she could, didn't mean she wanted to. "The internet was down again when I got home. If it's not back up, I'm heading into Lucy's."

No surprise, the connection at the house was still dead in the water.

She packed up her laptop and headed for civilization. Or Lucy's, at least, where she'd have access to free WiFi, and if she was lucky, a butter tart.

Lucy's ire was more subdued this morning as she set Faye's coffee and tart down and rang it up, so Faye took a rare stab at conversation. "I guess you'll have a new neighbour soon. Who's leaving?" The *For Lease* sign had been out front for a couple of weeks now.

Lucy frowned. "Me."

"What? No, Lucy, you can't go! Why?" While Faye guessed the coffee shop wasn't the most lucrative business in town, it has survived while other places had not. She hoped the landlord wasn't doing something crazy with the rent. She couldn't imagine Lucy not being there.

The little quiver that came with Lucy's sigh shocked Faye. It was the first time Faye had seen any sign of vulnerability in her.

"My mother's very sick, and needs a lot of extra care. I just can't manage the business and that right now."

"Oh Lucy, I'm so sorry." Faye didn't know what more to say, but then the wheels started turning. "What if someone took it over for you? You'd still have an income, which I'm sure would help out right now. And we wouldn't lose this amazing place you've built."

Lucy's eyebrows went up slightly, with an expression Faye almost might have called hopeful. "I don't know how I'd find someone like that."

"Well it just so happens…" *What are you doing, Faye?* "…That I'm looking for an opportunity."

Lucy's head tilted, like she was pondering the likelihood of Faye having the necessary skills. Faye tried not to be insulted. It wasn't as if Lucy could have any idea what she did for a living, or what her interests were. Faye just needed…something. Something more productive to do with her life than deciding who her next boy toy would be.

When Lucy didn't speak, Faye jumped back in. "I'm a business manager for some of the farms around here." Okay, glorified bookkeeper, whatever. She did have the degree that would qualify her for such a title, though. "And while my baking isn't as wonderful as yours, I've been doing it since I was little, helping my mom. Why don't you think about it for a while? Here's my number." She pulled one of Dean's business cards out of her purse, and scribbled her name and cell number on the back.

"Just give me a call, or, I'm in here enough, tell me you want to chat if you see me. I'll make the time."

Lucy actually smiled, all the hard lines of her round face softening so that Faye barely recognized her. "Thank you. I'll do that."

Faye nodded, and handed her a ten-dollar bill.

Lucy waved her away. "On the house."

"Thanks, Lucy. We'll work something out. Something to buy you some time before you give this up."

She parked herself at a corner table, opening up her laptop and logging into the WiFi, then looked around the shop. It was surprisingly big. The things she could do with this place, after a fresh coat of paint. She created a new Word doc, and started brainstorming ideas while they were fresh in her mind.

7

Two hours was too long to keep Dean folded into her little Corolla, so they took his truck to Fort Erie. Dean was like a kid, all but bouncing in his seat on the way down, as if because he wasn't running a horse in the big race himself, he didn't have to be serious. When they got there, he insisted on going to the barn first to see Liv and Chique. Faye couldn't protest; it was the right thing to do.

The Fort Erie backstretch had seen better days. Faye had never known those days, but walking around the run-down barns always made her want to find paint. Her father had always called it Saratoga North, but he'd been around in the days when the A meet in Ontario had shifted to the border track for the summer, much like Saratoga hosted a boutique meet in New York state.

Dean pulled up outside the shed where Chique had spent the last few weeks, and Faye immediately saw Liv outside the stall, fussing over the filly while Jo St-Laurent stood to the side with a controlled expression. *Yep, we're in the right place.* Liv was dressed up, wearing a pretty blue-print sundress – did she ever wear anything but blue? It covered her scary-strong shoulders, but not the flex of the just as scary muscles in her arms. It also left her well-defined calves in full view above blue flats – Faye had never seen Liv in heels. Ever. Just as well, maybe, because those calves in heels? She could probably do one of those swimsuit fitness model competitions, or whatever they were. The ones where the contestants got spray-on fake tans and wore tiny bikinis.

"Thanks for coming!"

Liv's words sounded artificially bright, like she knew she had to say them but was too distracted to actually mean them. Not that Faye doubted her sincerity, just her ability to focus on anything other than the horse. Faye navigated the uneven shedrow in her heels and wrapped her arms around Liv, making herself a human Thundershirt. Liv stilled.

"Now breathe," Faye instructed, and she felt the exhale. Chique snorted behind them, then yawned, and Faye dropped her arms and stepped back. "Better."

"Anything I can do?" Dean asked, probably dying to help out because he wasn't comfortable watching anyone else work while he stood by.

"Stick around in case I pass out or have a panic attack?" Liv quipped, which might be a legitimate concern.

On a normal day, it was easy to forget Liv had only had her trainer's licence since April, and this was only the third time she'd saddled a horse – but today the jitters of inexperience were putting on a parade. Liv had always wanted to be a rider – and had been, until a freak accident in Florida last winter had put her in the hospital. Faye didn't know all the reasons behind Liv's decision to take over as Chique's trainer of record in the spring. By then she'd been feeling a disruption in their friendship, suspicious something was developing between Liv and Nate, and it kept her from asking either of them. Now it didn't really matter.

"It's still a couple of hours till post time. You two should go over to the buffet," Liv said, crossing her arms and grasping her elbows. Chique tossed her head up and down, her long forelock flying, and Faye wanted to laugh. It was like the filly herself was telling Liv to calm down, because she was making them all nervous.

"If you were a normal trainer, you'd come with us, and leave Roger's very capable assistant to do her job and get the filly ready," Faye said with a smirk.

Jo snorted, and Liv shot her a look, but admitted, "Because I could eat right now? You can go with them if you want, Jo."

"I have strict instructions to stay right here in case you do, in fact, self-destruct."

"If that happens, Jo, call 911 first, and then call us. Dean can help you with the filly, and I can help resuscitate Liv."

Liv rolled her eyes. "Would you two just leave?"

Dean put an arm around Liv's shoulders and gave her a squeeze. "You'll be fine. See you over there."

Fort Erie was a happy place, despite its tumbledown state. It was a tighter community than Woodbine, made up of smaller outfits. The people here had to be in it for love, because there wasn't a lot of money to be made. Those A meet glory days were several decades in the past now, the present-day racing dates going from May to the end of October and offering an option for horses that weren't quite competitive enough for Woodbine. The eternal optimism shared by everyone who called The Fort home was at odds with a reality that couldn't help but depress Faye on those rare occasions she walked this backside.

That was another reason she'd been surprised Liv had wanted to spend a couple of weeks here. It was the last stop for some of those animals, and at the end of the season a number of them were sold to trainers who went south for the winter – but not to warmer destinations like Florida, New Orleans or Arkansas. The ones who survived the season at Fort Erie went to places like Pennsylvania and West Virginia where they could run on medications that weren't legal in Ontario. Dean never let his horses go like that. He retired them, and let Emilie and Nicole – who galloped and ponied for Triple Stripe but had a network of riding horse friends – find appropriate homes and second careers.

On Prince of Wales Day, though, Fort Erie shone, at least on the front side. Faye scanned the food trucks, patrons lined up as they waited to grab a quick bite before watching the horses in the nearby walking ring. The paddock was rustic, more intimate than Woodbine's, which had once upon a time been similar, but suffered modern upgrades. The old trainers liked it better than the new one at Woodbine; the younger trainers didn't know any differently until they came to the Fort and someone told them this is how it used to be. How it should have stayed.

While Dean grabbed a program, Faye texted Em. *We're here. Where are you?*

Em: *Upstairs. We have a table. Come up!*

Faye: *We?*

Liv's parents, perhaps. But Em didn't answer before Dean was swallowed by the grandstand and Faye had to pay attention and stay close, latching a hand onto his elbow so she didn't lose him in the crush of people packed on the lower level.

Faye didn't know this grandstand like she did Woodbine, relying on her brother to lead the way: up some stairs to where a buffet dinner was set up, tables crowding the room that looked out over the pretty infield. The lake there had a story, and the picturesque little bridge was a popular spot for weddings – at least racetracker weddings. Beautifully-maintained landscaping surrounded the old tote board that declared *Alive And Kicking,* the track's motto. Because Fort Erie had, indeed, fought hard to stay alive and survive in the post-Slots-At-Racetracks climate in Ontario.

Em waved as soon as they pushed through the door. There was someone sitting with her, but it wasn't her parents.

Oh. Will. Smiling a charming smile. That stupid humming started, overriding the din of diners' voices.

Well okay. She could do this. She could accept that not every guy was going to go for her. Nothing to be embarrassed about. Will stood as Faye and Dean approached.

"Nice to see you again, Will. You remember my brother, Dean?" she said coolly, as if Will hadn't already endeared himself to Dean by helping with the hay. Faye carefully took off her hat – because she never missed an excuse to wear a hat – and seated herself across from him.

Dean grinned as they exchanged a handshake across the table. "You're becoming a regular part of the gang now."

Like they were the Little Rascals or something. Faye caught an amused look on Em's face.

"I am sorry I missed hearing you play at the Plate Party." Dean settled into his seat. "I keep hearing how good you were. I hope we can get away with having you again next year."

"You have a horse in it next year?" Will said – sounding like he was just being polite.

"I hope so."

"You hope so every year," Faye said with an eyeroll, but Faye hoped so too. Dean's eternal optimism always brought out her fondness for her brother. Sometimes she had a hard time believing they were related.

"So who's that, Dean?" Emilie said.

"A son of Catch The Joy out of Avalanche. I doubt I'll even get him to the races this year – he's a big colt, awkward as anything. But he sure is bred for it."

Em looked suitably impressed. "Catch The Joy was trained by Dean and Faye's father, and won the Canadian Triple Crown, *and* was second in the Breeders' Cup Turf Classic, *and* was Canadian Horse of the Year for two years. He went on to become one of the top stallions in Ontario."

Will looked blank, and Faye had to take pity on the poor guy. "So you've heard of the Kentucky Derby, right? And if you've heard of the Triple Crown, it's probably the American one. We have one too. The Queen's Plate is the first race, and this race today – the Prince of Wales Stakes – is the second. Then in another three weeks, the third one is back at Woodbine. It's called the Breeders' Stakes, not to be confused with the Breeders' Cup, which is two days of races and pretty much accepted as the world championships of horse racing…even if it's mostly only horses from the northern hemisphere that compete."

"You really have missed your calling, Faye," Em interjected. "You should be volunteering for the Canadian Horse Racing Hall of Fame. You're like an ambassador."

"I'm not exactly looking for philanthropic opportunities right now, Em. If you hear they're hiring, though, let me know, all right?"

"So kind of like the World Series is really just an American thing, not a world thing?"

Dean laughed. "Kind of. Though a lot of horses from the UK and Europe come over."

"How do they get here?" He looked genuinely puzzled.

"They fly," Dean said.

"Do I want to know what that costs?"

At least he hadn't made a crack about Pegasus. "Best not to think about it," Faye said. "Are we having wine, Em? Or did you drive?"

"Will met me at Woodbine and I came with him. He drove." She smiled.

Faye nodded. "Wine it is, then."

Well, that was cozy. Faye stopped herself. Em wasn't acting like she was interested in Will, though Faye wasn't sure if she'd recognize if Em *was* interested in someone. In that way, the sisters were a lot alike; Em just wasn't systematically opposed to the idea of male companionship like Liv had been – historically, at least. She'd wondered early on if Em liked Nate – it was from Em she'd learned about him, not Liv, after all – but the two of them had fallen into a cute brother-sister type relationship. And though Em was the youngest of their group, sometimes Faye thought she had a better head on her shoulders than all of them combined, the common sense she'd demonstrated steering clear of romance with Nate Miller being a case in point.

Faye reached over and snapped the program from Dean. "What race are we on?" Will's presence had distracted her. She needed to check if Jiro had any mounts.

The buffet wasn't as fancy as what they'd had at Woodbine on Plate Day, but the atmosphere was down-home, and hey, it was free. It would have been better if Touch and Go had stayed sound, but it had been nice of Liv to invite them. Faye nibbled as Dean nattered about the race that had gone off, Will valiantly trying to follow what he was saying. His utter confusion was adorable.

"I need to stretch my legs. I'm going down to the paddock for the next race." Faye scooped up her hat and gave Em a pointed look. "You coming?"

She felt bad abandoning Will to Dean, but they were grown-ups. She was sure they'd find something to talk about. Dean could discuss things other than horses. Like hockey. Nate liked hockey, so probably Will did too. Like any self-respecting Canadian boy, right? Was it wrong to make that assumption? All Faye knew was she needed to get her mind off Will and back to a more suitable target.

"I don't know, Faye," Em began as they started down the steps. "I think you should give Will another chance. He seems so nice."

"First of all, it's him who would have to give me another chance, because it's him who turned me down. And second, nice is wasted on me."

"Are you really going to let what happened with Nate taint your view of relationships forever?"

"You're not exactly an expert, Em."

"Oooh, snippy!"

"Sorry." Really, Emilie didn't deserve to take the brunt of her frustration. "I think we need Pie In A Jar, Em. Yes? That might be the best food truck I have seen in my entire life."

"Caramel apple with ice cream? Count me in. I'll stand in line, you grab a spot."

"You're a good friend, Em. I do need to maximize my viewing time." Faye adjusted the angle of her hat. "Am I too old to play paddock girl?"

Emilie laughed. "You've been too old for years, Faye. When have you let that stop you?"

Few of the spectators gathering outside the walking ring were as dressed up as she was. She sidled next to a man with a *Form* propped in front of him, giving him a smile and a *thank you* when he made more room for her. Using her elbows to take up extra space, she typed a text to Liv while she waited. *How are you holding up?*

The response came in a remarkably short time. *Counting the minutes.*

Down to the seconds, no doubt.

Em squeezed in beside her, pressing a mason jar into Faye's hands. "Cheers."

"This looks like sheer brilliance." Faye dug her plastic spoon into its depths.

"I agree."

The pie was so good, Faye almost forgot to look for Jiro. It seemed wrong to be stuffing her face with dessert while ogling a guy whose survival at least partially depended on his ability to starve himself. With sunglasses and her hat, in the midst of the crowd, maybe she'd blend in. She almost laughed out loud. If Liv or Em had heard that thought, she knew how they'd respond. *You never blend in, Faye.* And did she actually want to blend in? No. She needed to keep Jiro aware of her. Maybe finish up the pie before he saw her, though.

"So why," Faye said, in between mouthfuls as she worked to scarf it down, "is Will here?"

Em shrugged. "Nate asked him. I told Nate I'd make the drive down with him."

"So he wouldn't get lost?"

"Or feel lost if he didn't get lost? He's being a good sport." Emilie gave her a sideways glance, her own spoon dipping into the jar with less frantic frequency. "There he is."

Both she and Em zoned in on Jiro. *The guy you're supposed to be interested in, remember, Faye?* She forced herself to admire the view in front of her, instead of contemplating the intruding thoughts of Will floating through her mind. Jiro's stereotypical square, crossed-arm stance, whip tucked neatly under his arm as he listened, nodding, to the trainer. The way he moved, fluidly, as he walked up to the horse, and hopped weightlessly into the saddle with only the slightest aid. His beautiful hands as he knotted the lines, then reached forward to stroke his mount's neck. There was no humming sound here though; no tremor that ran through her leaving her both thrilled and maddened. This fruitless attraction she had for Will was getting in the way.

Faye chickened out and ducked her head as Jiro went by, like a bashful teenager, but Em gave him a full-on smile. He knew Em from the mornings though; she could get away with it. Em got away with so much.

"We'd better go rescue Will from my brother." Faye nudged Emilie with her elbow as the horses headed for the tunnel under the grandstand on their way to the track.

Will and Dean looked as if they were doing okay; not best buddies or anything, but getting along as well as fish-out-of-water Will could be expected to with a horse-centric like Dean. Faye and Em's return didn't bring relief to his face though. Why would it? Em was a horse girl, try as she might to deny it, and he'd already shunned Faye. It didn't stop that damn humming sound from coming back, blocking her eardrums from everything else for an instant so all she heard was her own erratic heartbeat.

She still had wine, thank goodness. But she'd need another glass. She took a photo of the refill and sent it to Liv. *I'm having one for you.*

It was a few moments before Liv answered. *You're the best.*

Faye grinned at the phone screen, feeling the sarcasm through whatever magic transmitted SMS messages. *What are friends for?*

"You know what they're going to do, right?" Dean was starting in on his prediction of how the Prince of Wales would be run, his plate replaced by the program he'd reclaimed from Faye when she'd returned. He'd left his *Form* behind, at least.

Her brother needed to get a girlfriend; one who was into racing. Liv really would have been perfect. Sure there was an age difference, but Liv had always been too mature for her own good, and she got along so well with Dean. The two of them probably had one of those pacts; the ones where they promised if they were still both single in their 40s, they'd get together. That would put Faye's sexy spinster plan out the window, though, so she'd better root for Nate.

She realized Will was staring at her, and hated to think what weird expression she'd had on her face. She smiled at him, hoping the look she sent back was more, *I understand, I've always felt like an outsider too with these people;* a civilian hovering at the fringes of the frontlines on which they battled.

Faye had grown up in a horse racing family. She'd come to understand the ins and outs by osmosis; it couldn't be helped. It didn't hold her interest, but she felt obligated on some level to have some idea of what was going on. But Dean was the only one of their group who really paid any attention to the race that was going off. Em normally would have watched too, but she could at least set her interest aside and do her part as Will's escort as assigned by Nate. They were talking music, Will looking way more comfortable. Faye just observed, thinking about how he'd guessed what her musical tastes were, and for a moment, feeling just a little bit left out of everything.

When the race was over, she hopped to her feet, quickly draining what was left in her glass. "Okay. We all have to go down for this. And watch the race with Liv, so make sure you have everything. We probably won't be back."

The horses were already in the saddling enclosure, and there was no hope of seeing Liv and Jo and Chique with the crowd that had gathered. Well, Dean and Will might be able to; they were tall enough. Faye and Emilie squeezed up to the walking ring rail instead, leaning forward over the hedge inside it. Faye glanced over her shoulder under the brim of her hat, catching Dean's intent expression as the horses started to appear. She could feel Will, so close the heat of his body was like a warm shawl on her back. Maybe someone would run into him and press him against her. *Oops, so sorry!* Her pulse drummed in her ears. *Okay, breathe, girl, and at least try to pay attention to what's in front of you instead of who's behind.*

The early evening light hit Chique's bright white shadow roll first, then caught the glint of her eye against the cut of the blinker cups. Nate and Liv followed, spotting their cheering squad. A little four-fingered wave from Liv, a toned-down grin from Nate, then their heads were back together, strategizing.

"Chique's behaving," Em said. "Though with her, I'm not sure that's a good sign."

The little dark bay filly might be tough to manage, but her crazy seemed to enhance her performance rather than hinder it. It was really a credit to Nate she'd accomplished as much as she had. He'd insisted the pre-race treatment most trainers would use to settle an anxious horse was taking too much away from her. He was the one who had to ride her crazy ass, so Liv had gone along with it.

With the riders up call from the paddock judge, everything started to move. Trainers and riders, horses and grooms; their activity choreographed in the small confines of the walking ring. The outriders on their decorated ponies led the procession to the track.

"Aweille!" Em said the word like a war cry, shooing with her hands and pushing into Faye to get her point across.

When Em lapsed into French, you jumped first, and asked questions later. Faye stepped back quickly to get around the person next to her, and felt her pointy heel sink into something softer than pavement.

"Ow!" Will gasped.

Faye spun around in horror, seeing Will's scrunched-up face, and grabbed his arm. "I'm so sorry Will! But, um, suck it up, because we have to catch Liv. We can't miss this race."

With Em leading the way, serpent-like, through the sea of spectators, they reached Liv as she exited the horse path.

Faye squeezed her elbow. "Okay?"

Liv looked at her sideways with a smirk. *Right.* Don't ask a control freak that when things are out of her control.

"Filly looks great," Dean said.

"What do you think?" Em asked.

"It's Chique. Anyone's guess, right?" Liv answered wryly.

The sun was setting over the beautiful old track, giving everything an orange glow as the horses warmed up. Faye made sure she wasn't next to Will, wedging herself between Emilie and Liv.

When the gates opened, Nate didn't gun Chique for the lead. Dean, on the other side of Emilie, was nodding, muttering, "Good, good. Let that speed horse go. You don't want to get caught up in that." By the turn Nate had Chique tucked on the rail, saving ground behind the pacesetter.

"See, what did I tell you?" Dean nudged Emilie hard enough Em dominoed into Faye. "They'll try to keep her boxed in, spoil it for her."

Shut up Dean. But Liv would know that. Faye glanced at her just the same. Liv's jaw was set, but if she was worried, Faye couldn't tell.

"Nate's cool, though," Emilie said. "And Chique looks surprisingly chill."

"She's really grown up," Dean said.

On the backstretch, nothing changed, and Faye was starting to sweat. Her palms damp, she clutched Em's hand because Liv's were wrapped resolutely around her binoculars, fixated on every stride her filly took. But Chique bullied her way out as they turned for home, Nate threading her between horses the moment the sparest of holes opened up. And once Chique was clear, she was gone.

THEY WERE all on their feet, screaming, like everyone else there, so it made sense for Will to scream too, feel part of the excitement. And it was exciting, the way it looked like the little horse was stuck and wasn't going to get out, and then she was breaking free, and running away. The fact that that was Nate on her – that this fast and nervy sport was what he did for a living – was pretty cool. Nate had always had a bit of an edge; always been a bit crazy on a snowboard or on the ice, the scrappy little dude who everyone liked just enough to not punch in his perfect teeth.

Em was whooping as she and Faye enveloped Liv in a hug, then Dean hugged Liv too, though Liv was soon breaking out of it to push Faye in front of her and rush away. Will wondered if he'd thought quicker, if he could have gotten away with hugging Faye, but there'd been no smooth opportunity for it, because she'd stayed way on the other side of Liv.

Emilie reached for Will and dragged him behind her, with Faye's brother bringing up the rear. Down the stairs and right to the racetrack. Amazing how fast these women could move in their fancy shoes, through the deep sand of the racetrack that he was having enough trouble with in loafers. Emilie braced him, laughing and pulling again.

It had been sweet of Em to take him under her wing. She was easy to be around, too. She was cute. She was young. Too young. Plus, she seemed to be Nate's adopted baby sister, so that made her a definite no, even more so than Faye. Faye was still a no, right?

Liv broke away from their little conga line to meet Nate and the horse, reaching up to grab his hand, Nate pulling her close enough, and leaning over far enough, so he could kiss her. It was like something from a movie, and it did seem like all of it was coming together for Nate. He'd worked hard, professionally and emotionally, to make that happen.

Em led him to a semi-circle where they crowded with Faye, an older couple Will guessed were Liv and Em's parents, and the woman who had been with the horse at the barn, whose name Will had already forgotten. They stood in a line, waiting while Liv positioned the horse with them, a blanket of yellow and purple flowers now hanging over the horse's neck. A photographer captured the scene before Nate hopped off, all smiles as he undid things and took the saddle off the horse.

"We can go now."

Faye's sultry voice, and the very familiar way she looped her arm through his, unnerved him. He was tempted to lean over and whisper in her ear, *Where are we going?* But he kept the words to himself and the sensation of her touch at bay, obediently going along.

It wasn't until they were back across the track and Faye led them up to Dean that he realized Dean hadn't been over there. Dean seemed unfazed by the way Faye still had her hand on Will's arm, small and warm, the brim of her hat every so often brushing his bicep.

"We're going back to the barn, I assume?" Dean said.

"We'd better." Faye nodded, then looked up at Will. "You can come with us. We can drop you at your car afterwards. How's your foot, by the way? I can't believe I did that."

"It's all right." To be truthful, the excitement, and now her nearness, had distracted him from that pain.

"You sure? I could get a wheelchair for you."

Her cheeky smile made him want to scoop her up right there, in the middle of everything, and wipe it off her face with a kiss.

"I think I can make it," he answered dryly, though he did think about putting an arm around her shoulders, using the excuse of needing the extra support. She still had hers wrapped around his elbow. That was probably as much touching as he should be trusted with right now. "You going to be okay on those shoes?"

Dean had a beast of a four-door black Chevy pickup, parked far enough away he did become more aware of his foot. He didn't know how Faye managed not to be crippled in those shoes.

"Nice vehicle," he said as Faye released him to climb into the back.

"Are you guys going to talk about the virtues of Chevrolet now?" Faye peeked at him between the seats, her hat still poised on her head.

"Not a fan?"

"My choice of vehicles is evidence of my black sheep status in the Taylor family." Her eyes, like milk chocolate, went from him to Dean and back, teasing. "You never did guess what kind of car I drive."

"Toyota Corolla. Really not what I'd have thought."

"Of course you saw it at the farm. Well that's no fun. What should I be driving, then?"

He thought for a moment. "An Audi RS 5."

"Hmmm. I like that. Hear that, Dean? Can we buy me an Audi?"

Dean laughed, and drove up to a small booth. There was a security guard inside, and Dean just nodded as the man waved the truck through.

"So I don't have to write my name in blood?" Will quipped, remembering the paperwork and photograph Woodbine had required for him to gain admittance to play after the Queen's Plate.

Dean shook his head. "They're a lot more relaxed here."

Maybe that was because things were…dilapidated. Dean drove slowly down one of the rows between the barns and pulled up in front of one that bore a vague resemblance to the stable at Woodbine where Will had played the Plate party. He got out slowly. Except for a couple of scruffy-looking types down at the end of the barn, there was no one around.

"So –" He hesitated. "Where's the party?"

"I think you're looking at it," Faye said. She didn't seem to care how out of place she looked with the backdrop of the peeling green paint and weathered wood railings, the dirt on the barn floor hard and uneven.

"They're at the test barn," Dean said, as if that explained everything.

What the hell was a test barn?

Faye clarified as if Will had said it out loud. "That's where the winner of the race, and usually the second place horse, and/or maybe a badly-beaten favourite, go for drug screening. The horses are walked around in circles to rehydrate and cool out, and when they're done – which is basically when they stop drinking water – the attendants take a urine sample, and a blood sample for horses on Lasix, which is most of them, and also, randomly, a second blood to test for bicarbonate."

"So that was mostly a foreign language to me. How do they do that?"

"They take a blood sample from the jugular, which is pretty easy to access on a horse, and they whistle at the horse to get it to pee, and collect it in a cup."

"They – you're joking."

"Not one bit."

"They pee on command."

"Yep."

Will looked at Dean. "She's having me on, right?"

Dean shook his head. "We start teaching them that when they're just babies. Simple association, a conditioned response. Whenever they urinate, you whistle. Over time, for most of them at least, you whistle, they urinate."

"You'll never think of whistling the same, ever again." Faye grinned.

What a funny little world this was. Faye didn't quite fit; it was as if she was mocking it when she elucidated, while at the same time loving its weirdness. The more he listened to her, the more he watched her, the more she fascinated him.

Emilie joined them – had she walked here? It wasn't really that far, but she was all dressed up too, even if she wasn't wearing quite the heels on which Faye teetered.

"I don't imagine Chique will take long – she was barely breathing hard after that." Em said.

She and Dean started talking about things that were way over Will's head, like Dean had gone on about how the race would develop – and, apparently, had. Faye seemed to appreciate he was out of his element here, and gave him a quick smile.

"We should at least find some beer. We have to make some attempt to mark this as a celebration. There must be a bootlegger around here."

"A – bootlegger?" Where were they, the Wild West?

"There's always someone who will sell you beer on the backstretch." Faye elbowed Dean. "You've got to know who?"

"Sorry."

"Those guys will then." She tipped her head towards the other end of the barn, where the two scruffy guys he'd noticed still sat on overturned buckets. Then she started walking – on those high, strappy shoes, over the rough terrain.

He called after her. "Want me to come with you? They look kind of…"

Faye snorted. "Oh, please. I'm fine."

Will watched her navigate the dips and ruts expertly, hips with an extra swing, hair flouncing, hat still set just so on her head. Totally out of place, and completely at home. The two men didn't seem to be at all affected by her arrival, and Faye appeared to chat with them with the same ease she did anyone else. One of them gestured; Faye nodded and smiled, saying something with a laugh – and disappeared around the corner of the barn. Will took a step – did she really think it was safe to parade around here? But a hand on his arm stopped him.

"You don't have to worry about Faye. She can fend for herself." It was Emilie, a slight but very amused smile on her lips. "Of course, we'd be very worried about you, if you tried the same thing."

"I live in downtown Toronto, and I'm kind of intimidated in this place," Will admitted.

"You didn't catch the sign by the stable gate? Mostly harmless."

"What?" He'd found himself saying that a lot around here.

"I'm kidding. And, did you somehow miss reading *Hitchhiker's Guide to the Galaxy* growing up?"

Faye returned with half a dozen bottles of Molson Canadian. Em rushed up to help her, handing one to Dean, and one to Will.

"We can share, Em," Faye said. "I'm hiding the other three so we don't attract scavengers. Though I'm willing to bet Liv won't want one." She stashed them in a box in front of one of the stall doors, closing the lid then sitting on it as she cracked open the beer and took a swig.

So, that seemed to be how Faye Taylor operated. Sweep in, take charge, make things happen. Proactive, not reactive.

Everyone was quiet – such a different scene from after the other race, when this one seemed to be pretty important too. Faye took another sip of beer, then offered the bottle to Emilie; Dean stood with one hand tucked in the pocket of his dress pants and the other wrapped around his bottle. Then the horse appeared, with the short-haired woman who had led her to the grandstand and taken her away when Nate had got off her. Liv was right behind them, and with the influx came a fresh injection of energy.

"What's her name?" Will whispered to Dean, feeling awkward for not remembering, if he'd even been told.

"Jo St-Laurent. She's the assistant trainer for the stable Liv's father owns. Liv's been taking care of the filly while she's been down here, but Jo came to run her."

Faye piped up. "That means she brought Chique from the barn here to where Liv put the saddle on, then brought her back after the race. I'm guessing she walked her – to cool her out – too, because she wouldn't let Liv do it in a dress and unsafe shoes. Which Liv probably tried to do, despite the stupidity of it."

"Oh come on, Faye. She probably had running shoes in her car." Emilie grinned.

"I knew I should have brought one of the hotwalkers with me," the woman named Jo said, walking Chique outside. Chique looked at the scrubby grass and Will swore she gave her a look of disgust. It didn't look all that enticing, he had to agree. "Liv had to hold the filly for me to bath her."

"Track speak, Will. They bath – not bathe – horses. Never, never, 'wash'." Faye gave an exaggerated shudder. "Unless you want to stand out like a sore thumb around here, say bath not bathe or wash!"

"You should probably just stay next to me while I'm here to act as my interpreter."

Faye blinked before she smiled, like she wasn't sure. Was he flirting? Maybe he was. Or just trying to be funny? He hadn't decided yet. And she didn't come over to him, which he realized he'd been hoping she'd do.

Will recognized Nate's car pulling up, and the horse abandoned the grass hunt, her head popping up. Nate went right to her, feeding her something and scratching her neck.

"You're just in time, Nate. She's ready to do up," Jo said.

Nate laughed, and Will just automatically looked at Faye now.

Faye smirked. "So, first you have to know, that's a groom's responsibility, not part of the jockey's job description in any way, shape or form. But if you don't already know this Nate – which I kind of gather you don't – after the Plate, he helped Jo do up Chique. Liv took a photo and posted it on Instagram, and it went a little bit viral." She rolled her eyes. "What it means, literally, to do up a horse, is cleaning out her feet and putting some cool mud on her soles to draw heat out, then putting a similar kind of mud on her front legs for the same reason – all to help prevent or reduce inflammation. Then the legs are bandaged – you just have to look at those to know what that means, because I don't even know how to explain it. It's sure not what you'd put on a paper cut. Then for Princess Chique here, they'll bandage her hind legs too, likely with a sweat underneath, which is kind of the opposite of a poultice, because it creates heat so makes everything feel nice and warm after all that exertion. Anyway, all of it to say, for him to help do all that is a remarkable display of humility and his way of honouring Chique. Sound totally weird?"

She looked like she might admire Nate for all that, even if it killed her just a little.

"Now you're embarrassing me, Faye. But you should have a YouTube channel or something." Nate threw out that high-watt grin of his, and Faye pressed her lips together, giving him a withering look, apparently no longer affected by its radiance. "Put her in, Jo, and I'm there."

Faye's head turned to look at something somewhere behind Will. He glanced over his shoulder, and saw a very new, very blue Toyota 86 pull up. Nice. A guy, skinnier than Nate, and Japanese, climbed out.

Dean turned, "Hey, Jiro!"

Nate was taking off his suit jacket, and said to Liv, "I invited him to stop by before he drives back to Toronto." Then he gave Faye a pointed look.

Faye extracted the beer from the box. "We have domestic beer, or we have domestic beer." She passed one to Jo, and one to Nate. "I'm assuming you're not going to want one, Liv, which means I must've got this for you." She gave Jiro a winning smile.

A beer might take out a guy that size. But it looked like Will had lost his interpreter. Faye was casual about it, but moseyed over to stand opposite Dean, eyes settling on Jiro with that same look she'd given Will when they'd met at the Plate gig. So the last few hours had been a game for her, or the sense of obligation she'd felt to babysit the outsider fulfilled, and she was clocking out.

Dean tipped his head back slightly to take a swig from his bottle, and Will muttered at him, "I'm feeling like a giant around here." All the women were pretty much the same size, give or take an inch, so he and Dean seemed to tower over all of them. "Do you get used to it?"

Dean laughed. "I guess. I don't even notice it. Stings a little though when they always seem to get the women, though. Like what they lack in height they get back double in attractiveness."

Will looked at him sideways, and wondered what that meant. Was Dean trying to tell him something? Like *don't waste your time, buddy; my sister is going to end up with that guy, not you.*

Faye was engaged in what looked to be a slightly humorous, if a bit clumsy, conversation with Jiro, thanks to a language barrier. Nate and Jo were probably with the horse in a stall doing whatever doing up was, with Liv and Em close by. Why was he here again? Dean was friendly, but not exactly talkative when horses weren't a subject option.

It was a relief when Nate finally came out of the stall. He said something in Liv's ear before coming over with the beer Faye had left on the railing for him.

"I bet you're bored stiff." Nate looked apologetic.

Will shrugged. "Just out of my element."

"You think?" Nate laughed. "Sorry, sometimes I need someone else to remind me."

"Congrats though, buddy. On your success."

Nate touched the neck of his bottle to Will's. "Thanks. And I really do appreciate you coming out."

"So who is that guy?" Will motioned towards Faye. "And why did you invite him? I know his name is Jiro. And that Faye is obviously into him." He tried to keep the disgruntlement out of his voice.

"I feel bad for him sometimes. It must be tough, coming to a new country, especially one where no one really speaks your native language." Nate paused. "And you sounded a little jealous there. Just remember what I said."

Will narrowed his eyes, but took the hint. It was okay if the guy nobody really knew got together with Faye, but not him. How, exactly did that make sense again?

Faye was laughing, brushing her hair off her shoulder. She was obviously making sure she didn't misplace her hat tonight, because it remained securely on her head. Jiro was enjoying the attention; Will had yet to see him take a drink from the beer. Jiro nodded at Faye, saying something, then handed her the bottle and stepped back, waving.

"Thanks, Nate! See you!"

There was a collective "Bye Jiro!" chorus that Will didn't join in on; he was just glad the guy was leaving. Liv, Em and Jo joined their little circle, but Faye watched Jiro drive away, then turned and lifted Jiro's bottle to her lips, her eyes steady on Will as she did it. Was she trying to drive him crazy? Because it was working.

When she came over, she squeezed in between him and Dean, her elbow touching his hip, a bottle in each hand. He looked down at her, but she ignored him, scanning the circle.

"This feels a little kumbaya," she said, the usual wry humour in her voice.

"We could sing," Nate said, grinning, and catching Will's eye.

"Oooh, acappella!" Em almost bounced on her toes. "Would you?"

Nate had never needed much of an excuse to sing, and an invitation? He wouldn't turn that down. He started singing *Elements Combined,* a song by Fiction Family, and Will joined in with the harmony just because it was habit, and the song demanded it. Nate could hold a song on his own, sure, but it sounded that much better with the both of them.

Nate was singing to Liv, her face pinking under his attention. Will had been around for part of his relationship with Cindy, the girl who'd ripped his heart out. He was looking at Liv like that, which was maybe a brave thing for Nate to be doing. Liv, from what Will had gathered, wasn't nearly the open book that Cindy had been. Though when all was said and done, Will could argue a good case for her lack of transparency. What had she really been doing with Nate? Playing games. She was just more subtle about it than the likes of Faye Taylor. With Faye, it was more of a sport.

But was Faye over Nate? She'd latched onto Jiro like he was Nate's gift to her which was a little messed up all on its own. Will wasn't really sure he wanted to play this sport. Maybe Nate had been trying to protect him as much as Faye by trying to put Will off.

Jo was the first to speak into the quiet that followed the song. "The musical interlude was beautiful and all, but we should probably get your filly loaded and back to Woodbine." She glanced at Liv

"You're taking her back tonight?" Faye said.

Liv nodded. "Jo brought the van down."

"Let's do it, then," Nate said. "We'll have a real party after she wins the Breeders.'"

"Hush, Miller," Liv hissed, and Nate just laughed at her.

Nate and Liv looked like quite the couple, him in his suit, her in her dress, putting up the ramp after Jo had put the horse on the van. Nate grabbed Liv's arm and kissed her before she rushed off to jump in her car to follow the trailer as it pulled away.

"So that's it?" Will asked as Nate rejoined them.

"They're all up past their bedtimes," Faye said, that little smile toying with her lips.

"Exactly. Time to hit the road." Nate pulled his keys from a pocket.

Dean stared at his phone, then typed something. "Hey Faye, would you be able to catch a ride back with Nate? A friend of mine down here asked if I wanted to go for a drink. And if I do that, I'll just stay over and leave early to get to Woodbine."

Faye stared daggers at him. Will was a little stunned by how clueless her brother was.

"How about this?" Emilie chimed in. "I'll go with Nate, if you don't mind taking Faye, Will?"

"Not at all," Will said, probably a little too quickly, but Faye looked relieved.

"Have fun, Dean. Let's go then, Em. Drive safe." Nate raised a hand and Emilie followed him to the Mustang.

"We can go now," Will murmured, and Faye's eyes flashed to his. Now where was his car?

8

Her feet were killing her. Hindsight: she should have asked Nate to give her and Will a ride to Will's car. She could have dealt with being in the Mustang for that long. But thank you Em, for avoiding the prospect of two hours back to the farm with him. Sure she was over him. But that was asking too much.

"You okay?" Will said.

She was too stubborn to ask him to slow down. "I'm fine," she muttered through gritted teeth. One day she'd learn that comfort was more important to fashion. Too bad it hadn't been today.

"There it is." Will pointed into the darkness.

It wasn't hard to pick out the car. It was one of the only ones left in the big lot, and it was unusual enough that Faye remembered it. She folded into the passenger seat with a sigh, throwing a grateful look up at Will as he swung the door shut, and immediately unbuckled the shoes. So pretty, but so painful. Then she removed her hat, set it in her lap, and ran her fingers through her hair to put some lift back into it.

"You know how to get out of here?" she asked when Will ducked in the driver's side.

He nodded, zooming around to point towards the highway.

So here we are again.

But she was distinctly aware that, regardless of the little moments of zing she thought they'd shared today, he had yet to seek her out, and the only times they'd had contact was because of mutual friends. Well, Nate, specifically. The thought that Nate might have anything to do with Will keeping away made her seethe. Between her aching feet and watching the evening's exchanges between Liv and Nate – she hadn't wanted to let them get to her, but they did anyway – she was exhausted. Just drive, she wanted to say. But she wasn't good at silence.

"So what did you think of the whole Prince of Wales experience?" She tucked a foot into her lap and started kneading it.

Will turned down the music on the radio – it hadn't even registered with Faye that it was playing until he did.

"It was different, being there. I've seen big races on TV, but it's like hockey, you miss so much. Miss hearing and noticing things, because all you ever see is what the cameras decide to show you."

"But this wasn't your first ever time at the races. You were at the Plate."

He shook his head. "Nate arranged whatever credentials we needed to get in, and we went right to the stables."

"Just as well. I love the Plate, but for an authentic racetrack experience, Fort Erie on Prince of Wales night is a better bet."

"It's kind of – shabby," Will said. "But it was cool. Except maybe for the last part at the barn."

"The Fort's backstretch has seen better days, that's for sure."

"So how big a deal is it they won that race?"

"It's pretty big. Liv isn't the first female trainer to have won both the Plate and the Prince of Wales, but she will be the first to win the Triple Crown, if Chique wins the Breeders'. We might be more progressive here in Canada than in the States – we have a number of successful female trainers – but it's still a man's world."

Faye stole a glance at him, when she could have easily stared for the whole two hours home. He was that good looking. It was such a shame things weren't happening between them. She'd tried her best to chat up Jiro, but even that hadn't been satisfying, because she'd kept wondering if Will was watching, and if it bothered him in the least.

"So what was with Dean ditching you like that?"

Faye laughed quietly. "My brother is the most solid, reliable guy on the planet, ninety-nine point nine percent of the time. If on occasion he wants to play, I don't say anything. It's good for him. He needs to do it more. But he could plan better." She sent Will a half-smile, and tried not to think of how valiant it had been of Will to realize how awkward it would have been for Nate to drive her home. "Thank you. How many times have you rescued me now?"

"If he'd done it like half an hour earlier, you could have gone with that Jiro guy."

Oh, well, that was interesting. That wasn't an innocent comment. It was a good thing she was sober, and tired enough not to be firing off-handed comments. "Jiro's just an amusement."

"Like me after the Plate Party?"

Ouch. But guilty. "Is that why you didn't play along? Because you thought that?"

"That, and I wasn't about to trust your judgement when there was cheap champagne flowing, and your ex – my friend – making ground with someone new. Not to mention that that friend would kick my ass if I behaved dishonourably."

Ah, so, Nate did have something to do with it. "Why would he do that?"

"Because despite how things turned out, he cares about you."

She snorted. "What a guy. You're both too kind. I can take care of myself." This was going famously. Maybe she should have gone with Nate. At least a fight with him would feel good.

"So why are you so mad at Nate? You broke up with him, didn't you?"

She knew exactly why she was mad. She also knew, if she was honest with herself, she wasn't mad at Nate. She was mad at herself. It just made sense for that to manifest as anger towards him. It wasn't exactly a new strategy in the history of the world. "Why do we always end up talking about Nate?"

"To help you get him out of your system."

"Therapy isn't really my thing, if that's your angle. I can think of a far better way to get him out of my system. And I'm sober this time, so you can throw out that excuse. Nate can deal with whatever objections he has to it. I promise not to hold either of you responsible." She switched feet.

"You have another hour and a half to think about it. And just to prove I'm not holding a grudge against Nate, the two of you, that acappella duet – wow. Please tell me you're going to do something more than backstretch parties with that."

"I've been trying to talk him into it. We do kind of have opposite schedules. At least our days off match up." He hesitated, fiddling with the volume on the stereo again. "You should come down sometime and hang out while we play. Bring Em with you if it'd be too weird because of Nate."

"Now that I am mad at Nate about. That he never brought me down. But he never really shared the best parts of himself with me, so I shouldn't be surprised." Maybe just as well, because what he had shared had been hard enough to let go. "He never sang to me, like he sang to Liv tonight. That was sweet, you know?" So it had hurt, burned, pierced, wounded.

Will didn't respond to that. She was opening up too much, bringing Nate right back into it when she'd been so determined not to.

"I don't even know what you do," he said, thankfully steering away from anything that involved Nate. "For work."

"Likewise," she said, a little cheek coming back to her voice.

"You first."

"All right. It's very glamourous. I'm a bookkeeper. It started out just being for the farm, and Dean – payroll and taxes and such – then he got me a few more clients. I always thought that I'd get a real job after graduating, but…I don't know. Maybe I'm just an underachiever."

"What's your degree?"

"Commerce. Your turn."

"Almost as glamourous. I work in a restaurant."

"What do you do?"

"Sous-chef."

"A sous-chef with a degree in music. At least my job is remotely related to my education."

"Working in the restaurant business seems to go hand-in-hand with working in the music industry." He grinned, and the hum fluttered back up through her. "But I actually find I like working with food. So I'm thinking about sticking with that."

"Like going to school for it?"

"Yeah. And we need to talk about something other than food, or we're going to have to stop somewhere for something to eat. That buffet was hours ago."

I could eat, she almost said, wanting to prolong this, because hovering around the hum of attraction was something less familiar: contentment. He was going out of his way again to drive her home, though, and she didn't want to take up even more of his time.

"So you aren't a horse girl at all?"

"Oh hell no." Her laugh was automatic. "Everyone thinks I must've been born into the wrong family, because the horse gene skipped me. I let Dean deal with the hands-on. The books – and the odd bale of hay – is as close as I get."

"Guess I can't use the horse girl excuse either, then, can I?"

She smirked. *Don't toy with me.* "What restaurant do you work at? Would I know it?" Food was something she could talk safely about. While Liv was always too busy for forays into the city, Em was usually up for it.

"Mysticus. Right downtown?"

"Ooh, fancy. I have never been. I don't quite frequent those circles."

"I thought your family owns racehorses."

"Parts of racehorses, remember. There's a joke about owning horses. Do you know how to make a million dollars in horse racing? Start with two million."

"That doesn't –"

"Make sense. I know. You're supposed to laugh, not think about it." He laughed easily, and it fed the little happy feeling in her chest. "Dean usually ends up having to take on partners in the best horses to keep things going."

"So did your father retire?"

"My parents and middle brother were killed in a car accident eleven years ago." She was so used to saying it, she never felt the need to sugarcoat, but Will went very still.

"I'm sorry," he said, when his reaction made her feel as if she should be apologizing for being so blunt.

She'd never wanted anyone's pity for the loss. And only Dean might understand how much it had made her the person she was. A psychologist would probably have a field day with her. But sometimes she felt she was hanging onto it all – the grief, the guilt – because who would she be, really, without it? Her identity was built around it.

"Please tell me your parents are alive, or the rest of the drive is going to be unbearably awkward and depressing, and I'm going to end up wishing I had gone back with Nate, as tortuous as that would have been."

Will made a sound that was trying to be a laugh. "Alive and well. My mom's a doctor and my dad's an Environmental Engineer."

"How do they feel about a son who works in a restaurant?" She would definitely not want to be the girl who met the overachiever parents.

"They're those parents who say, 'as long as you're happy…'"

"And are you?"

He glanced at her, then back to the road. "Good question."

"So if you're not…what would you change?" She didn't usually ask this many questions of the men she wanted to sleep with. She didn't usually care to get to know them that well beforehand. But sex wasn't a foregone conclusion here – Will didn't seem inclined to pull over to the side of the road and ravish here there. Was that legal? So they'd be in this car for a while yet.

"My job. The head chef is an ass. He treats the female staff like shit. I just want to pound him."

"So why do you stay?"

"Because I haven't figured out what else to do with my life, and I have bills to pay."

Huh. They had that much in common. "That can't be fun, standing by when he's treating people badly."

"It's even worse that they put up with it."

"I wouldn't last very long in a place like that."

His laugh was looser this time. "No, you would not."

"So do you have a plan? You're all educated in music, is there something you could do with that? Besides teaching?" She remembered that.

This time when he looked over, there was a little furrow in his brow, a crease between his eyes that flickered with uncertainty. "Music's tough. It's a hard way to pay the rent. And I've always worried that I'd love it less if I had to make money with it. The restaurant biz has grown on me. And this may sound stupid, but I have a thing for pastry."

"I have a thing for pastry too," she quipped.

He chuckled, the deepness of it strumming her strings with a vibration that resonated deep.

"I've learned a bit about it at the restaurant. If I do go back to school, it would be for that, but throwing money at yet more education…I don't know. My mother would insist on paying for it, and I don't want her to do that. So I'm doing what I can online, and practicing at home, and sometimes I get to do stuff at work. What I'd love is to have my own place. Not a restaurant; more a cafe, with books and music and espresso and original art by local artists on the walls. Not necessarily in the city. The city gets kind of old."

"What a great dream," Faye said quietly, thinking of her offer to Lucy, and the brainstorming it had inspired. More common ground. She didn't want to like him as much as she did. She hadn't even liked Nate that much by this point. He'd just fit the profile.

She kept asking questions because it spared Will having to query her. He was probably too scared to, afraid of any more awkward revelations. Did she have more? He knew about Nate. He knew about the car accident. Her approach to relationships wasn't exactly a secret. Maybe all the skeletons were out.

"Do you have siblings?"

He shook his head. "Only child. I grew up down the street from Nate, so he and his brothers were like family to me. I was pretty happy when I found out he was moving east too. Until this whole racehorse thing swallowed him up."

"That's exactly what it does." It was all-encompassing, leaving room for nothing – and no one – on the outside. Racetrackers worked together. They played together. They dated and married within the cult, and made more racetrackers. Sometimes that next generation had the common sense to escape. She'd been one of those. She was most definitely not a racetracker; the backstretch just provided her with a few bookkeeping clients, and a consistent supply of prospects for her non-relationships. Things never would have worked out with Nate long-term.

She'd known that, but let herself believe otherwise for a while. She was always surrounded by racetrackers, how could she expect them to be rational? She'd needed someone like Will to come along to make it obvious.

"What about you?" he asked. "The dream thing."

"I'm excelling at being an underachiever, so I was planning just to go with it. We should all do what we do best, right?"

"Oh come on, there's got to be something."

"Then my dream is to be a sexy spinster to my brother's genteel bachelor."

Will snorted. "So basically a cougar?"

Faye looked at him wryly. "I can't quite decide if that's supposed to be an insult. If so, I'm going to reclaim that word for the greater good of middle-aged women everywhere."

"You're definitely not middle-aged."

"No, but we're dreaming here, right?"

He laughed. "So you'll have, like, gentleman callers?"

"Yes. And Dean will continue to do whatever Dean does. Which none of us really knows."

"Try to be serious for a moment. They say the thing you wanted to do as a kid is what you're supposed to be."

"I'm betting you didn't want to be a pastry chef."

"It's no fun when you don't play."

Faye sighed, and wracked her brain. She'd tossed out the idea of dreams so long ago, she couldn't even remember if she had any. She'd always envied that about Liv – that she had such a big dream, to become a jockey, and she'd gone after it. Even if she never went back to riding races, at least she could say she'd done it. Faye had nothing.

"I just wanted to get away from the kind of life I was raised in. I didn't care where, or what took me there. But I'm not going anywhere."

"What's stopping you?"

"Everything. Dean needs me. I mean, look at him. He's closing in on forty. If he found a wife, I'd be off the hook. I could get out of that damn house." She loved and hated that house, somehow. "I don't see that happening, though."

"I bet Dean can take care of himself. We can do that too, you know."

"But the bookwork…that's our deal. I take care of that side of the business, he does the horses and the face-to-face with the clients."

"I'm pretty sure in this day and age you could do that from anywhere."

He wasn't letting her out of this, but she was at a loss. "Clearly I'm going to need help with this big dream thing. We have another hour to figure it out, so let's go."

"Can you sing? You could do vocals for our band. We could use a female voice. I'm envisioning you and Nate doing Gotye's *Somebody That I Used To Know.*"

It felt good to laugh that hard, to throw her head back against the headrest and let go of tension in her chest she hadn't even realized she'd been holding there. "That's a good one."

"So you can sing?"

"I can carry a tune." She couldn't tell him about the painful memories associated with it; how she and Shawn had put on silly mock concerts, how he'd always been the star of the high school musical. How when he'd died, she'd left the singing to others, like her voice had died with him. "All right, that's one. I need more than one."

"Hmmm…" He drummed his fingers on the steering wheel. "Craft brewery? Boutique winery?"

"That would be fun. I could move down this way. Or Prince Edward County."

"Or maybe you could roast coffee beans."

"For your café. You could have your own proprietary beans. To go with the perfect tiny pastries you're going to make."

That sounded a bit too much like they were doing things together, and a little too close to what might be kindling for a dream with Lucy's. If only Lucy would call her.

She needed to redirect. "What do you do for fun, besides play music and bake things? Are you into sports? Please tell me you're not a runner like Nate and Liv."

"No. I played hockey with him growing up, but was never really that good. Used to ski back home. Used to climb."

"Like mountains? You are a badass, then."

"Nope. Not anymore."

His voice was a little flat. There was probably a story behind that, something more personal than she wanted to get into right now. "Just as well, we probably don't have what you'd call mountains around here."

"Your turn," he said, pushing them past the awkward.

"What do I do for fun? You mean, besides getting dressed up and going to the races? I cook. I read." *I pick up bug boys and have my way with them. But in the absence of one of them you'll do nicely.*

"What's your favourite book?" he asked.

The perfect segue. He was well-read, and it kept the conversation going until they were on the sideroad home, and she realized he hadn't asked her to direct him to the farm.

"Do you have a photographic memory or something?" she asked, an eyebrow quirked.

"Just a good one."

He crept up the lane, and for a moment she considered perhaps she should be concerned her remembered where she lived, that his jumping in to drive her home – so far, far out of the way for him – was just a convenient opportunity to execute a plan to slit her throat and leave her to bleed out in her own driveway. Then she remembered he was Nate's friend, and regardless of her antagonism towards Nate right now, would he really have a friend who was a murderer? And if for some crazy reason he did, would he let that murderer drive her home?

She picked up her shoes in one hand – she would suffer those few feet of gravel before she got to the back deck before she'd put those wretched things on again – and reached for the door handle. "Thank you for doing this. On my brother's behalf. For saving me from a fate worse than death." He followed her across the deck. Had he really been a murderer, would she still have been thinking it preferable? What was worth that death? "It's far too soon for me to be civil in private to my ex. I'm impressed with myself for being able to be civil in public."

"And we made it so long without talking about Nate."

She wasn't expecting that look, the light by the back door catching the upward twist of his lips on one side. His hazel eyes reminded her of champagne, and she let herself feel just a little drunk by them. He leaned in, and it was all the permission she needed to meet him, and his lips did exactly sizzle when they connected with hers.

"Come in," she breathed against his mouth. "Don't make me beg."

9

Four AM brought the realization of what should have been there that was not, and what was there that should not have been.

Faye was always aware, if not fully conscious, of Dean rising before dawn, brewing coffee, making toast. He'd eat, then go out to feed the horses on the farm so his manager could sleep later, then she'd hear the roar of his truck starting, the crunch of tires on gravel as it rumbled out the lane. She'd roll over, and sleep to a more civilized hour.

The house was strangely devoid of those sounds. For a groggy moment, she thought she'd better make sure he was up. He never slept in, but there was a first time for everything, right? Then she remembered, he'd stayed in Fort Erie. He'd probably gotten up an hour ago, wherever he'd ended up, and would be on the road to Woodbine to make it by his usual time.

There was an unfamiliar sound in its place, however. This time when she rolled over to reclaim the slumber luring her back, it was to the sight of Will's head pressed into the pillow, hair falling across his forehead, beautiful lashes dark against his skin. The sheet rose and fell with his breathing, his arm free of it millimetres from her own. For a moment, she let herself feel it, the strangeness of it. Any man who had shared this bed had been gone by this time – to risk their necks on those crazy horses. The fact that this one was still here was a reminder that he wasn't one of them. There *was* a first time for everything. But that, in and of itself, was dangerous. Because it would be harder to find excuses to push him away.

If she closed her eyes again, and went back to sleep, he would probably be gone too. That's how it went. And how she wanted this to go. But she watched him a while longer, to enjoy the novelty of it, however brief it might be.

IT WAS LIGHT OUT NOW. He was still here.

As was Gus, the Golden Retriever, cold nose on her elbow, tail thumping softly against the hardwood.

She put a finger to her lips, *shhhhh*...the least she could do in appreciation of Will not only bringing her home, but also ending her painfully long dry spell, was let him sleep. She threw on a robe and padded downstairs to let Gus out, then back in, then fed him his breakfast before climbing back up to the bathroom. She stopped to look at her reflection in the mirror – the messy hair, the colour in her cheeks – and smiled at it before slipping out of her robe and into the shower.

Oh yes, she was back. For real now.

The man could sleep like a rock. She almost took a photo of him, dozing all cute and dreamy, to send to Em, but thought better of it. That would just be crass. Damp hair soaking through her t-shirt, she pulled on jeans and left him there in search of coffee.

Coffee. Another reminder Dean hadn't been around. The little bit he always left in the carafe, even if it was burnt and nasty, was how she always started her day. It was one of those little things she loved, because he'd thought to leave it for her.

It got worse. They were out of coffee, period, so there would be none of the French press magic that routinely followed that first cup. Oh well, even less reason for Will to stay. But she couldn't exactly leave him here while she went off in search of some. There was a jar of Nescafé of unknown origin in the back of a cupboard. It would depend on just how desperate he was for that first hit of caffeine.

" 'Morning."

She jumped, and spun around, bracing herself against the counter. Then recovered, holding up the jar doing her best display model impersonation. "Coffee?"

"Are you serious?" He laughed, eyes still sleepy, his smile lazy. And he was shirtless.

It was almost enough for her to change her mind about this being just a one-time thing. She could put up a case for it still being part of a single event and meander to him, run her hands over that chest, and help him back out of those pesky slacks. Right there against the doorframe would do.

No, no. He'd served his purpose.

"Normally I'd say no, but apparently we're out of real coffee. The little Prince of Wales foray meant Dean missed his usual Tuesday grocery shop."

"Is there a Starbucks around?"

"Hardly. We don't have them on every street corner around here. There is a coffee shop in town though."

"Do they serve breakfast?"

"Of a fashion. Follow me there? My treat." When he looked like he was going to protest, she waved him off, with a coy smile. "I owe you. You'll need to put on a shirt, sadly."

Getting him out of here was the right thing to do.

Lucy did serve limited breakfast options to go with the only slightly better coffee. Faye wondered if Lucy would be offended if she made some suggestions in that department. If Lucy ever called her, that was.

"What's good here?" Will asked, standing slightly behind her at the café's counter – close enough she could remember the heat of skin to skin.

She took a breath to steady herself. "Everything tastes the same," she whispered, with one eye on Lucy herself, who pressed out from the kitchen, wiping her hands on her apron, her permanent scowl in place. One did not insult Lucy by saying such things within earshot, because those butter tarts were the best in a fifty-kilometre radius, and quite possibly wider. They made up for everything else.

Faye's smile wasn't reciprocated. The reception she was getting made Faye wonder if she'd just dreamed that moment of vulnerability she'd seen in the café owner.

"I'll have an egg sandwich on a biscuit –" she started.

"We're all out of biscuits," Lucy snapped.

"An English muffin then?"

Lucy nodded.

Faye glanced back at Will. "What do you want?"

"That sounds good," he said, his tone hesitant.

"Two of those, then. And two coffees. And half a dozen butter tarts?" she added hopefully.

"Last ones." Lucy nodded, setting the styrofoam tray of tarts on the counter. She rang up the order on the old cash register, and waited while Faye pulled out her wallet and found some bills.

"Well she's terrifying," Will muttered as they sat down, the round metal table tilting when they set the food on it. He pried the plastic top off the styrofoam coffee cup, peering at it suspiciously before dousing it with cream and sugar. He hadn't added anything to his cappuccino on Plate night – that would have been gauche – but Lucy's coffee definitely needed help.

He replaced the lid, took a sip, and shrugged. "I've had worse."

Faye drank hers black, because it would make her appreciate the butter tarts all the more. Will watched her with eyebrows raised as she scarfed down the egg sandwich.

"What can I say, I worked up an appetite last night."

He grinned before he bit into his own, chewed…swallowed…and gave another shrug.

"Had worse?" Faye suggested.

"Yes." He washed it down with coffee.

"Are we food snobs?" she whispered.

"You are, for sure."

"And you're not, Mr. Sous-Chef?"

"Occupational hazard," he agreed.

Faye made a show of opening the butter tarts, then removed two and set one next to Will's plate.

She plucked the other from its tin. "This is why we endure the mediocre."

The filling was crystallized on top and soft in the middle, caramelly-sweet on her tongue, with a touch of sea salt. The flaky pastry melted on her tongue. She closed her eyes and sighed, holding the flavours in her mouth before swallowing.

"Should I leave the two of you alone?"

"You jest," she said, taking a sip of the bitter coffee. "You'll see."

He set the foil to the side, appraising the tart for a moment before presenting it to his mouth like an offering. Would he demolish it in two bites, or three? Would he balance the sweet with bitter coffee? No point in that part, probably; he'd added enough milk and sugar to obliterate the coffee taste.

Two, and *no*.

"You're right," he said, licking his sticky fingertips after the tart had disappeared. "That might be the best butter tart I've ever tasted." He sipped some of his coffee, glancing at his phone. "You should come down Monday. When we play. Nate doesn't usually show up on Mondays."

Little things like that threatened her intent to let this go at last night. He didn't judge her for not wanting to be around Nate. He got that it would be uncomfortable. He didn't expect her to just get over herself and play nice.

"Thank you for the invite. I'll think about that."As much as an alien part of her brain wanted to follow him home, crawl into his bed, make herself a permanent fixture there…no, she would not.

He pushed himself back from the table and stood, coffee cup in hand. "I've got to go. Thanks for breakfast."

She almost said *the pleasure was all mine,* but felt strongly it had been mutual.

"I'll call you," he added

She wasn't going to mention that he hadn't asked for her number, or given her an address. She let him say the things, even if he didn't mean them. He leaned over, his free hand snaking behind her neck as he placed a kiss on her lips that felt anything but chaste. Then he grabbed two more butter tarts with a grin, and walked out. Thief. And he's stolen more than just pastry, he'd nabbed a chunk of her resolve.

"Hi Will."

Oh. That voice was familiar. So familiar Faye could see the dark eyebrows raised, the hair pulled back in its perpetual ponytail, the amused twist to the lips. Faye turned slowly as Liv walked in, rolling her fingers at

Faye in a small wave. Will wasn't in view, but he must have held the door open for her.

Liv ordered a coffee, so Faye stayed put. When she asked for a butter tart, Lucy magically found one. She always had a butter tart for Liv. It was like she was trying to fatten the girl up. She almost even smiled when she presented it on its white china plate.

"It's like you knew I was here," Faye said when Liv settled across from her, the seat probably still warm from Will's very fine butt.

"I saw your car out front. And, doing better, right?"

"I think we are. How's the filly this morning?" It was more than rote; she was feeling renewed, the world a brighter place today.

"Good." Liv bit into the butter tart. She was a *three* and *yes*. Faye could tell she was letting those flavours linger before she reached for the coffee. "And how are you this morning?" She drew the words out, eyebrows arcing again.

Faye turned the styrofoam cup slowly, contemplating another butter tart because she was feeling indulgent. A kittenish smile tweaked her mouth. "Good," she said simply.

"It's eleven AM and you're just having breakfast. You never let them stick around that long."

"That's simply circumstance. They always had to be at work before dawn. He doesn't have to be at work till later."

"But you didn't chase him away. And you had breakfast in public."

"You're right. I also shared my butter tarts with him. It might be serious."

Liv's eyes narrowed, like she was trying to glean if there was any truth in the crack.

Faye laughed at her. "So I know one thing for sure. I got more action than you last night."

A tinge of crimson rose in Liv's cheeks. "He caught up with the van and helped unload."

"Is that foreplay? For weird horse girls?"

Liv stuck out her tongue before taking another sip of coffee. "So when are you going to see him again?"

"After the Breeders' Stakes, if things follow their present pattern. Maybe he'll propose then," she quipped. "He did ask me to come down next Monday and hear some music. But no. This was a one and done, sweetie. Mission accomplished. I am back on track."

But a little voice in her head whispered, *the same track? Or a new one?*

WILL HAD NEVER BEEN to Nate's apartment, but for some reason, now seemed like a good time. They were old, old friends; he had to be honest. He wasn't going to keep this from Nate. He texted first, instead of running the risk of wandering aimlessly around that big farm, because that was probably discouraged. Nate texted back, with directions to keep that from happening.

There were gates, which opened as he drove up – no security code needed, though there was a keypad. Tall maples in full plumage on either side of the driveway created a canopy overhead. Nate had said to turn left after the big house – which was mostly hidden by more big trees. He parked the Chevy next to Nate's Mustang and left them there like old friends, catching up.

It was cool inside the barn, and it seemed to be empty. He found the stairs, tromped up, and rapped on the door, balancing the two butter tarts in his cupped palm. Nate's familiar voice called to him to come in.

"Cool space, dude," he said, closing the door behind him. There were shoes on a mat there, so he left his with them. "A real piano, even. How did you get that up here?"

Nate's initial expression of mild surprise at Will's appearance narrowed. "Wait – are those Lucy's butter tarts?" In no time flat he was snatching one, flashing a quick glance up at Will, and heading for the kitchen.

"What happened to the whole jockey weight thing?"

"I'll tack a pound over for one of those. Or put time in the sweatbox if I have to. It'll be worth it." He set the tart on a plate with reverence. "You have to warm them up a little. Make the filling a bit runny." He set the plate in the microwave, beeping in a time. "Here, give me the other one."

Will obeyed, exchanging it for the hot tart Nate handed him. He parked himself on one of the stools at the kitchen counter.

"You slept with her, didn't you?" Nate said, not entirely without accusation, before biting into the hot pastry he'd just nuked, blowing out and fanning his mouth.

It seemed pointless to answer when Nate had clearly already figured it out. Either way, he didn't want to be grilled about it, so he ignored it, deflecting with his own question. "So do I remember you saying you actually don't pay rent here? I'd think you'd actually have to be sleeping with the owner's daughter to get away with that." Will grinned.

"What can I say, they like me." Nate's tone was abrupt "So are you here just to tell me about Faye?"

He wasn't just going to let it slide. "What's there to talk about, really? I wanted you to know first hand. Because the way things work in your tight little world, I'm sure you'd hear about it soon enough. You might already know."

Nate opened the fridge, grabbing two bottles of water. "No. Did you think Faye was going to text me or something? Like, 'take that, you bastard.'"

"You think she's using me? It was some kind of revenge move?"

"No, actually, I don't," Nate responded quietly. "And I should probably just keep my thoughts to myself. You're both adults."

"Why are you so out of sorts about this? You look like you're happy with Liv."

"I am, okay? I don't know why. Just be careful. For both your sakes."

"You could say we'd been on three dates, so except for the part where you have a bug up your ass, it's perfectly acceptable, isn't it?"

"Three dates?" Nate nudged one of the bottles of water over the counter then opened the other one.

"I drove her home after your Plate Party, which was your idea, as I recall. I came and helped with the hay. I hung out with her and drove her home after the race yesterday. It's more normal that you and Liv. Do you guys even see each other outside of work? I think I have the potential for a healthier relationship with her than what you've got."

That made Nate laugh. "You may be right. Damn, I need to work on that."

"Seriously." Will grinned. He picked up the water, and turned back to the room, scanning the space. "So you think we could come here sometimes? It would give you a break from driving into the city all the time."

Nate shrugged. "There are three of you, and only one of me. Plus not sure the noise would be welcome, with the horses and all. And along the same lines, the only thing that gets me off this place is work, so, balance?"

"Why don't you bring Liv down sometime?"

"Maybe I'll ask her. That doesn't mean she'll come."

"How come you never brought Faye down?"

Nate met the look Will gave him, looking a little grim, a little regretful.

"She told you that, did she?" He paused. "I wasn't really coming that often when I was seeing her anyway, I guess. My career was new. She was new. Maybe it was something deeper, I don't know. Like I was keeping her in her own compartment, because of what happened with Cindy. What if you two had hit it off then? She would have ditched me a whole lot sooner than she did."

"Would have saved you both a whole lot of grief though, right?" He finished off the tart in two bites. Nate was right, it was way better warm, but that wasn't news.

Nate smirked, like he didn't appreciate Will stating the obvious. "You're a jerk. Can you get out of here? I have to ride tonight, and after being so late last night, I'm exhausted. I need sleep."

Will walked to the door, Nate following. "Oh, one more thing. My dad's in town, to get married, believe it or not. He invited me, and you, and whoever we want to bring with us. It's in a few weeks. Please, please, *please* say you'll come?"

"You're really testing this friendship, you know."

Will slapped him on the arm, and reached for the door. "You're the best, buddy. Talk to you soon."

WILL CHECKED his texts as he towel-dried his hair. Monique asking for a ride to work. His neighbour three doors down saying she was away for a few days, could he feed her cat, for the millionth time in the last month. *Yeah, absolutely*, he responded to both. Nate was doing him a huge favour, saying he'd come to the wedding; the least he could do was pay it forward.

The cat's name was Clementine, but Will just called her Lemon. She was a little tabby with white on her chest and extending down her front legs, and was waiting with meow on repeat when Will unlocked the door. He scooped her up and scratched her behind her ears, and she vibrated against his chest.

"What would you like for lunch, *chérie*?" He opened the fridge, found an open tin of wet cat food, and portioned out a couple of spoons into a small dish. "Et voilà! Tuna *tartine*." Not exactly, but it sounded better than Fancy Feast, which probably had little to no tuna in it anyway. *"Bon appétit."* His entire French vocabulary was related to food.

He filled another bowl with kibble, gave her fresh water, then leaned up against the counter to watch her eat. He found himself wondering if Faye liked cats. Maybe they just had barn cats. They had a dog, a goofy bear of a Golden. Which led him to wondering if Dean had stayed in Fort Erie to get laid, or just to go drinking with his buddies. Either way, it had worked out just fine as far as Will was concerned.

Lemon finished the wet food, took one sniff of the dry, and wafted over to him, rubbing against his legs with fresh pleas. He lifted her again. "Sorry, *chérie*. Your mom says you have to watch your waistline. It sucks, I know. He placed her back down, and tried not to trip over her as he headed for the door. "I'll see you later. Some of us have to work for a living."

Work. That talk of dreams last night was getting to him. Actually being in that plain old café with the for lease sign, imagining what it could be. What would it be like having a partner? Someone smart and bold like Faye to handle the business side, which he admittedly struggled with. He'd bet she'd do a business plan, and have spreadsheets, and all that stuff that made him shudder. Then he could focus on the creative side. The menu. The right beans. He could handle the kitchen equipment they'd need. Sourcing it. Setting up an SOP. Training staff – when they got that far. Live music nights, a bookshelf, local …he needed to call that number, and find out more.

Enough of that. Better get Monique. It would be a bad thing for both of them to be late. Chef would explode.

He was the guy with the car. Few people in the city had them. It made sense – parking was a nightmare, and transit was so readily available. But he'd come east with his, and needed to hang onto it, for the same reason Nate hung onto that Mustang: because it was part of his history. But it meant he was the one his co-workers called on when their usual rides fell through, or transit wasn't going to work, or they didn't have money for a taxi. He was the guy with the car. How did you say no?

Monique was waiting, her blonde hair in a bobbing ponytail, her makeup perfect. She immediately started chattering away, and he tried to act like he was paying attention, while mostly tuning her out. She seemed extra-superficial today.

"So how was your race thingy? How did your friend do?"

"What?" The race thingy seemed like a different lifetime now. "Good. Great, really. He won."

"That's amazing! My little sister loves horse racing. She probably knows all about it. What was the race name?"

Will relayed the info – actually remembering Prince of Wales because he'd associated it with the Princess of Wales Theatre. Monique keyed something into her phone. Googling it, probably.

"Oh, here it is," she chirped. "He's cute, the jockey. If you like short guys."

Some women do, apparently. Like Faye. Nate, Jiro…that was her thing. And Will had gone ahead last night knowing that. Knowing also he was the rebound, and her way to get past a breakup she'd been clinging to…with his best friend. Maybe he should have heeded Nate's advice.

"That's your friend?"

He glanced at her. "Yeah. Nate. We grew up together, in Calgary."

"That's pretty cool. It says it was like $400,000. Did he win all that?"

"Well – I don't know exactly how it works." Faye could tell him. The way she'd played liaison last night had been pretty damn adorable. "The horse wins it though. But he gets some. He still drives the same old car though, so it can't be that much." Or else he really was just as attached to that old Mustang as Will was to his old Chevy.

Why did everyone want to talk about Nate? Monique didn't even know him, and she'd latched onto the subject. But what else were they going to talk about? No one wanted to talk about work. And he'd never had a conversation with Monique about life dreams or the best books.

He was going to be cool about Faye. He was going to accept that it had been, only, a one-night stand. It wasn't his first. Except…he couldn't shake hoping it was his last.

10

"Coffee's ready." Dean closed the door on the darkness outside, Gus bringing a current of air with him as he rushed to Faye's feet, like the particles were trapped in his thick coat.

Faye stumbled into the brightly-lit kitchen, eyeing the gurgling brew Dean had initiated before he'd gone out to feed. He poured, then handed her a cup, and she breathed the rich vapour in, wishing she could inhale the caffeine until it was cool enough to drink.

"Toast?" Dean asked, setting up a couple of slices in toaster slots.

Faye waved a declining hand at him instead of speaking, and sipped her coffee gingerly. It burned her mouth a little, but the tradeoff was worth it. She consumed enough of it while Dean ate his toast to help her brain cells start to fire, when by rights they should have still been directing dreams.

Once she was in the passenger seat of the truck, she leaned back and closed her eyes, because Dean, thankfully, wouldn't be looking for conversation. She wasn't likely to find REM sleep in the next forty minutes, but it didn't mean she couldn't rest. Two strange mornings in a row…it was taking its toll on her equilibrium. She let her mind go back to yesterday's more preferable scenario, her bed kept warm by the tasty Will.

Just because she was done with that didn't mean she couldn't indulge in some fantasy until someone took his place in her head, did it?

She'd never thought about the future before Nate. It had always been just here and now, because anything could happen to rob you of your plans. She'd gone to school and finished her degree because her parents had set aside money for it, and she'd felt obligated to follow through on the wish they'd had for her. But she'd never thought about what she might do with that degree. What job she could find. As the other students in her program job hunted fervently in the final semesters, she'd rolled along, keeping one disinterested eye on them. Sometimes she scanned the posts on the employment sites, but when she'd graduated, she'd continued to help Dean, who was having a good enough few years to support her under-achiever lifestyle. She took on some local and track bookkeeping jobs to stay out of trouble. Well, mostly out of trouble.

Then there had been Nate. She'd let herself imagine things with him she'd never allowed to enter her head before. Not things she'd ever shared with him – she knew better than that – but they'd worked their way in all the same. A house together. Kids. She'd joked to him once, on the beach in Florida, about being a kept woman. Nate's success probably would have let her be just that. They'd never talked any more seriously than that about it, because about the time she'd realized that's what she was thinking, she'd also realized he'd started thinking that way about someone else. And not with just anyone else. With her best friend.

And truth was, she didn't want to be kept. Like Liv, she didn't want to stop being who she was, and wasn't sure how that would work within the confines of a relationship. She'd told herself, and believed it, that that was why she preferred short-term liaisons. She had Dean to keep her company. Dean had help to work the farm. What did Faye need a man for, but entertainment? Except the older she got, the more it wore thin. The more she wondered if it was actually a subconscious safeguard, instead of what she liked to think of as a feminist stance. That by keeping things brief and unemotional she got out before she exposed herself to the seated fear of losing them like she'd lost Shawn, and her parents.

Liv doing the unfathomable, finally getting together with Nate, left Faye feeling she'd lost her one ally when it came to her perspective on men. Emilie might be single, but there was no doubt in anyone's mind she would have a normal, stable relationship one day. She was the sensible, sane one in their group. She'd take her time and be choosy, and end up with Mr. Right, while Faye continued with an endless stream of Mr Right Nows.

She hadn't answered Will Tuesday night when he'd asked her why she was so mad at Nate, because that would have meant letting it go. Part of it was because she could never be truly mad at Liv. Liv had fought it so long – not just the idea of Nate, but the idea of anyone at all – that it was hard to deny her the prospect of someone who saw her. A someone who wouldn't have ever legitimately been happy with Faye. For some reason that seemed to make her extra-mad at Nate. The nerve of him, making her fall for him. Like it had been all his fault. If she let herself, though, she saw that the relationship with him had opened her up to the possibility of such a thing. So here she was, at a crossroads. Did she close herself back off, or push ahead?

Where had all that come from, when Will had been nestled so nicely in her head? She was not thinking of a future with him in it. She'd established that already.

Will stirred something else in her, though, like he'd inadvertently issued a challenge. A *dare to dream,* when she'd been so committed to not letting herself do that. To not think *what if.* It was bigger than her relationship goals, or lack thereof. Will had made her aware that she was, just under the surface, dissatisfied with her life. That this was not enough.

How dare he rouse her out of her stagnation, make her think she could have more. More than taking care of her brother. More than being taken care of by him. More than maintaining her parents' legacy. Wasn't that important, though? Who said she got to have her own dream? She'd given that up, accepted it wouldn't be her lot in life just like Dean had given up on his education, something he'd dedicated a lot more to than she had, before the accident that had reduced their family to just the two of them.

She liked her life. How had Will come along, and in one night, made that a lie?

Faye stirred when the truck slowed, and opened one eye as Dean pulled up to the security booth at the east gate. He held his hand out for her license, and she fumbled through her purse, and planted it in his palm. The guard scanned them and sent them on.

"Why are you having Nate breeze Wampum?" Faye mumbled, trying to remember why last night it had seemed important for her to come. Except for some reason the colt's work seemed significant, like it would unlock this future she was so worked up about.

"Because I want his opinion. He knows the colt. He's ridden him every time he's run."

Dean had thrown everything into that horse's rehab, investing money Wampum had earned back into the colt. Faye had worried he might be rushing Wampum by bringing him back when he had – stress fractures usually meant a solid three months of stall rest – and while Dean wasn't one to take chances, maybe this year had made him feel the pressure. On the farm Wampum had received body work, magnetic therapy, and these funky new patches – so much woo Faye had wondered if they might have some sort of weird interaction and cause more harm than good – but when Dean had sent Wampum for scintigraphy to check how the shoulder was healing, the nuclear scan had come back miraculously clean. Now with any luck, the colt would reimburse him for his diligence. Not many trainers would micromanage like that. But that was Dean, through and through.

"Well he can't ride him this time," Faye felt the need to point out. Because Dean had dog-eared the Breeders' Stakes in the condition book with Wampum's name scribbled on it, and everyone knew exactly who Nate would be on that day. A certain filly with a chance to win the Canadian Triple Crown.

Dean laughed. "I know that. I can't always make my rider choices based on your latest love interest, you know."

"That was almost mean, Dean." She smirked. "Who will you get to ride him?"

"Probably Steve. We'll see how Jiro does with She Brews, but if he doesn't win with her I'm putting Nate back on. The bug might be hot right now, but he is still pretty inexperienced, and the Breeders' isn't just any race. "

Faye nodded. Steve Gordon was a nice, uncomplicated choice. A veteran rider who had ridden for their father. Neutral, in the grand scheme of things.

The shedrow was a chaotic, scary place this time of morning, when you were just a little afraid of these unpredictable animals. Sure, some horses walked around quietly, but there were enough crazies to put the fear of God into her. She stood with her back pressed against the metal Dutch doors of Wampum's stall while Dean leaned causally on the bar, looking in. Faye caught Nate's arrival out of the corner of her eye.

"'Morning," he said, his tone businesslike. No smart-ass comments about her unexpected presence.

"Hey." Her eyes didn't quite meet his.

"How's our boy?" Nate asked, and Dean shuffled over so they were both looking in.

"He's been training great," Dean said. "If he breezes well, I'll prep him for the Breeders'."

"He's gonna love the turf," Nate said, nodding. "Not the first time I wish I could ride two horses in the same race."

Last time Chique and Wampum had run against each other had been the Fountain of Youth at Gulfstream Park last winter. *Bet you wish you were on our colt that day.* Wampum had run third, while Chique floundered up the track, letting everyone know her disdain for the sloppy conditions.

"I'm going to watch from the bleachers," Faye said as they went to the track, walking far enough out to the side that she was out of harm's way. She split off from them before Dean led Wampum through the tunnel, and stayed on the paved road, giving little smiles and waves when someone would call out to her. Then she cut across the horse path and up the steps, coming out at the backstretch of the turf course.

She was alone here, and it was a better vantage point than at the clocker's stand where most of the trainers gathered. It was more elevated, and further east, so she had a better view. Not that it really mattered to her; her understanding of the finer points was minimal. She just recognized the extremes. The two-year-olds galloping slowly but eagerly in sets; the older, fitter horses on the bridle, their exercise riders with strong holds; the bad actors, crow-hopping sideways, riders cussing into their ears; the workers flying smooth and rapid on the rail.

Nate would be jogging Wampum, going the wrong way on the outside fence, to the wire over on the front side of the track. She didn't try to follow their progress, just observed the horses going by, gazing down towards the turn by the on-gap, trying to recall what Nate had been wearing. He had a navy and red helmet cover, navy jacket, stone-washed jeans. Wampum was a plain bay, and from this angle she wouldn't see the red and white saddle pad, so she looked for a plain bay, red and white helmet, red polo bandages. There they were.

Wampum was still galloping in the middle of the track, relaxed, Nate perched nonchalantly. Then Nate eased him to the rail, his body position changing, and Wampum's ears went up, like he was saying, *oh, really?* His stride quickened, so when they reached the red and white half-mile pole he was taking flight, all business now with his neck stretched in front of him and legs firing as they headed into the turn.

Faye didn't really know if this was fast, or slow, just that it looked like a joyful thing, and Nate wasn't doing much, which meant Wampum was going the way he should.

She didn't wait to watch them gallop out, stepping carefully down the bleachers, looking both ways on the horse path to make sure she didn't spook anyone. She glanced over at the Triple Stripe shed just across the road – a horse grazed on the lawn, and there was activity apparent on the shed – but she didn't see Liv or Em. Then she hurried along the road so she was there by the time Dean, back at Wampum's head, emerged from the tunnel. She heard him ask for the colt's time, saw Nate nodding, and Dean's satisfied smile. That's all she needed to know. They were happy. She followed them back to the barn.

"Where do you have to go next, Nate?" Faye asked, making it sound like she was trying to be polite.

His eyebrow twitched, like he'd caught himself before it got too high, and he dunked the bit in the water bucket. "Trixie Bigsby's."

She nodded. Not Triple Stripe. Good.

"Listen," he said, and Faye froze. He set the tack on the rail. "I'm having a…thing, next week."

"A thing?" Dean looked perplexed, and Faye exhaled. She'd thought he was going to say something about Will.

"Like a get-together. At the farm. Because we couldn't really do anything after the Prince of Wales. I hope you'll both come."

Faye's lips tightened.

"Thanks for the invite," Dean said. "But I'm off to Saratoga for a couple of days."

"Seriously?" Nate said. "Now I'm jealous. If you're running something and didn't ask me to come, especially."

"No. Just getting a couple of days away."

"Jiro said he'd come. To the thing." Nate was gauging Faye's response, like it was a test, but that carrot wasn't as enticing as it would have been a few days ago. Had Liv told him? Unlikely. Will? Would he do that?

I'll have to check my schedule. I think I have plans. Like oral surgery or something more pleasant than your little get-together. But she forced a smile, without answering at all.

"Have fun at the Spa, Dean. Bye, Faye." And then he was, thankfully, gone.

"I'm going to see Liv," she said to her brother. "I should be back before you go, but don't leave without me unless you hear differently."

Liv wasn't in the tack room, so Faye headed straight to Chique's stall, right beside the office. Because where else would Liv be, if she wasn't on a horse?

"Hey." She was cleaning out the filly's feet, the little metal pick clinking against the aluminum shoe as she cleared edges, then scraped out the deeper parts. Faye knew what the frog was, but that was about it. Liv gave the foot a quick brush so there was probably not a speck of dirt left in there, painted it with oil, then placed it down gently in the straw before reaching under to slide her fingers down the right leg. Chique lifted, Liv picked and brushed and painted. She straightened, then moved closer to the door, to Faye, and Chique's hindquarters. "What are you doing in this morning?"

"Dean worked Wampum. First time since the accident. Felt like I should be here, for some reason."

"Oh yeah. Nate mentioned he was working him. How'd he go?"

"They were all happy. One day at a time I guess, right?"

It always was, with every horse. The horse who was going great one day could pull up sore the next. Or blow apart into a million tiny pieces.

Faye's phone buzzed with a generic tone, and by the time she glanced at the screen, the notification had faded. Some spam text probably. While

Liv finished Chique's hind feet, Faye opened the phone, and found it in the unknown senders file. It was an address in Toronto. So very random.

She was going to delete it, when a second text came through from the same number.

This is Will, BTW. Come down Monday if you can make it. 2pm.

A silly, happy, warm feeling flowed through her as a smile spread over her face. She seriously needed an antidote for that, because she was not… repeat, NOT, going to fall for this guy.

11

The big black tom twirled between her legs, hopping into her lap when she sat down outside on the deck with a cup of coffee, his motor running at steady RPMs. Faye stroked his sleek coat. He popped by every so often, making like he was homeless when he was clearly well-fed. This is how she liked her cats – just like she liked her men. Short uncomplicated visits, enjoy each others' company, no commitment or expectations. No hard feelings when the visits stopped.

Which is why she probably shouldn't be going down to Will's this afternoon. She was going off-script. She could call him, now that she actually had his number, and tell him she couldn't make it. Stop this thing before it went any further into dangerous territory.

Her phone rang and she grabbed for it, sending the tom scrambling to the deck. Local number. *You were hoping it was Will, weren't you?*

"Hello?"

"Hi Faye. It's Lucy. Is your offer to talk still open?"

Faye stood abruptly and rushed for the door. "It is, definitely. Would you like me to come over?"

After they talked, Lucy sent her off with a fresh half-dozen butter tarts, and the rare feeling that for once, things were going her way.

"How do you get away with a place like this in downtown Toronto? It's fabulous!"

Faye looked up, and around, mouth gaping at the old hardwood floors and brick walls. It was one big room, with a curtained-off section where she assumed the bed, and probably bathroom, were; a simple kitchen; a sitting area; and the music studio. He had everything: guitars, a keyboard, a drum set, and it didn't end there. Inspiration and creativity filled the place. *I could live here,* she almost said, but caught herself. That might sound like she was thinking this was more than it was.

"Thanks," Will said, his expression invitingly uncomplicated.

She found her eyes drifting towards the curtain, and snapped her head back to him. "I come bearing gifts." Faye held out the butter tarts, and grinned.

Will swept them away. "Do I have to share?"

A cat pushed out from the curtain, a pretty little tabby with a white chest, and it piqued her curiosity further. *Music, Faye. He invited you here for music.* Not the things she could think of doing with him behind that curtain.

"I never would have pegged you for a cat person." She crouched down to distract herself again, finding a spot behind the kitty's ear that made her purr. Maybe she wasn't exactly a cat person, but this one seemed sweet. It shouldn't have surprised her that Will had a nice cat.

"I'm not."

"Then why do you have a cat?"

"I don't."

Faye laughed at him, watching as not-his-cat drifted directly to him, rubbing against his leg. "Are you sure about that?"

"It's my neighbour's cat. I feed the cat when she's away for work. She's away so often, this time I asked if the cat could come here instead of me going to her apartment. I'm usually getting in so late, it's just more convenient."

"Looks like you've been adopted. What's her name?"

He picked the cat up, and ruffled her head fondly "Lemon. It's really Clementine, but that's what I call her."

"You renamed her cat?"

"Just extrapolated."

"So you have a part-time cat, and a part-time band…how do you have time for a full-time job?"

"You ask a lot of questions for a guest, you know."

"Just making conversation."

"Do you want something to drink?"

"What are you offering?"

Not alcohol, as it turned out. Restaurant worker, it wouldn't be responsible to serve her when she'd driven here, would it? He brewed tea, set two butter tarts on mismatched plates, and offered her a seat at his little, wooden, kitchen table. He really was too nice.

"This is all very civilized," she said, sipping.

"I'm glad you came."

She could only hold his gaze for a moment before hers dropped to her cup, fingers curled around it. "I want to be clear about this, right from the start." She squared her shoulders, pressing them against the back of the chair, and lifted her eyes again. "I don't do long term. Perhaps you've already heard that. What happened with Nate was an unexplained blip in the space-time continuum, and I don't intend to let anything like it happen again. I like you. We've spent several hours in a car together and not killed each other. The other night was amazing, but can we agree not to ruin things with feelings?"

His eyes lit with amusement. "Sure. I'm good with that. I'm not looking for some happily ever after here, Faye. I'll leave that to guys like Nate."

Faye tilted her head, the corner of her lips curving up. "It might be too bad though, because I think you could be my soulmate." She grinned right back at him, and almost broke into laughter, except the door opened, and two of his musical friends shuffled in.

"Better make quick work of that butter tart, or things might get ugly in here." Will popped his into his mouth whole, and got to his feet.

He introduced her to the others as a friend. She recognized them from the Plate Party, and wondered if they knew how he knew her; knew about Nate. They didn't seem to care, though. Balancing her cup of tea in one hand, and stroking Lemon with the other, she settled into a battered leather love seat to listen. She could think of worse ways to kill a couple of hours.

After thirty minutes, Will stilled the strings on his guitar. Faye hadn't missed the keyboard one bit.

"What'll it take to get you to sing with us, Faye?"

She set the empty cup carefully to the side, and continued to attend to Lemon. "I'm occupied here, so nothing, I'm sorry." She smiled her best fake-sweet smile.

"Pick a song. Any song." He strummed a chord, then paused, his mouth twisting up as he thought. Then he started playing *Brown Eyed Girl.*

So not fair. She loved that song, but it's not like he could know. It was just an obvious choice.

*Sha-la-la, la-la...*she couldn't help joining in on that bit. And she hoped he didn't notice her blush when he sang the bit about...

"And on that note...thanks," she said, waving her fingers airily and pushing out of the cushions when the song was over. "I'm going to go before I wear out my welcome."

"We're just getting warmed up!" Will protested, still smiling a somewhat victorious smile.

"It was so nice meeting you all, though!" She sashayed towards the door, when she really wanted to stay. She felt so light and floaty. It was ridiculous, and wonderful. They sounded amazing. Especially because Nate wasn't there.

So why was he approaching her on the sidewalk outside the building? There was no way she could duck him, even though she'd seen him first. He looked up, and slowed, stopping the same time she did – a distance away from each other; slightly offset instead of exactly opposite.

Anger was really just a way of keeping harder to accept emotions at bay. Disappointment. Sadness. Shame. She'd thought sleeping with someone else would remove those feelings, let her shove them aside, and maybe it had, for a while, but seeing him, like this, brought them back. Will had known her three weeks, and he'd asked her to come down. *You never once brought me. You sang for her. You never sang for me.*

He didn't ask what she was doing down here. And he wasn't blocking her way, so she could just step aside and move on, not say anything; leave before he spoke. What was there really to say anymore, outside of social situations? She had no obligation here.

It became a weird little face-off, and she'd missed the window where walking on past would have been acceptable. Or less childish, because, really, it wasn't a very mature plan of attack at all.

"Hey," he said hesitantly, and she read his feelings like she was analyzing a wine. A little bit guarded, a touch uncomfortable with a hint of apprehension and what's that last bit? Oooh, irritation.

"Will said you didn't come down on Mondays."

"I usually don't."

She could tell he was going to say something else, explain it, but that it probably had something to do with Liv, so he stopped.

"Well. I'm leaving now. Perfect timing."

"What are you doing, Faye?"

"What are you talking about?" It was more fun to pretend she had no idea what he meant, when she knew exactly. So much more satisfying to make him spit it out than to second-guess.

"With Will."

She shrugged. "Getting to know him. Is that wrong? He's attractive, he's nice, he's interesting." *He doesn't work at the racetrack, his job doesn't involve him risking his neck, he's not in love with my best friend.* "Why can't you just stay out of it?"

"Because he's my friend. And you're…"

"What?" she challenged. But maybe she wanted to know herself, because she wasn't sure what she was right now.

"Hurting," he said.

It was unexpected, the compassion on his face. He wasn't supposed to make her cry. She was supposed to hate him.

"Goodbye, Nate," she said, and pushed past, feeling a jolt of pain as she brushed his arm. She could feel him still watching her, but didn't look back, rubbing a tear off her cheek and looking up at the sky hoping to quell any more.

Where did Nate get off suggesting she didn't have any business getting involved with Will because she was…a mess? She didn't want to marry the guy, she just wanted a change of pace.

He didn't think she was doing with Will what he'd done with her, did he? Gotten invested, involved, when his heart wasn't right. She didn't intend to let her heart play a part in this at all.

There was a stupid saying, *love is not enough.* But lust was. It was spicy and salty; sharp edges and hard surfaces; bites and bruises, motel rooms and kitchen tables. Nate had said sex was easy, like that was a bad thing. What was wrong with easy? What was wrong with just sex? Not everyone wanted to find the love of their life. She wouldn't be fooled again by thinking she might.

She relied on an insecure world to give her security – the racehorse business, a family farm that needed just one bad season to go under, one year of more losses than gains – more injuries than runners, more owners leaving than staying on. Lost layups, lost foals. The ways it could fall apart were endless.

She needed to be proactive. Personally, and professionally. And that meant constantly adjusting to what life threw at her.

12

Emilie and Lucy stood elbow to elbow, the two of them patting unbaked pastry into tins. It still amazed Faye how the woman had softened since she'd officially stepped in to help. Dragging Em with her had been a good move – not that Em had complained. She was in her happy place. The whole shop smelled heavenly.

The bell on the door rattled, announcing a customer's arrival. Faye swept up a tray of fresh tarts, because who could resist them, fresh out of the oven?

"Oh, it's just you," she said, a slight delay to her smile, a tinge of the disquiet she'd been feeling since yesterday afternoon returning.

Liv grinned. "I feel so welcomed."

"You want one of these, I suppose." She shielded the tray with mock protectiveness.

Lucy appeared behind her and scowled before selecting a tart, setting it on a plate, and presenting it to Liv. Then she turned to Faye. "Are you all right if I leave now? You know how to work the cash?"

"Yes, and I have Em for backup."

Lucy nodded. "I'll be back in an hour."

It was like Faye was a puppy Lucy was leaving out of her crate for the first time. If she couldn't handle an hour, she deserved to be fired.

"Come back here, Liv. It's where the magic happens." Faye ushered Liv into the kitchen and set her up with a stool.

Liv snapped a photo of the tart on its plate, then of Faye and Em, the latter dusted with flour.

"Are you going to manage our Instagram account?" Faye asked.

Liv rolled her eyes. "You set up an Instagram account?"

"Of course I set up an Instagram account."

Liv had started keeping one for her riding when she'd been laid up with a broken arm, and surprisingly, it had taken off. She would never admit that she liked doing it. Now of course, it was mostly about Chique and the filly's journey.

"Maybe that could be my contribution. You two seem to be in your element. How are things coming?"

"Lucy is teaching me how to make the tarts," Em said.

"You look as happy – and as messy – as you did when you were six, helping *Maman* with the baking. I think you were about eight when you started to take over."

"Clearly this is what you should have gone to school for, Em," Faye said. "Not all that science stuff."

"Baking is science," Em insisted.

"That's my kind of science," Faye said. "Science you can eat."

"Everything going smoothly with Lucy?" Liv asked.

"So far, so good." Faye nodded.

"You're coming over this afternoon, right?" Liv took another bite of her tart. Faye didn't know how she could make it last that long.

"Oh…I don't know about that. If Dean were here, it might be okay." Faye turned away from her, and fussed with some dirty utensils.

"I get it. But I don't want to be hanging off Nate all afternoon, so I really hope you do come."

Faye sighed. Liv would not easily fall into the role of hostess for this little to-do, and Nate wouldn't expect it of her. Her anxiety over it wasn't reason enough for Faye to voluntarily put herself in Nate's company after yesterday's encounter. Surely Nate had told Liv about it, and Liv would understand that she was asking a lot, requesting Faye's presence for support. Shouldn't this be a loophole in the "do better" pact? Surely Liv could ghost if it became unbearable for her.

"No promises," Faye said.

Liv nodded, excused herself and disappeared, muttering about getting in a run.

When Lucy returned, she shooed Faye and Emilie away, assuring them she'd be fine for the afternoon – because apparently Em had thought it helpful to tell her about this thing. Having the excuse of Lucy needing her would have done quite nicely to get Faye out of it. She didn't want to explain why to Lucy, though.

Just because she was leaving didn't mean she'd go. When she got home, she might not want to leave. This seemed like a great time to binge-watch something on Netflix. The truth was, she didn't want to be alone.

Gus's boisterous welcome at the farmhouse didn't make Dean's absence any less obvious. Why did Nate have to have this thing while Dean was away? If Dean had been here, they could have gone together, made an appearance, and got out, because Dean wouldn't want to stay long. And why hadn't she heard from Dean? He should have made it to Saratoga by now; he'd left early enough.

She'd worry until he remembered she'd worry and finally send her a text saying he'd gotten there okay. She kept herself from texting him to check in; never mentioned to anyone how much it affected her, those long drives her friends took – like Nate and Liv to Florida every winter – all the things that could go wrong and leave her even more alone in this world. Saratoga was only six hours, and it was summer, but anything could happen on the road.

"Come on, Gus. Let's go for a walk." She didn't want to be in the house right now.

At times like this she wished she ran, but she'd never been athletic. If only they could bottle those endorphins Liv lived on. Liv probably created enough of them she could share.

Before the accident, she hadn't really known Dean. With eight years between them, he'd always been in a different stratosphere from her. He'd been away at university before she was even in high school. He might as well have been a cousin – she'd see him on holidays, mostly. He rarely came home for weekends. He was fully invested in his studies, always got good grades, made their mother proud, and their father content he would not end up a slave to the racetrack. Ironic, that.

Their middle brother, Shawn, she'd been close to. Shawn was funny. Shawn made her playlists of great music. He looked out for her when she started high school. Vetted her potential first boyfriends. He was the quintessential big brother. When he'd decided to go to Queen's for his undergrad, she'd felt abandoned.

He kept in touch, sending her texts of funny things, sharing new music, writing her emails, sometimes even sending snail mail. And unlike Dean, Shawn always came home whenever he could, even though he was three hours away. He'd take a bus, or a train, or catch a ride with one of his school friends who came from the area. But Faye was still harbouring anger towards him for going so far away, so she hadn't joined her parents that February weekend, when they'd picked him up and gone on to visit cousins in Ottawa.

They didn't make it there.

They should have stayed overnight in Kingston and left in the morning, waited for the snowstorm to pass.

Faye should have been with them. But then Dean would have been alone. She felt guilty for not being with them, and guilty for wishing she had.

Gus bounded past the barns – he knew their route – and Faye called him every so often so she didn't lose him. She was pretty sure he'd return, but wasn't about to risk finding out. She couldn't bear the thought of anything happening to him, either.

Dean could easily have shipped her off to the cousins in Ottawa, her rightful guardians, but while he'd presented that option, he'd offered to move back. Faye was sure both affection and responsibility had contributed to that, but she was willing to bet the horses had been a big part. It was his chance to train; what he'd wanted to do all along.

In the bigger pasture out back, the foals, sleek with their new grown-up coats, galloped up and raced Gus along the fenceline. He barked once and Faye called him away – fun and games with young horses quickly turned to vet bills, and possibly, permanent damage, if one of them slipped, or ran into a fence. Those foals were the farm's future. Whether Dean decided to sell them as yearlings, or kept them to race and sold pieces of them to partners…they were commodities. It was the only way Faye could let herself think of them. They were beautiful, but they were fragile, and one freak accident could break your heart and kill the hopes you'd piled upon them.

Faye kept it all as numbers. She would let the others lose their souls to it. She didn't know how they stayed sane. That was just it, though – were they?

SHE HAD BERMUDA SHORTS ON – leaving not nearly enough of those gorgeous legs bare for his eyes – and a loose, long-sleeved shirt tied over a tank top. Hair blowing around her face, sunglasses giving her an air of mystery, until one side of her mouth curved, pushing her cheek up, creating a dimple. How had he not noticed that before?

"Hello," she said. "You might be trespassing, you know."

The big Golden Retriever gambolled over, ears flopping with each stride, and landed in a sit at Will's feet. He held the paper bag he was carrying to the side, and reached down with his other hand to stroke the dog's head. "He seems happy I'm here."

"He's not the best judge of character. Gus would welcome an intruder and make him tea." She crossed her arms, one hip jutting out, the dimple disappearing and a hint of aloofness creeping in. "To what do I owe the honour?"

"I was in the area."

"Right."

She obviously wasn't buying it, even though it was true.

"I'm headed over to Nate's."

"Oh. His thing." Disdain dripped off her words.

"Aren't you coming?"

"No, I think not."

"Why not?"

"You are not that dense. I got blindsided yesterday when I left your place, and ran right smack into him. You said he wasn't coming."

She was simmering, looking as if she was yearning for a fight, and Will felt a little blindsided himself. Nate hadn't told him that.

"I didn't know he was coming, Faye. He just showed up. I guess because we couldn't get together this afternoon. I'm sorry, all right? You have to believe I wouldn't set you up like that." He wished she wasn't wearing those sunglasses so he had some hope of reading her, because right now she was a wall; her voice, her face, her stance, everything.

He sighed. "So you would send me on my own. Among those weirdos without my interpreter."

An eyebrow crimped, but there was no smile accompanying it. He wanted that dimple back. "I don't work for free, you know. The Prince of Wales was just a sample of my talents."

"Do you accept payment in pastry?" He held out the bag.

She rushed up to take it, tucking the hair on one side behind an ear as best she could in the breeze, the dog bouncing out of the way. *So, that's all it took.* First she peeked in, then she peered over her sunglasses at him through her dark lashes.

"I'll have to sample the currency." Her voice was like honey on toast, smooth and sweet on the surface, crisp underneath.

"I have cappuccino in the car."

Finally the corner of her lips pulled up on one side, but not quite enough to create the dimple. "Let's have the cappuccino, then I'll make my decision."

She wasn't following him closely, but he could feel the heat coming from her, sense her eyes on him as he leaned into the Chevy and lifted the tray. After closing the door he rested against it. Let her come to him if she wanted it.

Her lips were playing a game, but her eyes were hidden again, not visible to give any clues. She stepped in, resting a hand on the tray as she worked the cup free. She lifted the lid open a crack, as if she didn't believe it was what he'd promised, and followed her visual inspection with a deep whiff. Finally satisfied he was telling the truth, she turned on her heel and marched up the steps to the deck.

"I don't really want to go to this thing either," he said.

She paused, glancing over her shoulder. "So why are you going?"

He wasn't going to tell her that. Because while Nate hadn't mentioned running into Faye, he had asked, before leaving, if Will would come, and if he might see if Faye would come with him and that had been enough. A chance to see her again, and with what might be construed as Nate's blessing? He'd started making the pastry as soon as the guys had left.

He watched her drift to a chair and plop into it, crossing her legs. She opened the bag and reached in, then lifted out one of his little creations, fingers pressing into the creamy mousse as she put her lips around it and closed down. Her eyes closed, and she went still.

"If you keep me in these, I'll do just about anything." She slid him a loaded glance over the shades, sipped the cappuccino, then finished the other bite. "Though I'm not sure I'd call that pastry."

"It's just easier to say than *petit fours,"* he explained.

"Liv or Em could help you with that. Details, though. I'll have to save the others as my reward for after."

She rolled the top of the bag, gave him a smirk, and ducked into the house, but didn't invite him in. He thought about following anyway, because really, neither of them wanted to go, and they could have considerable fun right here.

When she returned, the bag was gone and she'd done something with her hair. Because he'd missed his chance to get his hands on her, he'd just have to enjoy the visual as she closed the door – the way her lines smoothly curved from the hint of her ribcage under her shirt, in to her waist, and back out to her hip. She locked the door and turned, the outer screen door shutting with a click behind her.

For a beat he was pretty sure she was doing her own examination, the sunglasses propped on her head, eyes roving from the top of him to his toes and back again, as if she were mentally mapping his body. When her gaze returned to his, she held it for another beat, then dropped the shades.

"So?"

He shook off the involuntary tremor that fired through him like some kind of energetic residue from her perusal. "Are you coming in my car?"

"Sure," she said, and started walking towards it. "If you decide to ditch me for one of the cute farm girls, I'll understand. It's not that far of a walk."

"So you don't think Nate invited me to distract me from you?" He grinned at her, catching up.

"Hmm, it's like that, is it? Interesting."

He wasn't sure it was, anymore.

"He's been very much an enabler with Jiro, now that I think of it,"

Faye continued. "Which means we should totally go together. And be all over each other. Just to drive him crazy."

Will laughed. He wasn't going to have a problem with that plan, except the part where it was supposed to be an act.

It was a modest gathering. While Nate put on a good show, he didn't really like people much more than Liv did; he just had a higher tolerance. Reason number three-hundred and ninety-nine why they were so suited to each other. At least they'd finally admitted it.

Faye really, really hadn't wanted to come. She was blaming the pastry. The way to her heart, apparently. No, not her heart, exactly. But she needed to be on her guard, keep that heart in check, just in case all that sugar was weakening it. Stick to the script. No ad-libbing.

Nate lived in an apartment over the smaller barn that also housed Triple Stripe's office. While Faye had been to the farm many times over the duration of her friendship with Liv, she'd never spent time with Nate here when they were together; he'd always come to Northwest. Which was understandable, because while the farm wasn't the track, there was overlap, and it still felt like being on display, when he was high enough profile to want a break from that. Now Faye wondered it had just been him keeping a sanctuary, never quite letting her in.

She'd always thought Triple Stripe a strange name for a farm and racing stable, not that there was any shortage of strange names in the business. Liv had explained it to Faye once – it had something to do with Acadian heritage on her father's side, the Acadian flag based on the French flag of blue, white, and red. Their silks didn't exactly copy the flag, just the colours, and the idea, to an extent. They weren't as boring as the Northwest silks. So many things she could do with those silks, given the okay.

It wasn't as fancy as some of the big farms in Ontario, but it was definitely less rustic than Northwest, and larger. Outside money, that's what it took. Liv's father was an investment banker – which Faye probably should have leveraged into some kind of internship that would have provided her with a more substantial income. Given that, the farm was modest – the house was big, a custom design– but the barns were practical instead of showy. It was all well kept though. Things seemed to get fixed a lot faster than Dean managed at Northwest.

But Faye wasn't looking for sympathy. It was that whole, be careful what you wish for thing. Bigger farm meant bigger responsibility. She had a hard enough time with the idea of leaving their little farm. Part of why Liv had dropped out of school was because she was trying to get away from the expectations associated with being part of that family. Her mother had wanted her to be a vet, and control freak that she was, Liv would have taken on the farm's work, and the track work, and made herself miserable, because track work was more about injecting joints and jugulars than problem-solving.

Faye fully expected Liv to take over the farm one day; she was already so involved with the management of it. She wasn't about to oust the Lachance's trainer out of his job, so if she didn't go back to riding, short of going back to school and finishing that veterinary degree, what was she going to do with herself? She didn't suffer from the whole underachiever thing Faye did. She'd get restless. The girl needed to learn how to relax and enjoy life.

And maybe Faye could use a touch of her seriousness and drive. Whatever.

Will pulled up next to Nate's Mustang, and waited for Faye to climb out before locking it. She gave him a look.

He shrugged. "Habit from living in the city."

He fell into stride beside her, and she toyed with the idea of taking his hand. Too much? She'd decided not to change her clothes for that reason. All she'd done was brush the tangles out of her hair and sweep it up off her neck.

A couple of picnic tables that weren't usually there had been set near the paddock fences; a spread of food just inside the open end of the barn, a clean muck bucket filled with ice and loaded with soft drinks. Horses were everywhere at this place, and Faye even recognized Claire, the mare who, as a two-year-old, had taken Liv to New York promising to jumpstart her riding career. Reality hadn't been as smooth as that. It rarely was.

No alcohol. Interesting. A small crowd. The Triple Stripe crew from the track stood in one group, the farm staff in another, and as promised,

Jiro, off to the side with Em. Then, of course, Nate and Liv. Nate was dressed not unlike Will, jeans and a neat polo shirt. Liv had donned a skirt and white blouse, her default simple, pretty, always elegant, though she never looked entirely comfortable out of jeans and a t-shirt.

"Dean sends his regrets," Faye said. She'd finally had a text from him on the drive over. There was a faint odour of horses and manure wafting through the air. It barely registered for her, but she wondered if it bothered Will.

"We're not feeling sorry for him, getting to go to Saratoga." Nate grinned.

"Saratoga?" Will asked.

It was so cute when he got that mystified look. He was so wonderfully out of place with these people. Faye had gotten used to being the black sheep – in both her own family, and the greater racing community. It was nice to have someone more displaced around.

"Saratoga Springs, New York," Faye said, falling into the expected role, earning her sweets. She glanced up at him, and caught his eye, part of a smile, their little shared joke. *Oh no, now they were sharing jokes.* "For about six weeks in the middle of the summer, the racing meet in New York State shifts there. Everyone who knows anything about horse racing in North America wants to go. It's a big thing."

"Are you included in that? Or…"

"On the fringes, perhaps. It's not just about the horses. It's about what happens to the town when they're there. I'd go for sure."

"You've never been?"

"No. Somehow I've never pulled it off."

"Have you guys?" Will looked at Liv and Nate.

Faye did too, finding Liv's eyes appraising her. Faye tried to give her an *it's not what you think* look back.

"Twice, very briefly, myself," Nate said.

"I rode there the last three summers," Liv said.

"Like doing the jockey thing?" Will asked.

Liv nodded. "Seems like a long time ago now."

"Chique, next summer," Nate insisted, capturing Liv's attention with that grin of his.

Liv laughed. "Maybe we can focus on trying to win the Triple Crown first?"

They did balance each other. Liv so cautious, Nate gung-ho for the next great accomplishment. They seemed to manage to meet in the middle and make the best of it, professionally. Maybe, in time, Nate would draw Liv out more. Faye hadn't been able to get too far, but guys always seemed to get women to change in ways they'd never thought possible. He'd already managed to do that, without scaring Liv off. That was an achievement, with Liv.

"So, does that mean we could go?" Will was still stuck on Saratoga. "I don't need a horse passport or card or something?"

It's we *now?* She caught herself. She'd forgotten for a minute this was a performance "Sure. No horse card needed. And I hear there's an amazing French bakery there."

"Mmmm, yes." Liv nodded. "It's worth the trip just for Mrs. London's."

"What are we waiting for?" Will asked.

The idea was so tempting. *I would go, in a heartbeat. If this were only real.* Would she? "We'll have to figure that out. Now all that talk of a French bakery has me hungry, and no pastry in sight." She gave him another sideways look, then felt the beginnings of a flush tingeing her flesh, thinking of him in her kitchen last week, and the *petit fours* she'd left there not long ago, and how both those things held so much potential deliciousness. Later, perhaps. She glanced from Nate to Liv. "Where's the food?"

"This way." Liv swept an arm to the side, dropping a sweet but subtle look to Nate before stepping past him towards the barn. Faye didn't have any trouble picking up on the signal.

"You're safe with Nate, I trust? He can interpret in my absence." Faye leaned in, touching Will's arm, then murmured, "I bet he'll do it for free." She caught up with Liv, and scanned the table in the barn.

"Couldn't wait for the Breeders'?" Liv said, looking at Faye pointedly as she stuck a carrot stick in her mouth and chomped off the end.

"He showed up at my house with pastry. What can I say."

"I don't know, Miss Taylor of Northwest. I think you're being courted." A teasing smile tickled her lips.

Faye looked at her skeptically. "What have you been reading? That sounds so Regency."

"I had a lot of time when I was in Fort Erie."

"I bet you did. If you're looking for an instruction manual, I'm not sure that's the way to go. I could make suggestions. Though I bet that's about the right speed for you two."

"Ha ha." Liv handed Faye a plate before taking one for herself and selecting more veggies and some dip – like she was calculating calories as she went. Old habits died hard. "I'm glad you came."

"Thank Will."

"You seem to like each other."

"We've spent quality time stuck in a car together. We bonded." So there had been sex. So there might be more.

"And you get on me for being cautious. You're one to talk."

Faye glanced at her, then focused on the food. With no alcohol, she'd better go right for the sweets. "Em's been baking again, I see." Better take two of those brownies. "I'm not being cautious. I'm simply remembering to keep men for what I most need them for. My amusement." She'd better take Will one of the brownies, in case they disappeared. Liv scooped up a couple, and restored Faye's faith in her ability to take care of herself.

They walked back into the sunshine, both of them seeking out Nate and Will. Faye hated the pinch left in her heart for Nate, but the squeeze that followed when her eyes rested on Will took her pulse up a notch for a few beats. Fondness, that was all it was. She was allowed to feel that. He was nice. He was cute. He was funny. Attractive, of course. He was good in bed. There would be time for Jiro. He was a project for another day.

Though Em was still chatting with Jiro. She'd have to quiz Em about that later. They looked cosy, but Em had that effect on people, made them feel comfortable with her cheery, relaxed demeanor. Oh-so-opposite to her sister. The physical resemblance was strong between the two; the emotional, not so much.

Faye re-established herself next to Will, making sure their arms touched, and held up her plate. "The brownies are amazing. Em made them. You have to try." Before he could reach for it, in an inspired moment, she broke off a piece, holding it up to his mouth. He grinned before opening it, and she popped it in, then made sure she carefully licked her fingers.

Neither Nate nor Liv looked terribly upset, much to her disappointment. Oh well. It was still fun. And she did like Will. And Liv. And she'd liked Nate well enough to spend nine months with him. She'd like him well enough again. It might be good, the four or them. Liv and Em were the closest things to sisters she had, so this could be nice. Maybe not if Em was interested in Jiro. That might be a little awkward at the moment. She wasn't into two guys starting to throw around testosterone over her. Em had to find herself a man that would fit.

Em seemed to be introducing Jiro to the farm girls, leaving them to gush with him. She flashed a grin at Faye, then sidled up to Will. Emilie was definitely on Team Will when it came to Faye's future prospects, keeping Jiro away like that.

"Great brownies, Em," Will said, the two of them falling into conversation about baking, which Faye kept one ear to, so no one tried to talk to her about horses. Liv had drifted over to visit Claire, and been cornered by Jiro, who had escaped from the farm girls. Liv made introductions to the horse better than she would a person, and was obviously telling Jiro more about the mare, because it was one thing she could converse happily about. He was a captive audience, looking more comfortable himself.

"Do you really like him?"

Faye's head snapped to Nate, finding his eyes on her. Why did the question make her feel defensive, scrape up her irritation like petting a cat against the hair? His words had been soft, a genuine question –that might have been why. That was the Nate she'd fallen for. He felt stuff – maybe too much sometimes, maybe for the wrong reasons.

"Would that be a problem?" she asked, her lips locked in a line, her own eyes thankfully behind her sunglasses once again, so she didn't give too much away.

"Not if you really like him."

She took a bite of a cookie – more aggressively than she should have. "I get why you don't want him to get involved with me. I don't do relationships. It might not end so well for him. I don't get attached."

"But that's not true, is it?"

It's not like she could deny it, standing across from him, because he knew, first hand. He'd been there. They'd been there.

"You're not my keeper. Or his. But it doesn't matter. I'm not interested. It was just a game, to get on your nerves. But I don't even want to do that. I am so over this feeling."

"You know I understand that, right?"

"How could I know? You never told me anything."

"I'm sorry about that, I really am. And I don't really want to tell you that whole sordid history right now. And maybe never, because it would kind of still feel like I'm hanging onto part of it. And maybe I am, and should acknowledge that. I don't want to rehash us, either. I mean, if you do end up being serious about Will, it would be kind of nice if we could sort of get along."

"For Liv's sake, I assume."

"No. For your sake. For my sake. For our sake. I don't want to hate what we had. And I don't feel bad for breaking your pattern."

"You only interrupted it."

"In that case, that's too bad."

"It's so much more satisfying to be snarky. I'm not serious about Will. This *is* just a game."

"You might want to believe that, but I don't. That's one of the things I liked – like – about you. You're totally authentic. I didn't have to guess. I still have to guess with Liv."

"Oh, this is early days with Liv yet. No fast moves, and you'll be fine."

He laughed, and it was a good sound, a healing sound.

"I am tired of hating you," she admitted. "It's exhausting. You're hard to hate."

"Thanks. I think." His smile looked a little tired of it all too. "We were pretty good together, Faye. But maybe we needed each other to be ready for what was to come."

"You're not suggesting Will is my Liv, are you?"

"Could be. If you let yourself believe it."

"Sounds so easy when you put it that way, doesn't it?"

"But it's not."

She didn't know if it was weakness or impulse or cleansing, but she put her arms around him and squeezed. "Thank you. I didn't know how much I needed this."

Finally, instead of the pain of a hot poker, she felt a little closer to whole.

"This looks serious. Should we be worried?"

Will had snuck up on the conversation, Liv with him. Liv didn't look worried about anything. It was nice to see her looking happy and secure. She wasn't threatened. That's how it should be.

And Will seemed to be adapting to his role readily. Nate was full of shit, saying he didn't believe she and Will were simply performing. He thought he saw through it. He thought she was incapable of playing this game; that she was ready for something deeper, but she might never want more than entertainment from the opposite sex.

She should probably go talk to Jiro. But seeing as she almost hadn't come at all, and the unexpected conversation with Nate had worn out what benevolence she had, it felt about time for her to excuse herself. She was even willing to let Will off the hook. It was a nice day for a walk.

"You look tired," he said. "Want me to drive you home?"

Was he actually paying close enough attention to her, that he noticed? She could like this guy, if she let herself.

"Yes, if you don't mind." She glanced from Nate to Liv. "Sorry for ducking out early. It seems wrong to complain about being tired to two people who get up at an ungodly hour every day. Thanks for the invite. We'll get together soon, okay sweetie?"

She saw the look Liv gave Nate before stepping in for a hug. "Are you okay?" she said quietly.

"Just too sober," Faye answered, conjuring up her sense of humour. "I'll be fine."

Will was silent during the short drive to Northwest. When he pulled up next to her Corolla, he met her questioning gaze.

"I need a drink," Faye said. "You in?"

He nodded. "Sounds good to me."

He followed her to the door, waiting while she fumbled for keys. Gus was on the other side, slipping past them and around them before bounding out to the lawn. He lifted his leg on a tree, then bounced back and ushered them into the kitchen.

"What did Nate say to you?"

Faye glanced over her shoulder, kicking off her shoes and shuffling across the old hardwood to the cupboard where she kept the glasses. "I guess, just, things that needed to be said. Nothing unkind, don't worry. I'm good."

She reached in for a couple of tumblers, setting them side by side on the counter, then felt his arms go around her, his face in her hair. He held her against him, his heartbeat steady behind the firmness of his chest, the rising and falling of it grounding her. It was a foreign sensation, that sense of comfort, free of judgment. A small part of her wanted to stay there, let herself feel it. But it was easier, more natural, to pivot to face him, slide her hands to his shoulders, to his neck, and pull his head lower, catching his bottom lip between hers, feeling him respond. She went deeper, making his mouth hers, fingers running down his ribcage to yank his shirt free, breaking apart just long enough to grab a breath and drag the shirt over his head. He dipped back in to reconnect, deftly unknotting her shirt, his calloused fingertips smooth on her bare shoulders as he pushed it off, sending a shiver through her. And now she couldn't wait to feel skin to skin, peeling her tank top off as his fingers tickled her back, undoing the clasp of her bra – which was not a sexy bra, because she really hadn't anticipated her afternoon going this way. She shrugged out of it and arched into him while his hands traced down her back, along her hips, tucking into the back of her jeans. Why were they even still on?

"I know you bribed me with pastry," she murmured, "But I'm the one who should be thanking you. Here, or upstairs?"

13

This time, when she woke up, he was gone.

It was daylight. She'd slept right past her usual four AM wake up, so she didn't know if Will had left before, or after that. It didn't matter. It meant they were on the same page. So why was she disappointed?

More importantly, where was Gus? He was supposed to be her alarm clock, one who tended to go off much too early. She rolled out of the rumpled sheets and wrapped herself in her robe. When she reached the first step, she was greeted with smells that made her stomach growl. And made her stop in her tracks, skitter back to the bathroom, and brush her teeth.

Downstairs, there he was, his bare back to her, nothing but boxers under what looked to be a long lost apron, standing in front of the stove with Gus flopped at his feet. So much for loyalty. *Can you blame the dog, though?* Gus scuttled up as Will tossed him a piece of something, snapping it from the air. *Nope. Can't blame him one bit.*

She wanted to drop the robe, walk up behind Will and encircle his exposed torso with her arms, then dive her hands into those shorts. They'd made it to the bedroom last night; they could do the kitchen this morning.

He'd picked up his jeans from where he'd discarded them last night and folded them, and his wallet rested on the kitchen table. She'd bet he kept the necessary accessories in there, just in case, like she maintained a supply in the end table next to her bed. A hot frying pan, though. And a persistent unwillingness to jump into the fire.

"Make yourself at home," she said, standing in the doorway and leaning against the jamb. A little part of her brain lit up that liked that idea. Of him, in her home, and part of it.

He glanced over his shoulder and gave her such a buoyant smile, he made the thought of that fire seem oh-so-tempting, but she managed to control herself, stuffing her hands in the robe's pockets and sauntering over. Gus thumped his tail a couple of times; that was all she got from the Golden. She wasn't much competition for the bacon collected on a plate.

Will reached for a glass of orange juice on the counter beside the stove, and handed it to her. "'Morning."

Nice, cute, funny, good in bed, and he could cook. Someone needed to give her a slap. Couldn't she make good use of all those things?

"I see someone's been shopping." He turned back to the stove.

"Dean very kindly got groceries before he went to Saratoga. I'm not sure he believes I'm capable of doing it myself. And I'm not about to tell him I am." She sipped the juice, half expecting it to be freshly-squeezed. It wasn't. So the guy couldn't magically transform concentrate. "Can I do anything?"

"Just have a seat and relax." He poured coffee from her French press, and brought it over. Honestly, the man got major points for not just defaulting to Dean's calcium-encrusted coffee machine.

Bacon, eggs, toast with butter melting into it. No one she wasn't related to had ever made her breakfast, not even Nate. If she hadn't come down, would he have brought it to her in bed? Feelings threatened again. She tightened an imaginary lid on them to keep them safely stashed, and tucked into her spot at the table.

"So much nicer than Lucy's," she purred.

"No butter tarts, though."

"We could still go for butter tarts." The words were out like reflex. She should be chasing him away, but instead she was prolonging contact.

Lucy's face almost brightened when they showed up. It was still so unexpected, it took Faye a second to smile back. Will was close enough behind her she had an impulse to reach back and grab his hand and play along like they were all shiny happy people in a shiny alternate universe.

"What can I get for you? And are you going to introduce me to your boyfriend this time?"

Faye caught herself before she said *he's not my boyfriend.* He wasn't, and she didn't know what to call him, but no need to find a label for it right now. "Of course. This is Will." She glanced up at him conspiratorially. "I've got him addicted to your butter tarts now too."

Will nodded solemnly. "True story."

"We'll take half a dozen," Faye said, seeing a loaded styrofoam tray in the display. When they were available, it would be silly not to grab them. "We had coffee at home, so we're caffeinated for now."

Will had a funny little look on his face. *Yeah, yeah. We? Home?* It was becoming too easy to play this game.

Lucy took the bills Faye offered, and gave her change. "I'll see you tomorrow?"

"Yes, absolutely." Faye nodded. "I'm meeting with a friend of Emilie's who's an artist to see her work. Hopefully we'll come to an agreement about hanging some of it. And I have a couple of other ideas to run past you."

Will was staring at her, but not like she'd lost her mind. That's exactly how he should have been looking at her. Not like…that. Like something she'd said had started up a ferris wheel in his head.

"Bye Lucy!" she called, and herded him back outside. She had work to do, and imagined he did, too.

"Are you going to tell me what that's about?" he asked.

"It's nothing. I just offered to help her out a bit, so maybe she doesn't have to give up her business."

"I saw the place is up for lease."

"I hope she'll change her mind about that. The sign makes me nervous, like someone will come along and grab it before I convince her it doesn't have to happen."

There was that look on his face again, but he didn't say anything, didn't give her any clues as to what it was about.

"I'd better get going," he said. "But I will call you."

"Don't leave without your butter tarts."

She stacked three of them in his hands, and thought he might kiss her, but he didn't. That was fine. He wasn't *really* her boyfriend.

Something in his chest had swelled, when he'd heard Faye talking to Lucy. It was like fate had a finger on each of their shoulders, nudging them closer together because of their shared interest in that plain little café.

He wished he hadn't had to leave, but maybe it was for the best. It would have been too much, everything he wanted to talk to her about. The way they seemed so easy together made him brave, and that might not be a good thing.

He would call her…but some things he didn't want to say on the phone.

Lemon was waiting for him, on an extended stay. Really, the cat might as well be his. He attended to her, feeding and cuddling her as his job as her loyal liege demanded. Once she was satisfied, she went slinking away. That's probably what it would be like with Faye, too.

He needed to shower and get ready for work, but he picked up the phone and dialed her.

"Miss me already?"

Even miles away on the other end of the phone, that voice of hers did things to him. He cleared his throat. "So, are you going to tell me more about this arrangement with Lucy?"

There was a beat of silence before she drew out her response. "Why?"

"I don't know. I just thought you could possibly use my expertise. Given my restaurant experience and all."

"Does that mean you're offering to help?"

"I guess I am."

"Hmm. Does it involve pastry?"

He laughed. "It could."

"Well then. Perhaps this requires a meeting."

"I think that could be mutually beneficial."

There was a long pause. Okay, that comment did leave a lot up to interpretation, but he'd leave the direction it went up to her, entirely.

"Fine. As you heard, I'm at Lucy's tomorrow at eleven. If you think you can pop by, we'll chat."

So he had been hoping it might go another way, but hey, that was good too.

14

It had taken self-control. She did have some.

Three times made a habit, isn't that what they said? Maybe it was three weeks. Either way, she was going to have to do something about him. Usually her relationships were good for a couple of months or so, but she couldn't let it go that long with Will. Because he was breaking the rules.

So, yes, best that he met her here. She could see what he was thinking, and what he could offer by way of his restaurant experience. Those baking skills of his were clearly valuable. She had ideas, but they'd been fed by his ideas, so why not put their heads together?

Lucy looked extra stressed, and relieved to see her. It would have been a good feeling, if it hadn't been so concerning, and it put seeing Will right out of her mind.

"Busy morning?" Faye asked, fearing it was something more.

"My mother had a bad night. My neighbour was able to stay with her for a few hours, but I'm worried."

"Go," Faye insisted. "I've got this."

"Thank you, Faye. Call me if you need me."

It was a good feeling, that Lucy trusted her enough to go. She really was serving a purpose. She could adjust her schedule to be here all day. If

Lucy needed her to be here more often – if her mom was on a steady decline – Faye would step up, do more food prep. Get Em to help when she could. It was just a matter of re-prioritizing. Faye was winding things down with the MacIntosh Stables account, so it was time to shift her focus to this place.

Lucy must have been up as early as any racetracker to get all the baking done. There was a healthy supply of tarts (butter tarts were healthy, and no one could tell Faye differently; mental health, right?). Not that there were ever enough; they sold out each day. There were little quiches that made perfect, quick, lunches. A few uninspired breakfast wraps remained. Those were things Faye could easily make, with a little help from Lucy to get her started, because the quantity required would be more than Faye was used to preparing. She poured herself a coffee, managed to resist the butter tarts – she didn't want to eat all the product, after all – and opened up her laptop to take advantage of the window of time where it was typically quiet, between the morning madness and lunchtime.

The coffee was harder to take when there was no butter tart sweetness to help it out, and it was even worse when it got cold. Maybe just one tart? Then voices outside distracted her, and she shut the laptop, rising to see Emilie entering, Liv behind her with a box in her arms.

Faye arched an eyebrow and crossed her arms. "This looks suspicious."

"My friend who does the artwork should be coming by shortly," Em said. "That's the real reason Liv's here. My friend also wants a job on the farm, so it made sense to have her meet both of you here. You can talk to her first, before Liv kills her dreams." Em grinned.

Faye laughed, and Liv said, "I'll try to be nice."

"I don't suppose you stopped for cappuccinos on the way home from the track?" Faye asked hopefully.

"Sorry," Liv said. "I was at the farm before Em let me know about the plan."

"Somehow I don't think an espresso machine is in the cards here." Faye sighed. "Lucy can't both take me on and have an income and also buy that. One day, maybe."

"Where can I put this?" Liv asked, her chin indicating the box.

It looked heavy. "What is it?"

"Book donations. For your burgeoning library."

"Oh! Perfect. Right over here." Faye ushered her to the corner where she'd set the bookcase Dean had found, a shelf already stacked with paperbacks.

The bell on the door jangled, and a tiny, young, blonde woman stopped just inside with a thin, black case.

"Now I really feel old," Faye whispered. "That must be Em's friend."

Liv nodded. "I've met her. Em's had her to the farm before. She looks like a young Julie Krone, don't you think? Cuter, even."

Faye hadn't missed learning who Julie Krone was growing up. Her father liked to tell the story of how she'd come to Woodbine in the 80s to ride in the Queen's Plate, when he'd been just starting out working on the backstretch.

"Hi Cory," Liv called, her tone impressively welcoming.

Cory was even tinier than Liv. Her hair was cut in a practical bob but not styled, the ends flipping every which way, a ready smile on her lips. Rubbing one palm on her black jeans, she tugged nervously on the corner of a bright blue t-shirt. Em scampered from the kitchen and hugged her, directing her to one of the tables to spread out her work.

"You've had Lucy's butter tarts before, right?" Em said. "Want one?"

"Yes, please!" Polite, too. Her voice was as bright as her smile.

"Go ahead and pull out your work, and I'll grab it. This is Faye, by the way. Faye, meet Cory."

First Cory laid the portfolio flat on the table, then her hand jutted out in front of her. Faye closed her fingers around it, getting a firm squeeze back.

"Nice to meet you, Cory. Let's see what you've got."

Cory spread out a series of painted panels. "I have some photos of my larger work on my phone."

Liv looked over Faye's shoulder. "These are good, Cory."

Cory flushed at the praise, her grin widening. The kid was good, Faye had to agree. The subject matter was heavy on the horses, of course, but given the area, that was okay. An equine theme seemed like an appropriate place to start with this art initiative.

"What are they?" Faye asked, trying to sound like she knew something about art when all she really knew was what she did and didn't like.

"Acrylic," Cory said. "I'd have to frame these panels. The larger ones are on stretched canvas, so they can hang as they are."

Faye nodded, scanning. "Why don't we start with three months. We don't want anything – no commission. We'll just pass anyone interested on to you. Em can rep you when she's around."

Em grinned, Cory's champion of the moment.

"Thank you, Faye!" Cory said, and set about putting the work away.

Faye didn't know how the kid's smile could get any broader, but it did. "Just let me know when you're ready to hang some stuff. Em, can you give her my cell? She's all yours, Liv."

"Why don't you start on that butter tart first?" Liv suggested. "Em can grab you a coffee, or whatever you'd like to drink."

Cory was excited and chatty as she sat with Liv. Faye imagined working at Triple Stripe, helping start yearlings, would be any horse girl's dream job. What better mentor for a girl with riding aspirations – because that was no doubt, with her stature, what Cory was dreaming of – than someone like Liv, who had lived and breathed the struggle of a female apprentice jockey.

Faye served a few customers as Liv and Cory talked, Emilie working away in the back. Her phone buzzed with a notification, and considering the two people most likely to text her were with her at Lucy's, she was guessing it was either Dean, still in Saratoga, or…

Will: *Still at Lucy's? If so, will be there shortly. - Will.*

As if she hadn't set him up as a contact after the first time he'd messaged her. She responded: *Still here. I hope you brought real coffee.*

He didn't answer, so she set the phone back down, looking up to see Liv was finished with Cory and coming over.

"Hey Em," Liv called. "Cory's all yours again."

Em popped out from the kitchen. "Did you hire her?"

"She earned herself a working interview." Liv gave her sister a sly smile, then turned to Faye. "I haven't worked with the yearlings since Chique."

Faye tilted her head, her mind going back. "You were such a mess then."

Liv didn't deny it, but neither of them took the topic further. So many emotions were tied up in those days now. For Liv, because she'd been trapped in the wilderness after losing her mentor, Triple Stripe's old farm manager, who had died suddenly while she'd been away in New York. And for Faye? On the one hand, Faye had wanted to strangle Liv for her behaviour at the time, but that had been just a tiny bit hypocritical, because Faye had been there once herself, wallowing in her own loss a few years earlier. That was also when she'd finally met Nate, and she very clearly recalled the day, one afternoon as he and Liv were working with the yearlings. Not that they'd gotten together until the following summer, because Faye hadn't been convinced Liv didn't like him then. *Hindsight.*

Liv's phone started a tune now, and even Faye knew who it was, because it was a clip of a Switchfoot song. *Speak of the devil.* Of course she had a ringtone for him. She had to stop herself from sending a text of her own to see if Liv had a custom ringtone for her, too.

Emile was saying her goodbyes to Cory, and Liv still had traces of a mischievous smile on her lips as she put away her phone. Faye didn't want to know.

"So I'm assuming Nate told you about our little conversation?"

Liv raised her head and nodded, meeting Faye's eyes. "So very grown up of you both."

"At this rate, we're going to be old and in rocking chairs in no time."

"I said grown up, not growing old, Faye." Liv smirked.

"YOU'RE sure in a chipper mood. Please don't tell me this is to do with Faye again."

Will didn't think Nate was being completely serious with that comment; it was actually starting to feel as if he'd softened to the idea of Will and Faye getting together. If that's what was happening. "Yes, and no."

"Just tell me."

"You know Faye is helping out Lucy."

"Yessssss?" Nate drew out the word, an eyebrow raised.

"So that's something you could see?"

"What do you mean? I'm pretty sure she's capable of figuring out a cash register and taking people's money."

"I mean, what about, if Lucy decided to give it up? Could she take over?"

Nate squinted at him, questions collecting behind those eyes. "For sure. She's smart, she's got a great business brain, and her degree is along those lines. And she can cook. I've always thought Faye's undersold herself. It would be great for her to sink her teeth into something like that. Give her a bit of space from Dean, too, and maybe Dean would get off his ass and find himself a girlfriend." He laughed at the last bit.

"Okay. I need a hand with something."

"With, what, exactly?"

"Physical labour. You can still do that, right? It's not below you?"

"You think my job isn't physical?"

"Not what I meant. I just need half an hour. Follow me. Maybe drive your own car."

Will made sure Nate was in his rear view mirror as he drove out the maple-shaded lane of Triple Stripe, turning up the music. This plan was falling together so easily, he felt guilty.

He pulled up behind the plaza, to the back of Lucy's. Nate climbed out of the Mustang, looking even more distrustful.

"What are we doing?" he asked.

"Nothing nefarious, I promise." Will grinned. "Text Liv or Em and let them know we're here."

"So they're in on this? But I'm not? What's with that?"

"Don't take it personally, it's just the way it worked out."

With only a little more side-eye, Nate pulled out his phone. It wasn't long before the back door popped open and Emilie's head peeked out.

"Now help me with this." Will waved Nate over.

"Ahhhh," Nate said, a smile taking over his face. "Why didn't you tell me in the first place? I can totally get behind this. Might be a little overkill though, y'think?"

"Just grab an end, all right?"

Emilie held the door for them, and they set it in the space she'd cleared.

"Hey, Faye!" Emilie called. "Can you come here for a second?"

Liv grinned over Faye's shoulder as they came through the door. Faye's eyes landed on Will, a solid gaze, but as much as she was trying to control it, she couldn't hide that she was happy to see him. At least that's what he was going to tell himself.

"Is there a party you forgot to invite me to? What are we celebrating this time?" she asked.

"I brought you something," Will said, motioning to the gleaming machine resting on the kitchen floor.

Faye's mouth fell open, then the corners of her lips curled upwards, the lift reaching to her eyes, then brows. "An espresso machine! That's amazing! But –" Her face fell slightly. "I really should run this past Lucy."

"Already cleared it with her." Will smiled.

But there were complicated gears churning behind the look he got back, and he wondered if he'd overstepped.

"How soon can you set it up? It looks complicated, like I might need a degree to operate it, too."

"It just so happens I have such a degree. Or the equivalent experience, at least. I've got it covered."

There was the slightest tilt to her head, and no one was speaking, until Emilie saved the day and spoke up. "I can't wait till you get it fired up. This is going to be the best!"

Nate pulled his car keys from his pocket and tossed them in the air. "I'm guessing that's going to take more than a few minutes, and not something I'd be much help with, so I'm going back to doing what I was planning to do before I was shanghaied into this mission. Sleeping. Wednesday night racing, yay."

"I'll see you later too, Faye. Call me when it's up and running." Liv smiled and gave Faye a hug. She went out the front, while Nate slipped out the back. The timing of their departure, just after Nate said *sleeping,* was that a coincidence?

"I'm guessing this is part of the grand plan," Faye said finally, holding her hands out to the espresso machine. "Thank you. It's amazing. The coffee we'll be drinking while we talk is going to seem even more horrible than usual, knowing we have that to look forward to."

"I'll make you guys some fresh, at least," Emilie said. "You two go ahead with your meeting."

She didn't wink, but she might as well have, with the look she gave Faye. *No, it really is just that…but I'm hoping too, Em.*

"Really Will. This is…amazing," Faye said again as they sat at a table out front. "It must have cost a fortune."

"I got it from a buddy who was upgrading, so he gave me a good deal. It'll pay for itself in no time. I told Lucy not to worry about it until it does."

"I can't believe she didn't flip out."

"Are you mad I didn't tell you about it?"

She leaned back, pressing her lips together as Emilie set cups in front of them. "A little. But the prospect of being able to get cappuccino right here in town makes up for it."

"So this was my big idea. What have you been working on?"

Faye wrapped her fingers around the hot ceramic cup. "Emilie's friend Cory came by with her artwork, and she's going to get some of it ready to hang. We've started our little library…" She nodded toward a bookshelf. "And there are a couple of things you could definitely help with. I'd like to think about a few new menu items. Nothing too extravagant. And…" She took a careful sip of the coffee. "I want to do a little music night."

"I see."

"I hope you know what that means."

"I do. I'll talk to Nate."

"Tell him Em asked. It'll improve the chances of him saying yes."

"And I'll do some thinking about the menu."

"You're being very helpful."

"I might have an ulterior motive. For all this, and rescuing you the other day."

"You rescued me? You came, you bribed, I went with."

"Fine. I'll just go with the espresso machine, then."

"That is pretty huge." Finally, a slight lift to the corner of her mouth. "Okay. Spill."

"I saw my dad last week. He's in town…with his brand new fiancé."

There was mild surprise on her face. "So your parents are divorced, obviously."

"They're getting married Friday night. Here. Like, in the city. And well, he wants me to be there."

"Oh." She shifted in her chair, eyes darting to the side.

"Yeah. You know what I'm going to ask."

"I don't know about that, Will. That's like family."

Will snorted. "Barely. Trust me on that. Here's the deal. He's invited Nate, and whoever he wants to bring which means Liv."

"You don't know her that well, do you? She's not big on social things."

"That's why you'll talk her into it. It works both ways. It'll make Nate happy so he doesn't hold this over me forever for making him come, and if Liv comes, you won't feel like you're there with me, exactly. Then I can be present at this thing, when I'm not even sure I should be, and not feel like a fool."

"United we stand?"

"That's what I'm hoping. I have to give my father credit for thinking allowing my own little team there might convince me to actually come. Plus he didn't ask me to be his best man or something ridiculous like that, thank goodness."

"Team, huh?" She hesitated, bringing the cup to her lips again.

"Please? I don't want to go to this thing alone."

"All right. If I can get Liv to go, Nate will go, or if you get Nate to go, he'll find a way to talk her into it, probably. So we go at it from both sides. But we're a team, not a couple. Got it?"

Will sighed, and nodded. "Got it."

"And, you have to talk Nate into the music night."

"Deal."

15

The wedding would be fine. It would be a way of thanking him, for being such a nice guy. And she could be nice, for five minutes, and let him down there, instead of on the phone, or in a text, because that was just wrong.

It was time.

She was on the verge, she could feel it. The verge of falling again. She recognized it, this time. Him standing in her kitchen, half naked, making her breakfast, had almost pushed her over. The espresso machine was her wake-up call. It jolted her back to her senses as much as the first cup of coffee in the morning brought clarity.

Even beyond her history, it was a logical decision. He lives in Toronto, and she was out here, so it wasn't exactly convenient for them to get together. He had his own life; she wasn't going to drag him into hers. If he wanted to continue as a consultant for Lucy's, that was up to him.

She poured over the numbers, analyzing. Lucy made a modest income from the business. Faye wasn't in a position to do a complete overhaul – it's not like she had financial resources to draw on – so she'd have to make changes slowly. Being able to offer espresso was a big deal, so she hoped Will came through getting the machine set up before the wedding, in case, well, things went south and he took it personally. She'd talk to Em about helping with the website. Faye was fine with maintenance, but the design part was not her thing, and smarty-pants Em did them for fun in her spare time. She'd probably take payment in butter tarts. In time, they could add e-commerce, start to sell online. Butter tarts for all!

It kept resurfacing, over and over, that a café like this was Will's dream. All the things she was doing, he'd talked about. She shook off the thoughts invading her headspace about how nice it would be to have him work side-by-side with her on this. He wouldn't want to leave the city anyway. And it would be too complicated, because they were definitely headed into something, if she didn't put a stop to it right now.

Look what she'd achieved. She'd never felt so…alive, dammit, as much of a cliché as that was. She'd grown up wanting to get away from the farm, and landed herself right smack in the middle of it. With this project, she could keep her commitment to Dean and her parents' memory, and have something that was hers. Something not based on the unpredictable world of horse racing. Except for its tie to something very reliable: this area was populated with horse people, and horse people ran on coffee.

THE TONE REPEATED in Will's ear, and finally Nate picked up.

"Everything okay?" he grumbled.

"Sorry, I know," Will said. "You weren't actually asleep yet, were you?"

"Close enough."

"Just want to bring you up to speed."

"And it couldn't wait till say, five o'clock?"

"You're here now." Will grinned into the phone, but was met with silence. "So. Faye agreed to come to the wedding, if you guys go. It's up to the two of you to convince Liv to come, because I'm guessing it would be awkward if it was just you, me and Faye?"

"If it came to that, I'm pretty sure Faye wouldn't come, no matter how much ground we've made up. But I'd be your Plus One, dude."

"Good to know. Next favour."

"Here we go." Nate's sigh was audible. "What?"

"This one's for Em."

"I don't even need to know what it is, then. I'm in."

"That easy?" Faye had been right.

"For Em? Absolutely. She's always there for everyone. She's social convenor and team therapist. She should be a mental health coach instead of studying to be a physiotherapist. It's what she does anyway."

"Great. This one will be fun. She wants us – you and me – to do a little duo thing at the cafe. They're going to do an evening event. Her friend Cory is hanging some art; we'll do the music, they'll serve cappuccinos and dessert."

"Sounds great. Acoustic?"

"Yep."

"Count me in."

He couldn't wait to tell Faye. Maybe he was trying too hard, when he hadn't intended to try at all.

FAYE LEFT Emilie in her happy place, fists kneading flour into pastry dough. Liv unpacked a second box of books, slotting them neatly into the shelving unit. Probably alphabetically.

Yep.

Liv scowled at her when she started pulling out titles. "Here you go, Liv. Em knows good romance. Read this one!" She waved a Kari Lynn Dell paperback.

"Cowboys?"

"It might help you figure out what to do with your own cowboy. Better than this, for sure." Faye peered at one of Liv's thick contributions. "Was this even written in this millennium?"

"Not sure he'd appreciate being called a cowboy, even if he is from Calgary. Or maybe because he's from Calgary."

"Well no one's saying you have to call him that to his face."

Em emerged from the kitchen, pushing a loose strand of hair away from her face with her little finger. "We need to convince the world that gallop boys and jocks are the new cowboys of romance."

"Is that going to be your next thing, Em?" Faye teased. "Romance writer?" Faye unloaded more of Liv's box, which was dramatically lacking in romance in any way, shape or form. Suspense and thrillers and big, fat historical fiction. No wonder the poor girl was so lost.

Faye's phone buzzed. It was Will. All it said was, *Nate's in*, with musical notes.

Awesome, she fired back. This would not shake her decision about breaking things off with him. She'd been up front with him from the start. She was not responsible for his reaction. He'd probably be relieved, and wonder why more women couldn't be like her.

"Em! Let's start getting the word out. The boys are going to play."

"Yes!" Em shot a fist into the air. "What if we make it a fundraiser for New Chapter?"

"That's a great idea. I know we won't have a lot of lead time, but let's make the best of it."

Faye's phone buzzed again. Will. *I'm sending someone to get the espresso machine running for you. I gave him your number to set up a time, hope that's okay.*

A clench of disappointment squeezed her stomach. But she couldn't tell him she'd been hoping he'd come, when on Friday night she was going to push him away.

16

"Well, this is quaint." Faye's lips curved with her trademark sarcasm as her eyes roved around their table.

Will reached for one of the bottles by the centrepiece. A drink was long overdue. "Red or white?" he asked Faye first.

"Red," she replied coolly.

Will looked to Liv next, and she nodded. "Same."

As he poured their glasses, Nate nudged his forward. Red all round it was, then.

Will settled back into his chair, raised his glass, then drank, giving Faye a sideways glance. There would be enough toasts; he wasn't going to make them wait for one of his own. "All the same, I'm grateful for you guys coming. I mean, Nate I could guilt into it, being my oldest friend and all, but you two are going above and beyond." Will's gaze went from Liv's careful smile to Faye, whose expression had been behind a curtain since he'd first laid eyes on her this evening.

He was still awestruck she was actually here, and then there was that dress. It had made him forget everyone else in the room. He didn't know any of those fashion terms about necklines and waistlines and hems. All he knew was it was distracting, and she was beautiful. If she intended that veneer to put him off of something, it wasn't working. No, it was having the opposite effect.

She'd come down with Nate and Liv, and seemed to be making sure she wasn't alone with him. Will had no idea what that was about. He'd endured the service, complimented the bride on how lovely she looked, introduced his troupe to her and his beaming, fake-as-hell, father. It wasn't a big wedding, but there were enough people around that after that formality, dear old Dad was kept busy enough with people he wanted to be around that he left their group to themselves.

"At least he picked a good spot," Will continued, leaving his sentimental thoughts and moving on to something less awkward. "They put on a good spread here. I'd hate to have to miss a night at work for bad food."

Faye stuck close to Liv when they went to the buffet. Maybe he should have just had Nate come solo, because this was almost as awkward as coming alone would have been. He decided against asking Nate if he knew what might be going on. It might be bad form, given the history between them. He didn't want to push things when Nate had really done him a solid by being here; bonus points for getting the two women to cooperate. Things seemed smoother between Nate and Faye since the afternoon of Nate's thing at the farm, but that might not include Nate being willing to provide frank insight on her state of mind, if he even had any.

None of them moved when the dancing began, the formal ones not something Will wanted any part of joining in on. Nate seemed to feel the same. Will was happy just to scowl openly at the bride and groom's first dance, and blocked out the father of the bride one as soon as he noticed the bride's father was probably the same age as her new husband, her mother looking more appropriately matched with Will's dad than his own, new wife. It had to be ridiculously uncomfortable for all of them, but that wasn't Will's problem.

When they got those out of the way and the DJ started something more upbeat, Faye popped to her feet and stretched out her hand.

"You're up, Miller," she said.

Once Nate got over the shock, he grinned and scrambled up, shedding his jacket and going with her. Will stared after them feeling like he'd been socked in the gut.

"What just happened?" he said to Liv. "Are you okay with that?"

"Relieved, actually. Better her than me." She smirked, reached for her wine, and sipped. "I'm happy they've come far enough that they're okay with that."

"So we don't have to be worried?"

Liv laughed quietly. "I don't think so. And if there were something to worry about, what would be the point in worrying?"

"I'm not sure I know what that means, but it sounds wise." He took a slug from his own glass.

"I don't know what exactly is going on with you and Faye, but I didn't think you were yet in a position to merit feeling that way."

Well. That was direct. This one didn't pull punches. "Maybe I'm not." So, he didn't feel right about asking Nate for his thoughts, but Liv might be up for sharing intel. Considering her own position, she seemed remarkably neutral. And she was Faye's best friend, so she might know better than anyone but Faye herself. "But with that outlook, you're either very secure in your relationship, or…indifferent."

"I'm not sure I'm either of those things. Sure I care, but if that –" She inclined her head toward the dance floor where Nate and Faye were working up what Will had to admit looked like a very innocent sweat, "is actually the rekindling of something between them, and they're both convinced it's real, it's not going to do me any good to fight back, is it? Seems to make more sense to cut my losses and go back to what was working just fine for me before."

"Is that what Faye's doing, then?"

"She's trying."

"I guess that'll make Nate happy then. He wasn't impressed with the whole idea of the two of us anyway."

"I do get that, though. You know what happened to him. You two are close, right? From what I understand, you're practically the fourth brother in that family."

"Yeah? So?"

"So his brother went and married his first girlfriend after she broke up with him. Now his next girlfriend breaks up with him, and starts seeing you. Maybe it's not exactly the same, but there's enough similarity that on some level he might not even be aware of, it triggered him."

"There's a big difference. He was still in love with Cindy when she married his brother. I don't know how deep his feelings went with Faye, but either way, he's not in love with her. He's in love with you."

"No such declarations have been made," she said, glancing down at the wine glass with one of her small smiles. There was a fresh pinkness to her cheeks.

"Only because you are how you are, and he's going to be extra-careful this time. It's going to be excruciating for the rest of us to watch." He grinned.

She laughed quietly. "It might be just as excruciating watching you and Faye trying to sort yourselves out, so, *touché."*

He chuckled, and contemplated pouring himself another glass. The wait staff had replaced the empty bottle with a new one. He wasn't sure he'd figured anything out talking to Liv, except that Nate was in good hands with her.

Faye returned laughing and breathless, the energy that surrounded her a contrast to the quiet calm of the discussion at the table. Will's chest tightened with jealousy he, as Liv had pointed out, probably didn't have the right to feel.

Nate gulped down half a glass of water, fit enough he'd hardly turned a hair, then nudged Liv. "C'mon. I let you off the hook for the fast stuff, but you're not getting away with sitting at the table the whole night." He lifted her to her feet and slipped his arms around her, taking the time to kiss her before sweeping her away.

"Would you dance with me?" Will's voice was wobbly. He hadn't intoned it like he'd thought in his head, had he? Would you dance with *me?* Like he was suddenly second rate.

Faye turned her head swiftly like she'd forgotten he was there, her dark hair swinging from her shoulder in waves and layers. Their eyes met for a moment, hers still frustratingly cloaked. She set the water glass she clutched back on the table.

"Of course."

She couldn't say no, but his arms just made what she had to do harder. They transmitted that unicorn feeling that had fallen on her when she'd stood in front of him at the Plate party, looking into those magical eyes as she swayed, and he sang. But there was no destiny between them; that had just been the cheap champagne in her blood that night, amplifying misdirected feelings.

She'd put it off for a moment, and just rest her head against his chest, pretending this was everything it wasn't. The music was all oldies, classic rock. Which had been fine when she'd been out here with Nate, bopping to Crocodile Rock. That had been cathartic, like the history between them was finally documented and archived. Unlike this, a full-fledged war raging inside her as she tried to resist the feelings that assaulted her when he held her against him. And he was *singing*. She didn't even like the Eagles, so why was it getting to her? She needed a new rule. No guys who sang.

Okay now, Faye. Do it now.

She lifted her head and looked up at him, and her neck kinked. See? Again. That was why she didn't date tall guys. Not that it had mattered when they'd been horizontal.

Stop it.

She rested a hand on his chest and tried a wry smile. "So after tonight, we're even, right?"

His eyes fell to hers, a slight furrow to his brown. "Yeah. Tonight carried a lot of weight."

"The espresso machine is a big deal, of course, and I'll always be grateful for your part in the recovery of my sense of self. That one was priceless to be honest." She fingered his tie, letting her smile persist. How did she do this again?

She'd never found it hard, before Nate. Her script had fallen apart with him, but she'd been fed by her desperation and dismay. There was none of that here. All there was, was…senselessness.

Oh, please, Faye. This was the deal, all along.

"And dragging me to Nate's thing, even if it was to our mutual benefit. If you hadn't talked me into going, I never would have talked things out like that with him. I feel like I've got a clear head now. Being part of Lucy's is…I mean, I'm sad for her, but I'm happy I can help. And maybe this is going to be my thing. Like today is the first day of the rest of my life, and all that."

She felt his chest rise and fall against her hand.

"I have to tell you, though." His tone was too serious, and it was robbing her of the vibe she'd been trying to create. "I like you, Faye. For real. I think we could have something."

He'd figured her out. Her rambling little speech had been too obvious a set up. And fine, she liked him too, more than the passing amusement she'd intended him to be. Because he made her think of Shawn, and what it was like to have fun. The music. The silly songs they would do for their parents on special days. Her voice had died with him, and she'd traded passion and adventure for duty. With Nate she'd felt a glimmer of its return, but as a sidekick, future trophy wife. Will made her think of combining their talents to make something bigger and better. He'd made her sing again. But that didn't change what needed to be done.

"If there's one thing I learned from my time with Nate, it's that it's best to get out while things are still good, instead of waiting till it all goes bad. And Nate is probably right about you and me anyway. It's a bad idea."

"Did he say that to you?"

"It's not exactly a secret, is it?" This wasn't the time for honesty, for the revelation that Nate had backed down on that stance, *if you really like him*. "Besides, I was up front about this. I don't want a serious relationship. I had one of those. Except it wasn't serious. I just let myself believe it was, for a heartbeat. And I never want to have that feeling again. So let's quit while we're ahead, all right? If you still want to help with Lucy's, that would be great, of course. We may have hit our personal expiry date, but that's something we could have."

"Like a consolation prize?"

The lines around his eyes and mouth were tight, and she had to look away.

She glanced across the room to where the bride and groom stood, chatting with their guests at one of the tables. "Your father's a good-looking man," she said. "You have good genes. It's kind of a shame; we'd have beautiful children." Not that she'd ever imagined it.

She closed her fingers around the tie and pulled his lips to hers, hoping the kiss sealed it. So long, and thanks for the pastry.

He didn't say anything. Because what could he say? She'd been honest with him from day one. No more means no more, right?

When she stepped away, the space between them generated a strange emptiness in her chest, and she quickened her pace, hoping more distance would make it go away. It didn't, and Will caught up anyway.

Nate and Liv looked wilted, and Faye put on a bright smile to chase away the melancholy and doubt invading her mind. "It's late for you two. We should probably go."

Liv straightened hopefully, and Nate looked past Faye to Will. "Is that okay with you?"

Faye didn't turn, because she didn't want to see his face. She just wanted to leave before she rushed back to him and started babbling silliness like I *think I've just made a big mistake.*

"Of course." His voice, even speaking, still struck that chord deep inside of her. "I totally understand. I could get out of here myself. I don't think I'll be missed."

The four of them walked out, Faye and Will deflated bookends to Liv and Nate. Faye stood back next to Liv as the boys embraced and nodded about needing to talk about their plans for Monday night. Faye had totally forgotten about Tuesday night, thanks to her chaotic brain. Their music night at Lucy's. Em had been doing all the legwork.

It would be all right. As long as Will didn't back out, now that she'd said her piece.

"Do you want me to drive, Nate?" she asked hopefully. None of them had had more than that early glass of wine, but she hoped he'd appreciate the chance to doze. "If you trust me with your cherished rust bucket, that is."

He surprised her by agreeing. That just proved how tired he really was. He climbed into the back seat, letting Liv ride shotgun.

"What happened," Liv said, her voice hushed. "Are you okay?"

It wasn't all that surprising Liv had picked up on it; she could read animals, and in Liv's mind humans were just another animal, albeit predators.

Faye nodded firmly, as much to convince herself as Liv. "Yeah. It was time. He's a nice guy. He needs to move on and find himself a nice girl."

"You are a nice girl," Liv said, quietly. "One of these days you're just going to have to admit it."

Faye wouldn't look at her. Eyes on the road only. She liked herself the way she was. She would never call herself nice. She could be civil enough in social and business situations to give people that impression, but no, she wasn't nice, below the surface. But Will had made her question that, too. Not because he'd suggested there was anything wrong with her; in fact, he seemed to appreciate her outlook on life. But because he'd made her think there could be more. And there could be, to herself, at least.

17

"What's all this?"

Nate peered around Will's elbow, watching him mash butter and flour together, fingers buried in a bowl.

"Pastry. French pastry."

"You should have warned me you were stress-baking. I'm not sure I can be in the same room as that stuff." He leaned over a rack of cooling croissants and inhaled. "I'm sure even the smell of them has calories."

"I thought some stuff was worth it," Will said, looking at him sideways.

"I know what kind of volume you can create when you get on a roll. I have to be sensible."

"Sometimes sensible interferes with your ability to be supportive."

"My job interferes with my ability to be supportive, not to mention a bunch of other things. What are you stress-baking over, anyway?" Comprehension overtook his face. "Hannah. I'm sorry, man. I forgot."

Will stepped back from the counter before he abused the delicate mixture. Hearing the name stopped him, even if the thought had been in his head all day. "That's okay. It's been a long time. I should be over it."

"No one gets to tell you how long it should take."

"So does that mean you're still holding onto old stuff?"

"Well – if by stuff you mean a certain amount of anger, and a sense of betrayal…yeah. I know I am. But isn't admitting that a step? And I'm not letting it hold me back from believing there can be something different anymore."

"But not better."

Nate grabbed an apple from a bowl on the counter with obvious frustration – and probably not just because he'd rather have had one of the beautiful buttery pastries.

"It's not that simple, is it? If I said it was better, I'd be admitting that things with Cindy were a mistake. And I'm not ready to do that."

"Does it have to be a mistake to just be not the right thing?" Will swung open the fridge.

Nate laughed then. "Funny, that's kind of what I said to Faye." He set down the apple in favour of the bottle Will offered him. "Does beer go with French pastry?"

Will wiped off his fingers, encrusted with flour and butter, before twisting the cap off his own. "It is hard to believe it's been nine years."

Nate held the bottle out. "To Hannah."

Will tapped it, and they drank, then he leaned back against the counter. "My mom called this morning."

"Ooh."

"My dad said he'd tell her he was getting remarried. Which I guess he did, after the fact. He's lucky I didn't talk to her sooner, assuming he'd done it already. If I had, and I'd said something about it…" He shook his head slightly, and set the bottle to the side, returning to the counter. "It's not like I can do anything for my mom except agree my father is a jerk. And I'm not going to hop on a plane for that."

"She wasn't asking you to, was she?"

"No. But I still feel as if I should." Even though he knew if he did, he'd get to Calgary and find his mother submerged in her job like she'd always been. That was how she dealt with unwanted emotions.

"There's more though, isn't there?"

"More? More what?" *More poking around in my head?*

"To this." Nate waved his hand over the accumulating baked goods.

Will filled the tart shells he'd formed and slid them into the oven. "What's up with the psychoanalysis?"

"The sooner we get it over with, the sooner we can focus on tomorrow night. You haven't cared this much about anyone since Hannah, have you?"

"I don't know what you're talking about."

"You can't lie to save your life. You never could."

"Fine, all right? It's true. You warned me though, so I'm gonna be graceful in defeat and just accept it."

"Nah, nah. This ain't over. Just sit chilly and let her think she knows what she's doing. We'll go there tomorrow night and you'll take piles of pastry, obviously…" Nate looked at the counter again, a bit longingly, Will thought. "Then you'll melt her some more with the music. You'll act like you're cool and not say anything to her about it, and in a few days, she'll make the right choice."

"You're funny. Where did you get all that from? She seemed pretty confident about her decision last night."

"Hardly. You forget I know her. She'll come around."

"Promise?"

"Well that would just be stupid, wouldn't it?" Nate slapped him on the back and walked over to the piano.

He probably shouldn't be taking advice from Nate when it came to Faye. The guy's overall track record with relationships was, technically, better than Will's, however. Even if the first two hadn't ended successfully, at least they'd had some length to them. It wasn't a bad plan, really. Pastry and music? It could work.

"Em, you're a genius. You seriously should go into event planning. It's such a shame you want to do that physio stuff. Helping people," Faye scoffed light-heartedly.

"This is helping people. And by people, I mean horses," Liv pointed out.

Em nodded. "Every donation of $10 to New Chapter gets a ticket for the draw for that painting Cory donated; 10 for $50. Song requests for the guys – $20. And we have a little silent auction. Next time we do this it'll be way better. There just wasn't enough time."

Volunteering for New Chapter Thoroughbred Retirement was another of Emilie's side projects. While Faye would gladly support the group, aligning with them could be valuable PR for the café.

"We should auction off a private show with the boys, with coffee and dessert here at the cafe. A live auction, of course," Faye suggested.

Emilie laughed. "That would be great, but we'd better run it past them first. And have very strict conditions."

"Probably wise," Liv agreed, her gaze landing on Faye. "For people like you who might have unwholesome ideas."

"The fact that you mention that gives me hope for you, sweetie."

"The guys should be here any time to set up," Emilie said.

Faye was not going to think about seeing Will for the first time since Friday night. "How about Cory? We should have had her paint live."

"Oh, I tried that. No go. She says she could never paint in public. In fact, she's too terrified to even be here."

"That's a shame," Faye said.

"Not that I don't understand," Liv said, "but she's going to have to get over performance anxiety if she wants to be a jockey."

"See, you really are the best mentor for her." Emilie nudged her sister with an elbow, then pressed her hands together. "All right, let's go. We have half an hour."

Em had outdone herself, decorating the little room. Strings of fairy lights surrounded them, little flameless candles on all the tables – Faye had really wanted real ones, but Liv had pointed out it was an unnecessary fire hazard and Faye agreed it wouldn't do to burn the place down. Dean and the guys had gotten together and sent them flowers, and Em had plucked some from the generous arrangement to put in vases on the tables. The lighting might not be best for Cory's artwork, but the paintings had been placed in such a way that they caught the available illumination.

"It looks fabulous, Em. You really are the best." Faye captured her in a hug, then released her to continue her scurrying.

She needed something to do herself – Emilie was far too efficient. Was it going to be weird with Will? He hadn't called her, begging her to reconsider, telling her they were meant to be. That was a relief, not a disappointment, contrary to what a very stubborn part of her brain kept suggesting. The important thing was he hadn't backed out of tonight.

It wasn't like she could hide anywhere to avoid him here. She busied herself lining up cups for the hot drinks. Maybe, after all, Will agreed it was for the best. He had sent someone else to set up the espresso machine, so he'd probably been feeling it too, even before the wedding. She helped Em place the last few butter tarts on plates, and Liv joined them to set them on tables. Emilie had sold tickets because they had limited seats – each guest would get a tart and the espresso drink of their choice – and they'd sold out.

The guys came in the back, with just a couple of guitars, no speakers, because they'd decided the room was small enough the sound would be fine. Em planted water bottles by their stools as they unpacked the instruments, and Faye stayed out of the way until everything was ready. They all gathered in the kitchen.

"This is great," Nate said, stealing a butter tart from a nearby tray.

Em scowled at him, then just shook her head with an eye roll. "Go ahead, Will. Consider it part of your payment."

They weren't getting paid, even though Em had offered. They hadn't asked for anything, of course. All of it was very sweet. Very *nice.*

Liv glanced out the swinging door to the front. "There are already people waiting outside."

"It's only ten to. Should we let them in?" Faye asked.

"No!" Emilie gasped. "Make 'em wait."

Emilie gave a short nod to Liv, and Liv nodded back. She pulled a tray of flutes from under the counter as Em ducked away to the refrigerator, reemerging with a clean white dish towel and bottle of champagne. Real champagne.

"We might not be serving alcohol, but we most definitely must have a toast." She held up the bottle and grinned.

"Here, Em, I'll open it for you," Nate said.

"No! Don't let him!" Liv warned, then their eyes met, like no one else was in their universe, and they both started laughing.

"This place is clean enough we could eat off the floors, so definitely not going to happen." Emilie angled herself away from Nate and opened it conservatively, a quiet pop followed by a whisper of released pressure.

"Here's to you, Faye," she said once everyone had a glass, "and this new adventure."

"Here's to all of us," Faye replied.

Will's gaze pinned her before the glass made it to her lips. Faye had to look away, quickly tossing back a mouthful.

Everything about the evening was perfect – the gentle music, the soft lighting, the muted hum of voices – but she managed to feel lonely in the midst of it. This new adventure, as Emilie had called it, was supposed to fill her up more than this. That's what she got for stealing Will's dream, and only letting him be a tiny part of it.

An hour had passed when Dean slipped in – late, but Faye was more grateful than ever to see her brother. He stood just inside the door, eyebrows up and eyes wide as he scanned the packed room. His gaze finally rested on Faye, and he weaved through the tables and pulled her into a hug.

"This is extraordinary, little sister. You have done an incredible thing here."

"Couldn't have done it without these two." She tilted her head at Emilie and Liv with a smile. *And those two.* She didn't say it out loud, but cast a gaze at the Calgary boys.

Dean gave Liv and Em a squeeze in turn, and Em rushed away, presenting him with a cappuccino and a golden butter tart when she returned.

"Want to make a request, Dean?" Emile said, turning on her fundraising charm. "I have to warn you, though. There are bidding wars over them. This one went for $100 on the secondary market."

"Secondary market?" Liv choked back a laugh. "You'd definitely better plan to do this again."

"What's it going to cost me then, Em?" Dean asked. He finished off the tart, balanced his cup on the empty plate, and pulled out his wallet. Faye was awed by Emilie's ability to draw out that behaviour in people. Dean handed her cash, and she gave him a slip of paper and a pen, on which he scribbled something Faye couldn't see. Emilie took her fistful of slips to the front and waited till they finished the current song to present the fresh requests.

"They really are amazing, aren't they?" Faye said, swaying slightly to the next tune. All the requests so far had been pretty generic, things it seemed they hadn't had to think twice about to play.

"Do I detect a note of regret there?" Liv leaned closer, so Faye heard her words despite how softly she'd uttered them.

"It never would have worked. He lives in the city. He works evenings and weekends."

"He seems to have found ways to see you despite that. Maybe it's not such a bad thing to have to work at finding time."

Faye's eyebrows raised. "Everything all right with you and Nate, sweetie?"

"Yes, totally. Can it be too perfect?"

"No, it cannot, so shut up. You're just so used to being dark and twisty, I realize accepting happiness must be a challenge." Faye hadn't meant for it to sound caustic, but Liv didn't seem offended. She just sighed.

"It's hard to keep my own identity, when our lives are so intertwined."

"You were someone before he was, remember."

"But how quickly do people forget that?"

"Um, hello. You train a filly who's just one win away from the Canadian Triple Crown. If you pull that off, you'll be the first woman to do it. You are still someone. You are remarkable."

Liv's sideways glance was part grateful, but part dubious. "Sometimes I just wonder where work ends and we begin."

"Has anyone told you that you think too much?"

Liv laughed, quietly. "Oh yes. I don't seem to be able to stop, though." She was silent a moment, listening. "We should request a song."

"How much do you think that will cost us?" Faye asked.

"Shouldn't we get special consideration?"

"Em's a hardass when it comes to raising money for a cause."

Liv laughed. "True. What would you request?"

What would she give to hear Will play *Brown Eyed Girl* again? But that would send the wrong message. "Let's see. It has to be a little obscure. Something no one else would think of, but the two of them will know."

"Like, *The Sand and the Foam,"* Liv offered.

"That's obscure enough I don't know it."

"It's Dan Fogelberg. Don't ask me how I know."

"But now I must."

"Emilie!" Liv called, blatantly ignoring Faye. She grabbed the pen in

Em's hand and scribbled the song's name on one of the blank tickets. "I'm pulling strings."

Em grinned, plucking the ticket from Liv's fingers and reclaiming her pen. "It's only right."

The next song Faye knew well, from the first note Will picked with the guitar. Dean nodded in time, so it must have been his request, but Will was looking directly at her as he started singing, *Where Are You Going?*

Had he and Dean plotted this somehow? *It was just a song.* But oh, that damn hum, made worse by all the emotion that came with the memories the music conjured up. She shut down the feelings, opening the camera on her phone. Lifted it, hitting record, forcing her thoughts to content for social media. They would pass, those feelings, fading with the melody as it ended. The next song, and the one after, would free her of them, except the intoxicating resonance of his voice kept stirring it all back up.

Faye glanced at the time as Em passed Liv's ticket to Nate, Em leaning over, her lips moving close to his ear. He looked at it, looked up…found Liv, and smiled. Faye gave her a little squeeze. Liv would master this happiness. And Faye would not envy her for it. She'd figure out her own.

"Last one." Nate spoke into the crowd and was met with a restless rustle that indicated they all would have stayed long into the night for more. Faye would have.

Nate passed the slip to Will, who nodded, his gaze travelling over and around heads till he found them, again settling uncomfortably on Faye. Faye had long ago perfected a benign smile for moments such as this. But as they began, she couldn't keep herself from studying every motion, every nuance in his expression, hopelessly entranced.

"That is a beautiful song," she said softly, head tilted towards Liv, and she tried not to assign personal meaning to the words. They were nostalgic, a little sad, a place to which she didn't want to return.

The guests were slow to leave at the end, the boys flooded with compliments and back-slaps. Liv had disappeared, probably hiding out in the kitchen to avoid any unnecessary conversation with strangers and vague acquaintances. Faye and Emilie cleared cups and plates from the emptying tables. Liv assumed dishwasher loading duties in the kitchen, and they disappeared into the machine as quickly as Faye and Em brought them.

Emilie shooed the stragglers out and locked the door, and they gathered again in the kitchen. Nate set down his guitar case and slipped an arm around Liv, kissing her cheek then resting his head on her shoulder, looking beat. Liv barely even squirmed.

"That was incredible," Faye said, trying to keep the tremor of emotion from her voice. She wanted to say, *I hope we can do it again,* but needed to let it all sit right now. She couldn't shake that it felt so natural for Will to be part of this, but she wasn't ready to figure out how to make that so. Every time she invited the thought, fear roiled back to the surface.

18

The café's Facebook page was alive. She'd shared photos and the video clip from last night, and the post was going wild with comments and reactions. Half the video plays were probably hers, though. She kept listening to it again, and again. She'd thought she'd known where she was going. She'd been happy to go there alone, while occasionally enjoying company along the way. It was probably time to revive Operation Jiro.

She sent Em a text to try and dislodge the heavy lump in behind her ribcage. *Races tonight? I need a fix.*

It was a frustrating few minutes before Em's response. *Sorry, I can't. We've got a horse in, though, so try Liv.*

Being a Wednesday night, Liv wouldn't necessarily be there, but Faye could hope. *Are you going tonight?*

The little reply bubble popped up immediately. *Good girl, Liv, replying so fast.* The text whooshed in. *Yes, saddling the horse in the second. Roger's in Saratoga. Why did I not go to Saratoga this year?*

Faye: *I can think of one very good reason, about five-six, blond, killer grin and hot as hell.*

Liv: *I don't think it would be hard to convince him to come along. Don't think it's going to happen this year though. See you tonight?*

Faye: *You know where to find me.*

The excitement she should be feeling was missing, though. Of course Liv wasn't as fun to hang out with at the races as Em, and having saddling duties would make her even less so. It was Will. She'd only known the guy for five weeks, and she was miserable. It was almost as bad as after she'd split up with Nate, only this time, the only one she could be mad at was herself.

She let the aroma wafting gloriously from the kitchen distract her. Lucy must've pulled a fresh batch of butter tarts from the oven. Time for a break. These days, Lucy offered a tart without Faye having to ask. She hadn't gotten Lucy on to drinking cappuccinos yet though. Faye set up the machine to make one. Will had taught her. It wasn't as difficult as she'd thought it might be, and last night she'd had lots of practice.

"I have to tell you something, Faye."

Uh-oh. Lucy's tone caught her attention. Faye poured the espresso into a cup, and topped it off with the steamed milk. She took a sip, telling herself the sense of foreboding she had was ridiculous. Lucy would have told her as soon as she'd arrived if her mother's condition had changed.

"What's up?"

Lucy rubbed her hands together, then slid them down the front of her apron. "I have a buyer for the business."

Faye's mouth dropped open, and she quickly took another drink to hide her dismay. "Wow!"

"It's not a done deal yet, but it's just a matter of details, really. Everything you've done in the last while clinched it for him."

So, she'd shot herself in the foot. Perfect. Faye couldn't even fight back the way she wanted to, couldn't beg for a chance to see if she could buy it instead.

Lucy continued. "Would you be willing to help with the transition?"

A small sigh escaped Faye's lips before she could stop it. "Of course. That's great for you, Lucy. You've been stretching yourself thin trying to keep it going and take care of your mom, even with me around."

"Thank you for all your help. This wouldn't be happening without you." While Lucy looked sad, the tension that had riddled her features had softened a little. "It will be strange, not coming here, but it's time to let it go."

"Just let me know whatever you need. You can give the new owner my number. I'm happy to meet with them." Maybe she could still finagle a job out of it.

Gus was the only one to greet her when she got home. As much as she loved the silly dog, she could have used Dean's ear right now. She didn't know where he was. It didn't look as if he'd been there since he'd left before dawn. Something was going on with him; he'd been away more than usual lately. Maybe he had found a girlfriend. Maybe he was going to leave her. So much for her life plan. Sexy spinster was turning into lonely old maid.

FAYE HAD GONE to the races alone many times in her life, and never felt uncomfortable, but as she leaned on the rail across from where Liv saddled a horse named Just Jay, she found herself glancing from side to side, wishing someone were here next to her. At least with the Triple Stripe horse in the race, she didn't feel conspicuous, but what was that? She never felt conspicuous. She was Faye Taylor, damn it. She'd been scouting short men in this paddock for a decade. She was a fixture here as much as any of the horseplaying regulars.

Nate joined Liv in the stall as the groom led the horse away to start walking him. He greeted Liv professionally, the affection he'd shown last night put on the shelf here, probably because Liv would kill him if he tried anything. Liv said something in his ear, and he looked out at the crowd. He gave Faye a quick wave and a smile, which was nothing like the smile he would have given her a year ago. Faye smiled and waved back, and realized, finally, she was fine with that. If she admitted it, it was because someone else had taken up the space that had been left. But that didn't change reality, that she'd pushed that someone away, and found herself with a new trench to fill.

Liv threw Nate up on the horse after the riders up call, and instead of following the horses and keeping her eyes peeled for Jiro, Faye waited by the gate. Liv wasn't as keyed up as she would have been with Chique, but her mind was still solidly on the horse. It was comfortingly normal, when Faye's own life had stopped being so.

"This is his first race back?" Faye asked, falling on the little bits of knowledge she'd retained about this horse. Last spring, Just Jay had been one of the most promising two-year-olds in the Triple Stripe barn. He was a half-brother to the nicest horse they'd ever had, Just Lucky – now on his way to being a successful stallion, Chique the most notable of the offspring from his first crop – but, in one of those promise versus reality stories, injury had kept Just Jay from actually making it to the races until now.

Liv nodded as the escalator took them to the next level of the grandstand. "Now we get to see if he might still be everything he's supposed to be."

They navigated through the spotty Wednesday night crowd on the second floor to the outside seating. Liv was good at silence, and if she found Faye's unusual, she didn't question it. Faye sat back and followed the post parade and warm-ups, something she only ever half-watched – a contrast to Liv's binocular-aided scrutiny.

Faye was happy when the horse won, even though it had been expected – as much as one could ever expect a horse to win a race. It was encouragement for everyone with horses whose careers hadn't gone the way they were supposed to, and it renewed Faye's hope that Ride The Wave might get there one day; that not getting to the races as a two-year-old wasn't the worst thing that could happen.

"Coming down for the picture?" Liv asked, her mouth lightened from the serious line of moments earlier now that Just Jay was galloping out, still far ahead of his foes.

"Sure," she said. "And congratulations."

Liv shrugged, far too restrained as usual, and headed for the stairs down to the apron. "I'm just the stand-in."

"But this was Jay." Because Faye remembered that part about the colt, too; that he was named for Geai Doucet, and it always meant a little more when a horse you named for someone special turned out to be special too.

Liv didn't comment, focusing harder than she needed on the steps, and fingering the pendant at her neck.

Faye almost ran into Jiro as they walked against the traffic of jockeys headed for the scales; the also-rans who had finished behind Nate and Jay. He lit up in recognition, and it should have thrilled her, because that's why she'd come, right? But all she mustered back to his cheery hello was a lukewarm *hey, Jiro.* Those aspirations were vexingly dead in the water. The heart wants what the heart wants. *Stupid heart.*

After the photo, when Nate dismounted, Liv released some of her professional guard and hugged him, and let him kiss her. Faye stood out of the way, keeping well clear of the horse, who seemed a sensible type, but exuded enough triumphant energy to rattle her.

"I have to go back and check on him. Do you want to come?" Liv asked once Nate had gone to weigh in, the groom and horse test barn-bound.

Faye didn't blame Liv for sounding so unsure – not that the offer wasn't genuine. It was more that she was bewildered she felt it was necessary. Where was strong, *laissez-faire* Faye?

"Sure," Faye said. She had officially begun to resort to monosyllabic responses.

"I think mad-at-Nate Faye was better than sad-without-Will Faye," Liv said quietly, eying her carefully.

"I'm not sad without Will." Faye scowled, which was a sure sign it was, at least partly, a lie. She did agree that post-Nate Faye was better than post-Will Faye, though she didn't particularly like either of them.

They reached the test barn just after the horse, in time for a *so far, so good* response from the groom to Liv's "how is he?" Liv watched as they bathed Jay, and waited while the hotwalker took him a few turns.

"Want a ride back to the barn with us, Michel?" she asked the groom once they were both satisfied everything was under control. The hotwalker would bring Jay once he was cooled out and the necessary samples had been acquired.

The Triple Stripe barn was deserted when they got there, nothing but the rustling of haynets and snoring of horses. Liv went straight to Chique's stall. Considering how close the big race was, Liv was remarkably calm right now; either that or she was hiding it well.

Faye stared outside the front of the barn at the bank across from it. The glow of the main track lights rimmed its top, the announcer's voice coming eerily from the distance. She heard a deep rumble.

"Was that thunder?" she asked. She hadn't looked at the forecast all day. Not like the people around here, who followed it obsessively because it had such an impact on racing and training.

"Probably," Liv said from behind her. "I think the turf is going to be soft for Sunday. A storm rolling in tonight, and rain predicted for the next couple of days."

"Is that good, or bad?"

"For Chique? Who knows. First time on the grass for her, so it's anyone's guess."

That phrase was used a lot with Chique. *It's anyone's guess.*

Faye glanced at her phone to check the time, and saw she'd missed a text. Dean: *I'm staying down here tonight.*

There he was. So maybe this time his absence was about a horse, and not a woman.

She Brews was a little colicky earlier, and with this weird weather, I'm worried about the others.

And by the others, he meant Wampum, four days out from his return to racing.

All racetrackers were superstitious. Even the one who insisted they weren't. For all she knew Dean was sleeping in a stall next to the horse. You'd think he was running in the Breeders' Cup, not the Breeders' Stakes. She probably wouldn't see him again until the day of the race.

Faye responded. *Have you been here all day?*

Dean: *Yeah.*

Faye: *I came for Just Jay's race. Liv was saddling him.* That wasn't why she'd come, just how it had worked out. *I'll get Liv to stop by on our way out.*

Once Jay returned to the barn, Liv was content to leave him under Michel's care. They checked in with Dean, then Liv drove Faye back to her car on the front side.

"Are you waiting for Nate?" Faye asked.

Liv shook her head. "I'll see him in the morning."

"Should I be worried about you two?"

"We're fine, Faye. Sunday's kind of a big deal. We'll get a breath of normal after that."

Until the next big race drew near. A relationship made up of breaths.

19

What a miserable night.

The rain had started as she'd driven home, a wind-whipping, driving kind of downpour that forced her to go slowly so she could keep the car between the lines. The low-slung clouds left everything under the cloak of premature darkness.

It suited her. She was happy Dean was staying close to the track tonight because he was worried about his Breeders' horse. Happy for her brother's weirdness. Happy to be alone. Misery loves a rainy, stormy night.

She'd made herself this person. The woman who saw men as something to be used. It made her just as bad, just as sexist, as any man who treated women that way, didn't it? *I deserve to grow old and die alone.*

If one was ever really alone with a bottle of wine. And a Golden Retriever.

"C'mon Gus. This definitely calls for a bottle of red."

She didn't care about the weather. She didn't care how Wampum ran. Win or lose, as long as no one was hurt, it really didn't matter to her. The money took the pressure off, then got used up, and something else broke, and it was like it had never been there. Wampum wasn't connected to her fresh start, because there was no fresh start.

A brilliant flash lit up all the windows, stopping her short. The crack that followed – within seconds – almost made her drop to the floor, it was so loud. Everything went dark before the windows had even stopped rattling.

That was close. Really close. But there was no way she was going out to have a look around. The way that gale was gusting, she and Gus would end up in Oz. She preferred to get her ruby red slippers the traditional way, with a good, old-fashioned shopping spree downtown. Not that her credit card would appreciate such a thing. Now where were the candles? *Kitchen counter, I think.*

The next flare of lightning was gentler, the interval between light show and rumble farther apart. It gave her a glimpse, and she saw her phone on the kitchen counter. There was already a text from Liv. *You get home okay? Power just went out here.*

She sent Dean a message before answering. *If that horse wins on Sunday, first thing you're doing Monday morning is calling the electrician and getting that damn generator wired into the panel.* She'd watched Dean hook it up before, but it had never really stuck in her mind. She should have paid more attention.

Dean: *Hydro out, I presume.*

Faye: *Good guess, genius.*

Dean: *Have you heard from Stacy? If it's out for long, you'll have to get it running. The horses will need water.*

With any luck Stacy, the barn manager, had done night check early, anticipating the possibility of this happening. But Faye kept that comment to herself. *I'll text her.*

First Liv. *Yeah, home and okay. At least nothing a bottle of wine won't fix. Power just went out here too. Do you know how to start a generator?*

Liv: *You need help? I'm sure someone on the farm could do it. I'll ask Nate. He just texted saying they cancelled the last two races, so he's on his way.*

Faye: *Because that's just what I need, Nate coming to my rescue.*

Liv: *Really? You want to be picky like that now?*

Faye: *Why is there not a tongue-sticking-out emoji? Because I could use one right now.*

She got a rolling ROTFL one for that.

Now, Stacy. *Do you need help with anything? I'm at the house. Horses have water?*

Stacy: *Good for now. I'll let you know if that changes. I'm just going to make sure everyone outside is okay.*

Thank goodness for small mercies. Faye opened up the bottle of wine, counted to ten – long enough for her to breathe, if not the wine. Glass filled and in hand, she padded into the living room. Dean always made sure there was kindling and wood for a fire, even in the summer *because August can get cold, you know.* And so it could. And tonight it was.

She felt a hundred times better once it caught, flames spreading from the paper and cardboard to the pile of dry branches, and she sat in front of it, staring, until she was convinced it was ready for a larger log. Then she waited until the fire was committed to its consumption, and pushed herself up, grabbing the wine again – because it would not be far from her side tonight – and began the search for candles.

They were never all in one place. A couple in the kitchen cupboards, a couple in the rarely – as in, almost never – used dining room. Striking a match, the wick on the first one hissed to life, settling into a steady, comforting flame. She lit the others, until little flickering lights dotted the kitchen and living room.

What now?

Well, she would drink wine and feel pathetic so that tomorrow she could put it all behind her and figure out how to move forward from here.

THE RAIN WAS PELTING against his windshield like it was personal. Like he shouldn't be driving up the 400 at this time of night, on an evening when there were wind warnings, maybe even tornado warnings, going to see a girl who didn't want to see him. At least the weight of his old domestic car kept him on the road; kept it from hydroplaning over the glassy sheet of water that covered the asphalt.

A headwind fought him when he left the highway, pushing back as he drove along King Sideroad. If it had been words, it would have been saying, *don't you see, any rational person would not have left the city on a night like this?* And why were there no lights? Anywhere.

He turned up on the sideroad Faye's farm was on, creeping. Everything was so dark. But he was almost there now. No turning back. She couldn't turn him away, could she?

Thunk.

He braked, hard, pressing into the headrest, back braced against the seat. His knuckles were so tight on the wheel his hands hurt. What the hell was that? The windshield wipers tried to beat back the rain as he peered through the glass, trying to figure it out. He climbed into the soaking downpour, and stepped towards the front of the car. A tree! And not a small one. Right across the road. A matter of seconds had been the difference between it landing on his Camaro, and where it had ended up. Except now he was stuck here.

There had to be a way around. Or maybe this was a sign from God. *Hello, idiot, you should have stayed home. She doesn't want to see you. You're too tall, or nice,* or…something. Cripes.

So…now what? Faye's house was literally a hundred feet away. He could text Nate, and see if Nate could help with the tree. Or, it wasn't much of a walk to the apartment. Maybe back up the car and get it on the side of the road before he abandoned it. And pray another tree didn't fall on it.

Were things ever dark. Had he told himself that already? He climbed back in the car, and punched a message out to Nate. *Hey man, crazy question, but do you have a chainsaw?*

Sending it into cyberspace felt a little like setting a message in a bottle to sea. Who knows when Nate would see it; it was nine PM on a Wednesday night. The guy was probably asleep in bed, and would be pissed off at Will for waking him up. This wasn't exactly an emergency, was it?

The logical thing would have been to text Faye. But that would ruin the surprise. Ha. That element might not work in his favour right now. Showing up at her door on a night like this? He wouldn't put it past her to own a gun. Farms had shotguns, didn't they? He'd bet Faye knew how to handle one.

But, he was committed now. And that tree wasn't going anywhere. So, if he was doing this, he was doing it on foot. He retrieved his backpack from behind the front seat, slung it over his shoulder, and pulled up his hood, which really didn't do much to protect him from the angry elements.

It would probably be smarter to ask to sleep on Nate's couch. Instead he climbed through the downed branches, snagging his jacket on something and hearing the tear as he pulled it free. Sheets of rain stung his eyes. A southeast wind never brought good things. But he was fighting it, pushing into it, come what may.

A LIGHT OUTSIDE THE WINDOW – was she seeing things? Faye sat bolt upright, clutching the glass, heart hammering against her chest. Gus slept like the dead at her feet. *Great, Gus. You'll be lying there passed out as some ax murderer is slashing my throat and leaving me to bleed out.*

The rain still beat against the window pane. She set the wine glass on the coffee table, stepped over Gus – that dog was unbelievable – and crept into the kitchen, like her footsteps might, what, alert whoever was out there to her presence? She should probably be hiding in the basement, instead of investigating. Except the basement of this old Victorian was scarier than whatever might be out there.

It was times like this she wished they had a shotgun – but Dean was too nice a guy to shoot coyotes like most farmers. She had nothing with which to defend herself. Except – yes. That's what she'd grab.

The light flashed around the back door. Then the ax murderer knocked. Did they do that? Wouldn't they just barge in? She closed her grip around the wooden handle, and opened the door a crack.

"Will!" He was soaked, hair plastered to his face, his jacket clearly not waterproof. "What the hell are you doing here?"

"If you put down the rolling pin and let me in, I'll tell you. I do love your weapon of choice, though."

She backed away from the door, leaving the wooden pin on the kitchen table. Then she grabbed him with both hands, pulling him against her, his clothes so wet they made hers damp as she clutched his waist. Her heart finally started to temper.

"You need some dry clothes." She reluctantly peeled herself from him. "Take off your shoes."

He did as he was told as she lifted the backpack from his shoulder, holding it, dripping, out to the side. It took him so long to get his coat off she thought it must've been adhered to his skin.

Will reached for the backpack and glanced around before setting it on the floor. Gus lumbered sleepily between them, sticking his nose into it and wagging his tail.

"Sure, Gus. Now you decide to make an appearance. Lucky for you, there's no blood to clean up." Faye rubbed the Golden's ribcage.

Will looked at her strangely, then reached into the bag and withdrew a paper bag.

"What is that?" she asked suspiciously.

He handed it to her. "I brought dessert?"

"I didn't know you were coming for dinner."

Accepting, she placed it on the counter. The paper bag was so wet it tore, so she just ripped it the rest of the way off to reveal a white paperboard box. She eased open the sodden lid. Four small, perfect pastries. They looked part chocolate, and part tart, and totally melt-in-your-mouth.

"They're prototypes. For the shop. Your shop."

She'd let herself forget when she'd seen him. She looked at the perfect little confections with a sad smile. "I don't have a shop."

"Sure seems like your shop."

"Lucy's selling it. I'll help with the transition, then, I guess I'm done. These look delicious, though." She pushed them back from the edge, because Gus was known to counter surf on occasion. "Come on. About those dry clothes. You're about the same size as Dean."

It was just plain human decency to bring him back from the verge of hypothermia. She'd decide if she was going to jump his bones after he'd had a chance to warm up by the fire. Nothing had changed, but she certainly wasn't sending him back out into that horrible night.

Will could hear his phone buzzing, he just had no idea where it was. He was warmer, sure, but the effort his body had put into reheating had left him exhausted, and his head hadn't caught up.

Then there was another ringing, and it wasn't until Faye went dashing toward the next room saying, "If the landline rings, it has to be serious," that he realized that's what it was.

He found his phone on the counter, and glanced at the screen. *A chainsaw? I don't understand.*

He chuckled at Nate's text. *Go back to sleep. I'll tell you about it tomorrow.*

Wednesday night racing, dude. I just got home. Where are you? Are you okay?

NVM. I'm fine now.

Nate seemed convinced enough to leave him alone. He disconnected in time to hear the tail end of Faye's conversation.

"Okay. We'll be there in a few minutes."

We? "What's up?" he asked when he reentered the living room.

"That was Stacy, the farm manager. One of the outdoor horses managed to slice her leg. She saw it when she was doing one last check before going to bed. Can you start a generator? I'm totally hopeless at remembering how to do it."

"Where is it?"

He followed her to a laundry room off of the kitchen. "It's outside. Dean got as far as building it a little shed. I know you have to take this long cord and attach it - unplug the dryer and use that outlet, then the other end goes in the generator."

Will walked to the electrical panel and flipped off the circuit breakers and the main switch. "So we don't blow the place up."

"See, this is why it petrifies me. Here, take one of Dean's jackets." She pulled on a proper Gore Tex raincoat and led the way out.

The generator had gas, thank goodness, and was soon chugging away with ear-piercing determination.

"So what do you want power for?" he asked, back in the house where they could hear again.

"Water. Lights in the barn might be helpful too. Barn one on the panel.

Then we'd better go see if she needs any help. Not that I'm much good as far as horses are concerned."

"Well I don't know much about them, but they don't terrify me, so I'll do what I can. My grandfather had cows. Now they're terrifying." He flipped on individual breakers for the barn and the pump, hearing the pump run immediately. "There you go."

Faye keyed in a text to update Stacy, then started blowing out candles. "Do they bite?"

"Cows? I don't know, but they sure can kick."

FAYE DIDN'T RUN – except sometimes, through the rain, when it was gushing down like this. Nervous whinnies travelled through the barn as they ducked inside. Simple bulbs illuminated the aisle – and Stacy filling a bucket with warm, soapy water.

"Thank you! Of all the nights. Horses!" she said, but with a laugh in her voice that carried more affection than Faye felt for the species at the moment. Love is patient, love is kind, love is stupid, love is blind. It should be the horse girl mantra.

"They know how to pick 'em," Faye agreed. "This is Will. If you need help, he says he's your man." She stopped short of saying, *he's actually my man,* because he wasn't, and wouldn't be. No amount of pastry and heroics was going to change that, not even on a night like this.

"Perfect." Stacy was too engrossed in preparing to doctor the horse to give Will more than a quick glance. "I've almost got stuff ready, then I'll bring her into the aisle – if you can hold her for me? She's a sweetheart, she won't give you a hard time. One of the barren mares."

Will held the leather lead awkwardly as Stacy tapped bubbles out of a small syringe. She put pressure on the mare's jugular and deftly slipped it in, pulling back the plunger so the colourless medication was quickly turned a deep red before easing it into the vein. Faye had watched it enough times she could probably do it herself, if she could ever get over her fear enough to be that close. Even as the shot took effect, the mare blinking before her eyes began to droop, Faye was glad Will was here to hold that shank so it hadn't been up to her.

"I don't think she'll need stitches," Stacy said, standing with hands on hips as she waited for the injection to kick in further "But I want to clean it up and put a bandage on it. I'm sure the vet would love to come out on a night like this."

"He's probably dealing with a bunch of colics," Faye said. "Dean had one at the track today, Mild, thank goodness, but it put him on edge."

"Oh – there's a tree down on the road," Will said, breaking out of what seemed to be intense concentration on the job he'd been given. It was cute.

"Really? Where?" Faye asked.

"Right before your driveway. Between here and Triple Stripe."

"So that's why you were soaking wet? You left your car and walked?" She hadn't even not-seen his car.

"Do you have a chainsaw?"

Faye looked at Stacy. "We do, right? I am feeling very much like a useless woman tonight."

"We do. But I think it's best you call the township and have them remove it. It's kind of dangerous."

"I can do that," Faye said. "Just not in a steel barn. You two okay?"

"Yep," Stacey said, grabbing a little stainless steel pail and carefully dousing soapy water over the wound with gauze sponges, the scent of the air tinged with iodine.

FAYE LEFT THEM. The horse was really quiet, her eyes droopy. Every now and then her head would twitch, and Will would jump, but the horse didn't move.

"You can relax," Stacy said. "She's got good drugs on board, and this won't take that long."

The suds pooled on the mat under the horse's hooves. Once Stacy seemed satisfied she'd cleaned the gash enough, she ripped open a small packet and placed a pad over it, then wound a gauze roll over that, then a longer roll of something that covered the lower leg.

"That's quite a production," he said. How she managed to do it so that it wouldn't fall off, he didn't know.

"Done it so many times I don't even think about it. Horses like to hurt themselves. It's like every day is a fresh chance for them to find a new way to die."

"That's a morbid way to look at things."

Stacy grinned, and glanced up at him. "True horse people are in a constant love/hate relationship with these animals. There's a fine line between how they help us stay sane, and how they drive us completely *in*sane."

"So why do you do it?"

She paused, like it was justifiable to question it. "Because they're everything, wrapped majestically together. Power and fragility, strength and vulnerability. Honesty and bravery. They can literally kick your head in if you let your guard down, but they can lift a peppermint from your palm with such gentleness. Once they're in your blood, there's no getting out." She was applying another, thicker, pillow-looking layer, then held it all in place with a red bandage like the white ones Jo and Nate had put on Chique after the Prince of Wales.

Stacy's soliloquy was just more proof the whole horse world was beyond his comprehension. "She's not looking so majestic at the moment," he said, convinced now she wasn't going to cause any trouble. He stroked her long face, and the mare's lids slid over her glassy eyes.

Stacy laughed, securing the end of the bandage and smoothing the whole thing with both hands.

"Does Dean know about this, Stacy?"

Will glanced over his shoulder. Faye stood at a safe distance, snapping.

"No, I didn't want to contact him till I knew how bad it was. And it's not that bad, so it can wait till I'm done."

A few flicks of her fingers later, Faye said, "I just sent him a text."

"Thanks. One less thing for me to do." Stacy stood, reaching for the lead. "She's done. Here, I'll take her."

Will stepped back, and Faye inched up to his elbow. "Good job, cowboy."

He laughed, and resisted a very strong urge to put an arm around her. "I had the easy job."

"You know, there is one thing about you Calgary boys that disappoints me. Like, where are the white cowboy hats? Isn't that part of the uniform?"

"Right." Will laughed. "For the Winter Olympics, maybe."

"You'd look good in one," she said, sliding him a wry grin and turning away. "I don't know about you, but I need wine."

GUS SCRAMBLED to his feet in a clatter of nails when Faye pushed open the door, behind which he'd been right behind, worrying. Somehow he wasn't afraid of thunder or fireworks, but the noise of the generator outside unsettled him enough to temper his usual enthusiasm.

She dragged off her rubber boots and shuffled to the wine bottle, gauging its contents. "Do you want some? Would you prefer beer? Or I can make coffee or hot chocolate." He was looking chilled again, after standing still holding the mare.

"Wine is fine, if you have enough."

"I always have enough," she assured him. She divided what remained between two glasses, handed him one, and wandered into the living room, settling on a cushion in front of the fire. Will dropped into a nearby chair.

"How do you know when the power comes back on?" he asked.

"Stacy will tell me, if she's still awake. She said she's okay with her electric lantern if it's just short term. Her apartment is wired separately. If it were winter and she needed heat, I'd have invited her to the house."

She'd invited Stacy anyway, but Stacy had shot a look at Will and declined. Having Stacy there would have provided assurance Faye would not stray from her resolve with him. Now, she'd have to just rely on self-control, which was an unpredictable thing. She kept her eyes on the fire, because watching the way the light moved over his strong features would tempt her too much.

"I have to tell you something, Faye. It's major.'

Well that was scary.

"I'm the one who's buying Lucy's."

All she could do was stare at him while she tried to process his revelation. Because how should she react? She was angry, like he'd kept an affair from her. She was happy for him, because that had been his dream, right? She was relieved, that someone was buying it who would do right by Lucy's legacy. She wanted to be hopeful, but that was a precarious emotion at the best of times.

"Congratulations," she said, trying to keep all of it out of her voice, waiting for him to fill in more details. "You could have told me."

"I am telling you."

She rolled her eyes. "You could have told me sooner."

"It honestly just came together this week. Okay yes, I've been communicating with her. And you ending things between us should have ended that, too, but it seemed to have the opposite effect. So I might have just taken a way bigger risk than I'm entirely comfortable with."

"Why didn't Lucy tell me?" Faye was just wondering out loud with that one.

"To be honest, she never made the connection. And I didn't help her make it. So to her I'm still some random guy. We've never met in person to discuss anything. It was always over the phone."

"How are you even affording this? You work in a restaurant."

His smile was elusive. "A little help from my mother. A little help from my friends."

The pieces started to slot together, one by one. "Liv."

"Nate too. Not a huge investment, because Lucy's letting me pay for it over time. So she gets a decent lump sum, then a monthly income for a while. Liv's dad is helping her set the money up in investments so she can focus on her mom and not worry about trying to pay the bills."

"All of you. All of you kept this from me. I can't believe it." She pushed up from the cushion with one hand, turning away and taking a slug of wine to try to calm herself.

"Please don't be mad. Listen, Faye. The last five days have been hell. I know you don't do this. I think there's more to the why than you let on. But I do know one thing. I want you in my life, and not just as a guy on the periphery, the friend of your friends."

She dared a glance over her shoulder. His expression was so…earnest. The hair on the back of her neck had risen, little bumps manifesting on the skin of her forearms. Will set his glass on the end table next to the chair, coming over, hovering behind her for a moment before turning her gently. She relinquished her glass against her better judgement, letting him set it aside. Then he grasped both her hands in his, and she wanted to drink in whatever coloured his golden hazel eyes. She was in trouble.

"Faye…will you…"

Oh, no way. No. Way. He was going to ruin everything, wreck any chance she had of reconsidering him and a future. But she couldn't speak, needed to hear it anyway; like maybe that would convince her that it truly was not meant to be.

"…help me run Lucy's?"

She blinked, then felt a warmth spread through her like that first, glorious sip of a steaming cappuccino. Her lips spread so wide she was sure the corners were in her ears, and she threw herself at him, laughing with a ridiculous sob as she attached herself to his shoulders.

"I will."

She reluctantly detached herself, pushing him away with a smirk. "Smart ass."

He caught her arm, and pulled her back in. "This probably isn't the best way to start a working relationship, but…" Keeping one hand on the small of her back, he pressed her into him, brushing her hair away from her face. Then, curling his fingers to the back of her long neck, he met her lips, carefully, until he was convinced she wanted to find out what this thing between them was as much as he did.

He finally made himself pull away, and she very nearly fell into the small space he'd created between them. "Could this be considered sexual harassment?"

Her head tilted slightly as she answered. "You haven't actually bought the place yet, so if this happens before you do…"

"This being?"

"Us," she said, her voice a low tremor.

"Do you want to try that? Us?"

"I do." She looked up at him with a very impish grin.

"I will. I do. Those words carry some serious intent. Are you sure?"

"As long as right now they only mean I will help you, and I do want to try something that doesn't have an expiry date, then, yes."

"I'm happy to hear that."

He started kissing her again, but she ducked out of his hold. "We need a toast. We have all night for the rest of it. I'm not letting you go back out into that." The room lit up with a flash for emphasis, followed by a crack of thunder that made them both jump.

After throwing a log on the fire, Faye parked him there before going to the kitchen, returning with another bottle of wine. He sat cross-legged, resting his refilled glass on one knee, staring into the flames. When she joined him, he tucked her under one arm. Truth be told, it was physically uncomfortable, but cosy and right.

She sipped, nestling closer. "Part of why I was attracted to Nate was because he was so obviously wounded. I probably should have pushed, to find out why. Hindsight and all that. I just never expected to be with him long enough for it to matter. And as it went along, I think I just didn't want to know. Maybe he never opened up to me, but I never asked. So I have to know, with you. Something happened to you, too, to make you leave. Something deeper, submerged. His was right there, only barely contained. If I'd been brave enough to uncover it, I would have known far sooner that I had no chance with him."

"Nate was blameless in what happened to him, unless you can blame him for being naïve. He fell in love with the wrong person."

Just like she had. "I'm not asking what happened to Nate. What happened to Nate doesn't matter to me anymore. I'm asking about you. Because if I really am going to do this, I need to know if I have a better chance with you."

He sighed, letting the wine and her hand, reaching over to touch his chest, draw it out of him. "It wasn't really one thing. More a combination." He filled his lungs with air; released it slowly. "There was a girl on our street named Hannah, growing up. She was a tomboy, one of the guys. She used to play street hockey with us, could climb trees better than anyone else, ride her bike just as hard. She'd come out to my grandfather's farm and hop on horses bareback and ride around with Nate. We'd go climbing in the summer, skiing in the winter. We were best friends. Then things changed in high school, of course. For me, anyway. But she didn't change, she still played just as hard, so I never told her how I felt. Which is all fun and games until someone gets hurt. Or dies."

"Oh Will – no…"

"Climbing accident. So I think she's forever suspended in my memory, as the ideal, because we were so close. I just wanted to be closer. She didn't though, and then she was gone, so it didn't matter."

"How old were you?"

There was so much dark tension in Faye's voice he glanced down and tightened his arm around her, but she wriggled slightly, and he eased off. "Fifteen. It was around the same time my dad decided to leave my mom and move to BC with his then-girlfriend. Father of the year. So he was gone, and my mom was so upset she threw herself into her work twice as hard. It didn't leave a lot of time for me. Sure she did all the things she thought was right, getting me counselling, and the Millers were amazing. But none of it set me up for success when it came to relationships. Then when I met you, and you were so open and life goes on about losing your parents, it made me think I should be able to get over it, too."

She laughed. "Ironic, though, that maybe life goes on, but mine has been totally dysfunctional."

"Do you try and figure out why?"

"The therapy thing never worked for me, probably because I didn't care why. I figured I deserved it. You know the weekend my parents went to visit Shawn, I was supposed to go? But I was mad at him, and I had a new boyfriend. He'd always vetted the guys who were interested in me because we had a one year overlap in high school – his last year was my first. When he was around, none of them were good enough, in my eyes, even if he'd think they were okay. Because I was always comparing them to him. When he left, I started dating a guy who was totally the opposite, who he never would have liked. And that weekend, I stayed home, because I could have the boyfriend over, and they would never know. And then they were all killed. And I've never been able to shake the thought that it was somehow my fault."

"You know that's crazy, right?'

Her shoulder lifted and fell under her arm. "Hasn't stopped the feeling, though. I don't think I really realized, till Nate, that my pattern might be a little game I've played since then. Getting involved with these men with high-risk jobs, to feel something – anything – and getting out before it got serious enough that I cared. None of them have died, thank goodness…but that day at Keeneland, when Nate went down with our colt, Wampum, was like a trigger. It was a reminder that the relationship had gone far beyond its best before date. Beyond safe."

"So it was more complicated than just Liv, and Nate falling for Liv."

"It was, wasn't it? But it's all turned out okay. Nate was fine. Wampum is ready to run again. Liv and Nate got together. And I'm happy they're happy, even if it's hard to tell with Liv sometimes, she keeps her feelings so close."

Will nodded against the top of her head, and kissed it. "I think of Nate, and Liv, and how much of a risk their life holds. How they have to live with that every day. I don't want to be completely sheltered, but I'm done with needing that level of adrenaline to feel alive. That kind of physical challenge, where the threat of death is always looming…it's not worth it. Hannah was like that. She and Nate were always egging each other on. Neither of us were there when she died, though. Nate was spending more time with horses by then. And some of the crazy climbing shit she did, I just stopped going. I don't want to be with someone like that again. This right here is risk enough for me."

"Seeing if you can break my pattern of dysfunction?" She tipped her head back, hair falling from her face as her eyes met his.

He leaned in and kissed her. "You read books and cook. You play with numbers. You run a café. I think the biggest danger will be that you won't have time for me. If I can get you to sing more than the vocables in a song, you're my perfect woman."

"Well, you're going to have to work on that." A smile twisted her lips, and she brushed a still-damp lock of hair from his forehead, stretching up to kiss him back.

20

Dean had ventured home the next afternoon, Faye luring him with a proper meal after he'd consumed more takeout than she deemed good for him. He was out in the barn, getting the rundown on the horses from Stacy. The mare was fine, and thankfully no one else had found trouble during the storm. At the track, She Brews seemed to be back to her old self, though Dean was still playing it safe with her. Wampum was fine too. This had been entry day for the Breeders', so Dean was worked up, though he would never admit it.

She yawned, peering into a fridge that was looking too sparse this soon after grocery day. She had to pull dinner out of it, somehow. Time to use up bits and pieces before they went bad. She set out the wok, tipped in some oil, and when it was hot, threw in all the veggies she found, sliced and fried up the last bit of chicken breast, cooked some rice noodles. Simple, but it smelled delicious.

"Mmmm, looks great," Dean peeked over her shoulder, inhaling happily. He pulled a bottle from the fridge, one of those nice honey-brown craft beers she'd found for him last week. "Want one?"

"No thanks." While she wasn't hungover after last night's wine, she was tired enough alcohol would just make her drag more.

She hadn't been able to sleep with the generator running. Will, on the other hand, had passed out in front of the fire, back to back with Gus. The noise hadn't bothered him, used to constant sound in Toronto, whereas anything more than country silence kept Faye awake. The power had come back on sometime in the middle of the night, at which point she'd roused Will and Gus out of their slumber long enough to shepherd them to her bed.

Dean parked at the kitchen table and unfolded the *Form*, spreading it out and immersing himself; studying of a different sort from what he'd done during his formal education. He took it as seriously as he had his degrees: poring over pages of past performances, filing away names and numbers and combinations. Trainers had to be handicappers too, even if they never bet.

Dean stopped reading, his head at an angle. "What's that?"

Faye could hear something out of place too, beyond the sizzle as the stir-fried veggies became tender. She pushed them around, added more soya sauce, and stirred. "Someone having a party? Sounds like music."

"On a Thursday?" Dean pushed himself to his feet and went to the screen door. He grinned, then looked over his shoulder at Faye. "Come here."

She turned off the heat, wiped her hands on a towel, and padded over, peeking around him. Then she grinned too.

Will. He stood on the deck with a guitar, picking and strumming and tapping…and singing, in that voice. Her hand went to her mouth, because her lips didn't know what to do. Smile, wail, because she had to smear away a tear. The guy was singing to her.

"I don't know, Faye," Dean said, "but I think you'd better ask him to stay for dinner."

He moved out of the way, pushing her forward gently with a hand on her back, and turned back to the table, his *Form*, and his beer.

Faye swung open the door, holding it so it wouldn't slam shut, and stood in silence listening to the sweet words and melody…more than words…and watching the champagne eyes, the curve of his lips as he sang, the movement of his hands. Part of her wanted the song to go on forever. Part of her wanted it to be done so she could kiss him silly.

She crept closer, until she was a few feet from him. He was winding down, the notes fading into the summer breeze.

"Dean says I have to ask you for dinner."

"I like Dean."

"Now what are you going to do with that guitar? Because I don't want to hurt it."

His lazy smile turned the warm fuzzies she was feeling into something red-hot, but she stood her ground while he lifted the strap over his head, and, grasping the guitar by its neck, leaned it carefully against the deck's railing. Just in the nick of time, because she was on him, coming short of jumping up and wrapping her legs around him…but only just.

"You are a glutton for punishment," she breathed into his ear.

"Don't flatter yourself."

"I could rip off your clothes right here."

"Dean's probably hungry."

"Who's Dean again?"

He pried her arms from his neck, but it took longer for them to pull apart. Faye straightened her shirt, smoothing the front, but there was no calming the bounce of her heart.

"The serenade was nice," she said, trying to compose herself. "But I hope you brought dessert."

THE CLOSER THE BREEDERS' Stakes came, the more stressed Liv got. Pressure building on pressure. Faye had to intervene.

"You're not going to sleep, so just come over. We'll get a little bit drunk, eat junk food, and talk about boys. Like normal girls do as teenagers. You missed out on that, so we'll do it now. Bring Em."

Dean came out of the office and eyed them with raised brows, the three women camped out on the floor of the farmhouse's living room. The fire roared, a bottle of wine soon empty. They each had their own cartons of Haagen-Dazs. Faye guarded a plate of Will's decadent creations from the nose of Gus.

"Ice cream and wine? Does that work?" Dean asked.

"Go away, Dean. Girls only," Faye scolded, scraping her spoon around the edges of her carton to collect the softest ice cream.

"Fine." He tried to grumble, couldn't keep the smirk off his lips. "I'm going to get some sleep."

"No chance of that here, so get some for all of us!" Emile called.

He turned for the stairs. "See you in the paddock, Liv."

"Shut up, Dean," Liv growled. "I'm trying to forget about that right now."

Faye laughed, and topped up the wine glasses. "You know he adores you."

Em shot her a look, but Faye just threw her irises up into her eyelids.

"Don't even joke about that. He's like the brother I never had, Faye." Liv sipped a bit too much wine, and it caught in her throat, making her cough. "Like you're the sister I never had."

Faye laughed. It didn't take much to get Liv a little drunk.

"Um, hello?" Em said.

"The older sister I never had," Liv corrected.

"I don't know, I think Em fills that role quite well. For both of us."

"True." Liv had her wine glass in one hand, and ice cream in the other, and seemed to be weighing the relative benefits of each.

"How's Jiro, Em?" Faye asked, reaching for one of Will's perfect confections and popping it into her mouth, whole.

"Jiro and I are just friends. Letting people think otherwise keeps us both from the wolves."

"Wolves like me. Or what used to be me."

"I'm so proud of you, Faye. I'm so proud of both of my girls." Emilie grinned, looking from Faye to Liv.

"One day, Mom, it will be your turn," Faye said. "Your perfect man is out there."

"Is he, though?"

"There's a brother," Liv said.

"That's right," Faye said. "Nate has a younger brother."

"I'll need a picture."

"I have seen one," Liv mused. "He's taller, with dark hair. Just as good-looking. But still in Calgary."

"Calgary boys do seem to be the way to go, though, Em," Faye said. "We'll just have to figure out how to entice him here. Unless you want us to set you up with Dean. Because it may come to that."

"Poor Dean," Em said.

"Why poor Dean?" Liv asked. "He could be perfectly happy alone. I was perfectly happy."

Faye snorted. "You were not."

"Well if Nate had never existed, I would have been."

"Ah, but he does." Faye grinned. "And your life will never be the same."

"When does it stop being scary?" Liv asked.

Faye held out the plate, because Liv clearly needed chocolate to amplify the wine and ice cream. "I don't know. I'm not there yet. Fun, isn't it?"

"There is something that's even more terrifying."

"Which is?"

"Tomorrow," Liv said solemnly. "Tomorrow, I have to saddle a potential Canadian Triple Crown winner."

"If Chique wins, you'll be the first female trainer to pull it off." Like she likely hadn't heard that how many times since the Prince of Wales?

"Shut up, Faye."

"Snappish."

They laughed at each other.

"Either way," Emilie interjected, "I need to raise my glass to both of you. Liv, turning things around to get your trainer's license, and have a relationship with something other than a horse –"

Faye snorted again.

"– And you, Faye, to chance another relationship, and to take on a new business, making yourself a pillar of the community…"

"I'm blushing now, Em."

"Cheers to both of you. You're inspiring. No matter what happens tomorrow."

"Gah, tomorrow," Liv moaned. "Pour me some more wine."

Liv stared into the fire, fixated on the flames, having set her ice cream aside to wrap an arm around Gus. Em sampled a chocolate mousse bite, closing her eyes as the ecstasy of it hit her taste buds. Faye leaned back against an armchair, legs tucked underneath her, grateful for the warmth of the fire, and friends.

"This is how I imagine the night before your wedding," she said.

Liv sputtered out her most recent mouthful of wine. "My wedding?"

"I'd better be your maid of honour," Faye said.

"Fine," Em said. "As long as you have at least one bridesmaid. Me."

"My wedding?" Liv repeated.

"So that means no eloping!" Faye warned.

"Unless you take both of us along," Emilie said.

"And Will," Faye added. "And the brother. A destination wedding might be nice."

"When do I get to meet the brother?" Emilie asked, looking at Liv.

"My wedding?"

"Yes, he'd come, wouldn't he?" Faye said.

"That's not what I meant!" Liv groaned.

"Well that took your mind off the race, didn't it? Yes, your wedding. Don't worry, we'll help you plan it."

"Of course we will," Emilie agreed.

"Will's restaurant can cater it. I mean, he'll be too busy to do it himself, as Nate's best man, but his in with Chef Gerry will come in handy. I'm sure he's got a favour or two to call in with that monster."

Now Liv was laughing, like the idea was totally absurd to her. "You'll definitely be married before me."

"Wanna bet?"

"Careful now, you're looking a little lovestruck," Liv whispered, leaning into her ear.

Faye batted her away. She needed to stop looking so obvious. "It's happening again, isn't it?"

"Who would have thought, eh?"

"So lightning can strike twice?"

"Statistically improbable, but not impossible." Liv grinned.

"You know, I really wish you had become a vet, or gone and got a PhD or something, because it just feels like we should call you Dr. Lachance."

They weren't new, these feelings, but this time, she hadn't been caught off guard. If she was careful, she'd see them through. Make something tangible from them….like a future.

21

Dean held Wampum as Nikki gave him a bath, steam rising and blending with the cool grey sky. The colt had just walked, casually touring the shedrow. Chique had trained.

Faye had walked out to the track to watch, following Liv on the Triple Stripe stable pony, Paz. More evidence of her fresh start, a continuation of their promise to do better: she'd risen with Dean to come in, not to set up a not-so-chance meeting with a hot bug, but to stand by her friend in the anxious morning hours before the race. Her friend – the trainer of the horse Dean was trying to beat with Wampum.

She could cheer for them both, couldn't she? It would be amazing if Liv's filly won. It would be great for Northwest if Wampum won. Then again, this was horse racing, so maybe neither of them would win. All that mattered in the end was that they both came through safe and sound. Losing a race was disappointing. Losing a life was devastating.

Chique had galloped an easy mile – easy relating only to the speed of her effort. It hadn't looked anything close to easy for Nate up there as he held her, his weight balanced against her fire, the puffs of vapour from her nostrils like smoke from a dragon. Liv had escorted her protectively off the oval, Chique vibrating in the uncharacteristically chill August air. *Filly weather,* Faye's father would have called it – though it was supposed to show up in October, conjuring up talk of Florida departures and the speedily approaching end of the Ontario season.

A groom called for Dean from a stall, and Dean glanced around as Nikki began the rinse, clearing the layer of suds with alcohol-laced water. Wampum gave a little shudder, when a horse like Chique would have likely erupted from the tiny sparks the brace sent over sensitive skin.

"Here Faye. Hold him." Dean waved her over.

Faye blinked. "Uh…" She glanced around, sure there must be someone else who could step in. Dean knew better. Dean knew why.

"He's quiet as a pony, Faye. He won't hurt you. I promise. You don't have to walk him, just stand here until Nikki's done his bath."

She inched forward timidly, taking the long length of leather with both hands, but standing back. Wampum's ears flipped closer together, his big, soft eyes penetrating skin and bone to see inside her. Her trembling didn't seem to bother him.

She still had the scar, and the misshapen nail on the middle finger of her left hand – the one a broodmare had taken the tip of. She'd been five, feeding the huge animal a carrot. Her father had likely only blinked – things like that happened so quickly. Wailing in the back seat of the car in her mother's arms, he'd driven to the emergency room. When she'd been older, she'd learned from her mother that her father had struggled to forgive himself for that incident. To Faye, it was just an indication she lacked the horse gene. He'd stopped trying to foster a love of horses in her after that. She'd kept a safe distance from the animals since.

Wampum lipped the shank, his neck telescoping, somehow getting closer without moving his feet. Faye stood her ground, though her heart was racing. She held out her other hand, palm flat, and grinned as he licked it like a huge dog. A big, kind, gentle giant. Her fear eased just a little with the tiny connection she felt. She wasn't in any danger of becoming a horse girl, but it felt somehow like moving forward.

The colt's comeback, his second chance to show who he was, matched her own, didn't it? They'd both gone down that day at Keeneland. They'd both been broken. And now they were both healed, and stronger than before. If she could do this – stand here, this close to a horse, and not get bitten – maybe lightning could strike twice, and set her on fire again. Fire wasn't always bad – especially when it came with pastry.

THE END

ALL GOOD THINGS

BOOK 3

Out of suffering have emerged the strongest souls. The most massive characters are seared with scars.

— EDWIN HUBBELL CHAPIN

1

Voices, nervous laughter, peripheral movement; on the fringes of her consciousness, none of it important. All that was worthy of her focus was skin sliding over muscle, muscle extending and contracting. Liv analyzed every stride down to each footfall, and tried to gauge the ever-unknown unpredictability factor in the sleek filly before her.

Chique was light years away from the unraced two-year-old she'd been a year ago. There was a swagger to her step now, the glint in her eyes behind the blinkers self-important, if you could say that about a horse. With eight races under her belt, at five different tracks — five of them wins — the professionalism she displayed here in Woodbine's walking ring, willow branches whispering overhead, wasn't unexpected. Liv just didn't trust it.

A touch disrupted her concentration, her head snapping to the side like the wind whipping from the northwest had picked it up in a gust. She didn't bother to fix the dark hair flying around her face. She should have put it up. She was usually practical about such things, like the "turf shoes" on her feet — flats, when heels would have punched through the rain-soaked carpet of grass. Not that she ever wore heels.

She extracted a hand from the depths of her trench coat pocket, and

Nate returned the firmness of her grasp, the amusement playing on his features a contrast to the seriousness of her own. She could tell what he was thinking. *No, Miller, it would not be appropriate for the rider to kiss the trainer in the walking ring.*

"So?" He crossed his arms, stick tucked under his elbow.

"Stay off the inside," she responded, though she wasn't saying anything he didn't already know. They'd discussed strategy ad nauseam, walked the full mile-and-a-half of the rain-sodden E.P. Taylor turf course that morning, and he'd ridden over it in an earlier race. The course was soft, but safe.

"Breathe," he said. He squeezed the elbow of the arm that was now folded over her chest in a less-assured reflection of his posture.

"Sure, Miller. It's only the Canadian Triple Crown on the line. But if you're cool, that's what matters."

This was the first possible first in her fledgling training career. A woman trainer had won the Queen's Plate before her. A woman trainer had won the Prince of Wales, the second jewel of the crown. A woman trainer had won this, the Breeders' Stakes, third and final jewel. But no woman had won all three in the same year with the same horse.

The paddock judge gave the riders up call. Liv glanced at Nate.

"Let's do this," he said with a nod, trying to be serious before he let go the grin that was the only thing with any hope of distracting her from the stormy sky, the very un-August-like cool, and everything that was on the line.

"*Bonne chance.* Don't screw up. Come home safe." She threw him up onto the moving filly, and felt the too-familiar helplessness seep in.

He was so sure about Chique. Like he was so sure about them. Liv envied that, but now wasn't the time to think about it.

"DON'T WORRY, princess, you don't have to run in this," Nate said.

Chique balked at the on-gap, as if she didn't believe him, her ears swiveling to the grey slab of sealed track in front of them, a wet gloss to its surface.

Nicole nudged Paz into a jog to lead them up for the post parade, the stable pony happily punching through the surface like a kid playing in the mud.

"You worried about the turf?" she asked.

"Nah. Just worried she might hate me after warming up."

The filly minced over the bog, and actually seemed happy to downshift to a walk while the announcer introduced the starters. Thank goodness they were running on the grass. Chique might have overcome her differences with the slop enough to win the Plate, but she was in a mood today.

Nate glanced at Nicole as soon as the roll call wrapped up, eager to get the filly doing something constructive. "Turn us loose. We'll see you behind the gate."

The slop slapped up onto her belly and soaked her tail, backing her off from her usual pre-race enthusiasm. At least it wasn't raining. Despite the conditions, this was almost Nate's favourite part. Just him and his little big filly out here, leaving the others behind — like she'd leave them behind in the race. It didn't matter that she'd never run on the grass before. She'd trained over it like a bear.

Six other racehorse and pony pairs approached the metal barrier looming in front of the grandstand. Nate wasn't in a hurry to join them, but it wasn't as if he could postpone it. When he steered the filly onto the turf, she dropped her head and let out a shuddering breath.

See? Would I lie to you?

Nicole slipped her long strip of leather through Chique's bit, Chique brushing up against Paz. The hairy eyeball she gave the asphalt to their right was a remnant of Nate's wild child — the one who had tried to lie down in the gate in her first start. And refused to run a jump in her second start. Or blown the turn so badly at Gulfstream in January she'd very nearly sacrificed a win in her fourth start.

The apron was bigger, so it didn't appear half as packed as Fort Erie had been the night she'd won the Prince of Wales, but there was a different anticipation in those who congregated at Woodbine. They were here to see which side of history Chique would land herself on. The Breeders' Stakes was a well-established graveyard of favourites — and the Canadian Triple Crown demanded greater versatility of a horse than its American counterpart. But behind the gate, there was no room for doubt.

She loaded without even a hint of hesitation. *So grown-up.* Nate felt her square herself beneath him as they both narrowed their vision to the stretch of blue-green ahead. With the crash of doors and clanging bell, the starter turned the seven runners loose.

Chique's launch projected them to the lead, letting Nate place her exactly where he wanted, just off the inside. The E.P. Taylor turf wasn't a traditional oval, the clubhouse turn's angle obtuse, more like something seen in the UK. Chique's ears flipped forward, eating up the short straight that followed as she sized up the next turn. It would be easy to blow this one — acute and on the home side — but Chique seemed to relish the chance to show off how handy she was. She dropped closer to the rail, hugging it. The turf did have more give there, and though Chique handled it okay, Nate steered her back out as they straightened into the long backside. He didn't think the others were anywhere close to him, and resisted the temptation to glance back.

Chique cruised along like she was on a morning gallop, setting a pace she'd have no trouble carrying to the wire. It was hard not to get cocky up here; hard not to think how close they were to achieving a feat that was still rare, despite a smattering of Canadian Triple Crown winners in the nineties. But she was moving so easily, happy with the springy footing, happy with the cool air, happy on the lead.

Happy, happy, happy.

The final turn was the complete opposite of the other end of the course — gradual, sweeping downhill to the long home stretch. If Chique had been a kid, she'd be squealing *weeeeee* as she reached out with her quick forelegs, thrusting with her powerful engine, accelerating down the incline. So she drifted a bit in the lane. Liv wanted them off the rail, right?

A flash of bay to the inside caught the corner of his eye. *What the…?*

Wampum slipped up next to them — still out from the rail, on that choice path Chique had abandoned.

Where the hell did he come from? That was way too easy.

Wampum looked good, big and strong and fit. And Chique? Chique was suddenly acting like she'd checked out. Still happy, but galloping alongside the colt like she was appreciating the company. Steve Gordon let Wampum out a notch, and Chique didn't fight back. Memories of the

Florida Derby flooded Nate — when Chique had let the same colt go on to be third as she finished up the track. *Not today, Cheeky Little Bitch.*

He chirped and threw the lines at her, and her ears flipped forward like she was saying *yeah, I see him*, but she wasn't interested in gunning for the lead again. Like she enjoyed playing this stalking game with the Northwest colt. *Kind of late in the race for games, Cheeky.*

He steered her closer to Wampum, hoping she'd re-engage. But she moseyed along with his tail billowing beside her like she was admiring its flowing length. A heartbeat later, the rest of the field closed in on her, leaving her blocked in tight quarters with limited options.

Oh, she didn't like that. She was back on the bit, her will to run resurfacing thanks to the surge of energy around her. She pinned her ears at the horse next to her and tried to drift over, and Nate hoped that horse would back off so they could break out of this pocket and chase down Wampum on the outside. Except that was Dave Johnson, his main rival for the Woodbine riding title, smiling back at him. It wasn't a friendly smile.

Chique eyed the hole on the inside.

She was dangerously close to Wampum's heels. Nate blew out a breath like it would lighten the weight of his decision. *Liv is going to kill me...*

The filly shot up the inside before he'd even sent her — apparently reading his mind — and caught Wampum in a couple of jumps. Her progress wasn't as smooth on the softer, more tiring ground though, and now that she was back up beside Wampum, she was content to match strides with him again, albeit with ears laced back. Or maybe the Northwest colt was digging in, holding his own. *Didn't think he had it in him.*

Nate took a chance — a big one given Chique's history with such things — and reached back with his whip to smack Chique on the haunches, hoping to jar her out of her complacency. Chique pinned her ears again and pressed against Wampum instead of shooting forward. Wampum crowded back, the two of them fused like conjoined twins.

He gave up on the whip, relying on hands and voice. Finally Chique broke away from Wampum, pushing her head in front, then her neck. *Yeah, that's my baby*. He exhaled in relief, half a length up, then a length. The colt was game, but Chique would prevail.

Except now Chique was coasting, with a sixteenth of a mile yet to run.

Her ears flicked forward, her stride less urgent. Nate flashed his stick, waving it without making contact, but she just swooped closer to the rail. *So much for being grown up.* He switched hands and waved her back off the inside — carefully, because all he needed was for her to encroach on the path of the horse behind them, the freight train breathing getting ever closer. Wampum, fighting back.

All he could do was growl at her and scrub the hair off her neck. Wampum wore down their lead faster than the wire was coming. The colt drew even, and Chique nailed her ears to her head like she was saying *how dare he?* Nate would have laughed if he hadn't been feeling so helpless. *Well, Cheeky…you let him. And it's up to you now.*

She wasn't letting him by, but Wampum matched her, stride for stride, breath for breath. Nate pleaded with his hands, the pop of Steve Gordon's whip in his ears. They drove straight through the wire, Chique still eyeballing Wampum as they galloped out.

"Sorry, Miller!" Gordon was grinning broadly.

Nate looked over sharply. "Don't be so sure!"

Gordon laughed.

He'd better be wrong.

LIV RUSHED TRACKSIDE, furious. What the hell had happened out there? What was Nate thinking? If he'd lost this race…

Her best friend Faye Taylor, and Faye's brother Dean — Wampum's trainer — clustered next to her, the three of them huddled on the apron near the scales. Liv searched for Chique as the other finishers returned and were stripped of their equipment. Both Chique and Wampum were still out of sight, held somewhere on the far side of the track with the outrider, who would escort the victor back.

"Your colt ran a hell of a race," Liv said, forcing a smile.

"It's gotta be close," Dean responded, pacing two steps, back and forth like a tall, wiry, broken toy soldier until Faye grabbed his arm to stop him.

Acid churned in Liv's stomach, and she wrapped her coat around herself to keep from shaking. She tore her eyes away from the PHOTO declaration blazing from the tote board, not wanting to know if the filly's number didn't come up first. When a furtive glance showed INQUIRY lit up in red, she turned away and stared up at the grey clouds. Which would be worse? Losing because Wampum had out-nosed them, or losing through disqualification?

The grandstand was humming, a swarm of restless bodies. Liv's chest hurt, and she pushed out a breath when she realized she'd been holding it. Dave Johnson walked by with his tack to weigh in, a smirk on his face.

"I don't know, Liv," he said, and Liv pressed her lips together to keep from snapping.

A surge rose from the crowd, and she heard Faye's squeal.

Liv didn't really need to see the board to know the result, but she turned and stared at Wampum's number on top. Dean crushed Faye in his arms, rocking her back and forth.

"Congratulations, guys," Liv said, not even attempting to muster enthusiasm. It wasn't like they wouldn't understand. The shoe had been on the other foot on Plate Day when Chique had just got up to beat Dean's Touch and Go.

Dean released Faye, and pulled Liv into a hug and kissed the top of her head. "Sorry, kid."

Liv pushed him away. "Don't be. You deserve every bit of that."

Dean and Faye rushed across the turf course, Liv stepping down more carefully in their wake, dropping her eyes to the boards making a path to the main track. She lifted her gaze to the clubhouse turn, Chique a dark smudge cantering back slowly as the other also-rans began returning to the barns. The filly looked fine. When Nate slowed her to a jog, Chique's toes flicked, her ears up, looking frustratingly fresh.

Someone bumped Liv from behind as Jo, the barn's assistant trainer, snapped a lead shank onto Chique's bit. Emilie, Liv's younger sister, squeezed her arm.

"Let it go, Liv."

She glanced at Em. Did she really look that mad? Liv nodded curtly, and took a step toward Nate as he dragged the tack off Chique's back.

His eyes met hers, wary. "Don't speak," he said, and she left him to walk away to the scales, turning on her heels toward the parking lot.

People just showed up.

It wasn't unexpected — racetrackers could smell free beer from the other side of the backstretch. They didn't care that this wasn't going to be a stake party after all. They'd made the assumption the Triple Stripe barn would've been prepared. They'd assumed right.

Two of the grooms, Michel and Sue, were unloading cases of beer from the back of Sue's VW Golf, surrounded by moochers ready to lighten their load. The cases were emptying before they had a chance to set them down. Roger Cloutier — trainer of all of the Triple Stripe horses but the one who had just lost the Triple Crown — watched with a frown. Nate came up behind him and gave him a nudge.

"I'll fix this. I'm sure I'm going to hear it's my fault anyway." Nate didn't look back to check Roger's expression, pushing himself through the cluster. It was time for the scavengers to move on.

"Okay, stop," he called to Michel and Sue. "Put them back. We're taking them over to Northwest. Party's over there, people!"

It didn't keep him from grabbing a bottle for himself before he sent them off. He twisted off the cap and took a swig. He was probably going to need it.

Chique came ambling around the corner as he walked onto the shed. She stopped and gazed over the dispersing horde like she was offended by their departure, then snorted, ducked her head to snatch a mouthful from the haynet hanging on the rail, and dunked it unceremoniously in the water bucket hooked to the post next to it. Munching, she dragged the hotwalker over to Nate.

"How is she?" Nate asked, backing to the inside of the sandy path. Chique poked her nose along his arm, still dribbling freshly brewed hay tea, until he produced a peppermint from the pocket of his suit jacket.

"Finished drinking in the test barn after ten minutes. Was afraid she'd miss the party."

The snort that reached Nate's ears was unmistakably Liv's.

"So sorry to disappoint her," she said. "You can take her out for some grass, Marc."

Nate removed the bottle he'd tucked in the crook of his elbow as he'd attended to the filly's demands, and half-heartedly brushed at the smear from her body search before holding the beer to Liv. Liv crossed her arms. Would he call that a grimace? Yep, it was going to be like that.

"Let's go in the office. I don't want to do this out here."

"What are we doing?" He actually said it out loud. He gulped another swallow from the bottle, and caught the screen door after she breezed inside, softening its landing as it closed behind them.

"You're mad at me, aren't you?"

She gave him a tired look as he dropped onto the small couch next to her. Well. He had to give her an opening, didn't he?

"What was the only thing we talked about?"

He shrugged. "I had no choice, she was getting snarky. I had to take her inside."

"There's no way you should have let her get boxed in."

"She wasn't really boxed in. The rail was wide open." The grin he flashed her did nothing to dislodge her cool expression. "Can you stop being a trainer for a minute and remember what it's like to be out there?"

She sighed, then grabbed the beer and took a swig, features screwing up as she handed it back to him. "I don't know how you can drink that."

"Don't you have some champagne stowed in there?" He nodded at the small fridge behind Roger's desk.

"I wasn't going to jinx us."

"Maybe if you'd had a little faith things would have turned out differently."

She scowled at him, then pressed her lips into a line. "Maybe we underestimated Wampum. Maybe we were over-confident."

"And by we, you mean me." He drained what was left in the bottle. *Should have grabbed two. "We* should get out of here."

She glanced at him sideways. "Chique's not even done up yet."

"Jo's doing her up, right? We'll come back later to check on her."

"We have to go to Dean's barn."

"Sure. Token appearance. Unless you really want to hang out there."

"No."

"Didn't think so."

Liv got up and walked to the door, peering through the screen, then turned back to him, her grey eyes warming a little closer to blue as she met his. "Let's go."

He left the empty bottle on the desk and grabbed her keys, tossing them to her with a smirk. “Probably best if you drive. I might not do it right.”

It was hard to find a spot to park at Dean’s barn, with cars jammed everywhere. They probably should have walked. Liv locked the Nissan with a beep, and Nate grabbed her hand, meeting her eyes when they turned to his, but she didn’t pull away. Not until they were closer to the crowd outside the shed, at least.

No one had to remind him he’d had the mount on Wampum once. He’d been up when the colt had broken his maiden. Been up, only to come crashing down, in the BlueGrass. That had been Wampum’s last race before this, the colt injuring his shoulder in the accident. It was a day forever imprinted on his memory; a *this changes everything* day. Faye breaking up with him. Liv giving him a glimmer of hope, only to figuratively slap him in the face. It had stung, but he’d deserved it.

“Sorry, buddy,” Dean said, shaking his hand with a self-deprecating shrug. Dean had always been good to Nate, and the BlueGrass spill had knocked Wampum out of Plate contention, so he couldn’t begrudge the trainer the victory.

He moved on to Faye, resting a hand on her elbow as he pecked her on the cheek and backed up to stand next to Will. It still felt strange that Faye had hooked up with his best friend. The four of them sure didn’t double date, unless you counted an awkward evening at Will’s dad’s wedding. It had been more of a mercy mission. If Nate were honest about the last seven weeks, could he really even call this thing between him and Liv dating?

She was talking to Dean now, but glanced over, and Nate had no trouble reading that look. *Have we been good enough sports now to leave without looking like we’re skulking off with our tails between our legs?* Nate’s nod was slight, the corner of his mouth rising just enough to second the motion.

“Sorry to be party poopers, but we’re going to go sulk now.” Liv wasn’t a fan of pretense. Her eyes shifted sheepishly from Faye to Dean. “Congrats again.”

Dean squeezed her shoulders — a little too comfortably for Nate’s liking — and Liv gave Faye a quick hug before they slipped away, back to the car.

"Where to?" she said once she settled behind the wheel.

"I just need to eat something. And I'd bet you do too." He paused as she directed the Nissan toward the east gate. "Turn right."

"And then?"

"How does Wendy's drive through sound?"

"I like your style, Miller."

Salads to go with plastic cutlery under the weeping willows along the track's back access road — not quite the celebration they'd been hoping for. Liv peered up at the grey sky, her eyes reflecting its colour. Serious and sombre was her default. In so many ways, she still felt elusive, a mystery to be solved.

"Do you think this is it for summer? Hard to believe how hot it was in June," she said, cross-legged on the navy night sheet they'd spread to sit on. It was clean, but still smelled distinctly of horse. Neither of them was ever very far away from that scent.

Nate leaned back against the tire. "Is it too early to start thinking about Florida?"

She laughed. "A little, maybe. Soon enough, though."

It might be Florida before they had a shot at some semblance of a normal relationship. Florida would give them the time and freedom they didn't have here, when sometimes it felt they were under a microscope. Liv had taken Chique to Fort Erie to prep for the Prince of Wales after the Plate, leaving him at Woodbine with his riding commitments. Her judgment had paid off — Chique had taken the second jewel handily, bouncing out of it looking for more. After that, the tension of a possible Canadian Triple Crown win had kept her preoccupied. He had to remind himself regularly it was best to take it slow, no sudden moves, all too aware how quickly she might spook — and knowing full well how prone he was to making mistakes when it came to relationships.

"So what do we do with her now?" Liv sipped her water.

"Take the blinkers off for sure," he said.

"Do you think the turf had anything to do with it? Back to the dirt?"

"It wasn't the turf. Trust me on that."

"Trust you? You totally blew off my instructions out there."

"Are we doing this again?" He shot her a sharp glance. "Cheeky blew *me* off out there."

"I'm sorry," she said, the warble of a laugh in her voice. "I guess it was only a matter of time before she started playing games with us." She produced a white booklet from the pocket of her coat, unfolding it and pressing it open to a page he couldn't see.

"What was that, almost an hour before the condition book came out? I'm impressed." He smirked before stuffing a forkful of lettuce in his mouth.

Liv rolled her eyes. "Where do you think we should go next?"

He didn't hesitate. "The Mile."

"Breeders' Cup *Win and You're In.*" There was no missing the incredulity in her tone. The winner of the Challenge race was guaranteed a spot in the Championship, with entry fees paid and a $10,000 travel award that would more than cover transport. "She didn't deign a restricted race at home worthy of an honest effort, and you want to think about the Breeders' Cup?"

He laughed. "It's at Keeneland this year. She loved Keeneland."

"You seem to be filtering out some details. Like when she got knocked to her knees. Or when I had to pull you off Ricky Acosta in the jock's room."

"That was pretty hot." His grin was crooked and bold.

She shook her head, shoving him with her elbow, and went back to the condition book. "In between the Mile and going a mile and a half again in the Northern Dancer Stakes is a nice little mile and an eighth race restricted to fillies. With a $250,000 purse."

"Cutting back to the Mile after today's mile and a half, she'll win for fun."

"That doesn't sound overconfident at all, Miller. But I'll think about it."

"Does that mean I'm forgiven?"

Her criticism rattled him more than he was ready to admit. Her eyes steadied on him, then she wrapped her fingers around the collar of his jacket, and pulled his face to hers. A smile played with her lips before she kissed him.

"I'll think about that too."

2

September brought with it a heat wave and a flood of memories. The hot spell was almost welcome, after a cold and wet August. Some of the memories were too. Others, not so much.

Liv closed her leg and the yearling colt dropped his head, moving into the bit like he'd been doing this his whole life instead of just two weeks. Chique's full brother, heir to the throne. He never put a foot wrong. He was perfect.

Like Nate, who had just walked up to the ring. He leaned on the top rail, and she returned his trademark grin with a more reserved smile. Thankfully Feste was so easy-going his rider's temporary distraction didn't phase him; he didn't react to the slight tension that overtook her body, or the subtle amping up of her heart rate.

Nate's gaze shifted to the other yearling and rider. "Hey Cory."

Cory wasn't so lucky. With the break in her concentration, the little bay she was on faltered and ducked, leaving the petite rider a dusty heap in the sand.

Liv pulled her colt up as Nate ducked into the ring. Cory's little bay snorted dramatically at his downed rider, one eye bugging out at the loop of rein hanging off the side of his neck as Cory climbed to her feet. Nate's voice came low and lyrical, the bay's eyes flicking toward him, his legs locking long enough for Nate to grab the lines.

"You okay?" he asked, scratching the bay's neck as Cory sheepishly dusted herself off and shuffled over.

She nodded, a bright pink flush rising in her cheeks beneath the brim of her helmet.

"Get Nate to tell you about the time he came off Chique as a baby," Liv called.

Cory straightened, eyes darting to Liv like she couldn't believe her idol had ever suffered such an embarrassment. "Really?"

Nate smirked. "Never going to live that down, am I?" He turned to Cory. "Let me throw you back up."

Cory sprang lightly into the tack, looking only a little less mortified as she thanked him, her voice a squeak. Liv set her dark bay colt in motion again, picking up an easy jog. When she was satisfied with the day's lesson, she parked him in the middle, and waited for Cory to join her.

Nate approached and rubbed the patch of white in the middle of the colt's forehead — a larger star than Chique's mixed swirl, like their dam Sotisse had been more generous with the paint this time. "He seems a lot quieter than his big sister. 'Big' being a figure of speech, of course. He's already as tall as her." He had the same inky coat as Chique though, a colour anyone outside of horse racing might label black.

"I'm not going to complain about either of those things," Liv said, dropping to the ground and running up her stirrup irons before she loosened the girth a hole.

"What do you call him again?"

"Feste."

Nate looked the colt in the eye. "You've got some big shoes to fill, Fester."

Trust Nate to think *Addams Famil*y instead of Shakespeare's fool in Twelfth Night. Liv couldn't help the wash of affection that came with her smile — freely, for the yearling. Helplessly, confusingly, for the man.

Cory trailed silently behind them as they walked to the barn — totally out of character for the gregarious eighteen-year-old.

"The new kid working out okay?" Nate asked.

Liv nodded, happy to discuss Cory and offset the conflict in her head. "She's a decent rider. And she works hard."

"Let me guess…"

"Of course. She wants to ride races. I'm thinking of asking her if she wants to come to Florida this winter."

They exchanged a look, and Liv tried not to overthink that. What would a winter in Florida mean? Would he expect to stay at the condo? He'd been giving her space, but she feared for her much-needed solitude in such a concentrated environment. It felt way, way too soon to be living together. But how practical would it be to live apart? As usual, she was getting ahead of herself. Time to steer the conversation away from that. "You should bring your boots and helmet next time and get on him."

"Does that mean I get to ride this one?"

"We'll see."

He held her eyes just a moment too long. Damn that grin of his.

It was cool in the barn, Feste snorting contentedly as Liv led him to his stall. Nate rested against the doorframe while she pulled off the saddle and bridle, and slid the door shut behind her.

"Hey Cory, when're you going to start coming into the track and helping us out? Now that Em's spending so much time with Faye at the café, we could use an extra rider." Nate caught Cory's eye as she emerged from the little bay gelding's box.

Cory froze, her lips parting slightly. "Are you serious?" she sputtered. She looked at Liv.

"It's up to you." Liv shrugged. "Even just get on the pony a few times."

"Oh hell, Liv." Nate choked back a laugh. "Paz? Jay would be easier to gallop."

"Jay? Just Jay?" Cory was gasping again.

Liv resisted the urge to elbow Nate. Like they'd put Cory up on the nicest three-year-old colt in the barn. A colt who was on the cusp of a promising career after a late start, and probably heading to California in a few months with her father's US-based trainer. "That two-year-old filly is super quiet."

Nate grinned. "You're right. Good choice."

He stepped in with the saddle pad and cloth after Liv knocked off the next four-legged student, brushing close to her as he moved out of the way. He slipped around to the other side while she settled the exercise saddle in place, then buckled the girth for her on the off side.

"So how are you feeling about the Mile?" he asked, his tone casual.

He was beside her again, handing her the bridle, their fingers touching as she took it, and she cursed the little tremor that ran up her arm and tingled along her spine. "I'll tell you on entry day." She'd nominated Chique to both the Mile and the fillies-and-mares-only Canadian Stakes — in case she chickened out on the whole Breeders' Cup *Win and You're In* thing.

"Thursday."

She didn't need him to remind her, to state it so affirmatively. Yes, Thursday. Three days out from the race. They'd agreed they'd decide after Nate blew Chique out that morning. Together, though the final word would be hers.

"Still game for blinkers off?" she asked.

"I'm always up for an adventure with the Cheeky Little Bitch."

She snapped a lead rope to the halter she'd left under the bridle, turning the yearling towards the door. He wasn't exactly blocking her way, but he was there; so, so, present.

"Don't you have to be somewhere?" she said quietly, unable to control the amusement playing on her lips. "You're distracting the help."

"Fine. I'll leave. I don't want to be where I'm not wanted," he said, feigning hurt that smile of his belied.

He leaned in, but she pushed him away before he could kiss her. She had to maintain some kind of decorum at work. Backing away, he held her eyes, his grin still taunting her, then sauntered out the end of the barn, leaving her standing there considering his silhouette.

"You are so lucky."

She hadn't realized Cory was behind her, the words a sigh. Liv glanced back. Why couldn't she just agree? Because this was good. This was fun; the back and forth, the teasing, the banter.

But it couldn't go on indefinitely. She knew his history; knew what he wanted. He wanted more, and she wasn't sure how she felt about that. Nate was patient. He'd never push her physically. But that wasn't the part she worried about.

Chique torqued her neck, one eye rolled back far enough Nate could see a crescent of white as she tilted her head away from Paz. The object of her contempt was directly in front of them in the post parade — Youthful, over from France for the Woodbine Mile, his straight-backed jockey cloaked in cobalt blue.

Don't they know that's not how we do things here? Chique seemed to huff.

Nate laughed and reached forward, running a hand down her crest, her mane defiantly flopping halfway to the wrong side of her neck. She shook off his touch, bouncing into Paz for good measure. Youthful strutted, bunched powerfully against his lad's hold. They didn't use pony horses across the pond. One of the outriders hovered nearby, ready to swoop in if the big horse got to be too much.

"You'd think this would be a 'when in Rome' kind of time, wouldn't you?" Nicole, atop Paz said, gently pushing Chique away now that the filly had pushed her nose against Paz's withers to get a good look at the offender with her other eye.

Nate shrugged. "Maybe he doesn't like other horses." Though it was pretty common for runners who came over for the big turf races at Woodbine to go solo to the post. Youthful was favoured to win, so they probably knew what they were doing.

Chique's odds were more a reflection of sentiment from the hometown crowd than logic — she was third choice in the betting, but no one in the *Form* had picked her in the top three. She gawked freely with her blinker-free view, but not once had Nate seen her check out the tote board.

The post parade wrapped up, and Youthful shot away from his lad, settling into a steady but energetic gallop. Nate glanced at the lad — red-faced but eyes still on his charge — as Nicole initiated a jog with Paz.

"You can turn us loose. Maybe keep close though, okay?" He flashed her a grin.

Nicole looked doubtful, as always, but let the long strip of leather slip through the bit. Chique surged forward, shaking it away, her ears shooting up and zeroing in on Youthful as the big horse swept around the clubhouse turn. The filly zipped past the other North Americans, who cantered conservatively next to their ponies. They looked like they were getting ready for a hunter flat class, not a horse race.

This might be fun.

The crowd pressing against the rail was a blur, the current of warm September air lifting Chique's unruly mane as she reached over the track, each stride quicker than the last. At least her fixation on Youthful kept her from the antics Nate had expected — or maybe she was grown-up enough for *blinkers off* to be a non-issue.

"You're determined to get me in trouble again, aren't you filly?" Nate muttered through gritted teeth, picturing the look on Liv's face behind the binoculars that were most certainly taking in his struggle to temper Chique's momentum. "Remember I had to talk her into this, Cheeky."

He pulled her up on the backside, Chique snorting with satisfaction as she finally caught up to Youthful. Nicole was close behind, and reattached herself to the filly, Paz blowing from the effort of keeping up.

"Don't laugh at me," Nate said, his heart still thumping against his chest, a warm ache in his arms.

"I don't know why you do that to yourself. One of these times it's gonna come back and bite you in the butt."

"This was almost the time." He grinned.

Nine starters filed through the gap from the main track to the turf course. Breeders Cup hopefuls, including some of Europe's top milers, and the two best middle-distance horses from south of the border. *Why did I talk Liv into this again?*

"Good luck, Nate," Nicole said when she transferred Chique to the assistant starter.

He chased his apprehension away as the doors slammed shut behind them, and focused between Chique's ears: a mile from here to the wire.

Chique bounced out when the starter released them, ears flickering as she assessed the footing and the horses around her, the same way Nate did. She wasn't gunning for the lead though. *Why the hell not?* What was she up to today? Youthful glided easily to the front, and Nate felt Chique line him up again, but she was content to let him go on. No sense trying to figure out what version of crazy was occupying her pretty little head. *Ride the horse you're on, Miller* — even if you don't recognize her. Chique skimmed over the turf, biding her time, one eyeball still locked on the dark bay horse on the lead. Maybe Nate shouldn't question. Maybe she had this under control. Now that was a scary thought.

They cruised into the big sweeping turn, the only one they had to contend with today. Chique naturally quickened with the incline, the field bunched behind them, the sense of their collective presence enough to press her closer to Youthful. She hovered just off his flank, ears flickering forward as they straightened into the wide stretch. Chique was in the game now, taking a hold, asking to run instead of waiting to be told, but Nate didn't move. It was a long way to the wire yet.

A horse surged up to their right, and Chique pummeled the turf, moving faster…but Youthful accelerated too, holding her off. She pinned her ears and Nate started to ride, rolling out arms and hands, Chique gaining inches, shadowed by the challenger to her right.

He glanced across — they were part of a four-wide charge for the wire. Youthful hung tough on the rail, Chique wearing him down with fervor, two closers creeping up insidiously on the outside. Nate cocked his stick, flashing it on the filly's right, coming short of actually hitting her. Chique scooted beneath him, veering towards Youthful.

Youthful's head swung towards Chique with a flash of teeth, and Nate's jaw dropped as he stood instinctively to check his filly — but Chique merely swapped leads to rebalance and drove on with a fresh burst of speed. The big horse's rider dragged him away, and Chique shot past, bursting ahead with her ears still pinned flush to her skull.

Nate thrust his arms with each extension of her neck, but it was just for show — Chique was doing it with or without him, jumping clear of her rivals, streaking under the wire alone.

There was a maniacal lift to his laugh as he stood in the irons, the filly charging on beneath him, the trailing thunder of hooves lost in the wind whipping past his ears. Chique careened around the clubhouse turn, ears flicking forward. A bounce finally returned to her gait, Nate able to separate the footfalls of her stride as she eased.

"Did you see that?" Nate said before the outrider could get a word in, picking them up as the also-rans exited the turf. "That bloody French horse tried to savage her! He don't know who he's messin' with, eh Cheeky?" Nate grinned, slapping her heartily on the neck. Chique snorted in agreement as they started towards the grandstand.

Liv was the one coming forward to meet them, taking the white lead shank from the outrider, reaching up to grasp Nate's hand. He wanted to hop off right then and there, throw himself around her. *Keeneland, here we come.*

Nate scrubbed Chique's neck as Liv made the requisite tour for the wall of snap-happy photographers, then they travelled across the main track to the infield winner's circle.

Then somehow, Liv was always where he wasn't. She passed Chique to Jo before his feet hit the ground, pulled away by her parents as he dragged the tack off and went to weigh in. She was distracted as Jo led the winning filly back to the barn; impatience thinly veiled during the presentations, mounting during the post-race interviews. Nate could see it so plainly, but if the reporters recognized it, they didn't care. She broke away before he did — extracting herself from the clinging media, giving Nate an apologetic half-smile.

The back-slaps and high-fives in the jock's room came one after another. Everyone liked to see one of the local riders win. It didn't happen often. Breeders' Cup *Win and You're In*. They were in.

It sucked he had the rest of the card to ride. These big races were broadcast on NBC and the telecast messed up the order of the afternoon, making the Mile the fifth. He grabbed his phone before he changed for the next race.

Wait for me, he typed.

THE SHEDROW WAS DESERTED, the afternoon's warmth giving way to a cooler evening. Chique's head hung over her webbing, staring out as if she was wondering why Liv was still there, staring back.

One phrase, filly: Breeders' Cup Win and You're In. It taunted, and Liv envied the filly's inability to comprehend the ticket this afternoon's victory had handed them.

"Do you have any idea how much stress you've caused me?"

Not that Chique causing her stress was anything new, but this was on a totally different level. *Yeah, I'm sure there are eight other trainers tonight who wish they had your problem.* It's like Nate was next to her, she heard his voice so clearly in her head.

She'd told him to go home, leave her here alone with this crisis. He was understanding about so much, but he wouldn't comprehend her reservations. Who would? Who would even consider not going, especially when it was Keeneland and not Santa Anita? Entry fees covered. Transportation covered. All they had to do was get themselves there, and keep Chique peaking for another six weeks. Keep her healthy. Keep her sound. Get her to the race in one piece, and pray she performed. Pray she belonged.

We ask, and we ask again. When was it too much?

The buzz of her phone startled her, Chique's ears swivelling forward.

Are you still there?

It didn't feel like an intrusion when he checked in on her, but she still wasn't used to it. She wondered how long he'd put up with her, with her fickle ways, her uncertainty. *You don't even know what you'd be getting into,* Miller, she'd told him back in May. When she'd put him off — again. He'd given her space — again. But he'd never given up. His conviction terrified her.

She couldn't ignore him, so she answered. *Yeah.*

See you soon.

So he hadn't gone home. She shouldn't be surprised. He wasn't that easily put off; not prepared to let her struggle alone. He never had been, though at times in the past she'd given him no choice. But this was right. They would talk. They were a team. Even before things had evolved into a relationship, they'd been a team. The three of them.

It wasn't long till she heard the beat-up Mustang's rumble. Chique echoed it with her own before Liv even saw Nate appear. Then he was at the end of the barn, backlit, his expression hidden, though it wasn't hard to imagine. She rose as he drew closer. Chique nickered again, vying for his attention, but he went first to Liv. Unspeaking, hand resting on her hip, lips meeting hers, lingering just long enough to grab wisps of her breath, trip up her pulse. When he went to greet Chique, he left a void.

He glanced over his shoulder. "It's okay. I'll give you a couple of days to process it."

She looked from Nate to the filly, the two of them emanating confidence. Chique's was cocky…Nate's was just sure. Steady. A foundation on which she could build things she'd never thought she wanted.

He returned to her, slipped his hand into hers, and pulled her back in. This time he just held her, arms enveloping her. She buried her face into his neck and breathed, his scent calming.

"Go home. Get some sleep. Okay?"

The voice of reason, in her chaotic brain. He made her doubts seem foolish, and at this moment, the two of them, together, made perfect sense.

3

Everything was finally aligning for Just Jay. It felt good to be part of that journey, seeing as Nate had always felt to blame for setting that cascade of one thing after another in motion. If Chique hadn't gotten away from him the day she and Jay had breezed as two-year-olds in Florida, maybe Jay wouldn't have developed tendonitis, the first of a string of minor injuries and ailments that had prevented the promising colt from getting to the races until last month. Now Jay had put together two impressive wins in a row. In the Durham Cup this past weekend he'd faced some tough older horses, and there was talk of him heading to Keeneland with Chique for a race the week before the Breeders' Cup.

But Nate hadn't expected all the good things in his career could turn the rest of his life upside-down.

He set the phone down, staring out the picture window behind the piano in his apartment. He almost hadn't picked up. He hadn't recognized the number, and assumed it was a scammer. It hadn't been, though it felt as if someone was playing a joke on him. He should be dancing around the room with the opportunity the call had presented. Instead, it felt as if the high he'd been flying on had propelled him into a mass of grey clouds.

He glanced at the photo he'd never been able to put away — he and his brothers, and the first girl who'd ever gotten to him. Cindy was so very different from Liv. He hadn't seen her since the night he'd left Calgary, the same day she'd gone and married his older brother. He'd been pretty messed up that night, but found himself wishing he could talk to her now. She was rational. Heartbreakingly so.

You home? he texted Liv.

Liv was one of those people you only called if someone was sick or dying, and showing up at her front door unannounced wouldn't be any more welcome. Sure this seemed like an emergency, the way it had set his world off balance, but she still might not see it that way. No immediate reply, but that was normal. She didn't live with her phone glued to her hip like some people.

The Lachance residence wasn't far. The walk there did nothing to settle his brain. Liv's Nissan was parked beneath the trees at the side of the building, so he'd guessed right. She must be finished with the yearlings.

It was only the second time he'd been to the house, the memory of the first hitting him with a ripple of melancholy as he trudged up the front steps. Liv's father, Claude Lachance had invited him here to break the news of the death of Geai Doucet, two years ago. Nate wondered if he and Liv would have handled the farm manager's loss better had their relationship been more what it was today. Back then, when he'd reached out, she'd pushed him away. Now, just when she'd started to accept she could count on him to be there, whatever the reason, he was going to put a fresh wedge between them.

Liv's mother, Anne, answered the door, stepping back and welcoming him in. "Hello, Nate."

Anne would genuinely inspire compliments that she could be an older sister to her two daughters. She reminded Nate so much of Liv — in looks and mannerisms and reserved demeanor. The same wry humour, once you got past the shield.

"Olivia's in the pool. I'm assuming that's who you came to see." Anne smiled as she ushered him across the sunken living room. There was no doubt Anne was on his side.

"Does she ever stop and relax?" Nate asked.

"Perhaps you can help with that? Sometimes I think the two of you are so wrapped up in that horse and your careers, you don't even know who you are apart from it."

That was exactly what they were supposed to be figuring out this winter. He thanked her and stepped through the sliding doors onto the patio.

The long, narrow lap pool was practical instead of fancy, his eyes going straight to it. Splashes of colour from purple and white petunias filled planters on the terra cotta stones, but they only remotely registered in his vision. Liv was in the water, a clean crawl stroke pulling her through to the far end. Her turn was seamless, and she came back toward him, her face only partially leaving the water to breathe.

He felt guilty watching her, though he told himself he was merely admiring her athleticism, not thinking about that supple body and what he could do with it. When she came to the near end, she stopped, starting when she saw him, though her expression quickly changed to a smile — even if it was a vaguely suspicious one.

She climbed out and he handed her the towel draped over a nearby chair, his eyes falling to the wet one-piece suit clinging to her torso before snapping up. She pulled off her cap and goggles and pressed the towel to her face.

"Thanks," she said, wrapping it around her shoulders, long hair falling stringy and damp about them. She still looked wary of his presence, like he was pushing the boundary too much and infringing on her cherished alone time. "Everything okay? I thought you were going down to Will's."

"Something came up. I did try to text you." He followed her lead and sat on the edge of one of the patio chairs, thinking she was going to get chilled if she stayed out here too long. He should have taken her out to dinner or something, instead of showing up like this. "Your mother let me in."

Liv rolled her eyes. "Next thing you know she'll be out here with refreshments. Asking you to stay for supper."

"Just because you shun guests doesn't mean it's normal behaviour." He grinned, and Liv laughed.

"So what's up?"

"I just had a call from Don." Nate paused. Don Philips trained a few horses for Liv's dad in New York. Liv and her filly L'Éclaircie had been based with him for most of Claire's career, though Liv had never wintered with him. She'd always chosen to go to Florida with Roger and the Canadian string instead. "He invited me to come to California this winter."

There was the slightest hesitation, a shadow passing over her features. Her voice was soft and careful when she responded. "That's great, Nate. You've always wanted to go to California, haven't you?"

He'd hoped for something different, some kind of protest; some indication she was as thrown as he was by the news. Because even though it was true, he'd always wanted to ride there — it was the pinnacle wasn't it? — he was torn by the prospect, because now, he wanted to be with her more.

"I haven't given him an answer yet. I had to talk to you first."

She nodded, but didn't offer anything; didn't rescue him from his predicament.

"Any chance you'd consider bringing Chique to Santa Anita?" It was a shot in the dark, though he didn't have to tell Liv what would be available to the filly there. There were a number of big stake races; rich purses, the best horses. Chique would have no trouble fitting in.

Don had confirmed he was taking Just Jay, hoping to build the colt's appeal as a stallion prospect. The trainer had dangled that information in front of Nate like a bright chestnut carrot, assuring him he'd keep the mount.

But Liv shook her head, slowly. "I'm taking Chique to Florida, Nate. She's had a long, hard season, and she'll deserve the break, especially if we go to the Breeders' Cup. And it's not like I could take Feste, is it?"

Of course — Feste. He'd let the yearling slip from his mind, neglected to assign importance to him, because he wasn't working with the colt, didn't see him daily like Liv did. He'd been living in the here and now, while Liv always, always, skipped ahead, sometimes to her — and their — detriment, mapping out worst-case scenarios. Feste was her insurance, the next in line, the one who would give her purpose once Chique retired. Liv planned to run the filly as a four-year-old, but Nate suspected that would be it.

"You should go, Nate. Don's got nice horses. You'll do well with him."

Every time she said the trainer's name, it twisted his heart. "I was looking forward to this winter."

"You should still be looking forward to this winter. Even more so. It's California."

"I was looking forward to this winter with you."

Her eyes dropped, hands wringing the edges of the towel. "This is your career, Nate. You can't make your plans around me."

"Damn it, Liv! Why the hell not?" He stood up and turned away, finally showing his frustration, because making plans — around her, with her — was exactly what he wanted to do. And this winter was supposed to be where she caught up with him, with those feelings. But like Cindy, Liv was ruled by logic — even more so. At least with Liv he knew his competition, and her allegiance to Chique and Feste wasn't a betrayal like Cindy's marriage to his brother had been.

He blew out a breath, and turned back to her, sighing. "I'm sorry. You're probably freezing. I should go."

Liv followed him through the sunken living room to the front door. Anne Lachance had discreetly disappeared. They should have come in where it was warm a lot sooner.

She faced him in the foyer, seeming as much at a loss as he was, reaching for his arm, her touch tentative. "When we're both back here in the spring, if nothing's changed…we'll start over, okay?"

It was like a slap to the face. "If nothing's changed?"

"A lot can happen over the winter."

He wanted to argue, but last winter, and how things had fallen apart in his relationship with Faye Taylor despite his intent to prevent it, came sharply to mind. This was different, he was sure, but it was too early to convince Liv of that. "So you want to put it off. Again. Now?"

"Don't you think it would be harder, staying together for the next two months, just to be apart for five?"

"It's going to be hell either way."

"What do you want me to say?"

"I want you to say you'll come too." He dislodged her hand from his arm, lacing his fingers with hers, but knew he was being unfair, no matter how much he meant it. The pain in her face was genuine, but it only amplified his own.

"You're the one who says everything happens for a reason." She countered his plea with a stoic gaze. "Good things come to those who wait?"

And all good things come to an end. "You would throw that back in my face."

He couldn't win. If he forfeited this opportunity, he passed up on a dream. But if he followed the dream, he did it without Liv. There were no guarantees he'd get such an offer again. He'd had a hell of a year — Eclipse Award for North America's top apprentice, Sovereign Award for the same in Canada; Queen's Plate, Woodbine Mile, maybe a trip to the Breeders' Cup — but this time next year there was a chance no one would even remember his name. The racing game was capricious that way.

If he had to make it through the winter without her to prove his point, so be it. He'd waited this long…what was another seven months?

SHE RAN ALONE TODAY, shoes crunching on gravel, heading towards the sideroad instead of the usual route around the farm — a change of scenery when her head was in desperate need of clearing. Nate's absence would have been more obvious through the trails. Damn him for wiggling into things she'd always been happiest doing alone.

She'd only seen him briefly this morning, when he'd come by first thing at the track to check on Chique. Cue awkwardness, thanks to the status update she'd inflicted on them. His usual end-of-the-morning visit hadn't happened, so apparently he'd taken her words yesterday to heart. It had been what she'd asked for, but she hadn't anticipated how disheartened she'd be that he'd accept it so abruptly.

The unpaved road was quiet, and she ran just off the shoulder where the repeated passage of tires had left a smooth path. She'd go farther today — maybe that would sort her out, bring order back to her brain. But it wasn't going to change reality.

Everything had been too perfect. Scary-perfect. Too smooth. A bump, a hill, or in this case, a roadblock, was inevitable. She pushed herself harder, not wanting to think.

On the way back, she turned up the lane to Northwest instead of going home. Faye's car was parked beside the old red brick Victorian farmhouse, Dean's pickup gone. Liv slowed, walking to let her breathing normalize, hands on her hips. She stretched before skipping up the steps to the back door.

"Hey! Come in!" Faye held the door while Liv walked through. "Forgive me for not giving you a hug. Can I get you a…towel? You're drenched."

Faye was allergic to exercise. It felt good to laugh, augment the endorphins.

"Hungry?" Faye said as Liv mopped her brow. "Will gave me pastries. Coffee?"

"No thanks on the coffee — I think I'm dehydrated enough. I won't say no to pastry, though."

Faye poured her some water and ushered her out onto the deck, setting a plate on the round glass table between the metal chairs. Liv drank half the glass before sitting, propping her legs out in front of her, letting the sun prolong the warmth of exertion.

"From dating a jockey, to a pastry chef. How did that happen?" she asked, grinning as she perused the plate. Maybe protein would have been a better option right now, but carbs would restore her depleted glycogen, right?

Faye closed her eyes as she bit into a flaky brioche. "I think it suits me."

A sigh escaped Liv's lips as the first buttery-sweet mouthful of an almond croissant melted on her taste buds. "This is divine. You'd better keep him."

"I do believe that's worth considering. He is multi-talented." Faye's mouth twisted slyly. "I hope he and Nate find another excuse like the Plate Party to play. Their little unplugged gig at the café was wonderful, but they need a bigger venue so the whole band can be there."

Liv shoved another piece in her mouth to put off a response. The night of the Plate Party had been dreamlike. Champagne on the shed with Nate after the race. The dance that had turned into a kiss. And another. Later Nate had joined the band for a few songs, the crowd loving the Plate-winning rider contributing vocals, Faye and Emilie heading up the dancing. The music had gone on longer than any of them had hoped before backstretch security had shut them down. And Faye was right, the evening at the café — which was now Faye and Will's café — had been magical. All of it had been a wave she'd been riding, but yesterday she'd been knocked off the crest, sucked into the undercurrent.

"You really should come when they practice at Will's," Faye continued.

Liv reached for her water, still not ready to bring Faye up to speed on Nate's bombshell. "That would be too much the doting groupie-girlfriend for me quite yet."

"Please." Faye waved away the protest.

"I think it's important we have our own things. He has his music. I have — "

"What, exactly?" Faye quirked a perfect eyebrow.

"I swim. And I'm starting yearlings." It sounded lame, even to her. "We work together. I don't want us to get sick of each other."

"You'd better not be sick of each other yet. You're still in the dreamy early stages. You seriously need to relax. You know what's good for relaxing?"

Liv smirked, then sighed, shoving another piece of croissant into her mouth, trying to convince herself she was savouring it, but it might as well have been sawdust now. She stared at the paddock across the driveway where a mare and foal grazed.

"What's up, sweetie?"

That's why she'd come here, wasn't it? To do what she was always disinclined to do. Talk about it. It would be all over the backstretch soon. Faye would never let her hear the end of it if it came second-hand. "We've kind of — I don't know. Broken it off."

"What?" Faye was immediately upright, the plate almost falling off her lap. "Why? What happened?"

Liv glanced at her, and set her own plate aside. It seemed a shame to waste the rest of her croissant on her churning stomach. "He's going to ride in California this winter."

Faye looked confused. "Okay. So, that sucks, sure, but why does it mean you have to break up? Especially now? That's like…weeks away." Faye paused. "I thought things were good."

"They were. Just — too good."

"That's not a thing, remember," Faye scoffed. "You being you, of course, didn't say anything to sway him."

"How could I? I had two choices. Either shut up, or go myself."

"That doesn't sound like a bad option."

"I can't, Faye. Chique's brother is a yearling now. I can't take a yearling to Santa Anita, no matter who he is."

"You know in this business horses come and go, Liv. Guys like Nate Miller don't. You let those horses get in the way of everything." Faye finished her brioche, and reached for her coffee cup. "It makes me want to slap you sometimes. You have no idea."

Liv felt guilty expressing her fluctuating emotions to Faye. Nate was the first guy Faye had really let herself care about, and if it hadn't been for Liv — as unintentional as her part had been — she wondered if the two of them would still be together. But Faye had found Will, battling her own resistance to give him a chance, while Liv kept struggling to do the same with Nate.

Faye's hard gaze hadn't left her. "It's not too late to at least change your mind about now."

"That would just make it all more difficult. Ending things before — " Faye's eyebrows went up, a self-satisfied smirk on her lips. Faye would never understand it wasn't about sex. Liv shook her head, twisting her fingers together. "This is the way it's always going to be. One of us is always going to be where the other isn't. It's part of the job description. So if we can't deal with it now, for one winter, I want to know before we get in any deeper."

That, at least, Faye didn't dispute.

"How are things with Will?" she asked, reaching for her water just to have something in her hands.

"Change the subject, why don't you."

"Not exactly." Liv grinned.

"Besides the fact that this pastry is amazing, and I'm going to have to start exercising too if I keep eating it like this…good. Really good. But if it doesn't work out with Will," Faye continued, "I'm moving to Calgary, because they seem to breed them right out there."

4

Nate stood back, observing silently with what he could only call resignation. Chique was tied to the stall's back wall, her sleek hindquarters bearing witness to absolute fitness, the definition of her hamstrings a sharp contrast to the soft sweep of tail that nearly touched the deep straw. Liv knelt at her left foreleg, quick hands wrapping the lower limb in a white polo bandage — oblivious to his presence.

Chique's head cocked ever so slightly, the low rumble escaping her throat exposing him. Liv glanced over, a half-hearted lift to the corners of her mouth when she saw him.

"Hey, Miller." Her tone was soft, almost apologetic, as she finished with the bandage and ducked under the filly's neck. She set herself by Chique's right leg, wrapping it to match the left.

"How is she?" he asked, coming to the doorway. Best to keep his mind on business. A month out from the Breeders' Cup. He could still be excited about that.

Liv straightened, coming closer, and he held out the martingale and girth as if they could shield him from the draw of her. She shrugged. "Everything looks fine, but you'll have a better answer after you gallop her."

It was so familiar, their motions rote as they got Chique ready, like they had most mornings this year. He liked to get the filly out first. It had always been the best part of his day. Now it was just a reminder that this emotional separation would be physical, to the degree of thousands of miles, come November.

"I'll take her a turn," he said, breaking the silence once they were done.

It wasn't common knowledge yet, the news that weighed on him — he'd seen no reason to share with anyone other than Liv at this point — but he still felt as if all eyes were on him, judging him. *Deserter*. But Liv had told him to go. Sent him away. Selflessly? Taking one for the team. Or was it defence? It didn't matter. It didn't change anything.

She waited in front of the tack room with her helmet on, taking the shank while he automatically checked the tack, even though he'd been there as it went on. Habit. When she wrapped her hand around his left ankle to throw him up, her touch, even through the leather of his boot, made him want to let go of the lines and grab her by the shoulders, demand they come up with a better answer than the one they'd settled on. But there were more appropriate times. A move like that would no doubt give Chique an excuse to go dashing down the shed without them — not something to even joke about with Miss Breeders' Cup *Win and You're In*. He mustered the inspiration to brace against Liv's hold on his leg and bounced, easing lightly into the saddle. The significance of *getting tied on* seeming deeper each day. Seven months was already feeling like the longest ride of his life.

"Right behind you," Liv called after turning him loose, and he was vaguely aware of her disappearing into the pony's stall.

Chique was uncharacteristically quiet, like she was picking up on his mood. Liv didn't even take her head as they walked to the main track, Nicole on the other side of her with an unraced chestnut three-year-old filly named Happy Together — a name which seemed a bit too ironic at the moment. The silence was painful.

Liv didn't back up with them, and didn't need to speak for Nate to know they'd meet after at the five-eighths pole. Chique settled into a jog next to Happy, and Nicole glanced over.

"You okay?" she asked. "You're not singing. With the way you're riding these days, I expect you to be singing."

He snorted, lightening up a bit and breaking into the first bars of Wild Light's "California On My Mind." It wasn't an endorsement for the place.

Nicole looked at him strangely, so he'd guessed right thinking she wouldn't know the tune. In an attempt to break out of his wallowing, he shifted to "More Than Fine." Switchfoot usually worked to get his head out of a funk, but it was a hard sell today. At least it kept Nicole from asking more questions.

They turned in at the wire like they always did before setting off to gallop. He noticed it immediately. Chique didn't feel right. It was more than her not grabbing the bit like she wanted to take him for a joyride, her usual MO; there was a subtle hesitation, a less than solid sense of her beneath him. She swapped leads a beat too early as they hit the backstretch, and her ears didn't flip forward like they always did at that point. He shook his head when Nicole glanced back as he pulled his filly up, letting Happy go on without them. Chique shook her head too, annoyed with being left behind.

Liv was already coming toward them, maneuvering Paz to their left. Nate wished he could rub the furrow out of her brow, but it probably matched his own.

"What's wrong?"

"She's off. Left fore."

"Damn it," Liv muttered. "Let's get her back to the barn."

He wouldn't have thought the silence could be heavier heading home than it had been walking out, yet here they were, Liv holding Chique protectively by the bridle like she hoped she could somehow regain control when things were fragmenting like cracks in an old teacup. Chique danced lightly, no doubt wondering why she hadn't been allowed to finish her gallop, even if Nate wasn't convinced she'd been into it today.

The vet wouldn't be around until after training hours, but he still felt bad leaving after he'd removed the tack. Not that there was anything he could do.

Work was only so much of a distraction. It didn't help that everyone asked about Chique. *How's the big filly?* He tried to go along with the fantasy that they were, in fact, Breeders' Cup bound, when he was sure in the pit of his gut now they weren't.

He hadn't noticed Cory earlier, but when he returned, she was there, putting a walker away. Chique waited in her stall, pulling at her haynet, rumbling for peppermints as soon as she saw him. He indulged her, glancing down at her bandageless legs. Open, for x-rays.

Ducking past a mass of bridles hanging on the hook in the doorway, he found a little huddle in the tack room — Roger's assistant trainer Jo sipping a coffee, Liv with her helmet still on, Nicole pulling off hers and hanging it on a nail.

"All out?" he asked.

"All except for Lacey," Jo said. "Liv's going to get on Paz and take Cory out on her."

"I'll take her," Nate offered. "You'll be more useful around here than I would be." He flashed his eyes to Liv with a restrained smile.

"I don't know, Miller. I'm sure you remember how to do tack, and you're pretty good with a bandage. But I do think she'd appreciate your company more than mine."

Nicole sputtered. "True. Though it might affect her ability to focus."

"Other than that she should be fine," Liv said. "The kid evented. She'll look better than most of the exercise riders out there."

Liv's grin was cute, tugging at Nate's heart, all he saw as Jo brushed past him and called down the shed.

"Cory! Get your boots and helmet on."

Cory was tiny. Saying that in a place where his five foot six was considered tall was quite a statement. It didn't mean anything, of course. It wasn't her size that would determine if she turned out to be a rider or not. Lacey was on the small side too — a late-maturing two-year-old filly who was just in for the experience. She'd go to Payson with the others this winter. The others that didn't include him.

"Ready to go, kid?" he asked.

Cory's head looked too big for her body now that her helmet was on, her tiny feet shifting back and forth, elbows clutched by white-knuckled hands. Liv stopped Lacey next to her.

"First thing? Check the tack," Nate instructed. "I'm not saying Jo didn't put it on right, but never assume the person who did knows what they're doing. It'll save your ass one day."

Liv's smile was encouraging, watching Cory do as she was told. Then Nate legged the kid up, and hauled Paz out of his stall while Liv led the filly off, quietly coaching as she went. *Yes, check your girth again. Got your lines knotted? We call reins lines. She's not tough, but shorten the irons up a couple of holes. Nate will have you, so you can work on standing up. Try it now. Take a cross — like a bridge. You know how to do that, right? That's it. Good.*

Nate swung into the pony tack unassisted. Liv hated it when he did that on Chique, even though Chique didn't care. He'd bet by this afternoon the filly would be at the farm, out with Claire, grazing in the warm fall sun under Triple Stripe's colourful maples. Why had he even bothered to let himself plan? This crazy job didn't lend itself to such things.

Outside Liv walked Cory right up to him, not letting the kid try to get there on her own. He rolled his eyes as he freed the long leather strip from where it hung on the pony's saddle and looped it through the D-bit Lacey wore. It wasn't till then Liv unsnapped the shank. *Not overly cautious at all.*

"Have fun," she called, retreating into the barn.

Nate squeezed Paz forward, holding Lacey with his arm loosely at his side. He ran his eyes over Cory — helmet secured, safety vest in place over her long-sleeved t-shirt, hands clenched on the reins in the same death grip she'd had on her elbows before she'd got on.

"You comfortable?" he asked skeptically.

"Except for being terrified!" she squeaked. "Are we really going to the track?"

"Yeah. The training track. It'll be fine."

Her face suggested that was a ridiculous thought.

The track was practically deserted this time of morning — just the usual assortment of babies like Lacey, and inexperienced riders like Cory. Nate stopped just before the on-gap. Lacey stood like a pony, while Paz dropped his head, mouthing the bit and starting to prance. *Chill, old man.*

"We'll back up to the five-eighths pole, then go once around as long as you're okay. Do you know what all that means?"

She gave a short nod. "Em told me some stuff. You're not allowed to trot going counter-clockwise, so we have to trot the other direction, and stay on the outside rail to keep out of the way of the gallopers and workers."

"Pretty much. Just don't say trot. We say jog." Not that anyone would mistake her for anything other than a newb. At least they hadn't subjected her to an orange vest. "All set?"

Another short nod, and Paz led the way as soon as Nate eased his hold on the reins. He let the pony gelding jog as soon as they were past the clocker's stand, Cory posting automatically to Lacey's lazy gait.

"Plant your cross at the withers and try standing up."

"That's easy," Cory chirped. "It's like cheating, resting my hands on her neck like this. I could do two-point for hours."

"Perfect," Nate said. "I'll make sure Liv knows, so she can send you out on those three-mile jogs we do in Florida." *We*. There would be no *we* this winter.

On the backside he pulled them up and faced the infield. "And then we spend a few moments watching the world go by. We like to teach the horses to relax — but you'll see a lot of people just turning around and taking off, or coming on the track and galloping right away."

He started them at a hobby-horse canter. "Stand up again, and leave your hands down there. You won't be able to do that with every horse — you've got to hold a fit one, and that's a bit different — but don't worry about that for now. Right now just worry about your balance, and stay out of the horse's way. Stay quiet. Not too far forward, or some rat that likes to drop its shoulder will have you eating dirt. With the babies, your balance is important because they're just finding their own, so they need a little more support. But you probably know that from the yearlings."

The kid was a natural, really. Liv said she was chatty, but she'd barely uttered two words. She was concentrating hard. It made him laugh.

"What?" She glanced over, then set her eyes back on Lacey's poll.

"You're taking this very seriously."

"Why wouldn't I be?"

"Well…you've ridden cross-country, right? Like galloping through fields and jumping stuff? This — at least this here, this filly — is a piece of cake next to that. Breathe."

Her cheeks puffed as she blew out a gulp of air.

"Better," he said. "Why do you want to do this, anyway?"

"You're a jockey. You have to ask?"

"Well, okay. But I hope I'm not the first one to tell you — getting an education and a real job is an easier way to go."

"I'm not smart like Em. I'd never get into university. And even if I did, my mom could never afford it. If I have to pick between this or working at Tim Horton's…I'll take this, thanks."

"You know you're pretty lucky Liv agreed to it, right? Most people have to start at the bottom. Walk hots. Learn how to groom. Beg someone to let them get run off with on the pony."

Her serious expression finally cracked, and she caught his eye with a bright smile that lit up her face. "I guess I have you to thank for that, don't I?"

"Maybe you do. You owe me big-time, then. I'll have to remember that." Her body was looser now, her knuckles on the lines not so white. "Once we get past the on-gap, I'm going to turn you loose. Worst case, Paz will run off with me, and you'll have to rescue me. You might get to pay me back sooner than you think."

Her grin only got bigger. The little gallop seemed to work her tongue loose, because she chattered all the way back to the barn. He tried to act like he was listening — and it had given him more of a distraction than hanging out on the shed waiting for the vet to show up would have. He tried to remember the first time his boss back in Calgary had put him up on a horse, that feeling. Even on the old war horse Al had let him gallop, he'd been hooked. Likewise, Cory was hooked.

Liv held Lacey while Cory bathed the little filly. The kid sloshed suds and water about, wearing a third of it, helmet off but her kerchief keeping her short blonde hair back. Now he saw what they were all talking about. He didn't think she'd stopped yakking. Liv stood patiently, tickling Lacey between her nostrils with the end of the shank.

"Thank you," she mouthed.

He shrugged, and had Paz hosed off and out grazing before Cory finished.

NORMALLY LIV WAS all about geeking out over cool diagnostics, but today she resented the expensive imaging that pinpointed the source of Chique's problem. Dr. Koval, surgeon at the nearby equine hospital, took the time to go over the report with her, even though she already knew the verdict.

He'd called as soon as he had the results, but due to the nature of nuclear scintigraphy, it was necessary for Chique to remain in isolation at the clinic until the radioactive isotope had decayed to safe levels.

They were pretty pictures, like colourful pointillism, with the darkest area marking the highest concentration of the isotope, at the site of concern. It wasn't a large area, but it indicated subchondral remodelling — what lay people were calling bone bruising — on the distal articular surface of Chique's left third metacarpal, the cannon bone. Liv was sure only Nate would have noticed Chique was even off, it was such a mild injury. But thank goodness he had, because when something like this went undiagnosed, it could lead to catastrophic breakdown.

She dressed Chique in clean white flannels and cottons, and the clinic staff helped her load the filly onto the Triple Stripe gooseneck, set up with a box stall. Liv didn't drive the farm truck enough to have her phone connected to Bluetooth, so she located the local alternative radio station and listened to its selection of tunes and commercials for the solitary drive home, keeping an eye on the filly with the trailer cam.

Once she'd unloaded and led Chique into her stall in the office barn, Liv drew tranquilizer into a syringe, returning to inject the small dose before removing the filly's travelling gear. It didn't take long for the intravenous drug to take effect. She led Chique to the small paddock where Claire lingered with interest at the gate, and turned the younger filly out with her old friend.

Chique dropped her head and the two of them grazed, nose to nose. Liv extracted her phone, snapped a photo, and texted it to Nate.

JUST JAY WAS the bright light in all this. When it came to Nate's career, it wasn't a bad thing to fly to Lexington, steal a win with the Triple Stripe colt in a Grade Two stake at Keeneland at the beginning of Breeders' Cup week; put his name more firmly in the consciousness of the American trainers. That was as close as they were going to get to the World Championship of Horse Racing this season.

In the eternal words of the sport: *maybe next year.*

5

More than fine…

The ringtone jolted him into consciousness. He grappled for the phone, managed to hit snooze on the second poke, and rolled over.

This isn't what he did. He didn't hit snooze. He always got up with the alarm. He got up before the alarm. Just not this morning.

Downstairs, he could hear Chique's low rumble, echoed by Claire's sing-song. He usually fed them before leaving for the track, but this morning, Liv had beat him to it.

More than fine…

Twisting and sitting up, he stabbed at the screen, leaning back against the headboard. He pushed himself out of bed, got dressed.

More than fine…

This time he made sure he hit stop. *Sorry, boys, not feeling it.*

The big picture window was a rectangle of inky black. Maybe he'd go back to bed after they left. Why not? Thursdays were dark; he might as well take advantage of this rare break. Guys booked off all the time for sketchier reasons. Why couldn't it be his turn?

The coffee maker gurgled when he pressed it into action, and he pulled two mugs and a glass out of the cupboard, pouring himself some juice while he waited for it to brew. After distributing coffee into the mugs, he added milk and sugar to one and gave it a stir, and left them on the counter as he shrugged into his jacket.

Three more weeks till the meet ended. He should be anticipating what came after that — the west coast, riding at Santa Anita — but California dreaming wasn't going to help this morning. He felt as hollow as the sound of his boots as he descended the wooden stairs.

Chique nickered at him, and he mumbled "Sorry," as he gave her merely a glance and opened the office door, balancing the mugs. He pushed it closed with his butt, the room's warmth doing nothing for his heart.

The oil painting of Chique's sire and dam — Just Lucky and Sotisse — grabbed his attention every time he walked in that room. It wasn't just a tribute to two great racehorses, but also to the man with them. Two and a half years, Geai had been gone, left standing between horses in a painting — and ever-present around the farm, in Nate's head, in Liv's. He didn't know if they'd quite achieved what Geai had hoped for them, and this winter wasn't going to do anything to change that. What he'd give to sit down with the old man right now for some encouragement. At least the colt they'd named for him — Just Jay, half-brother to Just Lucky — was a shining reminder of his memory.

His eyes dropped to find Liv watching him silently from behind the desk, the painting looming behind her. He set the sugar-enhanced coffee in front of her. The smile that drifted over her face twisted at his gut.

"Thanks," she said quietly, remaining focused on him instead of reaching for the mug. "Shouldn't you be on your way in?"

"You thought I'd leave without saying goodbye?"

A brief storm passed through her grey eyes before they fell to the papers on the surface in front of her. "The van's heading to Woodbine to pick up the rest of the load from here."

He knew that. She was missing the point. "They'll survive one morning without me." He slumped into the old overstuffed chair set at forty-five degrees to the desk and slurped some coffee — black because he didn't get indulgences like milk and sugar when he had to be sure to make weight. It was just a coincidence that it matched his headspace. "Thanks for feeding."

"I was here, figured I might as well." She fixed her eyes on her cup, steaming in front of her, and lifted it carefully to her lips.

"Isn't it time Chique had her portrait done?" He glanced from the curve of her fingers around the mug, back to the painting. Four years ago August, he'd sat here for the first time, sizing up this dark-haired, serious young woman as she scanned his resumé. *"I'm assuming you want to ride races."* First words out of her mouth, not counting the initial *Hi* with the handshake. Straight to the point.

"Claire too." Her smile was more convincing this time.

He hadn't cared to figure her out back then, too stuck in his own torment to acknowledge anything more than her demeanor and aesthetic. At least he didn't feel as low as he had then, but even though he was convinced now he'd left that mindset far behind, the current situation poked at a vague association. Cindy had pushed him away, because of his career. Now Liv was pushing him away for it too.

"Does Fester have a name yet?" he asked in a vain attempt to redirect his thoughts.

The way she reacted when he butchered the colt's barn name pecked further at his composure — the upturn of her lips, a subtle shake of her head as she sat straighter, tucking a loose strand of hair behind her ear. Again he had to wonder if he should change his mind, when she obviously wasn't changing hers. The fact that she was leaving now, with both Chique and Feste unlikely to resume training until January, said it all. She could have stayed behind with them, like she had with Claire that first winter; come down after Christmas. She could have stayed with him.

"*Téméraire*. We just got the name tag."

"Doesn't that mean 'reckless' or something? Kind of ironic for such a mild-mannered colt."

"Works with the pedigree, though." Liv placed the papers in a leather padfolio and stood up, zipping it shut. "Help me throw on some bandages?"

They functioned in the silence that had followed them around since that day in September— what had started as awkward had developed a character all its own. Liv would never comprehend why he would even consider not going. This is what he'd signed up for, getting involved with her. It was like they touched, then bounced back a distance from each other, always some peripheral force intervening.

"You want to get Chique?"

He nodded, and watched as she went to Feste, winding the chain over his sheepskin-trimmed halter, her face soft as she whispered to him. She never looked at Nate like that. Of course he would lose to a horse. Nate didn't know whether to laugh or cry at the irony. He could picture Emilie's amused face as she patted the back of a disgruntled Faye's hand. *"I hope you don't mind being second to a horse, sweetie."*

Nate led Chique out into the brisk November daybreak, the breeze lifting the filly's mane. Cory stood with the van drivers, hands deep in the pockets of her jeans, her short blonde hair curling around the edges of a red toque. Chique walked on without hesitation. *Damn it, filly. The least you could have done is stalled a bit.* He wasn't ready to let them go. Liv secured Feste across from the filly, and Nate followed her silently off the van. They watched the drivers dismantle the ramp, then climb into the cab with a wave. The transport rumbled slowly off. Nate trailed Liv and Cory to the Nissan.

"Have fun this winter, Cory," he said, and opened the passenger door for her while Liv waited on the other side.

Cory took that as an invitation, apparently, throwing her arms around his waist. "Thanks, Nate! Thanks for all the help! Good luck with the rest of the meet! And have a great time in California!"

He pushed her away and she ducked into the car. Too many exclamation points. He should be so excited. He shut in her cheer with a swing of the door, and shoved his hands into the pockets of his jacket as he returned to Liv.

"Guess this is it," she said.

"See you next year," he responded wryly.

"It sounds so far away when you put it like that."

"It is." There was so much he wanted to say, but he felt he'd lost his right to say anything. "Give me a call when you get down there, okay?"

"It's going to be strange without you around."

"Oh, come on." He laughed softly. "This is all part of your plan to keep Feste for yourself, isn't it?"

He reached out and brushed a strand of hair away from her face, his fingers lingering before he wrapped his arms around her and held her, not wanting to let go. Not for the first time, he felt like phoning Don, as soon as he returned to his apartment, calling the whole damn California thing off.

"Drive carefully," he said, kissing her cheek. He reached for the door handle, opening it, when he shouldn't be helping her leave. She hadn't moved yet.

Say something. Say something that will make this bearable.

Liv held his eyes, then blinked before folding herself into the packed vehicle. She glanced at him as she pulled on the seat belt. "Bye Miller."

She'd done it so easily. Maybe she was right not to prolong it. He watched her zip away to catch the van, and felt a chill as the wind hit the back of his neck. At least he thought it was the wind.

The barn was so deserted now, just reinforcing the encroaching emptiness he felt. He gathered the coffee cups, both of them barely touched, and locked the office behind him, trudging upstairs. He could wallow. Go back to bed. Watch Netflix all day. But something in him fought back, an idea taking shape as he dumped the cold brew and gave himself a warm cup. His phone camera, a tripod, the piano…he wasn't going to just fade away.

6

Chique's snort was loud and clear, the filly hanging her head over the fence of one of Payson's sandy paddocks. Liv ignored her, riding out on Feste, laughing at the filly's buck and squeal in protest of not being included.

Feste was sensible and bold, unfazed by things that would have set off his sister. Normally after sixty days the yearlings had a break until January, but hacking him about the grounds wouldn't hurt. In fact, it would be good for him. His swinging stride carried her down the laneway towards Route 76, small ears pricked with interest. Liv guided him left before reaching the office, to the trail that looped behind. *Over hill, over dale…*that's what Nate would have been singing, as they wandered in and out and up and down the gentle landscape.

Inspired by the training protocol they'd used for Claire two years ago — when Nate had talked her into doing things differently with the mare, who was a bad bleeder — Liv had dug out another of Geai's old books before she'd left: *Conditioning To Win*. It freaked her out to read how they'd trained yearlings back when the book had originally been published — breezing them so early, workloads that would bring PETA down on a trainer's head. Today's racehorses were treated like fragile birds, and one might think they were, because they sure seemed to break more easily. But

Claire hadn't, not from training hard. It had been a loose horse that had taken her out. So maybe Feste wouldn't either. Liv would monitor his progress down to the nth, of course, but she was determined to build him into the strongest, soundest athlete she could. Chique's issues just convinced her of it, rather than scaring her off.

She let him jog on the level ground, past Payson's unique turf course, where she envisioned them doing most of their work in the next months. The sun was hot, humidity amplifying its effect, leaving the t-shirt under her safety vest drenched. Nate had texted her a photo of Ontario's first snowstorm earlier. *Poor Nate.*

Michel met them in front of the open shedrow. No asphalt apron here, just sand, and grass, and trees. And fire ants. Liv sidestepped one of the mounds on the way to leaving her tack on the rail, and returned to hold Feste for his bath.

It was too early to know what Feste might or might not be. It wasn't fair to have any expectations, so she was determined to just enjoy the process of bringing along another hopeful. And Chique? For the first time in years, Liv wasn't preoccupied with what was next. There was no pressure, no big races looming. She could worry about that in January, when the filly would hopefully be ready to start back. The theme for the winter was self-care, for all of them.

Nicole had stayed in Ontario to gallop for Roger, Jo grooming what was left, while Liv and Cory, Michel and Sue, handled things here in Florida. They alternated afternoon feeding duties, and Michel and Sue were on today, so after finishing with Feste and bringing his sister in from the heat, Liv corralled Cory — who didn't have a car, and was living with her — and headed for the coast.

She hadn't told Nate about the condo on the beach. It would have seemed too much like rubbing it in. A friend of her father's owned it, and it was going to be empty otherwise, so Jo was renting her place this winter, while Liv shared this paradise with Cory. Maybe next winter she'd share it with Nate.

It felt indulgent, stretching out on the sand and gazing up at the clear blue sky. She loved the ocean; never tired of its power as the waves washed up on the beach. It renewed her every time she came out here. It gave her clarity. It made her want to see if her father's friend would sell this place. She'd happily let the one in town go.

Two thousand miles had put distance between her and her doubts. Everything with Nate was going to be okay. This is how things needed to be. It wasn't a bad thing, taking a step back from the relationship. The way she felt about him scared her. He was ready for it all, and she'd felt herself being swept along, in danger of being swallowed whole; run off with like a rank horse.

It was too much, too soon. Speed kills — Thoroughbreds and relationships. It was best to slow everything down, let him go — figuratively, literally. But she really didn't feel she was letting him go. They were always connected, somehow.

"Aren't you going to open this?"

Cory's voice, as bright and energetic as the kid herself, pulled her back from the drowsy edges she'd been fading into. She'd forgotten about the mail Cory had grabbed from Payson's office. A little bubble pack, with the farm at home as the return address.

She hadn't recognized the block lettering spelling out her name over Payson's address. Cory dropped to the sand beside her, wrapping tanned arms around equally-tanned legs crossed at the ankles, her petite frame decked in a bikini top and bright pastel-patterned shorts. Cory didn't hide her curiosity. Who got snail mail anymore?

A data stick fell out as Liv unfolded the lined three-ring paper. Liv recovered it from her lap, two fingers closing around it as the others held the letter — because it was a letter — open. The writing was more familiar: half cursive, half printing, perfectly legible, a quick confidence to it.

Dear Liv,

You're probably on the beach right now, roasting in the sun while I freeze my ass off.

She had to laugh, because, well, here she was.

I kind of think I'd trade the stupid riding title for the beach at the moment.

Things are falling into place for California, as much as part of me wants it all to blow up so I can tell you I'm coming to Florida after all. Jeanne's contacted me about an apartment. Will's got a buddy who's going to look after the Mustang for me. Do some work on the poor old girl so she might live to see another year, and store it for me over the winter. I'm almost going to miss her as much as I miss you, but at least I knew better than to ask her to make the trip.

He loved that damn car. She felt a pang of guilt, thinking the car, at least, would have made the trip with him if he'd asked.

Will keeps saying we should do a show next year. Me going away doesn't help much with that plan either, but we'll see. Might be kind of fun. I'm taking my guitar to LA, at least. Don't think the piano will fit in my carryon.

"What's the stick for?" Cory, still watching, said.

"I don't know yet, and I'm not sure it's any of your business." She gave Cory a wry smile, and the kid took the hint and wandered down to the waves.

I know you think we're doing the right thing. I'm familiar with the "I don't want to hold you back" argument. It just hits kind of hard, because, well…I thought we were in this together. You, and me, and Chique. And I know it's just five more months. It's just that right now, five months feels like forever.

I'll go along with the agreement, but that doesn't mean I have to like it. And that doesn't mean I can't fight it, old school. I'm going to pretend I have to win you over all over again, because clearly I haven't done a good enough job.

Yours — really,

Nate.

PS — If you want more, send it back. And give the kids a kiss and a peppermint for me.

More? He must mean the stick.

She folded the letter, returning it and the flash drive to the envelope. Gathering her towel, she returned to the house and Liv opened her laptop on the kitchen counter. She keyed in her password, and plugged the stick into the USB port.

A couple of movie files. *Okay*. Double-click. And there he was, at the piano in his apartment, no preamble as he started to play.

Some guys did playlists. Nate — well, Nate did this. Nate recorded songs. For her.

Hearing him sing wasn't new, but it was something else all together with the piano. It was like the piano was meant for him, part of him, the notes melding with his voice.

The music resonated in a way that was both enthralling and uncomfortable, exposing feelings she was trying to keep tucked away. This was hard. Hard to fight. She'd been so convinced things were as they should be. Somehow this rubbed off the protective coating she'd applied over the conflict that remained below the surface.

It was too late to change things. She wouldn't be the one to derail such an important career move for him, if that's what he was looking for. She had come to terms with the deal and was determined to see it through until they were back in Ontario.

But she couldn't help it. She scribbled a note to herself, to find an envelope and send the stick back tomorrow, hoping it would get to him before he left for LA.

7

"Ready?" Roger asked.

Nate didn't answer, just nodded, and stepped forward to meet Jay, hopping aboard from the trainer's legup. *Ready to be done with this season, sure.*

He pulled down his goggles and tugged up his mask against the bitter northwest wind as Jo led them from the paddock. Driving wet snow pelted his helmet, and somehow the base layer he wore under his silks and breeches hadn't put him overweight.

Closing day just as it should be, miserable.

It was enough to make him feel sorry for those who had to stay here for the winter. At least he got to go somewhere warm, even if it was the wrong place. Tomorrow, both he and Jay would be on their way to sunny California. It better be sunny, anyway.

Triple Stripe always seemed to have a live horse in the Valedictory Stakes, a marathon of a finale at a mile and three quarters. The last two years it had been Sans Défaut. This year, Just Jay was stepping up.

It always attracted a full field, many of them seasoned campaigners who so rarely got to run at this kind of distance. Jay was the young upstart, but Roger knew how to prep a horse for this race, and Nate was confident he was ready.

All the horses broke with a sigh instead of the usual bang. It was a long, long race. Jay was clearly confused by the lack of urgency. And it was fair for the colt to slow slightly, the first time under the wire, but when Nate asked — *a whole 'nother time around, buddy* — Jay responded with renewed confidence. They stalked the speed, sweeping around the clubhouse turn tight to the rail, and when the frontrunner started to falter midway down the backstretch, Nate worked his colt clear. Jay settled nicely, leading the way into the turn. Jay was smart, and Jay had gears. This was fun.

At the head of the stretch he asked for one of those gears, and Jay opened up a couple of lengths. When no one came at him, he asked for a little more for insurance, and Jay gave it. Nate didn't know how far in front they were when at the end.

He and Jay were going to be good friends this winter; this budding bromance would have to be enough.

WILL WAS DRIVING him to the airport in the morning, so when it was finally over — the card of racing, the season — he drove into the city.

"Can I get you a drink?" Faye took Nate's coat, and sashayed to the kitchenette. A year ago that would have been for him, the way her hips moved, that coy glance over her shoulder. Maybe that was a little bit for him. A little *you had that, bud, and you gave it up, and where's your girlfriend, anyway? Oh yeah, she dropped you because you're going to be 2,000 miles apart this winter. Hope you survive that separation better than we did.*

He shook his head, then stopped lest she think that was for the beer she held out, which he absolutely wanted. Faye was in the category of *been there, done that, screwed it up royally.*

"Please. Thanks," he said, watching her twist off the cap easily before handing it to him. "Where's Will?"

"On his way home from work."

"Home? You say that like you live here."

"Do I? Hmm. Yet, I do not."

"Staying over is a little too cosy for me when you're around."

"If you drink enough, you won't care. But, details. Sorry not sorry. Guess you're going to have to suck it up tonight."

"So I am." He swigged a good third of the bottle. "Better be prepared."

Faye returned to the kitchenette, steam rising over a pot on the stove. "Hope you're hungry." She dumped dried pasta into the rolling water.

"I'm always hungry." While he didn't have a terrible time making weight, he still had to watch what he ate. "And it's not like I can go crazy. I am going to California to ride."

The door cracked open, Will entering. Faye set a timer, and did her sashay over to Will, tipping her head back for a kiss. Nate looked the other way, and missed Liv all the more.

Faye wandered to the fridge for another beer, cracking it and handing it to Will, then passed Nate a bowl of salad and waved him towards the small table that was usually stacked with papers and music. Nate didn't think giving him the greens was coincidence, and he let himself laugh as he wandered over and set it down.

"So, are you ready for California?" Faye asked, dishing out the cooked pasta, now tossed with olive oil and garlic. "You know — besides wanting to get away from our weather."

Nate inhaled the steam rising off the fusilli before carefully loading his fork. She wasn't asking if he was packed. "Why wouldn't I be? I've wanted to get there for a long time. I almost went there in the first place, instead of coming to Ontario."

"You're not really sure about it right now though, are you?"

He met her eyes briefly. "I've got to do it. So maybe the timing sucks."

"Do you think you'll get to Florida?"

Nate shrugged. "I can't see Chique running down there, so it's not as if they need me."

"This has really got you down, hasn't it?" Faye set her fork next to her bowl. "You guys will survive. Besides, this is the best part, isn't it? All the silly maneuvering and second-guessing. You should enjoy it. Once you're actually together, that's when the hell begins."

"Hey!" Will interjected.

"I'm kidding." Faye smiled at him sweetly. Nate was happy they were happy.

He wasn't quite drunk enough to not care about sleeping on the couch, but he wasn't driving all the way back to his apartment. He still woke up at four-thirty, and dragged himself off the couch, folded the blankets and sheet and set them on the arm, and shuffled to the kitchen to pour himself some juice.

Liv would probably be at Payson by now, putting Chique out in the dark to give the filly as long as possible in the paddock while the horses trained. He opened the weather app on his phone, swiping left — he still had Indiantown in there. Hot and humid, chance of rain, like always. One further gave him Los Angeles.

Will looked wiped, but mustered a sleepy smile when Nate handed him a cup of coffee. Nate, on the other hand, was buzzing.

"I can't eat this early," Will said. "Want to go?"

Nate nodded. "Sure. I can drive there. Give you a chance to wake up."

Will didn't fight him on that, tossing Nate his keys. He folded into the passenger seat when they reached the Camaro, which was just as old as Nate's Mustang.

"Faye's right, isn't she? You're not really sure about this."

Nate scowled at him before refocusing on the road. "You're dropping me off at the airport."

"We're not there yet."

"I'm doing this. If she wants space, I'm giving her space." A couple thousand miles' worth of it. She hadn't asked for it, in so many words, but he'd deduced that was part of it.

"Big of you. Very understanding."

"But I don't want to give her space, damn it. I want her with me always and forever, like that stupid song in *Napoleon Dynamite.*"

"You're in deep, dude." Will chuckled.

It was painfully true. He had to stop thinking about it. "So what about you and Faye? You two seem disgustingly happy and shit."

"I'm going to ask her to come to Calgary with me for Christmas. Think it's too soon?"

Nate's eyes shifted over quickly. "I don't know. You're on your own with that one."

"Think you'll ever go back?"

And all of a sudden, this life of his, the one that seemed all shiny to an outsider looking in, showed a little more of its tarnish.

THE FARM in King City was appropriately covered in fresh snow, as if it had been special ordered for Liv. It was strange to be transported from the warmth of South Florida back to winter in Southern Ontario, but not nearly as strange as spending the holiday down there. Liv had only done that once, two years ago — officially her worst Christmas ever. But the memory made her think of Nate. New Year's Eve. A crazy night with a bottle of wine and an exchanging of woes. A first-class pity party, complete with dancing to a sad song. The kiss at midnight had been completely accidental. How different would things be now if she hadn't misread the entire evening and let it justify keeping him away? In a way though, this winter was about keeping him away. Again. Not in the dramatic, panicked manner of two years ago. This time she'd cited logic. It was a smoke screen.

"Thanks, Em." Faye peered approvingly at the label on the wine bottle Emilie had brought for their Boxing Day get-together at Northwest. "Mind you, it's the least you can do, deserting me like you are and running off to the Sunshine State with Liv."

"Are you really, Em?" Dean asked. "What about your Masters?"

"You're one to talk, brother," Faye chided. Dean had abandoned a Masters degree himself to take over training for his father's clients after their parents had passed away in a car accident.

"I will go back to it. I've changed educational paths so often, adding a few more months to finishing the journey won't matter." Emilie had changed majors several times in the course of obtaining her undergraduate degree before settling on the path that now saw her in a Masters program for physiotherapy. She handed a tin of homemade cookies to Dean.

"Forget all that, did you bake these?" Dean peeked into the canister.

"You know that's what Em does," Liv said. "Em bakes. I completely missed any fragment of the domestic gene."

"Clearly," Faye said.

Dean stayed for a drink, then disappeared with a handful of cookies, leaving the three women to catch up. The living room was cozy with its open fireplace, the house decorated with the same style and care Faye took with her own appearance. Light from the flames danced over the resident

Golden, Gus — flat out, soaking up the heat, his greeting duties complete. Emilie parked herself cross-legged on the floor next to him, running one hand over his long coat, holding her wine glass with the other.

"Did you talk to Nate yesterday?" Faye asked, settling on the couch with Liv.

"We texted," Liv said, looking into her glass and swirling the red liquid around. "I figured I'd talk to him tonight. Opening day at Santa Anita and all that."

"You're hopeless. You let Nate Miller go, on his own, to California, then abandon him. If some gorgeous little blonde movie star snaps him up, you completely deserve it."

Emilie laughed. "You're one to talk."

Faye glared at her. "That's enough from you!"

Liv raised her eyebrows and looked from Emilie to Faye. "Is one of you going to fill me in?"

Faye refilled their wine glasses, then sighed. "Apparently Will going back to Calgary for Christmas was enough to derail me."

Emilie laughed. "Only because he asked her to go with him, and she couldn't deal with that."

"And you're being hard on me for letting Nate go to California?" Liv said. "At least my derailing was about careers, not lack of conviction."

"Is it, though?"

Faye was calling her out. She was good — or bad — that way, her best friend. Liv stared at the fire. Avoiding. Which was what she was doing with Nate, right?

"Really, Liv what's the deal? Why are you so dead set on not giving it a chance?" Faye persisted.

"After what he went through in Calgary, I'm not sure it's fair to let him think we can have what he wants. I couldn't do that to him." The quiet declaration was laced with sadness.

Faye's eyes flickered, like she was feigning indifference. "He never did tell me."

"It was kind of harsh. I can't blame him for leaving."

Faye's gaze shifted to Emilie. "I suppose you know, too. He tells you everything."

Emilie shook her head. "Not that."

Faye and Emilie were going to wait until Liv explained, that was obvious. Should she, though? It wasn't really her story to tell. But maybe Faye deserved to know.

"He asked his girlfriend to marry him and she said no, then turned around and married his brother, in a matter of months."

It landed as it had for Liv, when he'd shared it with her — like a brick.

"Poor Nate," Emilie said. "That should make you feel better, shouldn't it, Faye?"

"Not sure about that, Em. I already knew I was Rebound Girl. That confirms we never really had a chance." Faye looked at Liv closely. "But I can see how that information wouldn't help you any."

Liv ducked her eyes to the wine, her words almost a whisper. "I would hate to end up hurting him."

Faye had another long drink from her glass. "I think we both need to make resolutions. I will call Will and apologize for my little meltdown, beg his forgiveness, and hope he hasn't written me off." She smiled wanly. "See, I get that Will is much too good a guy to let get away. And you, sweetie, will let yourself believe you can have a relationship with Nate, because we know the problems are all in your head and it's this talking yourself out of it that's the biggest issue. Time to move forward." Faye raises her wine. "You in?"

Liv frowned. "Kind of late for that, isn't it?"

Emilie scowled. "Like Faye said, hopeless." She removed her hand from Gus's side, and the Golden stirred, a nudge with his nose drawing her back to the all-important task of petting him. "I think you're both insane. I'm not saying you should have gone to Calgary with Will, Faye, but you kind of over-reacted, so you'd better fix that. And Liv, you and Nate are bigger than your precious independence. He had it bad for you long before even he would admit it — sorry Faye — and you're not oblivious anymore. We all want to believe in happy endings and Faye is right, it would be just wrong for you to throw that away. Take a deep breath and go with it. For all our sakes."

"So if it all falls apart, I've got that on my shoulders? Our collective hope for happy endings?" Liv smirked.

Emilie laughed. "I'm never going to suggest anyone has to have a relationship to be happy, but if I'm lucky enough for that kind of kindred spirit to fall into my life, I pray I have the common sense to grab him."

"Hear, hear," Faye said, grinning. "Nate's younger brother, remember."

"Wouldn't that be funny?" Emilie said.

"But far too easy. Shouldn't you have to go through hell like the rest of us?"

"The two of you just create your own hell," Emilie said, smiling with mock sweetness.

Liv let Faye refill her glass — Emilie declined, picking up her car keys to make her point, though they could walk home if they had to.

"Hey Liv!" It was Dean's voice, coming from another room. "Want to watch the race?"

Liv almost spilled her wine as she stood up, her eyes sweeping from Faye to Em, glowering. "I almost forgot thanks to you guys. Come on."

They crowded into Dean's office, his computer monitor full screen on Santa Anita as the horses came out on the track.

"Number six, Arosebyanyother, owned by Inspired Farm, trained by Don Philips, ridden by Nate Miller…"

It was just a glimpse, Nate ruffling the filly's mane with one hand while he held the lines in the other. Seeing him plucked a string in her heart — his familiar posture, the simple affectionate gesture for his mount. It fed her guilt. Did she lack the common sense Em talked about? She'd always thought herself so logical. But logic got in the way of love. *Love.* Where had that come from? And why did she feel like she had to choose between it and a career? Did they get to have both, in this world?

Arosebyanyother broke well and Nate settled her mid-pack, outside — out of trouble. The filly ran easily behind a pace that should set things up perfectly for her, given her come-from-behind form. Turning for home Nate picked her up and sent her, as calmly and cooly as he'd ridden the whole race. He merely waved his stick alongside her neck, the filly surging to the lead and beating her rivals handily.

He looked so good on a horse. But was that it? Were they just about the horses? Was there anything wrong with that, though? There would always be horses.

"I say this calls for more wine!" Faye declared.

Liv settled back on the couch with Faye. She'd call Nate later. A text wasn't enough, Faye was right. She had to make a better effort. She was the one who had put things on hold. Merely sending the flash drive back and forth over the miles didn't count.

She gave it enough time that he'd be done for the day, and sneaked into the kitchen, slipping on her coat and boots and stepping out into the sharp night air. Hit call, pressed the phone to her ear.

It just rang. Maybe he was out celebrating. An allowance race didn't usually merit anything special, but given it was his first win in California, maybe it was justified. Maybe that blonde California girl had materialized to help. As Faye had pointed out, it would serve her right. She didn't leave a message.

She went into the videos on her phone, and pulled up the latest one he'd sent, just to see him, to hear him, take solace in the sentiment. It was a cover of his favourite band, Switchfoot — *I Won't Let You Go.*

LIV HAD FLOWN HOME, but spent most of the twenty-one hour drive back to Florida behind the wheel of Emilie's red Civic, her sister sleeping through the music that kept Nate jarringly on her own mind. A combination of caffeine, separation anxiety, and too much time to think kept her going.

It was late enough when they arrived that she drove straight to the condo, despite a strong urge to check in at the training centre. Emilie was tired, but that didn't stop her waking Cory. Liv passed out gratefully in her own room to the hushed whispers of the two younger women.

Cory and Emilie were dragging but happy in the morning, and Liv left them to find their own way to Payson. It would be good to have Em around. She set off in the dark in her own car, navigating the way inland.

"I'm back," she called as she headed directly for Chique's stall, grabbing a thermometer from the nearby wallbox.

Jo poked her head out of the feed room. "We vaccinated everybody yesterday, so they're all walking."

Chique flicked an ear at Liv's arrival, but didn't move.

"What's the matter, filly? Your vacs not agree with you?"

She took hold of the filly's halter, but Chique resisted. After inserting the thermometer, Liv ran her hands down either side of Chique's neck, checking for swelling, then down the filly's left leg, feeling one hoof, then the other. The heat that met her touch sent her heart racing.

Curling her fingers around the filly's pastern, a strong pulse leapt under the pads. The other pastern was the same. Hind hooves normal. Liv stumbled to her feet, phone already to her ear as she called the vet — who wouldn't even be on the grounds this time of morning.

She found Jo. "Chique's trying to founder."

Jo sent Michel to the track kitchen for ice. Liv dragged the tub from the tack room. Even in these days of modern veterinary advances, the first line of defence for acute laminitis remained frustratingly simple: cold therapy, in hopes of arresting the inflammation assaulting the sensitive tissues of the hoof before irreversible damage was done. When Doc Beckett arrived, he confirmed Liv's fears, and administered supportive medication and fluids. She felt ill, watching Chique's pain escalate, the filly sweating, shifting uncomfortably from side to side, rocking back on her hindquarters as she tried to relieve the pressure in front.

"Maybe we'll luck out. You caught it early," the vet said. "Get her started on that footbath."

Everything seemed to swirl around Liv. Michel dumped bags of ice into the tub. Jo dragged the hose over. They lifted one foot, placing it gently in the freezing bath, then the other. Chique trembled in the doorway of her stall, swaying slowly back and forth.

Liv was only vaguely aware the others had gone back to work. Sometime in the middle of it all Cory and Emilie had arrived, and they helped walk horses, muck stalls, turn yearlings out.

Nate. He needed to know.

She didn't bother to calculate what time it would be in LA; just fumbled to unlock her phone again, finding his name on her most recents, resting her finger on it to initiate the call. She willed him to pick up.

"Liv — what's wrong?" His voice was thick with sleep.

She couldn't speak.

"You're scaring me." His voice came again; clearer, more urgent, this time.

"It's Chique. She had a bad reaction to her vaccinations." It came out strangled, shaky. "She's got laminitis."

"I'm on my way."

"Nate, you can't — "

"The hell I can't. I'll call when I get a flight."

The line went dead, the phone remaining pressed to her ear. Chique still swayed, back and forth.

It was Emilie who was waiting for him at the Fort Lauderdale airport, standing on the fringes of the crowd welcoming his flight — arms clutched around herself like she was cold in her t-shirt and shorts, brow creased as she scanned the arrivals. Fatigue lined her face and weighed down her shoulders. He scooped her up and squeezed her, her arms unhesitatingly returning the gesture.

"Sorry, Em. I should've rented a car."

She shrugged. "I needed something to do. Just help keep me awake, all right?"

"I can drive."

She didn't argue, handing him her keys and leading the way to the car.

"How's Liv?" he finally asked, pointing the Civic north on the Turnpike.

"How do you think?"

He could imagine.

He didn't care that he was driving too fast, pushing the little Honda through the falling night. Being in transit all day, it felt better to finally have some control over the speed of his journey.

Emilie stirred as he turned into Payson's familiar dirt drive, the place he'd spent the last three winters. The Triple Stripe barn was the only one lit up, Liv's Nissan parked out front. He pulled in beside it, leaving the keys in the ignition, climbing out.

Liv sat on an overturned bucket in front of Chique's stall. She rose in slow motion. She felt limp and powerless in his arms, her breath warm as she pressed her face against his neck. He pushed her back to look at her, but she ducked away, breaking his hold.

"You should go home and get some sleep, Em," she said. "Jo's taking over for me at midnight or so."

"Stay awake, Em," Nate cautioned. At least she'd napped on the drive. He turned to Chique and stroked her neck. The filly pressed her muzzle into his hand, but without her usual demands.

"She's loaded up with medication, so she's more comfortable, for now," Liv said. "A bad reaction, Nate. That's all it took. I can't believe it."

He caught the distress in her eyes before she slumped back onto the bucket, hands clasped over her knees, leaving him feeling even more useless. Feste pushed his head over his screen, and scratching the yearling's forehead seemed like the only productive thing Nate could do.

"How was your Christmas?" Liv asked out of the blue.

It seemed an oddly polite question. "Quiet would be an understatement," he responded.

"I should have called. Faye told me off for it."

"Did she." He laughed quietly. "I'm not sure I'll ever believe Faye is truly rooting for me."

Liv rose again, running her fingers through the water in Chique's footbath. "We should add more ice."

He nodded, and one at a time dumped in two of the partially-melted bags resting nearby. Liv picked up the plastic, pressing the empty bags into the old feed sac that hung on the rail for garbage. She touched Chique's nose and slipped into the stall.

Nate followed slowly, and slid down beside her in the straw, leaning back against the bank of bedding that provided cushioning from the cinder block wall. Every so often Chique's muscles trembled, her head hanging low over the crossbar, the tie attached to her halter only a formality. He wrapped his fingers around Liv's, and she squeezed back, resting her head on his shoulder.

"Happy Birthday to me," she murmured.

"Oh shit, Liv. I forgot."

"If you recall the other time we were together on my birthday, it's probably best forgotten."

He chuckled quietly. "That was a strange night."

"A bottle of wine would go down nicely right now."

"Promise tonight you won't run away if I kiss you?"

She looked up at him, and he wasn't going to tell himself it was wrong, when everything else about this winter was wrong. He tipped her chin up with his finger, and let his thumb graze her jaw as his lips met hers, lingering just long enough that when he pulled back, the ache in her eyes mirrored his own. It wasn't enough, but it would have to be, for now.

"I still hate New Year's." His hand drifted back to find hers. "At least we're broken up already."

"It's not like that."

"Isn't it?"

"I'm sorry, Nate. About all of it."

"Bygones," he said. Not that he was over it. "Just three more months, right?"

It might have been romantic — here together with the sounds of rustling hay nets, the occasional snuffle as a horse cleared his nostrils, someone else grunting in flat-out sleep in the stall behind them — if not for the distressed filly before them.

Liv was so still next to him, he thought she might be asleep. He glanced at the time. "Happy New Year," he said quietly. No champagne, no fireworks, no streamers.

A whinny rose above the ambient noise, and Liv stirred, climbing to her feet — breaking the moment.

"Jo," she said as headlights flashed into the yard.

Jo's eyes swept from Liv to Nate as he brushed straw from his jeans. "Get her out of here, Nate. I'll carry on. If anything changes, I'll call."

Liv insisted on driving, silence stretching like the lonely road in front of them until they began to reach civilization.

"Where are you going?" he asked when she drove past the familiar condo complex, where he'd lived just down from her the last two winters.

"You'll see."

They passed over the intracoastal, and he could tell they were near the ocean, the smell of saltwater hanging in the humid air. Liv pulled in beside Emilie's Civic, in front of a modern-looking detached house, right on the beach. He followed her to it, and she let them in.

"Wow," he said quietly, looking across a large room to the floor-to-ceiling windows opposite. He wandered over and stared into the darkness, just able to make out the ocean where it met the sand. "You've been keeping secrets."

When he turned, Liv was slumped on a stool at the island that dominated the kitchen, her head resting on her arms. The answers to his questions could wait.

"You should eat something. Any food here?" He drifted past her and took the liberty of opening the fridge.

"I don't think I could stomach anything, Miller."

"I see eggs. And cheese. An omelet, maybe."

She didn't move as he cooked, but lifted her head when he placed a plate in front of her. "Who knew."

He laughed. "It's not a five-course meal or anything. C'mon. Eat."

The other half of the omelet went down quickly — he hadn't eaten all day. Liv rose when she was finished, and took her plate to the sink.

"Want the grand tour?" she asked. "It won't take long. You've already seen the best part." She waved her arm at the big open room, and he followed her down the hall.

"Cory's room — now shared with Em," she said as they passed the first door. "Bathroom." She pointed to the door on the right. "My room."

Liv went straight to the queen-sized bed and collapsed on top of the covers. He stopped, stuck in the doorway for a moment, then pulled his eyes from her. More floor-to-ceiling windows facing the ocean on the left, an ensuite on the right.

"Nice," he said, drawn to the windows. It was quiet enough he could hear the crashing waves. He glanced over his shoulder.

Liv had rolled onto her side, watching him. "You should get some sleep too. You might as well stay here. It's more comfortable than the couch."

He hesitated, not sure how much he wanted to test his self-control. He came over, pulling out a pillow and propping it against the headboard to sit with his legs resting on the bed next to her.

"Everything going okay in California?"

He shrugged. "Living the dream." The furrow in her brow was evidence his sarcasm wasn't lost on her.

"What's the problem?"

Besides the fact you're almost three thousand miles away? Success had come quickly and easily for him when he'd started his career in Ontario, and he hadn't missed a beat when he'd lost his apprentice allowance earlier this year. The west coast was making it clear it wasn't going to be as cooperative.

"Competition's tougher there," she said when he didn't respond.

"I just need faster horses to ride." If he hadn't lost most of his sense of humour, he would have laughed.

"I tried to call you Boxing Day, after you won on that filly."

"I saw. You didn't leave a message." Or call back. But he hadn't called her, either. "Don took Jeanne and me out for dinner."

She didn't respond, and he noticed her eyes were closed. Soon he could tell she was asleep. He tried not to think about how nice it would have been to spend the winter here, with her, condo on the beach — as if that's how it would have been. He reached out, and almost touched her before pulling back, getting off the bed. The living room sofa seemed a safer place to be.

When he woke he felt disoriented, sitting up abruptly. Lights were on in the kitchen, Emilie pouring herself a glass of juice.

"Hey, Nate. Get some sleep?"

"What time is it?" He didn't feel very rested, no surprise.

"Four-thirty. When did you guys get back?"

"I don't know. One o'clock or something."

"Any change with Chique?"

"No. Good or bad."

Emilie came over and sat beside him, sipping her juice.

"Where's Cory?" he asked.

"She worked Christmas, so she's off New Year's Day. Her mom came for a visit, so they're doing tourist stuff. She wasn't sure about going, but Liv made her. Not like there's much she could do that's not already being done."

Nate nodded, and rubbed at the ache behind his temples. "There more of that in the fridge?"

"Help yourself."

What he needed was coffee, but he poured himself a glass. "You guys really need to do some grocery shopping." They'd bought the good orange juice, at least.

"Give us a break. We've been away, then came back to a sick horse. It hasn't been a priority."

"I know." He wasn't hungry anyway.

Emilie's eyes followed him as he returned. "Guess you didn't expect to find yourself here this winter."

He shook head, wondering if she questioned the way he'd just dropped everything in Los Angeles and hopped on a plane to be here. For some reason he thought of Faye. Faye would never get that he would do such a thing for a horse, and would think it only had to do with Liv. Of course, it did have a lot to do with Liv. He wasn't sure the two could be separated; that one could exist without the other.

"So did you two talk at all?" Emilie asked.

He shook his head, resigned. "It's not the time. In a couple of days I'll be leaving. Gotta stick to the deal, right?"

"Why? Seriously, Nate…do you have to go back?"

"What are you saying, Em?"

"I don't know. It just seems like you should be here."

"You're not really helping. This is hard enough. Coming here, especially under these circumstances…of course I don't want to go back. But now Jay won a race out there, and Don wants to point him to the Santa Anita Handicap, and it would look really bad to bail. For what, really? Liv is tough. It's not going to make a difference to her if I'm here or not, once the smoke clears."

"Do you actually believe that?"

"She's given me no reason not to."

"Wow, Nate."

He glanced at her, not really surprised by her reaction. He was always the optimistic one, trying to think positive, no matter what. Somehow he'd lost that this winter.

Em glanced at the clock on the kitchen wall. "I'd better get going. You two take your time. The longer Liv rests, the better. You too, for that matter. Go back to sleep."

Instead he showered, then dressed in shorts and a clean shirt before slipping out the sliding door off the living room and wandering to the beach in bare feet. There was no hint of the sun that would rise in a few hours, just pinprick starlight scattered in the indigo sky, the rhythm of the waves as they crashed against the shore luring him.

There was no sense in rehashing anything on this visit — Chique was the priority here, not his personal angst. Of course if the threat Chique was dealing with was bringing Liv face to face with their collective mortality, and showing her the importance of hanging onto — whatever this was — he would take that, but she needed to express it, not leave him to guess.

8

Liv shed her clothes quickly — the ones she'd fallen asleep in — and showered, pulling on clean jeans and a fresh t-shirt and sweeping her damp hair into a ponytail. She was angry with herself for sleeping so long; she needed to get back to the barn.

She caught a glimpse of Nate through the window, a lone figure on the empty beach, and paused. He'd come without hesitating, despite everything. She pushed open the sliding door, and instead of rousing him to hurry back to Chique, stood silently beside him, following his gaze to where the sky transitioned from cerulean to pink to orange above the horizon.

"Hey," he said, glancing at her. "Get some rest?"

She nodded, noticing the fatigue etched on his face. "How about you?"

"Uh — a bit. I woke up before Emilie left."

"You could have stayed on the bed, you know."

He raised an eyebrow and looked at her sideways. She flushed — she could still be so naïve — and quickly resorted to the first plan. "Better get back and see how the big filly is doing. You coming?"

He laughed softly, following. Inside she picked up her keys, waiting while he brushed the sand off his feet and slipped on his shoes.

"We are going to grab some breakfast somewhere, right?" he said as he settled into the passenger seat. "And coffee. You still drink the stuff, don't you?"

"Sure." She didn't think she was hungry, but Nate seemed determined to make sure she ate. "I generally am able to take care of myself, you know."

"Does that mean I didn't need to come?"

He was grinning, but Liv felt he was baiting her, rather than making a joke.

"Well — need? I don't know. But — I'm glad. And — grateful — that you did."

He seemed entertained by her stuttering attempt to verbalize her feelings. "You're cute when you're flustered."

Liv gripped the steering wheel and looked straight ahead, frowning. Was she overreacting?

"Something to go okay with you?" She pulled up to a doughnut shop.

"You're calling the shots."

She almost commented on his attitude, whatever it was, wherever it came from. It wasn't just him, though. It was the cumulative effect of this winter so far, for both of them. She heard Nate sigh, but looked away as she turned off the ignition.

"I'm sorry, Liv. I don't mean to give you a hard time. I had to come, as much for myself as for you or the filly. I need to be here, and I didn't want you having to deal with this on your own. Whatever else is going on… we're a team, the three of us, right? I don't know what either of us would do if anything happened to her."

Liv looked at him for as long as she dared before uninvited tears welled in her eyes. She blinked them back, and quickly got out of the car. Nate followed slowly, and she sensed his dwindling morale — or maybe she was just projecting her own emotions onto him.

They bought extra food and coffee, Nate handing the woman behind the counter cash before Liv could pay. Liv thanked him quietly and picked up the doughnuts and bagels, leaving the tray of drinks for him.

By the time they got to Payson, most of the horses were turned out in the small paddocks behind the barns, and stalls had been mucked. Chique nickered softly.

"That's encouraging," Liv said. She let the filly push her muzzle into her open hands.

"She was certainly happier this morning when I got here than last night when I left," Emilie responded. "I told Jo to go home and get some sleep."

"Thanks, Em," Liv met Nate's eyes. "Good news, so far."

He nodded and turned his attention back to his coffee, which was finally cool enough to drink. "Bagels and doughnuts, Em. Breakfast of champions."

Emilie laughed. "No, that would be the orange juice and leftover fake champagne Jo was drinking at six AM," she said. "There's still some in the fridge, if you're interested."

Nate glanced at Liv, but Liv shook her head. "No thanks. But you go right ahead. What's left to do, Em?" She needed something to keep her occupied until Doc Beckett made his rounds.

"Looks like we need more ice," Nate said. "I'll go."

Liv handed him her keys, and pushed out a breath. Emilie's brow furrowed, and she looked like she was going to say something, but Liv started off towards the paddocks to check on Feste. She didn't need one of Em's pep talks or lectures right now.

As soon as Liv started to take Chique out of the ice for the vet's assessment, she knew for sure the filly had improved. After his exam, Doc Beckett nodded.

"Keep up the ice bath for another twenty-four hours, and we'll continue with the medication. We'll do radiographs tomorrow."

Liv tried to take his guarded optimism for what it was, but Chique wasn't out of danger yet. Nate refreshed the ice, and helped Liv put filly back in the tub.

"How long can you stay, Nate?" Emilie asked, hovering.

"As long as I need to. Don knows what's going on, and I told my agent it was a family emergency. Nobody can tell me it wasn't." His gaze locked onto Liv. "Unless you want me to go."

It sounded like a challenge. If she wanted to be honest, it had been easier for her when he wasn't around. She'd had her emotions in check. Face to face, it fell apart. But she said, "No," simply, and held his eyes, wishing she could transmit feelings where words failed her.

Jo showed up as they fed lunch, and Liv let Nate and Emilie continue down the row, facing the assistant trainer with hands on hips. "You didn't need to come back so soon."

Jo waved her off. "Roger will be back tomorrow. I can take the day off then. Doc Beckett been by yet?"

Liv updated her on the vet's instructions. "How do you want to do this? I can do the night shift tonight if you want."

"You have to get on some horses tomorrow, so you need to sleep like a normal person. Come back at feed time, and stay the evening again. Take Miller to the beach this afternoon. He's looking a little pale."

"How about a grocery store on the way home?" Nate said.

Liv smirked. "Okay. But you're going to have to cook anything that doesn't come already prepared."

The supermarket was practically deserted, and Liv watched with curious amusement as Nate pushed the cart around, selecting items one by one. She threw in a few essentials — yogurt, some fruit. Back at the condo she grabbed an orange as Nate started putting things away.

"Make yourself at home, Miller," she said, walking to her room to change into a bathing suit. She could hear him laughing behind her.

Emilie was out on the sand already, lying face up on a towel, sunshine and contentment bathing her face. Liv settled beside her, and Em cracked open a squinting eye.

"Where's Nate?"

"Putting away groceries." Liv grinned. "I'm sure he'll be out shortly."

"It's a shame he has to go back so soon," Emilie said, both eyes narrowing on her. "He could come in handy around here."

Point taken.

Nate appeared in shorts, *sans* shirt. For once Liv had more of a tan than he did.

"Did you not find the man a towel, Liv? You really are a sad hostess. Here, Nate. You can have this one." Emilie scrambled up, tossing him her sunblock. "I'm going in the water."

He wasted no time dropping to the towel and lying back. "I've got to catch up on my sleep. Wake me up if I start to burn, okay?"

Liv let her eyes rove over him as his closed, his muscles lean under his light skin. She stopped herself from rescuing the lotion he'd ignored, the obvious possibility igniting her nerve endings. "Sure Miller. It's the least I can do in exchange for you making sure I don't starve."

She left him to doze, if that's what he was doing, and watched Emilie for a while before leaning back herself, letting the sound of the waves soothe her. It was easy to fall asleep, her dreams light and meaningless.

"Hey, Liv. It's three o'clock."

The softness of Nate's voice in her ear lured her back, his breath on her neck. When she opened her eyes his face was poised just above hers, blond hair falling over clear blue eyes that locked on hers. He smiled, just a quirk of his lips, and pushed himself away.

NATE PULLED down the ball cap he'd borrowed from Em — his rushed packing hadn't included one — and stretched his neck side to side. Sleeping on that couch was going to be the death of him, but even the couch was too close to Liv right now. He had to go back to California. He wasn't going to start something he couldn't finish. He wasn't going to screw this up. Their agreement, and all.

Feste galloped over Payson's turf course — ears forward, head down compliantly, striding out nicely. Nate remembered Chique at the same age, hauling him around with determination, eager to do more. So different, her full sibling; or maybe Liv was just better at keeping the young ones relaxed. She was definitely good at reserving calm for them when everything around her was upside down.

"He's looking good," Nate said as they walked back to the barn. "When are you going to breeze him?"

"When he tells me," Liv answered.

"He's so frigging polite, I don't think he's going to tell you anything."

The affection on her face dredged up feelings he'd agreed to put on ice. It was for the colt anyway, not for him.

Doc Beckett was on the shed when they returned, his assistant setting up the x-ray equipment in front of Chique's stall. Liv stopped Feste outside on the stretch of green.

"Cory! Where are you?"

"Here!" The kid's voice came in a soprano sing-song from behind the bridles hanging in the tack room doorway.

"Put your helmet and vest back on, and get on this colt to cool him out for me. We need the shed for Chique."

Cory didn't have to be asked twice. She bounced over, Feste not batting an eye at the kid's exuberance. Nate wished he felt an iota of that.

"Just take him on a little walkabout, then he can have a bath and some grass when you're done." Liv left Nate to leg the kid up, removing her own helmet and wiping her brow with an arm as she walked to the shed. Cory sauntered off on the dark bay colt, still grinning.

"Here, Liv, I'll hold her," he said when she pulled Chique out of the stall. She'd want to see the images as they popped up on the laptop; pictures that would determine Chique's future. Was he the only one obsessing over *their* future?

He watched distractedly, and the muscles in Liv's neck visibly relaxed as the views came up on the screen in succession. She glanced at him, the tension that had kept her lips in a resolute line easing, allowing a subtle upward curve.

"No sinking or rotation," Doc Beckett confirmed.

They'd managed to pre-empt irreversible damage, though careful management would continue. Nate steered Chique back into her stall, and Liv surprised him when he came out, wrapping herself around him. He pressed back, burying his face in her hair, breathing in the scent of her sweat like it was the sweetest smell on earth.

"I've got to go back." His words were muffled as he allowed himself to kiss the side of her head.

"I know."

Why had he thought — hoped — she would ask him to stay?

The airline was far too accommodating, finding him a flight that afternoon that would see him to LAX by evening. He wished he hadn't let his frustration get to him while he'd been here. He hadn't made the best of the little time they'd had together.

They reached Fort Lauderdale in plenty of time, but he couldn't deal with the thought of her waiting with him when he didn't know what more could be said. It would just inflame the wound in his chest.

"You don't need to come in," he said.

She didn't protest, pulling up to the curb outside the terminal. He met her behind the car as she opened up the back, and reached for his bag.

"Come out to LA for a few days. Once you're past worrying about Chique." It was a plea, out before he could stop it. But when would Liv ever stop worrying about Chique?

She searched his eyes, hers filled with conflict.

"Just a few days. No pressure. Maybe when Jay runs. Do that for your sad friend." He tried a grin, coming up short.

"Let me think about it."

She'd be reluctant to leave the filly again. An obscure set of circumstances had brought on Chique's laminitic attack, but from here on, the filly would be considered susceptible to another. He'd cling to the fact that Liv hadn't given him an outright no.

"I'll call to see how she's doing."

"Thanks, Nate."

"Family, right?"

She closed the space between them, but the awkwardness of their embrace made their limbs feel like wire instead of flesh; there was no comfort in it. Pulling away, he pressed the flash drive into her palm before scooping up his bag, and disappeared into the terminal.

"YOU NEED TO GO, LIV," Emilie said.

Liv kept her gaze fixed on the back of Feste's head.

"You need the break," Em continued, chatting as she posted on her own mount. "You've been stressing over that filly since it happened. I know, I get it, but you should really let yourself relax for a couple of days. Chique will be fine."

Emilie was right…as usual. Her little sister had somehow acquired all the interpersonal smarts she'd missed.

"Plus, you get to see Nate. Duh." Cory piped up from the two-year-old she jogged on Em's other side.

"Seriously," Emilie said. "Nate came all the way here when Chique was sick. You know how much this would mean to him."

"Plus, he's gorgeous," Cory warbled.

Liv had to laugh. No doubt Cory would be hopping on a plane without hesitation had she been in Liv's shoes. She probably would have followed him there in the first place. It was a relief to see Chique bounce back, but Liv still worried, every day, that she would get to the barn and find the filly in the corner, crippled and shaking again.

"She'll be fine, Liv," Emilie repeated. "You can do this."

"Who's going to get on Feste while I'm gone?"

"Oh! Me! Please? Liv!" Cory chirped.

She should have a fraction of Cory's enthusiasm. The kid put her to shame.

Liv had the beach more or less to herself that afternoon, Em and Cory off to Gulfstream to watch races. She'd added the most recent of Nate's songs to her phone, and the chorus played over and over in her head, even when she didn't have the earbuds in. He must have done this one in California, just him and his guitar — taking The Lumineers' *Ophelia* and changing it up.

Oh-oh-livia...

The sweetness of it squeezed her heart, but the last phrase of the chorus — which he hadn't altered and spoke, rather than sang — stopped it. Which one of them was the fool, really?

9

Nate grinned at her. That old grin; the one she hadn't seen, full on, since October.

"Some holiday, eh? You haven't even been here twenty-four hours, and Don's got you on the pony. Are you going to gallop a couple, too?"

"I'm not licensed in that capacity in this jurisdiction," Liv insisted, laughing. Not that she should technically be on the pony, either. Her credentials today were strictly that of *guest.* "How are you finding Don, really?"

"We get along fine. He's a lot like you. Wasn't much of an adjustment."

She rolled her eyes but had to smile as they reached the track. This felt right. So much better than when he'd come to Florida.

Nate and Jay left her at the on-gap, backing up, and she followed with her eyes until they jogged out of view — or she was distracted by the warm pink of the San Gabriel Mountains in the distance, she wasn't sure which. She refocused in time to find them on the busy racetrack, Nate holding the gleaming red colt to an easy gallop as they shimmered past. They would go once around, just a bit of light exercise to limber Jay up on the morning of his California debut.

"Those mountains are something, aren't they?" She glanced over her shoulder as they left the track.

Nate smirked. "Come to Calgary sometime, I'll show you real mountains."

Her eyebrows crept up. *Is that an invitation, Miller*? He rarely talked about his hometown; hadn't gone back since he'd left over four years ago. There was heartache there. Maybe he'd dealt with it now, but he still hadn't visited.

She put the pony in his stall when they returned to Don's barn, Nate setting the tack on the rail, leaving Jeanne and a hotwalker tending to Jay.

"I've gotta go," he said to Liv. "See you at the races?"

She nodded, then glanced at Don beside her as she watched Jeanne bathe the colt. "Looks like he's training great. He could be all right in there, eh?"

"He's got a shot," Don agreed. "But so does Paradise. A win would be nice."

Liv agreed. A welcome bit of good news, in a winter that had been sorely lacking.

THE GUEST ROLE was an odd one to play. Easier on the backside. Here, out front, in her sleeveless shift, unsettling. She watched the three-year-old filly Nate had won with on Boxing Day, moving up in class, come flying on the outside to catch the strong favourite at the wire. Next to her, Don looked over with his characteristic restrained smile.

"There's no question the kid can ride," he said. "He just needs a little better luck."

Liv controlled the twist of her lips. *Faster horses to ride.*

She followed the trainer trackside, remaining outside the winner's circle while the photo was taken. Nate seemed more satisfied than pleased by the effort, chatting with the groom as he pulled the tack off and gave the filly a pat on the neck.

"Lighten up a little," Liv said as he walked to the scales.

His smile was tepid. "One more before Jay."

It ended up being one more winner, a longshot for a small-time conditioner. Nate had controlled the pace, pulling away on the front end. She waited again on the fringes, feeling just a little bit paddock girl-esque as she scuffed her flats on the concrete apron.

"Looking good, Miller."

When he lifted his head, he grinned. "You'd better stick around. You seem to bring me luck."

"Since when are you about luck?"

"Maybe it's one of those things you don't believe in till it's disappeared."

"That might be profound if it wasn't so cynical." She crossed her arms, narrowing her gaze on him. "It seems so backwards for me to be trying to cheer you up."

"It is kind of sad." The grin resurfaced. "Let's see if we can make it a hat trick."

The San Pasqual Stakes, with Jay.

Nate wore the familiar red, white and blue Triple Stripe silks when he entered the small walking ring, going through the ritual of shaking her hand, then Don's. Don's instructions were merely a formality. Nate knew Jay as well as anyone.

"Good luck, Miller."

He suppressed a laugh before Don legged him up onto the chestnut colt.

They were the golden boys of the post parade, Jay's copper coat gleaming in the warm California sun, Nate's blonde hair hidden under his helmet. Once the race caller announced them — *"Just Jay, from Triple Stripe Stables, trained by Don Philips, ridden by Nate Miller"* — Nate broke him away from the pony to let the colt stretch out on a loose line, Jay bounding off powerfully.

Liv tightened her fingers on her binoculars, trailing them. When they came back to the gate, Jay had a dark sheen of sweat on his neck and a keen look in his eye. All eight horses loaded professionally.

A dark bay named Torrid broke from the one hole and shot to the lead, the field settling behind him. Nate parked Jay on the rail, and Jay rated comfortably for him, skipping easily over the track and waiting patiently for the race to unfold.

Torrid's fractions were quick — an honest pace that would set it up perfectly for the closers like Jay. On paper, the front-running gelding wasn't in the same class as the other five. Cheap speed. Not enough substance to go gate to wire at a mile and an eighth in this company.

Nate was biding his time, letting Jay gallop along the backstretch, maintaining his position on the rail. Torrid was already showing signs of fatigue. He only had to drift out a little to leave the hole that would give Jay a clear path to the wire, the perfect trip. They rounded the final turn and favoured Paradise moved up on the outside, his jock steering him a bit wider than seemed necessary, suggesting to Liv he expected Torrid to come out. The dark bay leader was giving everything he had, but he was tiring, unable to keep tight to the rail as they entered the stretch. Nate had Jay on the bit, ready.

Liv saw it — the awkward alteration in Torrid's stride — a split second before the gelding bobbled and went down, an involuntary gasp escaping from her throat. His rider toppled over his head, right in Jay's path. With no room to spare, Jay stumbled and went down with them, the rest of the field scrambling to avoid the spill.

Don didn't have to tell her to move. She was already rushing for the stairs, heart plunging from her throat to the pit of her stomach, the trainer close on her heels.

It was heartbreakingly obvious Torrid was in bad shape. Nate was up — thank God — holding Jay, a steadying hand on the trembling colt's neck as he watched the paramedics see to Torrid's unconscious rider. Liv left Don further behind, passing the trainer's assistant, Jeanne, and sprinting across the deep sand of the track.

She stopped short of Nate, sucking in erratic gulps of air to try and tame the adrenaline charging through her bloodstream. "You okay?"

Nate nodded, but his face was ashen.

"That horse isn't going to make it off the track." Don caught up, wiping his brow with a handkerchief while Jeanne took Jay's head, glancing at Torrid as the state veterinarian attended to him. "We'll get Jay a ride back to the barn and take a good look."

"We went right over top of him." Nate's voice quavered when he finally spoke, his attention more on the ambulance driving away with Torrid's rider than removing his saddle from Jay.

"There was nothing you could do," Liv said. "Go change and come back to the barn, okay?"

He nodded again, his eyes shifting to the tarps being erected around Torrid.

"Go," she prodded, and waited until he hitched a ride in a utility truck before jogging to join Jeanne in the van that would take Jay to the backside.

SOMEHOW, Jay seemed to have escaped unscathed, but the relief Liv felt was deadened by her sorrow for Torrid's connections. Nate walked on the shed with hands jammed in the pockets of chinos, a dark grey jacket over an open-necked dress shirt. He nodded wordlessly as he passed the departing vet. When he was close enough, Liv noticed traces of dried sand on his cheek. Getting here had taken priority over a shower.

"What's the story?" He looked directly at Don.

"He didn't find anything obvious, but wasn't convinced there's nothing wrong. We'll look at him again in the morning."

"Any word on Cook?" Liv asked, hoping for an update on Torrid's rider.

Nate shook his head.

"Get some bandages on Jay, Jeanne," Don said. "If you find anything we missed, let me know."

Nate glanced at Liv, his jaw set, agitation in his blue eyes. "Drive you back to the hotel?"

"Yeah." She turned to Don and Jeanne. "My flight's pretty early tomorrow so I probably won't see you again, but keep me posted, okay?"

She followed Nate to an older-model Jeep, a cheap vehicle he'd picked up for the winter, waiting while he unlocked and opened the passenger door for her. Once he was in, his fingers closed tightly around the wheel.

"You sure you're all right?" Liv nudged.

He turned the key with an unconvincing dip of his chin. "I could use a drink."

They left menus untouched and words unsaid at the hotel bar. Liv watched him carefully as he took a deep draught of his beer, fingering the stem of her wine glass. His eyes locked onto the television at the end of the bar.

"What is it?" she asked.

"Something about the race. About Cook." He flagged down the bartender, who had been closer to the screen. "What were they saying, did you hear?"

"Spill at Santa Anita this afternoon. One of the jockeys just died in hospital." He shook his head. "Crazy job." Then his expression changed, like he was noticing Nate's size. "Need another one?"

Nate drained his glass, setting it down resolutely and sliding it forward. "Please."

Liv sat in silence. Her presence and the knowledge she could relate to what he might be feeling was as much as he would expect, but it felt inadequate. It hadn't been her out there today. It had been over a year since she'd ridden a race. It didn't mean she'd left the risk behind — the metal rod in her thigh was a reminder that accidents happened during training too — but trading in her jock's license for a trainer's badge removed her a degree from the dangers of a profession she'd pushed him to pursue.

"What time is your flight?" he asked, going more slowly on the second beer, at least.

"Seven-thirty."

"I'll drive you. I think I'm going to book off tomorrow."

Liv looked at him sharply. Maybe she had no right to question a decision based on something more mental than physical, but if it got out, it would do nothing for his reputation around here — if people thought the accident had shaken his nerve. She was sure that wasn't the case, but many would make that interpretation. She didn't try to talk him out of it, though. She didn't feel in a good place right now to justify the argument.

He pushed his glass away. Half-empty, or half-full? "This isn't going to help anything. I should go."

"You sure?" She hesitated. "You could come up and hang for a bit." She didn't care what reaction the suggestion might draw. She wasn't sure being alone was the best thing for either of them at the moment.

His eyes were full of so many things, meeting hers briefly before he stood. Sadness. Regret. Appreciation?

"That's all right. But thanks." He reached into his pocket for a couple of bills. "What time should I pick you up? Five?"

Liv nodded, at a loss for something to say. He smiled faintly and touched her arm as he walked past.

There was luck and there was luck. Some days it just meant getting out alive.

Liv: *My flight's delayed a couple of hours. I'll get a cab.*

Nate: *Forget that. I'm already on my way. We can grab a coffee or something.* There was no way she was getting on a plane, back to Florida, without him seeing her again.

"Or something" ended up being a beach not far from LAX, coffees curled in their fingers. His was black, when he really craved what Liv had ordered. There was something comforting about the frothy warm milk of a cappuccino.

"Sip?" she said, proffering it, like she understood. Of course she understood.

He accepted the paper cup, closing his eyes as he savoured the fusion of creamy and bitter and thought about how her lips had touched the plastic lid. He hadn't kissed her since she'd come. Why hadn't he kissed her? Stupid agreement.

"Walk?" he suggested, relinquishing the cup, the flavours and warmth lingering. His seemed a poor alternative now.

Liv followed him to the sand. The dark waves of the Pacific appeared colder and more unruly than where the Atlantic met South Florida's shores. She shivered, gripping her cup between both hands. He slipped an arm around her shoulders, pulled her against him.

"So what will happen with Chique? Are you going to send her home?" he asked.

"I've offered to go back and manage the early runners at Woodbine for Rog."

"Feste too?"

"Of course, Feste too." She smiled, like it was ridiculous to think otherwise. "I'm going to start back riding."

"Really." It had been over a year since her accident. Chique's three-year-old campaign had provided a distraction, but with the filly's four-year-old season in question, it didn't surprise him she'd need something to occupy her. "So you are going to keep Feste for yourself. Can you train and ride too?"

"Maybe. We'll see." She sipped. "Sotisse had a filly this year."

"Just Lucky again?"

Liv nodded. "Another dark bay. I guess she's got a bit more white than Chique or Feste."

He didn't say anything; no reference to the next one in line, another one to keep them both going, something to look forward to in the midst of uncertainty. It was as if they were in suspended animation, strolling in another world, this beach so far removed from everything that was supposed to be.

He couldn't stand it, the small talk, and stopped abruptly, spinning in front of her. "This is crazy. This winter has been such a disaster. Chique… now Jay…what next? I want to tell you not to get on that plane. They say everything comes in threes, right?"

"Thanks for that." She laughed softly. "You've never been the superstitious one. Don't start now. One of us has to maintain some semblance of sanity."

"I'm not feeling so sane right now. That could have been me, yesterday. That could have been you. That's what we're a part of. I know it's not news, and I know we're not supposed to think about it except… what are we doing? Are we taking this for granted?"

The conviction in her gaze caught him off guard. "I'm not. Not anymore." Her voice was soft, sure. "And I know you never have. But you wouldn't like me much if you kept me away from that filly any longer."

"I'm not liking myself a whole lot right now, the way things are."

"And I'm supposed to fix that?"

His laugh was almost a sigh. "Yeah, I know. I just keep thinking something has to go right in the middle of all this; it may as well be us."

"We've got less than two months to go now. There's no point in second-guessing what's behind us — we'll both just drive ourselves crazy. What would we do, anyway? I still have to go back to Florida."

"I could go with you."

"Sure you could. And that might be great for us. But if you ever want to ride on this side of the border again, you need to show everyone that spill yesterday didn't rattle you — even though it did."

He didn't deny it — it wasn't as if his reaction wasn't obvious. At this point Liv might be the only one who knew, but if he didn't show up in that room later this morning, the first seeds of doubt would surface; initially amid his peers, then more significantly, among the trainers.

"Does it always come back to that?" he challenged. "What happened yesterday isn't going to keep me from ever getting on a horse again. It was just a blunt reminder that stuff happens so fast, and sometimes it seems we're just wasting time in a world where we might not have that luxury. I'm supposed to forget that and be worried about what everyone else thinks, to save my career?"

"Sometimes you have to. There's no guarantee things will work out between us."

He snorted. "That's what I love about you, always looking on the bright side."

"I never claimed to be an optimist."

"Maybe I'm just meant to be a Woodbine rider, Liv. Maybe I'm really not cut out for this."

"You don't believe that."

"Maybe I'm starting to. And what's wrong with that? I made a hell of a lot of money last season. What you're not saying is you'd think less of me if I abandoned this."

The way she paused — that had to be it. But —

"That's not it, really," she insisted. "I think you'd regret it. Running away."

Running away, like he'd run away from Calgary, five years ago. And had somehow continued to do, in some shape or form, since.

"But I'm so good at it," he retorted bitterly.

He broke away and left her behind, but she caught up, her hand sliding into the crook of his arm, hair blowing against his neck when she spoke, so quietly.

"Are you mad at me?"

He shook his head and laughed, then stopped and faced her, linking his arms behind her. She didn't push him away. "Only because you're so damn right."

"You do it to me all the time."

"What?"

"Read me."

"I'm not so sure about that."

"You do. It's aggravating."

"Well at least we know we're good at pissing each other off." He grinned.

"So, you're okay, then?" she said.

"I'll get through it." He brushed aside the hair that whipped across her face. "I know you've been working pretty hard to help keep my head above water. Thanks for that."

"Yeah, well, it's usually the other way around." Liv gave him a small smile. "It's hard to leave."

At the terminal, another curbside departure. Too many airports. Too many good-byes. This time, though, she kissed him, then held his face in her hands, arresting his eyes.

"Now call your agent. Salvage what you can of the morning. Then check into the room and ride this afternoon. That's the only way you're going to keep me from kicking your ass back at Woodbine. Right?"

All he could do was laugh, feeling like he'd been sent back into battle. But not before she'd said, like a shield maiden, she was going too.

10

The wind whipped, catching the quarter sheet covering chestnut haunches still sleek from more hospitable days at Payson Park. Happy Together skittered along the path from the training track, Liv holding the lines crossed in one gloved hand while she tugged the mask back over her nose, goggles protecting her eyes.

Was this dedication or stupidity, when she could have stayed in Florida till the middle of April with the rest of the Triple Stripe crew? Roger had been only too happy to let her have the job of prepping the handful of horses he'd decided would suit Woodbine's shorter early races. The main track wasn't even slated to open until next weekend.

She steered Happy onto the shed, her shoulders relaxing once she was out of the wind, and spotted Dean Taylor waiting with her groom Amy outside the filly's stall.

"Hey Dean," Liv said, smiling as she dropped her feet from the irons before ducking and directing the filly through the doorway.

"Welcome back," he said when she emerged with the tack, extricating the damp saddle cloth and girth cover for her as she took the equipment to the tack room.

"Am I crazy, coming back this early?" She hung the muddy bridle on the tack hook before pulling the mask down around her neck and setting the saddle and pads on their rack.

"I wasn't going to say anything."

"Because you're here too?"

"Probably. You have time for lunch?"

Liv took off her helmet and re-did her ponytail before unzipping her muddy chaps, glancing at the clock on the wall. "Sure. I've got to clean tack and do up Feste, but I can meet you after that."

"Sounds good. See you there."

Once the tack and Feste were taken care of, she ducked into the office to run a brush through her hair. That was as close as she'd come to being presentable — not that Dean would care. The restaurant they frequented was popular with racetrackers, so it wasn't like the wait staff weren't used to it either. A dark cloud released a random flurry of snow as she climbed into the Nissan.

When she stepped into the front of the pub, Dean waved her over from a booth off to the side. "Is it too soon to ask if you'll come work some for me?" He eyed her over the menu.

"That's what riders are for."

"Not even tempted to dust off your tack?"

"Maybe." She hadn't made her decision public.

"One of them would win a race for you opening day."

Liv smiled. Dean always liked his horses. Sometimes he was right about them.

He looked past her, and Liv turned to follow his gaze. "Faye!"

"This must be a record. You only just got home, and I've actually got you cornered." Faye slid onto the bench next to her and crushed her in a hug. "When does Nate get back?"

"I don't know. He's done okay this past while. Things kind of picked up for him."

Faye frowned. She was dying to ask more pointed questions, Liv was sure.

Her exchanges with Nate had been infrequent enough recently that Liv had begun to credit his fervor on the beach that morning more to his brush with death than impatience to see things between them progress. She missed him, wanted to see him, and now felt like she was the one waiting. That was a change; one she wasn't altogether comfortable with.

"So if Nate stays in California, who's going to ride your horses?" Dean interjected, then looked at his sister. "I was just trying to talk her into riding again."

"Are you thinking about it?" Faye asked.

Liv shrugged. "I need something to do, with Chique off. An unstarted two-year-old is a bit too eggs-in-one-basket."

"Normal people take up a hobby. How about crochet?"

Liv laughed, happy not to have to answer more questions about Nate.

"How's Chique?" Dean asked. "Do you think you'll bring her back?"

Liv shrugged. "That's up to her." And so far, the filly seemed quite content to spend her days hanging out with Claire in the paddock at the farm.

Dean picked up the bill before Liv could grab it when their server tented it on the table. "You can thank me by getting on my three-year-old for me tomorrow."

"Who is this horse?" she asked.

"Ride The Wave. Unraced, one of Catch The Joy's last foals. I'll even bring him over. Eight good?"

Liv rolled her eyes, but not without a smile. "Want to go in company? I can put Cory on Elemental." Cory had come back from Florida with Liv to start the final preparations for getting her apprentice license. The kid had worked hard over the winter, and even saved enough money to buy her own car.

"Sounds like a plan."

After paying the server Dean stood, but Faye kept Liv locked in the booth. "Dessert?" she said pointedly, her perfect eyebrows arched, then added low enough Dean wouldn't hear, "I require a more thorough update."

"See you in the morning, Liv." Dean pushed out his chin with a knowing smile, excusing himself.

"We had a deal, remember." Faye flagged down the server. "Can we have a piece of your cheesecake?"

With opening day a month away, Liv couldn't use the weight

argument. She was Faye's prisoner, and just maybe voicing her concerns would help.

"So?" Faye said, fork poised over the cheesecake the server set between them, as if the sugar would extract words like a buffer solution extracted proteins.

"Not much to tell, Faye."

"You've got to give me more than that."

Liv sighed, and stabbed her own fork into the slice, deciding it was for fortitude, not extraction. "I told him, okay? I told him I was in. But since then, I can't help but wonder if he's lost his conviction."

"You don't really think that."

"I do. I really do. Like I gave him this whole big speech encouraging him to stay there, but now I just want him to come back. I hate this."

"I, on the other hand, love it. It's progress, sweetie."

"It's sad and pathetic, and so not me."

Faye's laugh was low, and maybe a little bittersweet. "I remember that feeling."

"Well, I don't like it. It's distracting. It's not like I'm in love."

Faye patted her hand, and pushed the cheesecake closer. "You keep telling yourself that."

With time to kill before feeding the track horses, Liv went to the farm. The sun tried to shine, the temperature a few degrees warmer than it had been that morning. Chique and Claire lifted their heads as Liv approached. Chique nickered, but went back to munching her hay — just one of the things that told Liv she was at peace with her current existence. Maybe that spark would never come back. Maybe Nate wouldn't either.

11

Opening day.

What better way to announce her return to the saddle than a victory? Dean had been right: the solid older campaigner he'd told her would win lived up to the trainer's assurance, prevailing by open lengths. Faye and Will were in the winner's circle, their happy-couple-ness something she'd never thought she'd wanted until half of her own went AWOL in LA.

How about another win? Elemental, in an allowance race with a field of Plate hopefuls pointing for the first prep of the season in three weeks. Saddled by Dean, as Roger was on the way back from Florida with the Triple Stripe string.

And why not close out the card by piloting Dean's Ride The Wave to break his maiden, initiating the buzz that the rangy colt was also being pointed to the Plate? She would have to give up that mount, though. Her obligation remained with her father's horse, Elemental.

Dean pulled Liv into him once she was on the ground. "Great way to start off the year."

"Thanks, Dean," she said, extricating herself from his hold.

"Too bad you can't ride him in the Plate. It would make a great winner's story if the girl next door rode my homebred colt."

"Sorry Dean. I don't write the rules." It would be a conflict of interest for her to ride anything else, if there was a Triple Stripe horse in the race. Dean was going to have to settle for the boy next door, she thought wryly.

Dave Johnson, who had been the top rider at Woodbine for several years until Nate had knocked him out of that spot last season, was the first to congratulate her back in the room.

"Impressive way to come out of retirement."

Retirement? Is that what it had been? She was twenty-seven. *How about we call it a sabbatical?* "Thanks Dave."

"So, where is Miller, anyway?"

Everyone was asking her the same question, assuming she should have the answer. Sometimes when she heard snippets of the latest gossip floating around, she felt the rest of the backstretch was more informed than she was.

"Still in California. Can't say I really blame him for staying as long as he can."

"Well, let me know if you need me for any of those horses."

"Thanks Dave, I will." At least with Johnson she didn't have to worry about any personal connotation — he was only interested in what was to his professional advantage. "But between me and Cory MacDonald, even Nate might find there's not much left over."

She left him with a smirk.

It was a long drive home when she was especially tired. She checked on Chique and Claire under Nate's empty apartment, ate a light dinner at the house, and fell asleep trying to read.

NATE HADN'T SENT her any more songs, but Poe's *Wild* played through her dream, reminding her of him — and that she was, most certainly, in limbo. The buzzing bored in like a jackhammer, prodding her awake — the song part of her consciousness now, her current ringtone for him. She fumbled, knocking the phone to the floor before her fingers found it, and swiped to answer, pressing it to her ear.

"Hey Miller." She tried to clear her head, hoping the lingering fuzziness made her sound casual, non-committal.

"Did I wake you up?"

She glanced at the time. "It's nine PM, Miller." It would be six in LA. "But that's okay. It's good to hear from you." And it was, so good. He could have called her in the middle of the night, she wouldn't have minded. She propped her pillow up against the headboard and leaned back, closing her eyes like it would help her see his face.

"You had a good day," he said.

"They probably thought they'd have it easy without you around."

"Way to straighten them out." He laughed, then was silent a beat. "Listen — I'm going to stay a few more weeks."

"I figured as much," she responded, her tone softer. "It's the right thing to do."

"Is it?"

"We don't need to go over this again, Nate. Besides, I'd just kick your ass in the standings up here."

He chuckled quietly. "Thanks. Just don't get too comfortable. I'll be taking my title back."

"We'll see." She smiled.

"So — " She felt his hesitation. "Are we still on the same page? You…me…when I get back?"

"We are," she said, with certainty. "Though if we're supposed to be together, it does help if I know what you're up to. You know, so I can keep a step ahead of the rumours."

"Always so bloody practical," he said.

"Thanks for calling, Miller." She disconnected, holding the warmth of the phone between her hands because it was the closest thing to him right now.

THE PREDAWN SKY was a little richer; the April air a little warmer — and Chique's yell for breakfast a little louder. A little more like the old Chique. Thank goodness for that. It grounded Liv, saving her from feeling her head was a bad romance novel.

"Is today the day?" she asked as she turned the filly out. Chique snorted into the darkness, clearing the surroundings of goblins, and settled to munch hay nose to nose with Claire. Not a yes, but not a no, either.

It was the first dark day of the meet — no racing — so after a morning of working horses, Liv did up Feste and drove to the farm, boots still on, helmet tossed on the passenger seat. She tapped the steering wheel to Panic! At the Disco's *Collar Full*. Just another song that made her think of Nate, and the Plate Party last year. Time to hit restart — for them, for Chique.

She brought Chique in, then grabbed Claire, officially in foal to Just Lucky for a February baby. When Liv approached with the tack, Chique snuffled the armful of brushes and equipment. Liv freed a hand to grasp the filly's halter, and snapped the wall tie to a side ring.

Feet picked, a quick brush, pads and quarter sheet and saddle in place, bridle on. Liv secured her helmet and led Chique out to an overturned muck bucket to mount. Claire whinnied from the barn, and Chique didn't even respond. A little more like *yes*.

Just a hack — past the training barns, in between the broodmare paddocks, into the woods; following the trail that wove through the trees. Chique's long-striding walk didn't wait for anyone, ears forward in expectation. It wasn't as if she didn't know this path could lead to the training track.

They came out by the stallion barns and Chique's head shot up — but neither the filly's sire, Just Lucky, nor Starway, the other stallion in residence, were turned out at the moment. Chique cast a look in the barn's direction, but carried on without hesitation. She knew where she wanted to go.

She slowed at the training oval's on-gap, and Liv closed her leg to nudge her past. With a huff, Chique powered on. When Liv dismounted back at the barn, the filly didn't seem to believe they were done.

And Liv smiled. Tomorrow they would do more.

Convenient of Nate to return on a Wednesday, the flight from California late so Liv could pick him up after the races. She was early, and wandered distractedly past greetings of varying degrees of affection, not sure where she was headed, trying to work out the tension she felt. She jogged up the escalator to Pearson International's shopping concourse with no particular destination in mind, needing only to keep moving.

She checked the monitor again: Nate's flight had landed, but it would be a while before he collected his luggage and cleared customs. Gradually she made her way back down to arrivals, and paced through the bodies gathered to meet the plane from Los Angeles.

So, here she was. Now that she wanted it — did he still feel the same? Were they really on the same page? Or had California changed things after all?

By the time she saw him, he was moving toward her, bags in each hand, guitar slung over his shoulder. He looked like a kid coming back from a surfing vacation — tanned, hair a bit long and a bit sun-bleached — instead of a guy who rode racehorses for a living. Liv stopped where she was, rooted as he approached, feeling all the uncertainty built from months apart.

He stopped in front of her, dropped his bags and met that uncertainty, maybe with a little of his own. Then he was surrounding her, his lips catching hers, hands roving up her back to mold her against him.

He drew away slightly with a shuddering breath. "The winter from hell is officially over."

LIV STOPPED short on the doorstep. "That's not the Mustang."

"No kidding. Are you coming, or what?"

Nate leaned over the top of what she had no trouble identifying as a 911 Porsche Carrera. It managed, for once, to pull her away from that shit-eating grin of his. Her eyes ran over its sleek lines, compact and sexy and a colour that would match the dusky blue sky in a few hours. It might not be brand new, but it was mint.

"Seriously, where's the Mustang?" She stepped slowly down to the circular drive in front of the house.

"Just get in."

He'd come in to the track with her that morning, got on a few despite his jetlag, and she'd dropped him off afterward — she'd thought to pick up the old car from storage. Slipping into the passenger seat, she couldn't help caressing the dash. *Definitely not the Mustang.*

"So, I hate to ask…is this yours? Or did you steal it from somewhere?"

Nate laughed and put it into gear. "Mine, as of a few hours ago. What do you think?"

"I think this winter went way better than you let on. You must be making too much money." The interior was immaculate — it had obviously been meticulously cared for. "Other than that, well, it's gorgeous, and about time you got rid of that Ford piece of — "

"Hey! No dissing the Mustang, remember? I still have it. Will's buddy is going to do a bit of work on it. I'm thinking it could be my winter car."

Liv snorted. "Because those cars are so good in snow. And when was the last time you spent winter up here, Miller?"

"When was the last time it didn't snow before I left?"

He put it in gear, the rumble of its engine musical as it crept around the circle and onto the main lane. That rumble was soon drowned out by actual music, when he cranked the equally impressive after-market stereo.

"And this?" she shouted over the loudness.

"Biffy Clyro, babe," he called back, grin at full wattage.

"Did you just call me *babe?"*

"Oops?"

She'd let him get away with it, this time. She reached forward and adjusted the volume enough to be able to carry a conversation without hearing loss. "What inspired this?"

He kept his eyes on the laneway. "It's like I said to you in California. You never know when it's gonna be your turn. So why not?"

"I don't know." Liv smirked. "Maybe because it probably cost enough to cover the down payment on a house?"

"I got a good deal. One of the older guys had it sitting in his barn. Sold it to me to help pay for renos to turn said barn into a home for his new wife. Can you imagine?"

"Still."

"Please don't tell me you're going to kick me out of that apartment now."

"I hope you're planning on having a good year, Miller."

"I'm planning on having a great year." His perfect teeth backed him up.

Cory beat his ass, student besting teacher, to win with her first mount. He couldn't whine about Roger giving her that one; the trainer had done the same for him two years ago. Cory worked hard, was well-liked; she deserved the support. At least he still got to ride in the race. Since Cory was on a Triple Stripe horse, Liv had to sit it out. Just as well, because she could lie in wait in the jock's room for the unsuspecting kid.

"We did a good job with her," Nate said, standing beside Liv as they watched a grinning, flour-doused Cory jostled by the swarm of fellow riders after her initiation.

"Not so bright of us, really." Liv grinned.

"We should start a school, maybe. Something to do when we retire."

"I just came out of so-called retirement, Miller. You planning yours already?"

He laughed. "Not as long as Chique's still running. Are you going to bring her back in, or what?"

Liv nodded, still watching Cory. "It's time."

12

Nate leaned back in the overstuffed chair, feet propped on the edge of the desk in the office, the *Racing Form* in his lap. Liv, intent on paperwork, worked beneath the ever-present painting of Geai Doucet with Just Lucky and Sotisse. Geai had been right about a lot of things. It had taken some battles to get them to this point, but here they were. There were no more excuses; nothing left to get in the way.

He heard voices, and glanced up when Emilie pushed through the door. She had a weird look on her face. Then he saw who was behind her, and his heart seized. He staggered to his feet, the *Form* falling, his head spinning.

It seemed like Liv was moving in slow motion, coming around the opposite end of the desk, concern all over her face, like she must have put the pieces together. His resemblance to the man. The shock on his own face as he stared at the woman.

"Hi, Nate."

The timbre of her voice still resonated with every cell in his body. How, honestly? Liv stared at him now, waiting, her dark, determined reserve such a contrast to the invader's fair hair and warm features. He had to pull it together, because there was no escape. They had him cornered.

He offered a slight gesture with his arm, voice flat. "Liv, this is my brother Phil, and his wife Cindy." He paused, still stunned he was making this introduction. His eyes flashed to Liv. "This is Liv Lachance." He didn't add anything to it. "And I guess you've met Emilie — her sister."

Liv stepped forward to shake hands. Nate still couldn't move.

"Nice to meet you," Liv said politely, her face as guarded as ever. *I've heard so much about you,* her glance in his direction conveyed.

"What are you doing here?" Nate said bluntly.

Cindy's eyes flickered, from Phil, to Nate, to Liv. "Phil had business in Toronto. I decided to come along." She hesitated. "We thought we might have the chance to see you."

"You could have told me you were coming." It wasn't fair, their showing up like this. Ambushing him.

But if he'd known, he would have found some excuse to avoid them. When several provinces had separated them, he'd been sure he was past the feelings of betrayal and bitterness that had driven him east. Now that they were right in front of him, impinging on the new life he'd established, it all came rushing back. He didn't want them here.

Liv turned to him, a wave of sympathy crossing her face. "Why don't you take Cindy and Phil for a tour of the farm?"

Nate looked at her quickly. So much for compassion. *Great idea, thanks so much for the suggestion.* Not that she could really be expected to find him a way out.

"Yeah, okay," he muttered, gathering the *Form* from the floor and heading for the door. He needed to get outside, to try and find more oxygen. He glanced back at Liv, then Emilie, wishing one of them would come along to diffuse the tension. Clearly neither was offering.

It was bright out here, a clear spring day, nothing like the storm in his head. The nondescript rental sedan parked next to Liv's Nissan was out of place. It didn't belong. He looked over his shoulder at Cindy and Phil. They didn't belong either.

He inhaled deeply, swinging around to face them. "I'll drive you around. It's too far to walk." The weather was perfect for a stroll, but he wanted to get this over with. He pulled the keys out of his pocket and walked over to the Porsche, opening the passenger door.

"This is yours?" Phil said, eyebrows arching. "Nice, little brother."

"Yeah, imagine that," Nate said, not ready to play along, a sour taste at the back of his throat. Ironic he'd been the one to end up making that kind of money, though the new car was the only thing in his life that reflected it.

A shadow passed over Cindy's face as she ducked into the non-existent back. Nate turned away from Phil and walked to the driver's side, cursing himself for not going to Will's this afternoon.

He pulled the Porsche around and headed for the training area, forcing himself to matter-of-factly point out the buildings and tell the unwelcome visitors what went on around the farm at different times of the year. Driving slowly, they came to the mares and foals scattered in the two large paddocks on the right side of the lane. He shut off the car and got out, Phil and Cindy following.

"This isn't all of them," he explained. "Some of the mares are in Kentucky being bred. They stay there until they're confirmed forty-five days in foal."

"Mares with babies, too?" Cindy asked, and he knew she was thinking that was a long trip for a foal — one typically only a couple of weeks old when they left.

He nodded. "They have the babies up here so the foals are eligible for restricted races like the Queen's Plate. There are some pretty good incentives for Canadian-bred and foaled horses. There are also incentives for Ontario-sired horses, so some of the mares stay in the province and go to local stallions. Two of the top stallions in Ontario are actually on this farm."

He leaned on the top railing, a few of the mares grazing not far away. Chique's baby sister peered curiously over Sotisse's grazing neck. The foal was built like Chique, but bigger; the same smudgy dark brown, save for a star that dripped down to a stripe and ended in a snip between her nostrils. After that, they were nothing alike. Chique would have been totally in his face by now. Of course he'd encouraged her attitude. Something about being the one to breathe life into her newborn lungs had forged a connection, or so he liked to tell himself.

A few of the other foals approached, and Nate watched them transform the troubled look on Cindy's face as they nuzzled fearlessly. Cindy had always been comfortable around the horses. She understood the all-encompassing nature of the business, had encouraged him, and he'd thought they'd had the perfect balance, but somehow it turned out what she wanted for him, she hadn't wanted for herself. Now he was faced with the other extreme, with Liv — these animals so much of everything she was, he still couldn't be sure there was room for anything else.

"I'll show you the stallions," he said, returning to the car and leaving them to catch up.

Driving around the woods, he wished he was running through the trails and not caught here with the past screaming at him. The Porsche came into the clearing and passed Geai's cottage. It wasn't Geai's anymore, of course.

Just Lucky was in the first paddock, and the compact bay stallion sauntered over with the same self-assurance he'd passed on to his first daughter.

Nate introduced them. "He won the Canadian Triple Crown ten years ago, then sired a Queen's Plate winner in his first crop. Chiquenaude," he said. "My claim to fame," he added quietly.

"Is she here on the farm?" Cindy asked.

Nate reached into his pocket and offered the stallion a peppermint, then pulled Cindy back carefully so she was out of reach should Just Lucky decide to take a characteristic nip. Touching her stirred a dull ache, liberally laced with what could have been.

"She just shipped into Woodbine." He was glad Chique wasn't here. He wanted to keep her from them; keep that part of the new life he'd made — one they'd never shared — to himself. "She had an acute case of laminitis this winter — it's a disease that affects the tissue in their hooves. Very painful, and potentially life-threatening. She got through it, but we were pretty worried about her." *We* could have meant all of them, from Roger and the Lachances on down, but it meant he and Liv. Chique, the thing that bound them together, stronger than blood. Blood ties, as his present company proved, were easily severed. "She's doing well now, but we don't know yet if she's going to make it back to the races."

Starway was next, and kept his distance on the other side of his paddock. "This guy has one of the top contenders for this year's Plate, Elemental."

"Do you ride him?" Phil asked.

"No, Liv does." Maybe she'd get her Plate winner this year — when once upon a time she'd planned to be the one riding Chique — though Ride The Wave was going to be a serious threat. It would be a little ironic if Nate took another victory in the classic from her — he'd inherited the ride on Dean's colt.

He left the dark bay and moved on to the next enclosure. "This is Just Jay." The role of tour guide was coming easily, words rolling off his tongue, distracting him from the torrent of emotions he was holding inside. "Hey, buddy!"

The colt's head shot up at Nate's familiar voice, and Jay charged across the paddock toward them. Nate passed Cindy a mint. "He's all right."

Phil kept a respectful distance as Jay touched Cindy's fingers, blowing softly, and inhaled the candy.

"He's hardly like a stallion."

"He's always been a real gentleman. Still technically a colt," Nate explained. "He was undefeated, winning four races in a row, then went to California for the winter. A horse fell in front of him in a race there and we went down over top of him. Jay ended up with a hairline fracture and was on stall rest for a couple of months. When he came home they put him here, so I'm guessing they plan to retire him, even though it's healed completely now."

"You were on him?" Phil asked. "You're okay?"

"Yeah. I walked away." He felt cocky and fearless as he said it. How different his life was from his lawyer brother. "The other guy wasn't so lucky." An image of the spill at Santa Anita hurtled through his mind.

"Is he okay now?" Cindy asked, hesitantly.

"No. He died in hospital that evening."

He couldn't make eye contact with either of them, touching Jay's smooth neck in the silence, recalling the moment when he and Liv had heard the news, sitting in the hotel bar. It was one of those instants where he'd felt everything change, so aware of the transience of this life. He had nothing to lose, really, and everything right now was reflecting that. Buying the car, riding like it was his last day on the planet, bringing home the winners again as a result. Coming to the conclusion that his place was here, beside Liv, whatever the outcome. It brought his anger toward both

Phil and Cindy to the surface. He was tired of this little game. They didn't get to come disrupt it all.

"So what are you guys doing here, really? Is someone dying?" His tone was challenging, accusing, but if they were here to make amends, to put the past to rest, then they needed to get on with it and stop wasting his time.

"It's been five years, Nate. Isn't that long enough? Can't we get past this?" Cindy spoke, Phil silent. Phil, who Nate possibly held the most to blame. "You haven't been home once since you left. You know it's breaking your mother's heart."

Nate laughed, pushing past them. *What about my heart?* But the guilt he felt at the mention of his mother made him keep it to himself. He walked away toward the stallion barn, letting them to decide whether to come or not.

He felt a hand on his arm, Cindy appearing at his elbow. He flinched, but stopped short of pulling away.

"We have to talk, Nate. Please?"

Phil was ten feet behind her. Did she want to do this alone? Nate turned to face his brother, walked about halfway, and thought how good it might feel to throw a punch. He tossed Phil the keys to the Porsche instead.

"Take it for a spin."

Phil caught them and just nodded, forehead wrinkled above knitted brows. Nate started walking again, leaving Cindy to keep pace.

"So how are the kids?" he asked, with a sense of obligation, trying to suppress the accompanying bitterness. Twins, a niece and nephew he'd never met. "How old are they now?" He knew exactly how old they were, of course. Remembered the precise moment he'd gotten the text with the photo of their pinched, pink faces.

"Almost fourteen months." Cindy laughed in spite of the tension — that same sweet laugh. "How do you think they are, at that age?"

He let himself study her, despite the pain it caused. She looked the same as she had five years ago. Maybe her hair was slightly shorter, straight, a simple cut reaching just above her shoulders. Of course the last time he'd seen her she'd been wearing a white dress, that hair piled on top of her head, after the wedding where she'd married his traitor of a brother. He'd already had the Mustang packed, planning to disappear and get the hell out of Calgary once and for all. Cindy had caught him, tried to stop him — he was pretty drunk — but there was nothing left to say. At least nothing he wanted to hear.

What if she'd said yes to him, instead? He would have finished his degree, gotten a "real" job, been responsible. Maybe those would have been his twins.

"Neither of us meant to hurt you, Nate."

He couldn't help laughing, the sound of it choked, the taste of it acrid. "Really? You reject me, start seeing my brother, and within a couple of months you're going to marry him? And that's not supposed to destroy me?" He shook his head. "What the hell? How stupid was I? Were we even real?"

Cindy reached for his hands. He backed away, and couldn't look at her, her shining eyes killing him.

"You were going to give it up for me, this riding dream. I didn't want to be responsible for that, after always telling you you needed to follow it, even if it meant going against your father. This is what you were meant to do. I couldn't take it, this life. I'd be a wreck, wondering every day if you were coming back in one piece. And look at you. Awards and Queen's Plate and riding in California."

"So you were doing me a big favour. And Phil? What a sacrifice. He was always pissed at me for hooking up with you. I'm sure he was all too willing to sweep in and help with the plan. What a guy. How long had it been going on for, really? You know you didn't have to marry him to get rid of me. I was ready to leave anyway, after you ditched me."

It felt good to say out loud all the things he'd felt, and obviously still harboured. But her face made him falter, making him regret being so cruel when she was right. She'd had to break him to be sure he'd go. Some things had to be demolished so you could build something new.

"Don't ever doubt it was real," she pleaded. "I did love you —"

He wanted to hear her say *more than Phil*, and her hesitation made him hope it hung in her mind.

"But Phil was —"

Safe. He sighed, when he wanted to scream. "Yeah. I know. I get it."

He'd tried safe, following her lead, perhaps — with Faye. Safe hadn't worked out for him. He hadn't been allowed the easy way out.

"I won't apologize for it, Nate. We're happy."

"You settled."

"You would have been settling."

The comment knocked the wind out of him. He would never believe that marrying Cindy would have been settling.

"Look around." She swept a hand through the air. "Look at your career — that car. And you've found someone who's better for you than I could ever have been. She lives in your world, completely, not just as a terrified bystander."

"Liv?"

"I still talk to your mother, you know."

Nate rolled his eyes. Cindy and his mom had always gotten along — his mother loved her like her own child. At least his mother had still ended up with a great daughter-in-law. It was only him who'd lost out.

"There's nothing set in stone there," he said, finally. "She's a lot of work," he added with a smirk. He could feel the sting of the punch Liv would have given him for such a smart-ass comment.

"Is she worth it?"

He met Cindy's eyes, and found he didn't hesitate. "I'm pretty sure she is."

"I'm not sure it's supposed to be easy."

"We were."

"Maybe that's just it. It was too easy."

She searched his eyes, reached out and touched his face. He closed his fingers around her hand, then drew her in. Maybe it was wrong, but it was necessary. Cindy didn't pull away.

He wasn't sure yet he could trust how he felt about Liv. Cindy couldn't know she was the one, but there was no going back. Liv was his forward.

"When do you have to leave?" he asked, keeping her close, reshaping her memory into something different from what it had been for the past five years.

"In the morning. Early. You need to come home and see your parents, and your little brother. Meet your niece and nephew."

"I know."

"Of course, I may never see Phil again. You did give him the keys to your Porsche."

Nate laughed as he released her and led her to the picnic table beside the stallion barn. "Yeah. Maybe that wasn't so bright."

He let her talk, about the people he'd known back home, about his parents, about the twins. He didn't say much; spoke only when prompted. Phil would come back, return his car, take Cindy, and he would accept it all now, reminding himself a few hours ago he'd been content with his own life — excited, even. He would never be like Phil, working in an office, taking business trips. But Liv might never be the wife; there might never be kids; he might never have it all. He'd always wanted to believe it was there to be had, but now he wasn't sure. And he'd have to come to terms with that.

Finally they heard the Porsche, and wandered over to where Phil brought it to a halt. Cindy opened the door and peered in.

"Ready?" Phil said.

Cindy nodded, and slipped into the back again.

"You're looking a little too comfortable there," Nate said as he dropped into the passenger seat. Phil's gaze silently assessed him, reminding Nate so much of their father for a moment.

He didn't know what to say to Phil anymore but felt the need to put forth an effort, so he asked about their youngest brother Tim, though his mother always let him know what was happening. A few times Nate had even spoken with the kid.

"He misses you a lot."

"I guess Dad's happy, finally," Nate said. "He got his hockey player."

Phil laughed. "Yeah. You might not recognize the kid anymore. He's put on some serious muscle. And he's taller than me." Phil paused. "Dad's proud of you, Nate. He might have a hard time saying it to you — not that you'd give him a chance to try — but he is. You can stop thinking you're some kind of disappointment. You're anything but."

Nate looked ahead, dismissing the words as Phil drove. He had enough to sort through without starting on his father.

Liv paused next to her car as the Porsche approached. She couldn't just drive off. The interesting thing was, she didn't want to. She raised her eyebrows at Nate when he emerged from the passenger side. His brother was behind the wheel. Even she, who held fast to leaving others to things that didn't concern her, was curious. Or maybe it did concern her, because she was committed to this thing with Nate now, right?

"We need to be going," Phil said, coming around the car's sleek front to stand next to his wife. "I wish we could offer to take you both out for dinner, but I've got another meeting. There'll be another time."

Cindy reached for Nate, and it took Liv aback, protectiveness rising in her. But Nate seemed at ease, if not exactly cheerful.

"Promise me you'll come home soon," Cindy said.

"I will."

Phil held out the keys. When Nate reached for them, his brother pulled him in for a hug. Nate looked less convinced by this, a stiffness returning to his body, but he went along with it. Then he settled next to Liv, their arms almost touching, like he felt the solidarity she offered.

Phil held out his hand to her. When Cindy did the same, Liv took it politely but guardedly. She couldn't feel friendly towards this woman who had been so careless with Nate's heart — a heart that deserved better.

"Thank you," Cindy said.

Liv tried to read her brown eyes. Was there remorse there? An acknowledgement of what she'd done? "Why?"

"I think you know."

And maybe she did.

"Have a safe flight home," she said, Nate nodding in agreement without finding the words himself. She found his fingers and squeezed gently as they watched the rental car pull away. Nate was still watching when she shifted her gaze to him. "You okay?"

His eyes flashed to her. "It might be a while before I can answer that accurately. I'll buy you a drink if you let me, though," he said. "I think I need to decompress, and I could use the company."

Or maybe the supervision. She nodded. "Sure."

"I'll drive?"

She laughed with unexpected lightness. "Obviously."

YESTERDAY STILL FELT like a crazy dream. There had been something powerful about that moment when Liv had faced Cindy; what had been confronted by what would be; the past relinquishing to the future. Liv had stood by him, a silent constant, a steady heartbeat when his own had been raging. It had blown him away, made him determined to find the good in the past, incorporate those bits into who he was now, and let go of the crap that was holding him back.

Holding him back from what? He hadn't thought there was anything, until the visit.

At the pub, Liv hadn't pushed him to tell her about it. They'd talked about everything but, as if the afternoon's events had never occurred. He wasn't in denial — he knew better than to try and flee from it all again — but he still had to process it. Words didn't heal as much as time did.

Endorphins helped, a hard run at the farm, alone, after the distraction of a busy morning at the track. In his apartment he sucked back half a bottle of water then headed for the shower, grabbing his phone from where he'd tossed it. He absently checked the screen. He resented being so tied to it sometimes, but that was how it was. Texts from his agent were his career's lifeblood.

Voicemail was rarer.

He started listening to the message, cutting it short when he heard his mother's voice, the wobble in it making him disconnect and find the most recent call. She picked up too quickly. Her *Hello?* was small and unfamiliar.

"Mom, what's wrong?"

Her answer sent him into shock. He barely remembered calling Liv after hanging up, but there she was at his door. She reached for him and he clung to her, burying his face in her hair as he tried to deaden out the drone in his ears.

"Sit down. Tell me what happened." She gently guided him to the couch, and the grip of her hands around his was like a guyline, keeping him from blowing away in a gale-force wind.

"They were driving home from the airport." He started slowly, his brain fighting the formation of words because the scenario he sought to describe was too absurd to be real. "The roads were bad — freezing rain." That wasn't unusual for Calgary, even at the beginning of May. "A transport going the other way lost control, crossed the median…no contest. They were probably killed instantly." Better for them than a lingering death; not so for those left behind.

"Guess this is it, then. I have to go." He didn't recognize his own voice. He'd promised Cindy, but never thought it would be like this. This wouldn't be the family reunion his mother had in mind.

"Do you want me to come?"

Nate lifted his head, forcing his eyes to focus, her offer touching the darkness. "You'd do that?"

"Of course."

It was that simple to her. He never would have asked, knowing the position she was putting herself in. Their restart was just new, yet she was willing to throw herself in the middle of his first trip home since his frantic departure, for the funeral of the ex-girlfriend he'd thought was his soulmate — someone he'd hoped to marry — and where he could no longer avoid the father he'd endlessly battled on the direction of his life. Though it seemed contrary to Liv's nature, he'd begun to realize it was essential to what they were. It didn't matter what was or wasn't going on between them; some things were bigger than that.

"I can book the flight if you want," she said quietly.

"That's all right. I'll do it."

First he went to the kitchen, pulled the bottle of vodka out of the cupboard, and retrieved a jug of orange juice from the fridge. He dropped ice cubes into a couple of glasses, added juice to the liquor. The one he kept for himself was noticeably pale.

Liv accepted the glass from him, though she merely watched as half of his disappeared.

"You sure you don't want me to call the airline?" she asked again, the corners of her mouth drawn into a frown, her dark brows knitted.

He shook his head, finished the drink with another gulp, and glanced around for his phone — but hesitated before picking it up, like it was still radioactive with the devastating news. Finally he opened it, tapped and clicked and scrolled. YYZ to YYC, two seats — return.

Liv sidled closer, tucking a leg underneath her, her fingers reaching for his free hand. He curled his around them, tried to extract comfort.

"Do you want me to stay?"

Her grey eyes seemed almost blue in their earnestness. He did want that, more than anything, but the vodka was starting to have its sought-after anesthetic effect, and he worried in his impaired state he'd do something stupid; undermine this new level of trust.

"I'll be all right. But thank you."

She leaned in and brushed her lips to his, and he almost changed his mind. They could just sit on the couch all night; it could be harmless.

"Are you sure you're okay?"

He sighed, not feeling any more sure than she looked. "Yeah."

"I'll pick you up in the morning?"

He nodded feebly, and she left her glass on the coffee table, still half-full. It wouldn't go to waste. He followed her to the door, hands in the pockets of his nylon pants, vaguely aware they were still damp from his run.

"You never know, do you?" he said, meeting her eyes. The buzz from the vodka mingled freely with his anguish, but did nothing to dissolve it.

13

Nate gazed out the plane's window, transfixed by the clearness of the atmosphere above the carpet of vapour. Liv felt for what he must be going through, but was at a loss as to how to help him. Her only experience with death had been Geai, and all she had gleaned from that was that life does go on, but sometimes only after you crash. And sometimes you have to let someone else help you out. She'd been slow to learn that, but Nate had been her person. That's what made the decision to come an easy one, despite what she knew lay in store.

She'd never felt jealous of Cindy — even before meeting the woman, Cindy had seemed like a ghost. There would be comparisons made to the beloved daughter-in-law. Liv wasn't the open, warm-hearted girl that Cindy had been — not that any of those traits had done Nate any favours. Or maybe they had; maybe what Cindy had done was a greater expression of love than Liv was willing to give her credit for.

Nate touched her on the arm, returning from wherever he'd been in his mind, on that distant horizon line where the sky met the layer of clouds.

"It won't be much longer now. Do you want to sit by the window? I've seen it before."

There was no disdain in his voice — like he didn't resent the place, just the circumstances that had driven him away, and those that were bringing him back. She nodded, and they traded spots before the seatbelt light came on.

Liv looked out, putting the complications out of her head, anticipating the terrain as the plane began its descent. The land below was much flatter than she'd expected, and definitely less populated than what surrounded the airports in Toronto, New York City, Fort Lauderdale, or LA. There were still vast squares of farmland here. No sign of the Rockies, much to her disappointment.

Her nerves crept up as they landed, mocking her spontaneity. Maybe it hadn't been so smart, coming along, though Nate assured her his mother knew the details of their relationship. But mothers could see through things, past appearances to the more obscure and abstract kept beneath the surface. Nate didn't make his mother out to be someone anyone would be afraid of, but Liv wasn't sure how she would view the still-ambiguous nature of this bond between them.

He was on his feet as soon as the seatbelt light was off, reaching to the overhead compartment to retrieve their carry-ons, even though it would be some time before they could disembark.

She was usually a fast walker, but she matched Nate's uncharacteristically subdued pace through the terminal. He was dragging — he couldn't be looking forward to this reunion. The only experience she could relate it to was when she'd come skulking back to Ontario after letting her career fall apart in New York, but Nate really had no reason to be embarrassed or ashamed, except for leaving it so long.

She wasn't used to seeing him so serious, his face set like he was ready for a clash as he searched the crowd awaiting the arrivals. Then it softened, and he let his bags fall to the ground as he went forward and enfolded a small woman, dark blonde hair laced with grey, tired eyes weeping.

Liv stayed by Nate's luggage, tentatively putting down her own. Behind the woman stood a young man, dark hair, taller than Nate. He assessed her steadily, waiting just as she did, until Nate gently pulled away from his mother and threw his arms around him.

Nate took a step back, scanning cautiously. "Where's Dad?"

His mother answered. "He had to go into work briefly. He should be back by the time we get home."

Nate reached an arm toward Liv, encouraging her forward. "This is my mom. And my younger brother, Tim."

"Liv," the woman said, brushing away the hand she extended to pull her into a hug like she was family.

"I'm so sorry, Mrs. Miller," Liv said. "But I'm glad to meet you."

"Connie, please," the woman said, pushing a smile through persistent tears. "It was so kind of you to come."

Tim settled for the handshake before offering to take her bags.

Tim drove, heading west, his mother in the passenger seat next to him quietly asking about the flight and the weather in Toronto. Nate stared out the window. Liv could finally see the mountains, rising solemnly in the distance.

At the house Connie immediately busied herself, putting on a kettle and pulling plates from cupboards. "Would you like some tea? Something to eat? You must be hungry."

Nate smiled and glanced at Liv. "That's okay, Mom. Why don't you come and sit down?"

Connie scowled. "You're not riding this afternoon; you can eat something." She laid out some fruit and Nate grabbed an orange and started peeling it while his mother set out cups. "You can sleep in the spare room, Liv. Tim took over the basement after you boys left, so Nate, you can stay down there with him."

She looked distressed for a moment…*you boys.* Nate went to her, his embrace fierce. How much he must have missed her, restricting himself to only phone calls these last years. At one point he must have been close to his family; a piece of himself he'd left behind. Maybe cutting himself off had been more damaging than he'd let himself believe.

The click of the door was followed by a scramble of nails on tile, a whirl of energetic Golden Retrievers converging on the small space. Nate let go of his mother and laughed, the two Goldens circling his legs before bounding over to Liv at the table.

She leaned over and stroked their broad heads — a male and a bitch — and found herself speaking to them softly in French. Nate smiled at her before footsteps distracted him, his body turning rigid when someone appeared in the doorway.

It wasn't hard for Liv to figure out who the man was. The set of the shoulders and line of his jaw were the same, and she could imagine Nate's hair being that muted grey-blond in another twenty-five years. He was taller, though not as tall as Tim, and his face was considerably more serious — but the features were so similar. The man glanced at her first, then Nate.

"Welcome back."

The voice didn't sound particularly welcoming, but it seemed more neutral than judgmental. Nate met the man's regard, then walked back behind the kitchen table. The grim look on his face made him look even more like his father.

"Dad, this is my friend Liv." Nate's eyes flashed to hers. "My dad. Reid." He seemed to be withholding other sentiments that came to mind.

Liv rose as Reid Miller came toward her, hand outstretched. The Goldens scattered, the only happy ones left in the kitchen, tails wagging in defiance of the tension. The exchange was firm, businesslike. Unlike his wife, Liv thought Reid Miller's eyes were speculating, questioning her presence. Connie watched anxiously from behind her husband. That was it for the conversation, though. Nate wasn't offering anything more, and Reid turned to his wife and started talking about the funeral arrangements. Nate focused on the dogs, probably resisting the temptation to bolt, even though he'd want to hear what was happening.Then his phone rang, and he snatched it from the table, answering.

"Hey man." He paused, listening. "Will's coming on a later flight. Maybe we can get together after I pick him up."

Hearing Will was also returning for the funeral further cemented things from Nate's past for Liv. They'd grown up together, in this neighbourhood. Will and the racing industry in Ontario had been Nate's only destination when he'd departed. At least he'd had somewhere to go when he'd arrived in Toronto. He'd seemed so together when he'd come for the interview at the farm; there had been no indication of the hell he'd been through. Liv had always considered Nate one to keep his feelings close to the surface, but such a good chunk of his history he'd left buried deep.

After he disconnected, he pushed himself to his feet. "I'll show you your room." He slid past his parents, avoiding his mother's face.

Liv followed him, remaining by the door when he set her luggage by the bed. She scanned the walls. Hockey trophies of all sizes crowded shelves, and the same large win photo of Chique's Queen's Plate that graced the Triple Stripe office at Woodbine hung next to the bed — much to Liv's surprise. She felt him watching her, and wondered what he was thinking; how it made him feel, seeing some acknowledgment of his success. Maybe this room was low traffic, but they weren't stashed in a closet somewhere like he might have expected.

"Was this your room?" she asked, just to break the silence, edging her way in.

"Once. When Phil moved out in his second year of university I took over his space in the basement. Typical teenager, right?" His hands were in his pockets, looking from the trophies to the win picture before turning back to her. "Are you tired?"

"A little," she admitted, the time difference catching up with her, and she waited for him to tell her what was going on for the rest of the day. Another position she wasn't used to being in. Her time was usually so tightly self-regulated that the current state didn't help her feel any less out of place.

"I told Will I'd pick him up at the airport. Then I guess tonight I'd better be at the visitation."

Liv nodded, slowly. "Is it all right with you if I skip that?" That would be far too awkward.

"Yeah, of course," he said, his face softening. "It's just great to have you here."

THE KID HAD OFFERED to drive, but Nate didn't want to just sit there. He'd already had enough of that, and it wasn't doing him any good. If he could block out everything in his head, deal with it later, maybe he could get through this.

His mom's sedan was a step down — or five — from the Porsche, but probably just as well he didn't have that much power underfoot right now. He didn't want to think about where along this highway the accident had taken place. Better not to know. Didn't want to think about the niece and nephew he had yet to meet, who would grow up without their mother and father. Didn't want to get into anything with his own father while he was here, because it would just upset his mother more.

He switched his attention to Tim. His little brother hadn't changed that much, as far as he could tell — sure he was taller, and he'd filled out a lot. But he still didn't say much, still waiting for Nate to ask the questions.

"How's the hockey going?" Nate asked.

"Good."

Nate grinned, knowing — thanks to his mother — the kid was being modest. He was the leading goal-scorer on his team, but Nate could relate to the reservation. It wouldn't merit an answer of 'great' until he made it to the NHL.

"Still going to school part-time?"

"Yeah. I wanted to work, but Mom and Dad insisted."

"Probably smart."

"That's real great, coming from you." Now Tim threw him a wry smile.

"Yeah well…I've been pretty lucky." And should probably be saving more money in case that luck runs out, instead of spending it on expensive sports cars. He didn't tell Tim about the Porsche. He kept thinking about throwing the keys to Phil, like that was his last real memory of his older brother. It seemed symbolic, though of what, he wasn't sure. Giving in? Giving up? *You win*…though right now it wasn't looking much like a victory.

"Hopefully I'll get drafted this year."

It was the first thing Tim had said without prompting. That would put an end to his studies…but their father wouldn't have an issue with that.

"So…girlfriend?" Nate continued.

Tim scowled. "I'm not gonna let a girl mess up my head when I'm trying to get my hockey career on track."

Nate laughed, looking ahead to the road. "You and Liv have a lot in common. The two of you could discuss the virtues of being single."

Tim looked confused. "So you guys aren't together?"

"Ah…well…sort of, maybe."

"Sounds like one of those 'it's complicated' things."

"No. Not really. It's just…not simple."

"Isn't that the same thing?"

"It's a long story."

"You're making a lot of sense. So why's she here?"

Nate smirked. Tim was asking all the hard questions, for someone who kept quiet. He hadn't realized how much his little brother was like Liv. Maybe that's why he'd been able to get along with her the way he did — he'd had practice without really even knowing it.

"We've gone through some stuff. Maybe I've been there for her a couple of times. We're not sleeping together —" How did he explain the layers of that reality? "— but it's kind of…deep."

"Sounds serious. Is there something you can take for that?"

Nate choked on a laugh. "Your day will come. You go ahead and get that career settled, then give me a call. I've already got the girl for you."

"Yeah, don't you be setting me up. That's bound to go badly. Sounds like you've got enough to deal with already, with your own love life."

"Smartass."

They'd timed it right, so they didn't have to park, picking Will up at the curb. Will opened the door and threw his bag on the back seat, climbing in after it.

"Hey, Tim, how's the hockey star?"

Tim brushed off the comment as Nate pulled the car into the traffic flow.

"So how'd it go?" Will asked, tapping Nate on the shoulder.

Nate shot him a dark look and returned his attention to the road.

"They didn't kill each other, if that's what you mean." Tim grinned.

Will laughed. "That's a good start. Where's Liv?"

"Back at the house," Nate said. "She's not coming tonight. Just as well. I guess we've got some stuff to do."

"You going to be all right for that, buddy?" Will asked.

Nate grimaced. "I'll manage. Ben said he'd see us there. It'll give us a good reason to leave early." He was silent for a moment. "You hungry?"

"Sure," Will said.

"They'll have food at the funeral home, won't they?" Tim interjected.

"They won't have alcohol." Will chuckled. "You'd better plan on driving from here on in, Tim. I expect your brother needs to get on the drink program to get through this."

Nate shook his head. Not that it would surprise anyone if he showed up drunk. And part of him would really like to see his father's face. He wished now Liv had come, as if she would ground him to his new life so he wouldn't succumb to the failures of the old. He'd told her when she'd hit a low after Geai's death that alcohol didn't help. He needed to heed his own advice.

"I think I need to show everybody here I can deal with stuff sober," he stated. "I'm pretty sure the last time they all saw me I left them with a memorable impression that suggested otherwise."

"All right," Will said. "We'll just go get drunk after, then."

The visitation was busy enough he didn't have to worry about it being obvious he still wasn't talking to his father. He stayed next to his mother, focusing his energy on being her support. A good son, to make up for the one who'd run away. He was grateful things were sombre enough that no one said anything to make him feel badly for falling off the face of the earth as far as Calgary was concerned. All the same, when the time came he was happy to have that excuse to go.

"We've got some stuff to sort out for tomorrow, Mom." He drew her into a hug, and felt her nod against his shoulder as she squeezed back.

Worry lingered in her eyes as the guys gathered behind him. Even his mother expected him to go off the rails. Ben held up the car keys.

"Drive carefully," she said. They weren't just words.

At the restaurant he asked the server for water. Will's eyes went wide, and Nate just shrugged. It wasn't that he didn't want to be numb. And he didn't need to get up early in the morning, or make weight tomorrow afternoon. It was his mother's face, and his own fear, that if he started, he wouldn't stop.

Ben brought him back to the task at hand. "So we haven't played together since Will deserted us seven years ago, but tomorrow we're going to get up in front of a church full of people?"

Nate was having trouble thinking of Cindy coming up with songs to play at her own funeral. With the twins now, and Phil being a lawyer, of course they'd have wills. Phil would have made sure all that was in place. But the songs…the songs were all Cindy. Songs she knew he knew. And somehow he had to get up there and sing them.

"I should probably have a will," he said, trying to deflect his own thoughts.

"Sure buddy," Will said. "You do have a kind of dangerous job. You'll leave me the car, though, right?"

"Only if you agree to play at *my* funeral. Maybe we could pick out the tunes tonight."

Will laughed, but it lacked humour.

The house was dark when he returned, and he crept quietly downstairs. There was a light on in the TV room — and Liv curled up on the couch, asleep with a book in her lap. Rita, the female Golden, snuggled next to her; Dexter, the male, on the floor beside her. He wanted to curl up with them and bury himself there.

Liv lifted her head, eyes flickering open as she straightened and closed the book. Rita didn't budge; Dexter's tail thumped once. Clearly she'd been well taken care of.

Her head tilted slightly. "You okay?"

Maybe the question came because he hadn't moved from the bottom of the stairs, the scene giving him flashbacks of time spent down here. He shook them loose and walked over, leaning down, like his kiss was a breathalyzer to prove he was fine.

"Don't let my father catch that dog on the couch." He plopped down on the opposite end, his fingers weaving through the thick Golden coat to give Rita a scratch. "What are you doing awake?"

"I wasn't really awake." She smirked. "I slept for a while earlier. I'm all messed up between that and the time difference. How'd it go?"

"All right. A lot of people I hadn't seen for years. It's like a weird social thing, isn't it? Then Will and I met with our old band mate, Ben. We're going to play some songs tomorrow."

Her eyebrows crept up, a slight crease forming between them.

"Just another performance, right?" *Ride the horse you're on.* He shrugged, dropping his eyes to where Dexter's head now rested on his foot. "Cindy had stuff written out…" He faltered. "She was just like that. Always planning everything. Except me. I don't think she planned on me."

"I'm not sure anyone plans on you, Miller."

There was no response for that, the feeling it left him with one he couldn't pin down and put in a box. An admission on her part that he had managed to break through her well-constructed walls. *She's stingy with words,* he'd said to the old farm manager, Geai, when he'd first questioned her trusting him with Chique. She certainly didn't share feelings freely. And this, the two of them, certainly hadn't been part of any of her plans.

But now he felt he had to step back, when it would be easy to press forward, to take comfort there. It wouldn't be fair to her, after all this time, to use her to fight his memories — of that time, of this room; to put her in that position, competing with history. The irony was painful, after the long winter in limbo.

One thing he could count on — she wouldn't question it, wouldn't challenge the physical line they still maintained, her personal and emotional space something she didn't seem in any hurry to give up. They were still like a couple of well-behaved church kids. Crazy or endearing, he didn't know.

She finally broke the silence that had settled, extricating her legs from the sixty pounds of retriever that had held her captive. "Tomorrow's going to be a long day."

Leaning over, she kissed him, the touch of her lips light. The weight in her grey eyes was anything but. When she didn't quite pull away, he almost…almost…

Listening to her footsteps as she ascended, he hoped he was exhausted enough to fall asleep, because he was tired of thinking, and remembering, and trying to figure out what losing the past would mean for the future.

NATE'S VOICE NEVER FALTERED, fingers unfailingly striking the right keys, the three members of this unplanned reunion managing to sound like they did this every day. Liv could feel his pain though; his need to believe there was a reason behind it all. She swiped at her damp cheeks with the sleeve of her dress, and felt Connie press a tissue in her palm, squeezing, her own eyes shining as she met Liv's.

There was no shortage of speculative looks in the basement of the church after the service, Nate wrapping his fingers around hers as they stood on the edge of the gathering. He introduced her simply as a friend to a flurry of faces and names she couldn't hope to remember. The way he moved around her suggested there was more to them; that reassurance in his eyes she'd come to rely on, his fingers on her back as he presented someone new. She went with it. Maybe she could be who and what they might think she was. Maybe she was becoming it.

He caught sight of something across the room, and touched her arm. “I’ll be back in a sec, all right?”

Will appeared beside her like it had been staged so she wouldn’t feel abandoned. Not that he filled the void Nate left, even though he was physically bigger. Nate weaved through bodies to a man and woman, each of them carrying a child Liv hadn’t seen them upstairs.

“That’s Cindy’s sister Julie and her husband.” Will paused. “And I’m guessing those are the twins.”

It wasn’t hard to figure out. Nate embraced the woman and looked totally natural greeting the children, Liv guiltily relieved he hadn’t taken her over with him. She would have had no idea what to say. The thought of losing a sister was crushing, not to mention that of two kids who would never know their parents.

“You okay?”

Liv glanced at Will. Did she look that uncomfortable? Could he actually fathom how out of her element she felt?

“Come here a minute.” He inclined his head to the side. “This is someone you should probably meet.”

Will interrupted a middle-aged man who had the weathered look of someone who didn’t usually wear a suit and tie. “This is Al Wilson.”

The man grinned warmly, offering his hand. “Liv Lachance. I’m honoured.”

Liv smiled modestly. “Great to finally meet you.”

Al was the trainer, a family friend, who had given Nate his start with horses — the one to whom Nate had credited his broad range of skills, when most jockeys didn’t learn a lot of horsemanship before being tossed onto a Thoroughbred. She was happy to finally have someone she could relate to in a sea of people who would never understand her way of life.

“Glad to see the kid finally got his license,” Al said. “Would have been a shame for all that talent to go to waste.”

“It took him long enough.” Liv smiled again. “But maybe he knew what he was doing, taking his time. He’s done a pretty impressive job of making the most of things since.”

“You’ve been good to him.”

"He's earned it."

There was more assessing going on, given the mild look on Al Wilson's face. Then he looked over Liv's shoulder, his features lighting up. "And there he is. Good to see you, kid. Wish it hadn't taken something like this to inspire a visit."

Seeing the trainer threatened to chip away at the mask Nate was working hard to maintain. He recovered, deflecting the combination of praise and chiding with an ease Liv had seen time and again.

"How are you doing?" Liv asked after Al excused himself with the usual pleasantries.

"I could use a drink, or five, but thanks for asking," he responded, letting his weariness show.

They returned to the house before the others, Nate leading the way into the dining room, loosening his tie as he went. He opened the door to a hutch, peering in, and pulled out a bottle and a couple of tumblers, then looked at her.

"Want one?"

Liv looked dubiously over his shoulder. "That depends. What is it?"

"My father's scotch."

"No thanks," Liv said, eying him before going into the living room, open off the dining area. She hadn't been in here, and glanced around before sitting on the chesterfield. Nate came over and sat next to her, resting his arm on the back of the sofa and swallowing a healthy dose from the glass he'd poured. He looked as if he wasn't sure if he liked it, but it served the purpose.

"Is that your Eclipse Award?" Liv said.

Nate glanced at the bronze statue resting on a table near the window — the trophy that had been given to him as leading apprentice in North America in his first year of riding. "I guess it is," he said, laughing softly. "I figured it would be a doorstop or something."

"Thought about it."

Reid Miller stood in the doorway, Connie scowling behind him. It sounded so much like something Nate would say, Liv had to smother a grin.

"I'm taking the dogs for a run. Thought you might want to come along."

Reid was looking directly at Nate, and Liv couldn't help studying him as well, gauging his reaction. He stared back at his father, his prolonged hesitation making Liv think he was going to say no.

"Okay." He glanced at her. "That all right with you?"

Liv nodded quickly. "Yeah, of course."

"I'll need to change." Nate walked over to the dining room, draining the glass, and set it on the table with his eyes on Reid before disappearing downstairs.

Connie poured a measure of whiskey for herself, Liv trying to control the lift of her eyebrows as the older woman settled into the spot Nate had vacated.

"It was very kind of you to come with him, Liv. He's very lucky to have a friend like you."

After a day where she'd felt stuck for words, even more than usual, Liv didn't hesitate as she looked into Connie's careworn face. "I've always thought I was the lucky one."

NATE WATCHED THE DOGS PLAY, grabbing fallen branches and carrying them with wagging tails like the self-respecting Golden Retrievers they were. The walk to the park had been silent, and he'd found himself wishing that was good enough. He had nothing left, but this hadn't been an invitation he could refuse, not today. His mother deserved to have what was left of her family somewhat cohesive. It was unlikely he and his father would ever be close, but it could be a whole lot better than it was right now. Bygones.

Dexter came bounding over with his stick and a goofy Golden grin. Nate asked for it quietly, the dog releasing, sitting expectantly. When he sent it tumbling through the air, Dexter bounded off in hot pursuit with Rita on his heels.

"Sounds like Tim's doing great." He couldn't leave the silence, if anything was going to be resolved here. That seemed like a safe place to start. "Do you think he'll get drafted this year?"

"I'd be pretty surprised if he doesn't."

Stops and starts. This was either going to be a long walk, or a really short one.

"What's really going on with the girl?"

There was a trace of a smirk on his father's face, which was more than Nate had seen since he'd been back…and for a long time before he'd left.

"She's a friend, Dad."

Because first and foremost, she was. And wasn't that the best way for things to be?

"You like her, don't you?"

Nate sighed. "I do." That wasn't news, but he was aware his feelings were a whole lot more intense than that.

Reid shook his head. "You always pick the good ones, kid. Beauty and brains."

There was no use trying to explain the nature of his relationship with Liv to his father — like there was no "picking" her; it was a slow evolution over which he had no control. All he could do was see where it carried them, and hope it ended differently than his relationships had in the past.

"I know I was hard on you. It took a lot of guts to leave the way you did. I respect that."

Nate choked on a laugh. So they were going there. "Guts? I ran away with my tail between my legs."

"You did the right thing."

"Then how come you never let me feel that way?" He looked ahead to where the dogs were invested in some intriguing scent, finding he wasn't really angry anymore, just strangely reflective. "I couldn't do anything right as far as you were concerned. You know it was completely ridiculous to think I was going to play professional hockey, right?" He'd figured that one out himself, at about sixteen, two years after he'd started galloping for Al Wilson. No way was he ever going to have the size and weight needed to play the game at that level, but it just so happened those shortfalls came in handy for riding racehorses.

"I'm sorry about that. It's too bad, you were good. You're good at a lot of things." Reid paused. "And you went with something I admit I couldn't get my head around. I think you've made your point. You're the best in the country at what you do."

Nate grinned. "I don't know about that. Liv will probably kick my ass going head to head with me this year."

"That'll keep you humble. Probably not a bad thing."

Nate looked at him sideways. "Thanks. Anyone that can do that for you?"

His father laughed. "Yeah. You. That's why I kept that big old bronze door stop you sent us." He stopped and turned to Nate, his hands in the pockets of his jacket. "That was a pretty special thing you did today, standing up and singing like that."

"You thought Cindy and I were all wrong."

"And I was right. But that doesn't mean I don't appreciate what it took to do that."

He had to take the good with the bad, when it came to truth, and his father. It would be too much to have Reid become suddenly outspoken in his support. And now his mother would be happy. They were talking again — no small feat.

His mother was making dinner when they returned, Liv sitting behind the kitchen counter seeming almost at ease in her company. Both women looked up, as if they were expecting blood and broken teeth. Nate went to his mother and kissed her on the cheek, then wandered around the counter. He met Liv's eyes, and almost kissed her too.

THE DISTURBED SLEEP pattern of the last couple of days wasn't doing anything for his brain right now. He was beyond tired with fatigue more than physical. At least it seemed to have plateaued.

He poured himself a glass of juice in the kitchen and sat at the table. Nothing had really changed with the décor, though he imagined his departure five years ago had created a disturbance. His return might have given some balance, had it not been for the tragedy that had brought him here.

Liv appeared in the doorway — no surprise she would be afflicted with the same disruption of time, if not the full impact of the trauma — but it was like she was his totem, the thing that grounded him in this haze, reminded him that only part of this was reality. And as necessary as it had been to come, as grateful as he was to have held his mother, and set right the past with his father, her presence made him want to go home. It was official now. This wasn't home.

"Sleep okay?" he asked.

"Better than the night before, anyway."

Nate leaned on the table, hands folded as she joined him. "We should drive up to the Rockies."

Liv looked skeptical, but intrigued. "Do we have time for that?"

"Sure. If we leave now." Their flight wasn't until the afternoon. They could get to Banff and back. "I told you you needed to see real mountains."

He left a note on the fridge, and they headed out in the dark with his mother's car. The landscape emerged as the sun rose, foothills giving way to immense rock faces, blasted to create the highway. Liv was silent, peering at the vast peaks stretching to the heavens, catching the early light.

Nate didn't stop until they got to Banff. They found a coffee shop open but not much else, and walked down the quiet sidewalk with steaming cups, looking in shop windows. Every other storefront sold stereotypical Canadian souvenirs — plush moose toys, Mounties, beavers, red and white flags.

"This might be as close as I've ever come to being a tourist." Liv looked at him sideways, lips twisting up at the ends.

"In your own country, no less."

He held out his hand, and she took it, shyly. She could hop on a plane for him without a thought, but this simple gesture was a stretch, even so far away from their regular lives that it was unlikely anyone would recognize them.

"Let's go somewhere we can see the mountains better," he said, leading her back to where they'd left the car.

He ended up stopping on the side of the road because neither of them was dressed for a hike. They leaned against the car and looked up at the surrounding grandeur, ignoring the vehicles whizzing past.

"It's incredible." There was reverence in her voice. "Prehistoric, like we're close to the beginning of time."

Eternal, almost. Close to forever.

"I didn't spend much time out here, other than skiing in the winter.

Seems ridiculous to have something so amazing so near, and not take advantage of it." He probably left his eyes on her too long, his mind running parallels to this, to them. "But somehow it seems part of me, you know? I think if I lived out here now, I'd have to come up here all the time. As if it's where everything would make sense."

And maybe it did right now. And maybe she was why.

14

Elemental was the early Queen's Plate favourite. The Triple Stripe hopeful had two stake wins to his credit this season with Liv aboard, and looked to solidify his position this weekend in the Plate Trial. Dean was still on the fence about which race to enter his colt in — the Trial, or an allowance race, at the same distance, on the same day.

Faye, in jeans and a simple blouse, flashed Nate a smile as she set cappuccinos in front of him and her brother. She looked good no matter what she wore, hair and makeup always flawless. No wayward smears from a well-meaning horse on Faye; she didn't get close enough for that to ever happen.

"Have you made a decision yet?" Nate nudged Dean with his foot as he sipped some of the froth, and pondered whether he could indulge in a butter tart too. The little café had the best ones in this part of Ontario, something that hadn't changed when Faye had taken over running it last summer.

Dean doodled absently in the margin of a condition book. "Roger's entering Elemental in the Trial, I assume?"

"Yes."

"What do you think?"

"In three weeks, your colt will beat Elemental. On Sunday, I'm not so sure."

"That's quite the prediction. I hope this thing you've got going with Liv isn't affecting your judgment."

Dean's smirk was probably harmless, but Nate faltered a moment. Where was that coming from? "Absolutely not."

"Better not be, because I won't think twice about putting someone else on him if I'm the least bit suspicious."

Nate laughed, maybe too abruptly. "I'd love to win the Plate two years in a row — why would I mess that up? Your colt has a great shot. If we face Elemental Sunday, it might take more out of him than you want to be giving up right now — and that could affect his chances in three weeks. Give him an easy win instead. It builds his confidence, and sets him up perfectly. That's what I'd do, anyway. Whatever you decide, just name me on him."

He did find it difficult being in competition with Liv, but he wasn't about to say that out loud. She was unfailingly businesslike, and extremely fair when it came to the Triple Stripe horses, so that wasn't the issue. He had to go out there and forget who he was riding against, which wasn't always simple, knowing how easily one of them could get hurt. Their little rivalry did have a certain appeal, however…

The jangle of the bell on the door distracted him from that thought as Will shuffled in. Will leaned down to meet Faye's upturned face, heat there even in their simple kiss. A little reminder of what Nate wasn't getting. Or even asking for.

"Liv pulled in behind me." Will settled into a chair.

Emilie swirled in, and Nate caught Liv's eye and smiled when she appeared after her sister. Her quiet manner was a contrast to Em's energy, her fingers tucked into the loose jeans she'd had on for a morning of galloping and bathing and grooming. A dusting of alfalfa leaves still clung to her shirt, her hair loosely pulled back. She looked every bit as good as Faye. No, better.

"I've got news," Emilie said, her smile bright. "I'm helping revive the Plate Ball. And all of you are coming for moral support."

Faye laughed and clapped her hands. "Oh, can I help too?"

Liv scowled. "I put on formal wear for the Sovereigns, Em. I've met my quota for the year."

"You're going." Emilie pointed at her, then at Nate. "You're making sure, right?"

Nate grinned. "I got this, Em." He rose, making his way to Liv, and took her hand, going down on one knee. She stared at him, eyebrows knitted in what might possibly be horror. "Will you go to the prom with me, Olivia?"

"Please get up."

She tried to pull him, but he wouldn't budge. "Only once you answer me."

Faye drummed her fingers against the counter. "We're all waiting. Be grateful we're not videoing this, sweetie."

"We might, if you don't hurry up," Emilie quipped.

Liv looked at the ceiling, then dropped her eyes back to Nate with a smirk. "Yes, okay. I hate you all."

He popped up and kissed her quickly. "You coming, Dean?"

"To the prom? I think not."

"You can be my date, Dean," Emilie said.

"Save her the pain of going with whatever sack she might otherwise drag along," Faye quipped.

"Just come, Dean. It's for a good cause." Em was pretty convincing, with that sweet smile. "The money's going to New Chapter." Em was always coming up with fresh ways to raise funds for the local Thoroughbred aftercare organization.

Dean's scribbles became darker. "Some of us have horses to train for the actual race."

"Some of us have horses to ride, but they're not letting me out of it." Liv's arms were crossed, but she unfolded them and pressed her hands together. "Please, Dean. In solidarity."

He pushed himself up and grumbled, "Fine. Tell me how to buy a ticket, Em. I'll see you all later. I'm going for a bike ride."

Nate was starting to give her that look each day after galloping Chique: *let's get on with it.* He was right. After two weeks of training over the Woodbine oval, the filly was ready for faster work. She worried Chique might not be the same as she had been before the laminitis…but it was time to find out.

"Easy, Miller, right?"

"Yeah, boss, we can baby her a while longer. I'm okay with that." He grinned as he got tied on. "Don't worry. I'll take care of her."

Liv led Paz out of his stall, noticing Jo starting to walk out to the track with Roger, and decided not to underestimate the importance of moral support.

Nate made the usual casual conversation as they backed up on the outer rail, but Liv barely heard him, her senses analyzing everything about the filly. Chique's jog was businesslike and untroubled, and Liv hoped it was maturity she was seeing, not a decrease in the drive that had made the filly so competitive — and challenging.

Nate looked over as he stood easily in the irons. "I'm talking to myself, aren't I?"

Liv frowned sheepishly. "Sorry."

When they turned in and faced the infield, Chique stood alertly, ears forward, nostrils flared. That was the look.

Nate pulled down his goggles and let the filly start off, Liv keeping Paz close. Chique bounced, shaking her head and travelling sideways for a few steps before Nate straightened her and channeled her energy forward. The filly knew exactly what was going on.

Paz tossed his nose in the air when she pulled him up on the backstretch. She watched them gallop around until the tote board obscured her view, then picked them up again as they rounded the clubhouse turn. Chique galloped strongly, ears flickering back to Nate — asking, waiting. When he let her drop to the rail she switched leads, accelerating as they reached the half-mile pole. Liv hit the stopwatch and let Paz move enough to follow their progress.

Chique powered around the turn, eating up the first quarter before Nate gave her more of what she wanted. Another clean lead change as they straightened into the stretch, then steadily on to the wire. Liv stopped the watch and glanced down.

She spotted them through traffic again on the backside, Chique's ears pricked as Nate eased her away from the middle of the track, slowing to a jog. He parked Chique beside the pony gelding, running a hand under her tousled mane.

"She's grown up," he said.

"Just as long as you're sure that's all it is." Liv made a face. "That was slow for her."

"Well, that's what you asked for." He laughed as they started towards the gap. "Relax, Liv. Give her time. Don't forget what she's been through."

"You don't have to remind me." Sharpness crept into her tone, and she immediately regretted snapping at him. "Sorry."

He laughed again. "And this is only the beginning. Good thing I'm used to it already."

Roger and Jo beat them back to the barn, Jo ready with the filly's halter. It was warm enough for a bath, and Nate set the tack on the rail before returning to hold Chique while Liv put Paz away.

"See? She's not even blowing," Nate said when Liv came out to stand with Roger. "She's fine."

As if to reaffirm the statement, Chique's neck snaked, teeth grinding, and Nate grinned as he ducked out of her way. The black tail sprayed them all with soapy water, and Jo had to grab it to keep from being lashed in the face.

"Seems her old self to me." Jo grimaced.

Roger crossed his arms. "That was fine. Just what you wanted."

"I know, I know," Liv said.

Nate relinquished the shank to the hotwalker. "I think we'll probably get the filly back to the races, Rog, but I'm not convinced we can hold Liv here together."

Liv pressed her lips into a line. "Don't you have somewhere to be?"

"No, actually I'm done for the morning." That grin of his teased her. "I was thinking I'd make a run to the kitchen. Can I get you anything?"

He didn't wait for her answer. Roger chuckled beside her.

"He's right, you know. About the filly, I mean. She looked good out there. He had a stranglehold on her. And the two-year-old is training great.

You need to ride more races or something to keep yourself occupied, so you're not fretting so much. Then maybe you'll see how well things are really going."

She caught his eye as they walked onto the shed.

"You'll be all right. He's a good guy."

Liv ducked into Feste's stall and tied him to the back wall. That much was true — the colt was prepping like the racehorse he was supposed to be. With the winter's long, slow miles under him, the speed work was coming easily. She'd actually let herself start looking for a race. Chique stressed her constantly, but she was excited about Feste. He was trying on the sensible shoes Claire had left behind, while Chique danced to her own tune in knee-high spiky red boots.

"Looks like she's cooling out fine."

Nate leaned on the doorframe, holding out a bottle of apple juice. Had he run to the kitchen? Liv finished picking and painting Feste's feet before she came forward to accept it.

"All right. I get it."

She rested her shoulder on the cool cinder-block wall, aware of how close he was, and how that was okay. Regardless of the fact that they were no secret, she'd been clinging to a sense of propriety, her precious professionalism, but since they'd returned from Calgary it had started to seem less important.

He hadn't talked about the trip since they'd come back. He was different. Older, in the way that dealing with death couldn't help but age a person. More committed, which shouldn't have been possible, because he'd always been rock-solid, with his job. With her.

"Don't worry, we'll get her there," he said.

She laughed, surprised for once he hadn't pinpointed exactly what she'd been thinking.

She went to Feste, rubbing the star on his forehead, then looked sideways to Nate. "Can you breeze him tomorrow?"

He smirked, but there was a kink in one of his eyebrows. "I thought you might be keeping him for yourself."

Feste lipped at her fingers, and she tugged his upper lip gently. "I'm just asking you to breeze him."

"No you're not."

She met his eyes. "I did think about it. Keeping him. But when it comes down to it…I think all along I was planning to give him to you."

"Chique, Ride The Wave, now Feste…keep giving me your best horses, you're going to gift yourself out of a Plate."

"I am so beating your ass with Elemental this year."

"You keep dreaming." He grinned, held her eyes for a moment, and walked away.

"WELL. YOU'RE NOT MESSING AROUND," Nate said when Liv told him her plans for Feste's first race.

"You know how good he is."

"Oh I'm not questioning, just thinking I'm the one who's usually all high on the kids." His grin flashed. "Nice to see some confidence."

There was no sense denying it with this colt. Besides, the early two-year-old races were all short, so it would just be like another work…even if it was a stake race.

Her phone buzzed in her back pocket, and she pulled it out, glancing at the screen.

"Problem?" Nate asked.

She hadn't exactly hidden her scowl. She shook her head. "No. I've just — gotta go. See you tomorrow?"

She left him standing in the middle of the shed with a puzzled look on his face.

She'd forgotten about the Plate Ball until Faye asked her what she was wearing, and insisted a shopping trip was in order. Why had she agreed to this? Wasn't there enough to worry about in her life right now without making a big deal out of what should really just be an inconvenient social obligation?

"You gotta play the game a little," Faye insisted. "We need to make sure he's picking his jaw up off the floor when he sees you."

"Why?" Liv said, exasperated.

"It's all about power, sweetie." Faye's lips spread into that smug smile of hers.

"Oh come on. We're friends. I'm not getting into that."

"That's cute, but you really need to turn things up a notch or the two or you aren't going to get anywhere. He's probably scared to make any kind of move, so you've got to give him a little bit of an opening. Though we both know you'd never throw yourself at him."

"Yeah. Okay. I know better than to take advice from you."

"Just trying to help out," Faye said. "But you still need the dress."

"Téméraire..."

The colt began to dance beneath Nate as the announcer called an Anglophone's approximation of his official name. Liv wasn't watching this one in the room. It wasn't just that she was tired of the good-natured jibes, the "What are you doing letting Miller ride that colt?" She needed to be here, out front, binoculars clutched in a vise-grip next to Roger.

Nate left the pony behind to warm up, Feste's ground-covering stride a contrast to the easy gallops of the other entrants. The colt was the only first-time starter in the race, but he wasn't being overlooked. The position of favourite fluctuated between him and Way Too Normal, winner of the first two-year-old stake of the season. Reunited briefly with Paz and Nicole behind the gate, Feste loaded without incident.

Liv's hands trembled. Suddenly, she was terrified.

Terrified he'd hurt himself.

Terrified he'd run up the track.

Terrified he'd turn out to be everything he was supposed to be.

The gates crashed open, and Feste matched strides with Way Too Normal, gunning for the lead. Liv didn't want to look at the teletimer. Didn't really need to, to know they were flying — but her dark bay colt moved effortlessly, Nate quiet on his back. The two leaders opened up on the rest of the field, sizzling into the turn. Not that the others wouldn't catch up, if these two hit a brick wall mid-stretch, sustaining such a rapid pace.

Feste wouldn't. She knew how fit he was.

But Way Too Normal did — reaching his limit, going backwards. Nate calmly picked Feste up and urged him on by. Then steadily ran away from the rest of them, so it didn't matter who was coming on at the end.

Liv shook her head as Nate galloped the colt out. No flash, no drama — nothing like Chique — but Feste had set a track record just the same. Pure, uncomplicated talent.

This colt could be better than Chique. This colt could be everything.

15

Faye hadn't considered the high school formal a rite of passage the way some teenage girls did — she'd been more into going for the sport of seeing who wore what and came with whom. Liv hadn't shared her friend's fascination, refusing any attempts Faye had made to drag her along.

Now it seemed it had all caught up to her, with this whole Plate Ball ordeal.

Nate's mock promposal at the café that day had been a joke, right? Because this *was* just a professional obligation. It was in support of Thoroughbred aftercare, something both of them supported wholeheartedly.

So why was she so nervous? This was Nate. And neither of them was eighteen. They both had to make an appearance, so why not go together?

Well, of course there was the fact they were riding the top two Plate contenders. Elemental had easily won the Trial, and later the same day, Nate accompanied Ride The Wave to an impressive victory in an allowance race, matching Elemental's time. The Northwest colt was definitely going to be the one to beat — and Nate was being very close-mouthed about his mount. He had to be careful, especially if Dean, of all people, had voiced concern about his riding against her and a Triple Stripe horse, but Liv knew any loyalty dissolved out on the racetrack.

But tonight? They were old news. Surely the gossips would find something more interesting to talk about. Any occasion where the track community gathered had the potential for good stories. Someone would get drunk and do something stupid; somebody would leave with someone different from whom they came with. She and Nate would observe the indiscretions, pick at food, avoid alcohol; maybe he'd drag her out for a dance, but it wouldn't be them inspiring tales.

But it was their first public appearance, socially. And the dress…

The dress was exquisite. Faye had talked her out of her default navy or black, and into this sleek, deep aqua strapless gown that reached the floor with a subtle flare, a satiny shawl for later in case it got cool. Emilie had done her hair, sweeping it into an elegant updo, though Liv had drawn the line at makeup, because she'd no doubt smear it by mistake. How did people not do that all the time?

The pendant around her neck — the one Geai had given her, with the tiny painting of a horse that looked just like Claire, and, okay, a nun — would centre her. She'd scoffed at that nun, but it had become her way of keeping Geai close. And as much as this thing with Nate still managed to catch her off guard, Geai would have loved it. If he was looking down from somewhere, he had a big old smile on his face.

The doorbell made her jump, reverberating through the house, which was empty except for her. Her parents had left earlier, Em before that, because she was involved in organizing the event.

She stood in the foyer with her hand on the knob, eyes closed; made herself breathe. *Stop overthinking this.*

Then there he was on the front step, grinning, of course, one hand tucked behind his back. "Sorry I'm late."

"You're not."

It wasn't as if she'd never seen the tux, but…*well.* Standing there, all flawlessly turned out, he threw an irregular beat into her pulse, sending a current through her veins. Faye's so-called advice popped into her head: *we both know you'd never throw yourself at him.* But what if she did? That would get her out of this whole thing, of that much she was sure.

He pulled his arm from behind his back to present a single, long-stemmed, red rose. Most women would have melted, but Liv laughed as she accepted it, her tension easing just a titch.

"Wrong race, Miller," she said, immediately associating roses with the Kentucky Derby, then caught herself for being ungrateful. "Thank you. Come in for a minute?"

He sauntered after her to the kitchen as she found one of her mother's crystal vases for the delicate bud. When she turned with it, she glanced away from the look he was giving her, and brushed past him to the living room to set the vase on the coffee table.

I guess the dress worked.

She walked slowly up the two steps to the landing, making herself hold his gaze. "If you've changed your mind and don't want to go to this thing, I wouldn't complain." She didn't care how it sounded.

There was a definite beat before a laugh that was a little strained, the shift of his eyes telling her it wasn't her imagination. "That would attract more attention than showing up together will." He reached for her hand, pulling her slowly towards him. "We'd better get out of here. It would be a shame to miss it when we both look so good."

One touch. She could just reach a hand to his neck; kiss him, put an end to this silly idea. His eyes were on her mouth, fingers warm against hers. But he directed her to the door. She locked it behind them, and hesitated when he held out his arm.

"Why are you so worried?" Now he was laughing at her, looking, quite possibly, relieved that they'd made it out of the house.

His arm felt solid beneath his jacket as they descended the steps, which was a good thing, because she might as well have been wearing heels instead of ballet flats, as unsteady as she felt.

He stopped again at the bottom of the stairs. "Really, what's up?"

"This seems altogether too grown-up. You're making such a big deal."

"I'm not making a big deal. It'll be fun."

"Fun? Why is it that everyone but me seems to think these things are fun?"

"It'll be fun because you're with me." He rolled his eyes when she didn't lose the deer-in-the-headlights look. "Fine."

"Does this mean we don't have to go?"

"You need to stop saying that. We're going."

Then he dangled the keys in front of her with a tilt of his head. She snapped them up, leaving him standing there as she swept around the front of the Porsche. She definitely wasn't waiting for him to withdraw that opportunity.

He dashed to open the driver's side door for her, waiting as she slipped behind the wheel and tucked in the gown. Foot on the brake, depress the clutch, pop the stick into neutral. The engine purred at the turn of the key, and she almost purred with it.

"Well? Are you coming?"

*Humour me, it'll be fun...*that was the attitude, wasn't it? Of course, maybe this was all just an attempt to knock her off her stride for tomorrow — though two could play that game, and if the looks she kept catching meant anything, he was just as vulnerable.

He started singing along to the stereo, naturally. Van Morrison, *Moondance*. He always seemed to mix in some old stuff, but this song, and his voice, stirred everything inside her just a little more.

Liv glanced at him sideways, trying to get her head back in the game. "Did you curate this playlist specially for tonight, Miller?"

"Naw."

Right. The next song, *Hey Pretty,* was proof of his lie. The Poe was for her. And tonight? Oh yes, she got the gist of the song.

It was hard to resist the temptation to go faster when she reached the highway, though that only meant they would get there sooner. She needed to play the role for a few hours, make him happy. This was what most women would kill for. A sweet car, the enchanting music, a handsome, well-dressed escort. He should probably be driving, but that restyling of the fantasy might actually make it work for her. If it had to be, it might as well be like this.

The big white tent next to Woodbine's grandstand was already humming. Part of her was happy it wasn't in a fancy hotel ballroom, because that would have made it harder to keep her mindset of seeing this as a job. They worked on the backside in the morning. They worked on the front side in the afternoon. This was just more work. On the other hand, it was like a big fishbowl.

They gave up the Porsche to a valet, both of them looking longingly after it. Nate finally grabbed her elbow, steering her away and looping his arm through hers again.

"Ready for this?"

Liv squared her shoulders and sighed. "Okay. Let's get it over with."

"You're so good for my self-esteem."

"It's nothing personal, Miller." She grinned at him. *Play the game*. He could have this night. She would be that girl.

Eyes and whispers followed them when they walked in. Her imagination? She tried to feed off Nate's calm as her anxiety escalated again.

"Aha! Congratulations, Nate. You did it." Faye stood to welcome them when they found their table.

"I had to let her drive my car to get her here."

"Well then, I'm surprised you made it at all," Faye said.

Nate helped Liv into the chair next to her and she flashed him a look she hoped transmitted *don't stray too far*.

"Fashionably late for maximum impact." Faye leaned closer as Liv watched Nate drift over to Will. "How'd the dress go over? Fabulously, judging by the way my brother's looking at you."

Liv glanced at Dean on the fringes, towering over Emilie's bug rider date, Jordan Cooper. Dean's eyes dropped abruptly.

"Ooooh, I saw that." Emilie seemed to appear out of nowhere, all bright and flushed and pretty, like some alien thing Liv could never believe was related to her. "You are so right, Faye."

"Of course I'm right."

"Right about what?" Liv said, feeling lost, which was not all that unusual with Faye and Emilie.

"I think we need some drinks, don't you?" Faye spoke up, looking pointedly at Nate and Will.

They obediently excused themselves, Nate throwing Liv an apologetic look.

"You already know my brother's had a thing for you forever." Faye said, Emilie crowded in close beside her.

"Stop saying that," Liv scoffed. She'd never actually believed it. But the way Dean had averted his eyes…*just, please, no?* Why was she so bad at picking up on these things?

Faye continued her rambling. "I'd somehow forgotten how good Nate looks in a tux. If you don't make something of tonight I don't care, I'm leaving Will and going after him again. You've had your chance."

"Faye!" Emilie gasped.

"I'm kidding!"

"I did consider staying at the house and having my way with him," Liv quipped.

"Sure you did." Faye patted her arm. "I'm beginning to think you are hopeless."

Liv welcomed the wine Nate set in front of her as he settled next to her. So much for avoiding alcohol. His glass looked suspiciously like Perrier.

"Just so there's no question you know I'm driving home," he breathed in her ear.

The wine was going down too quickly; they needed to open up the buffet. She reached for Nate's glass as he eyed her appraisingly. Liv gave him her best attempt at a demure smile, taking a sip — yes, Perrier — and placing it back in front of him.

In reality the buffet was wasted on her, her salad merely picked over. Nate's plate didn't look much different. Faye couldn't even tempt her with cake. It was almost a relief when the music started up.

"I really wish we could have had you guys play," Emilie said, looking at Will. "I guess we'll have to wait until tomorrow." Will and the rest of the band would be setting up after the race for a repeat of last year's Plate Party performance — exact location to be determined.

Nate reached for Liv's hand. "Dance?"

"Do I have a choice?" She smiled as he lifted her to her feet. There was no point resisting, though when she got out there she realized she hadn't drunk nearly enough wine.

Nate found her eyes, locking them in, his palm on the small of her back anchoring her. "You really need to lighten up."

"Why did you want to do this, Miller?" she asked.

He didn't respond right away, not going with the obvious reply — the one she was trying to tell herself, that they had to be here.

"We're good at the day-to-day stuff. It works. And that's great. Last thing I want to do is mess that up. But…sometimes you just have to go out of your comfort zone. And I hope you don't think I've got any sort of agenda here. It's not like that." He met her gaze, and he didn't have to explain what he meant. "I never went to my high school formals. I guess I thought I was too good for that, with my older girlfriend, or that she'd think it was juvenile."

He hesitated, the not-quite-ghost of Cindy in his words, Liv feeling the sorrow waft over him. She moved her arm further up his shoulder, bringing them closer, feeling him inhale before continuing.

"I guess I'm a bit of a romantic, and I feel like I missed out. And you and I…we're around each other all the time. I wanted to do something… memorable. That probably sounds stupid, seeing as you find the whole thing tiring. But this is how it should be done."

"So you're asking me to buy into the fairytale?"

Nate laughed into her neck, heightening her awareness of every part of him. "Don't go all cynical on me, Liv. You'll ruin it."

The band drifted into the next song, and her laugh helped release some of the tension. "So you stacked the band, too? You are too much, Miller."

Of course he sang it to her, with his adjusted lyrics. When she should have felt singled out, like a spotlight was on them — because everyone had to be hearing this; everyone had to know — suddenly it was as if the two of them were dancing alone, barefoot on a beach with the sand between their toes, ocean crashing in even time to the punchy notes of the piano.

"Oh-oh-livia..."

It wasn't exactly a slow song, and she didn't even care that he moved her around the floor, somehow keeping them from bumping into others as he crooned the lyrics in her ear. But unlike his video, this time his clear blue eyes were right in front of her, arresting her somewhere between terror and thrill. As the notes died away, he simply mouthed the final words, his lips hovering over hers, their bodies unmoving, still locked in their stance.

"May I cut in?"

The voice jolted Liv out of her trance. Nate looked stunned — but he stepped back and yielded to Dean's request, much to Liv's dismay. She took Dean's hand awkwardly, and watched as Nate stormed over to Emilie and scared away Jordan.

"What are you doing, Dean?" Liv asked, her voice quavering.

He didn't seem to know what to say, appearing as uneasy as she did. She was lost without Nate's fluidity to guide her. Nate stared daggers over Emilie's shoulder.

"Faye said it serves me right, keeping my mouth shut all this time," Dean said, finally.

All spring…they had spent so much time together, and she had thought nothing of it. "Don't, Dean. Please."

"I have to at least feel like I tried. But it's too late, isn't it?"

This is what she got for being lukewarm. For not — as Faye so indelicately put it — throwing herself at Nate. It wasn't perfectly clear yet what she felt for him, but she had to find out, and Dean — Dean was supposed to be her friend, not another complication.

"Serves me right," Dean said again, when she didn't respond.

Liv ducked away, dodging couples as she rushed to their table. She gulped her unfinished wine, spinning as someone touched her back. Relief flooded her when she realized it was Nate.

"I'll get some more drinks," he said, his voice remarkably calm compared to the hysteria she felt.

"Don't you dare leave my side." She clutched his arm and glanced over his shoulder, finding Dean almost where she'd left him in the crowd.

"I'll be right back," Nate promised. "With more wine."

"I don't need wine."

"I think maybe I do."

Em appeared in the space he left, and pulled Liv to a chair. "Good thing Nate's riding Dean's horse in the Plate tomorrow. He has to behave."

"Who has to behave?" Faye swept up, Will trailing on the ends of her fingertips. "The guys go for drinks? Why don't you go find them, hon?"

Will rolled his eyes as he caught the dismissal.

"Just Nate," Emilie said. "I don't know where Dean went."

"So?" Faye leaned in further.

"Nate," Emilie said.

"What did he do? What did I miss?" She looked at Liv hopefully.

"Oh, no such luck," Emilie said. "Your brother cut in on him on the dance floor, and Nate just about lost his shit."

"Where the hell was I?" Faye stood back, tossing her arms in the air. "Trust my brother to keep it to himself all these years, then pick tonight to make a statement. I'll straighten him out, don't worry."

"No, Faye. I know how hard that must've been for him," Liv said. "Don't make it any worse."

Faye shook her head. "This should make things more interesting, at least."

Liv didn't care to know what Faye meant. She didn't want interesting. She didn't need Dean revealing hidden emotions, or Nate feeling provoked when he was on Ride The Wave tomorrow.

He handed her a new glass when he returned, reaching forward and clinking not wine but another Perrier to it. His composure was unsettling.

"I thought you said this would be fun. This isn't fun," she hissed.

"I agree. I'm sorry, I was stuck," he said quietly. "You should probably be proud of me for not decking him."

"Or really disturbed that you thought about it?"

"Do you think we've fulfilled our duty and can get out of here now?"

"Can we? Please?"

He nodded, setting his glass aside and rising. "When I beat Liv tomorrow afternoon, I don't want any excuses that I kept her out late, so we're going to duck out of your party early, Em. Sorry." He hugged Emilie, and tapped Faye's elbow, then folded his fingers around Liv's to guide her out.

A full moon hung in a darkening sky that matched the dusky blue of the Porsche, and she was glad he was driving this time, everything spiralling in her mind. She listened to the lyrics of his chosen songs — words of promises and broken dreams — wishing she could know what he was thinking as his eyes remained fixed on the road. Probably resetting. Focusing on tomorrow. Because it's what they had to do, wasn't it? The Plate was too big a deal to let tonight's fiasco interfere.

They left the highway behind, skirting up the rural roads that led to the farm, until they were creeping under the familiar old maples that lined the lane. He turned off the engine in front of the house, and she waited as he walked around, because he would want that. He didn't meet her eyes when he took her hand, helped her out. Didn't touch her as they walked up the stairs, staying slightly behind her until she turned to face him. Then he was as close as he'd been that moment on the dance floor — before the spell had been broken.

It was easy to recast it, expand it, their lips entangling as she laced her fingers behind his neck and molded herself to him. She couldn't tell if the drumming she felt was his heart, or hers, or if they were just synchronized now.

She'd been naïve to think she could manipulate this thing between them to her liking, to control it like the volume on the Porsche's sound system. Had she actually expected them to continue as they'd been, with sweet caution like they really were teenagers? There was no safety here, no halfway, not anymore.

With measured breaths he drew back, while her own respiration was wildly erratic. His gaze drifted from her lips, to her hair, like he was committing her features to memory before settling unwaveringly on her eyes.

"I love you."

The words had been diffused in the song, separated from reality. His outright declaration robbed her lungs of their remaining air, the sincerity of them paralyzing. What a risk he was taking, saying them to her, the model of self-doubt, knowing full well she wouldn't reciprocate the sentiment. But it didn't seem to matter to him. Did he know her that well? Well enough to understand — and accept — exactly who he was dealing with, and be willing to ride it out?

"Please don't freak out."

There was humour in his tone, but his eyes revealed his fear. She concentrated on re-establishing her breathing, regulating her pulse, though she still couldn't speak.

"I should go." His voice was soft, steady. "Unless you're all right with me camping out on your doorstep till morning. Just to make sure you don't run away in the middle of the night."

She had to laugh with him, her forehead resting against his, amazed and grateful for his ability to find levity. When his arms fell away, she would have grabbed him to fill the chasm he left, if she hadn't still been frozen.

"See you tomorrow." And he stepped away.

Tomorrow. Somehow she had to arrange her thought patterns to align that tomorrow with the one that included riding in her first Plate — against him.

Inside, she didn't bother to turn on the lights, the glow of the moon through the windows enough for her to see her way to the sunken living room. She dropped to the couch, curling her legs underneath her, and stared out the sliding doors to the pale light dancing off the surface of the pool. The subtle fragrance of the rose reached her from where it rested on the table in front of her.

The front door opened, and Emilie came in, starting slightly when Liv turned in her seat.

"Hey, Em."

Emilie came down and sat next to her. "How was your date? Are you going to tell me what happened?" She paused. "Should I just leave you alone?"

Liv sighed, and looked out the sliding doors again. What had happened? Nothing…and everything. She needed to articulate it, not hide from it.

"He said he loves me, Em."

It should have been good news, joyful news, but Emilie's initial silence was an indication she knew it wasn't that straightforward for Liv.

"Wow." Emilie hesitated again. "That's incredible, Liv. Unless you freaked out on him."

Liv laughed, remembering Nate's own plea. "Remarkably, no. Not yet, anyway." She paused, inhaling. "How can I ever possibly feel the way he does, Em? He's so sure. I still can't come close to knowing how to do that, without giving up too much of myself."

Emilie's expression was sympathetic. "I don't know, Liv. I haven't had to work through that yet myself. But it will sort itself out. He'll wait."

"I think he's been waiting a long time already."

"Don't do this to yourself, Liv. Just this once, try to live in the moment, okay?" Em patted her leg with a parting smile.

How did that work, living in the moment? How did she stop her brain from rushing forward, predicting disaster, where she didn't do him justice, where he finally got fed up and threw up his hands in surrender to her inadequacies?

It would be easier to accept if he had just been interested in getting her into bed, but with Nate, it went so much deeper.

16

Sure, going to the Plate Ball would be safe. Keep him out of trouble. He'd let himself forget that nothing would be safe with Liv. She was conflict, risk, emotional danger, and he had thrown himself into her abyss, fool that he was.

He didn't regret it, though. He didn't care if she never loved him back, as long as she didn't leave, or send him away. There was a term for that, wasn't there? Yeah. *Bat-shit crazy.*

Ironically, he was scheduled to work one for Dean Taylor at six AM. What the hell had that been, last night? On the one hand, Nate had to hand it to the guy — he hadn't thought Dean had it in him. On the other, he needed to back off. One thing: it had triggered his own impulse to leave Liv with no doubt where he stood. Maybe he should have left it at the kiss. It had been a hell of a kiss.

Dean's assistant was in the worker's stall, putting on the bridle.

"Hey Nikki. Where's Dean?"

"In the office. He'll be out in a sec. I'll throw you up and you can take her a couple turns, if that's okay."

That was perfect. Not that he expected Dean to do anything but give him instructions, especially within earshot of his staff, but it would be easier to be businesslike once he was on a horse.

Dean greeted him blandly and walked out beside the filly in silence. *Good.*

The worker helped get him back in the right frame of mind — one that would prepare him to ride in the Plate in eleven hours. Dean seemed pleased with how the filly had gone, nodding quietly and confirming Nate's estimation of time with the clockers. Nate joined him in the office after he got off the filly. He had a while before his next commitment, so there could be some discussion of race strategy.

"Last night everything you were hoping for, Miller?"

I guess we're not past that. "It was a nice evening, for the most part," he said carefully. "How about we talk about your Plate horse instead?"

"How can I be sure your mind is really on my colt?"

Nate had to control the tone of his laugh. "Because it's my job? And did you ever stop to think this might work to your advantage? I know her colt. I rode him last year. And I know Liv. I know how she's got to ride this race to have a shot, and it works out perfectly for us. Your colt is more versatile. Elemental has a ton of speed. She'll get him to relax — she's very good at that. She'll try to force a false pace, and we're going to need to stay close, to keep it honest, unless someone else does. Your colt can do that, and still win. That work for you?"

Dean nodded, slowly. He looked satisfied, if not happy.

"We're both professionals, Dean. Trust me, when we get out there this afternoon, we're not going to be thinking about last night." He rose, hoping to pre-empt any more off-topic discussion. "I'd better get going. I'll check in at the end of the morning."

He had another one to work before the break, then was due to get on Feste. Feste had come out of his race perfectly, sharper than before, and Liv had decided to breeze him this morning — a surprising move, so soon after the race, but she justified it by pointing out how easily the colt had won his debut. She hadn't yet decided what his next start would be.

The Woodbine backstretch always vibrated on Plate morning, but this time the hum of it burned his ears and churned his insides as he arrived at the Triple Stripe barn. It had all seemed so right in the moonlight, but the rising sun was uncovering all his doubts.

He touched Chique's nose briefly after her rumbling nicker announced his arrival, and the filly started her *tap-tap-tap* on the mat when he continued past.

Liv was in the stall with the colt, tacking up. Nate found the bridle hanging on the door and brought it in, trying to read Liv as she accepted it, but she was clearly set in work mode. He couldn't take it personally. He needed to be the same.

He watched her right hand curl around the bridge of the colt's nose to hold the bridle, left hand quickly slipping a thumb into the corner of the soft mouth and guiding the bit into place. He should just wait outside, because standing here next to her wasn't helping him feel professional.

She glanced at him and smiled — a very careful, neutral smile.

"I'll take him a turn," she said, finishing with the throatlatch and making sure the bit was sitting evenly before she crossed and tucked the lines under the seat of the saddle.

Nate followed them out of the stall and leaned back against the cool metal door, staring up at the rafters, trying to refocus on breezing horses.

"Where's Rog?" he asked when Liv stopped Feste in front of him. He shortened both irons and tightened the girth a hole.

"Ponying one on the training track. We don't need him with these two boys."

Liv didn't speak as they rode out to the track, which wasn't really unusual, and Nate tried to force himself to think about anything but how close he had held her last night, and how distant she felt right now. He responded to casual greetings as they went through the tunnel to the main track, and pulled down his goggles as they began to back the two-year-olds up.

Liv's colt was a leggy son of Starway named Astronomical, winner of his first two races and prepping for a stake. The two colts galloped around from the wire, and started out together at the five-eighths pole. Nate let Liv get ahead on the turn, Feste running easily at his stablemate's shoulder, anticipating further instructions. Chique at the same age would have been pulling his arms out, or just plain running off with him to get past the other horse.

He waited until they were inside the eighth pole to ask Feste, only needing a short chirp to send the colt on and effortlessly past Liv's mount.

They eased on the backstretch, and Nate slapped the dark brown neck as they turned in. "Just a little preview of this afternoon for you." He grinned at Liv.

"Really." But she didn't look offended, because how could she, after how Feste had worked?

"He's the one."

"Let's hope so."

Business as usual.

Liv glanced at him as they headed to the off gap. "So…last night…"

The drone in his ears came back, the rawness of his bold statement staring him down. But she was bringing it up. And that tempered all the misfiring neurons, diluted the adrenaline — her being brave in her own way, by facing it head on.

"I'm sorry. It was a lot. We'll talk, okay?"

"Okay."

"Lunch tomorrow?"

"All right."

"Loser buys."

Liv laughed. "You're assuming one of us is going to win?"

"Actually, I'm quite confident I'm going to beat your ass. I just hope you don't hold it against me."

He left her bathing Feste while he dashed off to get on his next worker. When they saw each other again, over there in the room, they would be back to being opponents, vying for the same prize. He was good now. Which was a relief, because if he screwed up this afternoon, his credibility would go out the window.

THE WAY LIV looked at him as they strode out to the walking ring for the Plate said it all. There was no careful smile left over from last night, just a professional challenge from a skilled colleague; a warning that he'd better be on his game, or he'd be eating this morning's bravado.

Nate greeted Faye and Will with a cursory nod before turning to Dean. Not that there was anything new to say, just some awkwardness to wait through. He was glad when the riders up call finally came. Dean legged him up on Ride The Wave and Nikki led them away through the fashionably-dressed throng.

It was a big field — fourteen horses, lots of traffic. Elemental had the four hole, and Ride The Wave the seven. Neither of them had anything to complain about there. His colt warmed up perfectly, loaded quietly, broke flawlessly. *Textbook*. Nate smiled as Elemental surged to the lead, and no one went with him.

He would let Liv have her way up there for a while, though when it came to race-riding, she wasn't naïve enough to think he'd be ignorant of her plan. Ride The Wave sat fourth first time past the grandstand, three-wide and out of trouble.

Nate let the colt accelerate around the clubhouse turn, fighting overconfidence as things unfolded just as he'd predicted. Liv glanced over at him when Ride The Wave appeared at her elbow. She smiled — and just sat there.

So you're gonna be like that. He flashed a grin back.

Liv didn't offer to go faster; in fact, she almost imperceptibly slowed Elemental, forcing Nate to make a decision. This wasn't Chique he was on — he had to remember that. Ride The Wave was talented, but relatively inexperienced, and not in the same league as his Cheeky. Going on with the colt wasn't really an option — he might as well hand Elemental the race right there. He had to hope staying up here with the slow pace wouldn't leave his colt flat-footed when the time came to turn on the heat in the stretch. He continued to let Elemental lead the way, and wondered if anyone behind these pedestrian fractions would be able to fool both of them.

Elemental remained perfectly relaxed under Liv's hold as they entered the final turn, when Nate would have expected Liv to be increasing the tempo. *Damn*. Ride The Wave was bored now, and getting distracted, ears flickering ahead to the big white tent, loaded with screaming voices. Nate smacked him once with the whip to get his attention, and Ride The Wave switched to his proper lead and surged to the front.

Elemental didn't take up the chase. There was no way that colt was done; Liv had to be playing mind games with him. But…*don't look back*. Ride The Wave's ears flipped forward again at the swarm of bodies on the apron, and he started drifting out.

He was going to have to drag all the potential out of this green colt. When Elemental came back on along the rail, Nate swore Ride The Wave was waiting for him. Liv's whip remained quiet — *how could that even be, mid-stretch?* Elemental drew even and hooked Ride The Wave.

Now Liv was extracting everything from her colt, Elemental refusing to back off, fighting bitterly with Ride The Wave. Nate cracked the whip once, twice, on the bay's hindquarters before doing some willing of his own with hands and voice, counting on his colt's basic instinct now to run; prove he was stronger, more courageous than his foe.

At the wire though, there was none of the uncertainty that had followed in those moments last June when Chique had staggered through the final strides, exhausted by her Herculean performance. Nate glanced over at Liv, both of them standing in the irons as their colts coasted past the clubhouse.

Liv looked back at him, wryness forced through the disappointment in her smile as she stretched out an arm to bump his fist.

"Just remember everything comes in threes, Miller."

He laughed and knew exactly what she was talking about. Same time, same place, next year — with Feste.

Liv leaned against the cool of the metal door, Chique and Feste picking the alfalfa from the timothy in their haynets on either side. There were people on the lawn, a Plate party in progress even in defeat, Roger doling out beverages from his usual post by the ice bucket. She watched the Porsche pull up at the end of the barn, Nate emerging, cleaned up in that same old navy suit he always wore. He could probably afford a new one, now. He quite possibly owned that tux he'd worn last night. She couldn't sustain her gaze as he approached, visions of that moment on the doorstep flitting left and right behind her eyes.

"Congratulations, Miller."

There hadn't been opportunity to put her arms around him like this after the race. He'd been detained, swept up in the revelry, parading the winner in front of a sea of photographers, gold and purple blanket of flowers draped over his knees, instead of hers; Ride the Wave's withers instead of Elemental's. By the time he'd been free of the media after the presentations, she was ready to ride the last race. At least she'd won that.

He wasn't content with a hug, his lips finding hers. "You scared me," he said.

"What, out on the racetrack?" She smirked.

"Well, yeah, but just now, more so. Why'd you leave like that?"

She looked down, arms dropping back to her sides as she took a step away, turning towards Feste and Chique. Because she had. She'd driven past the Northwest barn first. Seen him there, with Dean, who seemed to have forgotten last night's drama now that the offending party had won him a Queen's Plate.

"I don't know. Too many people, maybe." She let Chique nuzzle her hands while Feste craned his neck over the screen next door. "It was more fun last year." She looked at him sideways, one corner of her mouth turning up.

"You owe me lunch, remember."

"I guess I do. Though you're the one who made all the money this afternoon."

"You did make it pretty interesting."

Chique nibbled her net, keeping one eye on both of them in case they came up with treats. A year ago they'd stood here after the filly's win. It had taken twelve months for things to shift again as powerfully as they had that evening.

"I don't know what happens next, Nate. I'm not going to run away… but I'm not where you are. The way things ended last night was probably inevitable…but it still knocked me sideways."

He was close now, his back to Feste, a hand reaching to Chique by proxy maybe, like he was afraid to touch her in case she did bolt.

"I'm sorry. I mean…don't think I didn't mean it. And it's not like it just happened last night, like it just hit me, that I'm in love with you." He hesitated, the intensity of his gaze too much for her to take full-on, so she watched his hand instead, Chique's lips rubbing insistently like she could conjure up the peppermint he couldn't possibly have forgotten. "The timing was probably wrong. I let Dean get to me. But with everything that's happened this year…I was banking we'd come far enough you wouldn't panic on me, and would at least give me a chance to remind you nothing's changed."

"Everything's changed," she insisted, eyes matching the force of his, direct enough to keep him from countering. "But I know all the effort now has to be mine. And I am prepared to make an effort."

"Sometimes you have a way of making what might otherwise be touching sound so clinical." He slid his free arm around her waist to kiss her gently.

She drew in a breath, fingering the lapel of his jacket. Chique bumped her elbow like she was saying, *would you get on with it girl, so someone can get me a candy?*

"I think I get it now, what you've been saying all along. I know how much I've stalled about the two of us, but you know me, Miller. I'll never stop overthinking. There will always be some excuse. And then some disaster will happen, and this, *us*…it'll be gone too."

"You kind of live in a world of impending doom, don't you? I'm officially worried now."

Chique snorted in resignation, burying her muzzle in her haynet. *If you're going to continue to put this poor man through hell, I'll be over here when you're done.* He did look genuinely scared, prompting Liv to forge ahead.

"I want to take both Chique and Feste to Saratoga. I might be throwing Chique back into the thick of things, but there's a nice little turf stake there for her. The same day there's one going three-quarters for Feste. If he turns out to be everything you keep saying he is, we'll consider sticking around for the Hopeful."

He exhaled, a look of wonder taking over his face. "Wow. Okay."

"You know Don always ships some horses from Belmont with Jeanne. She has a house there — you might remember that." She frowned, wading through that memory. She could certainly say Nate had seen her at her worst. She hoped her best was yet to come. "We could stay with her."

"We?"

"Well, you could just fly down for the races, if you want."

"You're serious."

"You'd have your own room," she said, lips twisting.

"I don't know what to say. You're sure?"

"You can think about it. You might be giving up the riding title at Woodbine if you come." The jock's community at Woodbine was competitive enough that someone — like Cory, who was on her way to establishing herself as the season's hot apprentice — could rack up a lead in the standings that would be hard to top.

"Is this a test? Like, am I supposed to be thinking of my career here?" He grinned. "Give up the title at Woodbine…but ride at the Spa with you? I think I'd be crazy to turn that down. I'm assuming we'll both have to get to the Fort for a rematch of today in the Prince of Wales, but…hey, here's to Saratoga."

He raised an imaginary glass, and she obliged by meeting it with one of her own, their knuckles touching.

"What's the matter?" she asked.

"I'm just waiting for the catch."

"No catch. Leave the paranoia to me. I've got plenty enough for both of us."

"You could work on that, you know." He used it as another excuse to brush her lips with his. "Come on. I can hear the band starting up over at Dean's. They might need me. I'm a much better singer than Will."

17

"We made it, baby."

Nate grinned at Chique once she was settled, putting a hand on either side of her muzzle and planting a kiss between her nostrils. Feste took in the tranquil rows of viridian barns and terra verte trees with his usual class, helping himself to a drink from his bucket to test out the local water before tearing into his haynet.

Nate touched Chique on the nose before sauntering over to Liv and Jeanne. "I'm not going to want to leave."

"Welcome to Saratoga," Jeanne said. "No one ever wants to leave."

"You keep absorbing that atmosphere, Miller." Liv took one more look at Feste and Chique to convince herself they were fine. "I'm heading to the house for a shower."

"Right behind you," he said, but he wasn't. Not yet. He was going to give her a head start, and do just as she said: soak this up.

Jeanne crossed her arms and leaned against the rail. "So, you and Liv. How's that going?"

His lips twisted in a crooked smile. "Very cautiously."

"The winter didn't knock any sense into you, I guess. A little more complicated now that she's back riding. A whole lot of juggling there."

"Nothing I haven't already been dealing with in my career so far."

Back when he'd first started galloping at Woodbine and working daily with Liv, he'd told himself it was a bad idea, but he'd gone and done it anyway — gotten involved.

"Married to Triple Stripe, eh?"

He choked on a laugh. Liv wasn't ready to wrap her head around love, let alone the future. Wait — Jeanne was talking about the job. *Easy, Miller.*

"You sure don't like to pick easy spots, do you, Nate?"

"You're the first one to put it that way."

"Well, you let me know if I'm cramping your style around the house. I can make myself scarce."

He was kind of counting on her being an inadvertent chaperone, but he didn't say it out loud, pulling his keys from his pocket. Chique rumbled. *Yeah, of course I've got mints for you and your brother in there too.* "You need help feeding this afternoon or anything? I could come back."

"You're a rider, Nate. We let the grooms do their jobs around here. Go."

He vaguely remembered the way to the house — and more clearly remembered the time he'd been there, uninvited. A different picture greeted him this time when he pushed through the door from the garage that opened into the living room.

Liv, wearing shorts and a loose t-shirt, damp hair falling around her shoulders, standing by the counter with not a wine bottle in sight.

"Are you proud I left of my own accord?" she asked with a wry smile.

He grinned, kicking off his shoes and leaving his bag by the door to step up into the kitchen. "Right. You just didn't wait for Jeanne to chase you away like she did me. I know what she's like now too, you know. California doesn't make her any softer."

She didn't move away when he put his hands on her waist, resisting the temptation to slide them under her shirt, seek the smooth skin over the muscles of her back. He could think of a lot of things he wanted to do, but just kissed her and put his arms around her, breathing her in as she nestled against him — which was pretty incredible by itself.

"Do you think we'll pull it off?" he murmured into her neck.

She didn't try to deflect his question, or ask if he was talking about them, or success with Chique and Feste. "Guess we'll have to find out."

This was about more than the next week, or however long those two horses kept them in Saratoga. Complicated. Everyone kept saying it was complicated. But he was determined that it wouldn't be, if he was careful.

Nate didn't wait for a leg up, hopping lightly onto Chique in the middle of the shedrow.

"That's still the reigning Canadian Horse of the Year there, Miller," Liv called, settling into the tack on Feste after Jeanne had helped put her there.

"And she's still fifteen hands with shoes on." He knotted his lines and tucked his feet into the irons, slapping Chique on the neck as she began her march.

Liv had to smile. The two of them were still her idea of hashtag *relationshipgoals*.

"I'd say 'lead the way,' but she seems to have other ideas," he quipped once they were off the shed, Chique passing her brother like she knew where they were going.

"Have you broken it to her that she doesn't get to gallop today?"

With that reminder, he dropped his irons a few holes for security. Just because they only intended to let the pair stretch their legs with a walk around the grounds didn't mean Chique would be on board with that plan.

The equine traffic crossing Union Avenue this time of morning was heavier than that of the cars on the road, security monitoring and directing as needed. Chique assessed her surroundings alertly, unsure enough of where she was that she had to listen to Nate and keep an eye on Feste. The colt strode out boldly. Chique shuddered with a sigh, and dropped her head level with his.

"He's no fun, is he?" Nate tweaked the top of her crest, and Chique lifted her neck into his touch, shaking her head and dancing. Of course Nate couldn't just let her chill.

There was a timelessness to the Saratoga backstretch, the ritual one largely unchanged in the last hundred years. Grooms bathed their charges; hotwalkers turned left around the walking rings with steaming horses, stopping every few circuits to allow sips from water pails set on overturned buckets. Sheds were dressed up with hanging planters, hand-washed white flannel bandages hung alongside to dry.

The gallopers on the Oklahoma training track captured Chique's attention, her head flying up again. The filly started to jig, bumping into Feste.

"Tomorrow, filly," Liv promised.

They crossed back over Union Avenue, following the horse path around the outside of the main track, the shade of the trees scattering the morning light over the horses' coats. Liv glanced at Nate, then Chique, then Feste. There was hope here. So much good.

"Let's let them have a little jog around Clare Court. Her reward for not tossing you."

He laughed, scrubbing Chique under her twisty mane until she was on her toes again. "There's still time for that."

Clare Court reminded Liv a little of Woodbine's "field," just with more trees, and nestled within the heart of the backstretch instead of on the outskirts. The steady cadence of their horses' hoofbeats — Chique being remarkably compliant — added to the peace she felt, the sense of all being right in her world, at last.

Chique seemed satisfied when they pulled up, walking home full of happy snorts. Both horses would work over the track on Wednesday, a final old-school blowout before race day Saturday.

"I didn't think you were going to come back." Jeanne met them in front of the barn, Chique's halter in hand.

"Where did you think we'd go?" Nate quipped. "Isn't this the happiest place on earth?"

"I thought that was Disney."

"Same thing really, right? All the magic; where dreams come true."

He dropped to the ground, and threw a glance over his shoulder, catching Liv's eyes with a grin that made her believe.

In the haze of early mist that hung over the main track, Liv closed her fingers possessively around the strip of leather that connected her to Chique. The filly was sharp, there was no question. She didn't have to say anything to Nate for him to know he needed to be careful, not exploit that readiness. She probably didn't need to take him to the pole, but she did, of course, controlling whatever she could for as long as she could.

Chique shot away from the pony, dropping to the rail, but she was a different horse now, with maturity befitting the big sister. He didn't have to maintain a stranglehold to keep her pace steady as she swept into the stretch, though he didn't dare open his mouth, or she would have been gone. With his slight release inside the last sixteenth, Chique took advantage, seamlessly lengthening her stride. It would be the bullet — fastest three-eighths of the day — he was sure.

Liv didn't speak when they met up again on the backside, so if she thought it was too fast, he didn't know. It wasn't as if he could take it back now anyway. Chique had needed that; that last bit of speed to tighten the screws just so. Now she was ready for her comeback.

Next was Feste. *Just go easy*. Nate had never needed the pony to break the colt off before, but yeah, no point reminding Liv of that. When she freed them, he crouched, Feste putting down twelve-second furlongs as naturally as breathing. Just a kiss, and the colt would give him an explosive burst reminiscent of his sister, but that could wait till Saturday.

He didn't let Liv stay silent this time. "Okay?"

She nodded. "They can both gallop a little tomorrow, though. No days off, or we'll be rebuilding that barn."

Nate ran a hand over the colt's dark neck, the humidity an added layer on Feste's slick coat, damp after the effort, though he was barely breathing hard.

Liv's seriousness had started to rub off on him. One thing, it made it easier to stick to his resolve not to push the physical side of their relationship. That, and pounding the pavement in his running shoes for a few miles after dinner — alone.

Restless. Liv couldn't keep her nerves where she needed them, too many thoughts about the next day's card flying around her brain to focus properly on this one.

She didn't know. Didn't know if being here was the right thing for

Chique. Starting back at Woodbine would have been much easier. Feste, though, deserved to be here. Tomorrow he would prove it.

She was having a terrible afternoon. Her best ride was in the last, but Nate came out of nowhere with a longshot to nail her at the wire. Now that it was over, at least, her mind was free to run wild.

She stood beside him in the jock's room to watch the replay.

"Sorry, boss." A mid-afternoon downpour had left the track muddy, the outline of goggles creating a mask of clean around his eyes, his teeth looking especially white against the dirt spattered on his face.

"That's okay, Miller. Just keep that momentum going for tomorrow, all right?"

"Absolutely."

His confidence sparked boldness in her, and she thumbed some sand off his lips and kissed him. The way it wiped off his grin, changing it into something between amazement and shock, made the background chorus of whistles worth it.

"See you back at the house," she said, pulling off her helmet and kerchief and dragging the elastic out of her hair as she headed to the women's change room to shower.

She dressed dutifully in a navy print skirt and white silk tank top, brushing her hair back into its ponytail because drying it was too much work. It felt like a chore sometimes to maintain a professional image — one of those things Geai had insisted was important — especially on a night like tonight when she couldn't get out of here fast enough.

The grounds had quickly emptied out, only stragglers and clean-up crew remaining. A few tailgaters packing up their chairs and coolers noticed as she scooted under the administrative building's overhang, and she signed a couple of autographs. She didn't mind it so much anymore, was used to it, but just the same, was relieved to reach the refuge of her car. She and Nate probably could have shared the driving most days, but in some way, arriving and leaving in her own vehicle preserved some vestige of her independence. Silly maybe. Important, still.

Baked fish and a salad — honestly, it was like she was learning to cook. Nate usually made dinner for all three of them, and while she knew part of the reason he did so was because he had to be more careful about his diet than she did, she felt guilty always leaving it to him. And tonight, she needed something to do while she waited.

Table set, a couple of wine glasses on the counter…the bottle he'd promised to pick up would help take the edge off. She hoped he came home with it soon.

Home. It kind of made her shudder. Preparing this meal, however basic, was altogether too domestic for her. But…she was making an effort. And she wanted to, because he had said things, big things, and while it was still all scary, she didn't want it — him — to go away.

The door from the garage creaked when it opened, and Nate dropped his jacket over the back of a chair and set the bottle of red on the counter next to the glasses — then kissed her, the astonished look she'd left him with in the jock's room toned down to amusement.

"This looks dangerous. Where's Jeanne?" He reached into a drawer for the corkscrew.

"Don came up this afternoon, so she's having dinner with him and one of the owners."

A glass *now* was more important than letting it breathe, so Liv picked up the open bottle and poured. She didn't wait for him as she took a sip.

"Cheers." He crossed his arms with a smirk.

"Sorry." Liv looked sheepishly over the glass, but took another swallow.

"Are you really that worried about tomorrow?" He picked up his own glass and carried the bottle to the table.

"Apparently." She wasn't riding tomorrow, and needed to sleep tonight. The wine would help. It was straightforward.

"They're both doing great. It'll be fine."

Always reassuring, and always right. Was it pathetic she needed that? It was probably better to latch onto his positivity than the alcohol.

Liv forced herself to follow the unrelated discussion, every now and then shrinking from a look that let her know he wasn't fooled by her feigned attention, that his nattering was his way of calming her like he would a young horse She made the second glass of wine last, proud that there was still some left in the bottle when Nate started to clear the table.

"Thanks for dinner," he said, filling the dishwasher while she was content to watch. "I'm going to get out of this suit."

Maybe dressing as she had had taken effort, but changing seemed like more so now, when she'd probably be in bed in an hour. Liv eyed the bottle, and emptied what was left into her glass. The wine had done enough she didn't feel inspired to pick up the novel sitting on the coffee table. She turned on some music instead, settling on the couch, letting the melody lull her.

Nate returned with his running shorts on, carrying his t-shirt. Liv would no longer claim immunity to the clear cut of his muscles under smooth, lightly tanned skin, no fat getting in the way of their definition. He left the t-shirt on the armrest and came around behind the couch.

"Not something else you're good at, Miller," she murmured, letting her eyes close as his thumbs worked her traps, so tight they'd been close to seizing up.

He may have intended for it to be relaxing, but it triggered an element of intimacy she knew he'd been avoiding. She dropped her chin and tried to separate herself from it, then thought, why? Faye seemed to be able to remain detached when it came to sex, why couldn't she? It was, after all, just basic biological impulse, wasn't it? She had a rational, logical mind that thrived on science. It was the psychological aspect that messed people up.

He stopped and leaned over to kiss her softly on the neck, then reached for his t-shirt. Liv snatched the shirt away from him, dropping it on the floor, and curled her fingers around his wrist. She needed a distraction from thinking about tomorrow; maybe attempting her first seduction was a worthwhile one.

If she dissolved the physical barrier and proved it was just an evolutionary, hormone-driven exchange — leaving the emotion out of it — she'd be further ahead. Still in control. Power, Faye would call it.

Faye's voice niggled. *We both know you'd never throw yourself at him.*

Faye knew nothing.

But while Faye might have scoffed at Liv's lack of confidence, she'd also played the role of big sister and made sure Liv was prepared for the possibility. Saratoga, together…anything could happen, right? No excuse there.

Nate grinned as Liv dragged him down. It wasn't as if they'd never made out before, so he was allowed to be unsuspecting. His hands went to her waist as she slid closer, arms slipping to his bare shoulders. He tasted like minty toothpaste as she kissed him, while her own mouth was no doubt reminiscent of wine and fish — *ugh.* He didn't seem to mind.

She made herself aware of the strength of his back, feeling him flinch as her hands drifted to his obliques and returned to his shoulders. Those shoulders and arms were capable of containing the energy of a speed-driven Thoroughbred — holding it, guiding it, extracting every ounce of effort from it — but so were hers. When she laced her fingers through the softness of his short hair, he deepened the kiss, and she told herself not to back off, to enjoy rather than fear the unknown. *Mind over matter.* The music faded into the background, a soundtrack to someone else's story, aiding her ability to feel displaced.

He pulled her on top of him, like he'd picked up on the control thing and was willing to give that to her. All of a sudden her newfound assertiveness started slipping away — *what am I doing?* She tried to hide it when his eyes locked onto hers, battling with her uncertainty as he slid the elastic from her ponytail, her hair falling loose, still damp, into her face. She closed her eyes, concentrating on what should be instinct. She could be someone else, someone who fingered his collarbone, ran a hand over his chest, smiled as she admired the firmness of his abdomen beneath her palm. She could name each muscle group — keep it scientific, a study of the human form. His hand grazed the back of her thigh beneath her skirt and she fought the flight response, still so close to the surface, hoping he would misinterpret the tension in her body for arousal — not that it was completely absent by any stretch, but the conflicting parts of her brain weren't totally in harmony. The tips of her fingers reached the edge of his shorts.

His hand snapped to her wrist, arresting it there, and she flew to the end of the couch, feeling caught like a naughty child, as he rolled off. He was on his feet before she blinked — pacing like a caged animal, silent and not particularly friendly.

When words finally came, his voice was strained, the heel of his hand pressing into his forehead. "What is this, Liv? This isn't you. You need to stop letting Faye Taylor get in your head."

Flush crept up, heating her cheeks. He couldn't know her that well. Except he did. He'd seen right through her.

"I don't want this, not right now. You don't need to be anyone else. I love you. Damn it, I want to marry you." He glanced away. "You're going to have to figure out if you feel the same." He scooped up his t-shirt and pulled it over his head, all but diving for the door. "I've gotta get out of here."

Her heart found a new tempo, testing the boundary of her chest.

This was not how this was supposed to go.

He was dripping, the humidity so close he'd broken a sweat in the first strides — though he hadn't been far from that anyway. His running shoes crunched furiously over the gravel on the road's shoulder, skittering a step when he hit a rock. This was stupid. He should turn around. It made no sense to get whacked by a car in the dark and end up dead in a ditch.

A flash of lightning lit up the darkening sky, the crack of thunder on its tail a little too close for comfort. When the rain caught up, it came in sheets, soaking him to the skin.

True to form, he had overreacted to the night's bizarre development and thrown it all out there. Hey, love? Why not marriage? If anything could make Liv run, it was that.

He should have just gone with it. It wouldn't have been hard. He'd have put money on her backing off. Her defences would've kicked in before they got anywhere crucial. But it moved the line, changed the boundary, set the stage for next time — if there was a next time.

What if he backpedaled? Eased off on his initial conviction? That would be so much easier. No one waited anymore. It's not like he had before.

But his history stuck its tongue out at him. Sleeping with someone just seemed to scare them off. So this time, he was holding out, like some kind of twenty-first century freak.

Jeanne was sitting at the kitchen table and looked at him strangely when he came in, saturated. Liv was gone.

"Nice evening?" Jeanne asked.

He laughed abruptly. *Chaperone. Right.* "Yeah. You're fired."

It wasn't really sleep, the state from which he grappled to regain consciousness — more like someone was holding him just below the surface, not letting him come up for air. He crawled groggily out of bed. He had to catch Liv before she left. He should have knocked on her door last night, just to say something…something that might make him feel better.

No such luck. The house was empty, the Porsche the only car left in the driveway. This day…this day was already too long.

Chique stood tacked up on the wall when he got there. He cocked an eyebrow — he'd just assumed both runners would walk — but willed it back to neutral when Liv emerged from the tack room with a bridle.

She faltered — just a step — then dropped her eyes to the sandy shed, brushing past him into the stall. The air he sucked in to catch his breath was full of her, the memory of her on top of him flooding his senses, sending them haywire. He ducked in behind her, reaching for her arm before she made it to Chique's head.

"Listen, Liv, I'm sorry."

"You didn't do anything wrong." Her tone was flat as she broke free of his grasp, unsnapping Chique from the wall, slipping the lines over the filly's head.

"I did. I need to explain."

Her hands worked quickly, unbuckling the halter, looping it over her arm while she slipped in the bit and settled the headstall behind Chique's ears.

"We have to start talking, Liv."

"Not right now we don't. We can do that later."

"It's always going to be like that, isn't it?"

She stared him down, uncompromising.

He sighed. "Yeah. Of course. Later." He knew that. It was always later. After the Triple Crown. After the winter apart. Just when he'd thought they were finally working on *now.*

"You can get on her around the shed." She turned the filly toward the door, chasing him out. "I'll walk Feste."

Wow. He hadn't seen that…*veneer*…in a long time.

It was Jeanne who met him in front of the stall with Chique once he had his helmet and boots on. "Is one of you going to tell me what's going on?"

"Just throw me up."

Chique jigged down the shed once he was on, Nate letting his legs dangle while he snugged up the girth and knotted the lines. She seemed confused when he didn't direct her out to the track. They just kept going around and around, like the thoughts in his brain.

It was early yet, so he let her play, loose-lined, sometimes racing just shy of a canter with her head snaking all the while. It wasn't very long before the grooms working on the shed got angry with him, and he reeled her in and convinced her to behave. He tucked his feet into the irons and tried his best to think about anything but what was foremost on his mind, his energy wired into Chique's. He should be concentrating on this afternoon, Feste's race, Chique's post-laminitis comeback. Of course Liv was stressed. It wasn't as if he didn't understand that.

She was still walking Feste when he emerged from Chique's stall with the tack in his arms, the filly annoyed he hadn't left her with a flake of hay.

"I'll be back before I head over," he said.

Liv at least stopped in front of him, nodding. "All right."

That was it, nothing more. Getting away from her right now would be good. He had to get his focus back to riding. Screwing up those two races this afternoon would just compound the disaster.

FESTE LOOKED FABULOUS — the drizzle didn't do anything to diminish his lustre. He paraded confidently beside the stable pony, alert but relaxed. Nate reached across to stroke his sleek, dark, neck, and Liv pressed her eyes closed, trying to silence the words that swirled inside her head. Last night's declaration had made the Plate Ball seem like grade school.

Later. It was Feste's moment.

She let herself feel a touch of pride, even as the announcer botched Feste's French registered name: *Téméraire*. It was an accomplishment to get a Canadian-bred, especially a two-year-old, here. She wasn't alone in thinking he was the best colt in this field of very nice juveniles — the odds board reflected her opinion.

The horses broke off into their warm-ups, Nate taking Feste alone around the clubhouse turn, the starting gate waiting in the chute, six furlongs from the wire. Heavy dark clouds threatened more rain, but Liv hoped it would hold off until after Chique's race. Feste wouldn't care, but his princess sister might not appreciate it.

The start was clean, and Feste broke on top, Nate letting him stay in front, taking a gentle hold and settling the colt just out from the rail where the track would be firmest. Feste responded perfectly, showing sensibility Liv wasn't entirely sure Chique would ever develop.

Liv glanced at the tote board — for an off track, Feste was setting quick fractions. She wasn't concerned. After his morning times, splits like this were within the colt's ability. Longstreet crept up on his outside, staying close. *Enjoy it while it lasts*. Feste had gears.

Another colt gave chase, to the right of Longstreet — second choice, Market That. Nate let Feste maintain his pace, but wouldn't be coerced into going any faster. Neither rival offered to go by. The next tier bunched behind the three leaders.

Rounding the final turn, Nate still sat relaxed, the other two riders getting into their colts. Market That started to crowd, running a little green. Nate glanced over. Longstreet didn't like the pressure, his head going up, legs climbing. Feste's ears flicked forward, but the colt was only acknowledging the filled grandstand — something new and notable, but not enough to alter his course.

Then he swerved, connecting with the rail, tumbling into the mud like the ground had given way beneath him, Nate tossed over his head. The close-packed field was sent into a frenzy. Someone toppled and crashed over Feste; another leapt wildly. The rest somehow managed to avoid the pile.

Liv couldn't breathe.

Don had his phone pressed to his ear, dragging her with him, a frightened child terrified of what she'd find at the three-eighths pole. The crowd crushed on all sides, straining to see what was happening, oblivious to her dread. Their collective murmurs made her feel like she was in the middle of a hive, the drone of it filling her ears, its density suffocating her.

All the parts were in play before they reached the scene. Horse ambulance. Human ambulance. Tarp. Don made no attempt to stop her as she pushed past to her fallen colt.

The state veterinarian's words came from far away, only fragments making it through. *Can't be sure...aortic rupture...post mortem...*

Nate, unmoving, on a backboard.

There was nothing in her stomach — she hadn't been able to eat all day — and the force of her contracting diaphragm doubled her over. Don grabbed her as her legs buckled.

"Liv. You've got to go check into the room."

"What?" Her voice was reedy and foreign as she tried to straighten.

"Unless you want to pick someone else to ride Chique. Go. You don't need to watch this. There's nothing you can do. Chique still has to run."

She stared at him, then the slam of the ambulance doors jolted her back to — *Nate*. "No — wait."

Don grasped her forearms.

"Liv! Go. He's alive, all right? They say he's stable. By the time they get him to the hospital and actually know something, you'll be done with Chique. I'll call the stewards."

"I can't." All the times Nate had joked the only way she would get the mount on Chique was if he ended up in hospital. She didn't want it, not like this.

"Go!"

He sounded so callous. She didn't care anymore. It didn't matter if Chique ran, with or without her. But in a world that had spiraled so completely out of control in the last ten minutes, she needed a direction, and Don's words were the only thing on offer.

Mutters of sympathy met her in the room, but she tuned them out, shutting herself away in the women's area. She scanned the *Form* mechanically — not to size up the opposition, but to see who was available through exclusion. There were other, very capable riders who would jump at the opportunity to ride the filly, and given Liv's current state, would do a better job.

Nate's name kept leaping out.

She left the paper face down, because the cover article announced

Chique's return, a photo of Nate on her, winning the Mile — a race that carried more merit than the Plate on this side of the border.

It had to be her. Nate would never let her hear the end of it, would he? Nate, who loved her, wanted to marry her. She'd had no response for him last night, and refused to discuss it this morning, convinced it would wait. Her reluctance seemed so shallow now.

Breeches and stockings and paper-thin boots. Her hand froze on the red, white, and navy colours — the traditional ones, the silk-silks, while the day-to-day nylon ones were…where? Muddied from the spill, cast aside as the medics worked on Nate: assessing damage, attaching monitors, starting initial treatment.

A knock on the door jolted her back. It was time. She smoothed a clean kerchief over her hair, positioned her helmet, picked up her whip. Tried to shut out the noise in her head, because that's what she did. She was a professional, and that demanded she block out anything that might affect her ability to give her mount her best. Even this, impossible, thing.

When she stepped off the scale and handed her tack back to the valet, Ricky Acosta met her eyes, when no one else had dared, like he had been appointed spokesperson.

"Good luck, Liv."

His face was sincere, but luck had run out on her. The bullets had struck: one killed, one maimed. She needed more than luck. *Just let Nate be all right, and keep us safe*. Whether it was an attempt at positive thought, or a prayer, she didn't know.

The drizzle had turned to a more persistent downfall when the riders filed out to the paddock. Jeanne kept Chique under the shelter of the saddling stall, the groom playing with the filly's bit to keep her attention. The fat white shadow roll seemed fluorescent in the dimness as Chique swung her head, antsy at being asked to stand still. It took a moment for Liv to register that Don wasn't there. Jeanne must have put on the tack.

She refused to look at Liv at first. Both of them were adopting roles they hadn't planned on — Jeanne stepping in to saddle, Liv picking up the last mount she had ever really wanted.

"The turf is soft." Jeanne finally spoke, stating the obvious in an attempt to address the task at hand. She peered up at the dark sky as the rain came harder. It was a relief when the call for riders up came.

The downpour quickly soaked her in the post parade, and even though it was still warm out, Liv shuddered, chilled. She told the pony rider to let them go, and sent the filly off on her own. Chique didn't test her, galloping strongly but remaining manageable. They pulled up on the backside and turned in, both of them staring over the infield. Liv closed her eyes. Breathing in. Breathing out.

The pony met them to file onto the turf course, leading them up behind the gate and handing them off to the starter's assistant. Once they were in position, it was just her, Chique, and the lawn before them.

Chique flew out, Liv leaving her alone, waiting for feedback. The grass had give, but not too much. Chique, quick and catlike, skipped over it.

The others let her have the lead. Liv didn't have any illusions she'd get away with anything. No one was feeling sorry for her out here; any sympathy had been left in the jock's room. She shortened the filly's stride, conserving, but didn't expect to be left up here, dictating the pace, for long.

It was easy now to forget everything else — Chique absorbed it all. Liv hadn't felt anything like it since Claire. It was different in the mornings, even at speed — there was always something retained, held back, saved for the afternoon. While Chique was not in full flight, this was faster, freer, than any dawn trial. The best was reserved for the real test, when horses were matched against each other, and money and pride were at stake.

Around the clubhouse turn and coasting into the backstretch, they were still alone in front. Did the others think this pace, though slow, was enough in these conditions? Were they taking their chances, expecting the filly to tire? Or were the bigger, heavier horses just having more trouble than her compact filly? Maybe she was going to get a bit of luck today after all.

Chique powered through the final turn, relishing the inner course's tighter oval with something like authority — building momentum with strength Liv lacked. At the head of the stretch, the filly was in command with more left to give.

Grief hit Liv like a brick wall as they reached the spot where the accident had occurred, numbing her temporarily, leaving her deaf to the popping whips and riders' cries behind her. Chique pulled her past, rescuing her, and she left all of it in a little box somewhere in the corner of her chest.

Her hands and voice came to life, asking now, picking Chique up to keep her stride active when it might want to tire. The filly responded, ears laced back. Inside the eighth pole, twelve more seconds….

Beyond the awareness of Chique's exertion — each breath as she drew air into her lungs, oxygen into her bloodstream, blood to her heart — Liv was conscious of another horse. Like a train rushing up behind them, the rhythmic puffs of someone else, coming on. Chique pinned her ears and dug in, and Liv threw herself into the cause. She didn't look back. It didn't matter who it was.

The filly was dwarfed as her foe drew alongside, but Liv looked only at the green between Chique's ears and the pole that marked the finish. Another stride, another breath. Block out the dark image beside them, press on.

But somehow everything, every effort, all Chique's courage, wasn't enough today. A flash of light at the wire lit up for the photo the stewards would examine to determine the result, but Liv could have told them now, had they asked her. She stood in the irons, and for a strange moment felt as if she might fall, tumbling to the marshy turf beneath them. How easy that would be, if it could be like a dream where she never hit the ground. Maybe then she would wake up and find that's all this had been. She would go to the barn and find Feste waiting for her; Nate would show up and for once she would acknowledge they should talk *now,* because later might never be.

Liv galloped Chique back on the main track to the front of the grandstand. The groom and Jeanne were waiting, and Liv half-collapsed when her boots met the slop, falling against the filly. Chique sidestepped, agitated, as Liv's fingers fumbled to release the overgirth, then fought the billet under the saddle's skirt to unbuckle the girth.

Jeanne grabbed her arm. "Get out of here, Liv. Go to the hospital. You don't need to come back to the barn. We'll take care of Chique."

Or, she could just run away.

The version of Saratoga she'd climbed back from, those darkest of days when she'd fallen so far, and had done just that — run away — it closed back in on her now. They would take care of Chique, because she couldn't. What made anyone think she could do anything for Nate?

She had to get a grip. She had to go to the hospital, face what she might find there.

For better or worse.

That's what he was asking for.

She didn't shower, slipping back into her dress, the chill staying with her. Carrying an umbrella was more about hiding than shelter as she skirted through the crowd, finding her car under the staid old trees, leaves limp from the weight of the rain.

In the hospital parking lot she left the umbrella behind, letting the drops fall on her face, and drew her hands back over her braided hair to smooth it, but it was pointless. There was no hiding her distress. Just a moment, and she would go in. Geai's medallion felt heavy around her neck, not offering its intended comfort. *Ste-Anne, protector from storms.*

The triage nurse looked up as she approached, probably appearing like a prospective patient with her drawn and pale features, disheveled dress, arms hugged around her midriff.

"There was a rider — a jockey — brought in." She didn't expect they'd had any others. "Nate Miller."

The nurse nodded. "You are?"

"Girlfriend."

The knit of the nurse's eyebrows seemed to judge her — rightly so, because wouldn't a proper girlfriend have followed the ambulance?

"I'll call the doctor for you. You can have a seat."

It was a quiet emergency department, at least this evening: a mother and an uncomfortable child, another person holding a swollen wrist. The air conditioning made it freezing, a tremor beginning in her jaw that threatened to start her teeth chattering. She'd never thought to bring in her jacket. She wasn't thinking at all.

A doctor appeared only a matter of minutes later, scanning the room, catching her eye. It scared her that he'd responded so quickly.

She'd forgotten his name before he'd finished saying it, and his tight smile didn't reassure her as she pried her hand free from its grip on her elbow to shake the one he offered, his fingers much warmer and softer than her own. "Liv Lachance."

"I know who you are," he said.

She dismissed the comment, impatient. Apparently he was a racing fan, because why else would he know her? "What's going on with Nate?"

"What's your relationship? He's your boyfriend?"

Liv stopped herself from throwing her hands in the air. "Yes."

"What about family?"

"They're in western Canada," she snapped, exasperated. *Clearly I'm not enough.* "Are you going to tell me? I saw that spill. It was bad. He could have been killed."

"Then he got off lucky."

Getting out alive was the version of luck bestowed upon them today, but only in part, because Feste was dead.

She followed the doctor through doors, keeping up to his long strides, not letting herself feel any optimism until she had all the information.

"He was conscious when he got here. No internal injuries. He's broken his left clavicle, and a couple of ribs."

She could hear the unspoken *but...*

"We're concerned because he's experiencing paralysis below the waist."

The spinning started, and she had to reach for a wall. The doctor stopped short, but he continued talking.

"We did x-rays, and there are no fractures. We're going to have to wait until the inflammation reduces before we know more. Maybe that will be all it takes. In the meantime, we'll do more tests. All good news, really."

Liv wasn't sure Nate would see any of it as good news.

"In here." The doctor motioned to a doorway. "Let me know if you have any other questions."

A curtain was drawn around the bed, and all she could do for a beat was stare at it, her pulse throbbing in her ears. She glanced up at the doctor.

"Thank you," she managed, but it was so wispy, if he hadn't nodded, she wouldn't have known it had even been audible.

Liv could tell Nate wasn't sleeping, even though he didn't acknowledge her. She went around the bed, into his line of sight, and pulled the chair there to the edge, but it hurt too much to hold his gaze when it finally zeroed on her. Because what could she say? With the pain and uncertainty he was dealing with, how could she deliver any more blows?

"Did you ride the filly?"

She could nod. By comparison, it was the easy question.

"How did she run? Is she okay?"

"She's okay." That was the only positive news she had. "She got beat, Nate. Caught at the wire. But no excuses. She was game all the way."

His stare burned into her temple. "You have to tell me."

She shook her head, pressing her face into her hands, sucking air through her fingers. If only she could cry, curl up beside him…but he was too fragile, and she had nothing left, not even tears.

Distance would get her through this. She set aside the emotion, drawing on the person who'd be on her way to being a veterinarian four years ago. "They think it was his heart. Aortic rupture."

"Was anyone else hurt?"

She gave a short shake of the head, biting her lower lip before it started to quiver.

"Did the doctor talk to you?" he asked, finally, his voice toneless.

"Yes."

"What if they're wrong, Liv? What if this is it?"

She shook her head more assertively, sitting up. "We'll get you back to Toronto. My father has a good friend who's a surgeon. He'll be able to recommend a specialist. They'll sort it out."

She hadn't panicked when he'd told her he loved her; hadn't really even panicked last night when he'd put a thick and heavy layer on that, but now, seeing him like this, her anxiety was barely contained.

"I'll call him now." The chair scraped over the floor as she jerked to her feet. "And your parents. I have to go back and check on Chique — I'll update you in the morning."

The pressure in her chest made breathing seem impossible. What a horrible, horrible person she was, that she couldn't get over her own distress to sit by him. A fresh and clear reminder that she was incapable of being for him what he had always been for her.

When she reached the parking lot she broke into a run, drops streaming down her face when tears wouldn't. It wouldn't be much easier to go back to the track.

She walked to Chique's stall, past the empty one that waited, neatly bedded, for a colt who would never return. Chique rumbled in the darkness from behind her haynet.

Liv slipped in and put her arms around Chique's neck, pressing her face against the smooth, solid muscle of it. Chique pushed back, wrapping her head around Liv's torso, always in search of treats. How much could the filly sense of the day's devastation? Horses were such a highly social species. Racehorses spent so much time in relative isolation, their people a substitute for their own kind. The reverse was often just as true. This business was so all-encompassing, the horses were both co-warriors and friends.

She'd always thought equine bonds safer than human relationships, but today it was a toss-up, when her heart had been torn violently from her chest, scattered in pieces over the muddy racetrack.

18

And so it could happen, just like that. The life you knew, the one you told yourself you didn't take for granted — but did — could change, or disappear, for good. It was given, and it was taken away. Just like that.

Being back in Toronto didn't change anything. It was just bigger, and busier, with a world-class neurosurgeon and proper health care. He didn't let himself think about Liv. When he started to go there, things got dark in his head, fast. He would always be associated with the death of that beautiful, promising colt. There would be no redemption from that.

She had acted swiftly, facilitating the arrangements that had seen him transported to Ontario less than twenty-four hours after the injury, though he had yet to actually meet the specialist. On the outside, at least, Liv managed well in crisis — coolly taking charge to ensure the most favourable outcome — even if it was only a coping mechanism, her way of detaching herself. He envied her ability to separate herself from the barrage of feelings that had to be plaguing her, the same way they were him.

The door swung open, a cluster of lab coats gathering at the foot of his bed around whom he assumed to be the surgeon. Nate felt a bit better — at least it wasn't going to take all day to be seen by this guy. Liv slipped in behind them like she was late for rounds. She wouldn't have looked out of place in one of those white coats; hair pulled tightly back, smudgy shadows under weary eyes, her lips pressed together in grim focus. Nate, on the other hand, listened with about the same attention he'd give a TV medical drama. *How long till hockey starts up again?* All he wanted to hear was that they could fix him, and soon.

"I'll be back once we've got the results." The surgeon — Dr. Collier, he'd caught that much — nodded at Nate, and Liv ducked out of the way as he brusquely left the room with his entourage.

Liv glanced at Nate, a small, exasperated sound vibrating in her throat before she disappeared after them. He would have laughed if it weren't for his cracked ribs. Her reaction said it all — she was used to getting more consideration from the veterinarians she dealt with. He'd just sit back and let her do her thing — as if he had any choice.

She returned in a few minutes and sat next to the bed. "He wants to be a hundred percent sure there's no fracture, so he's ordered more diagnostics…but he still thinks it's probably just the inflammation causing pressure on some nerves."

"When are they going to do all this?"

"Hopefully this morning, but you know how hospitals are. Don't be holding your breath."

"Shouldn't it be just a little more urgent?"

"I'm sure if it was urgent, he'd be on it. If they decide they need to do surgery to release some of the pressure, they still want to wait till the inflammation's reduced. Time is a good thing here, Miller. You want to avoid surgery if you can."

"Did he mention surgery?"

Liv nodded.

"Were you going to tell me?"

"I just did, didn't I?" Her eyes flashed at him, not completely able to mask the hurt this time. *Nice job, Miller.* "I talked to your mother again last night when I got in. She's going to come."

There would be no stopping that, of course. His mother would be overwrought — it was probably killing her not to be here already. His father, on the other hand, would be grimly shaking his head in the background. *Great choice of occupation, son. Hell of a lot of good that Eclipse Award is doing you now.*

"Chique get back all right?" He made himself ask, to get away from the depressing subject of his condition — though it was all twisted together, a tumble of barbed wire that pierced his skin any way he tried to move.

"I haven't been in to see her yet."

That didn't fit. Nothing would take priority over Chique's welfare, for Liv — certainly not his sorry state. His first instinct was to make a smart-assed comment in his disbelief, but he managed to stop himself. "Don't you think you should have checked on her?"

"I followed the van from Saratoga and put her in the stall myself last night. All they have to do is walk her. I'm sure they'd call if something was wrong." She was back on her feet, halfway to the door, her gaze locked on the floor. "I'll call later to find out what's going on."

She hovered, eyes uneasily returning to him, maybe waiting for him to say something to stop her from leaving. But he just left it all there, in that messy mass of sidestepped emotions that simultaneously tied and distanced them.

He couldn't really blame her for wanting to bolt. Maybe she'd been right all along, and they weren't meant to be together, because if this was some kind of test, they were failing.

It was like the accident had left her heart paralyzed. There was no prospect of surgery to repair it, and she wasn't sure whether time would reduce that inflammation and bring the feeling back. There she was again, a horrible human, comparing her situation to Nate's. He was allowed to be a jerk, when she was being so remote.

She left the city, because she couldn't bear to go to the track. Seeing Chique would just remind her of Feste, his Woodbine stall emptier than the one at Saratoga, left that way out of respect. And there would be the inevitable questions about Nate. Jo and Em would make sure the filly was all right. There was nothing Liv could do to protect Chique. It didn't matter how right she tried to do everything, how much care she took. It could still blow apart, just as it had with Feste.

She didn't want to go home, either. She'd successfully avoided her mother, getting in late enough last night, and leaving early enough this morning, but that wouldn't last forever. She wasn't ready to endure her mother's concern, and again, the questions about Nate. Instead she found herself heading to Northwest.

There had been a time in recent memory she would have sought only solitude, today she needed Faye's ability to be no-nonsense but comforting without saying anything stupid. Of course, Faye would also drill her about what had gone on before the accident, and that would mean admitting what a fool she'd made of herself.

But Faye's vehicle wasn't there, only Dean's truck. It shouldn't be there, this time of day — he should still be at the track. Dean must've taken Faye's car into work to get it serviced for her.

The Porsche looked shiny and conspicuous next to Dean's dusty black pickup. She'd promised to drive the 911 back from Saratoga, leaving her own car behind, because heaven forbid anything should happen to the Porsche. She locked it in paranoia, even out here in the country.

The Taylor's Golden Retriever, Gus, bounded out the back door and across the deck, leaping off and shimmying up to her knees. She crouched and let him smother her face with his overly-enthusiastic tongue, burying her fingers in his thick ruff — a display of affection she could allow, when everything else was locked down. When she looked up, she saw Dean, towering from the first step with his hands in the pockets of his jeans, sad and awkward.

Liv shot to her feet, stepping backward. "I thought Faye might be here. I should go."

"Come on, Liv."

His tone stopped her mid-turn. Dean took the last step, reaching out slowly, and put his arms around her.

Liv let herself feel a shred of the grief and strain, setting aside, for now, the weirdness the night of the Plate Ball had inserted into a friendship she'd always valued. Maybe he held on too long, and she felt guilty for not stopping him, but she was so tired of pretending.

"Come in?" he asked.

She nodded, and followed him into the kitchen.

"Why are you home so early?" she asked. "Is everything okay?"

Dean opened the fridge and extracted a pitcher of orange juice.

"I had to be here for the vet — my manager had a couple of personal appointments today. Faye's having lunch with Will in the city. I think she was planning on going to the hospital. Thought she might see you there. You haven't talked to her?"

Liv shifted her attention to Gus, his big head resting conveniently on her knee. Faye was used to Liv being a bad friend, but not texting before showing up now seemed like a major oversight.

Dean splashed vodka over ice in glasses and topped them with juice, and planted one in front of Liv. Nate had served up the same drink after he'd told her about Cindy and Phil's accident, and she wondered if vodka and orange juice was a recommended tonic for times like this, or just something Nate and Dean held in common. She left the glass there. If she started drinking, there might be no end; the potential anesthetic effect was far too tempting.

"So…you holding up okay?"

The compassion in his voice made her eyes burn, and she bit her lower lip, reaching for the glass after all. She peered into the ice, but set it back down. "I don't really have much choice."

"How's Nate?"

She shrugged. "I'm sure he'll be a lot better when they sort him out. They're still doing tests."

"He'll be okay though, right?"

"That's what they expect."

She could talk about Nate, like a patient, careful not to let her confusion creep in. Nate had a right to be angry, and frustrated, but she would never have thought he would direct it at her.

"Do you think it's shaken him up at all?" Dean asked.

Liv choked back a laugh. "If you mean his confidence, no. I think as soon as he's walking and halfway right again, he's going to want to be back on a horse. Way before he should be. I get that. And I'll be glad of it. Or at least, remind me I should be, when the time comes, because right now, all this…" She finally took a swallow of the drink, the alcohol strong as it hit the back of her throat.

Dean hesitated. “The two of you, then. Is it for real?”

Liv looked at him critically, caught off guard by his timing and directness, his gaze a reminder that everything right now was wrong. She didn’t want this from Dean. She needed her friend back. And now that she was wondering what was going on in Nate’s head, she wished she could return to simple companionship. She’d been right about this romance stuff. It ruined everything.

“I don’t know,” she said. She’d thought it was. It was unraveling far too easily. “You and I were always the ones who wondered why everyone else put themselves through the hell of relationships.”

Dean settled into the adjacent chair, sizing her up like he knew a challenge when he heard one. “So why Nate?”

Liv sighed, pulling at the thickness of Gus’s soft ears. “I don’t know what to tell you. And it took a long time. He was ridiculously persistent.” The corners of her lips lifted, even if it seemed bittersweet now.

“That’s what I get for keeping it to myself all this time.”

She glanced at him, abandoning Gus to cup both hands around her glass. “I don’t know anymore if there’s any future to this thing with Nate. Maybe it was just a bad experiment on my part, a stupid attempt to be a normal person, and I’m really meant to be alone. And if that’s the case — and I have absolutely no problem with that — I don’t want to have lost two friends.”

She held his eyes this time, saw the words hit home, as hard as they’d been to find.

“All right. I hear you.” There was a trace of resignation on his face as he said it. “What are you going to do with Chique?”

She lifted the glass to her lips again and glanced away. It was a relief to get away from the personal stuff, but thinking about Chique right now was hard. “I haven’t even thought about it yet.”

“With Nate out, I need someone for Ride The Wave in the Breeders’.”

“Steve Gordon.” She didn’t want another of Nate’s big horses. Chique was guilt enough.

“I heard about Elemental. You know The Wave. Come breeze him in a couple of days. Winning the Breeders’ for me would go a long way toward easing the pain of you spurning me.”

"Fine." Liv met his smirk with her own, standing. "Let me know when."

She couldn't say no — fighting it would just sound absurd. Liv and Elemental had turned the tables on Nate and Ride The Wave in the Prince of Wales, but Elemental had pulled up sore in his last breeze. Not that the mile and a half of the Breeders' would have been the best spot for him anyway.

It wasn't even noon, and she was lost. She drove back to the farm, past the house to the small barn, and pulled up outside the side paddock. Claire nickered and ambled over, her distinctive roundness evidence of the life growing inside her in undaunted defiance to the surrounding catastrophe. Liv had been looking forward to this foal, a baby out of her rock by Chique's sire, Just Lucky, but now…now she was afraid to look forward to anything.

She ducked through the fence rails and slipped her fingers over the bridge of the mare's nose, pressing her cheek to Claire's, and tried to synch their breathing. Closing her eyes, she felt the first tear trickle down her cheek but brushed it away, and left Claire with a kiss on the soft skin behind her nostril.

The interior of the barn was cool, the door to the office unlocking with a click. She couldn't look at the painting of Geai this time, ducking under it to find the drawer with the spare key to Nate's apartment.

The air inside was still and stuffy, and she leaned against the door for a moment after closing it behind her, feeling like a trespasser. The piano was too silent, his guitar still in the back of the Porsche where she'd stashed his minimal belongings from Saratoga. She wandered around the room, taking quiet steps like she was afraid of disturbing something.

The photo of him with his two brothers and Cindy still rested on top of the piano, now accompanied by a smaller one that poked at her heart. It was from Florida, the winter Claire was three, when Nate and Michel had come to see her ride at Gulfstream, and the three of them had gone to eat afterward. It had been a joke, Nate dropping an arm over her shoulders, a shot Michel had snapped and posted on Instagram before she'd even known about it. A bit of fiction that had, in time, become reality. A reality that was breaking down.

His bedroom door was half-open, and she pressed it back, creeping in.

He'd left it neat, bed made, a couple of books on the nightstand. She crawled onto the bed, pulling out a pillow, and curled up, hugging it to herself and inhaling. It smelled like the old Nate; the one she'd last seen that moment she'd reached for his hand and pulled him down to her, unaware that less than twenty-four hours later, life would never be the same.

TESTS BROKE UP THE MORNING, but left him exhausted, which just added to his frustration. Lunch wasn't anything to get excited about. At least with the prospect of hospital food, he wouldn't have to worry about his weight. Not that he'd be riding any time soon.

Someone would be by to clear the picked-over meal tray — that seemed to be all he had to look forward to. Then Faye poked her head around the corner of the door. Nate laughed, and decided it was worth the stabbing pain in his ribs.

"Wow, I must be in bad shape for you to visit me."

"Ha ha," Faye said, wheeling the meal tray out of the way and chastely pecking him on the cheek. "I had lunch with Will, thought I might as well stop by."

"Where is he? My oldest friend can't even come see me in my darkest moment?"

"He had to go to work — couldn't get off. We weren't sure if we could visit this morning."

"Have you talked to Liv?"

Faye leaned her hip against the side of the bed, crossing her arms and looking down at him with a frown, picking up on the tension in his voice. "Just a text. She said she was going to have a nap and would catch up with me later. Which in true Liv form sounds all logical and healthy on the surface, but can't be trusted. I'm guessing she is not handling this."

"The two of us are like this massive black hole right now. It's just way too much grief in the same place. I can't take it."

"So, how were things going in Saratoga anyway? You know, before…this."

Nate squeezed his eyes shut, his mind going straight to that moment,

Liv being all daring and sexy, a bit of fun that had gotten bent so entirely out of shape. "It was great," he said quietly. "It was just starting to feel like we were finally getting somewhere."

"What happened?" Faye knew him too well. She hadn't missed that he was withholding.

"I'm not telling you, Faye. She has to be the one."

"Something did happen, then."

"She needs to talk to someone. She sure as hell won't talk to me."

Faye rolled her eyes. "Sounds like you're being altogether too dramatic. I know what happened to the colt is terrible, but why should that change what was developing between the two of you?"

"Why? Because I'm stuck in this hospital bed with more questions than answers, and she's running around all dark and tormented, chasing after doctors. I never really got to find out what she actually feels about us, and now we have to deal with what happened to Feste, and Chique getting beat, and this. If she has any kind of feelings, you'd think now would be a good time to say something, right? Instead she's just distanced herself. You remember what happened after Geai died. She shut herself off. I'm afraid she's doing it again."

Faye's eyes dropped — she'd been a casualty of that too. "You guys really need to cut each other some slack. You have to give the smoke a chance to clear. No dire predictions or major decisions right now, okay?"

"You'll talk to her? Please?"

She sighed. "I'll try. But you know there's no guarantee she'll talk to me either, right?"

There wasn't, of course, but he was reaching for any sliver of hope right now.

Her eyes narrowed, one edge of her lips curving into a familiar smirk. "It is so wrong, me playing counselor on this, you know."

He tried to grab onto the humour, but couldn't dredge up even a grin. "I know. Thank you."

Liv woke with a start, sitting up abruptly, blinking sleep away from her eyes. *Where…?* It took a second. Nate's apartment. *Damn,* what time was it? She was supposed to call him. She felt around for her phone, finding it under the pillow. Seven o'clock. And…notifications. Why hadn't she woken up? Somehow it had switched to silent. She hadn't done that, had she? Some warped, semi-conscious slip of her finger? Stupid phone, not doing its job when she actually needed it to.

The first one was from her mother. *Spoke with Mrs Miller. Flight AC447 23:37. His father and brother are also coming. Your father says you can take the Jag to pick them up.*

Talk about worlds colliding. She'd left Nate's mom with both her cell, and the Lachance's landline for back up. Figures she'd called the home number. Nate was more open with his mother than she was with hers. The thought of Anne Lachance querying Connie Miller to fill in the holes of what she knew of the relationship between their children made Liv uneasy. Of course, it might not matter anymore.

Faye next. She'd been just leaving the hospital after visiting Nate. *CALL ME!* That was five hours ago.

She fired off a quick response as she stumbled to her feet. *Just woke up! Ugh. Have to get ready to drive to the airport. Tomorrow, promise.*

It felt too weird to phone Nate at the hospital this late, but she had to. She needed to be up-to-date on him before she saw his family. The call was brief, information gathering only, the spaces between words tight and filled with the unsaid.

Her lack of nerves was bizarre as she waited at the arrivals gate for the flight from Calgary — a definite change from the first time she'd met Nate's family. With the calls she'd exchanged with Connie Miller since the accident, a strange bond had formed. Ironic, now.

She saw Reid Miller first, the man's stern, reserved face not much different from the last time she'd seen him. She'd met the man under tragic circumstances, and the situation with Nate that had brought the family to Toronto was hardly favourable; it wouldn't be fair to judge him on her time around him so far. She hadn't told Nate that his father and brother were coming — she hoped he'd appreciate it, but it was quite possible he would not.

Connie, in contrast, greeted Liv with open arms, holding her so tightly Liv had to fight back tears.

"Thank you so much for coming to pick us up, Liv. You must be exhausted. We could have taken a taxi."

Liv just waved her off and reached for Connie's bag.

"How's he doing?" Reid asked as Liv led them to the parking lot.

Liv glanced over. Even his voice was similar to Nate's. "I think he's just anxious to get the surgery over with."

"So they're going to do surgery, then."

She'd forgotten they wouldn't know, which was silly, because she'd only learned herself when she'd phoned Nate. "Tomorrow afternoon."

"They think that will reverse the paralysis?"

She nodded. "The surgeon seems confident, but it's not entirely without risk. It would probably resolve on its own given time." She could relay the facts. She just couldn't look at Connie.

"But far be it from my son to wait," Reid said.

The sarcasm wasn't lost on Liv, but waiting had gotten her into all sorts of trouble, so she wasn't going to judge.

THE NEXT MORNING at the hospital, she stayed by the door — not the picture of the doting girlfriend — watching Connie sweep straight to her son's bedside.

"Wow, everyone came." Nate glanced past his mother to his brother Tim, with a fleeting smile at his father. "Guess the career move isn't looking so bright right about now, eh?"

"You're going to be okay though, right?" Tim said.

"Yeah, for sure," Nate responded with confidence Liv wasn't sure he felt. "Sorry I probably won't be able to show you around while you're here. What do you think of Toronto?"

"Not much. So far all I've seen is the airport, a hotel, the highway, and a hospital."

"Maybe Liv's sister and her friend can do something about that while you're here. Is Cory still around?"

He found Liv's eyes, making her wonder what was going on in his head — and wishing she had the courage and the tools to find out.

"She's in Fort Erie for a few days."

She absently listened to the conversation, flowers next to the bed that hadn't been there yesterday dredging up her guilt for not coming back last night. After settling the Millers in a hotel on the airport strip, when she should have gotten herself a room, she'd driven all the way back to the farm and crashed at Nate's again, because it seemed to be the only way to feel close to him right now. Like maybe she could get herself used to the idea of a lifetime of that — and hope that in time, when he was better, he'd still want her there.

She hung back as his family had their parting words before inching to his side, still lacking any fresh ideas of what to say.

"Thanks for looking after my family," he said.

"It's the least I can do."

"Doesn't seem that long ago it was the other way around." He tried to smile.

"I wish I was better at this part."

"Hey — it's okay."

He opened his hand, and she reached for it, pressing her eyes shut as she squeezed.

"I walked Chique again this morning. I'll get on her tomorrow." How quickly she defaulted to talking about work. "Everyone was asking about you."

She relayed all the messages from the backstretch, wishes for good luck and promises of prayers. It had been silly not to go in yesterday. The whole Woodbine community felt the impact of the accident, aftershocks vibrating through it.

He didn't look at her as she spoke, like he'd shut a part of himself off, and that scared her more than the impending surgery. "Please tell me you're going to get through this okay."

He met her eyes, reading her face, which for once was transparent, when his was anything but. "I'm sure you've got the surgeon on his toes. See you on the other side."

It felt like a dismissal. She should have kissed him, except it wasn't enough to erase everything that was wrong, so she shrank away.

Liv left the Millers in a waiting room. She didn't know where she was going, but she couldn't just sit this out. Through halls, skipping down stairs, until she reached the lobby. Her eyes darted around. Flower shop, gift shop, coffee shop. Doors, with fresh air — as fresh as big city air could be — on the other side. She loped toward them.

Then there was Faye, in her face, stopping her in her tracks.

"Hey, where are you going?"

Caught. "I just needed to get out for a while."

"He's in surgery?"

Liv nodded.

Faye pulled her into a hug. "He'll be okay. Before you know it, you'll be fighting to keep him off horses."

The twist of Liv's lips wasn't a good approximation of a smile, if Faye's expression was any indication.

"Is there somewhere we can go?" Faye glanced around, steering Liv away from the door. "It's ironic hospitals don't have bars in them, don't you think? You could use a drink." Only Faye would make such a warped observation. She continued, her perfect eyebrows peaking. "I'm sure there's a bar close by."

"I'm not leaving."

"You looked like you were a minute ago."

Liv sighed. "I know. I guess you showed up just in time."

"Funny, that. Coffee it is, then. At least it's Second Cup."

Just the feel of the hot beverage between her palms helped. Cappuccino was her comfort food. Faye led the way to a nearby bench and pulled her down.

"His parents here?" Faye asked.

"His brother too. They're upstairs."

"You need to tell me what's going on. Something happened in Saratoga, and Nate's not telling. What the hell is that about?"

Liv shot her a look, brow furrowed. "What did he say to you?"

"Well that's just it, nothing. He said it had to come from you."

"Not now, Faye. I've got enough in my head without rehashing that. Why are you here, anyway?"

"You're welcome." Faye laughed. "I thought you might appreciate the moral support. Would you rather I leave you and your head alone?"

Yes, actually.

"C'mon. Whatever it is, it's eating at him, and by the looks of it, you too."

What had she learned? There was never going to be a good time… though talking to Faye was just another reminder of how she'd failed to clear things up with Nate. She popped the lid off her drink and blew on it before slurping some of the foamed milk.

"It's all your fault, actually. You and your stupid advice. It was the night before — the accident." Her heart started to pound in her ears just thinking about it. "I was stressing out and needed to distract myself. I probably drank too much wine. And attempted to throw myself at him."

Faye tried to smother her laugh, unsuccessfully, and Liv flushed, scowling. *Some friend.*

"And this was a problem?"

"Apparently, because he pushed me away and left the house."

"You're leaving something out."

"So it's not bad enough he wanted no part of me?"

"Oh, I'm sure that wasn't the case. How far did it go?"

"I really don't want to talk about this, Faye."

"Of course you don't. Seriously, what are you leaving out?"

She glanced back at Faye, then sipped from her cup, not caring it was too hot to drink. The sting as it burned the top of her mouth seemed a fitting punishment for her actions across the board. "Maybe the part where he said something about marriage."

At least Faye didn't laugh at that. Liv stole a sideways peek.

She was smiling. "Now it all makes sense."

"Great. How so?"

Faye slipped an arm around Liv's shoulders, and Liv felt the tremor of her low laugh.

"I know you don't think of stuff the way you need to sometimes, so let me try and help you out. Nate is a little bizarre. He seems to be able to show restraint better than any guy I've ever known, but it obviously comes at a price. He has this kind of sweet, very old-fashioned ideal that's never really panned out for him, but I'm betting he's pretty determined it's going to with you. I'm sure he thought it was going to be easier, because he counted on you not showing any initiative. Except, apparently, you did. Hence his major overreaction." She laughed again. "It's priceless."

"I'm so glad you're amused," Liv grumbled. "But marriage, Faye. Even if he was overreacting, it was obviously on his mind."

"Oh come on, sweetie. This isn't news to any of us."

"So what am I supposed to do?"

"Next time he asks, say yes, damn it."

Liv almost spat out the mouthful of coffee she'd taken, and Faye thumped her on the back as she coughed.

"Breathe. Take some time to wrap your head around the idea. You might surprise yourself. But in the meantime, the two of you really need to talk."

True, but that was proving easier said than done.

"I should probably go back upstairs," Liv said, sighing. "You can meet the family."

"Oh, I don't know about that."

"Don't be ridiculous. Connie is sweet. They know Will too, remember. At the very least, you can do it for me."

"The in-laws, eh? Well, all right." Faye grinned.

The Millers were where Liv had left them. Connie and Faye hit it off immediately, and Liv found herself thinking it should have been Faye Nate had fallen in love with; Faye he wanted to marry. It would have been so much simpler that way.

NATE KNEW the answers to the questions the nurses asked. He knew who he was, and where he was. He had a question for them, too, but wasn't coherent enough to ask it yet. It was all a bit foggy, but not enough to obliterate what he most needed to know.

Next time he woke up he was back in his room, feeling a lot more with it. He made his own initial assessment. *Yes.* Sensation. He closed his eyes, whispered gratitude, then waited to hear a more complete report from the surgeon.

Liv slipped in the room, approaching slowly. She reached out and touched his fingers tentatively.

"Hey," he croaked, the word catching in his sore throat.

"So?" Her eyes searched his face.

"So far so good, I guess. You okay?"

She shrugged, and looked away, and he wished he could sit up and hold her.

"Can you get me out of here?" he joked.

She laughed, just a small one, but it was good to hear.

"Just promise me you'll take it easy. Don't rush anything."

"I seem to remember throwing you up on Paz not long after you fractured a femur."

"That was different. This is your spine. Something goes wrong…"

The surgeon had already drilled it home — there would be no forcing this recovery, and Liv would do her part to make sure. She had all the power, really, holding the weapon that would be most effective in extracting his compliance — Chique. The realization caught him unawares. When it came down to it, he was just like Liv. It was all about the job; all about a horse.

19

Chique's ears worked like antennae, funneling information from her surroundings. A flick forward at the bad-actor up ahead, a pin and a wish to take up the chase when a worker dropped to the rail on her inside, surging by. Liv kept her hands set at the base of the filly's neck, silently telling her *no.*

They rolled around the turn, and the ears shot up again, Chique's lead change fluid. Liv let her gallop along, past the empty grandstand, under the wire, around the clubhouse turn. She wished she could let the filly go — it would help clear her mind of the clouded thoughts there.

Nate was being released from hospital today, the surgery a success, though his full recovery would take weeks. Yesterday after dropping off Reid and Tim at the airport, Liv had settled Connie into Nate's apartment — ending her little camp-out — but Connie had insisted Liv go alone to pick Nate up.

Being alone with Nate right now wasn't comfortable.

Chique dragged her into the backstretch before Liv reluctantly pulled her up, spotting Roger and Paz parked perpendicular to the outside rail. The filly snorted and tossed her head, the bright white shadow roll bouncing with it as Liv asked her to stand.

"She looks good," Roger said.

"She feels good."

Roger didn't take hold of the filly for the walk back. The days where Chique needed that were gone. Liv felt a pang in her chest, missing that Chique all of a sudden, because that old Chique was so tied to the old Nate — the *just relax and embrace the crazy* Nate. She was afraid the accident had erased the last traces of that version of him.

"Have you decided on a race for her?"

Liv shook her head, her eyes dropping to the twisty flop of Chique's mane. "Guess I should look at a condition book. The only reason I took her to Saratoga was because of Feste." Her voice tripped over the colt's name. She swallowed and continued. "I'm sure there's something for her here."

She needed to sit down and decide, now that Chique had made it successfully back to the races. But it was hard to do without Nate in the equation. He'd always been the glue that held their little team together. He hadn't asked about the filly since before his operation.

Jo met them in front of the barn. "I can do her up for you, if you want to go," she said, unbuckling the throatlatch as Liv dropped lightly to the asphalt.

She didn't, really. But she nodded, pulling off the tack. "Thanks, Jo."

WHEN SHE ARRIVED at the hospital, he was sitting on the edge of the bed in track pants and a worn t-shirt. She pulled clean black jeans and a short-sleeved shirt out of the plastic grocery bag she carried.

"Your mother sent them," she said, scrunching up the bag and shoving it in her pocket.

"She didn't come?"

Liv shook her head, but didn't explain.

He shrugged, and started to pull the t-shirt over his head with his good arm, flinching as it snagged on his right shoulder. Liv stepped in, gingerly easing it free, stopping herself from tracing the bruises on his torso, the grooves between his ribs that were a little too deep. Her fingers trembled, emotion flowing freely down her arms, being this close making all her nerves misfire. There was a little fire in his eyes, their pupils dark as he caught her quick glance. The tee fell to the floor and she groped for the shirt, trying not to look at him as she helped him into it. He started on the buttons, slowly. The lower ones he managed okay, but when he grimaced halfway up, she took over, resisting the temptation to close them all the way to the top to cover up as much as possible; get the memory of the feel of his skin under her palms out of her head.

"I'll come back in a couple of minutes," she said, and left him to figure out the jeans on his own, not before catching him smirking at her modesty. Yeah, fair. Not too long ago she'd been willing to rip his clothes off.

A nurse had a wheelchair ready — hospital policy, he had to go as far as the door in it. He hadn't bothered to tuck the shirt into his jeans, and reluctantly settled into the chair once an RN made sure he was wearing a sling on his right arm. The model patient act would probably last for about five minutes once he was in the car.

Many of the hospital staff interrupted on their way out. No surprise, really. Nate was a charmer, probably had the lot of them wrapped around his little finger. Liv had just forgotten, because he seemed so indifferent right now with her.

It felt strange to be driving him in his car, but now it was just one more strange thing on top of a mountain of weird. The last time — and first time — she'd been behind the wheel of the Porsche with him in the passenger seat was on their way to the Plate Ball. A lifetime ago.

The Bluetooth picked up her phone, because of course she'd added it to play music, but she felt self-conscious about it now, like she'd made herself too comfortable. He didn't attempt to change it, though. He didn't even poke through her playlist to find something to sing along to, like he would have in that other lifetime.

"Can we go by the track?" he asked as she merged into highway traffic.

"Sure," she said, glancing over, but he was looking straight ahead. She shouldn't have been surprised, but hadn't expected it, just the same.

She parked in front of the barn and watched him get out and head to the deserted shedrow with a careful stride that bore no resemblance to the confident, athletic one she was so familiar with. Liv followed as far as the doorway, but couldn't go any further.

He sauntered to Chique's stall, talking to the faces that poked out on his way, averting his eyes from the box that remained empty. Chique nickered multiple notes at the sound of his voice, and craned her head over her screen, her crazy forelock falling in disarray over one eye. The edges of Nate's lips turned up, but even his smile was reserved. He touched her muzzle with his good hand, then slipped in with her.

Liv closed her eyes, seeing the reunion like she was watching from the corner of the stall. Chique's head pressing into him, gently exploring hands that produced no treats, instead stroking her neck, pulling at her ears, straightening her forelock. None of it would alleviate the pain and emptiness.

He didn't stay long, Chique pushing her head out and staring after him. He didn't look back, his gaze dragging the neatly-raked shed as he came closer. He tried to meet her eyes, but they faltered, and he kept walking to the car.

"We could go get something to eat if you're hungry." It wasn't anything close to what she should be saying, but it was all that came to mind. A place to start, when she really had no idea where to begin.

"No, I'm okay. Kinda tired I guess."

"All right," she said, and started the car, feeling guilty for being relieved.

SITTING on the couch with a beer in his hand and his mother in his kitchen was not how Nate thought he'd experience the Breeders' Stakes this year. But here he was.

"You're moping," his mother said, setting a plate of sliced veggies at his feet on the coffee table. To offset the beer, probably.

"So what am I supposed to do?"

"Go in there?"

He'd needed to see Chique on the way home from the hospital, to know she was still there, and to give him a reason to look ahead, do his rehab, so he could get back and ride her again. But being at the track, in the meantime, was not something he wanted to deal with. All the condolences, the questions, the encouragement — he didn't need any of it. And he certainly did not need to be there to watch this.

"It's not as if I'd be any use to anyone. I can't even walk hots with this collarbone." Though that's the way it went in this business. One day you were riding at Saratoga, the next you could be back on the end of a shank, turning left. You never quit, you just downgraded. It was like Hotel California, you could never really leave.

"Maybe you're right. Maybe time apart is what both of you need."

He shot her a dark look. It wasn't what he wanted to hear, but maybe it was true, and he needed physical distance to figure out what was most important. Liv…Chique…riding — in that order? He wasn't sure they could be separated. Remove one element, and the whole thing fell apart.

Ride The Wave was on his toes in the post parade, Liv's long braid and straight-backed posture making them a contrast to the bored stable pony and his slumping rider. The colt looked even bigger and stronger than Nate remembered, like he'd grown and filled out in the last three weeks since the Prince of Wales. And Liv looked good on him. But she looked good on everything.

Between a pedigree that suggested he'd love the mile and a half distance, and the absence of Elemental, Ride The Wave stood alone as favourite. Nate hadn't had much to offer Liv about riding the colt that she hadn't already sussed out, but at least they'd talked about that. He set the beer bottle on the table and balanced on the edge of the seat cushion once the field was loaded.

The colt broke alertly but heeded Liv as she asked him to moderate his enthusiasm — he wasn't a front-runner, as much as he thought he wanted to be at the moment. He rated perfectly for her, sitting just behind and outside of the two speed horses who battled for the lead as they charged into the clubhouse turn. She kept him tucked there all the way around, and broke him out midway down the long homestretch of the EP Taylor turf.

"Wow," he muttered as the colt blew by the pacesetters and pulled away with authority, showing none of the immaturity he'd gotten away with in the Plate, but paid for in the Prince of Wales. *Such a nice colt.* Dean would probably want to think about running in the Canadian International after that.

He tried not to calculate what his paycheque would have been for that ride. The paycheque that was Liv's instead. Better her than someone else. He might have to talk her into marrying him for the financial support.

"Then there's that," he said, jutting his chin at the screen before sweeping up the bottle again and draining what was left.

His mother glanced at him, then the television, where Dean fucking Taylor crushed Liv in an embrace and planted a kiss on the top of her helmet.

THE PORSCHE WAS GONE. Liv checked on Claire before going up to the apartment, where Connie opened the door.

"So you let him have the car keys?" Liv smirked.

"Oh, he just went for a little drive. He'll be fine. He needs to do something — he's looking much too morose. He won't be long."

"Are you sure about that?"

Connie waved off her wry comment and set a bowl of cut vegetables and a glass of water on the counter in front of Liv as she sat.

"I need to start thinking about going back to Calgary soon. I can't stay around here forever."

"So who's going to keep him out of trouble?" The corner of Liv's mouth drifted up, but she wasn't joking, not exactly.

"He's old enough to do that himself. Wouldn't get him anywhere to push things, would it?"

If Nate's mother felt she could count on him to behave, Liv probably should too. There was nothing she could do to stop him anyway.

"It's been good to spend some time with you, even if things haven't been ideal," Connie said. "Maybe the two of you can come out to Calgary at Christmas."

"You're making assumptions," Liv responded, not quite frowning.

"And I shouldn't?"

"It doesn't seem safe to assume anything right now. But it's my own fault."

"Oh, I wouldn't say that."

"Why?" She couldn't keep the challenge from her voice.

Connie came around the counter and sat next to Liv with her cup of tea. "He's not handling this very well. He has the tendency to go off the rails a bit when something upsets him. He's done it before, I'm sure you know." Connie paused. "You need to stop being so hard on yourself and give yourself more credit. Don't let him off so easily. He needs to deal with this head on, not run away."

Liv sighed, turning on the stool so she could see out the big picture window. Who was she to talk someone out of running away, when she'd had the same thought more than once in the last three weeks? "I admit he's thrown me for a loop. He's the solid one. I'm the flake." She caught Connie's reprimanding eye and sat up straighter. "Okay. I'm the one who doubts. The only thing I know that would make him feel better, I can't give him — I can't put him on a horse. I wish I could."

"Have you told him that?"

"No. Give him an inch, you know? He'd probably talk me into it. And if something happened and he got hurt again, I'd blame myself."

Liv turned back to rest her arms on the counter. She never would have imagined Nate's mother being the one she opened up to. At least Nate knew how lucky he was to have her.

"Should Nate be worried about Dean Taylor?"

Liv almost laughed, because the thought seemed so absurd.

"Dean's a good friend, and I love him," she said, then shook her head gently. "But not like that. Not like Nate."

She knew what she'd said, and wouldn't look Connie in the eye. She could hear the unspoken *Have you told him* that? She could admit it, but saying it out loud, in context, to Nate…especially now, in the midst of so much uncertainty…

Connie leaned over and hugged her, Liv trying to extract all the strength and compassion she was so short of. If she were to have a mother-in-law, she could do a lot worse than Connie Miller.

The door clicked, and Nate came in, dropping car keys on a side table and kicking off running shoes.

"Hey," he said, the word casual but his posture guarded. His expression morphed into a smile for his mother before he kissed Connie lightly on the cheek.

"See, he came back in one piece," Connie said.

Nate looked sideways at Liv. "Were you worried I'd wrap the Porsche around a tree?"

"No, I think you love that car too much to risk that."

"True."

He reached past Liv and grabbed a carrot, then walked to the fridge, retrieving a bottle of beer and leaving the cap on the counter.

"I think I'll go for a walk." Connie stood abruptly, and gave Liv a motherly pat on the arm.

Both she and Nate watched her disappear out the door, the awkward silence that had become far too familiar descending. Nate took a long drink and set the bottle down on the counter. Alcohol was easy companionship when everything was disrupted. She'd been there, and, ironically, he'd been the one to tell her it never really helped.

"How's it feeling?" She inclined her head to his shoulder, grasping for conversation. As predicted, the sling was long gone.

"All right. I think collarbones and ribs ache forever, don't they? It still gives a pretty good stab if I try to move it the wrong way."

Liv couldn't help her scowl, but said nothing. She couldn't tell him what to do. He was right — she still felt an occasional twinge from the ribs she'd broken in the accident with Claire a year and a half ago.

"I'm starting PT this week," he added. "Maybe shifting gears is a good exercise."

Figuratively, as well as literally? *Don't overthink it, Liv.*

"Just take care of yourself, okay?" she said, quietly. "It would mean a lot if you were back on Chique before the end of the season."

She cursed herself for not being able to do better, say something more meaningful. He didn't comment, just looked back at the bottle — no doubt disappointed in her as well.

"I was thinking of the Canadiana for her next start." Because she was already being inadequate, she might as well settle back to default.

"Why not the Mile again? I watched the replay of the Saratoga race. First race back after such a long layoff, it's only fair she needed one."

"It's going to be tough."

"Don't duck the competition."

"If you think we're going to California if she wins, you're wrong."

His lips and eyes matched, impassive, removed, and he took another pull on the bottle. "Whatever. Not like you need my input. I won't be back by then anyway."

She stifled a sigh, and rose. "I should go."

He whipped around the counter and caught her arm before she made it far.

"Liv."

His touch was visceral, like a bite that tore flesh. It sent the cascade of events that had obscured their connection and driven this wedge between them flashing through her mind. *What doesn't kill you makes you stronger.* And this was killing her.

"I want to fix this. But I don't know how." There was a desperation in his voice that sent a chill through her, his fingers gripping hers.

"Time, Miller. There's no magic pill. It's going to take time."

"And space." His words came out mixed with resignation, and the bite she'd felt leveled off into a whole-body ache. He continued. "I'm going to go back to Calgary with my mom. Hanging around here isn't doing my head any favours. I can do my rehab there just as easily. It's just too hard to be around here right now. But I'm not running away, I promise."

He'd always given her both time and space — but it felt like failure to be going back to that, and for him to be looking for it too. Calgary was almost as far away as California had been. But what could she say? Admitting it was excruciatingly grown-up and rational.

His hands went to her face, his lips seeking something deeper than her mouth. She closed her eyes and tried to release it, to let go of everything that had happened since that last kiss, but she'd been far too efficient at locking it all up.

It hurt to push away, but she had to leave. And the words she needed to say, *I love you, don't leave me,* stayed stuck in her throat.

"YOU'RE GOING to hurt that thing if you keep pounding it like that."

Faye slipped onto the edge of the bench next to him and held out a beer.

Nate shook his head. "Got any water?"

She raised her eyebrows, then shrugged, but made no move to fulfill his request. "Have the two of you talked?"

"Not in a way that was remotely productive."

"You're such an idiot."

"Because this is completely my fault?"

"Well we know Liv is…" she paused, waving her hands around, "verbally challenged. You've got to do a bit more of the work."

"You say that like I don't know her. Like I haven't been doing that for —" He stopped himself from nailing down an exact span, because it overlapped his history with Faye.

"So no progress? At all?"

"She said she needs time. So I'm going back to Calgary with my mother tomorrow."

Will wasn't going to be happy about that, but he'd just add it to the list — it was one disaster after another right now. Will had finally booked their little band for an actual gig in a few weeks. It was just for fun, but Nate was looking forward to it. It gave him something different to focus on. The timing of his decision to leave was problematic. He'd joked about doing zoom sessions last winter, though it had never happened; maybe now was the time to test it out.

Faye was watching his hands, contrary to her earlier criticism seeming to find satisfaction in the way he was attacking the keyboard.

"Could you go do something else? I'm here to play music, not debate the sad state of my so-called relationship."

She didn't budge. "Emilie and Cory are coming tonight."

That wasn't unusual, but the comment felt like a jab, because Liv never had.

Cory was riding well at Woodbine — capitalizing on his misfortune, to be honest. The trainers loved a hot bug — at least those who weren't bothered by that hot bug being female. Roger was certainly making use of her. Dave Johnson was also all-too willing to help pick up the slack. It just got better and better. At least he could feel a little bit good about Cory, because he'd done what he could to help her out.

When they were finished, he watched Faye, Emilie, and Cory talking as the guys wrapped things up. It had been a productive session, and he'd managed to keep Liv mostly out of his mind, all the while sticking to water. Day one of pulling himself together. No more feeling sorry for himself.

"Just another two and a half weeks, and it's show time," Will said.

"I can't wait." Emilie did a little jig to imaginary music. "It's taken you guys long enough. It's going to be great."

"Not sure I can handle the pressure." Nate grinned.

"Says the guy who rides racehorses for a living," Faye scoffed lightheartedly.

Or used to.

Emilie glanced at her watch, slowing to a standstill, her face falling. "I guess we'd better go. It's getting late. Not that I have to get up early tomorrow; I have the day off."

"Why didn't you tell me, Em?" Faye said. "You should stay down here, and we'll go shopping tomorrow. Unless you've already made plans."

"Great idea, but I picked Cory up from the track."

"Nate can drive Cory back," Faye said. "Can't you Nate?"

"Sure," he said with a shrug. It wasn't as if he needed to get home in a hurry. "We'd better get going then."

Cory had gotten over her shyness around him, but she didn't say a word as they walked out to the car. He didn't question it, content to stay in his own head. He let her in the passenger side before getting behind the wheel.

"Such a nice car," she said, beaming.

He'd heard that enough times now to just smile and nod. "So how was your afternoon, anyway?"

"That two-year-old filly won for me, and I had a couple of thirds," she answered, her face lighting up all over again, then dialing back down. There was no hiding of emotions with Cory. "Ride The Wave ran huge in the Breeders'. Was that hard? I mean, you did win the Plate on him."

Her comment was innocent, but he didn't like the reminder after being happily distracted for the evening. By going to Calgary, was he opening the door for Dean? Is that what Liv needed time for? To compare and contrast horse trainer versus has-been jock?

"Sure. But I guess if there has to be someone else on him, I'd just as soon it be Liv. It's not as if she hasn't helped me through all this." Even if it wasn't on an emotional level. He glanced at the speedometer, mindful to keep the car within reasonable proximity of the limit.

All the things people had said to him about Liv came back to him.

Jeanne telling him he didn't pick easy spots. Faye *saying you've got to do a bit more of the work.* Cindy's voice asking if she was worth it. He'd said she was…but he was leaving without a valid attempt to breach the void. It hurt that she'd pushed him away, but he'd deserved it, thinking a physical gesture could in any way make up for all that was wrong.

"You're so quiet," Cory said, cautiously.

"Sorry. Just tired out I guess."

"You've had such a hard year."

"It happens." He didn't want her sympathy.

"I just feel guilty, having a good year, and it's partly because of you getting hurt. After all the help you've given me. I really appreciate that."

He laughed. "Firstly, don't ever feel bad for your success. You know how it is in this business. You hang onto it while you can, because you never know when it might disappear. Case in point, right? And despite everything, it really hasn't been that terrible a year. I won the Plate — how bad can things be?"

Traffic was light this time of night, and he was glad when he reached the exit for Highway 27, downshifting as they left the 427. All her apologizing and understanding only fed his self-pity.

"You parked on the frontside?" he asked.

Cory nodded, and when he saw her little VW he pulled up beside it. There were a few cars scattered in the area — not really unusual, no matter what day of the week. People left vehicles here, came back to pick them up later, just like this — or in the morning, if they'd gone home with someone. Sometimes people were too drunk to drive and slept in their cars. You saw it all around here.

He turned off the ignition, and Cory looked surprised when he got out. He just wanted to be sure she was in her car and safely on her way before he left. Things could happen in this parking lot at night, even though it was well lit and looked deserted at the moment.

"Thanks for trying to cheer me up." He watched as she unlocked the VW's door.

"The rest of the drive is going to be a step down, though."

"At the rate you're going, you'll be able to buy your own Porsche soon enough."

"You'll be back before that happens.

"I don't know, you've worked your way up pretty good. Plus you're a lot cuter than me. I can't compete with that." He was sure she blushed, though it was hard to tell in the light.

"Thanks for the ride."

Nothing felt right about the hug she gave him, as innocent as it was. He hated the thought that crept in. *This would be a much easier spot.* He wasn't even sure Liv wanted him anymore. But the affection he felt for Cory was only like what he felt for Em: they were his adopted little sisters, nothing more.

He watched until she was in the car and had started the engine, the lights flicking on, and didn't return to the Porsche until she was driving away.

A set of headlights lit up one row over, and a dark vehicle moved slowly toward the exit. His morale went from singed to full-on charred, because he'd put money on that harmless exchange with Cory distorting into something much different by the time it hit the backstretch kitchen tomorrow morning.

20

He'd forgotten how perfect the weather could be in Alberta this time of year. The heat in Calgary was dry, thanks to the altitude, a welcome change after the humidity in Toronto and Saratoga. It was the ideal climate — until something like a crazy premature snowstorm decided to arrive.

He headed for the mountains at daybreak — going further west, away from everything he'd failed to fix back east. Ironic, really, considering the drive he'd made to Ontario five years ago to escape all that had gone wrong out here. He didn't know any better now what he was going to do than he had then.

Al Wilson's farm was on the way, and when he walked from his mother's car to Al's office, he caught a speculative glance as one of the staff registered who he was. *Yeah, I don't know what I'm doing here either, buddy.*

"Look who it is." Al kicked back his chair and came around the desk to give Nate an embrace that was more fatherly than anything his real dad had ever given him. "Good to see you, kid. This is a surprise."

"Ah, well, I had some extra time on my hands."

"I heard about the spill. I'm sorry about the colt. Want a coffee?" Al stepped over to the machine on the sideboard. Nate shook his head.

He remembered Al's coffee. "You look pretty good now. How's it going?"

"I feel fine. You have no idea how much I'd give to get on a horse. This being hurt…it's doing a number on me."

"You'll get it back. You're not worried about that, are you?"

"I don't know. The longer I wait it out, the more doubts I have." It didn't matter that he did his rehab exercises with obsessive dedication. There was only one thing that would make it right.

"It ain't over yet. You'll be fine."

"Letting me get on the pony or something would go a long way to helping me out." Nate tried a crooked grin, but it was rusty from disuse, like the hinges of his jaw were a little seized.

Al laughed. "And I thought you'd stopped by for a visit. Not much has changed, eh kid? Still trying to talk someone into giving you a leg up." He smirked. "You're outta luck. Not gonna happen. Your girlfriend has my phone number."

The girlfriend he hadn't communicated with since he'd left; not so much as a text from either side. He should have called her to explain about Cory, instead of letting her interpret whatever skewed version was no doubt being gleefully passed around Woodbine's backside.

Al gave him a consoling pat on the shoulder. "Don't rush it, kid. It'll just make things worse."

Advice he seemed determined not to follow. He hoped the cool, clean mountain air would clear his brain; help him backtrack and find out how things had gone so far off course. Back in May, everything had made sense up there. Not anymore.

It was dusk when he returned to the house. He punched numbers into the microwave and reheated the plate his mother had saved him from dinner, listening to the hum and watching it rotate, and wished it was that easy to reheat his relationship with Liv.

His father surfaced, opening the fridge and emerging with a bottle of beer. Reid's unchanging gaze landed on Nate.

"Want one?"

Pretty sure that was a first. "All right."

Reid uncapped both bottles and surprised Nate yet again by sitting down at the kitchen table and sliding one across.

"Thanks," he said, settling into his old chair — trying his best to look grateful rather than suspicious.

"So why the hell are you here?"

Nate nearly choked on a mouthful of casserole. "If I knew, I'm still not sure I'd tell you." He grinned, chasing the comment with a swallow of beer. "How's Tim doing, anyway? Does he have a shot?"

"Maybe not this year."

Tim had been drafted by the Calgary Flames, but that didn't guarantee he wouldn't end up relegated to the farm team in the States.

"He'll be all right," Nate said.

"I know he will." Reid leaned back, hands around his bottle. "What about you?"

This was bizarre. Had his mom put his dad up to this? Well…while he didn't want to upset his mother, he wasn't all that worried about disillusioning his father.

"Me? Naw, you were right. Ultimately, I'm just a screw-up."

"Good of you to live up to my expectations. Did you actually do something, or are you just feeling sorry for yourself?"

Nate looked at him wryly. "Well, right about now everyone back there probably thinks I indulged a nineteen-year-old's crush — and I haven't called Liv to tell her it's not true. Meanwhile, Faye's brother, and Liv's long-time friend is probably going to make a play for her, if he hasn't already, and right now he's looking a hell of a lot better on paper than me. And Will is pissed because I've bolted, and our first gig is a week away. So when I go back, I'm guessing there's going to be just a little bit of animosity to deal with."

Reid nodded and tipped his bottle. "Nicely done."

"I always knew one day I'd make you proud."

Reid laughed. "So, what are you going to do?"

Nate felt suddenly sober. "I don't know."

"If Liv loved you enough to come to Phil and Cindy's funeral, she's gonna get over a bit of gossip. But sounds like you need to get your sorry ass on a plane back to Toronto and straighten that out."

If nothing else, he could count on his father to be blunt with the truth.

Someone would recognize him, despite his attempt at disguise: sunglasses, baseball cap pulled down over his hair — which was getting kind of long — an uncharacteristic shadow on his jaw. Dressed down in faded jeans and a black jacket over his t-shirt, he fit in pretty well with the crowd, the weather cool for a September afternoon. It wasn't the Plate; few people dressed up.

Why did he care if anyone noticed him? *This was stupid.* What was stupid? Being afraid of hiding in plain sight, or being here at all?

He watched the eighth race on a monitor, then pressed his way to the already busy paddock. He didn't go right to the rail, finding a spot behind the first row of people where he could still see.

Horses began to file in, and he spotted the filly between Jo and Sue. Chique looked alert, her dark coat gleaming, pretty face set off by the bright white shadow roll. All four legs were dressed in clean white polos, and she even wore bell boots on her front feet, Liv being her overprotective self. Then the filly skirted sideways, gawking at the crowd like a green two-year-old. Better to be a little cautious than risk catching a shoe or grabbing a quarter. It was good to see Chique being her old animated self, but he felt a strong pang of longing to be on her back again.

Jo led her into the number five stall. Someone waited there — tall, dark hair, lanky frame dressed in a suit — definitely not Roger, but familiar. Where was Rog? The substitute crouched down and helped Sue remove the polos, then stood, turning to Jo, so Nate finally saw his face. Dean Taylor.

Chique had settled, her ears flickering back, then out towards the crowd again. Nate ducked as her gaze shifted in his direction — silly, really. The filly wouldn't pick him out of the crowd, but he didn't want to risk her giving him away. He wasn't sure why. Why it felt wrong to be here. Why he felt out of place.

Liv emerged from the jock's room, relaxed as she chatted amicably with Steve Gordon. The paddock judge called for outside riders, so Nate jammed his hands in his pockets and shuffled away with the flow of the crowd. He cut across the horse path and decided to skip up the steps to the balcony. This really was ridiculous. But Liv had looked so much happier than the last time he'd seen her; maybe she wouldn't be glad he'd come.

Emilie, Anne, and Claude Lachance waited in the walking ring, Liv reaching them just before Dean and Sue. Liv maneuvered next to Dean, their heads going together. They weren't talking strategy. Liv would have determined that already. A hollow opened in Nate's gut. He was an outsider when he'd once been part of that.

He waited until Dean legged her up, Liv's focus switching to gathering the lines, knotting them as she tucked her feet in the irons. She reached forward and ran a hand along Chique's sleek neck, and Nate retreated into the grandstand, taking the escalator up to the second level, keeping his head down as he weaved through the punters. He found a spot to watch away from where the owners or trainers or grooms would be.

He felt displaced, observing Chique as merely a spectator. The filly was composed beside Paz, and it hit him — it had been a year since he'd last been on her in a race. He missed her, and it scared him that it was starting to feel like he'd lost them both as Liv took Chique away from the pony to warm up.

And who was he without them? Nobody. Liv and Chique had made him who he was. He didn't belong in the one place he'd come to let define him.

He forced himself to set emotion aside and studied the filly carefully, analyzing. Each stride was fluid, confident as they galloped around the turn. Liv pulled her up and faced the infield on the backstretch, and the filly stood, statuesque, before getting the cue to head to the gap for the turf course.

He glanced at the odds board as they gathered behind the gate — she was second choice with the hometown crowd. And Liv had, ultimately, decided to go with the Mile instead of the Canadiana. He wanted to think that meant something, that his words had played a part in her decision, but he was probably kidding himself.

The field sprang out cleanly, but Chique out-broke them all, surging to the front, looking every bit the bold filly he remembered. He found he was talking to himself, carrying on the discourse he would have had on the filly's back. *Easy baby girl. There you go. We'll just sit right here.*

Maybe she'd matured, and learned to rate, but the lead was still Chique's happy place. She traveled well within herself, going easily a length up on the others. She showed the way around the big, gradual turn, the slight downhill grade carrying them all along.

They came at her in the stretch.

Chique was aware as they drew closer behind her, ears pinning, begging to be released. Mid-stretch they were fanning across the width of the turf for the final charge.

Now!

"Come on Cheeky!" he yelled, forgetting he'd been trying to be anonymous.

Chique exploded, responding fiercely to Liv's driving hands. She remained on top, hooves skimming over green, light as a deer.

"You got this, Cheeky."

He stifled a victorious whoop as Liv wrapped up on her and they coasted under the wire, triumphant. Watching them gallop out, he swelled with pride Chique had turned those horses away with determination. She was back.

That didn't change that he wasn't.

The outrider brought her to the front of the grandstand, Jo snapping the shank to the bit then reaching up to grasp Liv's hand. Victory blanket of flowers draped over Liv's knees, Jo circled them on the turf for the photographers before heading across the track to the infield winner's circle.

He watched Chique pose for the win photo — you couldn't tell him she wasn't doing exactly that — then Sue dragged off the floral blanket and handed it to Em as Liv dismounted and removed the tack. Sue threw a cooler over the filly, and she and Jo started the walk to the test barn.

He could go back, surprise Liv there. Or he could catch her after she weighed in. He started to make his way through the clamour, losing tickets littering the apron, winners still waving their slips of paper, calculating spoils in their heads.

Then he saw Dean, hovering near the gate. And when Liv crossed over the track after the presentations, there didn't seem to be any reservation as she hugged him. Dean squeezed her back. His arm remained draped over her shoulders for a few steps as they walked.

It stopped Nate, like the asphalt under his soles had reached up and made his feet part of it. Any illusion he had of talking to her and ending this mess faded away. Maybe it was true then; maybe his gut was right. Dean looked too comfortable, and Liv, the joy on her face from Chique's success — he'd always thought it was something she shared with him. But it was clear now; she didn't need him. *They* didn't need him. They were self-sufficient.

He turned away, climbing the steps to the grandstand, letting himself be swallowed and spit out on the other side. Taxis dropped off and picked up the slots addicts. He slunk into one that had just offloaded its passenger, and gave the driver the address of the farm.

LIV EASED the truck and trailer to a halt outside the barn so as not to disturb her precious cargo. A glance at the camera monitor showed Chique's butt, her head up, ears swiveling. Then she let out a yell, to let everyone know she'd arrived. Claire called back.

Hopping out of the cab and jamming her phone into her back pocket, she reached for the shank behind the seat. The nice thing about the gooseneck was Chique rode in a cushy box — and Liv could unload the filly without assistance, so she hadn't needed to tell anyone on this end she was coming.

But — there was Nate. Where had he come from? He was supposed to be in Calgary.

"Is she okay?" he asked, his face showing worry but his words tinged with hostility.

Shouldn't she be the angry one? It was he who'd taken off to Calgary. Or had she chased him away? It was he who'd been caught with Cory MacDonald — even if Emilie insisted it was just another rumour spread by someone wanting to make Nate look bad. It wasn't as if he'd tried to clear it up. She didn't want to listen to Faye. *You need to*...add it to the mountain they had to talk out.

"Yes, she's fine. I just thought a few days on the farm would be good for her."

She was distracted as he helped unlatch and lower the ramp. His hair fell into his eyes, and she found she wanted to brush it back, run her hand over the unfamiliar scruff on his jaw, see if it burned her skin if she kissed him. But he stood back, hands wrapped around his elbows — a little cautious, a little defensive. She held out the length of leather and chain. An olive branch, of sorts.

He took it, silent, and walked up the ramp, removed the pins, and slipped in. Liv waited on the other side of the divider, his murmurs before the sound of chain against brass tugging at her heart.

"Okay," he called, and she opened it up.

He tied Chique in her old stall, sinking to his knees in the straw to start unwrapping the flannel from her legs. The position Liv took on the opposite side should have felt more natural than it did. She was still unsettled by this quiet, careful version of him, even if the whole rough, unkempt look that made him seem dangerous appealed to her on a primal level. It brought on thoughts of giving that whole throwing herself at him thing another go, like that's what was needed to set things right — but the memory of how he'd so effectively spurned her rushed rapidly back, drowning that fantasy.

"She ran great, eh?" he said, setting the bandage and cotton behind him and shifting to Chique's hind leg. He knotted her tail out of the way.

"She did," Liv responded softly, rising and ducking under the filly's neck. "If you can grab that last bandage, I'll get some polos and some tranq. I'm going to turn her out."

They watched the filly once she was in the small pen — Chique at first standing, surveying, sending a whinny Claire's way. Then she pawed, and collapsed in the sandy spot near the gate for a good roll. She came up exploding, like she'd just realized she was free.

"How was Calgary?" Liv asked when she was convinced Chique wasn't going to hurt herself, the filly dropping her head to nibble the sparse September grass.

He shrugged. "Quiet. My parents say hi." He propped a foot on the lower fence rail, leaning on the top one.

"I guess you had to come back to get ready for the big show next week." But not in time to come to the races yesterday.

"How long are you going to keep her here?"

"A couple of weeks maybe. She can train off the farm for a bit." It hit her that she wasn't consulting him; that she should be, that he could be back for Chique's next start. "We should —"

"Let me get on her when she's here."

Liv's mouth was still open with the words she'd hadn't got out…*talk about her next race.* She'd been on the verge of suggesting they go grab a cappuccino at Triple Shot — Faye and Will's café in town — because she had to stop putting off the long-overdue discussion, about everything. "When do you see the surgeon again?"

"A couple of weeks."

"When you get the okay from him, you can get on her."

"I'm not going to get hurt, Liv. I feel great. Please."

"It's just two more weeks, Nate. Just wait it out." She sounded more pleading than insistent.

He ran a hand over his jaw, and turned away, striding for the barn.

"Come on, Nate. You can't blame me for this. You have to think about the future. Is it really worth jeopardizing?"

He stopped abruptly, his laugh hoarse. "The future. Right."

Liv didn't recognize the reflection in the mirror, and it was more than just the short, strappy dress that skimmed her contours and matched her icy grey eyes, her long hair falling straight around her bare shoulders. It was the person wearing it, the one who found herself playing the game she'd been so sure was unnecessary with Nate. She didn't want to be that person. It disturbed her she'd sunk to that level.

"Wow." Faye strolled in and did a circle around her.

Liv crossed her arms, wrapping them around her torso. "I'm staying home."

Faye laughed. "No, you're not. Come on, we don't want to be late."

"Really, Faye. I don't think I should go."

"That's ridiculous." Faye took her hand, dragging her out of the room. "You didn't put on that dress because you want to stay home. You put on that dress because he's not going to be able to take his eyes off you."

Faye insisted on driving; it wasn't an argument Liv had any chance of winning. She probably would need alcohol to get through the evening, though Faye was an unlikely designated driver.

"As soon as it's over, we leave. Promise?"

Faye looked over at her sympathetically as she started the car. "Promise."

The club was packed by the time they got there, which didn't necessarily mean they slipped in unnoticed. Of course half the backstretch was there, watching every nuance. They'd be disappointed if they were expecting drama. She hadn't spoken with Nate since the morning she'd brought Chique to the farm, and there was no reason to do so tonight.

Faye led the way to a table — near the front but off to the side, apparently reserved for them — and, being a pro at these things, made sure the server brought them two drinks each. Faye lifted her first one towards Liv. Liv glowered in response.

They had a direct view of the stage, without having to deal with elbows and jostling up front. Of course that's exactly where Emilie and Cory were, chatting to each other excitedly. Liv felt bad for Cory, because those rumours hurt her, too.

Faye talked, and Liv tried to listen, taking a conservative swallow of the cocktail. She glanced at her watch. The sooner it started, the sooner it would be over so she could go home.

An opening act got the room warmed up with a brief set. It put Liv on edge. She wished they'd keep playing, because she'd heard Nate sing before, and it was never just a performance. There was a shuffle of equipment after the first band wrapped up; a hum running through the building that rose into whoops and whistles of anticipation. The lights fell, and the room went still.

Nate's voice came first, unaccompanied, an unfamiliar edge to it. It sent a shiver through her, and now she knew where he had put all his emotion these last weeks — all of it was channeled into that voice. It was clear and dark, the melody chilling; words that spoke a challenge, of meeting in another dimension, forgetting the world as they knew it…yet still questioning if it would ultimately make a difference. She felt Faye's eyes dart toward her. It wasn't her imagination. It was personal.

"…whatever it takes…"

That had always been Nate's stand, yet she'd accepted defeat so easily, while he'd put himself out there time and time again. No matter what Connie or Faye said, it was still her shortcoming, that she'd never been able to do that in return. It wasn't really any wonder he'd lost hope since the accident.

The music that followed was all hard edges and raw emotion; nothing like the fun of the Plate parties or the gentle coffee shop vibe of a year ago. Each note went straight to her core, leaving her ragged. If there was a game being played here tonight, she was losing badly. She would have fled, but she was supposed to behave as if she were unaffected by all this. What a joke.

It should have been a relief when the tempo slowed; kinder tunes, with Will on an acoustic guitar, Nate where he was most comfortable, at the piano. Familiar songs — ones he'd played when she was stuck on the couch in Florida after her accident. At the time she'd still been clueless that he wasn't just playing, he was playing for her.

They finished where they started, full of energy and attitude, and came back with an encore that had the whole floor bouncing, while she was drained, limp in her chair. Then finally, they were gone.

Faye sat down as the lights came back up, looking at her carefully. "I'm going to go say good-bye to Will, then we'll leave, all right? I won't be long. Wait here."

A DJ took over with recorded music, and the dancing started up — the night wasn't over. Liv needed another drink. She pushed her way to the bar, lowering her eyes in hopes no one would stop her and tell her how fabulous the show had been. Faye would find her.

"Are you okay?"

She looked up at the man who had spoken, and grimaced. "I'm fine."

He laughed. "Okay. Maybe I could buy you a drink?"

Apparently her stoniest glare wasn't enough to deter this guy. She shrugged, trusting Faye would rescue her before it became too unbearable. She ordered another cranberry and vodka and he paid before she could protest.

"I'm Kyle," he said.

He was tallish, dark hair and eyes, pleasant features, wearing a dress shirt and khakis. He probably worked in an office somewhere. Definitely not a racetracker. He might be nice enough. Too bad for him he'd decided to hit on her.

"Thank you, Kyle." She didn't offer her own name, or her hand. A drink wasn't enough to buy him that.

"All right," he said, and laughed again. "They were good, eh?"

"Yes, they were," she said, wanting to hit him for making her hear that one more time. Misdirected aggression. She didn't even know him.

"Complete fluke that I caught this. I didn't know there was anything going on, just dropped by after work to see if a buddy of mine was here. Somebody said the singer's a jockey at the track over there."

"He is. An exceptionally good one."

"You know him?"

She didn't answer right away. She had no reason to be honest with this guy, and he wouldn't know the difference. She was just some girl he was trying to pick up.

"Everyone knows him," she said.

She could tell he was sizing her up physically, though at least not in a leering sort of way. It still made her self-conscious. She knew her bare arms and shoulders were considerably more muscular than the average woman's, which threatened a lot of men for some reason, but he didn't seem put off. Or ready to give up.

"What do you do, then?"

"Back off, buddy. Can't you tell she wants to be left alone?"

She flinched. Nate. He was behind her, but she managed not to turn. She took a gulp of her drink and straightened her shoulders, trying to counter the chaos that rose inside her.

Kyle actually smiled, instead of taking offence. Is this what guys out there were like? Well, better that than a fight. Nate might very well be up for that if provoked.

She turned slowly to face him. "I'm fine, Miller. I'm just waiting for Faye, then I'm going home."

"Hey, you're the singer. You guys were awesome, man. You can play some serious piano," Kyle's voice travelled over her shoulder.

"Thanks," Nate said, flashing the guy an irritated glance. He zeroed back in on Liv. "Dance?"

"No, that's quite all right."

"Liv —"

He reached out to touch her elbow, but she twisted away.

"Hey, buddy, can't you see she wants to be left alone?" Kyle said.

No doubt he thought he was being funny, but Liv shook her head and walked into Nate, pushing him away before he did anything stupid. "Thanks again for the drink," she tossed back. *You should have just taken the hint and saved your money.*

"He bought you a drink?"

"Really, Miller?"

He didn't apologize, but dropped his shoulders and lowered his gaze. His hair was damp with sweat from the lights and the effort — mental, physical, emotional — and he still had that scruff of a beard he seemed to have mastered of late. *Rock star.* Dressed in black, of course. And he had effectively pulled the impression off.

She fought the chemistry, annoyed enough by her interaction with the guy at the bar to easily reengage her defences. Nate's whole adrenaline-rush confidence thing was fine, but she wasn't going to let him think this would be easy, like one of his choreographed schemes.

Resisting might look like she was angry, that she cared. She let him grasp her hand and lead her to the floor, and he pulled her in amid speculative glances. Liv braced her hands against his chest, trying to retain some distance between them as both his went straight to her waist.

And what was with the song? *"Strangers in the Night?* Ironic."

"Will has a sense of humour," Nate grumbled.

She was scaldingly aware of him — of his scent and the firmness of his pectorals under her palms, the bump on his healed collarbone, his eyes as she refused to meet them. The placement of his fingers on the small of her back was deliberate, but she steeled herself against its effect on her. When he leaned in, his rough cheek brushing hers, she pushed him back.

"What do you want, Miller?"

"Funny, I thought Dean might come tonight."

"Like Dean ever comes to these things. I'm regretting coming myself."

"You two seemed pretty friendly there after the Mile."

"Well, maybe that's because we're friends. How would you know, anyway?"

"I saw, okay?"

"Saw what? What are you talking about?"

"I was there, all right? I flew back for the race, like an idiot. And when I saw the two of you, well, I figured I probably wasn't welcome."

"You were there? And you didn't let me know? What's the matter with you?"

"You never said you wanted me there."

"I didn't think you wanted to be around! You went to Calgary! What was I supposed to think? And Dean? I don't know what you think you saw, but nothing has ever happened with Dean. I talked to him about it, to make sure he knew, because I — because of you." She couldn't help the exasperation in her tone, though now she was stunned. "Is that what this is about? Because if it is, you've just lost your excuse for screwing up. And I'm not taking the abuse for being the bad guy because I won't let you get on Chique. Maybe you need to go away again and not come back this time till you've figured yourself out."

"Is that what you want?" Then his eyes changed, transitioning from anger to fear. "Tell me what to do."

The quaver in his voice weakened her, but she couldn't back down. "Whatever it takes, Miller."

She shoved him away, leaving him standing there, and pressed blindly through the lingering crowd to the door. Outside she gulped in the cool air, and searched for Faye's car. She felt an arm slip around her, and Faye's voice in her ear.

"Come on, sweetie. Let's go."

21

Nate stalled outside the Triple Stripe shed, insulated by the darkness, and breathed. His emotions were firing all over the place. He hadn't been here since that day on the way home from the hospital.

He wasn't taking anything for granted, his helmet and boots left behind in the car. Honestly, if they put him on the end of a shank and told him to turn left, he'd do it.

Because Liv might just be mad enough to keep him off Chique. If that was true, well, it probably answered the question that plagued him; the one about whether or not there was any hope for the two of them. Maybe he shouldn't even be thinking about it. Maybe he should just be alone.

Jo noticed him first, hugging him with a rare display of affection, followed by Sue. Even Michel stopped what he was doing and came over. It was all strange, and embarrassing — because he hadn't stayed away for any good reason, just his own self-pity.

"Welcome back," Roger said.

Liv hovered in the background, a quiet but undeniable presence, her face a perfect mask. When the others dispersed, she remained.

"The surgeon gave you the right answer, then?"

"He did."

"Paz is tacked up. You want to come out with me?"

He nodded, the tension around his eyes easing. He'd take it. "Absolutely."

Back at the Porsche he exchanged running shoes for his boots, and pushed on his helmet. He had to lean back on the door for a minute, trying to nail down what he was feeling. Thankfulness, maybe. Relief, definitely.

He wanted to just vault into the saddle, but he took Paz a turn and let Liv leg him up. There was something symbolic in the gesture, even if there was no sentiment in it.

"Good to have you back, Miller."

He accepted that, and didn't search for anything more. It was enough that she meant it.

Waiting outside at the end of the barn, he watched Chique approach. The filly hadn't lost that swinging, sexy, walk, her head low as Liv held her on the knot. He'd missed that little thing, feeling guilty for his absence. As Liv came up beside Paz, Nate draped his hand over Chique's neck, patting her affectionately.

"We're working seven-eighths this morning," Liv said. "Don't worry, you don't need to take me to the pole. We'll just back up to the wire, gallop once around and go. I'll let you figure out how much you want to do."

A little jog, a little gallop — that would be a good place to start. No way he wanted to rush things now that he was in the tack again, even if it was pony tack. Funny, that, when he'd been in such a hurry a couple of weeks ago. He backed up with Liv and the filly, galloped with them to the backstretch, and convinced Paz to pull up there to watch Chique breeze.

Familiar faces on horses and at the rail greeted him, were happy to see him, and he tried to acknowledge their good wishes without losing track of Chique. The filly was galloping at a good clip now along the home stretch, disappearing behind the tote board, then Nate picked her up on the clubhouse turn as Liv set her down.

Now he didn't hear anyone, absorbed as the pair swept along the rail and past him, the drum of Chique's rhythmic stride in his ears. She switched leads cleanly as she approached the turn, rounding it snugly, floating down the stretch. Flawless.

He couldn't help reaching out again when Liv turned her in next to him. Chique leaned into his touch, then tried to rub her head on Paz. "She looks great," he said quietly.

"She'll work on the turf next time. Think you'll be ready to be back on her by then?"

It choked him up, keeping him from answering right away. "It would take an awful lot to stop me."

"We're not going to California," she said.

No surprises there. The Woodbine Mile that Chique had won was still a *Win and You're In* race, and the Breeders' Cup was at Santa Anita this year.

"But she's nominated for the International," Liv continued.

A mile and a half? That's just crazy. But definitely not ducking the competition.

"I think it'll be her last race, Nate."

Their eyes met, and he wanted to ask, *what does that mean for us?* He was going to have to play that one by ear.

He insisted on walking Chique, then Rog let him go out with a few more sets on Paz. At the end of the morning he started cleaning tack. Nicole shrugged and said she'd lend the grooms a hand. Emilie sorted through the saddles, separating dirty saddle cloths and girth covers for the laundry.

"How's Cory doing?" he asked.

"She's okay. She's been around long enough now she knows people will freely spread lies." Emilie looked at him, not unkindly. "How are things with Liv?"

He frowned, and attacked a bridle. "Status quo."

The next morning Liv looked at him strangely when he said he wasn't ready to get on Chique yet. He couldn't tell her it scared him, that as soon as he was up on the filly he'd be dealing with the memory of the tragic accident in Saratoga. He needed to overcome that, and reconnect with her, not only because of the upcoming race, but as part of the grieving process; the part where the inside of him started to heal.

The days were going by too fast. Just a week, and it would be International Day, the filly's career finale. Liv didn't know whether she should cling to every moment, feel every second as it slipped through her fingers, or give in to the inevitability of it all.

Nate hadn't questioned why she'd made the decision. Maybe he didn't need to, the way this year had gone. The filly had given them so much to come back after her New Year's Eve ordeal. Just one more race, and Liv would stop asking. But the last ask, at a mile and a half, was a big one.

Liv snugged the girth one more hole as he brushed past, and she watched him put the lines over Chique's head, remove the halter, and slip on the shadow roll before offering Chique the bit. He slid the headstall gently over the filly's tiny ears, clearing her bridle path before he did up the noseband and fastened the throatlatch. Liv unsnapped the shank from the screen and handed it to him, letting him take the filly a turn.

"I'll catch up with you," she said after throwing him up, and headed to Paz's stall.

Chique stood quietly, uncharacteristically so, just outside the barn when Liv emerged on the pony. Nate hadn't breezed anyone else since his return. He said Chique had to be the first.

"You okay?" she asked.

"Yeah. Let's go."

She didn't press him further. He had every right to be quiet and moody as far as she was concerned. It was part of re-entry into this world. She couldn't do anything to make it easier.

Out on the track, there was something poignant about the scene before her, as Nate sent Chique along the turf. The melancholy bounced between them, from Nate, to Chique, and back to Liv. Feste, Nate's injury, the fracture between them, and now the approaching denouement — it was all concentrated in their midst.

Nate and Chique were symbiotic, as if they'd never been apart, sailing through the stretch and heading for the wire. It was going to be hard on both of them once the filly retired. What then? With everything that had gone on in the last two months, would there really be anything left?

He turned Chique in alongside Paz, fondly caressing the filly's crest. "She feels good, Liv," he said. "But — I don't know. There's just something…different."

Maybe it was him that was different, or maybe she had missed something. Nate knew the filly better than anyone, and his comment painted on a fresh layer of concern. "As long as she's sound," she said. "She looked happy, anyway. How about you? Everything feel okay?"

Nate nodded, but didn't offer anything more.

HIS FIVE-THIRTY ARRIVAL on Sunday turned the grooms' heads because he was there even before Roger — though the trainer had asked Nate to work a couple that morning, He found Liv in Chique's stall, of course. It was mucked, the filly's bandages off, and Liv was running a soft brush over the dark coat, leaving it gleaming like ebony. She, on the other hand, didn't seem surprised to see him.

"Hey, Miller."

A hotwalker appeared beside Nate with a fitted cooler and shank, but Nate reached for both. "I'll walk her."

"Thanks, Nate," he said, raising an eyebrow at Liv. Liv merely smiled as she went through the filly's long tail, picking out a stray piece of straw.

"Meet me outside and I'll take that poultice off." She looked strangely amused, slipping past him as he ducked in.

It was as if they'd gone back, way back, when the thoughts running through his head relating to Liv were just unlikely romantic notions. That might not be a bad thing. Rewind to when things were simpler. Rebuild something stronger from the rubble.

Liv flaked away as much dry poultice as she could before removing the rest with warm water. Chique nibbled at Nate's jacket. He was having trouble visualizing her as a broodmare, fat and hairy. The thought of her babies romping with Claire's, though, were like little filaments of hope winding around his heart. He could convince himself he didn't care if he and Liv sorted things out, as long as they could keep working together, so he could be part of those foals' lives — and still be around Liv.

Because where would he go? If, when they finally talked, she told him to leave?

California, probably. Somewhere far enough away they wouldn't cross paths. Her pushing him to stay, after Jay's accident, had done one thing —

it had ensured he'd be welcomed back if he decided to ride on the west coast again. As humbling as the whole winter had been, there were worse places to be, but it would still feel like purgatory.

She probed the left front ankle carefully, and felt both feet. She probably did it a dozen times a day. Liv stood up and reached for the towel she'd left on the railing, drying both legs meticulously before wiping her own hands.

"She okay?" he asked.

Liv nodded, looking down at the black limbs. "I've x-rayed it, but they never find anything."

"But you're worried about it."

Liv finally looked at him, with a small smile. "I worry about everything, remember Miller?"

Chique pushed into him and swung her hind end when he didn't move. "All right, all right." He placed a steadying hand on her neck, and started toward the shed.

The filly was feeling good, a bounce to her step — nothing that would suggest she was less than right — but Liv's paranoia was contagious. It was just this year, the lingering dread, unbidden voices saying *everything comes in threes.* Phil and Cindy. Feste. That was two. Chique's every move defied his fears, however. She had galloped great, worked great, and dragged him around the shed now with mocking conviction. Still, he would be more critical when he got on her the next morning.

He forced it out of his mind, and thought forward to tomorrow afternoon instead. He had a couple of mounts, his first two since getting back. Was it too soon? If Chique weren't running next weekend, would he be in such a hurry? *Right.* Now that he'd made it this far, the weeks of frustration, driving everyone around him crazy, why was he second-guessing?

The filly started to settle next to him, slowing slightly from her power walk. He needed to think about something other than racing, or Liv, or Chique, or the future, before he drove himself insane. But what else was there right now? At this rate, the next week was going to be hell.

"Hey, Nate, hang on." Roger flagged him down. "Let Marc finish her. The first set is ready to go. Get your boots on."

Roger was grinning, and it broke Nate's tension. "All right, boss."

Roger put an arm around his shoulders. “Relax. You’re looking a little tight.”

He sighed, and took a breath. “Sorry. What’ve we got going first?”

Rog filled him in on Can’t Catch Me, one of three two-year-olds scheduled to breeze at six. He tugged on his boots in the tack room where he’d left them, looking up when Nicole walked in.

“’Morning, Nate.” Nicole smiled. She wasn’t dressed to ride. “The colt you’re getting on is a half-brother to Elemental. I’ve been on him most mornings. You’ll like him. He’s almost ready to run.”

“You get fired, then?” He grinned.

Nicole laughed. “Yeah, jocks only this morning I guess. I’ll come out and watch.”

She disappeared again. Nate put on his helmet and picked up his stick. He could guess who the other rider was. He and Liv were used to functioning with a low level of unrest, but he felt terrible Cory had inadvertently been dragged into their mess.

When he walked down to Michel’s stalls, the two-year-old he was supposed to get on was gone, so he stood in the doorway to wait.

Michel stopped the colt in front of him. “Everything seems quiet on the inner-city front.”

“It’s far too civilized,” Nate grumbled. “I kinda wish it weren’t, you know what I mean?”

“Yeah, a good fight would feel so much better, wouldn’t it?”

Nate laughed as he settled into the tack and Michel led him off.

“Good luck, Miller.”

Roger was coming out on Paz, and Nate carefully steered to the right of the stable pony, leaving Liv and Cory and their mounts on the other side.

“Hey Cory. How are you doing?” He wasn’t about to let things be any more awkward than they already were.

Cory had a determined smile, partially obscured because Liv was between them. “Hi Nate. You must be happy to be back.”

“I’m only part way back.”

Liv asked Cory a question Nate didn’t hear, and the two of them started talking. He tried not to think Liv was intentionally excluding him.

“All right, kids,” Roger said as they went through the tunnel. “Back them up down the chute, and gallop once around. You're going five-eighths. Nate, keep your colt behind the other two; let him eat some dirt and see how he likes that. Send him at the quarter pole and see if he's going to follow in his big brother's footsteps."

Nate nodded, and followed Cory and Liv off to the left, down the chute. The colt looked nothing like Elemental — his height was comparable, but he was chestnut, and rangier than his bay brother. Nate was quiet as he held the colt, galloping, content to focus on Can't Catch Me's stride while Cory and Liv chatted sporadically to his inside.

Liv glanced at him, calling over, "He's a nice colt."

"As nice as his brother?"

"Guess we'll see."

They galloped through the stretch and around the clubhouse turn, Liv dictating the pace and letting them move a bit faster. Nate started to let her and Cory inch ahead — his colt didn't like that. As they approached the pole he dropped Can't Catch Me behind them and let them go on, keeping within a length and a half. The colt shook his head as the first clods of dirt hit him, but soon put his head down and dealt with it.

As they entered the stretch again Liv was urging her colt, inching away from Cory. Nate let his mount go after her, steering him to the outside, and in three jumps they reached her. He restrained Can't Catch Me, slightly, letting him run alongside, and felt Liv's eyes. A couple of strides and he picked his colt up again, clucked once, and did, in fact, feel like yelling out, *can't catch me!* as the chestnut went right on by and had a length on the other two at the wire.

Roger waited for them on the backstretch. "There's a race for him next weekend. You want to ride him?"

Nate smiled, stroking the colt's neck. "Yeah, sure."

He came back at the end of the morning and ducked into the office to find Roger before anyone else saw him.

"Thanks for the distraction."

"I figured you needed it. You're under a bit of pressure right now," the trainer said.

Nate shrugged. "I guess. Nice colt."

"I'm hoping he's more than nice."

It wasn't until then that it made Nate think of Feste. Promising colt, next year's Plate horse…but it wasn't the same.

"So you should have a couple of live ones this afternoon, at least." Roger brought him back to the present. "That filly I'm putting you on is as close to a sure thing as I could find for you."

"Thanks Rog." Nate perched on the couch's armrest and came back to what he hadn't been able to push out of his mind. "So what's the story? What's been going on with Chique?"

Roger leaned back in his chair, and studied him. "Nothing, Nate. Every time Jake comes and looks at her, he can't find a thing. Liv's had him do radiographs more than once. Nothing shows up. You've been on her. She looks great. And it's not like Liv's given the filly anything or done any vet work. No medication. What you see is what you get." The trainer leaned forward, his forearms resting on the desk. "I know no one wants to see Chique retired, but I've got to admit it's going to be a relief. Then the two of you can figure out what you're going to do with the rest of your lives."

Nate met the trainer's steady gaze. "Whatever that means."

All Sunday afternoon, Liv watched Nate as carefully as she was watching Chique. He didn't have a lot of mounts, easing himself into it, but started the comeback with a win on a maiden three-year-old filly from their own barn. Liv had ridden the filly to a strong second in her last start. It was probably a little obvious she'd sacrificed the mount to give him the opportunity, but if Nate was healthy — and it was apparent he was — she wanted to see him return to form as quickly as possible. She wasn't sure if it was for Chique, so that the filly would have a rider with returned confidence, or something more personal.

"You're being far too nice to Miller," Steve Gordon said to her after the race when he came back to the room — where she'd been merely an observer.

"You were gonna get beat either way, Steve, so why does it matter who was on her? It's not like he's going to catch up with anyone in the standings at this point, is it? And I wouldn't want him to have to give up the Porsche because he can't make the payments." She smirked.

Nate endured congratulations and welcome backs before ensnaring Liv's eyes, working his way over. "You didn't have to do this, you know."

Yet she did — as if that was the only way she could communicate her feelings, by letting him ride a horse he knew full well she could have kept for herself. It wouldn't change anything, though. It wouldn't magically realign them.

Liv's quiet day-to-day demeanor was typical, merely professional — neither of them had made any attempt to initiate conversation outside of work. They would do what they always did, and wait for a more appropriate time, despite how that strategy had, in Nate's mind, proven so flawed. The letdown that was sure to follow Sunday's race was going to be difficult, so how long after that would it be before they were both ready to deal with everything they'd put off? If there was one thing he'd learned this year, it was that you had to say what you needed to say to make things right before it was too late. But he knew Liv. She didn't work that way.

As she put the tack on Chique Tuesday morning, the silence between them seemed so normal he wouldn't have thought of breaking it. He didn't leave right after the filly trained, standing to the side as Liv sloshed steaming suds over Chique from poll to tail, the sharp smell of alcohol in the rinse that followed biting his nostrils and making the filly skitter as it tingled over her sensitive skin. Liv scraped off the dripping water and ran a sponge over fine-tuned muscles and down tight legs, then dressed the filly in double coolers — one large square one, clamped high at the throatlatch; a second fitted one over top to help wick away the dampness as she dried.

"I'm having Jake do x-rays again this morning." Liv fiddled with the scraper once Marc had led Chique off.

Fanatic.

"Just a precaution," she said, like she had to justify it.

He shrugged. "I'll stick around."

When the vet came, Nate stood behind Liv and Jake as Jo jogged Chique down towards the middle of the barn, then back again. Nothing but an energetic head-shake from the filly. Chique stood patiently while the vet lifted and flexed both ankles, then radiographed the joints from multiple angles.

"Nothing," Jake said, flipping through the images. "Still clean. I don't know why you're not racing her next season. I think it's more for your health than hers."

Nate suppressed a snort.

Jake started packing up the laptop. "If something changes before entry day, let me know."

Liv gathered the filly's bandages, and Nate plucked a cotton and flannel from her arms and followed her into the stall.

"Listen, Liv, if your gut's telling you something, don't run her. It wouldn't be so bad, going out on that Mile win. So I don't get to ride her again. I'll survive."

Liv rubbed brace into Chique's leg, her face set. "You heard Jake. There's nothing wrong with her. How can I not run her? She's got a lot of fans. It's a big day. We can't let them down."

"What are you talking about? Your only responsibility is to this filly. Forget about the rest of them and do what you think is right. I never thought you'd ever let yourself be influenced by that stuff."

"I have nothing concrete to go on. I don't know if I can trust my gut right now, after everything." Her fingers wound the cotton against the leg, then fumbled with the flannel wrap. "If I don't run her, it's because deep down all I can think about is Feste, and you, and whether the universe has it out for me enough to have another go."

"So don't put me on her then, if that's what your warped superstition is telling you. You ride her, if I'm some kind of curse." He'd known it — known it all along. "If something goes wrong, that's what you'll be thinking. I'm doomed to forever be tied to losing Feste, aren't I?"

Liv looked down, her eyes riveted to the bandage as she secured it. "I don't know."

He laughed, bitterly. It wasn't the unwavering denial he'd been hoping for. "I don't want to be carrying that on my shoulders going to the gate on Saturday."

"Are you saying you don't want to ride her?"

"That's not what I said."

"That's sure what it sounded like."

"Liv —"

"Just make up your mind by tomorrow." She rose abruptly, going to the filly's head, waiting while he left the stall to slip off Chique's halter.

He told himself the stress was getting to her — to both of them. He might be back, but he'd failed to resume his role as the reassuring one.

Entry day.

Liv finished putting on the bridle and looked to the door, and Nate was there. She'd been worried he might not show up. Thankfully his loyalty to the filly was greater than the canyon between them.

He dropped the stall guard, but Liv stopped the filly in the doorway.

"If you feel anything…suspect anything…I won't enter. I want you on her. I want the two of you together again." She faltered. It wasn't the time to get into anything more.

They had a little following going out to the track, Liv escorting on Paz — Roger, Jo, Nicole, and anyone else who was free, coming to watch. Chique strode like a queen, alert but behaving, like it was only to be expected she would have an entourage.

"Let her gallop along a bit when you hit the quarter pole for about three-eighths," Liv said, staying alongside but not holding the filly as they backed up. Nate just nodded, his gaze fixed between the filly's ears.

The sadness she felt was everywhere, an atmosphere like the droplets of rain that created a mist around them. Chique rolled through the lane and around the turn and continued to gallop out strongly into the backstretch.

Liv searched Nate's face when he pulled up after a mile and a half, jogging over to Paz, turning in. How many times had they stood on this track like this?

"She still feels great, Liv. How does that ankle look?"

"Fine. Even my imagination isn't seeing anything. So…am I giving you the call?" Liv looked at him, begging him not to say no.

"Yes. Please."

Then he said what he'd said to her before, what he'd done every time he'd ridden the filly.

"I'll take care of her, Liv."

THERE WAS nothing fun about Wednesday nights. He won the featured allowance on a longshot that let him feel better about his abilities than those walks-in-the-park Roger had given him on the weekend. It lifted his spirits, at least temporarily.

"Want to pick up one in the last, Miller?"

"Sure, I guess. As long as it's not too crazy." Once upon a time, crazy had been his thing.

The four-year-old gelding in question, while not picked to win, had a decent chance. Maybe he could add another victory to the comeback.

Keep In Touch was the horse's name, and Nate assessed him as an honest sort as he put the gelding through his paces in the warm-up. Lower-level claimers weren't anything to get excited about, but the horse felt good, like it was possible he could outrun his odds.

After a clean break, the gelding rated kindly for him, Nate tucking him behind the leaders. On the turn the rail opened up, and he asked Keep In Touch to go. The gelding responded, though nothing like the horses Nate had been on of late. That moment of comparison cost him, as the horse in front of him faltered and lugged in. He checked the gelding hard, but Keep In Touch stumbled, and Nate was gone. He ducked, hitting the dirt with an *oomph*, then tried to tumble out of the way. Hooves whizzed by, and he gulped for breath, his heart pounding against his chest like the safety vest was the only thing containing it. Keep In Touch hadn't gone down, and Nate hoped he was all right.

He rolled onto his back, inhaling deeply, assessing. Everything seemed okay — toes and fingers worked, neck was sore, but moved, no sharp pains anywhere — so he sat up, slowly. The ambulance pulled up and the attendants rushed to his side, helping him off with his helmet, asking him questions. He assured them he was all right, but let them help him up, and he was far enough away, he figured he might as well get a ride back.

In the room he ignored all the questions about his own well-being until he had an answer about Keep In Touch.

"He picked himself up and galloped home ahead of the rest of us, Miller. Too bad you couldn't stay on."

Nate laughed, took the ribbing, and parked himself in front of his locker. Sure he was a little shaken — but he had walked away. Getting that behind him might be the most important step in his recovery to date.

"You're all right?"

He looked up, and Liv was standing there. Trust Liv — on the one hand so modest, but on the other, completely unselfconscious as she walked into this room of men in various stages of undress. She liked to show up when he came off horses, apparently. This time was a little less dramatic than when she'd pulled the same stunt. Keeneland, after the Bluegrass, when she'd hauled him off Ricky Acosta for the foul that had sent him and Wampum crashing to the dirt. The turn-on of it had been enough to distract him from his ire. But he liked his non-existent chances with her right now as much as he had then, and was too afraid to mess up this precarious state they were in by trying anything.

"Just ate some dirt, that's all."

"Good." Her face softened a little.

"What are you doing here?" he questioned, careful to keep his tone casual.

She wasn't riding tonight, and it was rare for her to come to the races just because. She tugged at the hem of a smart black jacket she'd layered over a white blouse, open at the neck so he could see the pendant Geai had given her. Dark blue skinny jeans hugged the hard muscles of her thighs, her sleek hair down. He wanted to run his hands through it, be done with this strangeness.

She didn't answer him. "Chique's going to walk tomorrow. I'll see you Friday at six to gallop her?"

If it hadn't been so late, he would have asked her to…have a drink with him? That was so not Liv. But the yearning was almost unbearable, to be with her. They didn't have to talk about anything, just sit there…and be.

"I'll be there," he said.

22

She woke drenched in sweat, sheets twisted around her legs, her pulse throbbing in her ears. Horrible, empty dreams faded with the sleep that had brought them. Forcing herself to the edge of the bed, she propped herself up. *Bad move.* A wave of nausea sent her staggering down the hallway to the bathroom, bile welling in her throat.

A cold dew coated her skin as she pushed herself back to rest against the wall. When she mustered the energy to climb to her feet, she stared at her bloodless face in the mirror. She must've eaten something funky a couple of days ago — back when she'd been able to eat anything. It couldn't be stress, *noooo.*

The fear from her nightmare crept back. It had just been a dream. But what if he did leave? What reason had she given him to stay after Chique was retired? She stripped off her nightshirt, climbing under the scorching shower stream to let it wash away the clamminess, willing the water to restore her equilibrium.

It did, a bit. It was four AM according to her phone. Close enough. She dressed and headed out.

It was like *déjà vu* walking into the office barn. Like Plate Day. She'd take that as a good omen, except the apartment overhead stayed dark. Nate didn't magically appear to appease her fears. What would Geai be saying to her now? He just regarded her silently from the painting behind the desk with that timeless smile. She fed Claire and her companions, and left a note in the feed room that it was done.

At the track, Chique stood at the front of the stall, surveying the activity on the shed, and locked in on Liv as she became part of it. The filly reached out, nose butting Liv's arm when she took down the empty haynet. Chique followed her to the corner as she unclipped the feed tub, like maybe this time Liv would give her a second breakfast. It raised a lump in Liv's throat. She unsnapped the water bucket with her other hand and slipped out, gulping it back down.

"Are you okay, Liv? You look like hell." Jo eyed her critically.

"I think I must've had a bit of food poisoning. I feel a lot better now than I did an hour ago."

Jo didn't look any more convinced than Liv had been herself. "You and Nate should just book after this, go on a vacation. God knows you both need it."

What a nice fantasy, she and Nate on a beach somewhere far away, like in his song that night. She closed her eyes for a moment, pictured a Caribbean ocean that matched his eyes, the sun warm on her face, and tried to cling to the vision.

"Liv?" Jo's voice, hesitant with worry, jarred her back to the reality of the cold October pre-dawn.

"I'm fine." She ducked the concerned stare and grabbed her straw fork, returning to the stall where she began carefully wielding it around Chique's flannel-wrapped legs.

Michel scooped up the filled muck sack before she could even protest, and Jo reappeared. "Once you're done in there, grab your helmet. I've got one that can go to the field. I'm thinking it's best not to leave you idle for too long today."

She nodded, kneeling to remove Chique's bandages. After she'd shaken them out and left them on the rail, she went back to the filly's side, and performed the daily ritual: examining every millimeter of those precious legs with hyper-sensitive fingertips, then placing a hand on each foot and blowing out a breath when all four were cool to her touch. Chique rolled an eye at her, just like everyone else had been doing each time her obsessiveness surfaced. Liv turned her loose.

It was an easy morning. Too easy. She wished she'd been run off her feet, left with no time to filter the flashes of her dreams and the intermittent pangs reminding her of the significance of this day. Emilie helped get the walkers out, then the gallopers, so they were done far too early. Chique was the only one left.

The filly displayed her usual exuberance, Liv smiling for the first time that morning. It was transient, of course, anxiety slithering back as Chique kicked out, nailing a bucket hung on the rail, the resulting splash and rattle sending her scooting forward with Liv skittering to keep control. It soon morphed back into sadness. This was the filly's last full day in the barn; the last time she'd get to try to tear it down.

She jogged Chique for the commission vet, Nate behind him when Liv turned her to jog back, appraising silently in the doorway at the end of the barn. He watched as closely as the official. Liv barely registered the vet thanking her and wishing her luck, her eyes tangling with Nate's before she walked Chique to her stall.

"All good?" he asked when she emerged. Chique pushed her head out, and he absently let her lip his hands.

Liv was close enough to see lines and hollows and shadows on his face she was certain hadn't been there before, and wanted to say *no, no it's not. Will it be?* But she answered, "Yes."

"I guess I'll see you in the paddock, then."

"Nate —"

He stopped mid-stride, uncertainty weighing down his features.

"Are we going to be all right?"

The question seemed to smudge away a few of the creases and etch in new ones, like a secret thought had tried to erase the gloom. His lips didn't quite lift, and there was a painful hesitation before he responded. "Yeah, Liv. I hope so."

It was an oat-sized promise, one she chose to curl into her palm and cradle to her chest.

Killing time in the kitchen, she abstractedly watched the undercard. Jo had chased her out of the barn because her anxiety was getting to everyone on the shed, equine and human. She felt the sideways glances, but other than acknowledging the odd *good luck today,* she ignored them, isolating herself in a corner.

A travel mug blocked her view for a moment, and she looked up as Faye set it down and nestled into the chair across from her. Faye was dressed for the races, reminding Liv she still had to somehow make herself presentable for the paddock.

"I did not slip a sedative in there. I was extremely tempted." Faye's mouth curled into a smile.

Liv eyed the mug doubtfully, but the scent of warm, frothy milk and espresso seemed worth testing her stomach's recovery. "Thank you." She sipped, and raised her eyes to Faye as the flavour of Bailey's hit the top of her mouth.

"I figured you needed something, though I decided pastry would've been wasted on you today."

"Sadly, yes."

Faye didn't try to start real conversation, instead joining Liv's silence. She let her mind drift, distracting herself by conjuring up the science behind the age-old wisdom of hot milk, embracing the anxiolytic effect of casein. Activating the analytic side of her brain seemed to settle it as much as the hot drink. It was a temporary vacation from her swirling emotions.

Outside it was drizzling now. The turf was listed as soft, but that wouldn't bother Chique. Nate won the Nearctic with Elemental — another one Liv should have been riding.

"Shouldn't you be getting ready?" Faye said. "You obviously decided against going home to shower."

Liv glanced down at her muddy jeans and smeared down vest, and ran a hand over her flat hair. "Yeah. Helmet head it is."

"Your hair is so straight, it'll be fine. Do you need help, or are you okay?"

Liv sighed, and drained the last of her cappuccino. It was a legitimate offer today. She pushed the empty mug towards Faye. "I'm okay. Thank you again for that. And for this." She met Faye's eyes with a small gesture of her hand.

"I'll see you on the front side. You're going to be all right."

Nate's words trickled into her head. *I hope so.*

She changed in the office. Faye was right — when she brushed out her hair and pulled it into a tight ponytail, it looked okay. The International didn't require the same finery as the Plate, so she'd get by with a pantsuit and her black trench coat. It was basically the same outfit she'd worn for Chique's Breeders' Stakes last year — which was fine, because this was Chique's rematch with Wampum, and today she'd have her revenge.

Jo had wisely left everything to her. Liv ritualistically set out four white Vetraps and cut four rundown patches exactly the length of the radius. Four, because she was taking every precaution today. Chique was waiting for her, standing quietly in the doorway, senses in tune to every vibe. Liv tied her where she stood, and started on the task that was second nature. The neat white polos she wrapped over them would keep the rundowns clean for the walk to the saddling enclosure.

When the call came, Liv dressed Chique in a quarter sheet and surcingle, and Jo put the bridle on. Liv watched Jo buckled the halter over it and lace the shank through its brass rings.

"You walking over with us?" Jo asked, Michel ready to escort on the off side.

Liv gave her a look. *You had to ask?* She nodded. "Let's go."

CLUSTERS OF BODIES gathered under the willows, more of them crowding the rail from the outside, trying to catch glimpses of the International field circling amid the connections. Liv homed in on her family, Faye and Dean and Will on the edges of her vision. She only glanced at Wampum. It didn't matter how good he looked. Chique was the right balance of composure and fire, sliding muscles and dense bone.

"She looks great, Liv," her father said solemnly, and her mother, next to Emilie, smiled. None of it could dissipate her tension as the minutes closed in on her.

She sensed Nate at her side, not needing to look his way to know he was there. No smiles, no joking, no singing, just eyes that shared her focus and heartbeat, at least in this moment. After months of division, Chique was the one thing that could bring them together.

"Riders up!"

Each step toward the filly was measured, one closer to the end of Chique's career. Liv wrapped her hand around Nate's boot and lifted him into the tack, walking alongside for two strides before she was able to let go. Did all good things have to end? She let that thought go with him, because right now none of it was in her control.

"*Bonne chance,* Miller. Come home safe." He might not have heard it, because it seemed to get caught somewhere in her throat.

In the box, she perched on the edge of her seat, pressing her binoculars to her eyes — dissecting each step as Chique completed her last post parade and broke away from Paz to warm up, just her and Nate. The gate waited on the wide green band of the E.P. Taylor turf, directly in front of the grandstand. When the time came, Chique went in, all business. One last dance.

Chique went straight to the lead. Now that Liv had ridden the filly herself, she felt every stride as the energy coursed through those limbs, to the turf and back again. Chique settled perfectly for Nate. No one else would realize it, but Liv did, especially now. The bond between those two was unmatched. And this was the last time she would witness it.

The rest of the field bunched a length and a half behind as they negotiated the irregular clubhouse turn, then straightened into the backstretch. Nate controlled the pace expertly, Chique content as long as she was showing the way. Liv glanced at the clock — perfect, equal quarters that obviously had the trailers spellbound, because no one was challenging. She let out a breath, inhaled again, and kept the binoculars glued as Chique entered the final turn, maintaining her length and a half advantage.

Wampum was stalking as Chique led the way into the long stretch, but there were no funny games for the colt to benefit from this time. When Nate let her out a notch, Chique propelled ahead to keep her advantage. The Europeans gathered like a storm cloud, but Chique started to draw away, quickening with a certainty that left Liv filled with pride and awe that overshadowed the heartache. The sorrow would return — tomorrow, when reality resurfaced — but this was a time to honour the bravery of their gutsy little champion. The crowd surged around her, cheering the sentimental favourite home.

Five lengths, then six. Nate glanced back uncharacteristically, as if he couldn't believe no one was challenging them. He wrapped up on the filly, and Chique's ears flickered forward to the wire as she coasted through.

Did Emilie and her parents follow her as she rushed from the box, down the stairs, to the turf? She didn't know; her focus was only for Chique and Nate as they galloped out. The outrider picked them up, and Liv stood rooted as they approached, wanting to hold onto this, wishing she had one of the powerful cameras the photographers fired behind her so she could freeze time, blow it up and hang it on her wall. Jo pushed her forward.

She took cautious steps toward them, like the turf would turn to glass under her feet and shatter the moment, robbing her of this. She took the shank from the outrider, registering his words of congratulations, maybe not quite able to acknowledge them, then kissed Chique between her billowing nostrils, the heat of the filly's breath warm on her cheeks. She couldn't look at Nate. Not now. Not yet.

Woodbine had revived the Canadian flag design for the blanket of flowers being draped over Nate's knees, halfway up Chique's neck because she was so tiny. Maybe the sponsor's name still dominated, but all Liv saw was the red and white against Chique's inky coat. Their little Canadian star. The Queen, relinquishing her crown. To whom?

There was the full sister, a scruffy weanling, like Chique had been four years ago.

There was Claire's unborn foal, with three months left in utero.

Both were so very far away from filling the deficit Chique would leave. As if she felt his eyes penetrating her skull, Liv glanced over her shoulder, up at Nate. Just a quick flick of her head, but enough to exchange a question. Could a human bridge that gap? Was there something left?

Their smiles for the win photo in the infield enclosure were sombre. Chique posed, of course. She would bask whole-heartedly in the glory. It was all hers. What were they, without her?

Liv hovered when Nate dismounted and pulled off the tack. She wanted to wrap herself around both him and the filly. He was safe. Chique was safe. Another exchanged glance, but he headed for the scales, following the rules to the letter while Michel threw a cooler over the filly, then joined Jo as she led Chique away. Liv almost went too —

she wanted nothing more than to bypass the formalities to follow her heart.

Or half her heart. Nate appeared at her side, and she offered him a slight smile, a brief interruption to her fixation on Chique. He slipped an arm around her shoulders, ignoring those who tried to rush them away for the presentation. Liv leaned into him, aware their heads touched as they observed Chique's departure like a ritual. She didn't let herself hope it meant anything other than the respect they shared for that filly.

The rest of it made her numb. The words, the trophies, the questions from the reporters. Nate was further away now, separated from her. *All good things must come to an end.* The phrase haunted her.

She was always better than he was at dodging the questions, checking on the filly a valid excuse to escape, but before she disappeared — remembering she'd walked over, and would be happy to walk back, have that time to herself — she captured his eyes, dragging them from the microphone stuffed in his face, and mouthed, *see you back at the barn?*

A question; a plea. Of course he'd come for Chique. Would he come for her?

He nodded, his expression giving nothing away.

THE SKY WAS GREY, the wind whipping up the tumultuous clouds rather than dispersing them. Everyone wore dark clothing and spoke in hushed tones, nibbling at their food and sipping their drinks. It felt like a funeral, though this time, no one had died. Requiem for a year, maybe. It had been a year.

But this should be a celebration. Sad could wait for tomorrow. At least for the sake of Chique, if nothing else.

He'd taken his time getting back. To rush would have felt as if he was trying to hurry it away. Now he stood next to the Porsche — which suddenly seemed indulgent, somehow offensive — and surveyed the subdued gathering. Chique was back from the test barn, tearing at the sparse grass on the lawn. She, at least, was free of the weightiness that hounded the humans.

He almost climbed back into the car. But he ducked in the end of the shed, avoiding the poor excuse for a party on the lawn. There were things that needed to be said before he turned that around.

Liv sat on the foot locker in front of Chique's stall, huddled in her black coat, like she was hiding from all of it. But there was no more hiding for her, no more running for him. Time to lay it on the line, once and for all. Time for them, apart from Chique, and this life.

She lifted her head, and he wondered if he had the same look of trepidation. It needed to be banished. She slid over, and he sat next to her, hip to hip, thigh to thigh. It wasn't enough. He reached for her arm, pulled it from the depths of her pocket, and closed his hand around hers.

"So, here we are," he said. "Can we talk?"

Only her fingers moved, cold within his, clenching and releasing. She didn't speak, her chin just dipped a little lower, a faint nod.

"I'm sorry for everything. I've been an ass," he started quietly. "I can't bring back Feste. But I should have done better, helped you through that, instead of feeling sorry for myself."

She shook her head, and cut him off before he could go on. "I didn't know what to do after the accident. You were so — different — and I didn't adapt. I was convinced you didn't want me around, especially because of that night."

He blew out a breath, resting his head against the rail. "I wish we could roll everything back to that night, so I could at least fix that. I overreacted. With everything that happened, I never got to explain."

"I made a fool of myself."

"Oh, no, no way. Is that what you think? You think I wanted to stop? I've just messed up enough times now to know there's no point if it's not right."

She inhaled, her palm warm against his now, but still restless. "Either way, I came up short. I couldn't blame you if you left. I'm grateful you stayed for today, and took care of her out there. But now — I understand if that's it, if it is over. Even if I don't really know what I'm going to do, without the two of you."

"Whoa — easy there." He chuckled, because he sounded like he was settling a fractious horse. "I didn't want you to stay away. You helped the best way you knew how. My head was messed up. I kept thinking, what if I couldn't ride? Why would you want me? I didn't realize how much I'd tied my whole identity to that. It was probably stupid, keeping that to myself, when you of all people would get it."

"But me, of all people, should have got it. I should have realized you'd be struggling with that."

"We were both just coping. And you were doing a way better job of it than me."

"No," she said. "I haven't been coping at all."

"I'm not going anywhere, Liv."

"I love you."

It came out breathless and precarious, like she'd tossed her heart into a chasm, where she might never see it again. Her expression was so intense, finally finding his eyes. And he started to laugh.

"What the hell, Miller?" she said, and almost pushed him off of the seat.

He wrapped himself around her, clutching her hard, his chest still rumbling. "I didn't ever think I was going to hear those words from you. Was it that hard?"

"Yes. Feeling it and saying it are such completely different things. It was terrifying." She clung to him, her pulse coming as hard as her respiration.

"That's all right. You scare the hell out of me."

He eased her back, his hands reaching to her face, holding it steady. He had to do it, dare the grand gesture, even when it might be the wrong call, might backfire on him. "So marry me."

She stared at him. Well, he'd said it. Might as well dig the ditch deeper.

"I'm serious. I love you more than you will ever know. We are not yet the good thing we can be. I can get down on one knee. I'll go ask your dad. Whatever you want. Trade in the Porsche for a house." He was grinning now, though his eyes hadn't lost their conviction. "I promise to love, honour and obey. Till death do us part. Forever and ever. Amen."

He could feel her shaking, and almost whacked her on the back as if she'd been drowning, because he was pretty sure she hadn't taken a breath. Forever was a hard thing to sell to Liv — not to mention the rest of it. She tried to pull back, no doubt to buy time, but he wouldn't let her go.

"All you have to say is yes," he nudged.

But what if she didn't?

"You can't just not answer," he insisted. "And don't tell me you need to think about it. You had a heads up."

She'd had three months — that night in Saratoga — but since the accident, everything had been wrong.

"You're crazy," she stammered. "I'm fickle and unstable."

"We're the perfect couple," he quipped, but he sobered. "Will you? Marry me?"

"Yes, damn it." she answered quietly, and her voice didn't falter, the tiniest of smiles gracing her lips.

He kissed her. It was a kiss that dressed wounds and faded scars, regenerating damaged cells like some miracle of biology; making promises that would never be broken, rewriting a future that only moments ago had seemed impossible.

"I'm not taking the blame for this," she murmured when they came up for air.

"I'm okay with that."

"Is it all right if we keep it to ourselves for a while?"

His eyebrow popped up and he leaned away, appraising her face. "So you have time to back out?"

"No. Everything between us has always seemed so public. It would just be nice if, for a little while anyway, there was something that was just between us."

He laughed. "All right. So, Las Vegas, then?"

She smirked. "Don't joke — that would suit me just fine."

"It's tempting. I'd get you on plane tomorrow, just so you don't bolt on me."

"I'm not going to bolt."

"Promise?"

"Promise."

Nate straightened when Marc brought Chique onto the shed, but Liv didn't move from his arms, even though Marc gave a start when he caught sight of them. Because when, ever, had the two of them been that entwined in this barn? Well…not since after the Plate. Not to mention that it was no secret they'd been at odds for a while.

"Thanks Marc," Liv said with a wan smile as the hotwalker hung the haynet. Another first, one of them not jumping up to do it. "Tell Jo we'll do her up?"

In other words, leave us alone.

"Sure thing." Marc nodded, the wag of his brows accompanied by an understanding grin.

Even Chique eyeballed them as she tossed her haynet, rolling it over her head before attacking it. Okay, Chique was always eyeballing them for one reason or another. She could wait a little longer. Even though this was a stupid uncomfortable spot to be sitting, he was afraid to break the spell.

"Would you have left?" she asked.

He just laughed again. "You couldn't get rid of me that easily. It would probably take an eviction notice. Maybe a restraining order. Besides, you know Chique's babies are going to be nightmares, and I'm the only one crazy enough to want to deal with that."

"True. You'd better stay."

"You probably have a stallion picked out for her already, don't you?"

Liv's smile was smug. "Maybe."

"So is it okay if I keep the Porsche?"

"Yeah. I kind of like the Porsche."

He dislodged himself reluctantly, lifting Liv to her feet, unable to stand Chique's scrutiny any longer. "Let's get her done up so she can have her dinner. Then we break out the champagne, and light a fire outside," — figuratively, of course — "to shake up the wake on the lawn."

He paused to brush back the strands of hair that had fallen into her face, and tucked them behind her ear. "We've put ourselves through such hell, maybe the rest of our lives will be easy."

"Happily ever after?"

"Absolutely."

Her smile was everything; love, and faith, and hope. "Count me in."

THE END

THANK YOU!

I hope you enjoyed *Good Things Come Books 1-3.* Reviews on your favourite retailer and GoodReads are always appreciated. They feed authors, which lets us keep writing more books for you. It doesn't have to be long — pick some stars and write a few words. Your input matters!

Book Four, ***This Good Thing,*** is now available in print and e-book format, continuing the story of Chique, Liv, Nate and their friends. Ask for it at your favourite retailer!

If you'd like to keep in touch, sign up for my newsletter at lindashantz.com/writes for sample chapters, updates, and more. Make sure you look for your confirmation email to be added. You can also follow me on BookBub. Or email me anytime at linda@lindashantz.com I'd love to hear from you. Thank you so much for taking this ride with me!

ABOUT THE AUTHOR

It was an eight-year-old me, frustrated that all the horse racing novels I read were about the Derby, not the Plate, who first put pencil to three-ring paper and started what would become this story. Needless to say, we've both grown up a bit since then.

I began working at the track before I finished high school, and after graduating the following January, took a hotwalking job at Payson Park in Florida. Once back at Woodbine, I started grooming and galloping. While the backstretch is exciting, I found I was more at home on the farm — prepping and breaking yearlings, nightwatching and foaling mares. Eventually I started my own small layup/broodmare facility, and in the last few years I've transitioned into retraining and rehoming. Somewhere along the way I did go back to school and get a degree. I should probably dust it off and frame it one day.

I live on a small farm in Ontario, Canada, with my off-track Thoroughbreds and a young Border Collie, and I'm probably better known for painting horses than writing about them — if you like my covers, check out my artwork at www.lindashantz.com

Printed in Great Britain
by Amazon

21247834R00424